Seeking Absolution

Shalisse Lewis

ISBN: 978-0-9903692-0-2

Published by Puck Was Here a division of Trading Oak Publishing
www.puckwashere.com

DEDICATION

To my family and friends. Without your support, none of this would be possible.

Maps

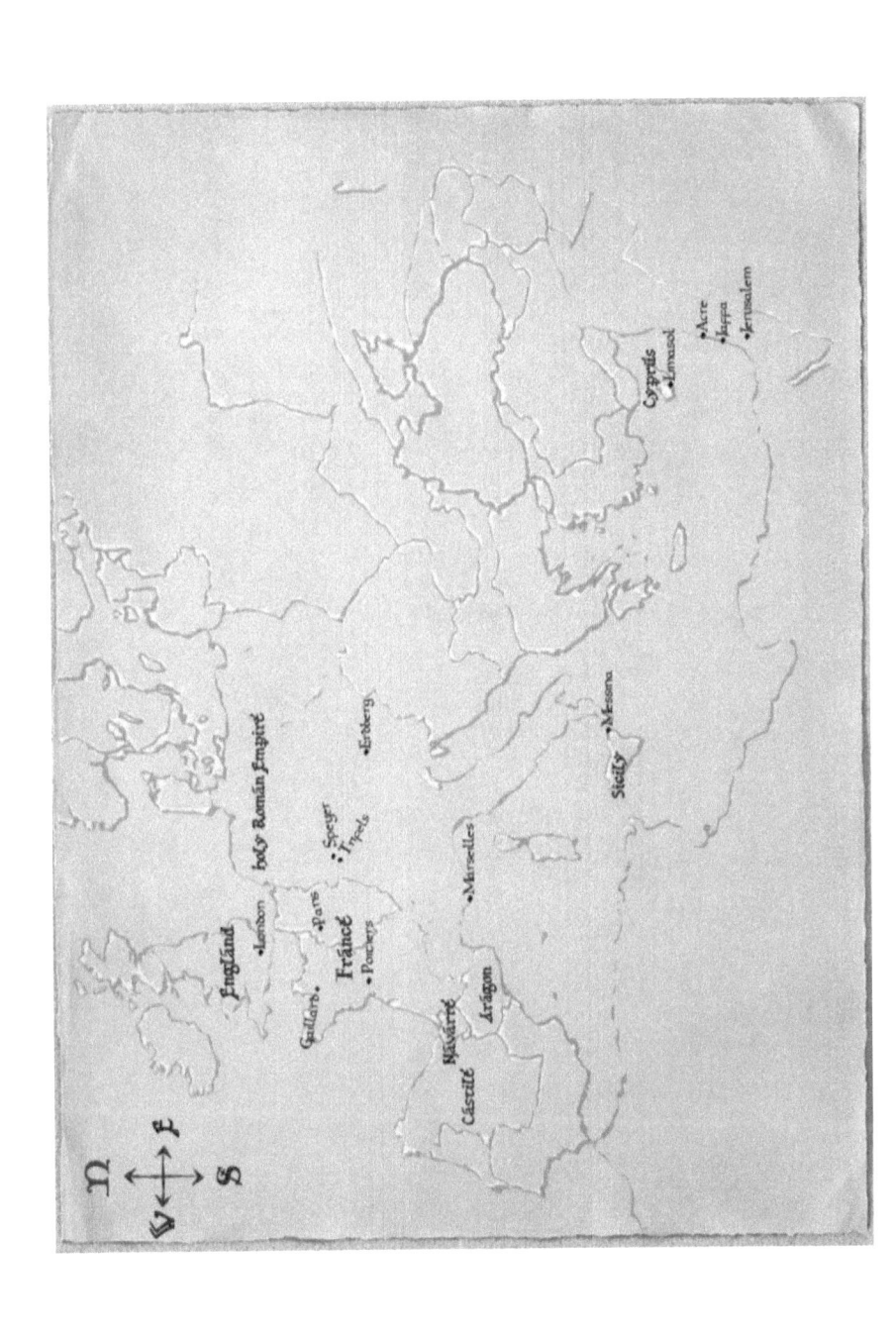

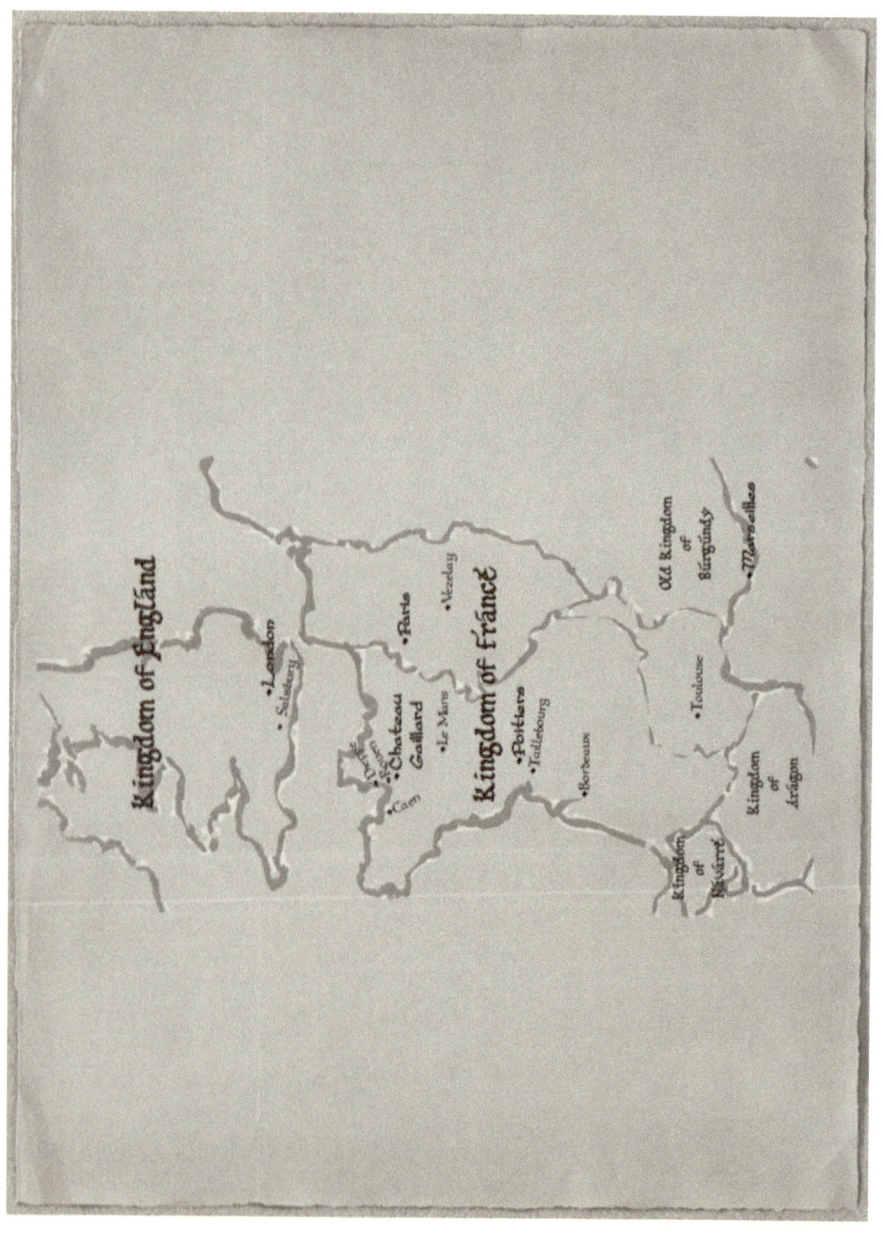

Prologue
March, Anno Domini 1204

The profane stench seared his nostrils and burnt his eyes until they watered. Bogis pushed backward against the uneven rock to force himself upward. With his fingertips, he could feel a rough ledge, but his whole hand slipped on the slime that coated it. Thrown off balance for a brief moment, Bogis thought he would tumble down the shaft taking the men below with him.

Reaching out to the opposite wall, Bogis used the pressure to stabilize his position. In an instant, he felt the burning sensation in his scraped fingers. He wasn't wearing any gloves; they would have only been a hindrance against the slime and refuse that coated the wall. Without thinking, he emptied the air from his lungs but regretted it, as he would just have to draw in more breath, ingesting the foul air around him.

Below Bogis, a man vomited, making his own reflexes spring into action. He clenched his throat, fighting it back down-he could not show such weakness to his men. Not only did his lungs burn from holding his breath and sucking in so much putrid air, now his throat was on fire from his own vomit. As he closed his eyes to compose himself, he remembered in detail why he, French King Phillip II's field marshal, was scaling the *gardez l'eau* drain of Chateau Gaillard.

Just hours ago he stood on the bank of the Seine looking up at the massive castle perched on the cliff high above him. The castle leered down at him, mocked him, grinned at him as if to say, "I shall never be taken."

Some men believed twenty-three too young for the job of Maréchal de Champ, but Sir Charles de Bogis proved himself time and time again. Coming from a minor noble family in the Vexin region, he rose to his present title rather quickly. King Philip took notice of the young man because of his ferocity in battle, his tactical skills, and his great loyalty. Bogis' military prowess spawned rumors that one day he might rise to the rank of Marshal of France, the commander of all the king's armies.

Bogis remembered the story of how, when Richard the Lionheart built Gaillard, Philip swore he would take it brick by brick if necessary. Richard replied that he would defend it even if it were made of butter. Right now it certainly seemed that Philip would have to take it brick by brick. Glaring, Bogis wished the chateau was indeed made of butter; then this siege would have been over months ago. Bogis didn't believe in ghosts; even with King Richard dead and buried, it seemed like he still protected his castle. Richard's brother, King John, certainly hadn't done much to defend Gaillard, the gateway to Angevin Normandy. The last time anyone saw John, he was sailing back to England, sulking the entire way.

Stones catapulted into the castle walls, and they made a thundering crunch as they hit and the earth shook. He wondered if they were the stones from the wall of the little peach orchard across the river, a reputed favourite spot of King Richard. It galled Bogis that in eight months the French only captured the orchard and the outer bailey. However, the outer bailey was not the first obstacle Philip and his men faced. The town fell with ease, but the besiegers dealt with what they now called the *Useless Mouths*.

When King Philip began the siege, Gaillard's castellan, Roger de Lacey, ordered all non-combatants out of the fortress. At first the French let them pass to the town below. The French found spies amongst them, and King Philip forbade any to pass through his lines. These people, old men, women, and children were trapped between the French lines and the silent walls of the castle. All winter, both sides watched as this hapless group starved in the muddy trenches. Shortly before the outer bailey fell, Philip took pity on the Useless Mouths, gave them food, and ordered them on through his lines.

The besiegers only managed to take the outer bailey a month ago, and then only when the curtain wall fell due to the mining underneath. Images of French men at arms trying to climb the outer wall with ladders flashed into Bogis' mind. The ladders came woefully short to reach the top, and the soldiers tried climbing up the rock wall. Many men plummeted to their deaths.

The mighty trebuchets below sprung loose another volley of stone projectiles. This time Bogis imagined them as they hit their mark, and stone splintered and shattered, leaving pockmarks in the gray walls, the damage on the face of the castle that Richard referred to as his daughter. It lifted Bogis' spirits. *If only Richard could see that*, he thought. Still, the French remained firmly shut out of the middle bailey. No doubt, Richard would have been as proud as any father of his citadel. Her defences performed exactly as designed.

Bogis ran his filthy fingers through his golden-red hair, pulling it out of his face. Thinking about Richard made him uncomfortable. At court people often whispered the only reason he rose to his position was because he reminded Philip of Richard in temperament, skill, and looks. Often times, people said the two men could have passed for brothers. Bogis never met Richard, so he didn't know if this was true or not. He did know that for years the French and English fought over the territory of Vexin.

A crash and a sudden spray of rubble brought him back to his task in the drain. He had his mouth open when the spray came, and his mouth filled with the taste of stone and feces. Bogis spat, scraped his tongue with his teeth, and spat again with no thought of those who were below, but he could hear that he wasn't the only one to do so. Ready to be finished with what seemed a sentence in purgatory, he made his final push upward.

Emerging into the open air, Bogis held his breath until he exited the garderobe and entered the chapel itself. Sharply, he let his breath escape, purging himself of the foul and breathing in the cleansing air. The man behind him, Eustache surfaced looking strange, freckled from head to foot in light and dark spots. A quick glance at himself confirmed that the sun did not cause the freckles.

Together they secured a rope around a heavy pillar, then tossed the rope back down the latrine for the other men climbing the drain. As Bogis looked around, he found what he was looking for. He ordered two knights to draw their swords, and he pointed to a grave. "There it is. Stand here with me and guard it," he growled.

More men poured into the chapel searching for a way to exit. "The door is locked," Gravier, a young man-at-arms moaned.

"Well, what did you expect, they'd leave everything open for us? Break a window!" Bogis grimaced.

"But it's a chapel, sir."

"Just break the window!" Bogis' face turned red. Time was vital, and this dolt wasted it.

Someone broke the window; Bogis did not see who, and the French swarmed onto the castle grounds. Bogis watched them go. From outside the chapel, he could hear the shouts and cries of battle, but he and the two other men remained at their post. Aggravated, he butted his head backwards against the wall. He wanted to be out there with the men, fighting, not in here standing guard at a grave.

Within a matter of moments, the French surprised and overpowered the English at the drawbridge, and another moment saw hundreds of King Philip's soldiers rushing into the castle, slaughtering Englishmen or taking them prisoner. A small group of English retreated to the inner bailey.

As the siege continued, Bogis remained at his post by the grave, assigned there by the king himself. He could not help but wonder just what he had done to deserve such an ignominious duty.

Once the middle bailey fell, it did not take long for the inner bailey to fall, and then the castellan, Roger de Lacy surrendered the fortress. Still, Bogis remained stationed at a grave.

Tall and graceful, the French King, Philip Augustus, entered the fortress to the shouts and cheers of his men, but he seemed to take little notice of them. He was a man in search of something.

Philip's personal priest, a rotund man named Guillaume le Breton, hustled toward the king. "Your Highness, I think I have found it!"

"Is it her grave?" Philip asked, his brilliant blue eyes sparkling.

Breton huffed, still a little out of breath. "Yes, my lord, I believe so. We have found the chapel. I will show you."

Without waiting for a reply, Breton turned and retraced his steps as fast as his stubby legs would allow.

They reached the chapel of Chateau Galliard with all the haste left in Breton. "There, my lord, there it is." Breton pointed a crooked finger toward a grave maker.

Philip entered the chapel reverently. Other than the broken window, the chapel was spared damage from the battle, and as of yet not stripped of its ornamentation. The grave lay in front of and to the right of the altar. Bogis and the two knights stood in front of the grave, swords still drawn. Philip went to the gravestone to which Breton pointed. The stone read:

Anne Baux

Viscountess De Marseilles

Philip dropped to a knee and tenderly touched the letters on the cold stone in the floor. Bogis noticed the king bite his lip and hold his breath. Then the King's chest quivered, and a small whisper escaped his lips, "Anne."

"Forgive me, sire, but I am puzzled." Bogis' voice broke the spell. "You have just won a great battle. This was King Richard's castle. They all said it could never be taken. Your men are celebrating! Yet, the first thing you do is come here to the chapel to find a grave. I am confused."

Philip's voice came with uncharacteristic compassion. "She was dearer to me than any sister."

"But, my lord, I thought she was Richard's mistress," Bogis griped.

Philip turned on Bogis pointing a shaking finger at him. "You and I would have been lucky to have been loved by half such a woman."

Bogis dropped his head and apologized, not wanting to incur any more of King Philip's wrath. "I am sorry, but I am afraid that I do not understand your meaning, sire."

Breton intervened. "Perhaps, Sir Bogis, it is best that we leave the king alone in the chapel. I am sure he could use this time alone with God, and you could use a bit of washing."

Breton ushered Bogis out of the chapel into the little entryway outside the chapel proper, and returned to get a chair. Looking back, Breton saw Philip take a seat on the cold stone floor next to the grave, prop his back against the wall, remove his sword and loosen his armor. Breton shut the door.

"I didn't mean to anger the king," Bogis protested.

"You did not anger him; he just needs to be alone." Breton set the chair down in front of the chapel door as if he guarded the door.

One of Bogis' men, who was now wet from head to foot, handed him a bucket of water. "This is maddening," Bogis said, scrubbing his hands and face to get the now dry freckles off. "He needs to be with the men in victory! He is not making any sense! He ordered me to stand here and guard a grave instead of leading the men to the gate." Bogis lifted the bucket and poured clean water over his head.

"That grave is very important to the king. He wanted to trust it to his most loyal knight," Breton tried to explain.

Bogis shook his head. "A grave?"

"Long ago, King Philip and Richard were friends—long before he became a king—long before the crusade. And Anne, she was always there with them; Lady Anne, the woman who could bring the mighty warrior Richard to his knees." Breton paused and gave a pained smile. "They met while Philip was still young. Richard was the Duke of Aquitaine then. Sit, sir, this will take some time."

With apprehension, Bogis took a seat in the narrow hallway.

Part One:
Poitiers

Chapter One

Queen Eleanor scurried through the unsettled *Grande Salle* in the palace of Poitiers. She directed the decoration of the great hall and made final preparations for the return of her son, Richard, the Duke. Eleanor, the formidable queen, was petite and a bit plumped after giving birth to ten children. Nevertheless, he queen's beauty and vitality radiated throughout court. Her once dark tresses now streaked with gray, but her soft brown eyes, long dark lashes, straight slim nose, and full lips presented her noble heritage. With a face that did not show the wrinkles that some of lesser years displayed, many people found it hard to believe Eleanor had entered her fifties.

The queen loved Poitiers, the birthplace of her ancestors, the town, her castle, everything about it. Poitiers loved the queen as well. The town's structures and the castle itself mirrored her beauty, charm, and poise.

Today, though, Eleanor found it difficult to complete the tasks at hand. Youths from throughout the kingdom and beyond filled the court at Poitiers to be trained in the ways of nobility and chivalry. With the coming tournament, the air at court sparked with excitement. Everywhere the youths found it hard to focus on their assigned tasks. Young women sneaked off to primp and fluff themselves while the young men practiced poetry recitations or dueled with cattails. All intended to notice and to be noticed– difficult and time–consuming work. One by one they fell prey to the atmosphere and left their other duties unattended.

The queen shook her head over the half-completed chores, but when she saw a pair of lovers fluttering their eyes at one another, she chuckled to herself. It was just a tournament, after all. It was not as if kingdoms rose or fell on this occasion. Even she could remember being young and filled with the same energy that now permeated the air.

Turning in place, Eleanor inspected the progress as one lady of the court made her way across the great hall, her footfalls muted in the cavernous space known as *The Hall of Forgotten Footsteps*. At one end of the long hall, light filtered in through arched windows carved like lace hovering over the raised dais. The sunshine landed upon a young lady carrying a bundle of deep blue cloth high enough to hamper her vision. She called out to the queen, "Your highness, here is the cloth you asked for."

Eleanor clapped her hands together. "Perfect!" She intended the bright blue cloth be used as bunting behind the head table. The hue would stand out against the gold earthen tones of the stonewalls, while making the yellow, pinks, and reds of the flowered swags pop and liven the room beneath its high timber beam ceiling. "Oh, bless you, Anne. I knew you'd be the one to find it." She leaned close to the girl and patted her on the cheek. "I am so glad your father chose to send you here to me. There are times that I wish you were my daughter."

Anne blushed. "My lady, I am among the luckiest creatures of Christendom."

Like Eleanor, Anne was a child of Languedoc, the area in France south of the Loire River. Her complexion was smoother and darker than those of her counterparts that came from the North. Anne wore her hair long in the fashion amongst the young ladies of the court. The queen called it cinnamon in colour, brown with touches of red in the sun, sometimes a "burning cinnamon." Anne's eyes, framed with dark lashes, shown an alluring hazel like her beloved father's. With high cheekbones, her slim nose came to a subtle point above her full pink lips.

Taking the bundle of bunting from Anne, Eleanor handed it to the nearest servant. She took Anne's arm and steered her toward the enormous fireplace. "My darling, I have grown to love you as if you were my own." Then she added with a twinkle in her eye, "Do not tell the Countess Marie; she will be jealous."

As if summoned by the sound of her name, Countess Marie

entered the hall. The Countess shared many of her mother's good looks and her mother's wit. She also inherited her southern French passion. The only thing that marred her features were her small eyes, coming from her father, King Louis of France. Countess Marie was blessed in many ways, but there was one constant irritant in her life, her husband. Like most noble women, Marie's father married her off for the best political advantage. The Count of Champagne, perhaps the dullest creature that God ever created, was only six years younger than Eleanor. In closed circles, the Countess often remarked, "A snail has more personality than that man!" So, Marie did the only thing she could; she fled to her half-brother's court at Poitiers. At Poitiers, Marie was, for the most part, responsible for the "Courts of Love," the arena in which the skills of *fin amour* were so aptly taught.

Eleanor caught sight of Marie as she entered the great hall. "What is it, dearest? You look rather fretful."

"He's done it again!" Marie threw her hands up.

"What? Who?" But Eleanor could guess the answer.

"Richard just arrived! Apparently, he left the main group behind, racing on ahead." Marie tried to narrow her eyes, but a smile escaped her lips.

Eleanor smiled in spite of herself. "Of course he did. That is so like Richard, but there is still so much to be done!"

"Not to worry, my lady. There are plenty of hands here to complete the work. I shall see to it that it is done, and we will be celebrating right on schedule," Anne offered. "Not to worry. If you wish, go and greet your son."

"I put my trust in your capable hands," Eleanor replied as she and Countess Marie left the great hall to welcome Richard.

When the appointed time for the banquet came, everything came together like a miracle. The decorated hall glowed, and the inviting smell of roasted meat and sweetbreads wafted from the kitchens as the court assembled ready to welcome the royal family. Lady Anne stood with a row of other young ladies waiting in the great hall. Millicent, another young lady of the court, fretted and fussed next to Anne. "What do you think, Anne? Are the flowers too much?"

Anne looked over Millicent. "Here. I think if we adjust these in front..." Anne plucked a few flowers from Millicent's golden head, " ... yes, that should do it."

" ... want to stand out, but I don't want to stand out too much. Do you think they are too much?" Millicent wrinkled her forehead.

"Your beauty does not need any more to augment it. You look fine. Besides, whose eye are you hoping to catch? I thought we agreed there is not a man here at this court that is of much interest." Anne adjusted her own dark green sleeves.

"Duke Richard, of course!"

Anne's brows lifted. "What do you mean, Duke Richard? Millicent, he is already promised to another."

Millicent rolled her blue eyes. "Dear, sweet, Anne, that does not mean that there is no fun to be had. I have met him before, and I must say he is a very agreeable person. Have you not met him?"

"Well, no. I have not."

"You will get your chance soon enough. If I were you, I would do something to spruce myself up at least a little bit."

"I did; I just chose not to put flowers in my hair." Anne narrowed her eyes at Millicent.

"You mean you did not have time to put flowers in your hair because you were too busy trying to be the queen's favourite." Millicent corrected her.

Anne smiled sweetly. "Oh, no. There was no *trying* involved."

Just then a trumpet sounded, announcing the arrival of the royal family. Looking down at one of Millicent's little white flowers she still held, Anne hastily tucked it into her own hair. Those in the great hall curtsied and bowed as the queen, the countess, and the duke entered. Curiosity should have driven Anne to look up and catch a glimpse of the duke, but after what Millicent said, she felt rather self-conscious. A lock of hair fell forward over her shoulder as she curtsied. She was glad of it; at least it would hide her ears. Anne hated her ears. Often times, she imagined that her ears were a bit on the pointed side. Anne always felt that she was plain, just plain Anne. People often told her that she looked like her mother, a renowned beauty, inheriting her mother's high cheekbones, and delicate nose, but there was just enough of her father in her to mar the look. Thinking of the silly flower she just put in her hair, she blushed.

After the royal family passed, those assembled found their respective places, Richard took his place on the dais, stood at the head table, and raised a glass. "I declare that the tournament festivities have officially begun. Here is to those who will attain honor and glory."

"Huzzah!" Many in the crowd echoed.

When the duke and company took their seats, page boys dressed in matching red tunics served dinner. Millicent, seated next to Anne, leaned over and whispered to her, "Well, Anne, even you must say that the duke certainly is handsome in an interesting sort of way."

"I am relieved to see that he does not have perfect shaped ears."

"His ears? What?"

Anne stole another look at the Duke. His looks were not the kind to make one's heart skip a beat, but not unpleasant to behold. His long, golden, red hair was the shade that came from spending time in the summer sun. Fortunately for him, he sat a head and a half taller than his mother. Lacking her delicate build, he possessed a barrel chest and a ruddy complexion. These must have come from his father, Anne surmised. His lips were also much thinner than his mother's.

Movement to her left captured Anne's attention, and she grumbled, "Oh, spite! Here comes Raymond." Anne caught sight of her least favourite thing about court as he stalked toward her. Raymond of Castile's black hair framed his face in soft curls. His pleasant shaped physique, muscular arms, and well-toned legs complimented his dark features. However, he carried himself with more arrogance than elegance, dressed as always only in the best clothes money could buy, the best fabrics, and the best tailoring.

Millicent tipped her head to the side. "Ah, yes, Raymond of Castile. He is the sixth in line for the succession to the throne of Castile, after the king, the Prince Alfonso, Ferdinand, Sancho, Don Carlos, Philip, Juan the cook, the master at arms, the pigs, the horses, the cows, and then Raymond—which makes him utterly useless. So, he came to Poitiers. Why?"

"Need I remind you that most of the young men here are the younger sons?"

Millicent shrugged. "Yes, but at least there is some hope for them that they will learn to be chivalric and honorable. I fear Raymond of Castile, on the other hand, despite the Countess' and Queen's efforts, will be neither."

"Shush, he will hear you, Millicent."

Raymond moved like a peacock to Anne's table, and addressed her as if he were going to give a command. "Lady Anne." He stopped and started again with a softer tone, "I mean, good evening, Lady Anne. I hope you are well."

"Very well, I thank you," Anne answered but avoided eye contact.

Raymond just stood there. Millicent looked away and stifled a giggle. The silence crushed Anne, compelling her to do something, say something. "Is there something else you wished to say?"

"Oh, yes. I just wish to inform you that I shall be singing a song which I hope you will find pleasing." Raymond lifted his chin higher.

"The Queen does enjoy a good ballad." Anne tried to deflect him.

"Come now, Anne." Raymond sniffed a little. "You know exactly what I am saying. I will be singing a song just for you."

Anne's eyes widened. "I assure you that is not necessary."

Raymond protested, "But according to the rules of the Courts of Love it is."

"No!" Anne almost shouted. "There are other ways of expressing oneself to a maid. Besides, I assure you that I am not worthy of such a performance."

Up at the head table, Richard signaled for the crowd to quiet. "Ah, good, the entertainment is to start!" With only the slightest bow, Raymond returned to his seat.

"Do you think he is really going to do it?" Millicent raised her eyebrows in concern.

Anne shook her head. "Heaven help us."

A series of boisterous jesters, sentimental singers, and lively dancers performed. So far Raymond failed to take the floor. Anne began to think he would not do it after all. Maybe he just made a strange sort of threat or a desperate plea for attention. As the night wore on, Millicent's unsuccessful attempts to catch the eye of Richard entertained her. Then, just when Anne began to relax, Raymond took the floor with a lute.

"It looks as though heaven is not on your side tonight," Millicent observed.

Raymond took a seat, not in front of the royal family as custom dictated, but on a stool in front of Anne. Accompanying himself on the lute, he sang a popular love song. Anne wilted as Raymond hit one off-key note after another, and she noticed other listeners grimacing as well.

At the head table, Richard watched the proceedings with

curiosity. Never hearing anything quite like it before, it affected his appetite, and he dropped the chicken leg he was eating on his plate. "Who is this?"

Eleanor replied, "Raymond of Castile."

"The poor fellow plays competently enough, but he brays like an ass!" Richard gulped some wine in a vain attempt to drown out the singer.

Eleanor smiled. "The youngest of six brothers, he is here for one reason and one reason only."

Richard hoped that it was something he could use to bribe Raymond of Castile to get him to stop singing. "What would that be?"

"Anne Baux de Marseilles."

"And who is she?"

"She is the heir of the Viscount de Marseilles, his only surviving child. His title is not so great as his wealth. I met him while on Crusade with Louis. The viscount is a good man and a very rich one. Anne arrived here while you were in Rouen. Of course, word spread, and suddenly many a young man pursued her riches. Raymond is, at least, the most persistent. If a good try were all required in life, he would have been successful a long time ago."

Richard winced as Raymond sang a high note. "If his personality is anything like his singing, I feel rather sorry for her."

Raymond finished his song as a collective sigh of relief filtered through the room. The applause that followed was for the respite from the agony. Raymond gave a bow to the head table, then turned giving a lower bow in Anne's direction.

Someone from the crowd shouted, "Give us a song, Lady Anne!"

"Oh, no. I could not possibly," Anne protested.

"Come now, Anne. We all enjoy hearing from you," Countess Marie called out.

Eleanor seconded the sentiment. "Yes, dear, favor us with

one of your recent creations."

"Yes, your highness." Anne stood and curtsied.

With a deep breath, Anne composed herself and took the lute from Raymond. She wrestled it from his hands as he remained there grinning at her. Taking the stool from where Raymond placed it, she seated herself in the appropriate place in front of the royal family. She stroked the lute with her long thin fingers and began to play her song. Her voice was not the high angelic type. Hauntingly, its deep rich tones resonated throughout the hall.

> *O shifting Fortune, ever-changing,*
> *Like the moon*
> *Always waxing, then collapsing*
>
> *But once this novel flame begins,*
> *It flares within*
> *And never shows a weakening.*
>
> *Love is not wrong because*
> *If it were a crime,*
> *God would never have used love*
> *To bind even the divine*

Richard watched Anne with a great deal of curiosity. The tone of her voice, the emotion in her words mesmerized him. "Money is not her only attribute," Eleanor whispered.

When Anne finished her song, the crowd applauded. The noise jolted Richard, and he desired a distraction lest he be snared by a siren's song. Calling for a dance, he rose to his feet.

In haste, the company sought partners, and formed up for the dance. Prince Osric of Sweden, who was only fourth in line to the Swedish throne, snatched Anne as his partner. Raymond glowered at Osric as he took a different companion.

With the dance, Anne experienced a sense of relief at being able to blend in. She allowed herself to have fun and enjoy the company of the other dancers. The dance was a carol, and through the course of it, partners were exchanged. That feature of this particular dance made it popular. Anne left her present partner, a boy younger than most, who made gagging faces at Castile's turned back while she tried to stifle her laughter. While still looking at the boy, she put her hand up to meet her new partner's. The touch of that hand made her tremble. Without looking, she sensed the hand of someone confident, and strong. As she turned to see this new partner, she found herself looking into the blue gray eyes of the duke.

Chapter Two

The next morning dawned bright and crisp. Many in the court took the opportunity to enjoy the beauty and the fragrance of the late summer gardens of Poitiers.

Several groups milled about the lavishly landscaped pathways or open patches of clean clipped lawn, some conversing, some listening to readings or songs. Walking amongst them, Richard nonchalantly searched the groups of courtiers. The bright colours of their clothing complimented the deep red, purple, and golden hues of the well-manicured flowers and shrubs. In front of a thick green shrub and two peach trees ripe with fruit, Richard spotted Anne sitting alone in a distant corner reading a letter. Her pale green dress camouflaged her against the shrub.

Without hesitation Richard headed toward her, but stopped short when he saw Raymond plant himself next to her. At that moment, Richard's own group of friends descended upon him, trying to engage him in conversation. Feigning interest, he eavesdropped on Anne and Raymond.

"I trust you enjoyed my tribute last night." Raymond stuck his nose in the air.

"I ..."

"You need not thank me. The blush on your cheek says enough," Raymond interrupted her.

Anne stood to leave. "Sir Raymond, I am sorry, but I promised the Queen to do an errand, and it almost slipped my mind until now. I must be going."

Raymond caught her hand, yanking her back to the seat.

"Please, I really must go."

"The Queen will forgive you. After all, you are a favourite of hers." Raymond leaned in close to her.

"Which is precisely why I must complete my task." Anne rose again, but this time Raymond grabbed her by the shoulders.

Raymond's eyes darkened. "Come now, Anne, you don't need to pretend and play coy with me."

"I mean nothing by my actions other than I must attend to the queen." She pronounced her words slow and clear.

Richard could wait no longer and stepped forward. "Lady Anne, I believe? My mother, the queen, is asking for you."

Anne excused herself, "I shall take my leave of you then, my lords."

As Anne rushed down the path, Richard and Raymond exchanged nasty scowls. Richard turned and followed her. It only took him a moment to catch up.

Anne whispered, "I thank you, your grace. Your timing could not have been better if I had planned it."

Richard couldn't help but smile. "In that case, I have a

confession to make. I listened in on your conversation, and thought I better do something or he might sing again."

Anne's mouth curved upward. "Yes, heaven help us, but you, sir, are the savior of ears."

"It took all my strength to summon my courage and face so terrifying an enemy."

"On behalf of all those at court, let me be the first to express my gratitude. May your path be strewn with roses and a laurel placed upon your head for saving us all from such a dragon." She swept her hand in front of her.

Richard tried to look serious. "Actually, my kindness does come with a price."

"So, that's the way of it then. Well, let's have it, how am I to repay you, my lord?"

Richard sighed. "It is simple really; I just request you sing another song this evening at banquet, or even read a poem, perhaps. I was... um... impressed with your performance last night."

"Were you now? There must have been other performances that made an impression on you. There were many good presentations." Anne's face flushed.

Richard laughed. "Yes, there was that one fellow with the dog."

Anne did not hesitate. "Did you also seek him out today and give praise to him?"

"As a matter of fact, that is the errand the queen sent me to ask you to do."

"Is it now? Then I shall find and congratulate him." Anne gave him a sly look and retreated into the castle.

Later in the week, a joust occurred. Richard and his two loyal companions, Andrew and Baldwin, prepared for an event in a field tent. Andrew and Baldwin were both tall and wore their hair to the shoulder like Richard's. Andrew's brown hair and soft brown eyes contrasted with Baldwin's light, almost white hair. Baldwin's clear blue eyes seemed to be in a constant state of laughter. Andrew's squire helped him dress, as it would soon be his turn to joust, Raymond of Castile entered the tent. "Good morning, your grace," his tone sounded brisk as always.

"Sir Raymond, let me introduce you to my two brothers-in-arms." Richard felt that niceties must be observed.

"Brothers in mischief is more like it," Baldwin chided.

"Yes, that would be Baldwin of Be'thune, and this fine fellow here is Andrew de Chauvigny."

"Ah yes, I remember you from the other night." Andrew extended his hand to Raymond. "You sang for a lady, I believe."

"Yes, well ... good Duke, I beg a word with you. I will take but a moment of your time." With a wave of his hand Raymond dismissed Andrew and Baldwin.

Richard's jaw tightened. "Here I am. What is it that you wish to discuss?"

Raymond hesitated a moment, but Andrew and Baldwin did not leave. Raymond continued, "The Lady Anne, my lord."

"What of Lady Anne?" Richard examined the blade of Andrew's sword.

"I am not blind, and I have noticed your attention toward her as of late. I have seen the way you look at her, and the other night I even noticed how you brushed your hand against hers as she passed you in the hall on her way to perform some errand for the queen." Raymond puffed out his chest as he spoke. "Now, as you know, my lot in life is to have a title, nothing more than a title, and a piss poor one at that. I came to this court to seek my fortune, and my fortune lies with Lady Anne."

"Oh?" Richard looked away from the blade and directly at Raymond.

Raymond attempted a smile. "Come now, let us not pretend you know nothing of her father's wealth."

"I have heard it rumored," Richard snapped.

Raymond spoke before Richard could say anything else. "I also know that for years now you have been affianced to Princess Alice of France. Therefore, I have a proposal for you regarding Lady Anne."

"What could you possibly offer me?" Richard shook his head.

"I shall make no bones about it. You want one thing from her, and then once you have had your pleasures, it will be over. Use her, my lord; let her satisfy you, and I will seek no revenge. In exchange order her to receive my attentions and become my wife."

"Excuse me?" Richard stepped back aghast.

Raymond clarified, "My lord, have your way with her, if you like. Just let me have her long enough to gain control of her inheritance and produce an heir."

Richard gaped. "You must be joking and poorly at that!"

"I assure you, I never jest about money."

Now Richard could no longer hold his tongue. "See here, *Sir* Raymond," he spoke the name with sarcasm, "as you clearly have pointed out, you really are no one of consequence, and your only hope is to marry well. I, on the other hand, am a duke and the lord of this court. I will attend to my own business. Your troubles in love and manners are not my concern. Do not make them such." He turned his back on Raymond. "Now, I bid you good day as I am sure you are needed elsewhere."

Raymond stormed off like a child just denied a toy.

Chapter Three

The court assembled in the *Grande Salle*, this time for a session of the Courts of Love, a popular game. Countess Marie presided over these games by bringing "cases" before a panel of fifty young ladies who decided the outcome of an issue. The ladies sat on tiers, placed on the dais, just under the great gothic arched windows, and Anne sat amongst them in an upper tier. An audience assembled to watch the exercises in etiquette. To the right of the "jury" sat a group of young men; Raymond being one.

Countess Marie stood and called all to order. "Ladies and gentlemen, before we begin this afternoon's court, I want to educate those of you who are here for the first time and remind those who have been here before as to the purpose of these proceedings. The objective of this forum is to instruct you in the courtly art of love. You young people are encouraged to bring your problems before the court here," she motioned to the ladies behind her, "to be judged by the panel of ladies you see before you. Remember these cases are to be submitted by proxy so as to not offend those actually involved, as many of these situations are of a delicate nature. By participating in these proceedings, you agree to abide by the judgments of this court. Let us begin. Bring forth the first case."

From the group on the right, a robust young man stood and took his place in front of the ladies. "Ladies of the court," he announced as he bowed low before them. "I bring you a complex matter as per request of a companion." He paused for effect. "It seems that for some time now he has shown favors to a certain young lady at court. However, the young lady spurned him, and he is deeply wounded. His intentions toward the lady are honorable. He cares so for the maiden that he is willing to put her happiness above his own. He suspects the young lady favors another knight, and he is even willing to turn a blind eye to any indiscretions. All he asks is that she marry him."

Someone in the court snorted in disgust at the idea of insult to the lady's honor. Countess Marie wrinkled her brow. "It sounds to me that love is not what he is after. I feel that he does not really love that maiden, or he would not be so willing to, as you say, 'turn a blind eye'. His protestations of love are merely for show.

There is no merit behind them. Let me ask you this: is there a particular quality about her which he loves so?"

"I do not know, my lady, but, as I have said, his intentions are honorable as to an end of marriage," the young man replied.

Countess Marie's expression grew stern. "I still believe it is not her he wishes to marry, but something that belongs to her perhaps?"

The robust young man held up his hands as if to stop her. "I cannot go into further detail or this knight's identity will easily be revealed."

"I see." Countess Marie shifted in her seat. "So, the question here is: should the lady relent and marry the knight she does not love. She can still carry on with the knight she favors?"

A young lady from one of the lower tiers stood and offered her opinion. "I believe that love and marriage are separate issues. What of the knight she favors? Is a match between them possible?"

The young man shook his head. "No, the knight she favors is from a station above hers and has been promised to another almost since birth."

Eleanor leaned over whispering to Countess Marie, "I suspect this has something to do with Anne and Raymond of Castile."

The Countess bobbed her head in agreement. She addressed the young man once again. "Sir knight, how does the lady's father feel about the situation?"

"I know not, other than he wishes her to marry well as she is the sole heir to his inheritance."

There was movement and whispering in the crowd, as many now figured out the parties involved. Anne rose to her feet. "Countess, your highness, with all due respect, I would like to address this issue." She did not wait for approval.

"As women of noble birth, we all know our purpose is to be a marriageable asset to men. By our marriages, alliances are formed, treaties are written; it is a heavy responsibility we bear."

Anne took a deep breath and continued. "As unmarried noble women, it is our lot in life to spend many hours praying to God that we will not be given in marriage to someone we revile. Alas, it is very rare to find love in marriage. I would even go so far as to say that I do not know of a marriage based on love. Love is not the purpose of marriage. Yet, a woman can be attracted to whomever she wishes. It does not mean that she will marry that individual. As to the lady in question, her most important duty is to preserve and strengthen her inheritance. Perhaps the knight who seeks her land and monies is unworthy of such a prize."

As Anne took her seat, another rumble erupted in the crowd. Raymond's face turned purple with anger. Someone gave an audible gasp as Eleanor stood. The queen always watched these proceedings with amusement but never gave advice. "I must whole-heartily concur that marriage is not love. One does not equal the other. It sounds to me as if the lady in question is perhaps a bit too much for the knight who pursues her."

Countess Marie cleared her throat. "I submit that the lady's duty is to protect that which will be entrusted to her and look to marry wisely in that regard. Love is not the issue here; duty and honor are."

The atmosphere at the evening meal buzzed. If any courtier was daft enough not to understand who the anonymous parties of the court case were, the gossips soon made it clear. Banquet was underway, but the dinner conversations remained hushed. The court scrutinized Anne, Raymond of Castile, and Richard. All three played their parts well. Anne held her head high and attended to the Queen. Raymond sulked and stabbed at his food rather than eat it. Richard acted as though nothing was amiss. He even started off the evening's dance with great grace and form. The excitement of the dance acted like a potion to help the courtiers forget the day's gossip and concentrate on the desired member of the opposite sex.

Richard had a certain loyal attendant, a troubadour name
Blondel. Tall, even wiry, Blondel carried himself with the
surpassing elegance that can only belong to an artist. Most often
Blondel tagged along in Richard's entourage. Tonight Blondel was
in comic form singing a song meant to be a duet. He took both the
man and the lady's part. In a low voiced, he crowed,

Sweet Lady, do you want a husband?

He leapt to the side, facing where he just stood. With a
flourish, he placed his hand on his heart. Then with a squeak, he
sang the lady's part.

No, for if he's not good, then I'd have no joy.
I'd rather have my chaplet then wed unhappily!

Blondel returned to the man's part, waving his eyebrows up
and down.

Sweetest Lady, I'll find you one, made just as you desire.

Grabbing his lute strung on his back, Blondel played the
chorus with fingers that flew over the strings. He finished the
verse by singing in a normal voice.

Kind, sir, then bring him to me here, down to this forest glade.
I'll be off now, but you'll find me sitting in the grassy shade.

The crowd roared in pleasure at the innuendo, and Richard
slipped out unnoticed. When Blondel finished his performance, he
sought out Lady Anne who remained rooted near the queen.
Master Blondel, as he was known, passed Anne with his great
poise and said, in a barely audible whisper, "My master, the duke,
wishes you to join him in the garden alone. He is waiting in the

spot where you first spoke."

Blondel made the request so quietly and with such discretion that at first

Anne wondered if he had spoken to her at all. She watched him take a seat in a corner, laying his lute upside down with the bridge pointed toward the garden. Eleanor startled Anne. "You are absolutely right to keep Marseilles from Raymond. He does not deserve it." She lowered her voice. "It is a lovely night for a walk in the garden, is it not?"

"Thank you, my lady. I will be brief." Anne rose and did not look back as she slid out of the great hall.

Richard waited on a bench. Sitting there in the warm summer evening air, listening to the music drift out from the castle beyond, worrying that perhaps she would not come after all, he stood up and paced. He turned his back on the castle and stared out in the garden. The wind tussled the leaves on the trees above him. Summer would be ending soon, and autumn would come. What would this new season hold? "Oh, dear Lord, let it be a good fall," Richard whispered.

"I beg your pardon, your grace?" Anne arrived.

Startled, Richard took a deep breath to regain his composure. "Good evening, Lady Anne. Thank you for coming. I wanted to speak with you."

Anne gave him her sly smile. "So you sent your troubadour to fetch me?"

"Who better than a man of words? Besides, Master Blondel and I grew up together. I can trust his discretion."

"My lord, I must know." Anne's smile faded. "Did you and Castile strike some sort of bargain?"

Richard sat down on the bench as if she pushed him back. "I am insulted. Do you think I would conduct any kind of business with that man? Why, I wouldn't strike a bargain with him regarding my dog!"

"Then, I must ask, where am I in your esteem compared to your dog?" Anne's smile returned.

"Well, that depends. How good a hunter are you?" Richard winked.

Anne let out a sigh and sat down next to Richard. "Oh, stop it. In all seriousness, today's court was completely humiliating for me."

"Castile's actions are deplorable. You, however, carried yourself quite nicely. You spoke your case with eloquence."

"I take my lessons from the best, your mother. The queen is a very wise woman, and I have a great deal of respect, even love for her." Anne glanced sideways at him.

They remained silent for a moment. Finally Richard felt brave enough to speak. "You intrigue me, Anne."

Anne knit her brow. "If this is your attempt at a compliment I am..."

Richard cut her off. "Don't play coy with me; it doesn't suit you. Anne, you are more intelligent than many of the men here at court. Tell me, where did you learn to read, speak so many languages, and the ways of diplomacy?"

Anne tensed and fidgeted with the end of her belt. "My father and my circumstance demand it of me."

Richard narrowed his eyes. "May I be frank?"

"Please do."

"Anne, the first time I saw you, I... I..." He could not find the right words, so he tried something else. "I know we have not spent a great deal of time together, but I feel as though I have always known you."

"I am sorry if I have been short with you. I am not a very trusting person," Anne explained.

"I honestly mean you no harm, nor do I wish to use you in any way."

"There is a great difference in intentionally using someone

and unintentionally using someone."

"Perhaps you could get to know me a little better. Tomorrow morning would you be agreeable to a quick ride before breakfast?" Richard asked.

"Need I bring a chaperone?"

Richard laughed. "You of all people do not need one. Heaven help the person who crosses you."

Anne stood up, gave Richard a little curtsy along with an encouraging smile, and took her leave of him.

Chapter Four

A luminous morning greeted Richard as he rose even earlier than usual, so early that when he made his way to the stables, the boys still slept soundly. Richard coughed, startling them. They scurried about trying their best to prepare Richard's horse, but sleep still clung to their fumbling hands. In exasperation, Richard took charge and saddled the horse himself. "Prepare Lady Anne's horse," he ordered.

"Yes, my lord," returned a boy with puffy eyes and bed-tousled hair.

Richard left the stable with his horse and waited in the courtyard for Anne. At last she approached from the stables leading her horse, looking as radiant as the morning in a ginger coloured riding dress.

"Good morning, Anne," Richard hailed her.

"Beautiful day for riding," Anne observed.

"That it is. Well, shall we?"

Anne grinned. "Why not? The court is already awash with rumors regarding the two of us, so I say why not… give them more fodder?"

Richard helped her onto her horse. "I like your spirit, Anne."

He mounted his own horse ready for the ride. "Let me know if I am riding too hard for you. I tend to ride too rigorously for others."

Anne gave him a mischievous look. "I doubt it shall be a problem."

She spurred her horse and launched out of the courtyard into the town that surrounded the palace. Richard followed, but it did not take him long to catch her. They rode on at an even pace, both enjoying themselves to the fullest.

Once they came to the edge of the village, they took a sharp turn to the road north.

They stayed on the road for only a short distance when Richard led them into a wood. Here they slowed the pace. The trees gave way to the riverbank where Richard stopped.

"This is one of my favourite places on the river," he told her. "Let us rest the horses here for a moment or two."

Anne nodded. Richard dismounted and helped Anne from her horse. Taking the reins from her, he led both their horses to the water.

"So, I take it you do a bit of riding." He smiled back at her from the river's edge.

"I very much enjoy the exercise it provides."

They stood in a clearing filled with deep green grass, and dotted with purple, yellow, and white wildflowers. A well-worn path led to the river. The bank was devoid of vegetation, but out in the river tall rushes sprang up and swayed in the gentle breeze.

The horses finished their drink, and Richard brought them back up on the bank. He removed the bits from their mouths, and hobbled them.

"You know, for someone whose father is a second son, you possess many qualities of a great lady." He spread his cloak down on the ground for her.

She smiled and placed herself gracefully on the cloak. Richard flopped down beside her.

"It is my father's fault, I suppose. He always insisted that I learn how to manage his estates, even more so when it became evident that I was his only heir." Anne picked a bluebottle flower nearby.

"What of your mother?" Richard questioned.

"She is dead, may God have mercy on her soul," Anne mumbled as she plucked off the purple petals of the flower in her hand,

Richard cleared his throat. "With you being from Marseilles, how is it that you came to be at my court here in Poitiers?"

"Surely the queen told you?"

"No, not really."

Anne took a deep breath then continued to slowly pick at her flower. "Well, my father and your mother met while they were both on Crusade. He was very... shall we say... impressed by your mother."

"Yes, I've heard the stories of how she dressed herself and her ladies as bare breasted warriors. That would make an impression on any man, I'm sure." Richard laughed. "So, your father sought his fortunes on Crusade?"

"As you know, he is the second son of the Duke of Northumberland."

"How is it that he came to be the Viscount of Marseilles?"

Anne shifted her legs. "Well, my father met my mother's father, the Viscount of Marseilles, in Jerusalem. My father was wounded while defending my grandsire. Grandsire nursed him and took him back to Marseilles. Some say there is a curse in my family to produce only girls, as my mother was to inherit Marseilles upon my grandsire's death. My grandsire, being the man he was, wanted Marseilles in the best of hands, so he gave his daughter in marriage to my father."

"And once again Marseilles is left to a woman," Richard observed.

"I'm afraid I am the only surviving child."

"Did your father send you here to find a suitable husband?"

Anne picked another flower and proceeded to systematically rid this one of its petals too. "No."

Richard waited for her to say more, but she remained silent. At last he spoke, "Oh, Anne, please tell me. No need to worry, I will not send you away, if that is what you are afraid of."

Anne gave another long sigh. "It is a very long story."

"I have the time."

"We shall miss breakfast."

"Not hungry."

Anne looked him over for a moment, as if trying to decide whether or not to tell him.

"Please."

She threw up her hands. "I don't know why you want to know so badly, but I shall tell you."

"My mother was much younger than my father. He was madly in love with her, but she detested him. He is a good man." Anne looked doleful.

"He has made himself quite wealthy, has he not?"

"Yes, he took advantage of the shipping market to and from the Holy Land. His business is quite extensive. He threw himself into this work, I think in part to forget my mother." Anne picked her third flower.

"My father was often away, but he made certain that I had the tutors and resources to learn all I needed to know. My mother constantly told him how she thought that this instruction a waste of time, and that I should be trained in the art of marriage instead.

"My father has a nephew from England, Etienne, who like himself is a second son. Etienne came to Marseilles and is Father's right hand in everything. Whenever Father is away, Etienne takes care of much of the business, and he also tutored me to that end. I trust him completely as does my father.

"On this last trip, my father was detained by business and

then fell ill. Too ill to travel, he was gone almost two years. My mother decided that he was dead and began to openly flaunt her lover, with whom she had been carrying on for years."

"Did your father know of this affair?" Richard raised his eyebrows.

"I think he did. Really, I do not know how he could not have known. Perhaps it was easier for him to ignore it. Anyway, her lover died in an accident at sea not far from Marseilles. Now you must understand, my mother was a very beautiful woman, and many men wanted to fill the void, so to speak. The most persistent was an abbot who obviously did not take his vows too seriously. My mother still mourned her lover and wanted nothing to do with the priest.

"Eventually, word came that my father was still alive and on his way home. The abbot made all kinds of threats to her. I do not know exactly what they were, but I am sure that he threatened to publicly expose her to my father. Perhaps it was the abbot's threats, perhaps it was the thought of having to continue life with my father, but my mother flung herself into the sea."

"She took her own life?" Richard's eyes widened

"Yes, she did. My father was delayed yet again, due to rough weather this time. In the meantime I needed answers, so I did what any Christian might do; I turned to the church for comfort. The answers I received only bewildered and haunted me with images of my mother burning in hell eternally. The same abbot who sought my mother became interested in me. I knew enough to know that his brand of repentance was not the pathway to redemption."

"He didn't?" Richard scowled.

One side of Anne's mouth went up in a crooked little grin.

"No, he found me a more difficult target than my mother. Soon I became the spawn of the devil to the church. I remained sequestered in the chateau for fear of retribution from the priests.

"Finally, my father arrived home. Traditionally the counts of Marseilles and the local priests have a rocky relationship at best. My father reminded them who truly holds the power in Marseilles. Then he wrote the queen and sent me here to serve her." Anne brushed the petals from her lap when she finished, and Richard said nothing.

Anne changed the subject. "Well, that's enough of that dreary talk. The day is too pretty to dampen with such nonsense. So, have you and Master Blondel written anything new lately?"

"I have hardly had time since I returned. I do find a certain satisfaction in poetry though."

Anne's demeanor brightened. "Perhaps you will find the time soon."

"And you, do you enjoy writing poetry?" Richard played with the petals she dropped.

"I am afraid I am not a good mistress of words." Anne shrugged.

Richard looked her straight into her hazel eyes. "I fear you do not give yourself enough credit."

"My lord..."

He interrupted her. "Richard, my name is Richard, and I would prefer you call me Richard."

"Richard then." Anne blushed. "So, do you pay this much attention to other young maids at court?"

"Only those who are beautiful." Richard looked away.

"Then it is no wonder you have little time to compose for there are so many beautiful distractions at court," Anne teased.

Her jesting made him feel bold. "Not anymore there aren't."

"Are you saying that your court is full of ugly women?"

"No, I am saying that I am only interested in one beauty."

He dared to look at her directly again.

Anne's eyes sparkled. "Oh really? Do tell me her name for I must warn her."

"Please, Anne. Do not tease me."

"I do not know how else to respond to you."

Richard sat up, picked yet another flower, and offered it to Anne. "It is easy enough; simply take a compliment when one is given you."

With a slight hesitation, Anne took the flower. She did not pick this one apart. After a moment she said, "Richard, I do enjoy your company, but there can never be anything between us."

"Alright then, Anne, why can we not be companions? Obviously there is mutual enjoyment of one another's company."

"Do you not care about the rumors that will be flying around court? They will be impossible to stop."

"Let them fly." He waved his hand in front of his face. "At the very least, it will be entertaining to see how imaginative the court can be."

"Well then, should we start back to court? We do have a full day of scandals to create." Anne winked at him.

Smiling Richard helped her to her feet. She tucked the flower into her belt while Richard gathered the horses. Once the horses were ready, he helped her back onto hers, and they rode back to court laughing and joking with one another.

When they reached the palace stables, Blondel informed Richard of some new problem the Countess desperately needed him to solve. He excused himself. Anne left her horse with the stable boys and crossed through the courtyard. She could not help but smile as she walked; the morning was pleasant. As she entered the hallway leading to the queen's bower, she found herself still thinking of the duke. In an instant she smashed against the wall. She gasped as Raymond stood nose to nose with her.

"See here, you little whore. I know what you've been out doing. Plotting against me will not work!"

"You flatter yourself, Castile. I had not one thought of you all morning."

Raymond pressed her harder against the wall. "You little scheming witch. I will not be made a fool!"

"You have no right to tell me what I can and cannot do," she shot back.

"You and Marseilles will belong to me." Raymond sneered.

"Not while I stand with a breath in my body. You will never have Marseilles!"

Raymond's face turned crimson. He raised his arm to strike her with the back of his hand.

"You do not frighten me!" Anne remained defiant.

Raymond coiled his arm further, this time to truly strike, but someone grabbed his wrist and pulled, spinning him around. It was Richard's companion, Baldwin.

"I suggest you leave the lady alone." Baldwin's manner was calm but forceful.

Several other young knights heard the ruckus and now joined Baldwin.

Again with a composed voice Baldwin warned, "Castile, now is the time to leave."

Raymond looked around and sized up the situation. Wrestling his arm free from Baldwin, he stormed off.

Baldwin turned to Anne. "Lady Anne, are you alright?"

"Yes, I think so." Anne's legs shook.

"Why don't you come with me?" Baldwin put out his arm to steady her.

Anne nodded and spoke again as if in a haze. "Yes, thank you."

Chapter Five

Word spread about the incident with Raymond, and it wasn't long before Anne's chamber flooded with visitors. Baldwin sent most away but dared not deny entrance to the Queen or Countess Marie. Anne sat on her bed as her lady, Marguerite, attended her. Eleanor swept past them all and straight to Anne.

"Anne, my dear, oh, come here. Are you alright?" She extended her arms to Anne.

Just then Richard burst through the door, and Andrew followed. "Is it true? Did he make to strike you? Did he threaten you?" Richard boomed.

"I saw it with my own eyes, my lord," Baldwin answered for Anne.

"This is an outrage! He must be banished from the court." Countess Marie stamped her foot.

Richard barked, "He should be horse whipped!"

"Castile and his entourage are preparing to leave as we speak." Andrew informed them.

"No one insults a lady in my court and is allowed to get away with it. This slander will not go unanswered," he snarled.

"No, Richard, no please! You will only provoke him more," Anne begged.

Richard shook his head. "I will not stand idly by while he insults you."

"Honestly, my reputation will heal. He has done damage to himself, to his honor."

Richard clenched his jaw. "Yes, well, my honor will not let him get away with this!"

Before Anne could say anything else, Richard stalked out of the room. Baldwin and Andrew followed in close pursuit.

In the courtyard Raymond and his men prepared to leave. Richard burst into the courtyard. "Castile!"

Upon hearing his name, Raymond spun around stirring the dust at his feet. He didn't hesitate, but drew his sword. In reaction, Richard quickly drew his. Richard lashed out at Raymond first, but Raymond skillfully deflected the blows.

By now, Andrew and Baldwin along with the Queen, Countess Marie, Master Blondel and Anne, all stood on the steps watching the brawl.

Despite Raymond's skill, Richard proved a challenging opponent for him. The two locked swords. "Such an effort is wasted on a good for nothing whore." Raymond narrowed his eyes and tilted his head.

"If she is so good for nothing, why do you pursue her?" Richard pushed hard against the swords causing Raymond to stumble backwards. "You will not have Marseilles!"

With an unsteady slash, Raymond knocked Richard's sword from his hand but lost his own in the process. Richard swung his fist at Raymond and made contact. As Raymond wiped the blood and sweat from his lip, he sneered. "I understand now. Aquitaine isn't enough for you. Your brother, Young Henry, is next in line for the throne, so you want as much land as can satisfy your greed."

Richard charged Raymond, knocking him to the ground. Raymond threw a handful of dirt in Richard's face. Frantically Richard tried to clear his eyes, but Raymond stamped hard on Richard's foot and used his shoulder to push against Richard's chest, causing him to fall to the ground. Before Richard could react, Raymond pointed his sword at Richard's chest.

"All your talk of honor... " Raymond leered. "Look here, good people of this court, at your lord and master." He yelled to the onlookers. "Yet, here lies your duke in the dirt, bested by a knight he considers lowly even though we are both princes by natural right. Where is the honor in that?" He paused. "Where is it?" Raymond screeched. "There is none!"

Baldwin and Andrew stepped between Richard and Raymond.

"I am willing to defend my most honorable lord to the death if necessary." Andrew drew his sword.

Baldwin seconded, "As will I."

Other knights of the court began to step forward.

Raymond glared at Richard. "Honor will not win you this prize."

Castile withdrew but not before turning to spit at Richard. Raymond and his entourage mounted their horses and flew out of the courtyard, almost trampling several people and animals on their way.

Baldwin helped Richard to his feet. Humiliated, Richard dared not look in the direction of Anne and the others. Anne fled inside, taking refuge.

Anne stayed in her chambers, refusing to see anyone the rest of the day and into the evening. The night air brought with it a chill, so Anne sat on the hearth warming herself by the fire. The day started off so pleasantly, but turned into a nightmare. She vacillated between worrying about Richard blaming her for his humiliation and sheer anger toward Raymond. Both lines of thought made her stomach churn.

She heard a soft knock at the door, and someone entered. Assuming it was her lady Marguerite whom she sent for some wine, Anne didn't bother to look up but stared into the fire.

"Anne." Richard's voice startled her.

Richard handed her a cup of wine. "I met your lady in the hall and took the liberty of bringing you the wine myself."

Anne took the wine from him. "Thank you, your grace."

"I take it you are not going to banquet either." Richard took a seat beside her on the hearth.

Anne shook her head. "After today's commotion, I am really in no mood."

"I must confess, neither am I. Countess Marie can take over my responsibilities, though I doubt it will be much of a merry one."

Anne set the glass of wine out of the way and took a deep breath. "I apologize for causing such an uproar today. Truly, I am sorry that you were forced into such a situation, and I would completely understand if you sent me packing."

"It is certainly not your fault that Raymond is such an ass. Your honor had to be defended." Richard shrugged.

"Well, I thank you for that." Anne fiddled with the hem of her sleeve. "How are you feeling?" slipped out.

Richard sat up taller. "I have just a few scratches, nothing that won't heal. My pride, however, may take a bit longer to recover."

"Yes, bruised dignity is a rather nasty wound from which to heal." Anne flashed her playful smile.

"How are you?" Richard questioned.

"I am fine." She paused. "Again, thank you for your kindness, my lord."

"Thank you for yours."

"But I have not done anything," Anne protested.

"Yes, you have," he answered.

Richard gently brushed some hair away from Anne's cheek. She jumped.

"Oh, I am sorry. Did I hurt you?"

"No just, you just, I just... "

Anne didn't finish because he kissed her with surprising gentleness.

Richard still held her face in his hand, studying her eyes to look for some sort of encouragement. She looked nervous, but he read nothing that told him to stop, so he tenderly kissed her again. At first she was reluctant, but then he felt her relax, seeming to melt against him.

"Richard," she whispered.

"Sh." With his forefinger he traced her jaw line from left to right, and then down her neck, brushing along the top of her collarbone studying the feel of her skin. She quivered against him, and he wanted to explore more. He had known other beautiful women before, made love to them, but Anne was different. When he kissed her again, he found that *he* was shaking. After reminding himself to breathe, he inhaled deeply taking in her spicy scent that seemed to be working a spell on him. Running his right hand up the back of her neck, his fingers wound around soft locks of her hair, and he drew her to him again, kissing her more forcefully. Again, she relented. Now he knew what he wanted, but as he began to loosen the laces on her gown, she became rigid.

Anne stood up and gave him a low curtsy. "I thank you very much for your attention this evening and the service that you rendered me earlier today. I must take my leave now."

Richard stammered. "I...I...I am a bit confused, Anne. For one thing this is your room."

"There is no confusion, your grace. I respectfully declined your offer."

"My offer? But Anne, I am in love with you."

"You hardly know me." Anne shook her head.

"Since when does that matter to love?" Richard stood up now ready to block the door if she intended to bolt on him. "I know enough to know that I want you."

"It cannot be."

"Why not?" He could still smell her, taste her on his lips.

Anne whispered, "It is wrong in the eyes of God."

"I thought you didn't necessarily agree with all the

teachings of the church," Richard argued.

"I believe in God and heaven and hell. I will not burn in hell just to satisfy your lusty desire!" Anne held her head high.

"Anne, this is how it is done. A man and a woman are attracted to one another, and they make love. It is a natural desire."

"People may do it all the time, but it is a sin."

Frustrated, Richard moaned. "What would you have me do, marry you? You know full well that I cannot!"

"Exactly! That is why we cannot be together." Anne's tone remained composed.

Richard slumped back on the hearth. Her calmness helped him regain some control. "Anne," he shrugged, "your meaning has escaped me."

"Think of it. Just as you have a duty and will marry Alice, I too have a duty to marry and produce an heir. What if I were to become pregnant?" Anne contended.

Richard placed his reeling head in his hands. "That is not a certainty," he mumbled.

"Can you assure me it will not happen? Sex is generally how babies come into being." She raised her tone of voice now. "Any child I have with you would naturally be illegitimate. It would hurt the child's claim to any inheritance. Who would marry me then? Granted my father's wealth would still be a bright asset, but I could never hope for a suitable match."

Richard pulled at his hair in frustration. "If you were any other woman, I would have taken you by now." He spoke through gritted teeth.

Anne shouted, "That would make you no better than Castile! Well, go on then! Do it and be quick about it!"

His head shot up. "Anne, you know I would never do that to you!"

Anne exclaimed, "No, I do not know that!"

Richard remained calm now. "You mistook my meaning." He spoke clearly and rationally. "What I am trying to say is that no one else would have stopped me or dared to say no. Few people question me."

"I apologize for my disrespect." Anne took a seat beside him.

"Look at me, Anne." He turned to her. "I am being completely honest when I say that I have never known anyone to captivate me so. From the moment I saw you, you were all I could think about. Ever since I met you, I have not had a decent night's sleep. All I can do is lie awake at night and think about you, how I shall be able to see you in the morning, hear your laugh, smell your fragrance, just be with you." He whispered, "You haunt me, Anne."

"Richard, please. I am not for you."

"Look into my eyes and tell me that you care nothing for me. If you can honestly tell me that, then I will never bother you again. You have my word."

Anne took his hand. "Oh, Richard, sex is so powerful. With sex, an empire can be built and crushed. Sex is a driving force behind history and legend, but sex outside the dictated confines of marriage can lead to nothing but disaster and misery. Look at Helen and Paris, or Cleopatra and Antony, even Guinevere, Lancelot, and Arthur. All those men were brilliant leaders, but they lost everything because of sex.

"Richard, you are just as talented as any of those men. You have the ability to become one of the greatest leaders the world has ever known. I will not have you throw it away for a moment or two of pleasure. I will not be the cause of your downfall. Let me help you, not hinder you."

"Nothing you could do would hurt me except denying me your affection." He pressed his forehead against hers.

"I will not deny you affection, but I will not make love to you. I do care for you." She paused again. "However, if you want nothing more to do with me, then I would understand."

"I cannot just change the way I feel." Richard shook his

head.

Anne shrugged. "Neither can I."

"Then what is to be done?"

"I do not know. I do not know."

"You are a stubborn one, Anne."

"Would you have it any other way?"

Richard tried to smile at her joke. "I think I shall take my leave."

He stood up and started for the door. Opening the door he stopped and turned back. "Despite everything you said, my feelings for you have not changed Anne."

Richard did not wait for a reply. He simply left and closed the door softly behind him.

As Richard slowly made his way down the stairs, he could hear the music and laughter floating out from the Great Hall, but he had no wish to be a part of it. Feeling as though something heavy had been placed upon his chest, he wanted to get outside where he thought it would be easier to breathe.

He stumbled out into the garden and worked his way along its paths until he came to the bench, that bench where he first spoke to her. He couldn't decide if it was a cursed place or a holy one. Sitting down upon the bench, he stared out into the night.

Chapter Six

Queen Eleanor's bower was just as lavish as the rest of the court. The walls were not like the bare stone walls of the great hall. These were lined with vividly coloured tapestries, the same tapestries Eleanor took with her whenever she traveled. No matter what castle she lodged in, these same cheery images greeted her every morning: birds, and unicorns, flowers, and fruit, ladies, and knights. Poitiers and this room were her favourite. When the tapestries hung on the walls here, both she and they were truly home.

Eleanor eyed these images as she pondered the message she received early that morning. Instinct told her that soon her tapestries would be pulled from the walls and packed away for another journey. Yesterday's events unsettled her, but with this message there were bigger problems to address. She sent for Richard.

Richard appeared with dark circles under his eyes. "You wish to see me?'

"Yes, I do. I have a great concern I wish to discuss with you." Eleanor motioned for him to take a seat.

Richard flopped down in a brightly painted red and blue chair opposite his mother. "What would that be?"

"First of all, I beseech you to let the matter with Castile drop... for now." She began.

Richard sat up straight. "But how can I? Honor must be avenged."

"Your pride is only bruised; you will recover, and there will come a time to repay Raymond of Castile. Right now there is something of more importance to which we must attend."

"Oh?" Richard raised his eyebrows.

Eleanor shifted in her seat. "A message arrived from your brother, Young Henry. As you know, he and your father," she said the latter with disdain, "have been at odds as of late."

"I thought it rather rash of Father to crown Young Henry king before he himself had passed." Richard sunk down in his chair again.

Eleanor stood and paced as she spoke. "Your father just wanted a smooth succession. He has done the same with all of you, given you titles but not let you exercise any real power. How else are you to learn to govern if you are never given the chance to do it?" She paused. "You, Richard, you are more fortunate than the others in that you have more freedom here in Aquitaine."

"So what is to be done?" Richard twisted in his seat to see her.

Eleanor stopped pacing and put her hands behind her back. "You and your brothers must take a stand against Henry, even if it means war. I did not work so long and so hard to see this realm collapse when Henry dies."

"Are you sure this has nothing to do with Rosamund De Clifford?"

Eleanor snickered. "Rosamund, your father's whore, well one of his many." Sadness shadowed in her eyes. "This one though, he's taken a different interest in her. I hear she presides over his court with him, and they live as if they were man and wife."

Richard looked down at his feet. "I have seen it myself but have never mentioned it to you."

Eleanor snapped her head up straight. "You needn't worry about sparing me. I have lived with Henry's numerous indiscretions for many years now, but that is not the issue. It seems that your eldest brother, Young Henry has been corresponding with his father-in-law, my dear old former husband King Louis of France."

"Louis the monk king? He hardly seems a fitting ally." Richard wrinkled his nose.

"Ah, but do not forget Louis has good reason to hate Henry. Henry took me, along with the majority of land in France, away from him." Eleanor licked her lips.

"Still, he is lacking in many qualities."

"You, your brothers, and I can help make up for what Louis lacks. Together we can create a power to which Henry will be forced to submit." Eleanor's eyes sparkled. "Henry has already grown suspicious of the Young King and tried to keep him close, but Young Henry escaped your father at Chinon and is now safely in Paris. You and your brother Geoffrey are also to meet Louis in Paris."

Richard stood. "I can be on the road within the hour."

"Good. I shall help you prepare." Eleanor put her hand on his shoulder.

"Mother, may I ask one thing of you?"

"What is it?" She patted her son's cheek.

"Will you watch after Anne?"

Eleanor gave him a warm maternal smile. "Yes, she shall be safe with me. I need to stay here in Poitiers, for now, but will join you in Paris as soon as I can. Anne will be with me. Besides, I hope to open some doors for her by taking her to Paris. After all, she is related to the French crown."

"Oh really, I did not know that."

"Yes, her grandmother on the father's side was the sister of King Louis' mother," Eleanor explained. "But do not worry about Anne. She will be well taken care of, I promise you."

"Right, then, I shall make ready."

Just as Richard promised, he prepared to depart for Paris within an hour. He dallied as long as he could in the castle, hoping to see Anne, but she never appeared. Maybe it was an omen that he should just forget her and throw himself completely into the task ahead. Yet he didn't want to leave like this. It might be weeks before they saw each other again in Paris. At length he knew he must leave, so he bid his mother and Countess Marie farewell then went to the courtyard.

Just as he decided to mount his horse, he took one more look back toward the castle steps. Anne's lady rushed out into the courtyard. "Your grace, please wait. I have a message for you from my mistress," Marguerite called out to him.

Richard wondered why Anne sent her lady rather than coming herself. "And what does your mistress have to say?"

"My mistress wishes you to have this. She says she hopes it will bring you luck on your journey." Marguerite handed him a red handkerchief with embroidered golden suns.

Richard took the token. "I thank your mistress, and I will be sure to keep it with me, for luck."

Marguerite added, "My mistress also wishes me to admonish you to be careful; it is a dangerous errand on which the Queen has sent you."

Richard tried to hide his smile. "Tell your mistress that my errand is not so dangerous as staying here and trying to capture her affections."

Marguerite gave Richard a dutiful curtsy and returned inside.

Chapter Seven

The weeks of separation that Richard envisioned turned into months. The Queen stayed in Poitiers to ensure the support of her vassals there while her sons went to war against their father. Anne remained with Eleanor. At length, the time came when the Queen knew she must travel to Paris.

The morning of their scheduled departure found Anne in the courtyard overseeing the trunks loaded onto a large cart. Two men grunted as they tried to lift hers. It was her father's trunk, but he gave it to her when she left Marseilles. The mere sight of it made her grin. The trunk carried a reputation. Painted white with blue geometric designs on it, the chest was large enough to serve as a coffin, and Anne's servants often referred to it as *The Reliquary of the Magdalene*. When the contents rumbled as it was being moved, they joked that those were the gardening tools that St. Mary Magdalene received from the risen Christ. Looking at the trunk now made Anne's heart ache for her father.

Just as the men finished loading it, two riders barreled into the courtyard. Before Anne got a good look at them, both bounded up the steps, and into the castle. Their haste sent a cold shiver down her spine.

Moments later Eleanor and the two men emerged from the castle. "Anne!" Eleanor waved her over. Anne walked to the queen. "The news from Paris is that my sons have met their father, but all is not going as well as we hoped. We need to get to Paris as soon as possible. Louis is not exactly a brilliant military commander."

"I feel the sooner we leave, the better." Anne added.

Eleanor grinned. "Unfortunately for Henry, my vassals resent his authority and remain loyal to me."

"I wrote my father to tell him that I will be doing some traveling in your service."

"Have you received a reply?"

"No, not yet." Anne shook her head. "There has not been time."

Eleanor took her arm. "Do not fear. All in Marseilles is well. After all, Henry is not there to muck it up. I plan to leave within the hour."

Anne raised her eyebrows. "So soon? Do you think the packing will be completed?"

"I highly doubt it," Eleanor lamented. "If we take only the absolute necessities with us, our load will be lighter, and we can travel faster. The King's troops have been spotted near here. As far as they know, I am at Poitiers and have no knowledge of their coming."

"How long until they arrive?"

"Three, maybe four hours at the most. We haven't a moment to lose." Eleanor turned to Anne. "Come, dress us. Then we must leave." She turned back to the messengers. "Make sure our horses are ready!"

Within an hour they were ready to ride. Their party included three more ladies, and four knights who served as escort. Also, a local priest drove a small cart, bumping and bustling its way along behind them carrying only the barest necessities of clothing and food.

The group started out from the castle, and as it cleared the large gate emerging into the town, Eleanor paused and looked back. She took in the sight of her beloved castle. In a quiet shaky voice, Eleanor whispered to Anne, "Of all the castles I know, Poitiers is my favourite. The *Tour Maubergeon* particularly tugs at my heart. My Grandsire, Duke William IX, built the donjon for his mistress, my grandmother, Amauberge, nicknamed *The dangerous*. Henry never, nor would he ever, build a donjon just for me. The rectangular keep is protected by four square towers that project from each of the corners." Eleanor pointed to each tower. "The four towers remind me of my four living sons. Three side with me, and the fourth, John, with his father.

"My lady?" Anne could see tears in the queen's eyes.

After a moment Eleanor sighed. "It is just that I love this place so dearly. When I return everything will have changed. Either Henry will have submitted to us, or I fear I will never see Poitiers again."

Their lead escort, a tall knight with the dark features of southern France, urged, "Your highness, we must be going."

"Yes, yes, I know." Eleanor rolled her eyes.

They rode on and left Poitiers for the uncertainty of the north and three of her sons.

The company of travelers rode hard for most of the day. Late in the afternoon, they stopped to rest in a clearing off the road. Suddenly, Master Blondel rode into the clearing.

Their escort gasped. "Master Blondel?"

"The king's troops discovered that the queen is on her way to Paris, and they are after her!"

"How far behind are they?" Eleanor gripped her reigns tighter.

"I'm afraid you haven't much time, your highness. I would only give you a couple hours' time. They are riding very hard." Blondel was still winded from his ride.

"Dammit!" Eleanor swore.

The exclamation took Blondel and the others by surprise. "My lady!"

Shaking his head, the escort offered, "There is a chateau nearby. We could seek shelter there and send word to your sons and King Louis."

Eleanor didn't hesitate. "No, that will be no good. That chateau is not easily defended, and our other forces should stay put."

"Your highness, I have an idea…" Anne started.

"Just a moment I need to think." Eleanor dismissed her.

The escort snapped at Anne, "Be quiet; the queen's got to think!"

Determined to be heard Anne raised her voice, "The king's forces are going to be looking for the queen and her ladies."

"Thank you for stating the obvious." The escort glared at her.

"What I am suggesting," Anne sounded more forceful, "is that they would not be looking for a group of young men traveling together."

The escort shot back at Anne, "Are you suggesting the queen dress herself as a man?"

"Well, yes, if it works! There will be many people on the road, and we can blend in more easily if we are disguised."

"Do you doubt our loyalty to the queen?" The escort looked like a threatened fluffed out cat.

"Oh, do shut up!" Eleanor interrupted their argument. "She is right. You are just angry because you failed to think of it first." She paused. "Alright, do we have enough clothing here to disguise ourselves as young men?"

The priest driving the cart replied, "Not really. It's just women's clothes that got packed in the cart."

Eleanor thought for a moment. "Here is what we will do then. I want Anne to come with me as well as two knights. The rest of you wait here for the caravan to catch up to you. When the rest of the company arrives, send them on the direct route to Paris. Those with me will take the back roads to Paris. You there," She motioned to the escort. "Give us your clothes. You too as well, Blondel."

"They can't very well go naked. If they were found, the king's troops would know our disguise." Anne recommended.

Eleanor nodded. "True. Well, then we certainly do have enough clothing here to make us a couple of well dressed ladies, don't we?"

"Ah! A woman! I am to dress as a woman?" Blondel protested.

"Master Blondel, remember it is in the service of your queen." Anne chided him.

With the help of the other three ladies, they quickly exchanged clothing, and within a matter of minutes, the escort turned to Master Blondel, who fidgeted in Anne's brown traveling dress. "This had better not be in any of your songs."

"I wouldn't dream of it," Blondel muttered.

Anne gave Blondel a grateful smile.

Chapter Eight

They rode harder than Anne ever rode in her life, but in the end it was not enough. Henry's troops soon overtook them. Henry's troops surrounded the little group and Henry's sergeant-at-arms bore down on Eleanor. "I arrest you in the name of King Henry."

"What on earth for?" Eleanor glared at him, doing her best to speak in a low voice.

Henry's large and sweaty sergeant-at-arms answered, "Treason, sir. You are helping the queen commit treason against our lord and ruler."

Eleanor feigned shock. "I have no idea what you are talking about. Now, we are on our way to a tournament in Chartres, and we would be most upset if we missed it."

"There is no tournament in Chartres," the sergeant-at-arms snapped.

Eleanor laughed at him. "How would you know? It seems to me that you are too busy making arrests on false pretenses to know if there is a tournament or not."

The sergeant-at-arms motioned to Anne, who had a lute strung on her back. "Come here, troubadour."

Cautiously, Anne moved her horse toward him. Without warning the sergeant-at-arms grabbed her by the scruff of the neck and yanked her cap off. Her hair tumbled down past her shoulders. "It seems to me that you are too busy inventing stories to be going to any tournament. Now, where is the queen?"

He lunged at Anne again, but in a swift move Anne produced a dagger and pierced him in the shoulder through a chink in his armor. Eleanor's company used the distraction to split in all different directions. "Follow them!" screamed the sergeant-at-arms. "Go! The woman will stay with the queen. Go after them! Go!"

All four of them rode in different directions, but Anne still kept the queen in her sights. Henry's troops pursued. One knight rode next to Eleanor and tried to grab the reins of her horse. Riding to her defence, Anne charged her horse at the knight. The knight knocked Eleanor from her horse, then turned his attention to Anne who rode hard at him. Anne put her horse between the queen and the knight. She drew a sword, unskilled with its use. With ease the knight knocked her off balance and to the ground. She remained between a dazed Eleanor and the knight. Snatching the sword from the ground, Anne swung awkwardly at the knight. He overpowered her, and soon Henry's other knights joined them.

The sergeant-at-arms rode to the scene. He pulled out the

dagger, as it had only pierced the outer layer of his hauerback under his armor. Dismounting, he approached Eleanor. "The king is very anxious to have a word or two with you."

He turned to Anne, grabbed her arm, and twisted it behind her back. "Perhaps this feisty one is up for a bit more fun."

Feeling his rancid breath on her face, Anne struggled against him. Eleanor shot forward. "No! If you hurt her, I swear I shall have your head on a pike." She stood tall and her eyes snapped. "I am still the queen, and you shall leave her alone."

The sergeant-at-arms let Anne go by giving her a hard shove to the ground. "Alright, your highness, as long as you behave until we have delivered you to the king, no harm will come to her."

Henry Curtmantle or FitzEmpress, by the grace of God, King of England, Duke of Normandy, Anjou, etc. stood on the deck of his boat in the Norman town of Caen, watching the female members of his family marched aboard as prisoners. The bitter smell of the sea wafted down the canal. Today Henry did not care for the smell; it irritated his nose.

Henry, a solid man with a barrel chest and a ruddy face, achieved more success at governing countries and provinces than governing his own family. As the women were led aboard, Henry made note of each one, his stepdaughter Countess Marie, this new one Anne Baux de Marseilles, and the crème, Eleanor, who by his grace was still alive to be the Queen of England. William the Marshal, Henry's most loyal knight and steward, brought the women to Henry.

Eleanor spoke first. "Oh, Henry, I'd say it is a pleasure to see you again, but it has been years since it was a pleasure."

"Marshal, look here. It is my long lost wife. See how she dutifully returns to the bosom of her husband." Henry rocked back and forth on his heels, enjoying the game.

"Ever so dutifully. So, Henry, tell me, what do you have planned for the weaker sex of your family? Is it to see us sacrificed on the altar of your self aggrandizement?" Eleanor mocked.

"Eleanor, it is so nice to see that you haven't changed a bit." Henry tipped his head to the side.

The king turned to Marshal. "Tell the captain it is time to set sail."

"I shall enjoy seeing England again. There are many whom I have not seen in quite a while. There is one young woman in particular, Rosamund de Clifford. I wonder how these years have been treating her." Eleanor failed to play the part of prisoner.

Grinning, Henry retorted, "Quite well, actually. Then again, how could she not be doing well? She has blossomed under the love of a king,"

Eleanor still held her head high. "It is a wonder that she has not died from your smothering nature."

Henry chose to ignore the comment and address all of the prisoners at once. "Ladies, you now find yourselves in a very precarious position. You all have been very busy of late. You would have done better to stick with your needlework. Countess Marie, your husband is waiting for you in England, and you will be obediently following him home. After meeting the fellow, I can think of no worse punishment than for you to spend the rest of your days with him."

"Next, we come to Anne Baux de Marseilles. I learnt of you only recently. Unlike the others, you, my dear, are more expendable. You would do well to remember that. For now, you will serve me and my family wherever and however I see fit."

Anne just stared at Henry.

Then Henry barked a command that made Anne jump. "Separate the women and guard them well, especially her." He pointed his stubby finger at Eleanor.

As his men led the women below deck, Henry and Marshal remained above. Marshal was an excellent soldier. In Henry,

Marshal found the father he should have had. In Marshal, Henry found the son he wished for. Marshal was fiercely loyal to Henry, and Henry trusted him wholly. Marshal's searching blue eyes lightened as he informed Henry. "My lord, news has come from the continent. It seems your sons are having second thoughts about rebellion. Taking the queen prisoner seems to have shaken their resolve."

"Good. Now they understand that if I am not afraid to lock the bitch away, then what am I not afraid to do to them? I only wish there was some way I could rid myself of the queen for once and for all." Henry stroked his beard.

"I'm afraid that would be impossible, my lord. There are too many of her vassals who are loyal to her and resent your rule," Marshal proffered.

"I do not need to be reminded of that." Henry rolled his eyes. "Then there is this whole puzzling problem of what to do with Lady Anne."

Marshal queried, "But what of her father? I hear he is very wealthy."

"Oh, yes, quite wealthy," Henry affirmed.

"Do you have your eye set on Marseilles then?"

Henry narrowed his eyes. "It is hard to say, hard to say. Marseilles would be a pretty prize, but it would be hard to defend because Marseilles would be cut off from the rest of my lands."

"Perhaps Lady Anne would be a candidate to wed one of your sons," Marshal advised.

Henry pondered aloud. "Well, Young Henry and Geoffrey are out, already married and allied. Richard is promised to Alice, and with Alice comes the Vexin. The Vexin is too important to me. It is more crucial than Marseilles. Of course there's always John. He is the only son who remained loyal to me. It would serve the others right if I declared John my sole heir and successor, something I seriously consider. Therefore, I must look to a more prudent marriage for John."

"Why not ransom Anne to her father? Certainly you could make quite a profit."

Henry leaned on the rail mulling it over. "I have heard it rumored that there is something between Richard and Lady Anne; even that while he was in Poitiers, she became his mistress. I need to know if she is a passing fancy, or if Richard really cares for her. I know all too well how a man can truly love his mistress."

"Your Rosamund, sire?"

"Yes, my Rosamund." Henry's expression softened. "Now there is a woman for whom I would do much. If Richard feels the same way about Anne as I do about Rosamund, then perhaps I can yet find some way to use her to my advantage."

Henry stood up tall and straight with the air of perfect authority. "For now, I will keep Lady Anne locked away with the queen."

Marshal added, "They should be grateful that you don't throw the key in the Channel or the Thames for that matter."

Part Two:
Henry's Will

Chapter Nine

Several of Philip's knights encountered Father Breton and Bogis outside the chapel door. Bogis silenced them with a hand gesture and Breton continued with his story.

"Henry and Eleanor— quite the match." Father Breton laughed as he stood and stretched.

Now Breton looked over as his new audience had grown from one to five. The stiff wooden chair was uncomfortable, and he needed to move.

"Well, what happened to Lady Anne?" One skinny knight complained loudly.

"Yes, when did she meet King Philip if Henry locked her away?" Bogis inquired.

Breton took his seat again and launched back into the story, "Well, King Henry returned to England triumphant over his family, for the moment. When his sons faced utter defeat, they all decided to repent and swore an oath of fidelity to their father. Naturally, Henry forgave them and welcomed them back into his good graces, as long as they behaved themselves.

"As for Eleanor, Henry locked her away in Salisbury Castle, a dreary drafty old fortress in need of much repair, closely guarded, and contact with the outside supervised.

"Henry consigned Anne to Salisbury with the queen. Her father, William, Viscount de Marseilles, wrote letter after letter to Henry. At first he offered a generous ransom, then resorted to making a plea to Henry's love as a father. Neither worked. At one point, William prepared to make a voyage to meet with Henry. To this, Henry finally replied that he, "could not guarantee the safe conduct of the viscount's personage through treacherous lands."

"Unfortunately, William lacked the military resources to threaten Henry, and his failing health prevented him from traveling. William continued to write and plead with Henry. He wrote constantly to Anne, but Henry kept the letters from her."

Breton paused for effect, and continued. "You must understand, Henry had a purpose in keeping Anne. At first he neglected to tell Richard about Anne. He concealed himself behind a curtain as Marshal let the information *slip* to Richard. Over the next few days, Henry observed how Richard grew sullen and pale. Finally the moment came when Richard begged for Anne's freedom, as he knew better than to ask for his mother's release. Henry promised to release her when he was convinced of Richard's loyalty. Richard acquiesced to Henry, but the months turned into years.

"During this time, Richard perfected his skill in war. As many of you are aware," Breton eyed Bogis. "He practiced on rebellious vassals. Any vassal foolish enough to go against Richard soon found himself on the losing end of battle. His reputation for fierceness and skill in battle grew.

"Anne remained imprisoned, and even on those rare occasions when Henry dragged Eleanor out for court or to fulfill some purpose of Henry's, Anne remained behind. One winter, Anne and Eleanor even shared a bed just to keep from freezing. Gradually, as Eleanor's sons' behavior improved so did Eleanor's provisions- food, heat, and clothing, for her household."

Several years passed like this, running one into another. Then as Christmas time came once again, Henry discovered he needed to prove to his vassals his power, and the power of his family as well. To put on a show of unification for all of Normandy, he summoned the family to Caen.

Impulsive Young Henry came to court, bringing his beautiful wife, Margaret. Henry and Eleanor's daughter Matilda and her husband, the Duke of Saxony, a large man, also attended.

Next, Geoffrey arrived with his wife, the Duchess of

Brittany, a handsome couple to look at, both tall and fair featured. John and Richard came, as well as the French Princess Alice, Richard's fiancé. Alice had been living all the while in Henry's court, and grown into a beautiful young woman with blonde hair and blue eyes. She replaced Rosamond in Henry's affections.

Away from the prying eyes of the Norman nobles, the family gathered in the solar. Even in this little room lined with tapestries depicting a hunt, dressed up with swags of holly and ivy in celebration of the season, a fire roared away in the grate, to provide warmth on such a cold occasion.

"Welcome, welcome to Christmas court!" Henry entered the room arms outstretched in warm greeting.

John, the youngest of the brood and exceptionally skilled at manipulating his father, piped up, "The whole family is to be here, isn't that right father? Well, the whole family less the girls who are married off."

Richard mumbled, "Not the entire family."

Standing close by, Young Henry overheard Richard. "Didn't father tell you *she's* coming?"

"The queen is coming to Caen?" Richard tilted his head to one side as John smirked at him. "When is the Queen to arrive?"

"Soon enough, believe you me, soon enough!" Henry rolled his eyes.

Richard sulked off to a corner, and Geoffrey followed him. Richard grumped to his brother. "If you ask me, it is just a ruse. All the nobles of Normandy are to be here, so we must show them our family solidarity."

"Sh, the old man will hear you," Geoffrey warned. He paused for a moment and then moved on to gossip. "My how the family has grown."

Richard watched as John laughed a little too loudly at a joke Henry made. John wasn't dressed in his usual slovenly manner, and Richard guessed that Henry had something to do with that. It would not do for Eleanor to have any of her sons put together haphazardly. He turned back to Geoffrey. "Yes, this is the first time I have met Matilda's husband, the Duke of Saxony."

"It would seem that he and our sister Matilda have been upsetting their overlord, the Holy Roman Emperor, so they fled here to Daddy's protection," Geoffrey mocked.

Richard shrugged. "Saxony is a powerful man himself. I trust he will soon reverse his fortunes."

Geoffrey continued his criticism of family members. "Then there is *the heir*, Young Henry. He has brought his whore of a wife with him— probably doesn't want to let her out of his sight. It is funny really. She is the half sister of your Princess Alice, and their father was such a monk; yet, they are quite the little pair of colourful women."

The Duchess of Brittany joined them. Geoffrey continued, "I assume you remember my wife, Constance, the Duchess of Brittany?"

Richard nodded. "So, what about the rumors of Young Henry's wife and William the Marshal?"

The Countess of Brittany interjected, "Oh, who knows for certain. But Marshal and Young Henry were thick as thieves, then parted company very suddenly. I doubt Marshal would act upon any desires he had. If he was not so damn good with the sword, he would make an excellent monk. Who can say for Margaret? She is young, attractive, and Young Henry hardly throws a look her way. Alice, on the other hand, would not make a good nun. Her list of lovers is a short but rather lofty one."

Richard glared at her. "Whatever do you mean?"

Constance batted her blues eyes at him. "Your father, my lord. She is your father's lover."

"Yes, it would seem the old man has replaced Rosamond since her death." Geoffrey's smile twisted to one side.

"Do you mean to tell me that Alice and Henry?" Richard scratched his chin. "Huh? What the devil is that man up to now?"

From the centre of the room, Henry clapped his hands,

commanding everyone's attention. "I have just been informed that the queen and her entourage are here. Let us make them welcome."

Dutifully the family followed him to the courtyard.

When Eleanor and her convoy entered the courtyard, servants buzzed around her. Henry approached her without hesitation, but the children stood off to the side watching.

The years in prison failed to dull her beauty or her spirit, and Eleanor greeted Henry first. "Henry! How pleasant it is to see you!"

"Do not pretend with me, old woman. It is pleasant to see Normandy again, and I am just a means to an end." Henry sparred with her.

She smiled widely at him. "You give yourself too much credit."

Henry extended his arm to her and Eleanor took it. "So tell me, was the crossing rough and hard?"

"Yes, just the way you like it."

"And so it begins." Geoffrey murmured.

Eleanor caught sight of the children. "My children are here! Now, that is pleasant."

"Something tells me that we fall below Normandy in the pleasant category," John grumbled.

A lady approached Eleanor placing another cloak over her shoulders— Anne. She glanced up for only a moment while performing her task, spotted Richard, and turned away giving directions to the servants unloading the cart.

Richard stepped forward, but Eleanor cut him off. "Richard, I am glad to see you in good health."

In an instant, John darted to his mother's side. "Mother, I am so glad to see you."

Eleanor patted his head. "I have no doubt of that." She turned to Henry. "Well, are we ready to eat? Traveling always makes me hungry."

"Give us a promise that you won't eat your young, and we

shall go into dinner." Henry taunted her.

"Give me an enticing alternative, and I shall not need to devour our young."

The royal couple entered the castle, as their children followed.

Chapter Ten

Henry meant to make an impression on the Norman nobles, and the feast's lavish menu was one way to accomplish that. He slipped away to check progress for himself, knowing that like in war, nothing encouraged men like the gaze of their master.

Down below the exchequer hall, the spacious kitchens roared like a vision of hell. Open, blazing fires, caused blistering heat, in which cooks worked like stout demons, sleeves rolled up, sweating and cursing. Under their orders little boys toiled, turning the giant spits. Gently roasting, whole deers and boars rotated, illumined by the flames, their basted meat glazing, tormenting the noses of boys and dogs alike with their savory smell. Kitchen hands and robust scullery maids hurried to and fro. Heaps of still rose-silver glittering trout, and snake-like black-coiled eel awaited gutting and cleaning. Baskets were piled high with braided sweet bread and dark loaves of the grainy variety. In the back, men with a dusting of snow on their hoods delivered rabbits, pheasants and ducks at the kitchen doors. Feathers blew in the air like snowflakes around the woman plucking chickens. Once Henry examined the most impressive item on the menu, peacock, he felt satisfied that all would be just as he ordered.

When it came time for the feast, the exchequer hall brimmed with people, as more than a thousand knights attended. So many tables were set up to accommodate them all that the serving boys found it hard to squeeze between them.

Amidst the merrymaking, Richard sat next to Constance, the Duchess of Brittany. After noticing Richard's empty trencher and that he seemed just to be passing the food by, she took the liberty of piling it high on his plate for him. Still, he did not touch the food, only sipped at his glass of wine and stared toward the head table.

Seated there were naturally the king and queen, as well as Young Henry, and his wife. Despite being of noble birth, Anne was not seated amongst the other nobles. Instead, she attended the queen. Richard did not know if this was Henry's doing or Anne's devotion to Eleanor. He wondered at Henry's motives for allowing Anne to come to court. Geoffrey gloated that while Anne was at Caen, she was to sleep on the dirty straw with the other servants, another show of Henry's power. Somehow though, Eleanor convinced Henry to let Anne sleep in her room with her, but still on the floor on a pallet of straw.

"Why, you've hardly touched your food, my lord." Constance tried to get his attention. "Do not tell me that the prospect of spending the season with the family ruined your appetite."

"Hum." Richard did not look at her, but kept watching the head table.

He studied Anne. Her face had changed making her look older and wiser, especially around her hazel eyes. They seemed sharper and to cautiously take in everything around her. The flames from the fire, candles, or torches occasionally sparked the red glow in her hair.

"My lord, your food." Constance urged him.

"No. I apologize. I find I am not really hungry." Richard pushed the plate away.

The queen sent Anne out of the hall on some sort of errand. Eleanor gave a discreet nod in Richard's direction, and he turned to Constance. "I beg your pardon, please excuse me."

He did not wait for an answer but left the hall, crossed the yard, and headed for the donjon after Anne.

Returning from her errand carrying a blue blanket for the

queen, Anne ignored the others coming and going from the exchequer hall. "My lady."

At the sound of Richard's voice she stopped. "Lord Richard!"

"Lady Anne, I have something for you."

Her hazel eyes were wide. "For me?"

"Yes, and we haven't much time. Quickly, come with me."

Richard led her away from the main traffic around to the side of the exchequer hall. The light from the hallway windows illuminated the cold, dark night enough to see their breath floating in the biting air.

"Here." He handed Anne a bundle of letters.

"What is this?"

"These are letters from your father to Henry," Richard explained. "I liberated them from him earlier this evening."

Tenderly, Anne took them in her hands. Her eyes filled with tears. "From my father?" she whispered.

"Yes, and not all of them are to Henry; some are written to you. Henry intercepted them and withheld them from you."

"But why would you do this?" Anne pulled her cloak more tightly around her to fend off the chill.

Richard tried to smile at her. "The queen told me how much you miss your father."

"I do not know what to say." Anne's voice faltered.

"I am afraid I cannot let you keep them. Henry would be furious. The queen will meet you back in her chambers in about an hour's time. I arranged for her to return the letters back to Henry's room."

Anne did not make a move; she just stared at the letters in

her hand. "Hurry, go read as many of them as you can." Richard prodded her.

Anne started off, but stopped and turned around. "Thank you, my lord."

"It is still Richard."

"Then thank you, Richard."

"Go!"

About an hour later as Richard made his way to his mother's chamber. Eleanor burst out of the room clutching the bundle of letters. "I am to meet with Henry. I must hurry and arrive at his chamber before he does if I am to replace the letters." She dashed past Richard.

After the queen left the hallway, Richard paused for a moment outside the door to her chamber. He knew Anne was inside, and he wanted to speak with her. Summoning his courage he opened the door.

Anne sat by the fireplace staring into the light, but jumped up when the door opened. Recognizing Richard, she put her hand over her heart. "The queen, is she alright?"

"I believe so. I just came from the banquet, and Henry was still there. She should have no trouble returning the letters." Richard did not invite himself to sit down, remaining apart from Anne.

"Thank God for that." Anne relaxed her stance. "I would not want any of you to get in trouble on my account. However, I do wish to thank you for your kindness."

"I am sorry the time was so short. Were you able to read many of them?" Richard inched a littler closer.

Anne teared up again. "Yes. So many years worth of letters in a short hour."

"Perhaps I could get a letter through to your father for you." Richard shrugged.

Anne blurted out, "I hate him."

"Your father?"

She wiped her eyes. "No, yours. He is cruel, heartless, maniacal, devious..."

Richard interrupted her. "He plays to his strengths."

Richard studied her face by the firelight and again noted how she had grown older but not old. Soft lines on her face captured shadows from the snapping fire.

"My father is ill. He needs me at home. Still, Henry keeps me locked away in prison with the queen." She gestured to the room around them. "What good am I to him? I do not see what possible use the king could have for me."

"Perhaps the king wants something from your father."

Anne shook her head. "My father offered Henry a ransom that is beyond generous, yet Henry still denies my freedom and refuses to list any demands to my father."

"Anne, I am so sorry."

She snapped back at him, "Yes, well, you are not the only one."

"I ..." Richard started.

For the first time since meeting again, Anne looked Richard in the eyes. "I do not wish to be rude, but I would really like to be alone right now."

Richard took a step back. "If that is your wish."

"It is."

"Then I shall take my leave." Richard left before Anne could respond.

In his chamber, Richard removed his gray tunic and plunged his hands into the frigid water. Concentrating on the sting of the cold, he stood over the basin letting the water drip down his face. Two days ago, Anne reentered his life when she appeared in the courtyard. Two days ago, he stole the letters, and she read them. That was the last time she spoke to him. He saw her here and there flittering around, but she refused to even look at him. He never expected to see her here at Caen, and the jolt he felt was at once both invigorating and depressing.

Looking around his room, he spied his favourite bright blue tunic clean laid out on his bed. This was a pitiful, small chamber, and its cramped space made him miss Poitiers. Perhaps he should just leave Christmas Court and go south. Of course, Henry would be livid because it wasn't his idea. Henry might even try to seek retribution through Anne, but what did that matter? It wasn't as if Anne cared for him anymore. Still, he couldn't seem to warm to the idea of her paying for his wrongs.

A frantic rapping at the door interrupted his thoughts. Irritated, he snatch up his tunic and pulled it on while calling out, "God's legs! I'm coming!"

The knocking didn't cease, only increased. Determined to give whoever was on the other side a solid tongue-lashing, he threw open the door. "What in the name of…" He stopped short because Anne stood in his doorway. "Anne?" He whispered.

Without warning she flew into his arms throwing her own around his neck. Using his toe, he managed to shut the door while at the same time pulling her farther into the room. She kissed his cheek then his lips. Richard wrapped his arms around her waist and pulled her closer. Despite his grip, she managed to step backward until her head softly thumped against the tapestry hanging from the wall. "Are you alright?" Richard reached out and brushed some stray hair from her eyes.

Anne gave a slight nod, but did not speak. Now Richard noticed her hair looked disheveled, and not from bumping against a tapestry or wall. In addition, the shoulder seam of her dress was split open at the top, green thread poking out in awkward directions.

Before he could inquire, Anne put her arms around his neck, placing her hands firmly in his hair. She kissed him again and gathered locks of his hair between her fingers. Richard bent down and buried his nose in the crook of her neck. As he inhaled, he felt her tremble against him.

Grasping her waist, he slid his hands up her torso. His right thumb brushed the side of her breast. To his surprise, she took his right hand and cupped it over her breast. Countless times, he dreamt of this, her here in his arms like this. He moved to kiss her again, but something wet landed on his nose. Drawing back, he noticed silent tears rolling down her cheeks, dripping from her chin. He took a step back. "Anne, what is it?"

Anne shook her head but couldn't seem to speak. She made to grab his hand again, but he caught hers. "Anne?"

Looking away she whispered, "I thought this is what you want."

"Yes, it is what I want. I would be daft not to, but obviously, it is not what you want."

"How would you know what I want?" She snapped her head around to face him.

Her hazel eyes, narrow and accusing, brought his frustration flooding back. "You have changed. Prison made you cold."

"Here I thought it was just the weather."

"You are not the person I once knew." Richard pointed at her.

"Neither are you."

"Well, it has been years."

"Exactly!" She glared at him. "It has been years with no word from you, not a sign."

"What would you have had me do, rescue you?" He threw an arm out in the direction of the fireplace narrowly missing a burning taper on the table.

She shouted, "Yes!" Then she lowered her voice, "I mean no. I mean at first it was hard, very hard. For a long time I kept the hope alive that if you truly cared for me, as you said you did, you would come for me."

"There was no way I could have come."

"I know; I am not a simpleton. It was just a youthful fantasy. It was unfair of me to expect it of you." Anne huffed.

"Anne, if there had been any possible way, you know I would have come for you," Richard hung his head.

Anne waved her hand to dismiss it. "Poitiers was such a long time ago. Sometimes it seems as if it were a different lifetime. We were very young then. I would not, I cannot blame you for placing your affections elsewhere."

Richard threw his hands up and groaned. "You are acting like such a... a... woman!"

"Well, thank God for that! I am a woman! Or perhaps you have forgotten," Anne snapped.

Richard shouted back at her. "Believe me, I have not forgotten. Do you think these years have been easy for me? I may not have been locked up, but I have been a prisoner just the same. At first, I tried so hard to forget you."

"Do not make any sacrifices on my account." Anne pouted.

"God's leg, Anne!"

She put her hands on her hips and took in a long deep breath. When she spoke she whispered, "Please, Richard, please. If you ever cared for me, even had the slightest friendly thought toward me, you will do this for me."

"Do what?" He folded his arms.

Anne stamped her foot. "Alright then! Sorry I bothered you. I am certain your brother will be happy to oblige." She turned to storm from the room.

Richard caught her by the arm. "What do you mean my brother will oblige? Which one? Anne, how did your dress get ripped, your hair mussed up, and why the hell are you crying?"

"You do not understand."

"Damn right. You are not making any sense."

"I did not come in here to argue."

"Obviously!"

Keeping a grip on her arm, with his free hands, Richard

reached around to the table behind him. He snatched the item, and in an instant held it before her face, the soft red and gold embroidered kerchief spilling from between his fingers. "Do you remember this?"

Anne gasped. "You still have it?"

"Yes, I still have it." He let it filter through his fingers and float down.

Anne caught it in her hands, but sank to the ground as if it were a weight she held. "After all these years?"

Richard shrugged. "Call it God, call it Fate, or Aphrodite, or even a curse if you will, but I do love you."

Anne buried her head in her knees. Richard crouched down in front of her and put his head up against hers. "I am sorry." Her voice was barely audible.

"Why?"

She lifted her head. "I just thought…" Staring past his left shoulder, she wiped her eyes with the back of her hand. "I just encountered John in the hall. He's a foul thing."

Richard chortled and sat down next to her. "You are being generous."

"Well, he was stalking virgin prey– tore my dress."

Richard's face flushed and he clenched his fist as he sprang to his feet. "I'll kill him myself!"

"No!" Anne grabbed his arm. "Please, I don't want to be alone right now."

Richard stared down at her. The wrenching anger in his gut told him to dart from the room and teach John a lesson he would not soon forget, but her eyes, pleading and wide, kept him rooted to the spot. At last he composed himself to speak. "So, you came here to…" She nodded. " I see. If you take away the prize, there will be no quest." He cupped her face in his hands. "Not like this, Anne. Not like this."

Chapter Eleven

Henry sat in his chamber warming himself by the fire, his mind racing over ways to reign in Richard. Lady Anne certainly held interesting prospects. Without warning, Young Henry burst into the room. "Father, a word please."

Henry snapped, "Well, what is it? I am busy building an empire or tearing it to pieces whatever your opinion may be."

"It has come to my attention that you and Mother were discussing giving some of Aquitaine to John." Young Henry grabbed up a candlestick.

Henry slammed his hands on the armrests of his chair. "Do people in this court not know of secret negotiations? Perhaps someone should educate them on the meaning of the word secret!"

The candlestick crashed down on the small table. "It isn't right, Father!"

"Yes, yes, I know. One can hardly take a piss without it being voiced abroad." Henry rolled his eyes.

"That is not what I am talking about, and you know it. I don't understand why you would want to give Aquitaine to John. There is no chance he would be able to take care of it properly. For heaven's sake, that is the richest land in the realm! You cannot give the Aquitaine to John." Young Henry turned on his father.

"And why not? Besides, what does that have to do with you? It is Richard's not yours."

"Think about how much work you put into having me crowned. I understand this was to insure a smooth transition, but really, it means nothing because you refuse to let me have any real power." The prince swallowed loudly and continued, "Richard and Geoffrey have their lands and titles, your daughters are married all over God's green earth, yet here *I* sit and wait."

"Need I remind you that you will be king when I am gone?" Henry's face flushed a brighter red.

"Of what, that dismal dark island? Who is to say that when you are gone my brothers will not rise up in rebellion against me and take England from me too?"

"Then pray tell, what is your solution?"

Young Henry lowered the volume of his voice, but his tone remained earnest. "Make them swear an oath of loyalty to me." He jammed his finger into his own chest for emphasis. "Make me their overlord."

"Ha! Now that would be a bold move." The king laughed.

"Indeed!" Young Henry's grey blue eyes were flaming, yet the king continued to laugh. "Father I am serious! This must be done," Young Henry entreated.

Henry shook his head. "I really do not see how it could be done."

The volume of Young Henry's voice rose again as he continued arguing his case. "Think of this then; it is pointless to persist in the naive belief that I will be king of anything. It is a fruitless struggle. Why, I might as well take up the cross and spend my days on crusade." He turned as if to leave the room. "Yes! That is exactly what I'll do, I shall take up the cross!"

"Do not be stupid. You would not dare. There is too great of risk of you being killed, or your pretty face maimed. It is not in your nature." Henry crossed his arms.

The son did not flinch. "A little price to pay for freedom. At least I would go to heaven being absolved of my sins on the Lord's errand."

Henry pointed a shaking finger at his son's face. "You forget young man just how powerful and persuasive I can be. My sphere of influence is very wide. I can see to it that no clergy will ever give you the cross."

"Very well." Young Henry backed away from his father. "Then you leave me no other choice. I shall kill myself and end this misery."

"You just spoke of heaven. Are you not afraid of hell?"

Henry laughed.

Young Henry yelled, "No! It shall be a welcome relief from this life. At worst, I would be trading one hell for another!"

"Oh, please!" Henry threw him a blasé look as he walked back to his chair.

"I'll do it. I am just as stubborn as you. I will do it, I tell you, and you will mourn me to your grave."

"Alright then, prove it. Here is my dagger, son. If you have the gumption, go ahead and do it." Henry unsheathed his dagger and dropped it on a table. "Well, what are you waiting for?"

Young Henry grabbed a large chair throwing it in Henry's direction. It flew, tumbling across the room.

Young Henry's eyes filled with tears of rage. He looked directly into his father's eyes and blinked one single large tear loose. It slid down his cheek. "Father," he choked. At that, the tears poured from the prince's eyes.

Henry's softened at the sight of his son's tears, but said nothing. Young Henry sank down onto the floor in a heap. "Father, this is not a life worth living." He looked up directly at his father again, and with trembling lip whined, "I no longer wish to live."

Henry felt a guilty pang for breaking his son. Kneeling beside him he stroked his son's golden hair as if soothing a baby. "Please understand that I am doing all of this for you. I work so hard to keep this empire together so that you will inherit the crown and thus be happy."

"I want to be happy, really I do," sobbed Young Henry.

Henry gave a long sigh. "I understand, and I will find a way to make it happen. Just remain calm and give me time to work. There, there, you've had a trying time. Go, gather yourself and leave it all to your father. I will... I will fix it. Go, my son."

Young Henry got to his feet, and moved toward the door. With a little sniff, he exited the room.

Alone, Henry spoke to himself, "Geoffrey will be easily persuaded; I can pressure him to it. Richard however, needs more persuasion."

A few minutes later, Eleanor and Matilda enjoyed some music as Anne played the lute. The women gathered in the solar for a pleasant moment away from the stress of the court below, and a lull in the incessant political battle that overshadowed them all. Unannounced, Henry entered the chamber. Matilda and Anne stood and dutifully curtsied.

"Good afternoon, Ladies and Eleanor." Henry greeted them.

"Henry, to what do we owe this um..." Eleanor coughed, "honor."

Henry put his arms behind his back and rocked back and forth on his heels. "Actually, I came to ask Lady Anne to accompany me on a walk."

Anne nearly dropped the instrument. Eleanor gave him a sardonic smile. "Would not Alice be better company for you?"

Henry protested, "Oh come now. The lady has been locked up in prison and not able to leave the castle walls. I simply thought a walk might do her some good."

While Anne looked at Eleanor in confusion, Eleanor glared at Henry. He chose to ignore her and instead address Anne directly. "Lady Anne, kindly accompany me on this beautiful afternoon for a walk."

"Yes, sire." Anne obeyed.

Chapter Twelve

Anne followed Henry outside where he extended his arm to her. She took it without trepidation. As he led her through the snow covered maze of castle gardens, the frosty December air filled their lungs, and their breath showed. Both wrapped themselves in fur-lined cloaks to protect against the cold. At length, he spoke to her. "Ah yes, Lady Anne, *the* Lady Anne. I thank you for tearing yourself away from the queen. I am glad to have this chance to talk with you. We have not spoken since that day on the ship to England."

Anne cleared her throat. "I beg your pardon, sire, but I believe you did the speaking on that day."

Her reproach made Henry smile. "Well, today you shall speak. I would very much like to hear from you on certain matters."

"I doubt that my humble thoughts can be up to your standards, my lord."

"I know they can, and that is why I shall come right to the point. I brought you out here with me to discuss my son, Richard."

Anne shook her head. "Please, I beg your pardon once more. I cannot tell you much of Richard. It has been a long time."

"Now, Anne, I have heard all about your *romance* in Poitiers." He said "romance" with a flourish.

"Once again I submit that was years ago."

"Yes, but I saw the way you look at one another now. I noted how he flushed upon the first sight of you again, and do not think that I failed to notice how you trembled when he approached."

"Perhaps I trembled; I cannot remember. Maybe it was the cold." Anne shrugged.

"Yes, my dear, you trembled, and you cannot blame the cold. Lady Anne, you are a very clever woman. In many ways you remind me of the queen."

"I take that as a compliment, sire."

"Well, having said that, I know that you understand there can never be a match between you and my son."

"My lord, I have no pretensions... "

"Yes, yes, I am fully aware of what you have told the queen." He stopped walking and looked her straight in the eye. "I have discovered your strategy, my dear."

Anne smiled. "My strategy? You make it sound as if we are at war."

"You are a beautiful woman, one that any man in his right mind would want to bed." Henry winked.

Anne added, "And a wealthy one. Do not forget my wealth."

"Lady Anne, your weapon is sex. Oh, do not look so shocked. I know your plan. You realize that once you give yourself to Richard the excitement and the mystery of the hunt will be gone. You will lose him. So, you use your denial of sex to keep him interested. Every so often, you show a hint, a glimmer of hope, dangle yourself in front of him like a toy, in order to keep his attentions." Henry nodded his head in triumph.

Without hesitation Anne laughed. "I was not aware of this plan, my lord. It is a risky plan at best, is it not? That is to say, without sex how am I to make the relationship a fulfiling one? Eventually he will tire of the game and look elsewhere."

"Do not tell me that you underestimate my son's love of the hunt."

"May I tell you something in confidence?" She squeezed his arm and drew closer to him.

"Please do."

"I will not deny that I have a great deal of affection for your son." She spoke in a mock whisper. "Indeed it is my greatest fear that he will tire of the game, as you call it; that he will became bored with me and seek another."

"Then why not just make love to the man?" Henry thundered.

Anne kept her voice quiet. "It is because I love him that I will not. I *cannot.*"

"Let me reiterate. You can never hope to marry him. I do not care if you are his mistress, but I will not have you do anything to ruin or prevent his marriage. You are of a lesser station in life than he." Henry waved his finger at her.

"Oh, I am willing to forgive his station," Anne grinned at him.

Henry chortled.

Anne continued, "You see, my lord, I am to inherit Marseilles and, above all else, must come duty and honor. I must, and will always, put Marseilles before any other desires. Now, I believe there is something I can tell you about Richard after all. Richard is also very concerned with duty and honor, even above me."

"And what if I were to say that Richard is freed from his obligation to Alice? Would you marry him then?" Henry queried.

"No, I would not." She nodded with determination. "It would be an unwise match for your realm, and therefore, it would be an unwise match for Richard. Besides, if I may be so bold, I do believe that as long as you hold Richard to his contract for Alice, you have an excuse to keep her close to you. I too am a keen observer of people, my lord. You are in love with the Princess Alice."

Henry laughed. "I may be an old man, but I am not dead yet." He patted Anne on the cheek and continued. "Well, Lady Anne, we have confessed our secrets. What now?"

Anne turned to look Henry in the face without fear and with sheer honesty. "Your highness, you have kept me prisoner for all these years, and I do not know to what end. I, however, have been completely forthright with you. Therefore, you should know that I mean no deception in what I am about to say. I do not pursue a marriage with Richard, nor will I ever do anything to prevent his marriage to another. I have duties of my own to fulfil. If at any time my relationship with Richard is interfering with him doing the duties bestowed on him by God, and yourself, then I shall end it. I solemnly promise you this."

Henry regarded her for a moment then replied, "For your part, I do believe you will keep your promise. You are just stubborn enough to do whatever it takes. Now I know that, I cannot release you. I must keep you close, my lady, because in doing so I will keep Richard close."

They rounded a corner and headed back in the direction of the keep. "May I at least send some correspondence to my father?" It sounded more like a request than plea.

"He would like to hear from you." Henry nodded. "I have been corresponding with him these many years now. Something tells me you know that though."

"Yes, I do. Your court can be very small."

"Yes, then you must know about the letters from a Raymond of Castile."

"No, I did not. Pray, is he still prowling about?" Anne shuddered.

"Oh yes, and he offered all sorts of outrageous rewards in exchange for you. I hear from that pain in the ass at least once a month. He even came to court a couple of years ago." Henry wrinkled his nose.

Anne shook her head. "You would think that by now he would have found some other rich woman to marry."

"You would think, but apparently not." Henry furrowed his brow. "He does not seem to have much help from his brother, King Alfonso. I believe his brother thinks Raymond is as worthless as I do."

In the distance, they could see Marshal hurrying toward them, his cloak billowing out behind him, his hand gripping the pommel of his sword. Everything about him spoke of urgency.

"Ah, here comes Marshal. I must see what disaster has befallen our happy season. Good day, Lady Anne. I shall see you later this evening, perhaps." Henry kissed her hand and left her.

The afternoon sun sank low now, but Henry still schemed. Outside, he spoke with Marshal about how Geoffrey's wife and Young Henry's wife screamed insults at one another, while the queen looked on very much amused. Henry instructed that the two women be separated and he would deal with each one. Marshal ran off to complete this unhappy task, at sword point if necessary.

Henry blustered into the castle bellowing, "Richard! Richard! Someone fetch my son!"

A young page scurried down the hallway and out of sight. Henry marched back to his chambers. He tossed his gloves, cloak, and hat onto the bed, and cleared the room of everyone. Then, he took a seat in a large chair, shifting a little, and once again until satisfied he had struck just the right pose. Presently a knock came, and Richard entered the room.

"You sent for me, sire?" Richard gave a curt bow.

Henry waved off the bow. "Cease with the formalities; I am, after all, your beloved father."

Richard remained stone faced. "Is something the matter?"

Henry gave his son a charming smile. "No, quite the contrary. I have reached a conclusion as to what is to be done with Lady Anne."

"I see."

"After much thought, I have decided she will be released into your custody."

Richard shook his head in disbelief. "My custody? Why? What is your purpose?"

"Now, that is painful." Henry bristled. "I simply wanted to reward you for your good behavior these past years. You have proved your loyalty." Henry pouted. "I thought you would like my gift."

After a quiet moment, Richard replied, "I am not sure what to say."

"Express your gratitude, then bear your news to the lady. I will go face the queen and inform her of my decision," Henry instructed Richard.

Richard warned, "The queen will not like it."

"She will get used to the idea," Henry sniped. "Now, go to the lady. I must be off to the queen before she hears it from someone else."

With apprehension, Richard left the room.

Within moments Richard sped into the queen's chamber. He found Anne there in the process of folding a blanket for the bed.

"Anne!"

"Why, Richard, where have you been? I had an interesting conversation with the king." Anne placed the woolen blanket down on the bed.

"You must pack your things and hurry." He picked up her cloak from a chair.

"I do not understand."

"Please, pack your things, and be quick about it."

Anne reached to take the cloak from him, but he grabbed both of her wrists.

"Anne, the king has given you to my custody, but I do not trust him. He is plotting something; I can tell. I have got to get you out of here and safely to Poitiers before he has a chance to go back on his word."

"But what of the queen? I do not want to leave the queen," Anne stammered.

Richard released her. "She will understand. I know she would want you to take this opportunity." Anne just stood astounded. "Please, Anne, just do as I say; trust me."

As his words sank in, Anne grew animated until finally she flew around the room gathering her few items of clothing and other possessions, tossing them into her trunk. "I will leave anything behind that I can spare."

"Baldwin and Andrew will accompany you and keep you safe. The courtyard is full with knights preparing to leave, and you can slip away unnoticed. Be prepared to ride hard to Poitiers. You don't mind that, do you?"

"Oh, no."

"I will join you as soon as is possible."

She wheeled around. "But, Richard, is it dangerous for you to stay?"

"I promise to be extremely cautious and leave at the first glimmer of trouble." Richard squeezed her hand. "Be careful yourself and stay close to Andrew and Baldwin.
You know I trust them completely. Now, I must go tell them to prepare, and make sure Henry is distracted so that you may slip away unnoticed."

"I guess I shall see you in Poitiers then?" Anne wrinkled her brow.

"Yes, soon. Goodbye, Anne." He pressed his forehead against hers. "Be safe, and I shall see you very soon." He gave her a departing kiss and rushed from the room.

Chapter Thirteen

That night Henry called all his sons together for a meeting in his chambers. Obediently, they all came: Richard, John, Young Henry, and Geoffrey. As hot flames licked at the large logs in the fireplace, Henry informed them, "Now that we are coming to the close of the season, we have yet more family business to conduct. It would seem that a formality has been overlooked."

Sitting at his father's feet, John piped up, "What would that be father?"

Henry cleared his throat. "Well, as you know, recently the King of France passed away, God rest his soul. Fortunately for Louis, he had only one son to succeed him. I on the other hand, have more than one."

"Yes, but you crowned Young Henry king" Richard narrowed his eyes at his father.

Henry waved him off. "True. However, I hear that Louis' son Philip is not in the least like his father. Somehow he seems to have learnt how to rule effectively. In order to curb Philip's appetite for our land, we must take precautions."

"Philip is hell bent on regaining land the French crown lost when our parents married," seated on his father's right, Young Henry added.

Henry looked up at Richard and Geoffrey who had chosen to remain standing. "Now, we did have a treaty with Louis; that still stands. Richard will marry Alice, and we gain the Vexin. It will not be easy for Philip to go against his in-laws. However, it is not enough; we need more. We cannot afford to show anything less than perfect family solidarity. We must do something."

"What do you have in mind, Father? Oh, I know. We all take a turn in the sack with Alice," Geoffrey smirked.

"Geoffrey!" Henry waved his finger.

Richard grumbled, "That is not funny!"

Geoffrey shot back, "What do you care? You've got your own tart!"

"Listen carefully!" Henry raised his voice. "You three, John, Richard, Geoffrey, must swear an oath of allegiance to the Young Henry." He pointed to each of his sons as he said their names.

Richard bellowed, "I have my own lands to think about. Let Young Henry solve his own problems. I will not sacrifice my independence to him!"

"Enough!" Henry thundered. "Stop and think about it. Put your pride aside for the good of the family. We can defend each other from our enemies."

John shrugged. "Well, I'll do it, Father. You know what is best, and I trust your judgment."

"Of course you do! You have no possessions, no land, no titles, nothing to lose!" Richard rounded on John.

Henry patted John's head. "Your loyalty will be rewarded. I promise you that."

"Oh, come now!" Richard gestured to Geoffrey. "Are you going to stand for this?"

Geoffrey stroked his beard. "He does make a strong case, and unlike you, Richard, my title comes through my marriage. I too will swear an oath of loyalty to Young Henry."

Richard's cheeks flushed. "I see. Now I understand. This is all just a ploy to take Aquitaine from me! Does the queen know of this?"

"The queen will do as she is told. Need I remind you that you received a gift because of your loyalty? I can take as easily, nay, more easily than I give. Relent and swear an oath to your brother!" Henry snapped at Richard.

Richard shook his head. "I was right. I knew you were after something when you gave Anne to me."

"You insolent puppet! You will do as I say or face the consequences!" Henry stood and to no one in particular and screamed, "Bring me Lady Anne!"

"She is not here." Richard threw open his arms.

Now normally ruddy Henry turned crimson like his son. "I beg your pardon?"

Richard spoke slowly and clearly. "She is not here."

Henry looked around the room at them all. John backed away. Richard continued, "I knew you were only scheming, so I sent her away the moment you gave her to my keeping."

"I shall send men after her." Henry spoke through gritted teeth.

Richard laughed. "You are too late. I have secreted her away to an abbey. What are you going to do, sack all the abbeys between here and Marseilles?"

Henry took a deep breath and appeared to have regained control of his temper. He still spoke firmly, but with urgency. "Richard, you must listen to me. Swear an oath to Young Henry. It is the best for all involved."

Richard turned up his nose at his father. "No, it is best for Young Henry. I inherited that land through my mother, not through my father. I do owe allegiance to an overlord, and he is the King of

France, not the King of England. Besides, do you really expect me to believe that once your beloved son has any claim to Aquitaine he is going to let me continue there as duke? I think not. The poor little prince is just lusting after the richest land in your realm. Well, you can be sure of one thing. If Young Henry wants land, then he is going to have to fight for it just as I have fought for mine!"

Richard stormed from the room, leaving the others in an awkward silence.

Even after she arrived safely at Poitiers, Anne did not sleep much. She spent most of her time worrying about Richard. This concern consumed her so that she hardly ate. Andrew and Baldwin tried to assure her that he was fine. At one point, she even begged them to go back after Richard. Finally they agreed that if Richard did not arrive in two night's time, they would go back for him.

Anne did have a pleasant surprise upon arrival at Poitiers. Marguerite, who had served as a companion and lady to Anne since childhood, now served at Richard's court in Poitiers. Anne's mood brightened at seeing such an old friend. While Anne enjoyed the happy reunion, she found it difficult to take any pleasure in her new found freedom. She did not feel free at all, but anxious to the point of being nauseous. She wanted Richard to come to her and reassure her that she was finally safe from Henry.

On the evening of the second night, Anne sat in her chamber, her brow furrowed in anxiety for Richard. Silently, she prayed for his safe and hasty return. Just as she finished, she heard a commotion outside the room. Opening the door to see servants scurrying to and fro, Anne caught sight of Marguerite. "Marguerite, what is it? What has happened?"

Marguerite grasped Anne's hands. "M'lady, it's the duke; he's come home. He is just arriving!"

"Richard?" Anne's eyes widened.

"Yes!"

Anne turned and sped down the hallway to the courtyard.

Dismounting from his horse in the courtyard, Richard spotted her. "Anne!"

"Thank God you are safe. I have been half sick to death with worry." Anne approached him.

Richard kissed her, put his arm around her, handed his reins to the stable boy, and gently guided Anne back into the castle.

"Oh, you know me; I always land on my feet." They kept walking toward *The Tour Maubergeon* housing Richard's apartments. Richard continued, "However, I was right in sending you here. Henry was conspiring."

Anne glanced up at him as they walked. "What did Henry want?"

"Me to swear an oath of loyalty to the Young King, and ultimately Aquitaine."

"And my purpose was to sweeten the deal."

Richard squeezed her hand. "Do not worry. I told him I sent you to an abbey."

"He will not believe that for long."

They arrived at the door to Richard's chambers. "You are safe here, Anne."

Richard opened the door and entered the outer room. He did not let go of Anne's hand, but pulled her along with him. Once inside, he took off his boots and gloves tossing them into a heap on the floor. While Anne unfastened his cloak and folded it over the back of a chair, Richard ordered a page to bring some food.

Richard and Anne entered the bedchamber where Richard removed his sword and belt. Pushing up his sleeves, he splashed his face, arms and hands with water from a nearby basin, and dried them on a towel. Then he jumped onto the bed and rolled over onto his back, his hands tucked under his head. Anne followed, picking up the belt, placing it on a nearby table.

"Anne, I have been thinking." Richard remained in the same position on the bed.

She picked up his sword and leaned it against the wall close to the bed. "You have had much to think on as of late, I am sure."

"What are you going to do now that you are free? I mean..." His voice trailed off.

"Well, I have not yet sent word to my father that I am here. I waited for your return."

"I suppose you will want to go back to the Marseilles."

"Yes, but... "

Richard interrupted her, "Anne, what do you think of staying here with me? Well, at least until it is safer for you to travel."

She grinned. "I think that would be wise. I appreciate your kindness very much."

He yawned. "Good. I shall enjoy keeping you close."

Richard closed his eyes. The bags under them showed his exhaustion. Anne gazed at him for a moment, then reached out and gave his face a couple of soft strokes. Gently she patted his arm and let her hand linger there a moment. When she turned to leave, he grabbed her hand and in one swift move pulled her onto the bed next to him. He still kept his eyes closed as he whispered, "Stay with me."

"Richard," she chided.

"I promise I shall behave appropriately. If I do not, you are free to give me a good whack with my sword and leave. Please, I just want to be near you tonight."

Anne thought for a moment, then lay down beside Richard. Gingerly, she placed her head on his shoulder.

"Do try not to snore; I am very tired dear," he teased.

"My snore is not nearly as dangerous as my kick."

Richard pulled her close, inhaling her spicy scent. "Well, goodnight then."

"Goodnight."

Both were quiet for several minutes until Richard spoke again. "I love you, Anne."

She put her arm across his chest. "Welcome home, Richard."

Chapter Fourteen

Just under a month passed, and Anne remained at Poitiers with Richard. Strangely, they did not hear anything from or about Henry. One morning Anne rose early and found Richard sitting alone in his solar chamber, letters strewn on the table before him. "Good morning." She kissed his cheek.

"And a good morning to you, my sweet Annie." He pulled another chair near for her.

Unsure she liked the new nickname, she wrinkled her nose. "Master Blondel told me you have been up half the night."

"Oh, I could not sleep."

"Is something the matter? Are you ill?"

He picked up the letter. "I have received word that a vassal, the Count of Bordeaux, is in rebellion against me. Part of me wonders if Henry is not behind this. Anyway, I will be heading south to remind Bordeaux exactly who his overlord is. Here," he handed her a letter as well. "The messengers came very late last night, and I did not want to wake you. This one is for you."

Anne took the letter, opened it, and began to read it. "It is a letter from my father and Cousin Etienne."

She read the rest of the letter. When she finished, she placed the letter on the table. "Richard, after the matter in Bordeaux is settled, how would you feel about a journey to Marseilles?"

"You've gone pale. Has something happened?"

"It would seem that my father's condition has worsened. It is very serious."

"Then I think it best that you not wait. You must leave for Marseilles as soon as possible. I could join you after I settle the matter in Bordeaux."

She nodded. "Yes, that would be best. I will miss you though."

"That goes without saying." Richard attempted to make her smile. "I am not looking forward to any time apart, but it will not be long until I see you in Marseilles."

"When do you leave for Bordeaux?" She questioned.

"The preparations are underway. I expect to leave by this afternoon." He sighed.

Anne hesitated. "Promise me that you will keep Baldwin and Andrew close. They are your best men."

"Maybe one should accompany you," he offered.

"No." She shook her head. "They should be with you."

"Anne, what is it?"

"It is silly, really."

"Tell me."

"I do not know why, but I have an uneasy feeling about all of this." She shook as if trying to rid herself of the notion. "Please, just keep Baldwin and Andrew with you."

He consented. "If it will put you at ease. I will, however, send for Mercadier to keep you safe."

"Mercadier, the mercenary?" Anne wrinkled her nose.

"Yes. I trust him. He serves me well, and I always pay him handsomely for it. He will get you to Marseilles safely." Richard flashed her a reassuring smile.

Anne kissed his cheek again. "If you trust him, then I shall trust him." She rose from her chair. "In the meantime, I better inform Marguerite of our plans."

She left the room with Richard still in the chair where she found him.

By early afternoon, Richard and his men were prepared to leave. The knights gathered in the hectic courtyard, some exchanging farewell kisses and goodbyes with loved ones. Anne accompanied Richard into the courtyard. Though still early in the spring, the warmer weather coaxed the hardiest of trees to bud.

"Mercadier should be here within a week," Richard informed her.

"Richard, do promise that you will be cautious. Please do not take any extraordinary risks," Anne urged him.

"Oh, come now. Since when have I been known to do any such thing." He batted his eyelashes at her.

"I am serious, Richard." She turned to Baldwin and Andrew nearby.

"Baldwin, Andrew, promise me to look after him."

Baldwin replied for the both. "We will, my lady."

Richard rolled his eyes. "Heaven and hell preserve us, woman! I will be just fine.
Now give your departing warrior a kiss."

Anne kissed him softly, and Richard mounted his horse. He bent down to her. "I shall see you in Marseilles."

Richard and his knights cantered out of the courtyard and galloped down the road toward the village. Without warning, Richard stopped his horse. Swiftly, he turned around and bounded back for the castle courtyard. Baldwin and Andrew exchanged entertained looks then followed.

Richard burst into the courtyard shouting, "Anne! Anne!"

Anne, hearing him call her name, emerged onto the steps. "Richard? What is it? What is the matter?"

Richard halted his horse next to the staircase. They were even with each other now, she at the top of the stairs, and he on his horse. Richard grabbed her and kissed her with intensity.

"Hang Bordeaux. I am not going. I'll not leave you!" He breathed.

He tried to kiss her again, but she stopped him by placing a finger on his lips.

"Richard, you must go. Besides, you promised we would be

together again soon. Take faith in that and go perform your duty."

Richard removed his glove and took a ring from his pinky. "Take this as a remembrance of me."

He kissed the ring and placed it in her hand, folding her fingers around it. "You gave me a token all those years ago, and it is about time I returned the favor."

"Have you got it?" Her hazel eyes shone.

"Here it is," Richard pulled the scarf out.

Anne took it from him and tied it securely on his arm.

Andrew called out to Richard, "What's it to be Richard, love or war?"

Richard looked at Andrew and Baldwin, sitting on their horses laughing to themselves. Then he glanced back at Anne. "Both!" He called out.

"Well, come on then. Let us go tear something down." Baldwin motioned to leave.

Anne quickly gave Richard one last kiss. "I will see you in Marseilles."

"In Marseilles."

He spurred his horse and called back over his shoulder, "I love you."

"You just cannot help yourself." She waved goodbye.

In just under a week, Mercadier and his men arrived. Their horses better kempt than they, the group appeared coarse. Mercadier reminded Anne of a wild boar, small and round, bristly and mean. An unusual scar that ran across the bottom of his nose looked like horns. Mercadier made Anne feel nervous, but she kept reminding herself that Richard trusted him.

The night before they were to leave for Marseilles, Anne and Marguerite stayed up late packing. "Are you excited to be going home tomorrow?" Marguerite placed another dress in the bursting trunk.

"Yes, I am. It has been so long." Anne watched Marguerite struggle to close the lid. "I am not looking forward to the journey, however. Mercadier and his men are a rather rough lot."

Marguerite pushed against the top, trying to latch the trunk. "They may be rough, but I do believe they will get us to Marseilles safely."

"Let us hope they sober up from their night's revels." Anne sat on the top of the trunk.

Marguerite finally closed the lid. She gave a long low whistle and shook her head at it. Then she turned to Anne to help her prepare for bed. "Has m'lady heard from the duke?"

Anne slipped out of her dress and into a shift and dressing gown with Marguerite's help. "Mercadier brought news that Richard arrived in Bordeaux and has laid siege to the Count's stronghold. Knowing Richard, it will not be long before he takes his target and is on his way to Marseilles."

"What if he were to arrive there before we do? Wouldn't that be a great joke?" Marguerite giggled.

"Then I better get some rest so that we may proceed to Marseilles as fast as possible." Anne climbed into her bed and snuggled under the covers.

"Goodnight, M'lady," Marguerite took the candle with her.

Anne called out to her, "Thank you, Marguerite, and good night to you. I will see you early in the morning."

Marguerite closed the door behind her and the room fell dark. With a new moon outside, there was no moonlight to give the room a glow.

Anne fell asleep fast. For a while, she slept comfortably and soundly. She dreamt of Marseilles and Richard. In her dream, Richard was in Marseilles waiting with her father. They walked along the coast when an owl landed on her father's shoulder. It confused her, an owl on the beach in the middle of the day. The sky around them turned black, and wind rushed in from the ocean. She had the sinking notion that someone was attacking Marseilles.

Anne tried to tell herself it was a dream, and to wake up. She struggled with this for a brief moment and then managed to roll over.

As she lay in the dark trying to shake off the lingering uneasiness, the door to her chamber flew open. Anne bolted straight up in bed. Several persons entered the room, and by their heavy footsteps Anne could tell they were men. One of the men yanked her out of bed and threw her to the floor. As she grappled to get up, the tallest man grabbed her by the arm with such force that she again stood upright. Then another man entered the room carrying a torch, the light slowly revealed his face, Raymond of Castile. "Hello again, Lady Anne."

The sound of his cold voice made her sick, but she quickly found her courage. "Just what do you think you are doing, Castile?"

A grotesque grin smeared his face. "Carrying out orders from the king."

Anne fought against the tall man's grip, but he simply restrained her further. "Your brother has no power here," she snapped at Raymond.

Raymond gave a sardonic sigh. "No, sadly he does not. However, good King Henry does.
It would seem that you are to be in my custody. Fortunately, for me, your precious Richard went too far."

"I do not believe you!"

He came very close to her and whispered, "Oh, believe it, my dear." He backed away and ordered, "Now come with me."

"No! I'll not go anywhere with you! Mercadier! Mercadier!"

Raymond let out an odd laugh, almost a cackle. "It will do you no good. We are acting on orders from the king. Even Mercadier dares not disobey."

"You are a wretch! I'll not go with you!"

Raymond yanked her forward. "Oh, yes, you will. If I must drag you by your hair, you are coming with me!"

Before she could respond, the tall man, along with others, bound and dragged her outside to the courtyard in just her shift and bare feet. She struggled in vain. The men tossed Anne into a cart. She tried to wriggle out and almost made it, but the men lashed her to it. Raymond headed toward his horse. The castle in chaos, Marguerite, Master Blondel, and Mercadier pleaded with the men to release her. "My Lord Castile, I beg of you, do not do this. Please, do not take Lady Anne. Surely something can be arranged with the duke." Blondel knelt before Castile.

Raymond turned on him. "Look here, you little gudgeon. I know that as soon as I leave here someone is going to tell your master what happened. In fact, I'm counting on it. Give this to him."

He handed Blondel a letter. Then Raymond went to Anne and yanked the green silk ribbon from her neck that held Richard's ring. "Oh, yes, and give this to him too." He tossed it to Blondel. "Tell your master that even if he were to come after Lady Anne, it will be too late; she is to be my wife."

Chapter Fifteen

During the years, Richard honed his skills at the art of war. When he reached Count Theobald of Bordeaux's castle, he immediately set up his siege machine. He started the assault by using the trebuchets to weaken the walls and the morale of those inside the castle. Next he brought up the siege towers, and archers assailed the men on the battlements. Miners tunneled beneath the walls to weaken the structure. The siege lasted only a short time before it was obvious that Bordeaux stood no chance against the duke. Still, the count held out in the hopes that he could inflict as much damage as possible on Richard's army before surrendering.

As another day of fighting dawned, the trumpets signaled, and Richard's army began their daily assault on the dismal gray castle. Richard, Baldwin, and Andrew watched the battle from a hilltop in the distance, positioned just out of range of any projectiles the count might lodge from his catapults. The trio watched a group of men beating on the gates with a large battering ram. Inside the stronghold, the count had run out of hot oil and had not had the foresight to obtain Greek fire before the siege began. Richard's men battered away at the gate with only the archers firing down on them.

"My lord, I dare say, it will not be long now." Andrew sat up taller in his saddle.

As they watched the scene below, a horseman came riding hard and fast toward them. With great surprise, they recognised Master Blondel. Blondel barely stopped his horse before he leapt from it, landing right in front of Richard. "My lord, I beg a word in private."

Richard laughed and turned to Andrew and Baldwin. "More orders from the king, no doubt." He looked at Blondel, "Well, let us have it. What does the old man want now?"

Blondel looked away from Richard and quietly said, "Sir, it is Lady Anne."

Richard jumped at the mention of her name. "What of Lady Anne?"

"Some men came with orders from your father, Raymond of Castile among them. They dragged her off into the night."

"Where was Mercadier? Had he not arrived?" Richard stammered.

Blondel swallowed hard. "He just arrived, but there was nothing he could do. Castile acted on orders from the king!"

Richard tightly clutched his sword in one hand, a gesture not lost on those around him. "Where did they take her?'

"Mercadier followed them, then sent word that Castile took her to Taillebourg. The baron there is hiding them. Mercadier said that according to those in the village, Castile has… married Lady Anne. Mercadier is waiting for your instructions."

Richard remained speechless.

"Is there anything more that you can tell us?" Andrew prodded.

Blondel shook his head. "Not really, sir. When Castile left Poitiers, he handed me this letter to give to the duke."

Richard stared at the battle before him, so Andrew took the letter from Blondel.

"It has the seal of the King," Baldwin noted.

Andrew ripped the letter open: it only took a second to read. "All it says is, 'This is the price you pay for your *pride'*."

They all looked to Richard for a response. Still he did not move. Baldwin spoke quietly to him, "my lord?"

Without saying a word, Richard turned to his horse. The others expected him to mount it and ride off; however, he suddenly threw whatever he could get his hands on. Anything hanging from his saddle was not safe. He even picked up rocks from the ground. They all had to dodge the flying projectiles, but Richard wasn't taking any aim. Richard grabbed his helmet and at a run threw it with all his might. He bent over grabbing his knees for a moment. No one breathed. Then, as suddenly as he started throwing things, he stood upright. His expression looked controlled.

Pointing toward the besieged castle and with a shaking voice he ordered, "I want that castle taken or burnt by nightfall, and that baggage inside to learn what it means to cross the Duke of Aquitaine.

"Yes, my lord," the men answered.

Richard could hardly have heard them because he mounted his horse and rode pell-mell toward the battle.

Built on a rocky outcrop overlooking the valley of the Charente River, the Castle of Taillebourg was thought to be unconquerable. In fact, no one had ever taken it. On three sides, mountains protected it with the fourth heavily fortified. Luckily for Castile, the baron there hated Richard almost as much as he did.

Another evening ended. Raymond attended another wedding feast, but Anne remained locked away in a room. As Raymond left the feast and headed to Anne, Taillebourg caught up with him. "Castile!"

Impatient, Raymond did not want to stay and dicker with the baron. "As soon as my escort from the king arrives, I will be able to take control of my wife's land. You will be rewarded handsomely."

Taillebourg, a large man, always wore a sour expression even in moments of great joy. "You know that I am not doing this out of the kindness of my heart, or because I like you, sir. The riches of Marseilles and the promise of the king that the rule of Pointu will be taken from Duke Richard and given back to the queen, are the reasons that persuaded me."

They arrived at the door to the bedchamber. "I understand. Just make sure you do your job, and you will have satisfaction. Now, to deal with my bride." Raymond licked his lips. "There really is nothing like a virgin is there? Alas, that time has passed."

Without giving Taillebourg the chance to respond, Raymond entered the bedchamber and shut the door in his host's face.

In the dimly lit room, he could just make out Anne sitting on the hearth. "Good evening, wife. You missed a wonderful feast tonight. It really is too bad that you've been ill and missed so many of our wedding festivities." He gave a patronizing sigh. "If only you would behave, I could let you have a little more fun."

Anne stood up, her hands behind her back. Raymond

scrutinized her. Her clothes were disheveled and smudges streaked her tear stained face. She had managed to put her hair back into one long braid.

"You look simply wretched! I find you a gown, and you let it become soiled and spotty. I give you a mirror, and what do you do? You break it." He continued his assessment. "You really must take better care of yourself. How do you hope to produce a healthy heir if you cannot? Tomorrow morning, I will have you waited on, washed and cleaned. I will have only the finest houses, horses, and women." He placed himself right in front of her. "You will not shame me, Anne! Is that clear?"

Anne answered with a glare. In response, Raymond grabbed her by the chin. "Do not look at me that way! You will kneel before your lord and master!" Raymond pushed her to the ground.

Anne gasped in pain as she landed on a bandaged hand, wounded when she broke the mirror.

"Well, my dear, we have been married nearly a month." His tone returned to sickening sweet. "Yet, there is no sign of your beloved Richard. It would seem that he traded you for peace with his father after all. What a shame. He *was* such a fine example of chivalry."

He walked away from her to the bed. "Ah, well, perhaps you are not worth his trouble. As for me, now that I have you and will soon have your riches, I want heirs from you, and then I will be done with you."

Raymond took off his boots, sat down on the bed, and patted the spot next to him. "Come, wife, let's to bed."

Anne obediently walked toward the bed.

"That's better. The more your conduct improves, the more I shall reward you. Now, give us a kiss." Raymond smirked.

Slowly Anne leaned down to meet him. Suddenly she pulled a long jagged shard of broken mirror from behind her skirts. She stabbed away at Raymond, making contact with his face and digging into his flesh just below his eye. Raymond cried out in surprise and pain, flinging his hands over his face to protect himself. Taking the opportunity, Anne bolted for the door.

Raymond's cries roused the guard who caught Anne before she could clear the doorway, knocking the glass from her hand. Baron Taillebourg also heard the commotion and joined in the fray. Together they managed to subdue Anne.

Raymond leapt from the bed still clutching his face, blood seeping out from between his fingers. "I'll kill her! I'll kill her!" He screeched.

"You have had but just a taste of what is to come!" Anne spat at Raymond.

"Silence!" Taillebourg ordered. "She goes in the dungeon."

The tall guard dragged Anne away as she screamed from the hall, "You will pay for this! All of you will pay! I swear before God, you will pay!"

"You first, bitch!" Raymond lunged toward the door.

Taillebourg cut him off. "Castile! You will be silent! She stays in the dungeon, for now."

Chapter Sixteen

Even though dawn approached, Taillebourg remained in bed, issuing forth a rattling snore as he slept off the effects of the evening's alcohol. The loud crash of stone hitting stone made him bolt upright. The sound resonated throughout the citadel, and the walls shook from the impact. Throwing on a dressing robe, Taillebourg ran from his bedroom.

His castellan met Taillebourg in the hallway. "What is it? What has happened?" Taillebourg cried.

"My lord, we are under attack." The castellan strapped on his sword.

"Is it Duke Richard?" Taillebourg's face turned pale.

His castellan could only nod. Taillebourg turned and ran through the castle with the castellan in hot pursuit.

They rushed to the battlements and looked over the edge to see Richard's siege machine lined up ready to attack. All about them, men scurried to prepare defences for the castle.

Raymond joined them on the battlements, his face twisted into an eerie smile. "Now it comes!" Taillebourg made a gesture toward Richard's forces.

"He is a fool to attack." Raymond laughed. "This citadel can never be taken."

Taillebourg turned on him. "Perhaps someone forgot to inform the duke of that little fact. Did he not try to make contact first?"

Raymond's eyes flashed with excitement. "Oh, yes. He sent an emissary late last night after you retired to bed. I refused to receive him."

"You fool, you damn fool! I knew you were thick, but I had no idea it was this bad." Taillebourg screeched.

"Sir, the villagers are already pouring into the citadel!" The castellan distracted Taillebourg.

"If they're not in by now, they are at the mercy of the Duke." Taillebourg shouted orders. "Fortify the main gate and prepare for a siege. In the meantime, Castile, you will send word to him that you mean to meet with him. Perhaps we can still end this with my castle intact."

"No! I refuse to meet with him!" Raymond stamped his foot. "Let him come; he does not stand a chance against you and your fortifications."

"That is precisely it, Castile! This is my castle!" Taillebourg pinned Raymond with his stare, veins bulging in his neck. "You will send an emissary, or I will throw you from these walls and send your head as a gift to Duke Richard. You have waged war with my men and my castle. You have used me and played me for a fool. It ends now!"

As Richard paced back and forth like a caged animal, Andrew, and Baldwin stood under a grove of trees a distance from Taillebourg castle, preparing to parlay with Taillebourg and Castile. "Now, Richard, I know you want to kill him, and I do not blame you; however, you mustn't do anything rash." Andrew rested his hand on the pommel of his sword.

Richard continued to pace. "I think we have Taillebourg's attention. Let us use that to our advantage."

"There. I see them in the distance." Baldwin pointed to three figures on horseback.

"Remember, they must meet every demand in order to avoid more aggression. Do not negotiate!" Richard grumbled.

Within a few moments, Taillebourg, Raymond and the castellan dismounted and entered the grove of trees. Taillebourg nodded toward Richard. "Duke Richard, we have come to discuss a peaceful outcome to this aggression."

Andrew took the lead. "My lord appreciates your coming, Baron Taillebourg. He asked you here to make his demands formally known."

Taillebourg made a slight bow, narrowing his eyes at Richard's arrogant expression. Andrew continued, "The duke demands that Lady Anne be released into his custody with the understanding that the Prince of Castile will not make any attempt to recover her. Taillebourg is to renew his oath of fidelity to the duke. In return, the duke is prepared to halt his attack on the castle. Also, he will graciously payoff Castile's debts and pay for his safe passage home."

Taillebourg snorted. "We all know that Prince Raymond has no intention of returning home to Castile to wait in line behind his six brothers. He has more important matters to attend to in Marseilles. Perhaps I must remind you that the Lady Anne and Prince Raymond are now man and wife." He paused to watch his words hit their target. "Oh, oh, maybe you had not heard."

"Take care, Taillebourg!" Richard growled. "Either you release Lady Anne and benefit, or I will take possession of your properties." He pointed to Raymond. "This craven lout is not worth the risk."

"And might I remind you, sir, that as of yet you have failed to capture the citadel. Try as you like, but your efforts will be for naught." Raymond gave Richard a contemptuous smile.

Richard scoffed at Raymond. "By the by, Castile, what unfortunate event did your face meet? Perhaps Queen Boudica herself? Now, that is the handiwork of my Anne. Who needs a woman skilled at making tapestries when you have one who can do this?"

"By heaven and hell, she is no longer yours!" Raymond stepped closer to Richard and taunted. "For all your titles and your swaggering boasts, I have had the one thing you could not, and I have had it over, and over, and over again."

Richard lunged at Raymond, but Baldwin and Andrew grabbed him. "Then we will take that as your answer." Baldwin snarled at Taillebourg and Raymond.

"I swear by all that is holy, if that is what it takes, I will see you in hell!" Richard roared.

Taillebourg stuck his nose in the air, turned and left. Raymond and the castellan followed.

Once they were out of hearing, Richard turned to his companions. "The small village located at the foot of the fortress, destroy it. Also, have the *boutefeux* raze the vineyards and fields. Make sure those in the fortress must watch their property destroyed. I want to anger those inside, drawing the men out. Then, we will rush the castle walls."

Richard's men destroyed everything in their path, the houses, the livestock, and crops. Due to the plentiful fires, a thick haze clung around the ruins of the little village. They spared one small part of the village that would only take a mere afternoon to destroy. Richard meant to draw out the besieged villagers, the peasants who abandoned their village for the safety of the castle walls, who now watched helplessly from the battlements.

Inside the castle walls, a grey doom settled on the inhabitants, many praying for a peaceful surrender. Taillebourg shut himself up in the keep and would not listen to the pleas of anyone. To him, surrender now was not an option. He didn't wish to spend the rest of his days a prisoner of the duke.

Taillebourg sat alone at the head of his table as Raymond sheepishly approached him. "When Duke Richard destroyed the crops, he took a great risk. While he did destroy the livelihood of the peasants and a great deal of revenue for you, he also put his own troops in danger. If the siege lasts a long time, he has no means to feed his army. Baron, the duke is just trying to lure the men outside the gates."

"Yes, well, I know a good many who are ready to go," Taillebourg snapped.

"We…" Raymond swallowed hard. "You mustn't let them."

The baron inhaled deeply to launch a fresh verbal assault on Raymond, but his castellan rushed into the room. "I beg your pardon, my lord, but the sentinels have spotted something."

Turning his anger, Taillebourg barked, "Well, what is it?"

"Duke Richard moved his camp. In his conceit, he placed it near to the walls." The castellan licked his lips as if the news aroused some kind of hunger in him.

"What is his purpose?" Taillebourg grumbled.

"It's obvious!" Raymond's expression lightened. "He plans to be close in order to facilitate a rush on the castle when the men come out to defend their property." Taillebourg responded with a disgusted grunt. Raymond continued, "At last, a stroke of luck. By moving his camp so close, he has made himself vulnerable to attack."

"If I might, sir, I have noted that the duke concentrates his efforts on destruction. He does this during the day forcing those inside the citadel to watch their property razed. At night his troops withdraw to their camp and all is quiet. Destruction is a taxing business," the castellan offered.

Taillebourg sat up straight as if lifted from a magical haze. "I see! We should attack his camp at night while they sleep. He wouldn't expect us to come out from behind the safety of our walls."

Raymond turned on the castellan. "Have your men spotted the exact location of the Duke's personal tent?"

He nodded. "Yes, I believe so, sir."

"If we enter the camp, we could capture the duke, and you could take a rebellious son to an appreciative father. With that cockered clodpole captured, I can be on my way to Marseilles, and you could have in your debt a very grateful king." Raymond clapped his hands together.

In the thick of the night, Taillebourg's troops crept through Richard's camp killing the first sentry who slept through his duty. If they looked more closely, they would have seen they slit the throat of a fresh corpse.

As Taillebourg's men penetrated deeper into the camp, through the rows of tents large and small, toward the centre where Richard's banner flew, they did not see Richard's men lying in wait. When Taillebourg's men slipped far enough into the camp, one of Richard's archers shot a flaming arrow into the air, the silent signal to attack. The crash of arms and men, screams and cries shattered the still night air.

Amongst Taillebourg's men, a ragtag group of knights and peasants, chaos ensued. Instinct called them back to the safety of the fortress. They rushed to its main gate, flanked by the curtain wall like a mother arms open ready to engulf her children in a protective embrace.

Richard perched himself atop some rubble to get a better view. His men rushed to prevent Taillebourg's from entering the gates and closing the portcullis. As he watched, his army suddenly rolled back toward him like a wave. Without hesitation, he leapt from his vantage point and rushed forward, his sword aloft, issuing a cry of *Mont Joie*.

At this, the wave of Richard's men rolled back towards the castle and crashed through Taillebourg's men like the ocean rushing into a ruptured sea wall.

As Taillebourg and Raymond waited in the keep for news from the battle, the castellan rushed in, "Your grace, they breached the main gate! The men are surrendering. Duke Richard is giving no quarter!"

Raymond turned on Taillebourg. "I thought you said this castle's defences would never break!"

"You stupid, simple fool! You have ruined me!" Taillebourg screeched. "I am going to flee before it is too late!"

Without further explanation, Taillebourg grabbed a flambeaux from the wall and headed to the dungeon below. He shouted for Raymond and the castellan to follow him. "You will pay all you have promised me plus my losses here!"

The dungeon, so Taillebourg called it, was actually little more than a large cavernous wine cellar. One small section was blocked off into a cell area, but Taillebourg rarely had occasion to use it. Anne was still locked behind the old rusty bars embedded in a stone wall laced with trails of rusty water dripping to the floor behind a straw mattress. Taillebourg headed straight for her, unlocked the cell, and bound her hands together. "We'll take her with us. We can use her as leverage, if need be." Taillebourg pushed her at Raymond.

Castile tried to pull Anne along, but she fought him. He struck her, and they grappled. Smashing Raymond's wounded face with both her hands, Anne used her weight to pull away from him. She slipped from his grasp, lost her balance, and slammed her head on the stone wall of the cell. Unconscious, she crumpled to the floor.

Raymond screamed in pain and gasped, "I think I've killed her!"

Taillebourg shook his head. "I'm leaving!"

Raymond panicked. "But how? Richard has us surrounded!"

"I have a secret passageway leading to the postern gate just beyond those wine barrels there. It goes to a cave that is well outside the walls. We can slip away unnoticed, but only if we hurry."

A large rope hung coiled on the wall, and Taillebourg slung it over his shoulder. As he turned and headed for the wine barrels, Raymond took one last look at Anne's crumpled body on the floor and followed him.

In the courtyard above, Richard's men now easily overcame the opposition. At the breach of the castle walls, most of Taillebourg's contingent surrendered as fast as they could. Richard let his knights take them hostage. Looking around desperately trying to see something that would give him a clue as to the whereabouts of Anne, Raymond, or Taillebourg, Richard could only see the chaos of the battle before him. As he sprinted for the keep, he shouted above the noise to his men. "Find Lady Anne and bring me Castile!"

When they entered the main hall, Taillebourg's servants fled before them like frightened deer. Baldwin disappeared to interrogate some of the captured servants, and Andrew left to search the bedchambers and tower rooms. Richard investigated the kitchen. There he found an old servant man cowering in the corner. Richard yanked the man to his feet. "Where is Lady Anne de Marseilles?"

The old man bowed his head in supplication. "I don't know, your grace."

Richard pointed his sword straight at the man's heart. "Listen very carefully. I have killed for less offense than this, so think really hard because when you take your last breath depends entirely on your answer. Now, I ask you again, where is Lady Anne?"

"Honest, m'lord, none of us has seen her since before the castle was attacked." The old servant shook his head in desperation.

"Where is your master keeping her?" Richard demanded.

The servant dropped to his knees and pleaded, "Mercy! I don't know! I don't know!"

As both Andrew and Baldwin rushed into the kitchen, Baldwin shouted, "Taillebourg has a secret tunnel, a posturn gate that leads beyond the walls to a cave. The entrance to the tunnel is located in the dungeons, and Anne is probably with them."

"It's true. It's true. I used to serve the Barron's father as groomsman." The old man cupped his hands together as if in prayer.

Richard turned back to the servant. "Do you know where the tunnel is?"

The wide-eyed man nodded. "It has been a long time, but I think I could find it."

Andrew cut in, "Richard, we haven't much time. They set fire to the keep."

"Follow me, m'lords." The servant motioned.

They entered the dungeons and ran past the cell where Anne lay unconscious. The servant stopped. "You must go behind the largest barrel of wine."

As they all began looking around for the large barrel of wine, Baldwin spotted Anne lying on the ground. "Richard!"

Richard rushed to her, and knelt beside her leaning his ear close to her mouth. The smoke from the fire above began to wind its way through the dungeon.

"She is still breathing," Richard cried out. "Anne! Anne! Can you hear me?"

"The fire is spreading; we must get her out!" Andrew warned.

"If I remember right, the other end of the passageway is locked by a heavy door or gate. Surely my master would have locked it behind him. Even if it is unlocked, we would need a rope. If we go that way, we could be trapped."

"Then we shall go back the way we came." Richard scooped up Anne.

They entered the kitchen again; this time Baldwin leading the way. The fire spread rapidly as tapestries, rugs, and dry wooden floors layered with rushes ignited in flames. The old servant aided them as they dodged falling timbers and groped their way through the smoke to the courtyard.

With Taillebourg's men being captured or killed and frightened villagers running to and fro, the courtyard was in chaos. Richard and the others finally made their way through the melee, and they continued their flight until they were outside the fortress walls where they were a safe distance away. Gently, Richard placed Anne on the ground.

"Fetch me some water or something!" Richard panicked.

They all looked around, and Andrew noticed a large horse nearby lazily grazing, oblivious to the destruction around it. Various accoutrements hung from its saddle. Running to the horse, he found a flask. Quickly, he brought it back to Richard. Richard removed his gloves and tilted Anne's head back. As he pressed the flask to her lips, her eyes flickered, and she moaned.

Chapter Seventeen

Three days later, Anne lay in a bed in a small chamber, still asleep. Marguerite slept on a pallet before the fireplace, and Richard dozed in a chair next to the bed. Slowly Anne began to stir. Richard sensed it and jumped. He knelt beside the bed and took her hand. Opening her eyes, Anne looked at him.

"Sh, do not try to talk. You are safe now. We are in the king's castle at La Rochelle." Richard turned to Marguerite. "Marguerite, she's waking."

"Richard?" Anne's brow furrowed.

"Yes, I'm here."

She looked around the room. "Oh, dear. I had almost taken the castle. Must you always steal my thunder?" In a hoarse voice, Anne attempted a soft joke.

Richard smiled in spite of himself. Marguerite brought some wine and handed it to Anne. With Richard's help, she sat up and took a sip. While she sat, Marguerite arranged the pillows to give her more support.

Richard put the cup on a nearby table. "Well, dear, I had to return something to you."

From under his tunic, he pulled out the ring on the ribbon and put it back on her neck. Anne lay back. His eyes red, Richard looked haggard, and he hadn't shaved for several days.

"Richard, I am so sorry," Anne whispered.

"You are not to blame. You are not to blame." Richard pushed some hair back from her face.

"But your father ordered..."

He cut her off. "Take no thought of him. He is here now, and I have reached an agreement with that damnable old man."

"What of Castile?" Anne pursed her lips.

"Castile and Taillebourg fled. Knowing that I would never stop until you were avenged, they promptly took up the cross and headed to the Holy Land on crusade. Now they are both under the protection of the pope, and I am forbidden to do any harm to them or their property. Do not worry; they cannot hide forever. They will be found,"

Tears rolled down Anne's cheeks. "Richard, I am married."

"I know." He stroked her hair softly. "We will find a way to get an annulment. But let us not worry about that right now." He took a deep breath. "Anne, I am afraid I am the bearer of bad news."

"There is something worse than being married to Raymond of Castile? I doubt it."

"Anne, it is your father. He didn't survive his illness." Richard said the words slowly and carefully, so they would not be misunderstood and would not have to be repeated.

Anne now sobbed, but with great difficulty, she managed to ask, "When?"

"Henry knew of it before the news reached Poitiers. He immediately claimed your guardianship. Then he struck a bargain with Raymond, and as soon as I left for Bordeaux, he sent Castile for you. He did all this to punish me. I am the one to blame. If only I had..."

Anne snapped her head up. "What? Sworn an oath of loyalty to Young Henry, thus jeopardizing Aquitaine and renouncing your true overlord, the King of France. No, Richard. That would have been even more disastrous." Another thought occurred to her. "Oh, Richard, you didn't give him Aquitaine did you?"

"No. There was no need. Fortunately for me, my brother is a fool. He allied himself with King Philip of France. They have actually gone to war against Henry, and the two of them are poised to invade my lands." Richard sighed. "But enough of this for now,

Anne. Anne?"

Anne did not respond. She had fallen back to sleep. Richard gazed down at her and shook his head in misery. "Anne, what am I to do?"

Breton wiped his brow with the back of his hand as if telling this part of the story was hard for him. His face now flushed had little beads of sweat breaking out on his wrinkled forehead. He took note that the growing number of men listening to him looked hungrily up at him. They wanted to know more. One of them brought him a cushion for his chair. "Thank you," he said as he took it, fluffed it, and sat.

Breton readjusted himself into a much more comfortable position. He winced a bit, for his left leg was asleep. Taking a deep breath, he continued, "So, Richard and Henry went to war against Young Henry, who was supported by King Philip. Then fate interfered once again, as fate so often does. Two events changed Richard's life; the first being the death of Young Henry. While fighting his father, he became very ill with a sickness in his bowels, and the bowels are linked to compassion. Some say it was his guilt about rebelling against his father that made him ill. He succumbed to the sickness and died.

Then Anne discovered she was pregnant. Now, Richard stood next in line for the throne, and Anne prepare to deliver her own heir to Marseilles."

An extremely pregnant Anne paced back and forth in the chamber. In recent days, her chamber had been turned into a proper lying in chamber in preparation for the birth to come. The windows had been covered and even the keyholes plugged to prevent light from entering. Traditionally, the only illumination came from candles, so the baby would not become blinded by light. Anne didn't care much for darkness and ordered extra candles brought in with the concession that half of them be extinguished when the time came.

A curtain partitioned off the area around Anne's bed. If she had the strength, she would have ripped it down, as she hated her chamber sectioned off like this. It made the room feel small and stuffy. The idea of the lying in chamber was symbolic of the mother's womb, but Anne decided she had already been in a womb once; she didn't want to be in one again.

The door creaked opened, and Richard poked in his head. Anne picked up a pillow and threw it at him. "You are not allowed in here. Men are forbidden from the lying in chamber," Anne snarled.

Despite her gruffness, Richard admitted himself into the chamber. "Well, I was planning on sneaking in to see you, scaling the walls if necessary. Then I ran into Marguerite. It seems you chased her away. She mumbled something about you acting like a woman possessed with a legion of devils, half full of hate and the other half full of sorrow, and that she would rather spend the rest of her days locked away in the cellar than be in here with you." Richard flashed a smile.

Anne gritted her teeth. "She refused to stop that damnable, unremitting chatter.

"Dearest." Richard took a small step in her direction. "I believe you are rather excitable right now. Perhaps you should lie down, calm down. Sleep would do you some good."

Her eyes wild, she snapped back, "Richard, I have had but very little sleep in the past two weeks."

"That is why you should just lie down and rest. It will not be long until the baby comes, and you will need your strength."

"I know that! I cannot sleep! I cannot eat! It hurts to sit, to lie down, to walk! And then there is this incessant kicking! Do you know this child kicked a book off my lap the other day? I have half a mind to become a nun after this. And what is that racket in the courtyard? Do they not know that there is a woman in confinement up here?" The tirade came all in one breath.

Anne gingerly placed herself in a chair and began to cry. Richard shrugged. "Is there anything I can do?"

Anne looked sharply up at him. "Yes! You can go through nine months of hell and get fat and swollen and miserable, and then give birth while everybody is telling you to be cheerful because you are bringing a life into the world."

Richard moved to make his exit. "Ah, I think I hear someone in the hallway, perhaps the midwife. I shall go see."

"Fine! Leave me here like this! Just go and do not bother to come back!"

Anne rose to her feet and tossed whatever she could lay her hands on at Richard. Richard slipped out with as much grace as he could.

When Richard returned to his own chambers, Andrew, Baldwin, and Blondel were there enjoying some wine. As Richard entered, they stood. Holding up his glass, Baldwin saluted Richard. "Here comes the returning warrior. We just saw Marguerite. She told us where you were headed, to the *forbidden* lying in chamber. Did the midwife toss you out?"

Richard took a seat. "Gentlemen, I am no longer anxious about dying and going to hell. I have just been there and met..." he paused, "seen something that would cause the devil and his minions to flee. God's legs, the next time I need an army, I would do well to use every pregnant woman in Aquitaine." Richard picked up a glass of wine and took a sip. "Let us pray that this child comes soon, or I fear that Anne just may tear the castle down around us."

A late autumn thunderstorm settled over Poitiers. The wind hurled cold sheets of rain at the castle walls while the lightening flashed and thunder rumbled about in the night sky, keeping Richard awake, in bed.

A quiet knock rapped at his door, and a half dressed Andrew entered. "My lord, the midwife sent me to tell you, it is time." Andrew tried to finish dressing as he walked and talked.

"What? She wakes you and not me?" Richard bolted from bed.

Andrew sheepishly grinned. "Not exactly, she woke Marguerite, and I happened to be in close proximity."

"Oh! I see." Richard gave him a slap on the arm.

After putting on a crumpled tunic that lay nearby, and setting off out of the room, Richard drilled Andrew. "How is Anne?"

"I do not know, sir."

"The baby, is it a boy or girl?"

"I do not know, sir."

"Well, what does the midwife say?"

"I do not know, sir."

"Hell, you are just a wealth of information, aren't you?" Richard grumbled.

Andrew shrugged. "I came straight from bed, sir."

Baldwin and Master Blondel joined them in the hallway.

"We thought perhaps you'd like the company," Baldwin offered.

"I am going to wait outside her room," Richard said over his shoulder as he raced down the hall.

The narrow hallway outside the lying in chamber grew crowded. Servants waited to perform various duties or came and went from the room, as well as Richard, Andrew, Baldwin, and Master Blondel. Baldwin and Andrew sat on stools, but Richard preferred to pace back and forth in front of his stool. Occasionally he paced over to the door, considered opening it, but after deciding against it, returned to the stool.

Baldwin tried to put Richard at ease. "My lord, we have the

finest midwife in all of Pointu. She has delivered hundreds of babies."

Just then a gaunt looking priest hurried down the hall to the door.

"Just a moment. Why are you going in there? Is everything alright?" Richard barred the way.

The priest gulped. "Yes, my lord. Lady Anne sent for me. She wants the baby baptized right away."

Richard shook his head. "But I am to be the godfather. I am to take the baby to church to have it baptized."

"It is my understanding that the Lady Anne wishes that you not acknowledge the child in any way. Excuse me, my lord, but I am needed in the room." The priest ducked under Richard's arm and into the chamber.

Master Blondel tried to hand Richard a drink. "Here, perhaps it will help."

Richard threw out his hands. "Get a woman to take it into her. I cannot go in the bloody room!"

"I meant it for you, my lord."

Richard seized the drink, spilling some on the floor. "Of course, I knew that." He drank it down in one gulp.

Andrew muttered under his breath, "I think the more he has, the better for us all."

As the night continued, the thunderstorm outside grew in strength, and the men remained in the hall outside the lying in chamber, a little tipsy. By now Richard took a seat while Andrew leaned against the wall and Baldwin sat beside him.

"I saw a cow give birth once, the most frightening thing I ever saw. It would be more pleasant to go into battle outnumbered a thousand to one than to see something like that again. Trust me, Richard, you are much better off out here." Andrew shuddered.

"Are you comparing the Lady Anne to a cow?" Drowsy from the alcohol, Baldwin looked up at Andrew.

Richard laughed. "No, my good man, he's just called us all

cowards."

Inside the lying in chamber, Anne's labor intensified, and she moaned with each coming contraction. The midwife and Marguerite assisted Anne while the priest cowered on the other side of the curtain. Marguerite brought Anne the candle, and the ceremonial hot wine sweetened with honey. Anne pushed it away. "No, enough."

The midwife scolded her. "You need it to keep up your strength."

Marguerite put the cup to Anne's lips and she begrudgingly sipped a little. After she put the cup down, Marguerite wiped Anne's brow. "It will not be long now, m'lady."

"Oh, good Lord, it hurts!" Anne moaned.

The midwife patted her leg. "There is a reason they call it labor, m'dear."

"Do not patronize me!" Anne lashed out.

She moaned through another contraction.

"Scream as loudly as you like, m'lady. No one would blame you." The midwife tried to soothe her.

"I'll give this storm some competition." Anne tried to make a joke.

The midwife checked Anne's progress one more time, and then looked up at her with a smile. "Alright, Lady Anne, let's bring this child into the world."

Outside in the hallway, the men still waited. The storm grew even louder, but Anne did not hold back either. They could hear her screams.

"Do you think she is alright in there? Childbirth is a dangerous thing." Richard looked pale.

"Ah, you know Anne. She'll pull through this as if it were

nothing at all." Baldwin shrugged.

"It does not sound as if it were nothing," Richard retorted.

Andrew tried to put him at ease. "Your mother gave birth to ten children and lived through them all. Anne is so much like the queen that I believe you have little to fear."

Anne gave a loud wail, causing the men in the hall to jump to their feet. Everything fell silent, then the quiet cry of a baby sounded from within, crescendoing until it filled the hallway. Stunned, they stood in silence.

At last, the door slowly creaked open, and a worn looking Marguerite emerged, shutting the door behind her.

"My lord, gentlemen." She gave them a tired nod. "Lady Anne has given birth to a son."

"And Anne?" Richard pressed her for information.

Marguerite gave him a drained smile. "Both mother and child are well, tired but well."

Richard asked, "When can I see her?"

Just then servants carried out the bloody linens and the midwife joined them in the hall. Richard gasped at the sight. "Lord in heaven! Is that natural?"

The midwife spoke with the air of a wise old mother. "Yes, it is. Not to fear though, Lady Anne is asleep. The first child is always the hardest. The wet nurse is attending the babe. He is a fine strong boy." She put a hand on Richard's shoulder. "Might I suggest that you yourself could use some rest? I will stay with Lady Anne. Please, my lord, send your men away so that they do not disturb her."

Richard snapped at the men in the hallway as if they had done something wrong. "You heard the woman! Be gone!" He turned back to the midwife. "You will tell me the moment I can see her, won't you?"

"Yes. Now go and get some sleep, sir." She shooed him away.

Chapter Eighteen

Later that morning, an exhausted Anne slept. The midwife and the wet nurse also slept on their straw pallets on the floor. Richard tried to sleep; he could not. Creeping into the room, he knelt next to Anne's bed. She stirred and slowly opened her eyes.

"I am sorry," he whispered, "I did not mean to wake you. I just could not wait any longer to see you."

The midwife heard him and jumped up from her bed. "My lord!"

"Please leave us. I will send for you if I need assistance," Anne ordered.

The midwife and wet nurse obeyed. Once they were gone, Richard spoke again. "How are you feeling?"

She took his hand, "Richard, I have a son."

"I know." Richard grinned at her, "and he will be the greatest viscount that Marseilles has ever known."

Anne tried to sit up, but Richard prevented her. "Now where do you think you are going?"

"I want to see my son," Anne explained.

"I shall bring him to you." Richard started toward the cradle, but turned back. "On second thought, perhaps I should call the wet nurse."

Anne gave him a gentle smile. "No, just pick him up and be sure to support his head."

Richard stood over the cradle for a moment then awkwardly scooped up the baby. With slow deliberate steps, he brought the baby to Anne. When the baby was in Anne's arms,

Richard let out a long sigh of relief.

Anne spread the blankets and examined her son. After a while she asked, "Do you think he looks very much like his father?"

Richard took another long look at the baby. He did have his father's dark features. "His looks may change, but his eyes; he has your eyes. That is the important part, you know. Eyes are linked to the soul."

Anne swaddled the baby back into his blankets and held him to her. "I feel badly because I did not want this child. I did not want any part of Raymond," her voice cracked. "But now that I have met him, held him, I know that he was meant to belong to me. Of all the things Raymond did, he at least gave me a beautiful son."

"At last you broke the curse of only female heirs for Marseilles."

Richard gave her a tender kiss on her head.

Neither said anything for a while. They simply looked at the baby. When Richard brought him to his mother, the baby opened his eyes, but he did not fuss. Now the baby closed his eyes once again and drifted off to sleep.

"Anne," Richard finally broke the silence. "I understand your reasons for not wanting me to acknowledge him, but do not forget that as his godfather, I promise you that he will want for nothing." He beamed. "Well, what did you name him?"

"William, after my father." Tears filled her eyes.

"Your father would be proud of his namesake."

"I know he is. I know he is."

Anne recovered quickly from giving birth, and Will, as she called him, grew strong. Before she knew it, he passed those childhood milestones of walking and talking. Richard kept his word and played his part of godfather well. He had a hard time refusing the boy anything. Every now and then, Anne found the need to intervene and remind Richard that she did not want Will to be spoiled like his father.

Had it not been for the fact that Will looked so much like Castile, people would have assumed he was Richard's son. Some just shrugged and declared that Will might as well have been Richard's son, the way he doted on the little boy.

Eventually, King Henry summoned Richard to travel with him to Gisors, the ancient meeting spot between the Kings of France and the Dukes of Normandy. They met there with King Philip under the pretense of discussing the Princess Alice and the Vexin; Philip, however, had other motives.

Philip sat in his tent, preparing to meet with Richard. The tent was decorated only to afford comfort, not luxury. The fabric throughout seemed as muted in colour as the pale canvas walls.

Settling himself in a large cross framed chair at a small oak table, Philip spoke to his short, blonde haired, blue-eyed attendant, Norbert. "The English King foolishly continues sending Duke Richard to deliver messages back and forth. Soon, I will have him eating out of my hand, just as I did his brothers."

"Yes, sire. It is tragic how both of them died, Geoffrey at a tournament and Young Henry while fighting his father. Some took his death as a lesson." Norbert adjusted his master's purple mantle for him.

Philip waved off his comment. "Come now, that is ridiculous. He just fought for what was rightfully his."

"Perhaps you can simply bide your time, and God will take care of the rest of your enemies for you." Norbert placed a goblet of wine before the king.

"Richard will be a challenge."

A French knight entered the tent. "My lord, the Duke of Aquitaine."

"By all means, let him enter." Philip's crystal blue eyes sparkled.

Richard entered the tent, bowed to Philip, then handed him a letter from Henry. Richard looked at Norbert, who stood behind Philip, and the two other guards stationed behind him. He glanced at the two visibly armed guards standing inside the doorway.

When Philip finished reading the letter, he looked up at Richard. "Your father is truly, oh, what is the word I am looking for?"

"Perhaps obstinate?" Richard's face did not register a joke.

Philip laughed. "Have a seat. Some wine for the duke, if you please."

Richard took a seat opposite Philip while Norbert poured Richard some wine. "Well now, this is a bit awkward, is it not?" Philip took a sip of his wine and continued. "Here you are affianced to my sister, the very issue that brings us to Gisors, and your future depends heavily on these negotiations."

Richard did not reply, and Philip studied him over the top of his goblet. "Now, here I go bringing a dark cloud over us. I want to be pleasant. After all, you are to be my brother-in-law. It will do no good to dance around the issues. Let us be honest."

"Precisely." Richard raised his cup to Philip.

Philip reciprocated, and took another drink. "Well then, where do you stand on the issue of marriage to Princess Alice? After all, the king is getting on in years, and you are his heir."

"I will do my duty, my lord."

"Your duty?" Philip looked amused. "Oh come now! Remember we are being frank with one another."

Richard grimaced. "It is exactly as I said, I will do my duty; regardless the king's age, for now, he is still the king."

"May I humbly submit that while he may be king, as the

Duke of Aquitaine, you are my vassal?"

"Then what is it you command of your vassal?"

Philip put down his goblet and leaned a little closer to Richard. "I sense that you don't trust me."

"Should I?" countered Richard. "There are very few people that I trust."

"So I have heard." Philip leaned back in his chair. "There is someone else I have been hearing quite a bit about lately."

"Oh?" Richard finished his goblet of wine and set it down.

"I have heard some interesting news regarding my cousin, the Viscountess de Marseilles." Philip pressed his fingers together as if anticipating Richard's reply.

Richard gave him a knowing smile. "Ah yes, Lady Anne."

"It was very smart of you and your father to snatch her into your custody. Marseilles is a rich prize indeed," Philip observed.

"Being a blood relation, you should know who controls Marseilles."

Philip recognised the compliment mixed with information. "Being a blood relation, I can only imagine. It is also rumored that she is too much for her husband to handle. I should very much like to meet Lady Anne. I understand she is here with you at Gisors."

"Naturally, I never go anywhere without her." Richard narrowed his eyes.

"Oh, right. You do not trust leaving her to anyone. That is rather odd." Philip frowned. "I do not think I have ever wanted to spend that much time with a woman, not a mistress, and certainly not my wife. Well, then, I guess you will just need to come along too."

Richard shook his head. "I fail to understand your meaning,

sire?"

Phillip shrugged. "I was going to extend an invitation to my dear cousin to accompany me back to Paris. Naturally she will accept, and so you will be joining her."

Richard looked into Philip's startling blue eyes. "Is this a command from my lord?

"No, oh, no." Philip waved his hand in front of his face. "I thought Paris might be a bit more lively than following dear old daddy around. Besides, you have not been to Paris since my coronation."

"I beg your pardon, but what is it that you want? I sense that my lord is up to something." Richard folded his arms.

"Why, Richard, I am surprised at you, surprised that you did not notice sooner." Philip threw up his hands, "Alright. In truth, you cannot deny your father is getting on in years. Let him make his empty promises here, for we all know they are empty. I simply wish for you and me to be amicable, even dare I suggest, friends? You've certainly got enough people to fight without adding me to the list." He paused. "Richard, you and I are going to be the real powers. I just want to ensure a smooth transition for all."

Richard raised his eyebrows. "My entourage is a large one."

Philip rolled his eyes. "Yes, you are traveling with a woman. Bring them all, my cousin, her child, the nurse, the servants, the whole lot of them. You will all be welcomed in Paris."

Chapter Nineteen

From the previous night's rain, a mist rolled through the morning air as Richard and Philip prepared to leave the camp for Paris. Standing near their horses, Philip and Richard prepared to be underway. Everywhere the camp was one large mud hole. Both man and beast wore down the grass, and rain only exacerbated the problem.

Philip turned to Richard and wrinkled his nose. "It is a fine morning for travel, don't you think?"

Richard's eye held a gleam. "Any morning is a good morning for travel, my lord."

"I suppose I will not have the pleasure of meeting Lady Anne until later today as she will be traveling with the other women," sighed Philip.

"Oh, no. She will ride with us. Her horse is made ready over there." Richard pointed to a nearby palfrey and as he did, caught sight of Anne. "Ah, here she comes now."

Anne gingerly picked her way through the mud toward them, her head bent down as she paid close attention to her muddy feet. The hood of her cloak obscured her face. When she reached the pair of them, she looked up, her hood sliding back to reveal her face. "Good morning, my lords." She gave a little curtsy.

"Richard, you have again deceived me, for this can be no cousin of mine but an angel sent from heaven." Philip rubbed his gloved hands together.

Anne flashed her disarming smile at him. "I assure you, sire, I am no angel. Alas, I was roused early this morning and informed two knights of most noble character needed my assistance. It seems they are in want of an escort to Paris. In truth, I have never been to Paris, so I do not know the way; however, I posses a good map, and by the looks of it, fine company, so to Paris I go."

"You see, we have most fortunate company, my lord." Richard's face beamed.

"And extraordinary one at that!" Philip licked his lips.

She shook her head. "Oh, no, my lord. I am afraid I am rather dull. In fact, I am afraid that before half a day's journey is through, you will have become so bored with me that you will send me packing."

Philip winked at her. "I will take my chances."

Richard noticed Phillip's covetous look. "I beg your pardon, my lord, but I would like to get the lady out of this muck."

"By all means." Philip made a wide gesture toward Anne.

Without warning, Richard scooped Anne up and carried her across the mud to her horse where he gently deposited her. Completely caught off guard, Anne giggled. Richard's page brought him his own horse that he mounted with perfect male gusto.

Philip watched this interaction with a great deal of interest. He too mounted his own horse. Once seated, he glanced back at Anne and Richard, watching as Anne tenderly adjusted Richard's cloak that was knocked askew. At that moment, Philip put a face on the notion of love.

In Paris, Philip tried to ensnare Richard. He had plans for Richard, but Philip found himself constantly distracted. However, in this distraction, Philip found Richard's flaw, a weakness. Inside Philip a conflict of *bellum intestium* raged as he discovered he was loathe to exploit Richard's weakness.

As he observed Richard and Anne, he learnt much about the nature of love itself. Love was not a horrible ugly failing in the human soul, as so many priests taught. Philip learnt of love in the little things that Richard and Anne did. Often Philip observed Anne absent-mindedly playing with Richard's hair, winding it around her little fingers. His glass was never empty; she always seemed to know what he needed before he could even ask for it. In turn, Richard frequently placed his hand on the small of her back, gently guiding her along. Sometimes when they rode horses, he reached over and discreetly took her gloved hand in his. When Richard looked at her, his eyes said a thousand things that could not be put into words.

Philip watched all this and took note. In time he found that he too loved Anne and was jealous of Richard. Nevertheless, he took consolation in the fact that he knew the chink in Richard's armor.

Several pleasant weeks passed in Paris, the trio forming a cautious friendship. Late in the evening of the fifth week Philip challenged Anne to a game of chess. She readily accepted and joined him in his solar.

When Norbert first showed her into the room, Anne noted the austere décor. Frugal Philip contrasted with Richard, who was not afraid to spend money.

The game waited for them on a small table, and Philip sat on the white side. When he motioned to her, she took her seat opposite him and they began to play.

"Well, cousin, how do you find Paris?" He casually tossed out his question.

"Very delightful," she replied. "And I have greatly enjoyed the hospitality of your court."

"I am glad to hear it and glad it has left a good impression." He studied her face for a reaction.

She stared down at her marble figures on the board. "And you have no interest in impressing Richard?"

"You are a forthright woman." Philip made his move. "Beat that move if you can!"

"I am sorry if I offend. Sometimes I am too candid."

Philip gave her a warm smile. "From you, I do not mind it. Although, I do wonder sometimes where your loyalties lie." He tried to gauge her expression. "Yours is an interesting situation, no doubt. Here you are, Viscountess of Marseilles, not technically under the ruler of the Kingdom of Burgundy but still ruling within the territories, kin to the King of France, under, shall we say, the guardianship of the English King, and for all intents and purposes, mistress of the future ruler of the Angevin Empire, and richer than us all."

"Do not forget, I am married," she added.

"Yes, but it is rather obvious that you have no loyalties to your husband. So to whom do you remain loyal, kin, lord, or lover?"

Anne made a counter move on the board that put Philip's queen in danger. "Well, with my complex relations being as they are, I cannot afford to be loyal to anyone. For if I am loyal to one, I make enemies of the other. Therefore, I am loyal to Marseilles."

"Pray tell then how following Richard around helps Marseilles?"

She leaned in a little closer and spoke softly, "Oh, I think you know as well as I that it does not hurt to have a truly gifted warrior as an ally."

Philip laughed. "I am relieved he is just an ally to you. Perhaps you and I..."

"Sire," she wagged her finger.

"You know I only jest." Philip rolled his eyes. "Yet, after watching the two of you, sometimes I wonder who is truly the master. It is clear that your influence on him is profound."

"Cousin, I do believe you desire me to use my influence to some purpose." Anne did not look up from the board.

"Ah! Now we are getting somewhere. You are good at this game, but perhaps not good enough." Philip made a move on the board that Anne could easily counter.

Anne looked him squarely in the eye. "Then what is it that you want?"

Philip sighed. "Oh, you know, the same old tune, Alice married, the Vexin, return of Brittany. Alas, I am a realist, and, for now, I want an ally against Old King Henry."

"You must not forget, Richard is his son."

"Yes, but it would not be the first time he rebelled against his father."

Anne made a feeble move that was an obvious setup for her to lose the game. "I will give you that. But suppose that Richard becomes your ally; eventually, he will become king. What then?"

"Now, you see that is why I must get what I want before

Henry dies. Then I will have what is rightfully mine, and Richard and I can simply rule as friends." Philip did not take advantage of Anne's weak move. He countered with an equally pathetic one.

"You do not really believe you will be able to remain on friendly terms forever, do you?"

"Why, Lady Anne, whatever do you mean?"

"Well, your highness," Anne took a deep breath then answered, "if Richard does become your ally, how do you propose to solve your differences? For example, you want the matter of Princess Alice and the Vexin solved. I do not believe it can be solved to either party's satisfaction. If Richard married Alice, clearly the Vexin would be his; but there is always the chance that he should at some point, God forbid, leave Alice a widow. Naturally you would contest that the Vexin belongs to Alice, as it is her dowry; therefore, it should recede back to French control."

"Naturally."

Anne made another pitiful move. "The Vexin is too important for either of you to lose. Now, say perhaps Alice is not married to Richard or even John, for that matter. Has she just been a political prisoner of the English crown for the past twenty-five years? Your family honor is most definitely at stake." Anne shrugged. "I really see there being no amicable solution."

"And what about you? Where does this leave Lady Anne?"

"I am not sure of your meaning." Anne tipped her head to the side.

"What if Richard does marry? Will you continue in your current... position?" He hesitated on the last word.

"I cannot say."

"What if your husband died while on Crusade? What then? Even if Richard were king, do you think he would marry you?"

"No. I would not let him," Anne gave firm nod.

"Let him!" Philip snickered. "You make it sound as though he needs your permission. Richard is not the type to seek anyone's permission."

Anne raised her eyebrows. "It would be an unwise match. The political ramifications would be too great." In response, Philip rolled his eyes again. "He has his duty and I have mine." Anne remained resolute.

"I can hardly believe that you would not distract him from his duty."

"If and when Richard marries, I am compelled to... "

"What? Leave him?" Philip interrupted. "Oh, do not be so naïve."

She shot back, "With all due respect, there is someone more powerful than any of us here, who demands our loyalty first, and that is God. He gave us our charges, our titles, our responsibilities. Just as it is your duty from God that you must be constantly fighting for the interests of your kingdom, it is Richard's duty that he must fight for his, and I Marseilles. If necessary, I would separate myself from Richard. Duty, my lord, is incumbent upon us all, no matter our station. The pawn, the knight, the castle, and even the queen owe their duty to the king," Anne thoughtfully, touched each piece in turn. "The king is duty bound to God and his kingdom. It has always been thus, and must ever be, so long as a king reigns."

Philip studied her for a long moment, still skeptical. "It would kill him, you know."

"Not as long as he had Aquitaine." She shook her head.

Philip's retort came out soft and sincere. "No, my dear. A hundred Aquitaines could never replace a life with you. To lose you would be a greater blow than any defeat I could deliver."

"Come now, that is not true."

"Vice versa. It would kill you too," he paused. "I must confess I am jealous. I also admire your courage. Anne, I know where your loyalties lie. You are loyal to love."

"If you say so, my lord."

"What do you mean, *if I say so?*"

"I do not know what to say."

"Hah! Speechless at last! I do believe I have accomplished a great feat!" He made the final move that won the game and looked at her triumphantly.

She gave him a gracious smile. "My lord, for me it is the Marseilles above all else."

"May I commend you in your resolve." He made a slight nod of his head toward her. Just then Richard entered the room. "Oh, Richard, just the person we were engaged in pleasant gossip about."

"I hope Lady Anne has not been too hard on me." Richard grinned.

Philip made a gesture for Richard to sit. Richard took a seat next to Anne. Anne looked back and forth between the two men and suddenly rose to her feet. "My lords, I must beg your pardon and take my leave. We have finished our game, and I need time to prepare for the banquet. The vanity of a woman, you know."

"I look forward to your company tonight," Philip replied.

As Anne curtsied and left the room, both men watched her go. "Now there goes a truly interesting creature," Philip remarked.

"That is one way of putting it." Richard's tone sounded stiff.

Philip ignored Richard's sullen glare. "I wondered why you continued to insist on her company. I reached the conclusion that her wealth contributed a large part of it, but now I understand. She is hypnotic! I would never let her go if I were you." He laughed. "Imagine that, a woman as such a great asset."

"I have no intention of losing Anne. If I may speak freely, I have seen a look or two you have sent in her direction," Richard rejoined.

Philip returned with a sardonic smile. "I confess, I have

feelings for the lady. Richard, as your lord, I must extract a solemn promise from you, that no matter what, you will always look after her. Take care of her. Protect her, even from yourself."

"You know I will."

"Swear it as my vassal!"

"I swear it, my lord."

"Good." Philip leaned back in his chair.

"Speaking as your vassal, I would like to know just why you have brought me here to Paris. I know Lady Anne was only an excuse."

Philip returned with an equally hard question. "In that case, I must ask you what your plans are for my sister Alice?"

Richard glowered at Philip. "You know full well that I have no power to make decisions for myself."

"That is just simply not true, Richard, and you know it!" Philip licked his lips. "Let me give you some advice. As a future ruler, you must start laying your foundations now. You simply cannot afford to wait."

"And don't I know it."

"Then demand what is yours!"

Richard shook his head. "It has been done before."

"With all due respect to both you and my late father, this time you have a more powerful, a stronger ally," Philip offered.

"Just what is it that you propose?"

Philip leaned in closer to Richard. "I wish for us to form an alliance against Henry. Together we cannot lose."

Richard reciprocated and leaned in so that both men whispered over the chessboard even though they were alone in the room. "And what exactly do you hope to gain from this alliance?"

Philip knocked some of the chess pieces over. He did not bother to right them. "It is simple really. I see Alice married and Henry humiliated."

"Ah, yes, Henry humiliated, now there is a happy thought." Richard smiled in spite of himself.

Philip continued, "He has offended many whom we both care for, and he will pay for it too."

Richard narrowed his eyes. "Yes, indeed he will."

"Let us strike a bargain then?"

"Agreed."

Chapter Twenty

Late morning found Anne in her narrow chamber with Marguerite and Will. Will had a wooden sword tucked into his belt, and he pulled a little toy horse on wheels behind him. He walked round and round in circles, all the while singing a little song Blondel taught him about a crocodile and a monkey.

"Will, perhaps you could sing something else, dear?" Anne suggested to him, as she loosened the braid in her hair.

Richard entered the room without knocking. Will's face lit up at the sight of him. "Uncle!"

"Good morning, Master Will." Richard ruffled the boy's hair. "Still singing about that old crocodile?"

Will nodded his head and beamed up at Richard. Marguerite held out her hand to Will. "Master Will, would you like to go outside for a little while?"

Will clapped his hands together. "Oh, yes, Mother, please, please may I go outside?"

"I don't see why not?" Richard gave him permission.

Anne narrowed her eyes at Richard. "As long as you stay with Marguerite, Will."

Will grabbed Marguerite's hand. "I know! You can be the dragon, and I'll be King Arthur come to slay you." Will continued his instructions to Marguerite as they left the room.

Once alone, Anne turned to Richard. "Richard, you must stop doing that. I am his mother."

"Well, if you do not wish for him to go outside, then I shall

call them back. Perhaps I could sing the crocodile song with him."
Richard grinned at her.

"Oh, you are awful." Anne pretended to be cross with him.

She rose from her chair, and Richard sat down in her place.
"Someday I will have to thank Blondel for teaching him that
song."

"You know Will, once he gets an idea in his head, he stays
with it." Anne shrugged.

"I wonder where he gets that from."

"Are you saying I am stubborn?" Anne put her hands on
her hips, and showed a tiny grin.

"I did not say the word stubborn. You did." Richard
gloated.

They both fell silent for a moment, and Richard fiddled
with Anne's comb lying on the dressing table before him. Then he
looked up at her and said with a slight pout, "Anyway, you
certainly seemed to enjoy yourself last night."

"Didn't you?" she asked.

Richard rolled his eyes. "Well, yes, but Philip kept you
pretty much to himself."

The corner of Anne's mouth turned up in a smile. "Why
Richard, are you jealous?"

"Jealous?"

"I believe you are." She leaned over and put her arms
around his neck. "Good, you should be. It will keep us all young."

"I know you belong to me, but I wonder, does he know it?
Tell me, what do you think of your cousin the king?"

Anne straightened, traipsed over, and sat on the bed.
"Generally I find him pleasant enough, but if I were you, I should
not trust him completely."

"And why is that?" Richard joined her on the bed.

"He has motives."

"We all have motives." Richard rolled his eyes.

"Precisely. You both want essentially the same things.

Think what you would do to obtain them, then plan on Philip doing at least as much." Anne raised her eyebrows.

Richard leaned closer to her. "That is an interesting theory you have, Lady Anne."

"You think on it, and you shall see that I am always right." She tapped on his chest lightly with her finger.

Richard chuckled and kissed her. "I believe I should like another one of those."

She kissed him back. He stood up and pulled her to him, kissing her on the lips, on the forehead, and on the neck. Sliding his fingers through her hair, he burnt with a kind of ravenous hunger for her, and she wasn't fighting or pushing away. He paused for a moment. "All you have to do is tell me to stop, and I'll stop," he whispered in her ear.

She nodded and barely spoke the word, "stop," before she kissed him hard on the lips.

A knock at the door startled them, and she jumped away from him. She immediately straightened his tunic, and he smoothed her hair, pushing a bodkin or two back in place. They were both flushed. He turned away from her, cleared his throat, and called out, "Um yes, come in."

As Marguerite entered the room carrying Will on her hip, they both gave a sigh of relief. She set the boy down, and he ran to Richard. "M'lady, the king is coming."

Richard and Anne exchanged wondering looks. Before they had time to do anything else, Philip and Norbert arrived at the door. Norbert took up a post by the door.

When Philip entered, Richard, Anne and Marguerite all bowed to him. "Good morning, good morning." He greeted them. Philip carried a letter in his hand, and he reached out to Anne with it. "This came for you."

"You did not need to go to all the trouble of bringing it to me yourself, my lord," she took it from him.

"No trouble, cousin." He smiled back at her.

She opened the letter, but dim light it the room made it difficult to read. "Excuse me, please," she offered, as she made her way over to the small window to use its light.

Philip sat down in a chair. Richard pulled another one over and sat facing him. Climbing up into Richard's lap, Will placed his head of downy soft brown curls against Richard's chest and stared at Philip with his large hazel eyes. "Is everything alright, dear?" Richard called over his shoulder.

Her brow furrowed. "It is from Etienne."

Richard looked back at Philip. Philip made a face at little Will who giggled. "And what have you been up to on this fine day, Master Will?"

Will showed Philip the wooden sword tucked into his belt. "I was going to slay the dragon, but Marguerite didn't make a good dragon."

"Funny, I know many women who make perfect dragons!" Philip smiled warmly at the boy.

Richard laughed at Philip's comment. "You shall have better luck next time; I am sure of it."

"Would you like to hear my song that Master Blondel taught me?" Will sat up straight.

"Let me guess, the one about the crocodile and the monkey." Philip leaned forward and tickled Will's tummy, as Will squirmed.

Anne walked over to the men. "Etienne sent some troubling news from the Holy Land." She began. She moved another chair over for herself before either of the men could react. "It would seem that Saladin has captured Jerusalem."

"What?" Both men sat up straight.

"That is what Etienne says." She handed the letter to Richard. He read:

The Infidel and the Saracen army have taken

Jerusalem and have taken King Guy hostage.

Will pressed himself back against Richard's chest. Sensing the boy's discomfort, Richard stopped reading. He looked up at Anne. She knelt down beside Richard and took Will's hand. "It is alright, son. There is no need for you to worry."

Will didn't look convinced. " Mama, what's a Sawa... a Sar... I" Will tried to pronounce the word.

"A Saracen." Richard helped him.

"A Saracen is a Muslim," Philip offered.

Will's little face screwed up in thought.

Anne tried a simpler approach. "Darling, you know how we go to mass to celebrate our Lord and Savior Jesus Christ?"

Will shrugged and nodded a little.

Richard tried to help. "Muslims do not believe in the divinity of Christ, Will. They ruled over many of the holy sites where Jesus lived. We Christians took back many of those places to keep them safe from ruin."

"What Uncle is saying is that Muslims and Christians do not always play nicely together." Anne brushed some of Will's hair from his face.

"Why?" he asked. "Mama, I thought boys should play nicely, right?"

Philip didn't look at Will; instead he looked at Richard. "Boys grow up into men, and men must defend what is theirs and keep other evil men from trying to take it. They fight over land, Master Will. They fight about who owns the land."

"Yes, arguments over land make men do mad things Will." Richard met Philip's look with a resolute one of his own.

"Are the evil men coming here, Uncle?" Will looked up at Richard.

Richard smiled at the little boy, trying to make him feel better. "No. They are in Palestine, and that is a very long way from here."

"Even farther than Marseilles?"

"Yes, it is across the sea from Marseilles." Anne rose to her feet.

Will thought for a moment. "Uncle," he asked, "will you go to fight them?"

"Will, I think you should go with Marguerite to the kitchen and get something for that empty stomach of yours," Anne said before Richard could answer.

Will slid off Richard's lap and obediently went to Marguerite. The two headed for the door, but Will turned around. "Mama, are they are mad about land and Christ?"

"Yes," Anne nodded.

"They don't go to mass?" Will tilted his head.

"It's complicated, dearest..." Anne began.

"Come, Will, I will make a much better dragon this time. I promise." Marguerite grinned at him.

Will hesitated a moment, then he ran to Richard again, jumped in his lap, threw his arms around Richard's neck and squeezed hard. Without saying a word to Richard, Will climbed back down and pulled Marguerite by the sleeve. "You must growl much louder this time."

Norbert shut the door behind them. Both Richard and Philip rose from their seats to offer them to Anne. Shrewdly she sat in the chair she pulled over.

"What else did Etienne have to say?" As he sat back down, Richard laid his hand on her knee.

Anne let out a long sigh. "Well, as you know, Marseilles maintains a church in Jerusalem. Etienne does not know the fate of that church, yet. My father worked very hard to build up trade alliances all over the Mediterranean, and Etienne is preparing to make a journey to shore up those associations and keep trade flowing." Anne rose from her chair, pacing back and forth. "There is more news. Pope Urban is dead."

"What?" Philip cried out in amazement.

"It would seem that when he heard the news of Jerusalem his heart stopped mid-step."

"Good heavens!" Richard leaned forward, "Are you sure?"

"That is what Etienne reports in his letter. If it is true, I am sure we will be hearing more of it. Etienne's letter goes on to say that the new pope is styling himself, Gregory VIII, and is calling for a crusade." She gave Richard a sideways glance.

Philip stood and gave Anne a slight nod of his head. "I believe I will see if my sources can confirm this information."

Anne curtsied and Richard bowed as Philip left the room. Norbert followed Philip. When the door closed again, Anne turned her back to Richard. "There is something else, isn't there?"

Anne's shoulders drooped. "He will take up the cross, you know."

"Who, Philip? Naturally he will."

"You will take the cross as well."

"I suspect every king, emperor, and prince will." Richard stared down at his hands.

Anne turned around and faced him. "Yes, but many of them will buy their way out of actually going on crusade. With you and Philip, it will be personal; it is personal. You will both take up the cross, and you will both have to see it through. It is going to turn into a private jousting match, and you know it."

Richard did not respond. Anne turned away from him again and went to the window.

Chapter Twenty-one

"Just as Anne predicted, both Richard and Philip took up the cross." Breton shook his head at the thought. "Without permission from his father, Richard took the cross from the Archbishop of Tours and had it sewn onto his surcoat."

As Bogis stood up and stretched his legs, some of the other knights shifted position. Breton did not speak while they moved. "How did Henry react to Richard taking the cross without his permission?" Bogis stretched his tired arms above his head.

"King Henry was livid when he heard what Richard had done." Breton smiled to himself.

Upon hearing the news that Richard took the cross, Henry shut himself in his room and refused to come out for days. Some, including Richard, suspected Henry of trying to get attention.

Richard used the cross for his own political gain. He pledged not to leave on crusade until Henry promised him the succession. This gave Richard two advantages. First, if Henry formally named Richard as successor, then he would not have to worry about John claiming the throne. Richard also knew that Henry was unlikely to do this, so he could delay leaving for Palestine.

Tensions mounted between Henry and Philip, and Richard aided Philip with men and arms. Finally in early 1189, they met for a peace conference in Bohmoulins.

Both factions met on neutral ground just outside of the town. Henry arrived first, and set up a large tent, hoping to impress the younger king. He sat in a bulky chair and mentally prepared himself for the negotiations as he waited for Philip's arrival.

Eventually, the tent flap was drawn back and the French king announced. Henry stood in greeting, but halfway up, he saw who accompanied Philip. Richard strode defiantly into the tent and did not give his father even a curt bow. Henry knew that Richard spent more and more time of late with Philip, but until that moment, he did not understand the extent. As he sat back down in his chair, he glared in Richard's direction. "Imagine seeing you here."

Philip's man, Norbert, brought in a large chair, and placed it before Philip. Philip took a seat. Despite the two empty chairs in the tent, Richard stood behind Philip, facing his father. "I am here in the service of my overlord and because these issues have much to do with me."

"Why don't you run along, Richard and let the kings conduct their business." Henry snickered at him.

"He will remain and participate in the negotiations. It is my request." Philip raised his eyebrows.

Henry continued, "Alright then, put forth your demands, boys."

"If you were any other man but my father, I would have killed you for that."

Philip put up his hand to stop Richard. "Our first demand," he stated loudly, "is that Richard be allowed to marry Alice, immediately."

"You do realize that one can only listen to the same tune so many times before it becomes downright boring." Henry rolled his eyes. "Well, do you have any other demands? If so, please hurry and state them. I know you both must be anxious to march off on crusade and prove yourselves men."

Philip stayed his course. "Now, Henry, even you must admit that you are not immortal. Yes, even you, the great Henry FitzEmpress will someday pass from this earthly realm. You must want to see a smooth succession for your empire. I am sure you do not want to see England plunged into chaos and civil war, as has been known to happen upon the death of a king without an appointed heir. Marrying Richard to Alice would go a long way in proving that you intend him as your successor. The only reason I can think of for you to not marry her to Richard is because you intend to marry her to John and name him as your heir." Philip rested his chin on his hands. "In short, the time has come for you to recognise Richard as the heir to the throne."

Henry firmly grasped the armrests on his chair. "That I will not do."

After a moment, Philip let out a long sigh. "I find it rather interesting; I took up the cross. You took up the cross, and naturally Richard took up the cross. Kings, princes, and noblemen all over Christendom are eagerly answering the call from the pope. In fact, I have a copy of the letter from the pope right here."

Richard pulled out a letter from under his surcoat and handed it to Philip. Philip opened it and looked as if he were going to read it.

"If you have a point, please come to it. I have my own copy, nay several copies of this letter." Henry put on his best-jaded facade.

Philip gave him a cynical smile. "Indulge me."

Noisily, Henry let out a long breath. "I do not suppose I shall get anything out of you otherwise."

"I particularly like this part." Philip read from the letter.

... WHEREFORE, TO THOSE WHO WITH A CONTRITE HEART AND HUMBLE SPIRIT SHALL UNDERTAKE THE LABOUR OF THIS EXPEDITION, AND SHALL DIE WITH REPENTANCE FOR THEIR SINS AND IN THE TRUE FAITH, WE DO PROMISE PLENARY INDULGENCE FOR THEIR OFFENSES, AND ETERNAL LIFE. AND WHETHER THEY SHALL SURVIVE OR WHETHER DIE, THEY ARE TO KNOW THAT THEY WILL HAVE, BY THE MERCY OF ALMIGHTY GOD AND OF THE

AUTHORITY OF THE APOSTLES SAINT
PETER AND SAINT PAUL, AND OF
OURSELVES, REMISSION OF PENANCE
IMPOSED FOR ALL SINS OF WHICH THEY
SHALL HAVE MADE DUE CONFESSION.

Henry fussed around in his seat while Philip read him the letter. First he leaned on one arm and then the other. Then he examined his hands, both front and back, several times. Finally Philip finished the letter and handed it back to Richard. "Yes, yes, forgiveness of sins and a pathway straight to heaven. It all sounds so tempting." Mockingly, Henry widened his eyes.

"I know of at least one prince who would find crusade very beneficial," Philip returned.

"There are not enough crusades to compensate for Richard's sins." Henry laughed.

"No, not Richard. Your other son, John, is the prince of whom I speak." Philip tilted his head. "John would benefit from crusade. Would you not agree Richard?"

"John does not need to go on crusade." Henry's face reddened.

"Pray tell, why is that Father?" Richard asked him.

"Yes, why hasn't your favourite son done his duty for God?" Philip added.

Henry spoke through clenched teeth. "I don't have a favourite..."

Richard interrupted him. "Oh, spare me! That is a lie parents have been telling their children since Adam. It did not do much good with Cain and Abel, now did it?"

Henry raised his voice, "Who are you to presume to tell me about my regard for my own sons? You do not have any sons! Thank God for it! You do not know what it is like to be a parent!"

"Some might argue neither do you!" Richard shouted back at him.

Philip spoke to calm down the father and son but with a feeble, halfhearted effort. "Just a moment. Shouting will do us no good. It will accomplish nothing."

Richard grew more animated, talking with his hands and arms. He pointed to Henry. "I am convinced that this conniving man refuses to name me as his successor because he intends to name John as his heir. That is why John has not taken the cross. He does not want his precious heir to be put in any danger."

"Richard, I am warning you!" Henry stood.

Richard placed himself right in front of Henry. "What? What are you going to do this time? Are you going to have Anne kidnapped again? You would not dare touch her because this time she is under Philip's protection as well as mine."

Both father and son seethed with anger, their fists clenched, ready to strike. "If I may," Philip forced himself between them, "I believe a simple gesture on your part, Henry, could end this argument." Henry only glared at Philip, as he continued. "Simply name Richard as your successor or give him some sign, some token that you do not mean to give the crown to John."

"No." Henry jutted out his chin.

"He means to give my rightful inheritance to John." Richard shook his head.

Philip tried again. "It would go a long way to restore your relations with Richard."

Henry sat down and spoke without shouting. "I have spoken."

Richard erupted. "Now at last I must believe what I had always thought impossible!"

Without warning, Richard dropped to his knees before Philip. "I do hereby swear homage for the Angevin lands in French territory to my sovereign overlord, Philip Augustus, by the grace of God, King of France."

When he finished, Richard rose to his feet, and without even looking in his father's direction, he stormed out of the tent.

Henry sat motionless in his chair. Philip picked up his gloves from where he dropped them. As he laid one on top of the other in his hand, he turned to Henry and quipped, "I do believe he just declared war on you, Henry."

Philip followed Richard.

Chapter Twenty-two

The rift between father and son ruptured into a chasm. In June, Philip and Richard launched a joint attack on Henry's lands. First they invaded Henry's county of Maine, but this time Henry's war machine could not fight hard enough to hold his territories. The towns of Montfort, Maletable, Beaumont, and Ballon rapidly fell to Richard and Philip. Henry was wearing down.

Richard wanted to find a way to force Henry to meet his demands, once and for all, so he feigned an attack on Tours to lure Henry's troops away from his asylum in Le Mans. With only the rear guard left to protect Henry, Richard's forces swooped in. Henry fled, leaving his faithful steward, Marshal, behind to command the rear guard.

Hearing that Henry abandoned Le Mans, Richard took six men, including Andrew and Baldwin and rode hard for Fresnay, hoping to capture the king. The June sun beat down on them, and to gain speed and time, the men rode without their hauberks or battle armaments. As always, Andrew and Baldwin rode at his right and left, respectively.

Their horses' hooves pounded their way down the road out of Le Mans. Up in the distance, Richard saw another group of men, the king and his guard. Richard spurred his horse onward.

Ahead of them, Marshal slowed his horse, turning to face Richard and the others. Only three men followed Marshal. They too were not dressed for battle. Henry took off pell-mell for

Fresnay with the rest of his knights.

Richard made out Marshal. Then, to Richard's horror, he saw that Marshal lowered his lance at him. "By God's legs! Do not kill me, Marshal! That would be wrong as I am unarmed!" Richard shouted.

Mounted in an attack stance, Marshal hesitated for a moment. His face flushed, and anger sparked in his eyes. Finally he screamed back at Richard, "No, let the Devil kill you, for I won't!"

With that, he charged at Richard. Richard instinctively put up an arm to deflect the blow. Marshal attacked, running his lance through Richard's horse. Richard fell to the ground along with the animal. He rolled out of the way of the dying horse. By the time he looked up, Marshal and his men were speeding away toward Fresnay. Andrew and Baldwin dismounted and helped a stunned Richard to his feet.

Henry temporarily escaped, but it seemed this time Richard and Philip had another ally, one that Henry could not defeat: time. Henry's age and health conquered him at last. It had been a long time coming, but it came steadily on, forcing Henry to face the fact that he was in a losing battle with his son. He could no longer carry on a war having narrowly escaped at Le Mans, and the enemy gained territory on a daily basis. Peace became the only option.

Ill and exhausted, Henry retreated to his castle at Chinon. Finally even the key city of Tours fell. The next day Henry agreed to meet with Richard and Philip at Ballon.

Richard stood watching in the direction he knew Henry would come, waiting for the moment his father would come down that road, a broken man. Philip joined him. "No sign of the old man yet?"

Richard shook his head.

"Do not fret. He will come. He has no choice." Philip wore

146

an odd frivolous smile.

Philip ordered a large tent erected in which to hold the negotiations. Many of Richard and Philip's faction gathered to see the English king brought to humiliation. They waited in groups off to the side. Anne stood in the tent's doorway, as the flaps softly fluttered in the breeze. She too watched the road for any sign of Henry.

Finally, three men on horseback approached in the distance. Henry rode in the middle flanked by his illegitimate son, William Longespee and Marshal. As the group came into view, it became apparent that Henry could barely ride his horse. Everyone fell silent as the trio stopped in front of Philip and Richard.

Marshal and Longespee dismounted and Henry followed. He faltered, but Marshal kept him on his feet. Still no one spoke. The gathered's astonishment was palpable as Henry tried again to walk but could not keep his balance. Once again, Marshal reached out and supported him.

Richard heard a rustle, and Anne appeared in front of him. She said nothing but stopped and stood before Henry, gazing at him with wonder.

Henry looked up at her; his eyes widened. In her hands, she held a cloak. Without saying a word to anyone, she turned and walked to a nearby elm tree and spread the cloak out in its shade. Marshal steered Henry toward it. Anne took Henry's other arm and helped Marshal place him on the cloak. Once Henry was on the ground, she walked back to the doorway of the tent. Philip and Richard joined Henry in the shade.

At length, Henry spoke in a raspy voice, "I agree to the terms you have set forth. I will pay Philip twenty-thousand marks; Alice is to be handed over to a guardian of Richard's choosing, and he will marry her as soon as he returns from crusade. We will muster at Vezelay during Lent next year to embark on your grand adventure." Henry stopped.

"And," Philip prodded him.

"And," the anger of the old Henry came back in the snap of his voice, " ... and my subjects both in England and on the continent will swear allegiance to Richard. Also, I grant amnesty to all those that have taken part in this rebellion against a *sanctified* king. Now, if that is all, the day is hot, and I intend to retire to Chinon." Henry tried to rise to his feet, and Marshal appeared at his side to assist.

Richard felt nauseous, and before he knew it he whispered, "Father?"

Henry looked his son straight in the eyes, "Richard, I am very tired. I do not care to do this right now." He and Marshal turned to go.

Philip stopped him. "I am afraid that is not all."

"What else can you possibly want, boy?" Henry turned back to Philip.

"You know as well as I that these negotiations must be sealed with a kiss of peace."

Henry only glowered at Philip.

"Give your son the kiss of peace, Henry," Philip commanded him.

Henry started to make his way forward to Richard. Marshal tried to assist him, but Henry shook him off. With what strength he could muster, he grabbed his son by the shoulders as if to plant the kiss of peace upon Richard's cheek. Uncomfortable, Richard tried to pull away, but Henry yanked him closer and hissed in his ear, "God grant that I may not die until I have had my revenge on you."

Henry released Richard, and on his own, walked to his horse and mounted it.
Marshal and Longespee mounted their horses, and the trio rode away in the direction they came. Richard and Philip watched them. Just before the men rode out of sight, Richard saw Henry's silhouette slump against Marshal, but they continued on.

Henry returned to Chinon, the castle of his ancestors. Marshal tried to make the king as comfortable as possible. As Henry lay on his bed, he motioned to Marshal. "I want that list of everyone who conspired against me."

"My lord, you need to rest now." Marshal protested.

"Good God, man! I want to know who thrust their daggers into me. The men who stabbed Caesar at least had the pluck to let him see their faces as they did it. Those daggers that are in me were put there by cowards, and I want to know every single one of them. I want to know the name of anyone who deserted me for Richard."

"As you wish, my lord." Marshal turned from him.

By late evening a page brought a list to Marshal of those who joined with Richard and Philip, either by conspiring or by simply not defending the king. He handed it to Marshal who took it over to Henry's bedside.

"Well, let's have it. Read it to me," Henry ordered.

Marshal looked at the first name on the list and stammered, "Sire, may Christ help me, for the first name is... is... is John, your son John."

Henry snatched the parchment from Marshal's hand and crumpled it into a ball. "Is it true that John, whom I loved beyond all my sons, and for whose gain I have suffered all this misery, has forsaken me?" Henry moaned in pain, his sweaty face contorted. "It is enough, no need to read the others. Let the rest go as it will. I care no more for myself, nor for aught in the world."

He turned away from Marshal, rolled over to face the wall, clutching the list to his chest. After a long moment, he softly cried out, "Shame, shame on a conquered king." Then he lay still.

A shaking Marshal checked for signs of life. Henry FitzEmpress, King of England, Count of Anjou, Duke of Normandy, Aquitaine, and Gascony, Count of Nantes, Lord of Ireland was dead.

Párt Thréé:

Sovereignty

Chapter Twenty-three

"Hum," Bogis snorted. "Good old spineless John betrayed his own father."

Father Breton replied, "I am afraid so. When Richard took Le Mans, John saw how powerful Richard had become, and he pledged his allegiance to Richard. To be honest, I think it disgusted Richard that John would be so disloyal to the man who championed him for so many years." Breton scratched at his throat. "Hearing that John abandoned him, was the final blow that killed King Henry."

Everyone remained quiet for a moment, as if they were paying some sort of respect to Henry. After a while, Breton asked, "Does anyone have something to drink? I am afraid all this talking is making my throat dry."

One of the younger knights sped off down the hall and returned with a flask. Breton took the flask. "What's in it?"

The young knight shrugged; Breton curled his lips in a smile then drank from it. The men waited for the priest to finish his drink. When Breton finished, he wiped off his lips with the back of his hand, set the flask down, and continued.

Philip left Ballon for Paris after Henry's departure; however, Richard remained in camp. The news of his father's death reached him there.

Anne went for a morning ride with Marguerite and Baldwin. When she returned to camp, she could sense something amiss. People spoke to one another only in whispers. She rode her horse straight to Richard's tent where Blondel greeted her and helped her dismount. "What is it? What has happened?" She looked around her.

"It is King Henry, my lady; news reached here just after

you left that he passed away," Blondel explained.

"May God grant him mercy." She crossed herself. "Where is Richard?"

Blondel took the reins of her horse. "When he heard the news, he did not say a word; he just walked over to a grove a trees and sat on a fallen log. He's been sitting there for a while now. We are waiting for Marshal to officially bring the word and the royal seal to Richard."

"Thank you," she called over her shoulder as she headed to find Richard.

She came upon the grove and could see Richard sitting still on a fallen log. Andrew stood off at a distance, arms folded, watching over Richard. She approached Andrew, who was out of Richard's earshot, and placed her hand on Andrew's arm. "He hasn't said a word," Andrew whispered to her. "He's just been sitting there."

"I can only imagine what he is thinking." She sighed. "Have any of the other men seen him like this?"

"No, he is pretty secluded here, and I've ordered all to stay away."

"Thank you."

She left Andrew and walked toward Richard; he did not even turn to look at her as she approached. She sat down next to him on the log, which bent with the additional weight. Without looking at her, he reached over, took her hand, and took a deep breath. "What was your wedding like?"

"My wedding?" Anne stammered.

"You know, I have been sitting here, and all I can think about is your wedding." His shoulders slumped. "My father is dead, and that is all that will come to my mind. Do you think I am going to hell?"

"That is a question for a priest."

Richard gave a snicker. "It has always been my experience that a man of the cloth rarely has anything good to say."

Richard arched his back and stretched his arms. "So, tell me about your wedding," he continued.

"Oh, Richard, I do not know." Anne rubbed her right temple. "It was a wedding. There was a priest, and Taillebourg, and Raymond, of course." She paused. "I was in a daze. I honestly remember very little."

"Oh." Richard fiddled with a loose thread on his sleeve.

"I do remember that after the wedding Raymond drank a lot of mead. I guess it was your standard *kidnap a wife and keep her for a month, hoping a pregnancy would result wedding*." She shrugged.

"I *will* have to marry now. The country will expect it. I will have to produce an heir, a son. I wonder if that son will feel the way about me the way I felt about my father." Richard's eyes looked empty.

Anne wrapped her arm around his. "Will loves you. Think of that."

"Excuse me, my lord." Andrew approached them. "Marshal is coming."

Marshal sauntered toward them with Henry's emissaries trailing behind. Feeling she had no right to be seated next to Richard in a moment such as this, Anne stood and moved off to the side. Marshal knelt before Richard and held out the royal seal to him. "The king is dead; long live the king."

Others around him knelt before Richard. He reached out and took the seal, then rose to his feet, and motioned for Marshal to rise. "Sir, you shall be rewarded greatly for your loyalty to the late king." Richard managed a smile. "Now take me to the body, Marshal."

They all turned and followed Richard.

Henry's body was taken to Fontevrault Abbey to be buried. Marshal accompanied Richard there, where they found Henry laid out in makeshift funeral vestments. As soon as Henry died and Marshal left the room, servants stole the king's clothing and valuables. An old sword and a makeshift scepter were placed in Henry's hand. Only a curt mantle could be found for a cloak and a fillet of gold embroidery from a woman's dress was fastened to his head for a crown. The nuns of the abbey performed their duty for Henry and held a wake for him. All that remained was for his heir to see the body, and then he would be buried.

When Richard arrived, the abbess escorted him into the abbey, and led him to the doorway outside the chapel. Richard paused. He turned to those around him. "Pray, please leave us alone for a moment."

The old abbess and the others silently obeyed, but when Marshal turned to go, Richard stopped him. "Not you, Marshal." Marshal's eyes widened. "I wish to speak with you for a moment. Marshal, you tried to kill me, and would have done it, if my arm had not turned aside your lance."

Marshal looked him in the eye and replied, "Sire, I had no intention of killing you, nor did I make any attempt to do so. If I can drive my lance aright when armed, I can surely do it when unarmed, as I then was, and it would have been as easy for me to strike you as to strike your horse. If I killed your horse, I do not think I did wrong, nor do I repent."

Richard could not help but smile. "Marshal, I pardon you. I pardon you, and furthermore, I hold no enmity."

"My lord... I..." Marshal looked down at his feet and shuffled them. "I thank you, sire. Please believe me when I say that I did by no means desire your death."

"I need men like you, who are loyal and brave." Richard clapped him on the shoulder. "In fact, I have an important task for you. I wish for you to speed to England to look after my lands and affairs until I come."

"As you wish, my lord."

Richard heaved a sigh. "It is time. The others may join me

if they so desire."

He put his hand out and touched the latch, hesitated, then opened the door. Marshal beckoned the others to join them, and they followed Richard to the funeral bier.

As Richard approached the body, everyone scrutinized him to see what emotion he would display. Richard remained in such control that none could read his sentiments. He knelt down before the bier and gazed upon his father's corpse. Richard only remained there for the space of a paternoster, then rose again. When he got to his feet, the abbess gasped in horror. Others around did the same. Confused Richard looked back down at the corpse astonished to see blood trickling from the nostrils of the dead king. The crimson flow seeped down onto the floor beside him.

Richard did not lose his composure. Instead, he turned and left the chapel. Outside he mounted his horse and rode off in the direction of Chinon. His stunned entourage followed.

Chapter Twenty-four

Richard made quick work to secure his succession. He started by taking possession of the royal treasury at Chinon. Next, he made his way to Rouen where he was invested as the Duke of Normandy. The ceremonies were carried out with proper pomp and circumstance. For many it was a joyous occasion, full of fun, feasting, and for some, frivolity. For Anne, however, it was a time filled with apprehension and doubt. She found that the closer they got to England, the less time she spent with Richard. Naturally he found himself bogged down with the daily responsibilities of running the kingdom; she understood that, but she felt she had become just another courtier or hanger on.

The night before they set sail across the channel she stopped and counted the number of words Richard spoke to her that day, three. He only bade her good morning; then she did not see him the rest of the day. The next day they crossed the channel in separate boats.

Richard's entourage landed at Portsmouth, where, to his surprise, his mother greeted him. When Marshal reached England, he found that the news of Henry's death traveled faster than he did. Eleanor's jailor released her immediately for fear of retribution from Richard. Eleanor was free to greet her son as he arrived on England's shore.

Eleanor's dark eyes sparkled as she watched the ship approaching the harbor. Her face had more wrinkles now, her hair turned silver, but her eyes could still enchant. When they pulled into the harbor, Richard did not wait for the boat to dock completely. He jumped down and swept his mother into his arms before those waiting had time to take the proper position of respect due to a king. The assembled scrambled to curtsy and bow. Richard let out a long

deep laugh at the sight. Eleanor grinned from ear to ear as she led him away from the docks.

Anne arrived at the docks just in time to see Richard and Eleanor leaving. She watched them go, until Baldwin got her attention. "My lady." He stretched out his hand to help her from the boat, and she took it. As he helped her down, he gave her a sympathetic smile.

Almost from the moment he landed, Richard began a Progress through his kingdom. Eleanor went to great lengths to prepare for his coming. Everywhere cheering crowds greeted him. Anne followed with the entourage. Without waiting to be asked, she resumed her duties as lady in waiting to Eleanor. Eleanor greeted her with cautious kindness, and before long Anne suspected that Eleanor resented her freedom all those years. The queen was not rude or mean to her, yet acted with a certain coldness toward Anne.

London welcomed its new king. Nothing about Richard's entrance into London was done by accident. Everything had been planned and choreographed by Eleanor, or by the participant hoping to gain favor with the new monarch. Richard would enter England's largest city, a triumphant king. For the first time in one hundred years, since William the Conqueror, the succession to the crown had gone unchallenged. Londoners and England gave a collective sigh of relief that this time there would be no civil war to accompany the new monarch.

Regardless of Eleanor's feelings toward Anne, she knew Anne's capabilities and delegated many responsibilities relating to the coronation and feast to her. Anne welcomed the diversion, satisfied with being busy. This coronation was to be the grandest show London had ever seen, and grand shows are time consuming and expensive to stage.

Two days before the coronation, Anne visited the kitchen to go over menus and order of courses with the cook. Just as she finished, one of the castle guards announced Master Thatcher. Along with Will's tutor came a thin middle-aged man also dressed in the robes of a scholar and an older, more gnarled man, but with a gentle expression on his face. In an instant, she could tell from their features, and their yarmulka's that the other two were Jews. All three doffed their hats and gave Anne a bow.

"Master Thatcher, is something the matter with Will?" Anne asked.

"My lady, I beg you forgive this intrusion. I have brought these two gentlemen to ask of you a special favor. Please allow me to introduce Jacob of Orleans and Rabbi Isaac."

Anne smiled at the mention of Jacob of Orleans' name. "Sir, I have heard your name mentioned often at home and abroad. It is said that you are one of the most learned men in London."

"My dear lady. I knew your father and always thought him

a most admirable man. I had the fortune of knowing him in my younger days, and I offer my sincerest of condolences on his passing."

"I thank you, but to what do I owe the honor of your visit?" Anne noticed the other man come forward. He was old but had a soft face, the kind that made a person feel instantly comfortable.

"Lady Anne, this is Rabbi Isaac. He is here as a representative of the London Jewish community." Jacob introduced him.

The Rabbi also gave Anne a bow. "Lady Anne, I have a cousin in Marseilles who speaks highly of your family. Let me personally thank you for the kindness and protection you have shown our people in your city."

"Rabbi, I have not been back to Marseilles for many years now, but let me say from one merchant family to another, I hope to keep good relations between us." Anne bowed her head at him.

"My lady, it is because of your fairness and understanding that we come to speak with you today." Rabbi Isaac looked at her with warm brown eyes surrounded by wrinkles.

"If you are like your father, I know that you will appreciate our being direct," Jacob added. "We know that you have a special relationship with our new king. We know that you have his ear."

"Well..." She blushed.

Rabbi Isaac gave her a look that reminded her of her father. "Lady Anne, we would very much like to present the king with gifts to honor him at the occasion of his coronation."

"I know you understand the art of diplomacy, as you are, after all, Sir William's daughter. You know as well as we that gifts can go a long way in helping to foster good relations. Since the Jewish community is under special protection of the crown, we must have the best possible relations with the king. This is a time of uncertainty for our people. Whenever there is a new monarch, we never know how he will treat us. It is most important that we start on a good footing with King Richard," Jacob explained to

Anne.

"Yes, but I fail to understand what I have to do with any of this." Anne raised her eyebrows.

Rabbi Isaac frowned. "We have made many requests, my lady, but all have been denied. We believe that it is not the king, but his man Marshal who repels us. We know that you can speak to the king."

"Good sirs, I do not mean to disappoint, but I cannot persuade the king to do anything."

Rabbi Isaac shook his head. "All we ask is that you try. As you know, there was another beautiful woman who had great power to persuade a king on behalf of the Jewish people."

Anne was embarrassed by their reference to Queen Esther, but felt for the men. "I shall try, but I cannot promise anything."

"I thank you, my lady. We thank you on behalf of our people. It is a great service you do for us." Jacob bowed his head again.

"Now come, gentlemen. We have taken too much of this good lady's time already. She is tremendously busy. We shall take our leave." The Rabbi gave Anne a warm smile and then turned to leave.

"Good day, Lady Anne." Jacob smiled at her and then he too left, followed by Master Thatcher.

Anne did not delay but went straight to find Richard. She arrived at his door, but Marshal blocked her way. As the days to the coronation drew nearer, Anne became aware that Marshal did not care much for her. Richard heaped lands and titles on Marshal as a reward for his service to the crown, even arranging a marriage for Marshal to the very wealthy, young, attractive heiress, Isabella Clare. Anne never dealt personally with Marshal, until now. His manner with her was abrupt and impatient. "I am sorry but the king cannot be disturbed, at present." He folded his thick arms and looked down at her.

She tried to give him a polite smile and told a lie. "The

King summoned me sir, and…"

He interrupted her, "The king is in there with his tailor at the moment."

"The cook is waiting on me to give final instructions for the coronation feast. This is a busy time for us all. The king has summoned me, and I have come." Anne rolled her eyes.

Marshal puffed out his chest in response.

"Marshal, is the King in a state of undress? If not, let me see what business he has with me, and then I shall be gone. Heaven knows he will not be happy if his coronation feast is a flop because you kept me standing here in the hall all day." She reached around Marshal and placed her hand on the door latch.

"Viscountess, it is not as if you are his wife."

His words made Anne stop. She had heard enough of Marshal's snide comments. She turned and faced him. "Do you really believe I do not know that?" She turned to the door again and pressed the latch but did not push the door open yet. "Besides, if I recall correctly, you found yourself accused of questionable conduct. Neither of us is perfect." She did not wait for his response, but entered the room and closed the door behind her.

Richard was, in fact with his tailor, but they had just finished. They stood at the other end of the long narrow room in front of a massive desk that seemed way too large for the space. His face lit up when he saw Anne. "Anne! I have got some wonderful news!" He dismissed the tailor with his hand.

"What? What is it?" She pushed some hair back under her wimple.

He sat her down in a chair. "You look tired, my Sweet Annie."

"Of course I am tired. But what news?" She prodded him.

"I have found the most wonderful new tutor for Will." Richard looked pleased with himself.

"What is wrong with Master Thatcher? He tutored me, and I do not think that I am any worse for it." Anne felt Richard invading her parental territory.

"Come now, Anne. Master Thatcher was a fine tutor to be sure, but the man practically has one foot in the grave. Master More is the best, and he is available." He smiled broadly.

Anne did not say anything.

"Well..." Richard prodded her.

"Well... Richard, I um..." Anne stammered.

"Anne."

"How have you possibly found time to worry about a tutor for Will?"

"By heaven, I am still the boy's godfather!"

"Richard, there is something else."

"You are just trying to change the subject." Richard grumped.

Anne shook her head. "No, no I am not. I promise. I came here because I just had a visit from two prominent men of the Jewish community."

"Jews? What would they want with you?"

"They knew my father, and that is why they came to me. It would seem they desire to bring you a gift for your coronation, but Marshal forbade them."

"Marshal has his reasons, dearest." Richard attempted to charm her with a smile.

"Richard, these men are in a very uncertain situation. They wish to gain your favor to protect their people," Anne argued.

"Yes, well, I am trying to protect my crown, so I can be there to protect them. I need to project a certain image to the people of my kingdom. They need to see me as an Arthur come back from Avalon to save them all and rescue the Holy Land for Christendom. With this new Crusade, Jews are not the most popular people to be seen with right now."

"It is only a gift." Anne looked down.

Richard glanced at her and sighed. "Oh, Anne, I wish I knew exactly what to do. When I think of all the money they have

loaned the crown, and how much I may have to borrow for
crusade, I know it is wise to keep good relations with them. On the
other hand, if I show them favor I will loose the support of others
that I desperately need."

Just then the door burst open, and John flounced in.
"Richard! Well, well, it is to be king at last."

"Ah, John the newly made bridegroom. Welcome!"
Richard clapped him on the back. "It is about time you showed
yourself around here."

John caught sight of Anne. "Oh, sorry, I did not know you
were... busy..."

"My lords," Anne stood and gave them a curtsy. "Perhaps
we can continue this conversation later." On the long walk to the
door, she could hear the beginning of their conversation.

"You remember Lady Anne de Marseilles." Richard gave
John a glare.

"You mean to say she is still around?" John laughed.

Richard redirected the conversation. "Yes, but enough
about Anne. Tell me, how do you find married life?"

John helped himself to a chair, tossed his hat on the desk,
and launched into a story.

As Anne passed through the door, she noticed Marshal,
who said nothing, but stood, arms folded, chest puffed out, with a
baleful smile on his face like a cat just about to eat a prized bird.

Chapter Twenty-Five

Anne and Richard, tied up in preparations for the
coronation, did not resume their conversation. They only saw each
other twice more in passing.

The morning of the coronation Anne watched from a
balcony as a solemn procession made its way to Richard's
chamber. The bishops, abbots, and a large number of clergy, all

wearing silken hoods came as far as the king's inner chamber door.

Richard waited at his door where his escort received him. From there, they traveled to the high altar at Westminster. Those in the procession walked on a red woolen cloth that stretched from Richard's door to the high altar. Fresh rushes on the ground marked the route, and garlands of brightly coloured flowers hung brightened buildings.

They made their way in a somber procession while singing chants of praise. The gathered crowd remained silent. They would cheer the king along his path when he returned from the ceremony.

From the balcony, Anne watched as they left the palace for the cathedral. As the procession filed past, she tried to remember who was whom. The clergy led the way, still carrying holy water, the cross, tapers, and censers. The priors, the abbots, and the bishops followed them. In their midst, walked four barons, each carrying a candlestick of gold. Godfrey de Lucy, the Bishop of Winchester, followed. He brought the king's symbolic cap of maintenance. The brothers John and William Marshal had special duties. John flanked Godfrey, while William followed immediately behind, bearing the royal scepter and a cross both of pure gold. William, now the Earl of Salisbury, bore a rod of gold with a golden dove perched on top. The Earl of Huntingdon, Richard's brother John, and the Earl of Leicester all walked in a row, with John in the middle. They each carried a golden sword from the king's treasury, their scabbards worked all over in gold. Six earls and six barons balanced on their shoulders a very large chequer, which carried the royal arms and robes. William de Mandeville, the Earl of Arumarle, bore the massive golden crown, decorated on every side with precious stones. As Anne watched them pass, it struck her how the whole procession gleamed in the sunlight.

Richard himself walked under a canopy of red silk, held up on four lofty spears, hoisted along by four barons. On Richard's right walked Hugh Bishop of Durham, and on his left, Iteginald, the Bishop of Bath. Large numbers of earls, barons, knights brought up the rear of the procession.

Anne noticed Richard didn't look nervous. As he moved in the procession, he played his part to perfection. Now was the time for the people to see their new monarch and to think of him as Arthur returned from Avalon.

Women were barred from a bachelor king's coronation ceremony, but Eleanor was so loved by all that she and two ladies were allowed to attend. However, they would watch the proceedings from behind an ornately carved wooden screen. Anne was shocked when Eleanor chose her for this honor, and she suspected Richard had something to do with it. Although Eleanor and her ladies were not part of the procession, they too dressed in their finest. The robes for Eleanor and the other women were made of five and a half ells of silk each, and all were trimmed with squirrel and sable. The Queen's dress itself contained ten ells of scarlet cloth, two sables, and a piece of miniver as well as linen.

Eleanor and her ladies left the palace after the procession, taking a different route to Westminster. They arrived before Richard and his procession. As the ladies were seated in the cathedral, Eleanor took hold of Anne's arm. "Lady Anne, come, be seated next to me."

A large weight suddenly lifted from Anne's shoulders, and she felt as though she could take flight. Perhaps the queen had forgiven her for being free. Suddenly, the already quiet crowd in attendance fell even more silent as they turned to face the new monarch. Anne thought to herself that Richard looked every part a king as he entered and walked as far as the high altar where he knelt.

Westminster was already richly decorated with gold, but the procession brought more. The candlelight sparked the gleam and the entire chapel glowed in a heavenly light, making the priest appear as archangels anointing God's chosen servant.

The Holy Evangelists placed many relics of the saints before Richard. He repeated the words that the Archbishop of

Canterbury instructed him to say. "I, Richard, do hereby solemnly swear before God and these witnesses, that all the days of my life I will observe peace, honor, and reverence towards God, the Holy Church, and its ordinances. I shall exercise true justice and equity towards the people committed to my charge. I swear to abrogate bad laws and unjust customs, if any have been introduced into my kingdom. I shall enact good laws, and observe the same without fraud or evil intentions. I do take this oath upon myself and my soul in the name of God."

He rose to his feet and two clergy came forward. They stripped him of his clothes from the waist upwards, except his loose open shirt and braises. Then they placed sandals embroidered with gold upon his feet. The Archbishop of Canterbury stepped forward bearing a vessel of oil. He anointed Richard as king in three places, his head, "that you may be wise as Solomon," breast, "that your heart may be merciful," and arms, "that you may bear a sword in defence of God and your realm." This was symbolic of glory, valor and knowledge. The archbishop was liberal in pouring the oil and the sheen from the liquid reflected the glow of the candles off Richard's bare skin. Next he placed a consecrated linen cloth on Richard's head then the cap of maintenance.

The Holy Evangelists then dressed Richard in the royal robes. First, a tunic followed by a dalmatic. The archbishop bestowed the sword of rule and reminded Richard that, "This is to crush evildoers against the church."

Two earls placed the golden spurs upon his feet, and, lastly, he was robed in a mantle. Richard stood and was led closer to the altar. Canterbury continued, "In the name of the Almighty God, I forbid you to presume to take upon you this dignity unless you have the full intention inviolably to observe the oaths and vows you have made here today."

Richard cleared his throat, and in a resounding voice that filled the cathedral, answered, "With God's assistance, I will, without reservation observe them all."

As custom dictated, Richard took the crown from the altar and handed it to the Archbishop, then knelt before him. The Archbishop held it aloft and slowly lowered it, placing it as gently as he could upon Richard's head. The extreme weight of the crown made it necessary for two earls to support it, keeping the new king's neck from harm. Canterbury gave Richard the scepter to hold in his right hand and the rod of royalty for his left. After all of this, Richard was led to a throne.

The dulcet tones of mass mingled with the chanting of the monks from the choir, created an ethereal atmosphere that enveloped the packed nave. As mass was celebrated, Eleanor and her ladies peered out from behind their screen. Anne noticed how stiff and still Richard sat. She studied his eyes to find a hint of what he felt. As she watched him, a small movement caught her eye. A bat fluttered above Richard's throne. Richard did not react to it, and the two earls who held his crown remained at their posts. Not even the bishops at his side stirred. It circled around once, twice and almost three times, when Richard rose to his feet. Anne realized that they had reached the offertory point of mass as Durham and Bath led him to the altar.

Richard offered up one mark made of the purest gold, as was fitting for a king to do at his coronation. He returned to his seat. The bat circled again. Suddenly, Eleanor grasped Anne's hand. She too noticed the bat, and her face grew pale. She leaned towards Anne, and Anne bent to place her ear next to the queen's mouth. "Pray that this shall not be a bad omen."

When mass concluded, Richard was escorted back to his chambers in the same order of procession that he had come. Once in his chambers, he changed into much lighter robes and crown before leaving to dine.

As a venerated queen, Eleanor was allowed to attend the coronation, but not even that was enough to obtain admittance into the coronation feast. Richard was unmarried and therefore all women, from the king's mother to servants, were forbidden. Instead, Eleanor and her ladies celebrated with a separate feast in her chambers, and in the end, she retired early. Anne spent most of the day on into the night in the kitchen overseeing the meal and attempting to bring order to the chaos there.

After the third course, a moist, delicious dish of roast goose, the king called for more wine. Anne noticed two large casks missing. She rounded on the head cook. "Where is the wine?"

"What wine?" The man questioned back.

"The wine in those two large casks brought here yester night! How do you misplace two casks of wine?" She demanded.

"Oh, yes. I had two o' the spit boys move it out o' the way." He tugged at his collar. "'Twas too crowded in here."

"Well then, where is it now? The king is calling for more wine!"

"I don't exactly know, m'lady. I'll find the spit boys and ask 'em."

She rubbed her forehead with the heel of her hand. "That would be a wise choice."

The cook scurried off, and Anne waited for what seemed an eternity. After a while, she decided she would not wait for the boys; she would find the wine herself. She looked around the kitchen and thought she might try outside. Many of the extra food items were stacked out there in large crates. On her way out, she passed three boars' heads ready to be taken to the banquet. She paused to give them one last visual inspection, and then continued on her quest.

Exiting through the door, she peeked around trying to see what was underneath or behind a rather tall stack of empty crates hurriedly thrown in a pile. In the distance, she heard a loud commotion, and she turned.

Outside the gates, the people of London gathered, hoping to catch a glimpse of the new king and the goings-on on the palace grounds. The palace guards let through a few of the invited guests. Anne could see by the light of the torches that the guards were pushing around about half a dozen men.

The head cook emerged from the kitchen. "M'lady, we have found the wine."

"Good. See that it is served to the king immediately." She did not take her eyes off the palace guards.

"Yes, m'lady." The cook scurried off.

Anne moved closer, and as she did, she recognised two of the men, Jacob of Orleans and Rabbi Isaac. She broke into a run. Just as she reached the guards, the Jews were tossed out to the other side of the gate. The guards screamed at them, but the crowd was so loud she could not understand anyone. Anne tried to push forward, but one of the guards stopped her. Out of nowhere, a rotten apple hit Rabbi Isaac on his left temple, spattering into bits as he staggered and fell to the ground. Jacob tried to help him, but was pushed away. "Stop it! Stop it this instant!" Anne screamed.

"These are Jews!" One of the guards shouted.

Another one added, "They tried to get in to see the king." He spat in the direction of the two men.

The crowd outside jostled the men as Anne tried to reason with the guards. "No, no! It is alright; they mean the king no harm. They only wish to bring him a gift!"

"The king forbade Jews at his coronation." The first one gave her a wild smile. The orange reflection of the torchlight in his eyes made Anne sick to her stomach.

"No, please! You must listen to me. That was not the king's order! Believe me, the king would not want this!"

Someone shoved Jacob up against the gate. Anne pushed past the guard and opened the gate enough so she could squeeze through it. As she did, the first guard yelled out to the crowd, "King Richard is a warrior for Christianity sent from God to deliver us from His enemies! Anyone who is an enemy to Christ must pay! God save King Richard!"

The crowd now a mob, stirred to an animal frenzy, pushed and pulled the Jews about, tearing their clothes off their bodies. Some in the mob spit on them, cursed them, and beat them. A cobblestone hit Rabbi Isaac in the chest. Anne tried to rush to the men to shield them and plead their case, but a woman tore Anne's wimple off and grabbed a handful of her hair. She screamed in Anne's ear, "Jew lover! Jew lover!"

The woman threw Anne to the ground and picked up the same rock that hit Rabbi Isaac. She drew back her arm to throw it, but she disappeared in the press of the crowd. Before Anne could react, someone grabbed her by the waist and pulled her up. Frightened, she kicked hard and thrashed about. Now, she was higher than others. She looked at Jacob, who saw her struggle, his eyes pleading, but she could not tell if it was for her help or to send her away. She realized that she was being taken back inside the gate and struggled to break free. "Anne, it is alright. I have got you. This is no place for you to be." It was Andrew. "You cannot be here."

Anne pushed down on his arms trying to pry herself loose. "No! No! We must stop this, Andrew! They will kill them!" Hot tears tumbled down her cheeks.

She broke loose for only a second, but Andrew grabbed her again. "Anne, listen to me! You must stop! There is nothing you can do! The mob will kill you if you go back out there!" Andrew tried to reason with her while still shouting over the crowd.

He forced her across the courtyard and into the kitchen. She fought him the entire way, trying to go back out into the melee. "For God's sake, someone help me!" Andrew barred the door.

Anne's cries sounded above the already boisterous din of the kitchen. The cook saw Andrew struggling and hurried to help. "You," Andrew shouted at a spit boy. "Go get Baldwin of Be'Thune!"

The boy ran off as Andrew and the cook made their way, with a panic stricken Anne, through the kitchen to a back hallway.

Baldwin came running for Anne. She was hysterical, screaming half intelligible curses. He grabbed Anne's face. "Listen to me, Anne. You must calm down. There is nothing you can do. That is a mob outside. They would tear you limb from limb and neither know nor care that they are doing it."

She pulled at his hands as he continued, "Think of Will. Think of Richard."

Anne stopped fighting the men. She moaned and began to sink to her knees. Baldwin caught her and held her against his chest. She sobbed, "I said I would help them."

"Lady Anne, come, let us take you to your chambers." Andrew laid a gentle hand on her shoulder. He helped her to her feet, but she only managed a few steps before falling to her knees again.

Without hesitating, Baldwin scooped her up, climbed the stairs and made his way to her chamber door. She still cried when they reached it. Andrew pushed it open and led them in. Marguerite jumped when she saw Anne at the door. "Marguerite, bring some wine." Andrew ordered as they helped Anne to a chair.

Marguerite brought a goblet forward, but Anne pushed it away. Clutching her stomach, she leaned forward and vomited. Baldwin grabbed for a nearby water basin, spilling its contents on the floor and handed it to Anne. She continued to vomit into it, holding it on her lap. Andrew pulled her hair back, attempting to keep the wild mess out of the way. When Anne finally stopped, Marguerite reached out for the basin and took it from her. Anne buried her face in her hands and continued to sob. Baldwin stood by her side, gently patting and rubbing her back, and Anne leaned into his stomach.

Chapter Twenty-six

Just at dawn the next morning, Richard crept into Anne's

room. Marguerite was up and in the outer chamber, gathering items for Anne to dress. She did not give Richard her usual friendly look. He knew she was still angry with him because he arranged a profitable marriage for Andrew. Marshal was not the only one rewarded with marriage. Andrew and Baldwin were married to an heiress and a wealthy widow, respectively. John had been allowed to marry his cousin, thus giving him power over many of the western lands near the Welsh border. Richard did not see what difference Andrew's marriage should make to Marguerite. The two of them still carried on their affair, the same as before.

Giving Marguerite a mischievous grin, he stepped into Anne's bedchamber. She was still asleep. He intended to wake her, but decided against it and just watched her.

As he studied her, he thought of how they were in the last days of summer, the same time of year they had met. She lay on her side, curled up into a ball, clutching the bedclothes in front of her. Because the nights still held much of the day's heat, she was nude underneath the covers. Richard knew she only did this when she was uncomfortable from the heat. Her bare shoulders rose and fell just slightly as she breathed. Her freshly washed, unbound hair lay heaped on her pillow. The light from the morning sun poured in from the window, and filled the room as it danced off the auburn in her hair, giving a radiant glow to her skin.

She stirred, and he knelt beside the bed resting his chin on it. He noticed her face, especially around her eyes, was puffy from crying. Also he observed some bruises and scratches on her hands, face, and arms. She must have sensed someone there, because she jumped up, grabbing the bedclothes to shield her. "Anne." He reached out for her, but she was already on the other side of the bed. He gave her a reassuring smile.

She pushed her hair back from her face and gathered the bedclothes more closely around her. "Richard." She relaxed a little.

"Good morning." He moved around the bed closer towards her.

Wrapping the sheet more tightly around her body, she scooted back. There was not enough bed, and she fell backward onto the floor. Richard walked around the side of the bed and helped her up while she managed to keep the sheets taut.

"I did not mean to startle you," he apologized.

"I am… I… Richard, what are you doing here? Are you the only one here?"

Richard laughed. "I am king, and this is my castle. I can go anywhere I please." He ran a finger softly back and forth over her left shoulder. "I am king, Anne."

She gave him a sour look and walked to the bedchamber door. She opened it, and Marguerite entered carrying a dressing gown. "Your highness, please turn the other way so that I may dress."

Richard gave her a tart look right back but turned around as requested. "I actually came because I heard about your rough time last night." He fought the temptation to turn around.

"Oh? Who told you?" Anne tied the belt round her waist. "I am finished."

Richard turned around in time to see Marguerite give him a scowl and leave the room. "I spoke with Baldwin and Andrew."

"You look as though you have not yet been to bed." Anne observed.

"From what Baldwin tells me, you have not slept much yourself."

"So, how much do you know?" Anne's hazel eyes were laced with red.

Richard lay down on the bed, his hands behind his head. "They told me about what happened at the gate."

"What else happened? Surely you must know what happened after Andrew forced me inside." Anne sat next to him.

He rolled over to his side and put his hand on her knee. Instead of answering her question, he stroked her knee. Leaning down to see his eyes more clearly, she gave him a questioning

172

stare. He looked up into her eyes. As he did, he again saw the physical effects of the previous night. "Anne," he whispered.

"Tell me all. Richard, I must know." Her voice sounded soft but impassioned.

He took her hand and played with her little fingers. "Several of the men were beaten to death. The mob turned on the Jewish community and houses were burnt, women and children…"

Anne's eyes welled with tears. Richard sat up but did not let go of her hand. "There is a group that fled to The Tower and locked themselves in. They will be safe there."

Anne looked away from him, but he could still see the tears roll down her face. "Jacob of Orleans, and Rabbi Isaac?" She asked.

"They may have been among those killed by the mob at the gate." He reached out to take her in his arms, but she remained rigid. He offered, "I sent out soldiers to stop the violence and decreed the Jews are to be left in peace."

Anne got up and walked away, turning her back on him to face the window. "They only wanted to bring their new king a gift," she whispered.

He shrugged. "These were my subjects, Anne. I feel for them, too. The leaders of the riot will be found and executed."

She did not respond, but stood with her arms folded, silently crying. He put his arms around her, and she pressed back against him, wiping the tears from her face with her hands.

In just a matter of seconds, Andrew swept into the room. He bowed to Richard. "Forgive the interruption, my lord, but I have an urgent message from your brother John."

"John is not someone I can put off. I really need to…" Richard started.

Anne nodded her head. Richard gave her a kiss on the head and began to lead Andrew out of the room. He turned back and said, "I will be back later. I promise."

Anne looked at him sideways. "You have a duty, Richard."

She looked away from him again.

He took one last look at her as he left the room. She stood still in the same spot with her arms folded.

"That winter was a long winter for Anne, I am sure," Father Breton remarked. "Richard kept very busy seeking benefactors for the crusade and putting his government in order before he left. By the time spring came, Richard had already sold just about everything he could get his hands on. He sold castles, estates, titles, and even offices and appointments to the clergy. If a person wished to remain in his present office, he bought the privilege, or it was sold to the highest bidder. Eleanor's jailor, Ranulf de Glanville, went bankrupt to pay for his office." Breton chuckled. "Oh, the stories that went around! Some said Richard would have sold London itself if he could find a buyer. I guess in a way he did. That is when the crown started selling town charters. London had its first Lord Mayor at that time." Breton looked down at Bogis who shook his head.

"Richard faced many political issues. He appointed, or more accurately, sold the office of Justiciar to two different bishops, William Longchamp, the Bishop of Ely, in charge of the South, and Hugh de Puiset, in charge of the North. These two men never saw eye to eye. Otto of Brunswick, Richard's loyal nephew, was left to govern Aquitaine. Then there was John, the most dangerous because he had a claim to the throne. I believe Richard gave him so many lands in the West Country to keep him busy and hopefully out of trouble," Breton explained further.

"'Lot of good that did 'em!" One of the knights grunted.

Breton raised his eyebrows. "Well, now, there is more to it than just that."

At Easter of the year 1190, Richard's fleet sailed from Dartmouth to rendezvous with him in Marseilles. At the same time, Richard, Eleanor, Anne, and the rest of his entourage crossed the channel so Richard could complete his business in his southern lands. After staying only a little while with Richard, Eleanor left him to go on a diplomatic mission of her own. Anne was not told the mission's purpose; she just knew Eleanor had gone south toward the Pyrenees and the little kingdom of Navarre, she supposed to strike some kind of alliance to shore up Richard's southern border.

In July, Richard and Philip mustered their troops at Vezelay. This was the first time Richard and Philip met each other as kings. They agreed on many of the finer points of rule for the crusade, including that the spoils of war would be split in half, equal shares. Long ago, Henry and Philip agreed that no women would be allowed on crusade. Philip cited the fiasco that women, especially Eleanor and her band of "Amazons," caused on the previous crusade. Now Philip held steadfast to this accord and demanded Richard comply. Richard knew it was a ploy to separate him from Anne, but he agreed to it. However, he informed Philip that Anne would be coming along due to the fact that they would be meeting Richard's recently widowed sister, Joanna, in Sicily, and Joanna, being a queen, would need to have a lady to wait upon her. To avoid complication, the women would travel in separate ships and not with the main army; therefore, they technically would not be traveling with him on Crusade. On this point, Philip finally conceded. He had a plan as well, for he knew why Eleanor traveled to Navarre.

Chapter Twenty-seven

Early in the afternoon on a hot windy July day, Anne sat in her tent at a large table next to Will. Light filtered from the canvas ceiling floating down on the books spread over the table. The flap to the tent flew open, and Philip strode in. With haste, Anne and Will rose to give the king a respective curtsy and bow. Philip took Anne's hand across the table and kissed it. "Cousin Anne, it is good to see you, my dear."

"Your highness, I am honored." Anne gave him a genuine smile.

"Sir Will, how have you been?" Philip addressed the child as he took a seat.

Will had grown over the past couple of years. He was taller, and it seemed as though the rest of his body could not keep up with his legs. Still, he was a beautiful, charming child. "I beg your pardon, sire, but I am not a knight," The boy remarked.

Philip laughed. "You may not be one now, but you will be someday. You will be as skilled in battle as your Uncle Richard I dare say."

"Sire, may I ask you a question?" Will's brow furrowed in irritation.

"Why, yes."

"What is the purpose of studying all sorts of different languages? I would think you would only need to know the language of your troops, and that would be the same language of the people you govern."

"Thank you, Will. That is enough. You will go and eat and be back here in half an hour's time. Do you understand me?" Anne spoke in a sharp tone.

"*Etiam matris*," Will said as he left the tent. His skill in Latin was beginning to pay off, for he could now begrudgingly drag out, "yes mother," in Latin as easily as in French.

Anne sighed. "He refused to do his Latin lessons for Master More. He thinks Latin is boring because Richard thinks Latin lessons are boring."

"I cannot imagine that any child of yours would be stubborn." One corner of Philip's mouth turned up in a smile.

Anne brought a chair around to sit next to him. The tent walls billowed in and out with the wind. "I was most sorry to hear of your wife's passing, my lord. May I extend my deepest condolences?"

"Yes, thank you, Anne." Philip tried to change the tone of the conversation from his wife who had recently died while giving birth to stillborn twins, and attempted to add some humor. "On top of everything else, I have got to find myself a new queen."

"Hum." Anne shook her head.

Philip looked at Anne. He found it hard to believe he had forgotten her beauty. She was not wearing a wimple as married women did. He knew she hated the things and only wore them when it was necessary. Now her auburn hair tumbled down about her shoulders and her face. "I shall be honest with you, Anne. You crossed my mind once or twice as a most pleasing candidate. I even petitioned the pope on your behalf for an annulment. As you know, he would not even let the subject be breached because your husband is on crusade and cannot speak his case. Besides, if you did get an annulment, then I would have to petition the pope to allow our marriage because we are second cousins. Then there is Richard. In the end, I came to the conclusion that were you and I to marry, he would find a way to ensure I would have no more heirs."

"Sire, I am flattered, but there are other women who would make a better queen than I." She tipped her head to the side.

"Or one that my marrying would not put my manhood in danger." He grinned.

Anne did not smile. She looked down at her lap and said nothing.

"Anne, you do not look happy. What is wrong? What can I do to make you smile?" Philip scooted closer.

"Oh, I am a little tired. That is all. Perhaps it is the heat and life in camp." She shrugged.

Philip cupped her chin in his hand and lifted it so her eyes would meet his. "I know you better than that, cousin. You have spent a good deal of time following Richard around in military camps. Camp life is nothing new to you." He let go of her chin. "I guess I can understand your mood when there is the whole business about the Princess of Navarre."

Anne narrowed her eyes. "The Princess of Navarre? What business?"

Philip hesitated for a moment. He knew his plan was beginning to work, and here with Anne, looking into her eyes, he regretted it. He knew she would be hurt, but he had already started down the path; he must complete it. He reasoned she would find out about it soon enough, and it was better she heard it from a friend. "Oh, no. You did not know? You mean Richard has not told you?"

"Regretfully, sire, I do not know what he should have told me."

"Really? Richard has said nothing to you about Berengaria of Navarre?" Philip felt slight surprised.

Befuddled, Anne only looked up at him.

Philip took both of her hands in his. "I should not be the one to tell you this. It is not my place."

"Your highness, *Cousin*—I beg you, please tell me."

"Richard should be the one to tell you this. Not me." Philip pursed his lips. "However, I will tell you because I care for you. My sources have informed me that Richard does not intend to marry Alice as he promised. He intends to marry Princess Berengaria of Navarre and form an alliance in the south to protect his borders there. That is why Eleanor went to Navarre, to negotiate the marriage treaty."

Anne relaxed. "With all due respect, you must have been misinformed."

"I wish I were. Believe me. I wish it was all a rumor, but it is not. Thrice I had the information confirmed." He studied Anne's face. "Richard does not know that I know."

After a trice, Anne exhaled. "Well, I was never born to be a queen."

"Naturally, I am angered by it all because of the whole affair with Alice, but to treat you this way, to not even tell you himself… Oh, dear Anne, I am sorry. Was he thinking, Eleanor would show up with the woman, and you would just understand or submit without any kind of warning? I am so very, very sorry you found out about it this way."

"No, I thank you for your candor, cousin." She pushed herself up out of her chair and began to stack the books strewn around on the table.

"I am worried about you." Philip stood and placed his hands on her shoulders. "Do not go with him. Stay in Marseilles with Will where you will be safe."

She reached out for a book on the other side of the large table and pulled it closer to her. "I am not going on Crusade with him."

Philip reached around her and firmly placed his hand on the stack of books, looking her in the eye. "I know why you are *officially* supposed to be going, Anne, but, in truth you and I know the real reason."

"My lord, the real reason is to see to Marseilles' interests overseas. We do a considerable trade all along the Mediterranean. Granted, we are no Genoa or Pisa, but we are still very dependent on trade from that region. I have an important duty to my son and his inheritance."

"Anne, I beg you. I do not want to see you further hurt."

She turned around and faced him. "My feelings are of no consequence in this matter. Duty is the important thing. I never hoped to marry Richard and knew this day would come, eventually."

"I realize that; however, the way he is going about it is not fair to you. He is treating you as a trifle. After all these years of loyalty and sacrifice." He was close enough to feel her breath on his cheek.

Anne looked into Philip's blue eyes. "I promise I will come out of this adventure unscathed."

"Anne, promise me that you will not hesitate to ask for my help, should you need it."

"I promise, my lord."

"Anne, I swear…"

"Don't," she interrupted him.

Philip gave her a tender kiss on the forehead and turned to leave. He stopped at the tent door and turned around. "Just because he is a king does not mean he has the right to act like… he should remember those who made him what he is." Philip did not wait for a response; he left.

Anne spent the rest of the day supervising Will in his Latin lessons. Night fell and the camp outside came alive with music. Anne sat in her tent and listened to the celebratory mood. The nervous laughter of men soon to go to war floated across the camp, men relishing but fearing the glory that lay ahead of them, ready to be taken.

Anne was alone. Marguerite went off on a tryst somewhere with Andrew, and Will dragged Master More off to look at fresh horses that arrived earlier that day. Richard and Philip were somewhere, probably in Richard's tent, going over war strategies, or something equally uninteresting.

After a while, Anne decided she would retire early. Sitting down at her dressing table, she loosened her hair, brushed it out with her fingers, and laid her hairpins neatly in a row on the table before her. Lost in thought, she felt the ribbon around her neck, which held Richard's ring; she still wore it after all this time. Wondering if Richard still kept his token as close by as she did his, she pulled the ring out to look at it.

Before she had a chance to examine the ring, she heard a ruckus outside, so she went to her tent door. Just as she reached out to pull back the flap, Richard burst into her tent. She could tell by his red face that he was livid.

"Be direct with me. Did you or did you not have a private audience with Philip today?" Richard boomed at her.

"Richard, keep your voice down." She tried to hush him.

"Do not order me about! I am your king! Answer the question, Anne." He spoke even louder.

She looked up at him, defiant. "I fail to see how that is any of your concern. I am *not* your subject, and I *will* conduct my business with whomever *I* see fit."

"You have embarrassed me, Anne. I spent all evening in parlay with Philip, and now Will tells me that you and Philip were alone together in your tent. There were others there and they heard." He pointed at her.

"You cannot possibly think that Philip and I…" Anne raised her voice slightly.

Richard picked up a blue pillow and threw it hard against a tent wall. "I know you did not, but others do not know that. Besides, it looks as though you are plotting against me with the French King."

"Richard, you are being ridiculous."

"I am being ridiculous? *I* am being ridiculous? What about you? You have moped around ever since my coronation. Everyone sees it! Everyone agrees!"

"Of course, they agree with you. You are the king."

"Do not mock me, Anne." Richard flashed her a look of warning.

"I would not know how to mock you. I hardly know who you are anymore. The Richard I knew would not have cared one bit for the latest rumor at court." Anne glared at him.

"That man was not the king."

"Do not worry. That is a fact I have not forgotten. How could I? You keep reminding me. You know that I am, and have always been loyal to you, sire."

Richard stood over her, his arms folded, and looked down at her. "Then swear an oath to me."

"*What?*" Anne's eyes widened.

"An oath. I want you to swear an oath to me that you are loyal to me and not to Philip."

Anne exploded. "An oath! I do not need to swear an oath to you, nor shall I. The fact that I have stayed with you, stood behind you all these years, that is my oath."

"Swear that you are loyal to me, and that you love me."

"No." She folded her arms.

Without warning, Richard reached out and grabbed her arm, hauling her out of the tent and into the camp. "I will have you swear it before a priest."

She pulled against his strong grip. First he went left and then he came back to the right. Quickly, he walked toward his tent, dragging Anne along with him all the while shouting, "Where is a priest?"

"My lord!" Blondel ran to him.

Still in Richard's camp, speaking with Baldwin, Philip heard Richard shout out. Returning towards Richard's tent, he found Richard standing there with Anne, both seething. Richard yanked on Anne's arm again as he started toward the Archbishop of Canterbury's tent. "Where is a damned priest when you need one? They are always fluttering and flitting around when it's inconvenient, but when they are actually needed, there is not one to be found." As he went past one tent, he slapped the wine out of the hand of one soldier and pushed another who stood too close to his path, sending the man reeling.

Philip stepped into Richard's path. "Richard, stop! You are hurting her!"

Richard bellowed back, shaking his finger, "This is none of your concern, Philip. Get out of my way!"

"Richard, I am not going to let you hurt her!" Philip stood firm.

Richard stopped and clenched his free hand into a fist. His face flushed red with rage, and he shook. "Someone find me a bloody priest!" He thundered.

"I am done with this conversation!" Anne shouted.

Her outburst shocked Richard enough to loosen his grip on her arm. She jerked free.

"Anne!" Philip reached out toward her.

Anne stepped out of his reach. "I am sick to death of kings. I have had enough of kings today to last me a lifetime, thank you very much. Good night, your highnesses! I am taking my leave of you." She turned and stomped back to her tent.

Richard tried to follow her, but Philip jumped in front of him. "As a blood relation, I would advise you to calm yourself and let her calm down before you approach her again."

The two kings stood face to face, each one silently daring the other to make a move. Baldwin rushed to Richard, "Your highness, there is a message from Marshal regarding your… brother." Baldwin lied, but he hoped it would be enough to distract the king. Once he got Richard away, he would make up something, but he needed to separate the two men.

"This is not over, Philip." Richard grumbled and stormed to his tent.

Chapter Twenty-eight

The English and French armies struck camp at Vezelay and left together. Both Richard and Philip rode in front of the marching column. At first everything seemed to be going well, but when the massive armies traversed the bridge across the Rhone River at Lyon, the crushing weight caused the bridge to collapse. The kings had already crossed the bridge; Richard's troops were sent tumbling into the river. Miraculously, only two men drowned. Richard took control of the situation and used a bridge of boats for the rest of the army to cross. After the bridge collapsed, the two armies split at Lyon. Philip took the northern land route to Genoa, while Richard took his troops south to Marseilles to meet his fleet there.

Anne did not speak to Philip again before the two armies parted company. For that matter, she spoke little to Richard and only when necessary. Richard did try to make amends, in his own fashion. He sent Blondel to Anne with a song he wrote. The parchment was tied with a red ribbon, and attached to a bouquet of purple and white sweet william. Anne sent no message back to Richard.

As they drew closer to Marseilles, Anne's spirit revived. She was going home for the first time since leaving to serve in Eleanor's court. Richard noticed a new glow about her that became more radiant as each day passed. Her eyes sparkled in anticipation of their arrival, and her smile held a new happiness he had not seen since before she was imprisoned.

Two days from Marseilles, Anne's cousin Etienne rode out to meet her and travel with her. Many dignitaries from the city came and went from the camp, and Anne's tent became almost as busy as Richard's.

Late the night before they were to enter Marseilles, Richard sent Andrew and Baldwin to Anne to discuss the next morning. She laid out a rough sketch of the city before them and showed the two men the route for the king to enter the city.

"His procession will end at the chateau here." She pointed to her crude map.

"That all looks agreeable, Anne. You have done a

wonderful job as usual." Andrew smiled at her.

"Be assured, he will receive a royal welcome." Anne spoke with little emotion.

Andrew and Baldwin exchanged looks. "As you know, it is customary for the local reigning noble to accompany the king on his journey through the city."

"Yes, Etienne will be there to serve as escort."

"Anne, he wants you to do it." Baldwin scratched at his neck.

Anne shook her head. "Ah, no. I am a woman."

"Marseilles is yours, and you are Marseilles," Andrew softly chided.

Baldwin interjected, "If you will not do it for him, then do it for us. Think of us having to go back to Richard and explain that you won't do it."

"Ha!" Anne blurted out. Regaining her composure, she looked at Baldwin and caught the glimmer in his eye. He was goading her to do it. "Alright," she threw up her hands in mock surrender. "For the sake of you two knights, who are, I might add, a constant thorn in my side."

"There is the Anne I know," Baldwin teased.

"Now, I must beg that you take your leave as I am tired and have a long day ahead of me tomorrow." Anne gave them a warm smile.

"Of course, Lady Anne." Baldwin picked up his cap from the table. "We will bid you goodnight. Come, Andrew."

Andrew turned to Anne. "Thank you, Lady Anne. I know this is not something you relish doing, but thank you."

"Goodnight, Andrew." Anne waved to him.

The royal procession entered the city in grand style with the people of Marseilles lining the route to see the hero crusaders. As the army made its way through town, crowds cheered the soldiers, offering them drink and food. Women lifted their babies up for the men to kiss and thus bless.

Richard looked more like a conquering hero than a visiting head of state. Anne rode on his right side and Will on his left. Etienne, Andrew, Baldwin, other dignitaries of the city, along with Richard's *conseil privé*, followed them. Richard at once saw the resemblance to Anne and knew that Etienne was her trusted cousin. He had light brown hair, hazel eyes, a prominent nose, and a bulky commanding build. Anne treated Richard with the dignity and respect due a king, but did not show any familiarity beyond that.

As they traveled the streets of Marseilles, Richard noticed Anne close her eyes for a moment just to let the sun shine on her face, so warm, unlike the grey of London, or even Paris, for that matter. It was a whole different world. The gentle Mediterranean breeze caressed her face and ever so slightly tugged at her hair behind her ears, gently blowing down her neck. This was home; she was home.

Richard also noted the influence of the many cultures that called Marseilles home. He could see the influence of the Greco Roman era, the Moors from Africa, and the more well known to him flavor of Languedoc. He remembered back to all those times Anne spoke of her beloved city. Marseilles fascinated him more than he imagined. It seemed only right that Anne came from such an extraordinary place. She was so like the city, made up of so many different ingredients, all blended together in a graceful, wondrous form. He felt a sense of belonging to that city too. In an instant, he fell in love with Marseilles just as he did with Anne.

They turned up a hill that overlooked the port, and the chateau crowned the hill above them. The procession entered the grounds through a large gate in a high wall that surrounded the chateau. The building itself, made of large golden brown stone, towered high above the spacious courtyard, and consisted of many different levels, making use of the slope on the top of the hill. On the grand steps of the chateau, a group waited to welcome them.

As Etienne helped Anne from her horse, he took her hand and kissed it. She laughed and embraced him. "You are most welcome to Marseilles, your highness." Etienne gave Richard another long bow.

"I thank you very much." Richard acknowledged him. He wanted to say more, but many people were preoccupied with reuniting with Anne. For the first time in a long time Richard was disregarded, and he felt both annoyed and delighted. Several men of the town greeted her even a contingent of clergy. Richard looked them over and wondered if the ancient one was the priest who caused Anne's hasty departure so many years ago. He also noticed an abbot about his own age who held back from the others.

From behind the crowd of Marseilles' dignitaries, an old woman pushed her way forward. Her face wrinkled and her back bent, she used a cane to aid her movement. Even with that, she seemed nimble for one so old and bowed. "Give way, give way! Allow a poor old woman to see her child!" She pushed her way past the men.

Anne turned at the sound of her voice. The woman walked right up to Anne. Lovingly, she took Anne's face in her gnarled old hands. The old woman's brown eyes twinkled as she gazed at Anne. "Nanette, my dear Nanette" Anne embraced the woman.

Nanette stood only to Anne's shoulder now, but she hugged her with surprisingly strong arms. Nanette pushed back and said to Anne, "Well now, let me have a look at my little Anne."

Nanette paid no attention to the others. She grasped Anne's hand in hers. "Now tell me, dear, where is that son of yours? I have waited a long time to see him. I shall not wait another moment."

Baldwin helped Will down from his horse. While his mother's relatives thronged her, Will hung back close to Richard. Anne now motioned for him to come forward. Holding his head up, Will went to her side. Nanette's eyes filled with tears, but only for a moment. "I see your grandsire in you, William. I can tell you will be a man to make him proud."

Anne patted Will on the shoulders. "Nanette was my nurse, dear." Will gave the old woman a shy smile.

Nanette smiled back, "Uh, oh. Anne, what have you done to this boy?" She spoke to Will again. "Dear boy, did you lose your teeth on the way here from England?"

Will grinned wider, exposing three teeth missing in the front. He shook his head at Nanette. "Well, what shall I call you? Will or William?" Nanette extended her hand to him.

"I am called Will."

"Well, then," Nanette gave a mock sigh. "I am afraid I shall be forced to call you William, for I cannot call you the same name as everyone else." She looked up again at Anne. "M'lady, pray excuse us. I need to get to know this young man better."

Nanette did not wait for an answer. She took Will's arm and steered him into the chateau. Etienne lifted his arms and beckoned the others to follow. "Welcome to Marseilles, my lords!"

All the leaders of Marseilles, Richard, and other important courtiers attended a festive banquet that night. They were seated according to rank. As the leading noble of Marseilles, Anne sat on Richard's right. A laverer placed a washbasin before them, and they both put their hands in it. Reaching out with his pinky, Richard caught hers. She looked him in the eye for the first time since they left Vezelay, allowing him to linger only briefly before withdrawing her hands and drying them on a towel before her.

Richard and his men were in for an enjoyable evening. The food was served, the wine flowed, and the entertainment amused. It reminded Richard of those days long ago at his court in Poitiers. He observed to himself how Anne directed the proceedings in such a subtle way that one thing seemed to flow smoothly into the next without much effort. Here she was in her element. This was her court, and she reigned over it with natural poise and elegance. At that moment he let himself imagine that this was their court, and she was his queen.

She stood to make a toast to the king and his men. Richard did not really listen to what she said. He felt as if he were in some sort of trance, as if he were someone watching. When the court all drank to the toast, she sat down but did not look at Richard. Andrew nudged Richard, which brought him to his senses. He rose and offered a toast of his own. "To Marseilles, her viscountess, and all those who inhabit this wondrous city, may she always be a jewel of the Mediterranean."

The crowd echoed his sentiment and drank to their hostess. Anne gave a gracious nod of thanks to Richard, and with the slight wave of her hand, signaled the next round of entertainment. The celebration continued long into the night.

When Richard woke the next morning, it took a moment for him to remember where he was, his senses conscious that he was not in a tent. He opened his eyes and recalled his location. A genuine ceiling hung over his head. The bedroom was light, warm, and airy. He watched the gossamer bed curtains float in the breeze that filtered in through the open window. Carried on the wind, the smell of the fresh sea drifted around him. He bolted upright. He wanted to see Anne and determined she would not put him off, not today.

After dressing, he strode into her room. Still early, the house was just beginning to stir. When he entered the chamber, he was surprised to see the bed already made. He heard a rustle and saw Nanette in the corner of the room placing some flowers in a vase on a dressing table. "Excuse me. Where is Lady Anne?" His voice sounded his disappointment.

Nanette made her way to a chair. "Forgive me, sire." Her body bent so much that Richard wasn't sure if she bowed. "My knees neither bend nor hold like they once did, so I must often rely on four other legs. I mean you no disrespect." She dropped down into the chair. "Anne is not here, my lord."

"Please, can you tell me where I might find her?"

"Love is a very confusing thing, your highness." Richard noticed that her voice had a gravely sound to it, although it was still quite strong. "I have lived in this house since I was a young girl. I have seen people in it love with a passion that is incomprehensible to many. Only someone who has felt that way can understand it. I know I am an old woman, but that does not mean that I cannot remember what it is like to love." She paused, holding the top of her stick with one hand on top of the other. "Love does change over time, because we change over time. That does not mean love is any less than before."

Nanette pushed herself up from the chair and went toward a window. She swung an arm in a wide motion for Richard to follow. "There." She pointed with a crooked finger. "Up there on a bluff overlooking the ocean. That is where you will find our Anne."

Richard followed the aim of the gnarled finger to a cliff in the distance. Nanette moved toward the door. She spoke to him without looking back. "As soon as she left, I ordered your horse be saddled. Your highness will find the stable boy waiting for you. He shall show you the way."

Chapter Twenty-nine

Following the directions the stable boy gave him, Richard rode to the cliff. Andrew and Baldwin followed him, but Richard gave them strict orders to stay out of sight. When he saw Anne in the distance, he stopped, dismounted, and walked his horse the rest of the way.

Anne sat on a rock near the edge of the cliff, overlooking the sea below. She held her knees close to her chest, and her hair floated back and forth in the gentle breeze. Nearby her hobbled horse gnawed on some vegetation. At first Richard was unsure if she saw him or not because she did not look at him. He noticed a basket on the ground next to her full, yet masked by a cloth. With caution, he approached her.

"Tell me, that song and the flowers, was that all of your own doing?" Anne didn't turn his direction.

"I confess, I had someone else find the flowers, but I told him what to get, and the song… that I did write myself, with some input from Blondel."

The sound of waves crashing on rocks below echoed up to them. "Then I guess I must confess that I have not read the song." She still gazed out at sea.

Richard kicked at a rock with his toe. "Marseilles is stunning, Anne," he said, changing the subject. "I can see why you love it."

"Hum, I do miss Marseilles. I may be an unfair judge, but I think the sea here is more beautiful than anywhere else I have been." At last Anne turned and glanced at him.

"I could not help but notice how your countenance changed when we arrived. This place is much more than just a town to you."

"My ancestors were Greek traders who came across that sea there." She nodded in the direction of the ocean. "They decided to colonize here because it was the perfect port from which to trade. The Ligure tribe already lived here ruled by King Naan. His daughter, Gyptis fell in love with Protis, the leader of the Greeks. They married, and that is how my family came to be Marseilles. I guess one could argue that Marseilles is literally in my blood."

"Thank you for taking me into the heart of Marseilles then." Richard tried to be poetic.

Anne let one of her legs dangle from the rock. He could see her bare foot. "I have not shown you all of Marseilles' treasures."

"I do not believe you have had enough time as of late."

Richard felt uncertain how to take what she had just said. Was she speaking of her heart, or was it the town?

"Yes, I think that you would very much enjoy the library at the Abbey of Saint Victor. It contains many ancient manuscripts, our own little library of Alexandria, if you will. I believe it was recently cataloged." She leaned back on her hands. "Etienne is very anxious to talk with you. He just returned from the Holy Land a couple of months ago. I believe he can tell you all about the fall of Acre and the siege efforts to regain the city."

"I would be most interested to speak with him about it. I am sure he has some insights to share. The sooner we take Acre, the sooner we take Jerusalem. The sooner we take Jerusalem, the sooner we may all return home." Richard waited for her to reply.

Anne just sat up straighter, her leg still dangling from beneath the folds of her green gown. Feeling uncomfortable with the silence, Richard looked around. He noticed the basket again and bent down to it. "What is this?"

He began to lift the linen cloth, but Anne snatched it away from him. She blushed. "It is nothing really."

"Please, you do not get that worked up over nothing, Anne. What is in the basket?"

She turned a shade redder. "Richard, I would rather not talk about it. It is something very childish and embarrassing."

"Come now. How long have I known you?" Richard winked. He was unsteady in his teasing, as their quarrel had been too long and too sore.

"No. I am embarrassed. I knew I should not have brought it up here at all." Anne looked to be on the verge of tears.

"Stop being so silly and tell me what is in the basket." Richard reached out and took hold of the cloth.

Instinctively, Anne pulled the basket further away, but Richard could see its contents. "Flowers?" He raised his eyebrows.

"Peach blossoms." She sighed.

Shrugging, he spoke in as soft a voice as could and still be heard, "Why do you have a basket of peach blossoms?"

She furrowed her brow. "It is a tradition. Oh, I cannot believe I am telling you this." She pushed some hair out of her face. "Every spring when the peach trees blossomed, I knew that it was traveling time. My father would either be coming or going from Marseilles. One spring I went to our orchard and tried to pick as many as I could. I reasoned if my father did not see them, he would not leave, and I tried to hide them in my room. Nanette found them and told my father." She smiled now. "My father told me that there was a way to make them last. He taught me how to preserve them, and he brought me here to this cliff. Then he told me that whenever I felt lonesome for him, I could bring the blossoms here and toss a few into the sea. He promised they would float across the water and find him no matter where he was. Whenever he was gone, Nanette brought me here to drop the blossoms in the water. When I got older, I figured out that they would not find my father, but I still came here and did this ritual all the same. It brought me peace."

Hair blew back into her eyes, and she tucked it behind her ear again. "Nanette has been saving blossoms for me ever since I left. I do not know why I brought them here today. Like I said, it was just a silly notion. Yet, here I am."

Richard just listened to her. She took the linen back from him and placed it back on top of the blossoms. "My father is buried in the chapel at Saint Victor's. I have not yet been able to bring myself to go there. It felt more natural to come here."

He reached out and tucked some hair behind her other ear. "I see why you have come here, Anne. You came here to toss those blossoms in the sea. Something about it gives you peace; you said so yourself. Do it with faith that the blossoms will be carried on the water to their intended destination. Don't try to reason with it. Some things in life defy reason." He pulled the linen cloth off again. "I do not think it silly, and I certainly would not want to restrain you from remembering and honoring your father." Richard took a step back to give Anne room.

With hesitation, Anne took a handful of blossoms. She walked to the edge of the cliff and held her hand out. Filtering them through her fingers, she set them free. Some instantly caught on the wind and soared about in circles. Others fell gracefully to the waves below. As she watched them go, Richard joined her. "May I?" He motioned toward the basket.

She nodded. Richard gathered a few in his fingers. "Let us think of it as my introduction to your father." He raised his eyebrows and then let his blossoms go.

Anne finished dropping the rest from the basket. When it was empty she watched the last of them fall. "Thank you, Richard."

They stood looking out to sea for a long while. Richard grew confident again and put his arms around her. She did not fight him.

Later that day Richard met with Etienne in the chateau's herb garden, and walked together into the orchard where Anne waited for them. Sitting in the shade of peach trees while the summer sun shone overhead, Etienne told Richard all the news from Outremer, as the Holy Land was commonly called. He spoke of the political mess now plaguing the Crusaders. "Queen Sibylla of Jerusalem died in the siege camp at Acre. Her husband Guy de Lusignan still claims the throne, but he was only king through marriage. Conrad of Montferrat, who saved the port city of Tyre from capture by the Saracens, feels he should be the next king of Jerusalem. Currently, he is ruling the city of Tyre and refused Guy entrance.

Sybilla's younger sister, Isabella, is considered by many to be the rightful heir to the throne, so Conrad had her marriage annulled, married her, and is now claiming that he is King of Jerusalem. He is cousin to Philip as well as Leopold, the Duke of

Austria, who as you know, is leading the Austrian contingent on Crusade. Sire, this is quite the political mess."

"Yes, the family relations make it complicated." Anne shook her head.

Etienne explained further. "Baldwin the IV of Jerusalem named his nephew, Baldwin V, Sibylla's son, his heir to he throne. Baldwin V died still a young boy. Baldwin V was not Guy's son, but his father was William of Montferrat, Conrad's older brother. That makes Baldwin V, Conrad's nephew. Baldwin IV stipulated in his will that if anything was to happen to Baldwin V, that his 'most rightful heirs' were to rule over Jerusalem until the King of England, the King of France, and the Holy Roman Emperor, could settle the matter of succession."

"It is enough to make a person's head spin." Anne rubbed her temples.

Richard had not spoken. He sat looking pensive and sullen. "To add another complication, Guy de Lusignan's brother is one of my most important vassals in Pointu, one more thing to create havoc with our shaky alliances. Philip will back his cousin Conrad, and I will of course want to back my vassal. The Holy Roman Emperor, Frederick Barbarossa died on the way to the Holy Land and the new Emperor, his son Henry Hohenstaufen, has no intention of going on crusade. He has too many other problems in his own kingdom with rebellious princes, including my brother-in-law, Henry of Saxony."

"What will you do, Richard?" Anne queried.

Richard stroked his beard, deep in thought. "I will have to give it some serious thought. That is for certain."

Anne knew better than to press it any further. She could tell he was frustrated and did not wish to discuss his plans any further with Etienne or with her, for that matter. "In that case, may I suggest we go into the hall? I planned another night of festivities planned in your honor, my lord."

Etienne took his cue from Anne. "Oh, yes, sire. I am sure

you will find this evening's feast most enjoyable. Lady Anne has really prepared something singular."

"Yes, that will be just fine." Richard responded as if he were someplace far away.

Chapter Thirty

Richard's fleet did not meet him at Marseilles as planned.

Instead, it stopped in Lisbon, and the crusading spirit got the best of them. The men were hungry for an adventure, and when they found Muslims living in Lisbon, they made that an excuse to pillage and plunder. As a result, they were late for their rendezvous with Richard and the army. An impatient Richard decided not to wait for them any longer than a week. He hired thirty merchant ships to transport himself and his army overseas. Splitting his army in half, he sent one group on ahead to Tyre with the Archbishop of Canterbury leading them. The Archbishop held orders to relieve the crusaders already besieging Acre.

The afternoon before they left, Richard's chambers were lively. A steady flow of people traipsed in and out, making preparations for the following day's journey. Some paid their respects to Richard, others consulted the king on various matters concerning the journey, while others packed and hauled the royal cargo to the boats. Anne visited a couple of times but did not stay long. When the crowd thinned, Richard was left in the room with Blondel, Andrew, and Baldwin. They heard a rustle behind a large chest, and Baldwin drew his sword. "In the name of the king, come out!"

To their surprise, Will popped out from his hiding place. "Boy, what are you doing there?" Andrew motioned him forward. "How long have you been there?"

Will stood up as tall as he could. "I came to ask Uncle a question, but I did not want to disturb him." He added, "I came in with my mother."

Baldwin approached Will. "Will, I am regretful, but the King is very busy at present. Can it wait?"

"No, Baldwin. It is quite alright. Obviously he has something on his mind, and it will be a long time before I see this young pup again." Richard motioned for Will to come to him.

Will came around the trunk and walked up to Richard. He gave a little bow to show proper respect. The men tried hard not to chuckle at his awkwardness. Will could read the expression on their faces, so he put on his most serious façade. "Now Will, what seems to be the matter?" Richard continued to gather papers on the table next to him. Andrew and Baldwin returned to packing weaponry in oilcloth. Blondel strummed his instrument.

Will hesitated for a moment then blurted out, "Are you my father?"

All the men stopped what they were doing and looked at Will. "I beg your pardon?" Richard was not sure he heard the boy correctly.

"Uncle, I wish to know if you are my real father. I heard people talking, and some say that you are." Will looked afraid to be punished for what he said.

"Oh, Will, I…" Richard pulled a chair over so he could be at the boy's eye level. "Will, what has your mother told you?"

"Mother says that you are my godfather, and that I am to call you Uncle. She also told me I am not your son, but because you are my godfather, you take care of me in place of my father."

"She is telling you the truth, Will. I am not your father, but I swore I would look after you like a father."

Will's eyes filled with tears, and his chin quivered. "What is it, Will?"

Will looked down at the ground. "I wish you were my father. If I promise not to want to be king, could I be your son?"

"Unfortunately, it does not work like that." Richard could see the desperation on Will's face. "Think of it this way; in a way, you are my son. You are my godson and always will be." He thought for a moment. "Will, what has your mother told you about your father?"

"She will not really talk about him. When I ask, she gets mad, and says only that he left us to go on Crusade, and you watch after us. She told me that we should not bother you with things because you are king and are busy with plans for the Crusade." Will sighed.

"Oh, I see." Richard wrestled with himself for a moment over just how much to tell the boy. In a way, he felt that Anne should be the one to do it, but he could not blame her for not speaking of Raymond. He decided that it was more important that Will know that his godfather was better than his real father. "Will, it is true. Your father has gone on Crusade, but the only reason he went on Crusade was so that I would not find him and take revenge on him for what he did to your mother."

Richard placed his hand on Will's shoulder. "Your father wanted to marry your mother because she was the heiress to Marseilles. He kidnapped her from my castle in Poitiers and forced her to marry him. He hurt her very badly, Will. I was able to rescue her, but I was not able to find him in time. He slipped away on Crusade. Every now and then reports come back from Palestine regarding your father. I do believe he is still alive, but he can never come back here, or he will be punished for his crime. Your mother does not like to speak of this because it makes her remember a very sad time in her life. Do you understand what I have told you?"

Will nodded. Richard looked into Will's eyes and worried that he had not conveyed the correct meaning to the child. "Will, your mother loves you very much. Everything she does is to insure you inherit Marseilles. In fact, your mother may have been able to annul her marriage to your father, but if she did, that would make you illegitimate. That means you would not be anybody's son, and you wouldn't be able to inherit Marseilles."

Will chewed on his lower lip for a moment. "Will you find

my father in the Holy Land?"

"It is very likely."

"If he finds my mother, will he take her again?"

"That will not happen. I give you my word."

"Will you kill him? If you did, wouldn't I be nobody's son then? Why does Mother have to go? Are you making her go with you? I heard someone say that she should stay here in Marseilles and let you handle her business, but you will not let her do that." Will fired questions at Richard.

"One thing you must learn about your mother is that no one makes her do anything." Richard chuckled. "And you must not listen to rumors you hear people say. They are jealous of her. Your mother is going because she wants to see to the interests of Marseilles overseas. She is doing this to strengthen your inheritance."

Will pouted. "I do not think it is fair. I should be able to come too. It sounds like an adventure."

"Believe me, it is not easy for your mother to leave you, but it is for the best. I agree completely with her there. Will, Marseilles, this city," he pointed out the window, "it is all to be yours someday. You need to learn of it. You must live here to understand it so you can rule it wisely. Cousin Etienne, Master More, and Nanette, they all want to help you. I know you will miss your mother, but you will be so busy here, that when she returns, it will seem as if she were hardly gone."

They heard a soft knock on the door. Richard nodded at Baldwin who opened it. Anne burst into the room looking frantic. "Richard, Will is…" she caught sight of him. Both he and Richard looked at Anne with the same expression of mischief. "Oh, Will!" She stamped her foot. "Thank heaven. I have been looking all over for you, son."

"I have been here, Mother," Will replied.

Anne took Will by the hand. "Come, you mustn't pester Uncle. He is very busy." She looked at Richard. "I am sorry, sire."

"It is quite alright," he responded, but before he could say anything else, Anne whisked the child from the room and the door shut behind them.

Not long after sunrise the next morning, Richard left the chateau. The men headed down the streets of the town to the port where Richard's private galley, the *Priombone,* waited for him to board. Once again citizens poured out into the streets to cheer the men along the way. All the way to the port, the crowd threw flowers and rushes in their path. Richard noticed a group of Muslim children huddled in an alleyway, staring with curious wide eyes at the Crusaders.

Anne's family galley, the *Madeline*, berthed next to the *Priombone*. She was slower getting out of the chateau than Richard. Taking leave of her relatives took a considerable amount of time. Etienne, Will, and even Nanette stood on the steps of the chateau to wish her farewell. Anne knelt down and gave Will a long embrace. Will tried to be brave. She pushed some of his black curls off his face. "You must mind Master More and Nanette," she admonished him.

Will only nodded his head, fighting back tears.

"Mind your Latin lessons now, dear. I know you find them boring, but they are very important. When I return I expect you to be able to read and speak fluently in Latin." She gathered him again in her arms.

Will managed to choke out, "I will, Mother."

"What is this?" Anne asked as Will held out a white kerchief. "Is this for me?"

With tears welling up in his eyes, the boy nodded his head.

She kissed his cheek. "I will miss you, son, but I shall return just as soon as I can. Promise me that you will always remember that I love you."

Will threw his arms around his mother's neck. She could

feel his tears on her skin. It was hard to bear, and she looked up at Nanette for help. Nanette hobbled forward and took Will by the shoulders. "Come now, William. The tide waits for no one, not even your mother."

Reluctantly, he let go of his mother and took up his brave stance again. Anne turned from the steps and, with the help of Etienne, mounted her horse. Turning back, she gave Will a cheery wave, and Will waved back. As she rode off, Anne looked back several times and waved in his direction until he was out of sight. Her heart began to ache, and now and then she held the kerchief up to her eyes to wipe away a tear. Then raised it up and waved it, hoping that Will could see her.

After Anne, Marguerite, and Gustave, Anne's new private secretary, boarded the galley, they set sail into the Gulf of Lion. She climbed to the railing at the stern of the ship and watched Marseilles grow smaller and smaller. She looked to the cliff where she would always go to bid adieu to her father, hoping that Will might be there, and she waved the kerchief again. She watched as the people on the docks became only tiny specks, and the town a blur in the distance. The red tiled roofs, and golden spires of Saint Victor's Cathedral melted away. Even when the earthen tones of Marseilles' building became a tiny dot, she strained to see it. When all she could see behind them was the azure sea, she gave way to tears and wondered when she would see Marseilles again, and prayed she did the right thing.

Chapter Thirty-one

The *Madeline* and *Priombone* put in at Genoa. Richard's other ships took nearly every available part of the harbor. Anne went right to work. She and Gustave made many business visits. Gustave worked with Etienne for several years and was skilled with keeping accounts. Tall and thin, with a long slim nose and blue eyes, his hair turned completely white at a very young age. Gustave also served as a liaison for those business contacts who refused to do business with a woman. Genoa competed with Marseilles, but it was important and beneficial for the two cities to keep good relations, a trade alliance being mutually beneficial. Both Anne and Gustave worked hard during their stay in Genoa, meeting often with a prominent Genoese merchant family, the Nuccios.

After leaving Genoa, the group of ships traveled down the Italian coast stopping almost every day to take on supplies and meet with dignitaries. Even though they were so close, Richard refused to travel into Rome. He had no desire to see the pope because he heard rumors that the pope made critical remarks about him.

The island kingdom of Sicily was the planned rendezvous point for Richard and Philip's armies. In Sicily Western and Eastern cultures met and merged. The king, William II, died just a few short months after Henry, leaving Richard's sister Joanna a widow. She married him at a young age, and they had no children. William's illegitimate cousin, Tancred of Lecce, snatched the throne, locked up Joanna and confiscated her dowry. Richard wanted it back. Also, he wanted the legacy that William left to Henry. William promised a golden table, a large silk tent, twenty-four gold cups and plates, and a hundred armed galleys for the purpose of financing the Crusade. As Henry's heir, Richard felt it was his right to inherit it.

Richard prepared for his grand entrance into the port city of Messina by having a platform built on the prow of his ship. Dressed in his finest armor, shined to a brilliant polish that reflected the sun with his white and red Crusader's tunic, he stood atop the platform as the galley sailed into the port. It was impossible not to notice his figure and many on the docks were in awe, the effect Richard hoped for.

As they were docking, Richard looked at the other galleys

in the harbor, irritated to see Philip's ships there. Glancing at the crowd on the dock, he spotted Philip waiting for him. Instead of showing his consternation, he leaped down from the boat and strode over to Philip with outstretched arms. The two kings embraced each other with forged smiles on their faces.

"I was beginning to worry you decided to stay in Marseilles, Richard," Philip chided.

"Oh, no. As you can see, I have come." Richard swung his arm wide back toward his galley.

"I could not help but notice." Philip glanced beyond Richard. "Pray, excuse me, Richard." Philip walked right past Richard. Richard turned to see where he was going.

A few galleys away from the *Priombone*, Anne was disembarking from the *Madeline*. Philip headed to greet her. "Lady Anne!" Philip called out.

Anne curtsied before him. "Your highness, it is good to see that you have arrived safely in Messina."

"And it is good to see you, cousin." This time his smile was genuine.

"Please allow me to introduce my secretary, Gustave." Anne explained the presence of the tall man behind her.

Philip gave him a nod, and the man gave Philip a low bow. Philip noticed that Gustave's face was a pale shade of green. He carried a handkerchief and wiped his face. "Gustave is not a man of the sea."

Richard's voice came from behind Philip. "Come." Richard extended his free arm to Anne. "Do forgive us, Philip, I must get settled before I meet with Tancred. As you know, we have much family business to discuss."

Anne took his arm but gave Philip a warm smile as she did so.

"I do hope to see you again very soon, cousin," Philip said.

"Oh, you can count on it. We shall have a grand time. There is nothing like old friends and an adventure," Richard answered for her and he steered her away from the docks.

Chapter Thirty-two

Richard was not welcomed into the city like Philip. Philip and his men lodged inside the city of Messina, but Tancred refused to let Richard and his troops stay in the city, so Richard set up camp outside the city walls. Richard sent his demands to Tancred, but Tancred was reluctant to meet with Richard and put it off as long as possible. Naturally, to placate him, Tancred released Joanna, but not her dowry, nor her husband's legacy.

Richard gathered with others outside his tent to meet his sister. He had a tent erected next to his to shelter her until other arrangements could be made. Joanna arrived accompanied by a royal escort, stopping her horse in front of Richard. Stepping forward, he helped his sister down from her horse.

Joanna was eight years younger than Richard. Slim with fiery red hair and deep brown eyes, she took after father in temperament. Richard's sister could prove useful. He could marry her to another man, using her to form a treaty or alliance.

Joanna did not smile at her brother. Instead, she frowned to show her displeasure. Richard tried to welcome her. "After all these years, it is so good to see you, dear sister."

She looked him up and down. "It has been so many years, I hardly recognised you. I would not have been able to, if you did not look so much like our father."

"Let me show you to your tent. I do apologize for the accommodations, but I assure you things will be sorted out with Tancred, and you will have a better place to lodge."

Joanna put out her hand for Richard. "Tancred is a louse, Richard. I doubt he will negotiate. He lacks serious intelligence when it comes to diplomacy." She let out a long sigh. "Alas, it is good that you are here, though. I feel much better knowing it is you that has come for me."

"I know you have had a rough time, but your fortune will change."

"Oh, Richard, he took everything from me, everything. Do you know that I couldn't retain even one of my servants?" Joanna pouted.

"There are plenty here to serve you, sister. In fact," he motioned Anne forward, "may I present Lady Anne Baux, Viscountess of Marseilles. She served our mother for years, even spending some time with her when Henry locked her up, and Anne has resided at my court ever since. She is here to be your lady."

Anne gave Joanna a proper curtsy. "Your highness."

Joanna pulled Richard aside and whispered to him, "Where have I heard her name before?"

"Her father was a very wealthy merchant in Marseilles," Richard whispered back.

"No, that is not it. I… oh, I know. She is your… Richard! You brought your mistress to be my lady? Really Richard, you are more like our father than I would have guessed."

"Joanna, she is the best, and as a queen, I thought you would appreciate the best." Richard scolded her.

Joanna looked down her nose at Anne. "Alright. I will give it a try. I am sorry; I am just so upset about this whole situation. I lost my husband, imprisoned, and the usurper is sitting on the throne. It is enough to make anybody feel out of sorts."

"I understand but keep in mind, I am here now." Richard flashed her grin.

They entered Joanna's tent and Anne followed.

Joanna kept a low profile, for the time being. She spent most of the day in her tent or Richard's, where she tried to advise him on the important players in Tancred's camp. Anne went about her new duties, sending Gustave to conduct the business affairs in

Messina. Joanna treated Anne with dignity, but she lacked the cordiality of her mother and brother.

The tensions in the city existed not just between Richard and Philip. The English did not find a friendly haven at Messina. The local Greek shopkeepers and the Lombardi citizens of Messina did not impress the English crusaders. The feeling was mutual. Shopkeepers inflated their prices whenever an Englishman was seen. Daily arguments broke out in the streets. Richard knew he must seek a resolution with Tancred for the situation to improve at all. It was too late in the season to cross the sea to Acre, so the armies were to winter in Sicily. Something had to be done to make it a livable winter for all.

Richard met with Tancred's representatives at his camp. For hours the negotiations went round and round with nothing accomplished, both sides frustrated and frayed tempers. Then Andrew rushed into Richard's tent. "I beg your pardon for the interruption sire, but a riot has broken out between the townspeople and your men."

"Oh, good hell!" Richard jumped out of his seat. "Excuse me, gentlemen. I must see to this."

News of the riot reached Anne and Joanna as they sat in Joanna's tent. Eventually, they heard noises from the riot, but remained where they were. About three hours after Richard left, a guard admitted Gustave into Joanna's tent. "Your highness, Lady Anne."

"What is it, Gustave? Your eyes look positively wild!" Anne put down her sewing and rushed to him.

"Lady Anne, I just came from the city and thought you would like to hear the news. As you know, I was meeting with the Signor Maurolico. All of a sudden, we heard a disturbance in the street. Seeing a riot, I thought it best that I come straight back here." He wiped his brow with his ever-present handkerchief.

"Yes, we heard the noise coming from town, but what is going on? What is happening?" Joanna pressed him for further information.

"Well, it was most difficult to get out of town. Everywhere was pandemonium. I did see King Richard, though. He rode into the middle of the fray on his horse, and shouted for everyone to remain calm. At first no one seemed to pay him any attention, but the crowd did start to quiet down, yet only for a moment."

"Were Andrew and Baldwin with him?" Anne interrupted Gustave.

"Yes, they were there too."

"Never mind Andrew and Baldwin, what did Richard do?" Joanna questioned.

"The crowd quieted slightly, mainly the king's troops, but the townspeople, they shouted at the king. They called him an English dog, a pig, a villain, and a coward. They used all sorts of abusive language towards him. Someone even threw rotten fruit at him."

"They didn't!" Joanna jumped to her feet.

"I am afraid they did, my lady." Gustave furrowed his brow. "The king did not stand by for such insults, and he called for his armor."

"You mean he went in unarmed!" Anne sank down in a chair and put her head in her hands.

"Yes, but he is armed now."

Anne looked up at Gustave. "Just tell me, is he alright or no?"

"The last time I saw him, he was leading his troops. They burnt down the city gate and poured inside." Anne's face looked pale with worry. "Lady Anne, I am sure he will return soon." He tried to comfort her.

"Thank you, Gustave. I appreciate your report." Anne stood back up.

"With your permission, your highness, I will take my leave

and return to my business."

Joanna gave a curt nod and giving them a polite bow, he left the tent.

Evening came and went, and night fell. The city glowed from the fire at the gate and other small blazes. The sounds of battle could still be heard as far away as the camp. In Joanna's tent, Anne clumsily performed her duties, driven to distraction with concern for Richard. Joanna sent for Blondel, and he entertained the ladies. As Blondel prepared to play, Joanna seated herself in a large chair filled with cushions. At first, Anne sat down on a smaller chair, but the instant she sat, she returned to her feet. "Lady Anne, you are making me anxious," Joanna spoke through gritted teeth.

"I apologize, my lady." Anne plopped back down in the chair.

Blondel started to play a song that Joanna requested while Anne resisted the urge to fidget. She studied the intricate design in the carpet that lay below her feet, concentrating on the golden hue that surrounded large scarlet flowers. Despite her efforts, her thoughts strayed to Richard, and her stomach ached. When Blondel finished his song, Anne was lost deep in thought. The sound of Joanna's applauding brought her around again. She gave Blondel a gracious smile. "Lady Anne, he will be alright. He always is." Blondel tried to make Anne feel better.

Outside the sounds of battle swelled, and the distinct sound of a wounded animal met their ears. Anne rushed to the door of the tent. She strained to see more clearly in the distance, but in vain. All she could see were the rows of tents before her and the bronze gleam on the horizon that met the purple twilight above. Before she even realized it, she was pacing back and forth in front of the tent.

Inside the tent, Joanna turned to Blondel. "Pray tell, is she always like this?"

Blondel nodded his head. "I am afraid she is always like this when he is at battle, my lady. She becomes quite agitated."

"Then this will be a rather long crusade." Joanna let out a loud sigh.

Hours later, Joanna lay in bed in her tent, looking at the ceiling and watching the lights of the fires throughout camp dance and form strange shadows. Anne remained outside but finally relented to Blondel and sat in a chair.

After becoming tired of tossing and turning trying to find a comfortable position, Joanna sat up and called out for Anne. Anne appeared in the tent door, looking exhausted and pale. "Anne, you really must try to relax. You will worry yourself sick and make me go half mad in the process."

Anne opened her mouth to apologize, but Joanna did not let her. "I know, I know, you are sorry." Joanna motioned for Anne to sit down.

"This is the part I hate the worst. It is the waiting and not knowing." Anne stretched her arms above her head. She looked Joanna in the eye. "I worry not just that he might not return but…" her voice choked, "but what if he is hurt or in great pain and here am I, helpless to do anything."

Joanna scrutinized her again. Anne's concern was about Richard's safety and not what would happen to her station, if he were not to return from battle. "Do you really love my brother, or is it the benefits that his attention affords?"

"My lady?" Anne sputtered.

Before Joanna could speak again, a trumpet sounded in the distance, announcing the king's return. Anne did not hesitate, but was up and out of the tent in a flash.

Outside, men poured into the camp cheering for the king. She could not see Richard; for that matter, she could not see much as the crowd pressed in around her. At last she caught a glimpse of Baldwin's blonde hair. She could tell he was next to Richard because she could see the top of his head, with Andrew on the other side of him. All three were on a path toward Richard's tent, but the crowd pressed in around them, cheering and celebrating. At first she felt relief, but then she noticed Andrew's clenched jaw. He shouted something at the people gathered before him. When they got closer, she could hear, "Make way! Fetch the surgeon! Make way, I tell you! The king is wounded!"

Chapter Thirty-three

Anne felt her heart stop, but she forced her way through the crowd to his tent. Just as the trio reached her, she broke through. Richard was on his feet and moving of his own accord. The men and his surgeon, Marchadeus hustled Richard into the tent. Anne stood wide-eyed, not knowing if she should enter. Just when she made up her mind to enter, Baldwin emerged. Glancing around, he saw her, took her by the arm, and pulled her into the tent.

Richard sat on his bed, as the men striped him of armor. "Really, this is ridiculous," he snapped.

Andrew yanked Richard's shirt off to reveal a gash in it just under his shoulder. The surgeon tried to blot away the blood that smeared down his arm. Richard jerked away. "Good God, man, it is just a flesh wound. I've had worse! Now, leave me be!"

"With all due respect, your highness, I must dress the wound, so it does not become putrid." Marchadeus turned and motioned to his apprentice who came forward bearing a small bowl of poultice.

"I said no! My arm is fine!" Richard knocked the bowl from the boy's hands.

Baldwin shot Anne a pleading look. Richard did not see her because his head was turned the other way as he glared menacingly at the surgeon, daring him to come close again. Anne placed a gentle hand on the forearm of his wounded arm and bent down to pick up what was left of the poultice from the floor. When she touched him, Richard jumped and tried to jerk his arm away, but she held tight and looked him in the eyes. He saw her and stopped fussing. "Leave us," he ordered.

"Sire..." Marchadeus protested.

"I said leave us." Richard did not yell this time but spoke with firmness.

The tent emptied, and Anne brought a chair over next to Richard and a basin of water. Dipping a rag into the water, she gently began to clean his arm. Neither one spoke until she had most of the blood cleaned off. Then as she daubed around the wound, she said to him, "Are you going to tell me what happened, or are you going to keep me in suspense?"

"Look at it. It is nothing really. They are overreacting like a bunch of silly old hens." Richard lifted his other arm to point in the direction of the tent door.

She looked up at him. "Well, you are the king, dear."

As Anne applied the poultice to the wound, Richard watched her work. When she began to rip some linen into strips, he inspected the wound more carefully. "An arrow grazed me before I got my armor on."

Anne scowled at him. "Before you got your armor on? You went in without armor, again?" She wound the bandage around his arm.

"Spare me, Anne. There was a riot. I had no time to lose."

"No time to lose... Just your life to lose, Richard." She tied the bandage and rose from the chair.

As she walked away, he caught her hand and pulled her back to him. She glared at him. He stood up, took both of her hands, and put his forehead on hers. "Oh, Anne, do not be cross with me. If you are going to be this angry with me about this, I cannot imagine how angry you shall be when..." He stopped himself.

"When, what?" Anne knew he slipped up and came close to saying something about the Princess of Navarre.

He let go of her and ran his hands through his hair. "When there is a bigger battle."

She narrowed her eyes and regarded him for a moment. She did not feel it worth picking a fight over at the moment. Besides, she wanted him to tell her of his own free will and not because she dragged it out of him. Instead she turned and emptied the water basin, then poured fresh water into it. "You are sweaty and covered in dirt." She tossed him a clean cloth.

Grinning at her, he caught it. "I *have* just come from battle."

"Battle or no, you cannot very well eat when you are in such a state. I will send for some food. I know you are always hungry after a good fight."

She poked her head out of the tent flap and said something to the men outside. Richard washed his face and hands, even running some water through his hair. By the time she came back to him, he was drying his arms and hands. "Food is not the only thing I am hungry for after a good fight."

Anne ignored his comment, and searched for a clean tunic for him. "Well, I would be willing to wager that you have got Tancred's attention now. I doubt that he will put you off any longer."

He laughed. "Oh, I think the negotiations have taken a whole new turn for him."

She found a tunic and helped him into it. "You really should speak to your page about your trunk. It is a mess."

"Stay and dine with me, Anne. You know a king never eats alone."

She gave him a smile but her eyes hinted sadness. "Within a few moments, this tent will be filled with ministers, clergy, clerics, pages, knights, and whomever else can fit. It will be no place for me."

As if her words summoned them, the tent flap opened and Baldwin came in carrying a tray of food. Several others meeting Anne's descriptions followed him. As the king was inundated, she slipped out of the tent.

Richard succeeded in getting Tancred's attention. Now Tancred would negotiate with Richard. Tancred would release Joanna's dowry and pay Richard twenty thousand ounces of gold. Tancred doubled the amount of gold when Richard agreed to a betrothal of his brother Geoffrey's son, Arthur, to Tancred's infant daughter. Richard gave Tancred his word that if he himself did not have heirs, he would name Arthur as his heir to the throne. That would make Tancred's daughter a queen of England.

In order to insure the locals behave themselves, Richard ordered a massive fortified wooden tower built just outside the walls of the town. Smaller than the Norman keeps back home, it was still large enough to make an impression of great power, in essence, an enormous portable tower keep. Richard called his tower *Mategriffon*, meaning *death to the Greeks*.

He also placated his own troops still angry about having to winter in Sicily, by giving them gifts of silver and gold and paying one hundred sous to each pilgrim willing to remain. In addition, he stopped the merchants from gouging his men and fixed the price of bread at a penny per loaf.

Philip did not participate in the storming of the city. He remained in his lodgings and gave strict orders for his troops not to get involved in the "local disturbance." When Richard concluded the peace settlement with Tancred, Philip demanded half of the spoils. He cited the agreement made at Vezelay, that the two kings split everything equally. Not wanting to have an argument with Philip when he knew that very soon he would break his engagement to Alice, Richard gave Philip a part of the gold and several of the English ships that had arrived from their escapade in

Lisbon.

A short time after this meeting between Richard and Philip, Anne received a summons from Philip. Anne knew it was better to tell Richard about it than to have him find it out after the fact, so she told him in passing. "He is up to something. Mark me, Anne, he is using you," Richard warned her.

That warning echoed in her mind as she made her way to Philip's lodgings in the city. When she arrived at the chateau, Norbert showed her into a large room filled with an enormous, intricately carved dining table. Philip sat at the end. As she entered, Philip motioned her over to him. "Good afternoon, cousin!"

"Your highness." She gave him a curtsy.

"Come, come, have a seat." He pointed to the chair next to him.

Norbert took Anne's cloak from her shoulders, and she sat next to Philip. A servant brought a small meal of fruit, cheese, bread, and wine. "I remember you do not take meat in the evening, cousin, so please enjoy these."

She gave him a gratuitous smile. "I thank you very much for the invitation."

Philip washed his hands in the bowl of water placed on the table. "I am glad you were able to come. I worried that Richard would prevent you."

Anne washed her hands in the bowl. "Yes, well, he is ill-tempered about it, but my cousin, the king, summoned me, so I have come."

"I hope you do not mind if Norbert stays. I thought it best we not be alone together, as I did not want a repeat of Vezelay." Philip took a bite of green apple.

Anne nibbled on a chunk of cheese and studied Philip. She still felt embarrassed about the incident at Vezelay, so she decided to change the subject. "Can you believe how warm it is? Here it is November, and it feels like springtime in Paris."

"I will wager it is most welcome after the cold winter in

England." Philip winked.

Anne laughed. "Your highness, have you brought me here to speak of England?"

Philip took a sip of wine. "How like you,Anne; straight to the point, no dancing around. Well then cousin, I shall follow your lead. Tell me, what do you know of the king's sister, Joanna?"

"Joanna?" Anne raised her eyebrows. "Well, let me see. In truth, I do not know her all that well. She has her own ladies back now to wait upon her. I fear I was more of an annoyance than a service to her."

Philip wrinkled his brow. "Surely you spent some time with her."

Anne shrugged. "A little. If I may be so bold, sire, why do you ask? What is it that you want to know?"

"You may be so bold." Philip turned his goblet in his hands. "I find her a rather attractive woman."

"Oh, I see. In that case I feel it only fair to warn you, her temperament is very reminiscent of her father's."

"Hmm… Interesting… pray, go on."

"Your highness, I will say this; *there* is a woman born to be a queen."

"Indeed."

Chapter Thirty-four

Anne returned to Mategriffon and headed straight to her chamber. Almost as soon as she entered, she took her cloak off and tossed it toward her little bed. It landed only part way on the bed, so Anne sighed and picked it up. She looked at the bed a moment. She hated that bed. Her room in Mategriffon was more undersized than usual, but that was only to be expected. She estimated a person could cross the length of the room in about six large strides, and the breath in four. Irritated, she placed her cloak over her trunk and called out for Marguerite.

"Marguerite is not here." Richard's voice came from the corner behind the door.

"Richard!" Anne jumped. "How long have you been there?"

"I waited here while you were gone." He sat in her chair that sat in front of her small dressing table.

"What on earth for?"

"I wanted to know the moment you returned."

Anne sensed the tension she often felt before he became angry with her. It seemed to surround her, pressing in on them. She tried to placate him. "You know I would have come at your bidding, my lord."

"Yes, but I did not wish to waste any time. So, tell me. What did Philip want with you?"

Anne knew better than to bring up Joanna, so she skirted the subject. "Oh, you know Philip; he wanted to gossip mostly."

"What about ,Anne? What was the topic of your conversation?"

"Marriage, sire. Philip wanted to talk about marriage. With the passing of his wife, he must remarry. He asked me what I thought of some different candidates. I know you may find it hard to believe, but he values my opinion on the subject." Anne sat down on her bed. "It sounds as if there will be weddings for both of you when you return from the crusades. Perhaps you'll make it a double wedding, you, Alice, and Philip and whomever he chooses." Anne watched Richard for a reaction to her mentioning Alice, giving him an opportunity to tell her the truth.

Richard studied her for a moment without saying anything. In a brisk move, he stood. "Well, then, I guess we should just be grateful, he did not seek to marry you. I need to be able to travel back through Marseilles when I am done in the Holy Land, and I would not want to have to cross hostile territory."

Disappointed, Anne managed to answer, "Yes, my lord."

"Do excuse me, Anne. I have other business."

Christmas time came to Messina, but not like other Christmas seasons. The mild weather reminded Anne a little of holidays from her childhood, but those had not been spent in a cramped fortified wooden tower.

In a gesture of friendship, Richard invited Philip to a Christmas court at Mategriffon, and Philip accepted. Anne suspected his eagerness was not due to his warm feelings toward Richard, but Philip's desire to spend time with Joanna. Anne noted Philip and Joanna's behavior towards one another. There were many exchanges and glances, and it did not take long for Anne to conclude their feelings were mutual.

The two kings attended mass together at *Annunziata dei Catalani*, an impressive cathedral completed during the reign of Joanna's late husband. Their various entourages accompanied them, and they sat side-by-side. After mass, they traveled to Mategriffon for a sumptuous holiday feast.

Ever aware of the importance of impressions, Richard provided all the exquisite food, wine, and gifts obtainable in Messina. As usual, the entertainment was spectacular. Richard treated his guests to an event worthy of the season. Even a Yule log blazed away in the fireplace.

Blondel sang carols and recited poems during the meal. Afterward, Richard called for dancing. Even in the cramped space, the atmosphere resembled those long ago days at Poitiers.

Richard sat at the head table with Joanna on one side and Philip on the other. Philip turned to Richard and asked, "Richard, do I have your permission to dance with your sister?"

Richard grinned. "I give you permission on the condition that Joanna can stand to dance with such a dangerous partner."

"Dangerous? You forget who I am, Bbother. I dare say I have faced down much more frightening partners than this."

Joanna's eyes sparkled.

"Drink your Christmas wassail, old man, and let the young folks show you how it is done." Philip teased.

Philip rose from his seat and extended his arm to Joanna. She took it, and they headed toward the space serving as a dance floor as Richard called after them, "Alright then. Do not come whimpering back to me when your toes are smashed and raw because your partner ungracefully stomped on them." He laughed. "Old man! Old man! I shall show you how an old man can dance circles around you any day! Anne!"

When Richard called for her she was deep in conversation with Gustave. Gustave did not share in the celebratory mood of the hour and wanted to go over some figures. When she heard Richard call her name from across the room, she did not hesitate but turned to him. He made his way to the crowded dance floor and beckoned her to come to him.

As Richard took his place on the floor, Anne joined him. "Play!" He commanded his musicians.

The musicians played a popular lively carol, and the dancers set into motion. While Richard enjoyed himself, Anne kept an eye on Philip and Joanna. They did not seem to notice anyone but each other. When Anne came in close, she whispered to Richard, "I do not think I have ever seen your sister so happy."

Richard glanced at his sister. "Yes, she does look rather joyous. The Christmas festivities must have brought it out in her."

They danced apart for a moment and then formed back in together. "Philip looks most content," Anne observed.

He drew her extra close. "I fail to see why. He is not dancing with you."

"Oh, Richard, it is not about me; do not be so thick. Give a moment's thought and you shall see what I am trying discretely to tell you." Anne followed the dance and glided away from him.

Richard looked at Philip and Joanna, then Anne. Anne raised her eyebrows. He looked back at the dancing couple. Just then the dance ended. Richard watched as Philip whispered something in Joanna's ear. She tossed her head back and laughed. His eyes wide, Richard looked at Anne again. She clapped for the musicians but watched Richard. His eyes questioned her, so nodded her head in affirmation. Richard reached out and took her elbow. "I wish for you to tell me more. Will you come to me after my guests have departed?"

"If that is your desire, my lord."

"It is not my only desire, but we both know that that one will have to do." Richard returned to the head table.

Anne waited until the last of the guests left Mategriffon then made her way to Richard's chamber. Richard occupied two rooms in the tower. One was his outer receiving chamber and the second his bedroom. Anne passed through the outer chamber where several pageboys lay asleep on the floor. A drowsy Andrew sat in a large chair placed in front of the king's door. His sword lay across his lap. "Lady Anne." Andrew acknowledged her as he stood and opened the door for her. "He told me to expect you."

"Happy Christmas, Andrew." She smiled at him as she passed through the door.

Anne found Richard alone, still up and dressed, standing near the only source of light in the room, a large candelabra situated in the far corner. His arms were crossed, and he was deep in thought. "Thank you for coming, Anne."

He pulled out a large chair for her and one for himself. She sat down in the chair and glanced around the room. Despite the darkness, she envied its spaciousness compared to her own. "Some wine?" He offered her a goblet.

"No, thank you. I think I have drunk more than enough wine for one evening, my lord."

Richard scooted his chair around to face her. "I guess it is best to come straight to the point. Pray tell, what do you know of

Philip and my sister?"

"I know that Philip finds her rather becoming and is very interested in her as a candidate for marriage." Anne leaned back in the chair.

"And Joanna?" Richard absent-mindedly put his hand on Anne's knee.

"You know she would never take me into her confidence, but think about it. Think about the way they have acted around one another. I think she is smitten with the King of France." Anne did not move her knee away from his hand.

"Shit!"

Anne laughed. "Richard!"

"This is not good, Anne. This creates a problem, a very large problem." He stood and paced before her.

Anne sat up straight. "Come now, Richard, this is not quite the crisis situation you imagine. They are in love. Do not take it so personally."

Richard gave her a nasty look. Then his expression changed to one of concern. "You do not suppose they have… have…" He shuddered.

"Have what?"

"You know." He widened his eyes and raised his eyebrows.

Anne chuckled. "No. Philip would never dare. He would not even dance with her without your permission."

"How long have you known? Was this what you two talked of that day you went to visit him? Why did you not tell me sooner?" Richard fired questions at her without giving her a chance to answer.

Anne bristled. "I did not want you to overreact, just like you are doing now."

"Overreact? Anne, you do not realize that this throws everything off. I cannot allow this relationship!" Richard's face reddened.

"What is so wrong with two people being in love? Why can

you not just let them be happy? It would be a second marriage for them both. It would give you and Philip another reason to play nicely with one another and form a solid alliance. What would be so bad about your sister being the Queen of France, Richard?" Anne bolted out of her seat.

"You do not understand the complicated politics involved here, Anne." Richard waved her off.

Anne raised her voice. "Then explain it to me. I believe I am more than capable of understanding if you just tell me. I would like to understand, but honestly, I do not."

"That is why you are not the king, and I am," Richard snapped.

Anne glared at him. "There was a time when what I thought mattered to you. I have never tried to tell you what to do about your own business; I have only tried to help you, to make you happy." She looked Richard squarely in the eye. "I may be just a woman, but at least there is still one man I know who values my thoughts. He invited me to dine with him and talk about your sister. I do not try to tell him his business either, but at least he respects me enough to be forthright with me."

Anne stormed from the room slamming the door behind her. Richard kicked at his bedpost but only succeeded in hurting his foot. He groaned then bellowed, "Andrew! Send for my sister. It is time we had a talk."

Andrew opened the door and gave Richard a short bow. "Your highness, I have sent for her."

In Richard's opinion, it took Joanna far too long. When she appeared in his chamber, she looked as if she had been roused from sleep, hastily dressed and rushed there. "What could possibly be so important, brother? You would think the tower on fire the way everyone is acting." She yawned.

"Joanna, I have just had a talk with Lady Anne," Richard

began.

"Lady Anne? You dragged me out of bed to tell me that you talked with Lady Anne? Really, Richard, your problems with your mistress are none of my concern."

"Do not speak so of Lady Anne." Richard snapped at her.

Joanna rolled her eyes. "Alright then, would you please be so kind as to tell me why I have been summoned here in the middle of the night?"

Richard pointed a finger at her. "Be straight with me. Have you or have you not been carrying on with Philip as of late?"

"Define *carrying on*." Joanna gave him a wicked smile.

"Do not toy with me!" Richard growled. "What is the nature of your relationship with the King of France?"

"Nothing, Richard. It is nothing. I find him attractive and eligible."

"Well put him from your mind. You are not to think of him as anything other than the King of France," he commanded her.

"And why not? I have to look after my own interests too. Richard, you convinced me that once I got my dowry back I should contribute it toward your Crusade efforts." Joanna showed that temper so famous to her family, and the higher her temper raged, the more shrill her voice grew. "You promised me that you would give me another upon my second marriage. I am single; I am free. Why can I not look to a good marriage? Have you forgotten how our mother married our father?"

"You cannot marry the King of France, Joanna. Do you not see that he is using you to get to me? Do not be a fool!"

Joanna slammed her fist on the table. "Is it so hard to believe that someone could fall in love with me and I with him? By some miracle we are both free from marital obligations."

"You may be free from marital obligations, but you have others. You have responsibilities to your family and to your station. You have a duty, and you must do it regardless your feelings for Philip."

Joanna glared at him. "Oh, I see now. Just because you cannot marry your little Anne, you think the rest of the world needs to suffer just like you. All hail the martyr King Richard. He sacrificed himself in the name of duty. Do the good people of England see how you writhe in agony for them, while you deny yourself marriage to your ladylove? I wonder how they would feel if they knew how you writhe in bed with her. You hypocrite! Do not talk to me of sacrifice for duty and honor!"

Richard swung his arm at the table, sending ink, quills and books scattering across the room exploding onto the wall. "I told you, do not speak of Lady Anne in such a manner. I swear to you, if I ever even hear the slightest rumor that you have defiled her good name in any way, I will personally see to it that you spend your days married to the most wretched man I can find. Your marriage will be the highlight of your pathetic life if you ever again suggest anything so degrading."

He turned around to face the opposite direction. When he did, he sensed Joanna heading for the door. "I gave you no permission to take your leave." He whirled back around and thundered at her, "Pack your bags. Pack them tonight. I am sending you to the Abbey of *Santa Maria of Bagnara*. You will remain there, out of Philip's reach. I forbid you to have any contact with him! Do I make myself clear?"

"Yes, sire." Joanna gave him a cold curtsy, looking into his eyes as if she were at that moment stabbing a dagger into his bowels.

"Go now!" Richard ordered her out of the room.

Chapter Thirty-five

Joanna obeyed and went to the abbey as Richard commanded. Richard and Anne did not speak again until after Twelfth Night. Anne did not find it difficult to avoid seeing

Richard, as she was so busy with Gustave and the business of Marseilles. Richard did not summon her because he simply did not know what to say to her.

Late the night of Twelfth Night, Anne sat alone in her room thinking she should call Marguerite and prepare for bed. There came a soft knock at the door, and before she could say anything, it opened. Richard entered alone still dressed from the evening's festivities. He seemed anxious. "Your highness." Anne stood and offered him her seat.

Richard shook his head and took her by the hands. He led her over to the bed, and it creaked as they both sat down on it. "Anne, I have something I need to tell you. I have a summit with Philip tomorrow."

"My lord, I wish you luck, and may your negotiations be smooth." Her tone remained flat.

"I am planning to do something tomorrow that will have deep ramifications for everyone, Anne." Richard reached out to touch her face, but she turned away.

"May I know of your plans?" Anne didn't look at him.

Richard let out a long breath. "Yes, but I am not quite sure how to explain this."

"I would imagine the easiest thing to do would be to just say it. If you have been planning to do it, it should really be no hardship to speak of the action." Anne stood.

She started to shake and took a couple of steps away from him keeping her back turned to him.

Taking another deep breath, Richard began, "After much consideration, I have decided to end my engagement to Alice. I realize that this will send Philip into a fit, but there are so many reasons that I simply cannot marry her. I will explain them one by one to Philip, and even he will not be able to deny the impossible continuance of this betrothal."

"He will fight you on this."

"Let me worry about Philip." Richard continued, "There is

more. For some time now I have been in negotiations with the King Sancho of Navarre. As you know, his kingdom borders mine in the south, and I need a strong ally there. I must protect those borders." He pled his case. "I made a treaty with Sancho, and I am to marry his sister Berengaria."

Anne's shoulders sank, but still she said nothing. Richard continued, "My mother is on her way here with Berengaria. We are to be married as soon as possible."

Anne clenched her jaw. She longed for him to tell her the truth, but now that the words were said, she felt sick. She wished they could somehow be undone.

Richard went to her and placed his hands on her arms, caressing them. Anne shook them off and moved away from him. "Anne, please, it is not as though I expect you to be her lady. I…"

Anne put her hand up to stop him. He tried to reach out again, but she shrank away, shaking her head. For the first time, she looked him in the eyes, but as she did so, she found it hard to breathe. A weight pressed down on her chest. All she wanted was to flee the little room. Flinging the door open, she hurried down the hall. Richard followed after her calling her name, but he sounded miles away.

Once outside, hot air burst from Anne's lungs. When she breathed in again, they stung. She ran through the camp and headed to the seashore, vaguely aware that Blondel followed her. The lights of the city and Mategriffon shone in the distance. Finding a strip of rocky beach, she sank down on it. Fervent tears streamed down her cheeks, and she put her throbbing head between her knees.

She could not pinpoint what made her most angry. Was it the fact that Richard was marrying Berengaria, or that he had taken so long to tell her about it? Anne knew of Berengaria; her beauty was widely renowned. Lately it felt as if she and Richard had grown apart. Ever since that day when they sat on that log together and Marshal came to give Richard the official news of his father's

death, Anne felt relegated to the life of a shadow. It seemed
Richard only paid attention to her when convenient for him. Would
Berengaria replace her in Richard's affections? That thought made
her head pound even harder.

From a distance, Blondel kept watch over her. Anne did not
seem to notice the cold evening air. She stayed on the beach until
well after sunrise, wandering until she was sure that the time
passed when Richard would have left for his appointment with
Philip. Then she started back to Mategriffon.

Worried about Anne, Richard did not sleep that night, but
trusted Blondel would look after her. When morning came and she
still did not returned, he was uneasy, but he knew he could not
miss his meeting with Philip.

As Richard returned to Mategriffon late in the evening,
feeling the physical effects of lack of sleep. He climbed the stairs
and made his way to his chamber. Passing through the outer
chamber, he handed his hat, gloves, and cloak to one pageboy and
paused only long enough to pluck his boots from his feet. He left
them lying where they fell and continued on into his bedchamber
sinking down into his chair in front of his desk. The door to his
bedchamber opened behind him and two servants came in carrying
a small meal on a tray. They laid it before him on the desk.
Without even raising his head to look at it, he sat with his elbow
propped up on the armrest and his head resting on a closed fist.

He could hear drink being poured into his goblet, and then
came the sound of someone shuffling the papers on his desk. "No,
that is not necessary; I am not hungry." He wanted whomever it
was to stop mucking with his papers.

"I do not know how well you have eaten today. I doubt if
either you or Philip had much of an appetite." Anne's voice
sounded hoarse.

"Anne?" Surprised, he looked up at her.

"Here." She handed him the goblet. "Have something to drink. I am sure it has been a very long day; at least that is what your face tells me."

He took the goblet from her but only sipped at it. "I am surprised to see you here."

"In truth, I am surprised to find myself here."

"Anne, last night…"

Anne cut him off. "I do not wish to talk about last night." Anne wore her wimple, something unusual for her to do when not in public.

Richard set the goblet down on the table. "Well, we cannot ignore it forever."

"How were negotiations with Philip?" Anne questioned him.

Richard snickered. "Oh, I am sure you can imagine; livid. That man's face glowed more crimson than a cardinal's robes. It was everything he could do not to lose his composure in front of the other dignitaries gathered there to aid in the negotiations."

"He does have a legitimate reason to be angry." Anne sat down in a second chair opposite Richard.

"That was most awkward, having to sit there and spell out my grievances while he glowered at me. If it was my sister, I would have wanted to slice off the man's head."

"He must have known that Alice was your father's mistress."

Richard sighed and rested his head against the chair back. "Oh, yes, he knew it. He knew it. What I fail to understand is how he could believe that I would… how I *could* possibly marry her after she had carnal relations with my father. By all that is holy, she bore my father children! Were I to marry her, I would be committing a great sin."

Anne ran her finger along the grain of the wood in the table. "Were you able to come to an understanding then?"

"Yes, but your beloved cousin is going to make me pay for

it. I am released from my engagement to Alice on the condition that I pay ten thousand pounds of silver for the privilege. After Crusade is over and we have both returned home, I know I can count on Philip to invade my lands. We have reached an understanding on the matter, but I doubt that it will ever be fully settled as long as both of us have a breath left in our bodies." Richard rubbed at his temples with his fingers.

"I understand your reasons for ending the engagement, Richard." Anne attempted to be stoic.

"Now you know why I could not let the relationship between Philip and my sister continue. He could easily have taken revenge on her. He could have strung her along for years, or refused to marry her until I married Alice. There was no possible way I could have demanded an immediate wedding. Sometimes I really do hate politics." Richard took the goblet and drank down its entire contents in one gulp.

"Richard, Philip knew." Anne confessed.

"How long did he know?" Richard scowled.

Anne let out a long noisy breath. "He has known since at least Vezelay."

"Vezelay! You mean to tell me he has known all this time. That deceptive, manipulative, son of a…" Richard stopped. "Just a bloody moment, how is it that you know Philip knew?"

"He told me when we were camped at Vezelay. That afternoon that we met in private, the one you were so angry about, that is when he told me." Anne looked away from him as she spoke.

"Anne! Oh, come now! Why did you not say something to me? Why did you keep this from me?" He slammed the goblet down on the table.

The noise made her jump. "Do you honestly think it is fair for you to sit there and lecture me about keeping secrets? Correct me if I am wrong, but you failed to tell me yourself until last night. I had to find out from Philip!" She pushed herself away from the table and leapt out of her seat. "Goodnight, your highness." She stormed from the room.

Chapter Thirty-six

As the early signs of spring began to appear in Messina, the days growing longer and warmer, flowers popping up from their winter beds, Anne kept her eyes on a peach orchard. She knew when the buds blossomed it would be time for sailing again, and that Eleanor would soon arrive with Berengaria. Richard and she were uneasy with one another. Once more, they rarely spoke.

Late one afternoon after the blossoms bloomed on the peach trees, Marguerite informed Anne that Eleanor was expected in port within the next couple of days. She also let Anne know that Philip planned on leaving in the morning, as he wanted to avoid Eleanor and Richard's bride to be. Furthermore, Philip sent a note that he wished to see Anne before he left.

Anne debated whether or not to go, and in the end decided she would. There was not time to tell Richard; he was off somewhere hunting with Andrew and Baldwin.

Norbert showed Anne into the same room as last time, but now the massive table was missing having been dismantled for Philip's impending journey. Two chairs sat before the fireplace, facing each other, and Norbert invited her to sit. The moment Anne took a seat, the door opened again, and Philip entered followed by a large brindle mastiff. She jumped to her feet and gave him a curtsy. "Your highness."

Philip reached out and took her hand giving it a gentle kiss. "Thank you so much for coming, Anne." He motioned for her to sit.

"I know that you must be hard at it preparing for your journey, and I do not wish to take much of your time. I was glad, however, for the opportunity to bid you farewell. It was most kind of you." Anne spoke as she took her seat.

"I could not possibly leave for Acre without seeing you." Philip sat down opposite her, and the dog plopped down at his feet. "Well, this has been a stormy winter, has it not?"

"Correct me if I am wrong, but I do not think my lord is talking of the weather." Anne gave him a wry expression.

He chuckled. "Always forthright, Cousin, always forthright."

"My lord, you must believe that I did try when it came to the situation with Joanna. I am so sorry if you were hurt in the process." Anne knew Joanna blamed her, and she worried Philip would too.

"I know you did. Believe me, I know you did. Do not worry yourself about my feelings. You know as well as I in matters of marriage I am not allowed to have any. On the other hand, I am most concerned about you."

"Me?" She dismissed it. "I am right as rain."

"Anne, do not … what I mean to say is…is… Anne, come with me. Leave Messina. Surely your business here is complete. If not, let Gustave finish it." Philip tightened both hands into fists, and the dog sensing his master's distress, looked up.

"My lord?" Anne whispered.

"I beg of you, do not stay here where you are being treated so unjustly. You deserve better. *She* will be here tomorrow or the next day, you know. Come with me. You do not have to face this. You do not have to be here for the wedding. There is an alternative."

"You know I cannot leave."

"*Will not* is more like it. Listen to me. I can escort you further to the Holy Land; you can conclude the business of Marseilles and then return to Will. Richard does not deserve you, and you certainly do not deserve how he is treating you," he pleaded further.

Anne stared into the fire as Philip leaned forward and laid

his hand upon hers. Anne's eyes welled up with tears. "They say she is very beautiful." A tear rolled down Anne's cheek as she spoke.

Philip wiped it away. "They also say you are beautiful. *They* are not wrong."

The mastiff rose up and put his head on Anne's knee. Philip went to push the dog away, but saw Anne scratching the dog behind his ears, so he let the dog remain. "She is younger than me."

"Come now, age has nothing to do with it," Philip tried to comfort her.

"But what if he falls in love with her?" Anne's chin quivered.

"Oh, my dear Anne! I wish I could promise you that he will not fall in love with her, but not even the King of France can control something as powerful as another man's emotions."

Anne could keep it in no longer, and she sank her head into her hands. Philip gathered her into his arms, and sobbing, she buried her head in the shoulder of his soft red tunic. "Anne, I cannot promise to take away any pain, but I can promise to take you away from that thing causing you pain." He held her for a few minutes while she cried, her body shaking against his.

Anne drew back away from him and looked up at him. "Thank you, cousin." Regaining her composure, she took a deep breath. "Thank you, for everything."

"You will come with me then?" Philip gave her a reassuring smile.

She shook her head. "No. I will remain here, but words cannot express how much your offer means to me."

"I know that I cannot change your mind."

"Remember this then, I shall keep my promise that I made to you long ago." She patted the mastiff's head. "Duty will always come first. If my presence ever impedes him from doing his duty, I will take my leave of him."

"Promise me this too. Promise me that you will never forget that I always offer you a safe harbor and will come to your aid, should you ever need it."

"I shall never forget it."

Philip kissed her cheek. Tears formed in her eyes again, but she held them back. "I beg your pardon. I must take my leave now. There is still so much to do to make ready for our voyage tomorrow." Philip stood and offered her his arm.

He accompanied Anne to her waiting horse and helped her onto it.

Anne bent down to him. "You will always be in my prayers, cousin."

"Then I shall have nothing to fear." He turned to two of his men who were mounted and ready. "Escort Lady Anne back to Mategriffon." He turned back to Anne. "Farewell, cousin."

"Farewell, your highness."

Anne rode off toward Mategriffon with her escort. Philip watched her go until she was out of sight.

If Richard heard of Anne's meeting with Philip, he never said anything about it to her. Philip left Messina the next day. Eleanor and Berengaria did not arrive until the following day. Richard assembled a welcoming committee for them, and brought Joanna from the abbey to see her mother. Anne was asked to greet the queen upon arrival, and her first inclination was to refuse. However, she finally decided to go, partly out of curiosity to see the Princess of Navarre, and partly to serve Eleanor again.

The party waited at the dock for those on the ship to disembark. Eleanor appeared first, followed by her ladies and attendants. She held her hand out to Richard. He took it and kissed it, then drew his mother in for a hug. Eleanor grinned not hiding her delight at seeing her son.

Joanna came forward next and greeted her mother with a

curtsy, and Eleanor embraced her daughter. "Oh, it has been so long, Joanna. It is good to see you."

"Welcome to Sicily, your highness," Joanna basked in her mother's attention.

Wrapped up in her joy of seeing her children, Eleanor suddenly seemed to remember why she came. "Richard may I present to you, Berengaria, Princess of Navarre." She turned and motioned to the young woman standing behind her.

Anne more or less hid behind a bishop but managed to peek around the man to catch a glimpse of the princess. The gossips were right; Berengaria was beautiful. Her golden hair glinted in the spring sun. The princess wore a light red dress embroidered with yellow on the sleeves and hem. Unlike Eleanor, Berengaria was not wearing a wimple as she was still unmarried. Her facial features were fine and she even had little ears. The dainty, petite princess possessed a flawless figure. Even the bracelets on her wrists showed off her tiny, delicate frame. When she smiled, she unveiled two endearing dimples. Anne wanted to throw a rock at her.

Anne watched as Richard greeted his future queen. He gave her a chivalrous bow as he welcomed her to Sicily. Lost in thought, Anne did not hear what they said. When the crowd finally made a move to leave, she started from her deep contemplation and followed along with the rest. A litter waited for each of the royal women to transport them to Mategriffon. As Eleanor began to climb into hers, Anne stepped forward and helped her into it. Eleanor's face lit up. "Why, Lady Anne!"

"Your highness." Anne gave her a curtsy.

"Oh, it is good to see you, my dear."

Anne felt better. Eleanor's demeanor was more receptive than it had been the last time they met. "I hope your journey has been pleasant, my ady."

"It will be even more so now that I am once again on dry land. You know I am not fond of the sea." Eleanor motioned for

Anne to come closer, then she whispered, "You and I must speak, Anne."

Anne acknowledged her by giving a slight nod.

Eleanor turned to Richard. "Well, your highness, let us see this portable castle of yours."

"As you wish, Mother." He signaled the party to move forward.

Chapter Thirty-seven

Richard held a feast that night to honor his mother and his new fiancé. Anne attended very little of the festivities. She was not needed. Instead, she took the opportunity to work alone in her room on documents regarding trade with some merchant families in Messina.

When she finished with her work, she checked to see if the queen's room was ready. She was only there for a few minutes when Eleanor entered. Anne curtsied. "Good evening, Anne." Eleanor took a seat before her dressing table.

Standing behind her, Anne took her jewelry from her as Eleanor handed it to her piece by piece. "Is the feast over, my lady?"

"No, but I am tired, so I will retired early." Eleanor took her pearl earrings out, first one ear and then the other.

Anne held out her hand and Eleanor reached back placing the earrings in her palm. "I hope your highness finds the accommodations acceptable. While this is not exactly a palace of pleasure, I have found it more comfortable than a tent."

Eleanor looked up at Anne with a mischievous grin. "So tell me, who planned tonight's festivities?"

"I believe Andrew and Baldwin." Anne could not help but smile.

Eleanor shook her head and laughed. "Well, it was evident

you did not have a hand in it; not that I blame you. I would not have wanted to plan a party for Berengaria if I was in your place."

"One could say that I have not been in a festive mood, as of late. Besides, I am engaged in business of Marseilles." Anne brought a night shift for Eleanor and laid it on the back of the chair.

Eleanor took her wimple off, and Anne unpinned her hair to brush it. "Good for you. That is the best thing to do, keep busy, see to your charge."

Anne finished brushing Eleanor's hair and pulled it back so she could put it in one long braid how Eleanor preferred to sleep. She felt nervous, even though she had done this so many times before.

Eleanor watched Anne's face in the small mirror. When Anne laid the brush on the table, Eleanor put her hand on top of Anne's. "My dear, you look simply miserable. Why, you are even trembling."

Anne knelt next to Eleanor's chair. "Your Highness, I am so sorry."

"What on earth for, child?" Eleanor turned to her.

"I was afraid you were angry with me for leaving you when you were in prison," Anne explained.

Eleanor sighed. "Well, to be perfectly honest with you, I was jealous at first, but then I realized, I would have done the same thing. If I was standoffish with you when Richard became king, it was because I unsure as to the nature of your relationship." Eleanor stood up. "But that is all over and done with. Now we must face the new task at hand."

As Anne helped her undress and get into a night shift, Eleanor continued talking to her. "I understand that you and Richard are barely speaking to one another these days."

"He has become more like his father." Anne pulled Eleanor's long braid from underneath the shift and placed it on her back.

"God help us and the kingdom." Eleanor crossed herself.

Eleanor sat and motioned for Anne to do so as well. Before Anne took a seat, she handed Eleanor her customary bedtime cup of mulled wine. "There is something I must confess. I am so relieved to be off that ship and away from Berengaria."

One corner of Anne's mouth went up in a smile. "I thought the princess a lovely girl."

"Oh, she is something alright. She is *so* infatuated with Richard. She could not stop talking about him the entire journey. They met once, long ago when you and I were still imprisoned. She claims love at first sight. Ha! What a load of rot. She is a silly girl who sees nothing but what she wants. Mark my words, Anne, you be careful of her. She is jealous and territorial, and will not take kindly to a mistress for the king." Eleanor sipped the last of her wine.

Anne took the empty goblet from Eleanor and placed it on the floor next to her chair. "You know I promised not to keep Richard from his duty. I understand the reason he is marrying her."

"She is not the diplomat you are. That is for damn sure. Richard will still need you, my dear. You are an asset that he cannot afford to lose."

Anne shrugged. "I mean no disrespect to you, my lady, but I do not feel I can be much of an asset to him. Joanna would agree. I fear she blames me for her misfortunes in love. She does not care for me at all."

"Rubbish again. Funny, I do not remember you talking this much rot. You must be around the wrong sort." Eleanor's eyes twinkled. "It is a bad habit you have learnt, Lady Anne, and I command you to break it. As far as Joanna is concerned, she looked up to Richard when they were young children. Perhaps she is feeling protective of him and sees how miserable he is whenever the two of you fight. Yes, she is probably just trying to protect him." Eleanor stood up. "Now, I am very tired. It took all my energy to pretend to have a good time at that banquet tonight."

"Yes, my lady. I shall turn down the bed for you." Anne fixed the covers for Eleanor.

Eleanor climbed into bed and sank her weary head down onto the pillow. Anne laid the covers over the top of the queen and said, "Is there anything else I can do for your highness tonight?"

"Anne, I still think of you as a daughter."

"Thank you, my lady. That means a great deal to me." Anne curtsied and turned to leave.

"One more thing Anne," Eleanor called her back. "Richard still needs you. He may not show it right now, but he will."

"Thank you, your highness. Goodnight."

Richard and Berengaria could not marry immediately as Lent was upon them. Eleanor did not stay long in Sicily; she felt she could not afford to stay and wait for the wedding but needed to hurry back to England in Richard's absence. After she left, Richard had Mategriffon dismantled, and the English army prepared for the journey to Acre.

As Anne packed what little there was in her tiny room, Baldwin arrived with a note from Richard. She read the note and then looked up at Baldwin. "He cannot possibly be serious."

"I know, I know." Baldwin shook his head.

"He wants to use my ship to transport Joanna, Berengaria, as well as myself! My people and I barely fit aboard it. There is not enough room for two royal women and their ladies. What on earth is that man thinking?" Anne blustered.

"He told me he wanted to send all the women ahead together. That way, he is not traveling with women; you recall that agreement he made with Philip and all. He wants you all on the same boat for defence purposes, and he feels your boat is the best choice in his fleet," Baldwin explained.

Anne shouted, "That is my boat! He does not have a right to it! Who does he think he is?"

"The King of England, Lady Anne." Baldwin flashed her a disarming grin.

"Alright, I will give him that, but he is not my sovereign." Anne sighed. "And what makes him think that Joanna and Berengaria are going to go along with this plan?"

"It is true. They have not been kind to you." Baldwin leaned against Anne's large trunk.

"Please. They huddle together—whisper to one another— point and giggle every time I enter a room. I have grown very weary of it." Anne folded her arms, causing the note to wrinkle.

"I am at a loss for what to tell you there." Baldwin raised his eyebrows.

"Well, you can go back to *the king* and tell him that he can find another ship to transport the royal women. I want nothing to do with it." Anne jutted out her chin.

Baldwin shrugged. "Alright, if that is your choice. I will go back to him and deliver your message. Then he will just come charging in here blustering and shouting. Naturally, you will shout back, and everyone will hear your argument, including the two royal ladies, who will then know that they have scored a victory against you. But, if that is your wish."

"No wonder he sent you. You are a silver tongued serpent!" Anne reproached him. "Honestly, Baldwin, I am certain that you must have been apprenticed to the devil."

Baldwin gave her a bow. Anne crumpled up the note and tossed it at him. By instinct he reached out and caught it. "Well, hang you both!" Anne fumed. She turned and headed toward the door.

"Wait, where are you going?" Baldwin called after her.

She turned around and faced him. "I am going down to *my* ship to find where we can store these vindictive royal persons."

"That's the spirit." Baldwin tossed the note up in the air and caught it again. "I will tell the king, and I am sure he will be most pleased."

"Oh, yes." She paused. "Tell his highness that the only way I will agree to it is if you are assigned as escort on my ship." Anne shot him an impish smile, batted her eyelashes, then turned and left the room.

"Now who is being vindictive?" Baldwin called after her.

On the day of departure, Anne boarded the ship early before the two royal women. Richard escorted Joanna and Berengaria to the ship but did not board himself. Once they were aboard, Baldwin came forward. He stood next to Richard looking up at the *Madeline*. Richard clapped him on the shoulder. "I shall see you in Acre."

Baldwin gave him a pathetic look. Andrew stood by watching the whole thing, entertained as Richard laughed. "She got you there, didn't she?"

"My lord, which one am I allowed to throw overboard?" Baldwin joked.

Richard beamed. "Come now. Do not tell me that a seasoned warrior, such as yourself, cannot handle three women. You are the Earl of Aumale for heaven's sake!"

"I beg your pardon, Your Highness, but I do not see you boarding that ship." Baldwin pointed up at the *Madeline*.

Richard slapped Baldwin's back again. "Consider it a benefit of my office."

Baldwin let out a long breath and boarded the ship. Once aboard, he looked back down at Richard, who still grinned. "Courage man!" Richard called up to him.

Baldwin shook his head, took off his cap, waved it in an

exaggerated deep bow, and turned away from the side of the boat to see to his own passage.

Four other ships full of soldiers and supplies meant for Acre accompanied the *Madeline*. Only a week out to sea, the little group of ships encountered bad weather and were tossed about on the waves. The farther east they traveled, the worse the weather became.

Anne's quarters were crowded. As Berengaria and Joanna were royalty, they could hardly be expected to sleep in the common quarters of the others, but Anne also refused to give up her cabin to them. It was, after all, still her ship. All three women had beds in the cabin, and their ladies, who normally would have slept in the same room, retreated to the common area. Baldwin set up a makeshift curtain for the ladies in waiting to sleep behind.

Berengaria and Joanna spent the majority of their time on deck during the day, but now that the weather turned stormy all three women found themselves in the crowded cabin together. Anne tried to ignore them as much as possible and sat in the corner reading. Berengaria and Joanna at first tried to play chess, but soon found that impossible as their pieces kept getting knocked off the board as the galley swayed back and forth.

Berengaria got seasick first. Joanna held out until the next day. The seas grew so rough that before long nearly everyone onboard, even the seasoned sailors became sick. The situation continued like this for what seemed like weeks, but in reality it was only a matter of days.

Before dawn, Anne awoke to the piercing pains in her stomach. She felt her stomach muscles tightening and her jaw clenching so she leaned over her bed just in time to vomit into her trusty bucket. When she finished, she wiped her mouth and face with a damp cloth. She looked over and saw Berengaria lying on her own bed curled into a ball with tears running down her cheeks.

Anne could not help but feel sorry for the girl.

Retrieving a small chest from underneath her bed, Anne opened it and took something out. Kneeling down beside Berengaria, she pushed Berengaria's tangled hair out of her face. "Here, suck on this if you can manage it." She placed a bit of ginger in Berengaria's hand. "Sometimes it can help."

Berengaria looked up at Anne with wide eyes, and then put the ginger to her lips. Just then, the ship gave a violent shake, tossing Berengaria and Joanna from their beds. Anne tumbled backward, and Berengaria cried aloud. Anne helped her over to Joanna who wrapped her arms around her. The ship shuddered again, and water seemed to be spraying from every direction. Berengaria moaned while Joanna soothed her. "Here, try to suck on the ginger, dear."

Anne and Joanna exchanged worried glances. Anne stood up as best as she could and grappled her way along the walls. With unsteady legs, she made her way on deck. Baldwin was already there, holding onto some of the rigging. Anne almost lost her balance but reached out and grabbed the same rope. He steadied her. "The captain says we have blown off course." He shouted to be heard above the storm.

"Does he have any idea where we are?" The rain beat down on Anne's face.

"Off there in the far distance." Baldwin pointed to something Anne could not see. "The captain thinks that is an island, probably Rhodes or Cyprus. He is going to make for it and land."

Anne pushed the wet hair from her face and looked around. "I do not see any of the other ships. Where are they?"

"We lost sight of them about an hour ago. Perhaps you should go back down below deck. Berengaria's personal priest is gathering people around him to pray."

Anne nodded her head and started to turn around, but just as she did, the sickening sound of wood splintering, and tearing sounded. The jolt caused the boat to list and Anne lost her balance.

Suddenly, Anne was in the ocean. She thought she could hear Baldwin screaming her name. A wave thrust her against a rock. In vain she tried to grasp it with her fingers, but there was nothing to hold onto, and the waves pushed her onward.

She saw cuts on her arms and hands, but did not feel any pain. As she cried out to an increasingly smaller Baldwin, the sea rushed into her open mouth causing her to gasp for air. Coughing and sputtering, she tried to calm herself and remember her days in Marseilles as a child playing in the Mediterranean with friends. She smashed up against another rock; the impact forcing air and water from her lungs.

Anne had been around the sea enough to know what happened. The ship was caught on rocks and probably sinking. She started pleading to the ship to remain in one piece, knowing that it would cost a small fortune to replace. She tried to swim against the waves to the *Madeline*, to somehow hold the ship together and save it and her crew. All her papers! They would be lost if the ship were destroyed! But then she remembered she sent Gustave on one of the other ships with all the trade documents, and she took comfort. The waves carried her further and further from the ship and into a field of dangerous rocks.

Chapter Thirty-eight

Vaguely aware of some strange repetitive sound crescendoing over and over again, Anne opened her eyes and looked around. Everything seemed to blur, but she finally recognised the sound of waves crashing. Realizing she lay in the shade of a rocky outcrop on the beach, it all started coming back to her. She remembered fighting the waves to avoid the rocks, and washing up on the beach. She dragged herself up the beach to lean against this rock and must have fallen asleep. Wondering how long she stayed unconscious, she tried to get up. As she pushed her body up, pain shot through her. She was sore, scratched, bruised, and battered. Tenderly, she managed to prop herself up against the rock and examined her body.

Her clothes were torn and one shoe missing. Despite being scratched raw, nothing *seemed* to be broken; for that she was grateful. She let out a long sigh and tried to take stock of the situation around her. Looking out over the ocean, she could see nothing of the ship, not even debris washed ashore. She realized that she was alone and had no idea where she landed. Then, a powerful thirst came over her. With caution, she struggled to her feet and looked about. Nothing seemed to be a source of fresh water. Then she tried to take a step forward but realized her ankle would bear no weight.

Terror overcame Anne. She thought of Will back in Marseilles and of Richard on his ship. She wondered if Richard encountered the same storm. Then another frightening thought came to her. What if she were the only one to survive the wreck?

Desperate and hopeless, she sank back down against the rock, and as she landed on the ground, something thudded against her chest. Looking down, she realized that by some miracle the ribbon with Richard's ring still hung around her neck. She clutched the ring in her hands, and as she did, she realized the ribbon must have been pulled on with great forced as it dug into her neck and left sores. She wasn't sure whether to bless or curse the craftsman. She lifted it, examining it more closely. The golden band gleamed in the sun as she turned it around, studying the pattern of a carved elongated lion, its tail wrapping almost the rest of the way around. The end of its tail looked almost like a tri-foil in an archway. The lion, a symbol of Richard's family, made her wonder where he was at this moment.

Unaware of how many days passed, Anne still curled

beneath the rock. She no longer paid attention to the hunger pains and the thirst. At this point, she only wanted sleep. She closed her eyes and yearned for numbness to overtake her.

Anne thought she could hear someone calling her name. Believing she now hallucinated, she groaned and slipped into unconsciousness again. She heard the sound of her name being called again in a man's voice that sounded a bit like her father. She wondered if she was dead; she must be because her eyes seemed too heavy to open. She heard her name again, this time it sounded like Richard's voice. Now convinced that she was dead, she reasoned Richard must be about to perish in the same storm and called upon her for divine aid. She tried to respond. No sound would come, so she held out her hand to try to calm the waves. The next thing she knew, she felt as if she were floating.

Anne awoke to a gentle breeze passing over her body. The man called her name again. She opened her eyes, and they took a moment to focus. Baldwin stood over her. He gave a broad smile. "You had me worried there. Richard would have had me run through if I lost you."

Anne heard a noise behind him. Berengaria and Joanna were there as well as others from the ship. "What is… Where are we?" Anne managed to say.

"We are on Cyprus," Baldwin answered.

"Oh, thank the heavens. We are saved." Anne gave a sigh of relief.

"Not necessarily," Joanna grumped.

Anne looked at Baldwin. "The boat is marooned on the rocks out there."

Anne turned her head to look, but she could not see beyond the sand and rocks of the beach. Baldwin continued, "We did not know how stable the boat was, so we brought supplies here to the shore. After that, we sent some men to scout our location. The first two were taken prisoner and the second two barely escaped. We hunkered down here hoping to negotiate with the Cypriot ruler, Isaac Comnenus."

"Did everyone from the ship make it out alright?" Anne asked.

"We lost three men and one of Berengaria's ladies. Then there are also the two men taken prisoner." Baldwin wiped the sweat from his brow. "We were relieved to find you. Marguerite has been beside herself."

"Where is she? Is she here?" Anne sat up a little bit, but dizziness and pains, sharp and dull, convinced her to lie back down.

"I am here, m'lady." Marguerite made her way past Joanna and Berengaria.

Anne reached out her hand and Marguerite took it. "I thank God for your safety."

"Forgive me, Anne," Baldwin interrupted them. "I realize you cannot feel well, but I was wondering what you know of this Isaac Comnenus. Has your family dealt with him before?"

Slowly Anne put her arm behind her head to prop it up. "I know that he has a questionable past. My family does not do business with him. Etienne told me the whole story once... oh, yes, I remember now. Isaac is a lesser member of the Byzantine Imperial family. He was governor of Cilice, I believe." She paused to gain more strength. "Then there was something about him staging a revolt against the emperor, and he wound up a prisoner of the Turkish ruler of Armenia." Anne groaned as she shifted positions. "By some unknown power, he convinced the Templars that if they ransomed him, he would return their money with hefty interest. He told them he had to collect the money from friends on Cyprus. That was how he got here."

"Can you think of anything that would help us negotiate with this man?" Joanna snapped.

"I doubt if he is the negotiating type. He came here with

forged documents, stating that he was to be the new governor, but the fraud was not discovered until it was too late. By then, he had taken control and declared himself emperor. If he is the tyrant they say he is, then I doubt we can count on help from his people either. They are almost certainly terrified of him." Anne's head ached.

Baldwin scratched at his beard. "I imagine that he saw a bunch of Frankish ships off his coasts and panicked, thinking the Templars or someone else acting for them came to collect their money, and that is why he has not come against us, yet."

"We are almost out of water. What we have will last us for only a week more, if we are lucky." Joanna narrowed her eyes at Anne. "We have no choice but to send an emissary to plead for help."

Baldwin remained with the women, as Richard expressly gave him charge over their care. He decided that Berengaria's priest would act as emissary, the idea being that a man of the cloth could make a less threatening appeal. The priest set out to meet with Isaac.

The marooned group waited together at the makeshift camp on the beach for five long days. On the evening of the fifth day, they saw the priest descending the dune that bordered the beach, his head hung low, and his manner morose. When he reached the group he looked at Baldwin and began wringing his hands. "Well, what news?" Berengaria urged.

The priest gave her a dejected look. "The other ships are here also. Comnenus has taken their passengers and crew prisoner."

"But what of our plight?" Joanna demanded.

"Comnenus agreed to let us remain here on the beach, for the time being, but he refused us any further aid." The priest dropped his head.

"Any further aid?" Joanna stood and stomped her foot in the sand. "What does that mean?" She bordered on hysteria.

Baldwin and Anne exchanged looks with one another. "It

means we will have to cut rations on the water," Baldwin explained.

"Can't we just go find a fresh water source and steal some?" One of Joanna's ladies looked to the priest.

The priest shook his head. "I am afraid that Comnenus warned me that he would post men to make sure that we stayed on the beach. If we leave this spot, it will be seen as a sign of aggression, and we will all be taken captive."

Berengaria began weeping. Baldwin turned to the priest. "Thank you, Father. Now, will you be so kind as to pray with the ladies?"

The priest nodded and took Berengaria by the shoulders, leading her under the canopy the men erected out of a torn piece of sail between two large boulders. Baldwin walked away from the group further onto the beach. Everyone but Anne joined around the priest. With the aid of some driftwood, Anne pulled herself up and hobbled over to Baldwin.

"You should stay off that foot," he scolded her.

"It is feeling much better. I believe it is healing nicely." She shifted her weight onto the stick. "Tell me, what are you thinking?"

Baldwin sighed. "I think that Comnenus wants to push us to the brink. He is hoping to starve us into submission. His plan is for us to have no choice but beg for his help. I am sure he will make us pay him a hefty price, and when we are weak enough, he will take us prisoner and ransom us."

The thought of being a prisoner again, anybody's prisoner made Anne's stomach churn. They both stood there in silence and stared out at the sea.

The next day, a general air of despair pervaded the camp. The following night few people slept. Four days later in the morning, they awakened to the sound of horses and men, and mass panic spread. As fast as possible, Baldwin organized the men into a defensive position, and ordered the women to hide themselves as best they could. Joanna and Berengaria turned to flee along with the other women, but Anne remained rooted. She picked up a rock the size of her fist and leaned on her driftwood stick. "What are you doing? Are you mad? You must come with us," Berengaria hissed at her.

"I have been a prisoner before, and I do not intend to be held for ransom quietly." She shifted her balance again, bearing a little more weight on her foot.

"Do not be a fool, Lady Anne. You and that rock do not stand a chance against armed men." Berengaria laughed at her.

"Perhaps not, but I cannot run, so I will remain here, and the first man that tries to lay his hands on me will soon discover a goose's egg on his head." Anne clenched the rock in her fist.

"Fine, be an idiot. I am going to hide." Berengaria followed the others.

Chapter Thirty-nine

Baldwin walked away from the women, the men following him, and they climbed to the top of the dune. He drew his sword from its scabbard, thankful that he had taken time in the morning and the evening of each day to keep it sharp and clean from the seawater. He watched as nearly two-dozen men approached from the distance. Squinting in the sunlight, he could make out a standard being flown. Then the muscles on his face relaxed, and his expression turned to one of joy. Recognizing the standard as Richard's, Baldwin gave out a shout, "It is the king! Thank God, it is King Richard!"

At first the men around him seemed confused, but then they too recognised the banners and saw the men on the horses dressed in white surcoats with a red cross emblazoned on the front. A least twenty soldiers on foot followed those mounted on horses. A general cry of joy went up from the men, and they shouted and waved to get the king's attention.

Richard led the party and spotted the group on the beach in the distance when the light reflected off their swords. At once, he spurred his horse forward.

When he reached Baldwin and the others, they were cheering. Baldwin sheathed his sword, and Richard jumped down from his horse giving Baldwin a quick embrace. "I should have you horse whipped for scaring me so."

Baldwin could feel his entire body relax from respite. "Your Highness, you have no idea how good it is to see you."

Richard laughed. "I can only imagine."

"The rest are on the beach." Baldwin pointed the way for Richard.

"Before I go, answer me this, is everyone safe?" Richard hesitated.

Baldwin did not know if he should report on the royal women or Anne first. He chose to speak of the causalities. "We lost three men and one of Berengaria's ladies."

"That is all?" Richard raised his eyebrows.

"Yes, my lord. The royal ladies are safe." Baldwin decided to stick with protocol.

Richard whispered, "And what of Lady Anne?"

"She is safe. She washed overboard when we hit the rocks, but we found her on the beach. She is scratched, bruised, and her ankle badly sprained, but she is well enough to move around with a staff."

Richard gave a nod of acknowledgement. "For God's sake, man! I did not give you permission to throw any of them overboard." Richard smiled at Baldwin and then started toward the beach. "And I certainly do not believe that I would have consented to Anne being the one."

Baldwin breathed a sigh of relief and followed.

The moment Richard reached the beach, Joanna rushed forward to him. Berengaria followed close behind. "Richard, oh thank the Lord!" Joanna called out to him.

When Berengaria reached him, she collapsed against him and buried her face in his chest. Caught off guard, Richard awkwardly began to soothe her. As he did, he looked around the beach to find Anne. He spotted her sitting on the ground. Andrew was close by embracing Marguerite. "There, there, it is alright now." Without enthusiasm, Richard patted Berengaria's back and stroked her hair.

Anne caught sight of him with Berengaria in his arms and looked away. Richard saw her do this, and he gently pried Berengaria away from him. "I must see to the condition of the others. You are safe now." He gave her a reassuring smile.

He did not go directly to Anne, but stopped to see some of the others that milled about the beach. When he reached Anne, he knelt down beside her and removed his gloves. With a tender touch he examined her ankle. "I will have my surgeon look at this as soon as we get you back to Limassol."

"I thank you for your kindness, your highness, but there is really no need. It is healing just fine. Baldwin took great care of me." Anne's tone sounded flat.

"Anne, I… am so relieved to see you," he whispered.

"She cannot hear you from here, Richard," Anne whispered back.

"Yes, well…I have news for you. Upon hearing of your treatment, I headed straightway for Limassol. My men and I took the port and Comnenus fled. It will not be long before he is captured. Many of the nobles and people of the island have joined with us to rid themselves of the tyrant. Our other ships and all of those taken prisoner have been recovered. I even recovered your secretary. He was a prisoner, but is really no worse for wear," he spoke at a regular volume.

"Again, thank you, your highness." Anne looked beyond his shoulder as he spoke. Her demeanor remained distant, as others made their way over to gather around the king. She glanced in their direction to hint to Richard.

When Richard understood, he rose up and gave orders. "We must recover everything we can from the *Madeline* before she breaks loose from the rocks. Baldwin, take a dozen men to help you with this. The rest of you will return to Limassol with me. Men, prepare to transport what is here on land with us now." He turned away from the crowd and back to Anne. He reached down, grabbed her by the waist, and helped her to her feet.

Just as Anne gained her feet, Berengaria's priest cried out from behind Richard. "Your highness, the princess!"

Richard turned around to see Berengaria on the ground surround by her ladies and Joanna's. "She fainted, Richard!" Joanna shouted to him.

Richard left Anne and strode to Berengaria. Marguerite went to Anne to give her bad leg more support. Andrew followed and stood on the other side of Anne. Marguerite gave her a sympathetic look, but Anne only shrugged.

Richard knelt over Berengaria. "Bring her some water," he ordered.

Someone passed a flask of water to him, and he put it to her lips. She coughed and sputtered. "Are you alright?" Richard asked her.

"I think so." Berengaria nodded. Then, with a great sigh, she continued, "It is all… just… so overwhelming."

"Let us get the ladies back to the palace at Limassol." Richard stood.

The knights helped the ladies onto their horses. Richard lifted Berengaria slowly to her feet. Berengaria took a step forward and then fell back onto Richard. He caught her. "Do you think you can ride? I do not have a litter."

"I shall try." Her voice sounded weak.

Richard lifted her onto his horse, and almost as soon as she had taken the saddle she swayed and drooped back toward Richard. "Hold her on!" Joanna instructed from a nearby horse.

A couple of men rushed forward and steadied her. Richard climbed onto his horse behind her.

"Oh, bloody hell," Marguerite hissed under her breath.

"It is alright, Marguerite." Anne tried to dismiss it.

Marguerite threw up her hands in frustration. Andrew took Anne's arm. "Come, Lady Anne, let us get you on a horse." Andrew, Marguerite, and Anne all leaned in close to one another. Andrew whispered to the women, "If you ask me, she is a rather poor player."

"That player is going to be your queen, Andrew," Anne murmured. "Now, let go. I can walk better than you two think." Anne hobbled along with her stick.

"Your highness, there are not enough horses," one of the men informed Richard.

Neither Anne nor Marguerite had a horse, and Richard looked around for another. "Well, my ladies are not going to walk. Neither are Berengaria's. They have been through enough," Joanna snapped.

"Joanna, she cannot walk," Richard protested.

Anne spoke up, "Your highness, with your permission, I would like to stay here and direct the process of salvaging my ship,"

"Anne, you need to rest and have that foot examined," Richard argued.

"My lord, I will stay here until my ship is unloaded." Anne remained firm.

Andrew chimed in, "By your leave, Marguerite and I will stay with her."

At last Richard said, "Alright, but I will send men back as soon as we reach Limassol."

"Your kindness knows no bounds, sire. Please also send carts to carry the cargo of the ship." Anne bowed her head as she could not curtsy.

"Lady Anne." He turned his horse and the others followed him.

When they were out of earshot, Marguerite criticised him. "I can't believe he left you here."

"Look on the bright side, ladies..." Andrew started.

Anne smiled and finished the sentence for him. "We do not have to be around the princess."

Chapter Forty

The party remained on the beach until nightfall. It finally became too dark to work much longer so the company headed to Limassol where Richard had taken over the palace as his headquarters. Anne was grateful to be assigned a room much larger than her quarters in Mategriffon. Much more open, it was decorated with colourful mosaic tiles.

With Marguerite's help she cleaned herself, and later Marchadeus examined her. When he finished, Anne went to bed. Sleep did not come as easily as she imagined it would. She tossed and turned, and every time she closed her eyes there was the image of Richard and Berengaria on the horse together, riding off. Sometime toward daybreak, she managed a fitful sleep.

In the morning, Marguerite entered Anne's room. "I can only guess where you spent the night," Anne teased her. "You probably did not get much sleep either."

Marguerite blushed. "No, not much."

"Well, I think it is best we get going for the day. I imagine

Gustave is chomping at the bit." Anne put her legs over the side of the bed and stretched her sore back.

Marguerite laid out a light blue dress for Anne. "You were lucky. Your trunk got very little water in it, Joanna's on the other hand thoroughly soaked."

"That has got her in a sour mood, more than ever, I would wager." Somehow it made Anne feel better.

Anne got to her feet. Her ankle felt better this morning, and she could bear more weight on it. "Try not to overdo it, m'lady," Marguerite warned her.

Marguerite helped her into her gown and Anne sat down at a dressing table. She began to comb her hair when a knock sounded at the door. "Come," Anne called out.

The door opened and Berengaria entered. Marguerite curtsied and Anne got to her feet as fast as she could, giving the princess an odd sort of curtsy. "Good morning, Lady Anne." Berengaria flashed her a smile. "Please sit." She motioned to the chair Anne leaned on.

Anne took the seat and Berengaria stood while Marguerite pulled another one over for her. She sat in it and then looked up at Marguerite. "You may go now."

Marguerite gave Anne a puzzled look. "Thank you, Marguerite. Please go find Master Gustave, and tell him I will see him here as soon as possible. We have much business to discuss." Marguerite nodded and left the room.

"There now, we can talk freely." Berengaria smoothed the silk material of her rose coloured gown, and light reflected off her jeweled frontlet. "I find that ladies in waiting are necessary, but sometimes their ears are too big, as they say. I came to thank you for giving me the ginger."

"Oh, you are most welcome. It is a little something my father taught me. He used it many times as he traveled," Anne explained.

"Well, it was a kind gesture." There was an odd silence for

a moment then Berengaria continued. "I was glad to see that you returned safely from the beach. I inquired of the surgeon about your condition. It sounds as though your ankle is on the mend."

"Yes, thank you for your concern, Princess." Anne wondered why Berengaria was here in her room.

Berengaria sat up taller. "Lady Anne, I have come here this morning to seek your advice."

"I doubt I can have anything to say which is worthy of advice for you, my lady." Anne raised her eyebrows.

"Yes, you can. I need to ask you about Richard," Berengaria continued.

"Oh, I see." Anne forced a smile.

Berengaria gave her a gracious smile back. "I do not want things to be awkward between us. In fact, I have a confession. I had hoped that we might even be friends. Until you gave me the ginger, I thought you hated me, but that gesture gave me some hope. After our ordeal on the beach, I feel that life is too precious to waste being enemies with one another." She wore her best repentant face. "Having said that, I know you love Richard and so do I. You can hardly blame me for falling in love with him. As we love him, I know that we both want only for him to be happy. If we are at odds, then it will make things harder for him. Do you not agree?"

Anne suspicioned Berengaria plotted something. "I understand what you are saying, your highness."

"Good. Then I came for your advice regarding Richard. What..." Loud persistent knocking at the door interrupted Berengaria.

"I am so sorry, my lady. That would be Gustave's knock. He is my secretary, and as we have been apart for so long, I am sure that he is frantic. If you will give me a moment, I will send him away. If I fail to answer the door, he will just knock louder. He is an excellent secretary, but he is also a very importunate man."

"Do not be silly. I will return and we can continue our conversation later. I know that you have your hands full with business." Berengaria stood to leave.

Anne rose again. "I thank you. It is most generous and considerate of you, your highness."

"Until later then, Lady Anne." Berengaria left the room smiling.

Because Comnenus no longer controlled Cyprus, Anne opened up negotiations for trade with Marseilles. She located an old friend of her father's, a nobleman of the city named Petane. Petane welcomed her warmly and anxiously resumed trade with Marseilles. To have an ally in Limassol, relieved Anne, somewhat. Petane even went so far as to invite her to lodge with him, but she declined.

Just when Anne began to wonder if she had escaped a second part to the conversation with Berengaria, she found she was sorely mistaken. When she returned one afternoon from a meeting with Petane, Berengaria waited for her. "Come, I want to show you the most enchanting spot I found in the garden." Berengaria did not wait for a reply but took Anne by the arm and steered her away.

Anne could walk better now but still had a limp. Berengaria led her to a bower in the garden where yellow flowered vines formed a little cave and a bench sat underneath the archway. "See, I told you. Is this not the perfect place to have a conversation between two friends?"

"Your highness..." Anne still felt unsettled by Berengaria's sudden move.

Berengaria grinned. "Let us sit here in the herber. I want to ask a question of you."

Both women sat down on the bench. "Now Lady Anne, you must realize that this is very hard for me to ask. But there is no one else. I need to know what it is like to become a mother."

"A mother?" Anne stammered.

"Yes. Now, I understand that this question may be a bit awkward for you, but my wedding night is fast approaching, and I am not so nervous about that as I am about bearing an heir for the king." Berengaria gave Anne a grave look. "I know you are thinking I should ask someone else, but none of my ladies has ever borne children and Joanna never conceived either."

"Uh…"

"Is there some sort of special trick that could increase my chances? You know as well as I, that as women, it is our responsibility to bear sons, and I am beginning to feel the pressure of that. You have done it. You were successful. Think how happy a son would make Richard. Please, I beg you as our dear friend, advise me on this matter."

Anne gaped at her in disbelief. "I mean no disrespect, but do you not know about how I married and conceived a son?"

"I just want to know how to bear a son. I am sorry if I hurt your feelings." Berengaria pouted.

"Princess, there is nothing I can tell you. I have no advice to offer you." Anne's head felt as if she had been walloped with a blacksmith's hammer. She was on her feet before she realized it. Her head smashed into the bushes above, knocking her wimple askew. "I… I… I have an urgent meeting to prepare for, your highness. I do hope you will forgive me," Anne mumbled.

As fast as she could, she sped away, imagining Berengaria with a smug look on her face, sitting there triumphant on the bench. Once she rounded the corner and knew she was out of sight, she yanked the wimple from her head, and her hair fell about her shoulders.

Anne decided to head to the stables. All she wanted to do was ride out of there. She did not care where; she just wanted to escape. When she entered the stables, she snapped at the stable boy, "Saddle my horse, and be quick about it."

As he scampered off to do her bidding, Anne closed her

eyes and tried to inhale in deep breaths. If Berengaria gave Richard a son…it was more than she wanted to think about.

"Anne?" Richard's voice made her jump.

"Richard?" Anne opened her eyes.

"I have been looking for you. Every time I send for you I am told 'the lady is not here at present,'" Richard complained. "I decided I would look for you myself."

"And now you have found me."

"Anne, we need to talk." Richard moved closer so he would only have to speak just above whisper.

Anne rolled her eyes. "I do not think I can survive another talk today."

"Tell me, why have you been avoiding me? Did Joanna or Berengaria say something to you?" Richard placed himself in front of her blocking her exit.

"While it is no secret that your sister would just as soon see me drawn and quartered, no, she nor anyone else said anything to cause me to *avoid* you," Anne huffed.

Richard threw out his hands. "Then why?"

Anne sighed. "Do not take it personally, Richard. I have my own interests here in Cyprus. Despite your war, I must still keep trade flowing. I do not intend to leave my son a Marseilles that has been neglected while I seek after more selfish pursuits."

"My, my, you are full of fire today." A stable boy walked past them. Richard ushered her to a more remote corner of the stables and continued. "Anne, you have always managed Marseilles quite well and never left me out in the cold in the process. Why will you not come when I send for you? I know you are there; you are just being stubborn."

"You are getting married, Richard."

"I fail to see how that changes anything. Your marital status certainly has not." He put his hands on the elbows of her still folded arms.

Anne shook her head. "No, no! It is not the same! You are

the king and she will be the queen. You have certain *obligations* to meet!" She ducked under his arm.

Richard spoke as she pushed past him, "I am getting married tomorrow, Anne. I thought it best I tell you myself."

Anne stopped. Realizing she still had her wimple in her hand. She crumpled it up and tossed it to the ground.

"I see."

"I did not wish to fight, Anne."

"Then do not fight." Anne saw the stable boy with her horse.

She took the reins from him and led her horse to the courtyard. She limped more now from her jaunt to the stable. Richard followed her. "Anne, do not walk away from me. I have not finished."

"Now is not the time," she snapped at him.

With ease, he caught up with her and put his hand on the horses bit. "When then? You tell me, when is the time?"

Anne made an abrupt stop and curtsied. King Guy of Jerusalem stood before them. The dark haired, blue-eyed Guy smiled down on them, looking at the two of them. "Guy! It has been a long time," Richard spluttered.

Guy bowed to Richard. "It is good to see you, my lord, not only because you are coming to save the Holy Land, but also I am here as your humble servant."

Richard acknowledged him with a nod. "You may be my vassal, but you are also a king, so I welcome you here." He motioned to Anne. "This is…"

"Anne Baux de Marseilles," Guy interrupted. "I would know her anywhere."

"My lord." Anne greeted him but did not smile.

"The last time I saw you, you were just a little girl. I knew your father and was sorry to hear of his passing. You look so like your mother. I knew her as well." Guy had a crooked smile.

"Oh, my…" Anne groaned. "I am so sorry, my lords,

but…" She could not finish her sentence. Instead, she tried to mount her horse.

"Here, allow me, Lady Anne." Guy helped her up.

Guy's hands lingered longer than necessary on her waist, and Richard swallowed hard to keep himself in control.

"Thank you, your highness." Anne's expression of gratitude sounded forced.

She said nothing further but rode out of the courtyard and into the city.

Guy watched her as she left. "Come." Richard motioned to him. "I long to hear all the news from Acre. How is the siege going? Tell me everything." Richard led Guy into the palace.

It did not take long for Anne to make up her mind, and she accepted Petane's invitation to lodge in his house, sending one of his servants with word for her effects to be relocated there. She did not seek Richard's permission, nor did she inform him of her choice. She just knew that she could not go back to the palace.

Petane and his wife welcomed her generously. They gave her a large room in their manor house that overlooked the street below. Once Anne's things were brought to her room, she sat on the bed staring at her trunk. Marguerite entered. "Do you wish for me to unpack for you?"

"No, dear. Just leave everything as it is. We can worry about that in the morning." Anne's shoulders slumped.

Marguerite brought a bowl of water to a little table near the nightstand. "Marguerite." Anne looked up at her with tear filled eyes. "How do you do it? I know you love Andrew, but he is married and you have to share him with another."

"Have you seen his wife?" Marguerite laughed. "I know he loves me, but he has a duty to perform, and that is enough."

"You do not have to stay with me. If you want to go back and be with him, I will understand." Anne smiled at her.

"He still loves you." Marguerite tried to reassure her.

"Thank you," Anne whispered, "thank you."

"What can I get you, m'lady?"

"Nothing. I just want to go to bed." Anne lay down on the top of the bed above the covers.

Anne knew that it would be hard to go to sleep, but she closed her eyes and prayed for the welcome reprieve to come.

Chapter Forty-one

Sunrise found Richard in his room preparing for the wedding, his page dressing him in clothing Eleanor chose for the wedding. He wore a rose coloured samite belted tunic. His mantle of striped silk gauze, decorated with gold crescents and silver suns, lay on his bed. Next to his mantle sat his red hat. It too was embroidered, but with golden beasts and birds. On the floor, his ceremonial buskins made of golden cloth and his gilded spurs, waited.

Andrew sat in a chair looking on, chatting away hoping to distract Richard. Knowing Richard well, he could see that the king was anxious. He barely stood still long enough for his page to dress him. Richard's arms were outstretched, and it made Andrew think that the king's crucifixion was coming. "At least your wife is fair to look at. The wife you gave me, well, let us just say, I consumed copious amounts of wine to get through my wedding night,"Andrew quipped.

Richard turned at the waist, arms still stretched. "You are not helping."

"Sorry, I was just trying to point out the positive." Andrew empathized with Richard.

"Where is Baldwin?" Richard burst out. "I sent that man to find her an hour ago!"

"If anyone can convince her to come, it is Baldwin, poor

fellow," Andrew reassured him.

The page helped Richard into his buskins. "All I want to do is talk to her. She left here with things so unsettled last night. What is worse, in my conference with Guy yesterday, he seemed very interested in her. Well, I put a stop to that right away."

"I understand, my lord." Andrew could wait no longer, and took a swig of wine. It was going to be a very, very long day.

The page struggled with the laces as Richard took several steps to the right, then back again. "I do not know what she is about. Here I am, I have kept her by my side all these years, and I have never gained a penny for it, only one scandalous story after another."

Baldwin knocked and entered the room, followed by Blondel.

"Well, where is she? Is *the lady not here at present?*" Richard growled.

Baldwin let out a long breath. "Your highness…"

Richard did not let him finish. "Do not tell me you could not convince her to come."

"My lord, she really is not here." Baldwin shrugged.

Richard moved away from the hapless page, who still tried to lace his boots. "What do you mean she is not here?"

"Sire, what I mean is she left the palace. Her room is empty. I have been trying to discover where she went, but it would seem she aided the memory loss of many with the glint of gold."

Richard moved again, and the poor page scooted along on his knees trying to follow and complete his task. When Richard started to pace back and forth the boy sat on the ground to wait for on opportunity to snatch up the laces again. "God's legs! I never gave her permission to leave!" Richard shouted.

Andrew stood now to aid Baldwin. "No. No, you did not. Perhaps Anne does not think she needs your permission. In principle, she is only a guest in your household, and she is not your subject."

"Think about how she feels," Baldwin jumped in. "I doubt today of all days she wants to be anywhere near the palace, my lord. I know she understands why you are marrying. That is not an issue for her. All the same, I fear this is hard for her to bear."

Richard still paced, flinging his arms about. "This is absurd! This is childish! What sort of game it she at?" He pounded his fist on a nearby table. "Find her and send someone to fetch her here!" He pointed to the ground.

Richard stopped for a moment, and the page pounced at his laces but fell short as Richard began to move around the room again. Andrew threw his hands up in the air. "Will you please try to reason with him Blondel?"

Blondel pulled his lute around from his back and plucked at it. "Love has no reason, gentlemen."

"Bloody poets," Andrew snapped at him.

"With all due respect, your highness, you must not worry about Lady Anne right now," Baldwin broke in again. "You are to be married in a few hours. You have a duty to your crown—to your people. You owe them a proper queen."

Richard stopped moving again and this time the page caught the laces. "Oh for hell's sake," Richard yelled down at him. "Let me alone, boy! I will do it myself!"

Numb and distant, Anne sat in a chair beside the shuttered window. She knew where Marguerite wished to be and sent her away. Anne longed to be alone. She could hear crowds gathered outside in the narrow street hoping to catch a glimpse of the royal couple as the made their way to Saint George's chapel. All at once, a cheer went up from the street below, and Anne knew the wedding procession was coming. On impulse she shrank away from the window and sat down on the hearth taking some consolation in the grey storm clouds gathering outside, a spring storm threatening the festive occasion.

The small chapel of Saint George brimmed with dignitaries from the city and the king's men. Richard and Berengaria knelt at the altar before her personal priest. Berengaria wore a mantilla of delicate white lace over her deep blue dress.

Overcome with joy, Berengaria shed tears. Richard, however, remained solemn throughout the entire wedding mass. At one point he noticed rain running down the stained glass window. As the sky outside darkened, the light from the candles and flambeaux on the wall made shadows dance about. Berengaria gave him a slight poke in the ribs, which brought him back to focus on the ceremony.

While John Fitzluke, the Bishop of Evreux, crowned Berengaria Queen of England. Richard pretended to pay attention, but his thoughts were not on the ceremony. They were somewhere else in the city with someone else.

When the sounds of the cheering crowd died away, Anne returned to the window. She sat in the chair and listened to the rain patting the rooftops and the cobblestone street below. After what seemed like an eternity, she heard it. The abrupt sound came and lingered, the peal of the church bells happily tolling the completed nuptials. To Anne their sound was no more welcome than the sound of funeral bells. For a moment, she wished they were funeral bells. Each strike of the bells of Saint George overwhelmed Anne all the more. Her head hung low until she could bear it no longer and dropped to her knees, her body shaking with sobs. She did not expect him to back out, but at that moment she knew Richard no longer belonged to her.

The extravagant royal wedding feast commenced with much

food and entertainment. The airy great hall decked in bridal garlands and fresh rushes, gave off a pleasant aroma. Richard saw that his guests enjoyed themselves, but, for his part, he had no appetite. Nothing appealed to him. He could still smile and laugh, but inside he felt empty and hollow, as if some part of him had been plucked out and taken elsewhere.

Glancing at Berengaria, he saw her beaming. He could not deny that she was a beautiful woman, but she was not the woman he wanted. As he looked out over the assembled guests, he thought to himself that there were many men present who would give their souls to trade palaces with him. Tonight, he wished he could trade places with them, or even with a peasant, for a peasant could marry for love.

Blondel strolled by playing a tune on his lute, stopping close to the royal couple. It took a moment, then Richard recognised the tune. It was the song that Anne sung that first night he met her at Poitiers. He had heard the song many times since, but never heard Blondel play it.

His first reaction was to be angry with Blondel for having such audacity, but he watched as Blondel gave a bow to the royal couple and sauntered off still playing the song. The troubadour wandered out of the great hall. Richard took this as a signal.

"Excuse me. I just saw a messenger from Philip at Acre wander into the hall and back out again. I must see to the man." Richard lied to Berengaria.

"It is our wedding night." Her blue eyes widened.

"And I am still a king, and we are still on Crusade. I will be but a moment." Richard did not give her a chance to protest further, leaving the great hall to the corridor beyond.

Blondel waited for him. "Andrew spoke with Marguerite. They are staying at the house of a nobleman named Petane."

"I know the man," Richard whispered back.

"Your highness, I believe it would be safe to assume Anne is there as well," Blondel continued.

"Is there any message?"

"Andrew reported that Lady Anne admonishes you to remember your duty above all else." Blondel finished and strolled off again, sending gentle strains of music from his instrument as he went.

Richard opened his eyes. He could hear Berengaria breathing next to him in the bed, and he knew she had fallen asleep. The sound made him feel sick. With caution, he sat up so as not to wake her, and as he did, he found that he shook. He got out of bed, and she stirred a little. He froze and watched her roll over, holding his breath, until certain she had gone back to sleep. He could hear rain pouring down like a waterfall against the castle walls as he dressed and left the room.

Outside a drowsy sergeant-at-arms snapped to attention. Richard shushed him with a signal. He waited until he was further down the hall to start speaking. He could hear strains of laughter coming from the great hall as the festivities continued. Andrew and Baldwin were in the hallway not far from his room. "Andrew, is she at Petane's or no?"

"Your highness, do you really think this is wise? Your guests are still here. What of your wife?" Andrew admonished him.

"To hell with the feast, and to hell with my wife!" Saying those last words made his temper flare.

Andrew threw up his hands. "My lord, she is preparing to leave the city, but she is at this moment lodging at the house of Petane."

"Bring me my horse!" He shouted.

"But, sire, the weather is dangerous outside," Baldwin interjected.

Richard's face turned red. He marched down the stairs towards the courtyard, strapping on his sword as he went. "Richard!" Andrew tried to make him stop.

Richard turned on them. "I said bring me my horse! God's legs! We are not even in battle and everyone is second-guessing my orders! Am I not the king?" His eyes were on fire now. "I said bring me my horse, and bring me my horse you shall, or you will suffer the consequences!"

Two nearby pageboys sprang into action and sprinted for the stables, while a third stood scared motionless. "Good God!" Richard screamed as he resumed his flight down the stairs, Andrew, and Baldwin trailing him. Blondel caught sight of the ruckus and followed.

Richard sprang forth from the building into the rain. Blondel shouted at him, "Your highness, we can send someone to fetch her. Please do not go out in this rain."

"Where is my damned horse?"

One of the pageboys led Richard's horse into the courtyard. Both were drenched from the rain, and the poor boy could hardly see through the water that ran from his hair to his face. The horse was still unsaddled as the second boy trudged behind through the mud with the saddle. Richard did not seem to care. He bounded down the steps and onto his horse. The restless animal did not wish to be out in the rain, and struggled against the bit. Still, Richard spurred him on and galloped out of the courtyard. Just as he cleared the gate, the second pageboy made it around with the saddle. His shoulders slumped when he saw Richard go, and like a dejected dog, he slunk back to the stables.

Andrew, Baldwin, and Blondel watched Richard go. Without saying a word, Andrew and Baldwin returned to the interior of the castle. Blondel descended the steps and headed to the stables for his own horse.

Anne experienced a miserable day. Petane treated her with generosity, and even returned after the ceremony, offering to escort her to the feast. He could not be to blame. He did not know. When

Petane learnt that his guest would not be attending the feast, he offered to stay with her, but Anne insisted that he go. She told him she was just tired and needed some sleep. Petane regarded her with his large brown eyes. His round head on his squat neck tipped to one side as he studied her. Then he bid her a reluctant good day and left for the palace.

That was hours ago. Day became evening, and evening turned to night. When night came, Anne would not let even Marguerite enter the room. She gave strict instructions not to disturb her, claiming that she only wanted to sleep uninterrupted.

Now she sat in a little chair next to the window and watched the raindrops plummet down the panes of glass. Her kerchief long since soaked through, she resorted to using her hem or sleeve to wipe away the tears. On the street below, she heard the sound of horse hooves and thought to herself that Petane was returning. Sighing, she wondered if she would have to speak with him. She knew her face looked puffy and red from crying, but there was nothing she could do about it. Still, she did not wish to give Petane cause to worry. She poured a small amount of water into a basin and washed her face.

It took Richard little time to remember where Petane lived. Petane was, after all, perhaps the wealthiest merchant in the Limassol and aided Richard in capturing the city. When Richard came to the tall manor house, he brought his horse to a halt. The animal slid on the wet cobblestones and very nearly fell as it struggled to do its master's bidding.

Inside, Petane's servants were startled by a visit in the night from the strange man. They could tell it was not their master. Marguerite, who sat by the hearth, knew who it was, and rushed to the gate. She opened it just in time for Richard to erupt into the enclosed courtyard. "Where is she, Marguerite? I know she is here."

"Please." Marguerite curtsied so low that she was almost kneeling. "I beg you, sire, have mercy on my mistress. She does not wish to see you."

In response, Richard unsheathed his sword, which sent Petane's servants scattering. Determined to find Anne, he marched into the house and rooms on the bottom floor. When he did not see her, he climbed the stairs leaving a trail of water behind him. Marguerite followed.

From inside the room, Anne heard a ruckus in the hallway. Instinct told her to lock the door, but just as she started across the room, the door burst open. Before she had time to think, Richard stood in front of her, his hair and clothes soaked through from the rain. He cared no more for his sword, and with a loud clang it struck the floor.

Without warning, Richard fell to his knees before her. "Anne, I have done my duty," he choked out.

She opened her mouth to say something, but there were no words. She looked down into his grey eyes. Grabbing her close, he pressed his face into her stomach, all the while mumbling, "I have done my duty! Oh, God in heaven, I have done my duty!"

Part Four:

Conduct

Overseas

Chapter Forty-two

Richard became aware of sunlight on his face. His arm rested behind his head; he must have slept on it that way, because it felt now numb. He moved it, feeling his way down the linen covered pillow. There would be hell to pay. He left his wedding bed to see another, but he did not care. Rolling over to stretch, he started up and found himself alone in the bed. Looking around he called out, "Anne?"

He got out of bed and spied a little basin of water on a table next to the bed. Richard splashed the cool water over his face to help drive away any left over sleep. When he finished, he leaned on the table and tried to gather his thoughts.

He thought she must have risen early and would be back soon, so he decided to wait for her. He sat down on the bed again and grabbed a boot, pulled it on, then searched for the other one. Peaking under the bed, he noticed it had been kicked underneath on the other side. Sighing, he went around the bed, reached under for it, and grabbed it.

When he came up again, he looked over the bed and noticed a letter with his name on it lying on Anne's pillow. It was her handwriting. Shaking he picked up the letter and stared at it. His mind raced as he looked around the room, a little more carefully. Her trunk was gone. He thought for a moment and realized that it had not been there last night. As he thought, more came flooding back to him. He remembered a piece of paper that lay on the table. Anne turned it over so he could not see what was written on it. That must be the same note he held now.

He dreaded opening it, but it had to be read. She had not sealed it just folded it over. Faltering, he opened it and read.

My much Beloved Lord Richard,
You must believe that what I have done, I have done

for the best.. The time has come for us to part ways. You must do your duty,, and I must do mine. I entreat you do not come after me.. On the subject of our separation,, I feel so strongly that I will take extreme measures if necessary.

Last night you told me that I was your true wife, the wife of your heart. Let me remain the wife of your heart, but do not lose your soul for my sake. Perhaps I am naïve in my belief, but I feel that in the next life we shall be rewarded for dispatching the obligations God gave us. In the life to come,, we will be able to love honorably. Until such time, remember me and faithfully do your duty.

My prayers go with you as you continue onward to the Jerusalem. Go with God. I wish you much success and happiness..

Your humble servant,
Anne

Richard crumpled the letter and sank down to the floor. For the first time in his adult life, he wept.

Anne boarded the merchant ship *Corday* bound for Marseilles. Gustave booked passage on it for her the previous day and saw her off at the docks. She and Marguerite waved goodbye to him from the deck and bid him good luck on his continuing journey to Jerusalem. With a deep sigh, Anne climbed below and saw the little area that would be hers for the journey. Marguerite and she would be the only women traveling on the ship, and the kind captain partitioned off an area for them away from the prying eyes of the crew. Captain Vasser was from Marseilles and Anne knew of him by reputation. She chose Vasser's merchant ship because she thought Richard would most likely look for her on a galley.

Anne knew the ship would be underway momentarily, so she sat down on the little bed Vasser fixed for the women. As she looked around, the cramped quarters made all too real the weight of her decision, and it pressed in on her mercilessly. She rubbed at her eyes with her forefinger and her thumb as if doing so would make things better. Without speaking, Marguerite sat down beside her and looked at Anne. Both women started to cry as they heard shouts above them then felt the ship move.

Blondel waited outside Petane's house with both his horse and Richard's. He spoke with Anne that morning and knew Richard would be leaving the house before too long. When at last Richard emerged, he looked a sullen, red-eyed wretched sight. Blondel said nothing to him, but handed him the reins of his horse. Richard mounted and both slowly rode away.

As they passed the docks, Richard paused looking out at the ships. The long banner of Marseilles blew in the wind over one ships as it slipped into the harbor. Instinct told him Anne was on board. He took a deep breath and held it almost as if to speak, but he did not. Slowly, he let it out and turned his horse to the palace.

When Richard reached the palace, Baldwin greeted him. He said nothing to Richard about the previous night, but briefed him on the situation of the day. "My lord, Sir Guy de Lusignan is here—or should I call him the King of Jerusalem, I am not quite sure. Regardless, he is here to meet with you this morning. The queen is entertaining him in your chambers until you return."

"Marvelous," Richard mumbled as he climbed the steps.

Baldwin followed Richard to his chamber door. Richard stopped, took a deep breath, then walked in.

Inside the sunny room, Berengaria and Guy sat at a table eating a light meal. When Richard walked in, both looked at him in shock. "Good heavens, Richard you look dreadful. Are you alright?" Guy stood.

Richard forced a smile. "Oh yes, just a little too much merriment with the wedding." Richard motioned for Guy to take his seat.

Berengaria threw Richard a disgusted look and turned away. Guy nodded in Berengaria's direction. "I cannot tell you how much I appreciate your meeting with me the day after your wedding. I begged your queen to pardon my intrusion, and she has been most gracious."

"I apologize for taking so long in coming. I had some urgent business." Richard avoided looking at Berengaria.

"Well, I understand that you and your forces are just days away from conquering the entire island." Guy smiled at him and popped a grape in his mouth.

"Yes, that is quite right. I expect Comnenus to surrender any day. In fact we have already begun negotiations," Richard gave Guy a terse answer.

"Comnenus cannot be happy about my being here, nor the Templars that I brought with me," Guy observed.

"I am sure it is preying on his mind." Richard looked at an empty goblet in front of him. He thought to himself that Anne would have filled it by now, but Berengaria had not made a move toward it. He sighed and filled it himself. Then he turned to her. "Thank you for seeing to the king's needs, while he waited for me. Madame, please excuse us now as I know this talk would only bore you."

Her expression fell. "As you wish, my lord." She gave him a curtsy and left the room.

When she left, Guy leaned closer to Richard. "Warrior by day and lover by night, eh?"

"King always."

"I understand." Guy gave a hearty laugh. "Well then, I shall come right to the point. Can I count on your support for me as king of Jerusalem?"

"It makes sense for you to continue in your current position, not to mention I rather like the idea of a vassal of mine sitting on the throne of Jerusalem." Richard brought the goblet up to drink from it but stopped. "Tell me, what do you plan to do about an heir? If you are recognised as king, you will need to produce an heir as soon as possible. Or, in the spirit of diplomacy, will you name Conrad your heir?"

Guy had a broad grin on his face. "Interesting that you should ask. I have been giving it a great deal of thought the past couple of days. Perhaps your wedding inspired me."

"Is that not what a king is all about? Producing an heir?" Richard cringed.

"Tell me more about Lady Anne de Marseilles. I think she would be a good candidate. I hear she is very skilled when it comes to statesmanship. Correct me if I am wrong, but is she not cousin to King Philip? Then, there is the fact that she could use those allies she has all over the Mediterranean to help solidify my position. Not to mention, she is a feast for the eyes." Guy tossed another grape up into the air, caught it, and flipped it in his mouth.

The more Guy spoke of her, the more every muscle in Richard's body tightened. Richard tightened his grip on the goblet and forced himself to take a drink. "She is taken," he finally managed. "That is to say, Lady Anne is already married."

"Oh, yes, to Raymond of Castile. I have met the man." Guy shrugged.

Richard blinked. "You know Raymond of Castile?"

"Yes. He is at the siege in Acre as we speak. In truth, I found him to be a horse's ass, but he is a skilled swordsman. Oh, he flitted around Jerusalem, for a while. He was not at the battle of Hattin where, as you know, I was taken prisoner." Guy gave Richard the pouting look of a martyr as he spoke of his captivity.

"He is still alive then? You are certain?"

"When Jerusalem fell, he was there. Some have whispered he tried to convert to Islam to save his neck."

"No?"

"Oh, yes! And it is that information I can use to convince the pope to annul their marriage. The pope cannot in good conscience allow a Christian woman to be married to such a man. It would not be hard to find *witnesses*, I am sure. If all else fails, it would not be unheard of for a man to fall in battle, now would it?" Guy spoke casually.

Richard's mind spun. He looked at Guy and informed him, "Lady Anne is no longer in Cyprus."

"Oh? Pray tell, where has she gone?" Guy's expression fell.

Richard shrugged. He wanted to look blasé and speak with the ease that Guy spoke of Raymond. "Away on business."

"I guess it is for the best. I should really be concentrating on reclaiming my kingdom first." Guy raised his glass. "Here is to success in Acre, and then on to Jerusalem."

Richard raised his glass in salute and they both drank, each man studying the other from behind his goblet.

When Guy left, Richard entered his bedchamber. He went to his looking glass and stared into it. The man he saw staring back at him looked strange, distant. Richard did not wish to see his reflection any longer, so he went to the window and looked out. Lost in thoughts of Anne, he did not hear his door open. Berengaria was there behind him, stroking his back. At first he tried to ignore it, but she began to play with his hair. He turned around to get away but was astounded to see she was stark naked.

He walked over to the bed and grabbed a blanket, hurling it

at her. "For God's sake woman, cover up!"

Richard did not give her a second look; he left her standing there thwarted as he strode from the room.

Chapter Forty-three

"The port city of Acre had been under siege for two years." Father Breton recounted. He knew many of them were too young to have been on Crusade. "Having taken a more direct route than Richard, Philip arrived in early spring. Philip's arrival breathed an air of revival into the crusading armies, but this was not sustained long as the siege continued to drag on. Many felt disheartened.

"Failure, sickness, and death plagued the Christians as they tried to recapture the Holy Land. Frederick Barbarossa, the Holy Roman Emperor was leading his troops overland to help relieve Acre, but he drowned in the Goksu River along the way.

"Richard's own Archbishop of Canterbury spent the winter with part of the English army in Acre, but he finally succumbed to one of the many diseases that raged through the camps.

"Still, the Christian armies hung on to the grim hope that God would send them a miracle. Many believed Richard would be that miracle."

Within a fortnight, Richard conquered the rest of Cyprus. Comnenus surrendered on the condition that he not be put in irons, so Richard had silver shackles made to hold Comnenus. Once he finished his conquest of the island, Richard again turned his sights eastward to Acre. As before, he sent Joanna and Berengaria on ahead of the others, only this time he followed them the next day.

When Philip heard the news of the arrival of Berengaria's ship, he did not delay, but went straight to the docks to greet the new English Queen. He seized the opportunity to put on a political show. In perfect chivalric form, he lifted Berengaria down from her ship and welcomed her to Acre. Philip saw to it himself that the women were made comfortable and waited for Richard to arrive the next day.

The next day, Philip and the rest of the Christian camp collectively held their breath, waiting for Richard to arrive. At last his ship appeared far off on the horizon. With his head held high, Philip prepared himself to greet Richard, dressed in his best, determined that Richard would not undermine all the hard work of the past few months. From the door of his tent, Philip had a wide view of the harbor and the sight that met him stripped his brashness.

Richard's galley glided into the port with Richard dressed in the awe-inspiring clothes he wore on his wedding day. The light played on the golden threads and danced off the blonde highlights in his hair. From certain angles, he sparkled like the sun. As if that were not enough, Richard sat atop a chestnut Spanish charger of the finest breeding. To make certain that everyone could see him, Richard had the platform erected again on his ship.

At first it was small, just a person or two, but as the news spread, a general cry went up in the Christian camp. Philip looked around him and saw men dropping to their knees, raising their arms, to give thanks to God for their deliverance. Some men ran for the docks, cheering and shouting along the way. Everywhere, celebrations broke out. Even some of his own French troops partook in the spirit of the moment. When Philip arrived at Acre, he felt welcome, but nothing like this.

Philip looked around him at the merriment and swallowed hard, taking a brief moment to collect himself. As he looked down upon Richard's arrival, Philip reminded himself that Richard now had a handicap; Anne had left him. With that comforting thought, Philip started for the docks to meet Richard.

From his high perch atop the magnificent animal with its gleaming coat, Richard could see Acre. Tens of thousands of people spread out before him, and they were just the besiegers. Inside the city walls, the Saracens waited. He could see Saladin's command centre in the distance, on the Hill of the Carob Trees. Looking back at the Christian camp, he noticed the banners waving in the breeze, and noted the vast numbers of noble families of Western Europe represented there. The Templar's Beau-Seant flag stood out in the sea of beckoning standards.

Also from his vantage point, Richard estimated around three hundred trebuchets and siege engines surrounding the walls. As the ship drew closer, the crusader's camp came into view more clearly. He ventured about two hundred or more tents housed the weary Christian warriors.

While Richard climbed from his horse and disembarked, Christians thronged the docks hoping to catch a glimpse of him, cheering and crying out his name. Several leaders of the camps, including Philip and Conrad of Montferrat, approached on their horses and watched from a distance as a page brought Richard his Spanish Charger. Richard held up his hand and the crowds quieted down. "No. No thank you." Richard said to the boy, but kept his eyes on the crowd. "I shall walk, for here we are all one. We are all Christians!"

From the distance, Philip and Conrad of Monferat watched as the crowd roared their pleasure when Richard marched passed, making his way towards them. Richard reached out and touched several of the men who were on their knees or extending their hands crying up to him. Conrad turned to Philip and whispered, "Who does he think he is, the bloody pope?"

"I should think Jesus Christ himself." Philip snickered then spoke with surprising grace, "Gentlemen."

Philip slid from his horse and the others followed suit. They walked and led their horses to meet Richard. When Richard saw Philip he looked up and smiled. Extending his arms he called out, "Brother, it is good to see you!"

Philip embraced him without outward malice. "It is good to see, my brother in arms, alive and well! Welcome to Acre." He turned to Conrad. "May I present to you Conrad of Montferrat."

"Ah, yes. The other contender for the throne." Richard puffed out his chest.

Conrad gave Richard a low bow. "Your highness."

Richard acknowledged him with a nod. Philip motioned another young man to come forward. "Richard, I have a surprise for you. Our dear nephew has arrived."

"Henry!" Richard's face lit up.

Henry of Champagne was the son of Richard's half sister Marie. Marie was also Philip's half sister through their father. Marie's dreadfully dull husband died. Her son Henry, now Count of Champagne, was handsome like his mother and carried himself with her air of grace and intelligence. Although Richard did not know the young man as well as he would have liked, Henry looked and acted a most worthy and chivalrous knight. "Your highnesses." The Count of Champagne gave his uncles an appropriate bow.

"Well, come. I am sure that you are anxious to hear all that is being done for the siege efforts." Philip beckoned Richard onward. As they walked Philip pointed. "As you can see, we have many siege towers operational. That one to the right is called *Bad Neighbour*, and the one to the left is *God's Own Sling*. In addition, we have miners tunneling under the foundations of the city walls."

"I am aware of all your efforts here, Philip." Richard cut Philip's elucidation short.

Philip bit at the inside of his mouth to stop himself from bursting out at Richard. He decided to take another approach, and leaned in close to Richard. "By the by, where is my cousin? I was most fortunate to welcome your wife and sister yesterday, but I have yet to see Lady Anne."

Richard's jaw tightened. "She is not coming."

Philip put on his best look of concern. "Has she been detained in Cyprus? I do hope that she is able to conclude her business and join us here in Acre. I so long to see her. She seemed so distressed when I left Sicily, and I have been worried about her ever since."

Richard glared at Philip. "Your cousin will not be coming to Acre. She has gone to Chartres, I believe."

"Chartres? What the heavens is she doing in Chartres? That is in my territory," Philip continued.

Richard forced a smile and spoke through gritted teeth. "Play nicely, Philip. Smile and wave. There are others watching."

No welcoming party greeted Anne at the dock in Marseilles. She never sent word ahead of her return. It just did not seem necessary to her.

When they reached the dock, Captain Vasser hollered to a young boy lazing about, "Go run up to the chateau and tell them the viscountess is home."

"The viscountess?" The boy looked confused. "She's gone to the Holy Land, sir."

"Look here, boy! The viscountess is on my ship, and you had better run yourself up to the chateau as I commanded, or you will find yourself hanging upside down from my mast for a fortnight straight!" Captain Vasser yelled back.

The boy scrambled off, and Vasser watched him go, laughing to himself. Anne and Marguerite appeared on deck. "I just sent a boy to the chateau to fetch them here," Vasser informed Anne.

Anne shook her head. "Captain Vasser, I wish to walk. I wish to feel Marseilles underneath my feet."

Vasser helped her down from the boat and a crewman helped Marguerite. Anne planted her foot firmly on the soil of Marseilles. As she did, she let out a long sigh, closed her eyes, and lifted her face to the sun.

Chapter Forty-four

Inside the city of Acre, the Saracen defenders watched the scene before them unfold. They witnessed the coming of the English King to Acre, and that night the Crusader's camp blazed bright against the black sky while music and laughter drifted through the air. The Christians celebrated as though they won a great victory. To the Saracens the transformation in the air was palpable, and they knew their situation would soon change.

Norman laborers were already well on their way to reconstructing *Mategriffon* when Richard arrived. He spent the first couple of days in a tent, but before long he was back inside his massive tower. On the way to his chambers he paused at the door to the room that Anne used when she was there. After a silent moment, he continued on to his room. It was late and he wanted to rest. He felt an unusual sleepiness.

When Richard arrived in his bedchamber, the same lonely room where he spent so much time in Sicily, he ordered, "All but my page leave. I am very tired, and I do not wish to speak to anyone tonight." He slipped into a dressing gown then sat down at his table with his papers spread before him.

Irritated with the fatigue tugging at him, he wanted to get more work done before retiring for the night, but after a few minutes at the table Richard noticed his body beginning to ache. He recognised the first stirrings of an illness; possibly a fever preparing to set in. Richard decided he would go to sleep early and try to head off any sickness coming. He blew out his candle and climbed into bed, not bothering to remove the dressing gown. It just seemed like too much effort.

When Anne arrived at the chateau, she felt as though she had stepped onto safe, almost holy ground. The house was busy with scrambling people trying to prepare for her. Etienne met her on the steps. "My lady! We did not expect you home. Word reached us that the King of England was in Cyprus."

Anne extended her arm to Etienne. "Do not trouble yourself, cousin. Gustave will see to the business, and I should like to see my son. Where is Will?"

"I sent for Master Will as soon as I heard you arrived. He finished his lessons early today, and Master More agreed to let him take a ride this afternoon."

"Good." Anne took his arm, and they entered the chateau.

Once inside, Anne removed her wimple. She felt torn between the joy at returning home, and guilt mixed with sorrow for all she left behind.

Anne noticed Etienne's hair had started to thin and lines of wrinkles spread across his face. "I am so very grateful you are here, Etienne." She wanted to bring a happy tone to the conversation. "Do you think I would have time to change before Will arrives home?"

Etienne nodded. Not knowing what else to do, Anne gave his shoulder a gentle pat and headed up to her room.

When she entered her room, Anne shut the door behind her. As she looked around, her emotions began to swell beyond her control. She leaned her back against the door. Before she knew it, she felt tears running down her cheeks. Her heart ached for Richard.

Anne only had time to remove her gloves when she heard Will calling her from the hallway. Wiping her eyes, she put on a fresh smile to greet him. She threw the door open to find her son, and she could not believe how much he had grown.

"Mother!" Will wrapped his arms around her before she had a chance to really get a good look at him, but Anne noticed she no longer needed to stoop down to embrace him. "What are you doing home? We did not expect you for months and months!"

Nanette made her way down the hall as fast as she could, giving a little cough for Will's benefit. Will let go of his mother. He gave Anne a graceful courtly bow. "Welcome home, my lady."

"Let me see now." Anne put her hands on her hips and inspected the child, all the while trying to feign seriousness. "Yes… uh hum… well…" She walked around him in a complete circle then stopped where she started. "I do not know, Nanette. I just do not think this will do. No, not at all."

"What? Have I done something wrong, Mother?" Will creased his brow.

"I should say so! I believe you will be taller than me within a year!" Anne could not hide her smile any longer. She grabbed him again, pulled him close, and tousled his hair. "Oh, it is good to be home, Will."

"Mother, where is Uncle?"

Anne gave Will the answer she practiced since she departed Cyprus. "I imagine Uncle is in Acre by now. Fortunately, I finished my business early, and I heard reports that you had been lax in your Latin lessons, so we both agreed I should come here straightway and see to it that you do not neglect them."

Will gave his mother an odd look, blinking his eyes a couple of times. She knew he wanted to know more, but out of respect he did not question her further. For Anne it was like looking into her own eyes, only these were younger. Suddenly, Will's eyes sparkled. "Mother, I want to show you my new horse!" He began to tug at her.

Nanette made a move to intervene. "Master William, your mother has barely had time to catch her breath."

"Oh, thank you, Nanette. It is quite alright." Anne laughed. "Will, I would love to see your new horse. Lead the way."

Will led her down the hall, chattering all the way.

Anne unsuccessfully tried hard to settle back into life in Marseilles. She was so happy to be home, but she felt hollow inside. She hardly ate and spent far too much time sleeping. Not even Will could rouse her from her doldrums. This continued for a couple of weeks, when Nanette decided to take matters into her own hands, and she entered Anne's uninviting bedchamber.

Anne lay in bed with the curtains drawn. Nanette pulled the curtains open and tied them back. "Nanette, you do not have to do that," Anne mumbled.

"Lady Anne, it is past noon and you are still wallowing in bed." Nanette opened the chamber windows wide, using her walking stick to aid her where she couldn't reach.

"I am not wallowing in bed. I am just tired from all the travel. That is all," Anne protested.

"Bah, travel. You have been moping around this house since you came home. As your nurse, I will not allow it." Nanette waved her ancient hand in front of her face.

"You forget, Nanette, I no longer need a nurse." Anne rolled over.

"No longer needs a nurse she says, no longer needs a nurse," Nanette murmured as she hobbled back toward the bed. She reached over and with surprising agility threw the covers off Anne. "If you no longer need a nurse, then why are you acting like a child?"

"Nanette!" Anne sat up. "I cannot believe you are…"

"I cannot believe *you* are acting like this. You are your father's daughter, are you not?" Nanette plopped down into a chair, leaning forward with both hands grasping her walking stick. "Now, tell me, what happened."

"Has Marguerite not told you?" Anne pouted.

"No, nor have I asked her. It is your business, and so you

are the one I want to hear it from." Nanette gave Anne a look that made Anne want to obey her.

Anne threw her hands up in the air. "Alright! I finished my business earlier than expected, and I came home."

"Were you *sent* home? Did he *send* you home? Because if he did, I swear…King of England or no I… he is a fool that…" Nanette shook her stick.

"No, no. It was not like that." Anne looked down at her hands.

Nanette spoke with a softer tone. "Then tell me child. What happened? What has happened to my Anne?"

Anne drew her knees up to her chest. "I left him in Cyprus."

"I say he is still a fool," Nanette grumped.

"I had to. He got married," Anne continued.

Nanette studied her. "I should think there is more to it than that."

"On his wedding night it was made clear to me that I was getting in the way of his doing his duty, and he was hampering me in mine. Duty comes first. That is something I learnt from Father." Anne rested her chin on her knees.

Nanette snorted. "Duty?"

Anne sat up taller. "Yes, Nanette, duty."

The old woman leaned her cane on the bedside table, folded her gnarled hands together and placed them in her lap. "I know you don't remember when my husband passed away. You were still a very little girl then. My heart broke. I thought that the most important thing I could do was to take care of you. I put all I had into it, becoming consumed with my task. One day your father came to me and said he was going to dismiss me—send me away. Sir William said that I was not taking care of you. As you can imagine I was upset, and in a rage of blustering tears I recited for him all that I was doing for my charge." Something like a smile spread across Nanette's face. "I will never forget what Sir William said. He told me that I neglected something. I neglected to care for myself. He pointed out that he took great care of his horses, his carts, his home, his weapons; he maintained them so they could perform to their best ability. Like those things he mentioned, we must maintain ourselves if we hope to be of any service. Just as a broken sword does a person no good, a broken nurse would do his child no good. Your father said to me, 'If you want to do your duty, that is admirable, but do not neglect that which makes it possible to do your duty.'" Nanette put both her hands on the armrest of the chair and pushed herself up. "Now, I am famished. I think I shall take my old bones down to the kitchen and see if I can't snatch something while the cook's head is turned."

Anne did not know what to say. She watched in amazement as Nanette made her way out of the room in her awkward gait. Once she was gone, Anne felt fortitude coming back into her. She got out of bed, washed her face, and dressed.

Richard could feel something touching his forehead. He pushed whatever it was away and opened his eyes. "Your highness, you have got yourself a fever." Andrew stood over him with a concerned look.

"Nonsense," Richard mumbled and tried to pull himself upright. The weakness that took hold of his body shocked him, and he fell back on his pillow.

"I sent for Marchadeus," Andrew informed him. "I came in early this morning because you did not show for our scheduled ride. You were sweating and moaning."

"It is nothing really," Richard protested. "I was just overly tired, but there just isn't time to rest today."

"All the same, I would feel better if you would allow Marchedeus to see you." Andrew handed Richard a cool cloth.

Richard took the cloth and wiped his own brow. The ache in his hands was unexpected. Still he tried not to let on to Andrew.

"How long ago did you send for him? I cannot wait around all day. I have got a siege to end. Lord knows if I leave it to Philip, this whole mess would go on and on."

Andrew fidgeted. "Your highness, the French king has come down with a strange malady. Reports are saying his hair is falling out—as well as his nails."

Richard let the news sink in. Andrew stepped to a chair near the bed and sat down. "I should think that with a little rest, you will be feeling yourself by this evening."

There was an awkward silence between the two men, but Richard could stand it no longer. "Have you heard from Marguerite?"

Andrew leaned on his elbows and shook his head. "No, My Lord. She cannot read nor write."

"Yes, I remember that now. Did she ever get the chance to bid you farewell?"

Andrew remained sulky and withdrawn since Marguerite left. "She came to me that night and told me that she and Lady Anne would be leaving the next day. Said she was afraid to leave Anne on her own, afraid she might do something drastic."

Richard licked his dry lips. "Do you know where they are? I was told she went to Chartres, but somehow I do not believe it. Did they return to Marseilles?"

Andrew looked up and furrowed his brow. "That is the odd thing about it. Marguerite said Anne was rather insistent that she was going to go to Chartres because it was in Philip's territory and you would not come after her there. Marseilles was too obvious a choice, I suppose. Chartres is also close to your sister Marie, and Anne wanted to see her." He leaned back in his chair and folded his arms across his chest. "Anne swore if you come after her, she will become a nun at the abbey there."

"Well, at least we know that Marguerite would never become a nun." Richard tried to joke.

"I mean no disrespect, your highness, but it sounds as if

Anne…" The door opened and Andrew fell silent.

Marchadeus swept into the room past Andrew to Richard's bedside. "Pray, give us leave." He turned to Andrew.

Andrew bowed his way out of the room.

Anne spent the rest of the day replying to some neglected correspondences. By the time she complete the task, it was well past the evening meal. Marguerite brought a plate of food for Anne to eat, and she ate but a very little. Anne reasoned the important thing was she ate. When night came, she went to bed with the intention of rising early and getting a start on the day's business, but her sleep was troubled.

Anne dreamt of Richard in the mountains somewhere in the cold. His body shook from the chill, and he could hardly stay on his horse. He wandered down a path alone. Although others called to him, he took no notice. Anne pleaded with him to stop and turn around, but no sound escaped her mouth. She tried pulling the horse from its direction, but it walked on. She tried pulling on Richard's leg, but he paid no attention. Looking forward, she could now see where he headed, a dark forest where the trees groaned as they swayed in the wind. She could only see the trees that rimmed the forest, not into a wood so black everything seemed to be swallow by it. Richard let his sword fall to his side and took off bits and pieces of armor, dropping them along the path. Anne tried picking them up and returning them to Richard, but the more she picked up, the more they fell from her arms and the more she fell behind him, trying to pick them all up.

Desperation closed in. Richard continued into the deep recesses of the wood, and then she could no longer see him. She screamed his name, but no sound came out of her mouth, and there was no answer.

Anne woke with a start. Once she regained her senses, she coughed just to make sure that she still had a voice, then laid her head back down on the pillow. She rubbed her eyes as if that would wipe away the visions in her head. Her eyes focused on an object resting on her large table, her peach blossom basket.

Blinking, Anne tried to make sure that she did not imagine it, that this was not another dream. She could not remember putting it there. She knew that she hadn't. The cloth lay on top, and it looked full. Rising from bed, she went to the basket. Pulling back the cover, she saw it was filled with peach blossoms. She put on a cote hardie, and with new found determination, snatched the basket and headed for her bluff above the sea.

Richard could not keep track of how many days he remained in bed as the fever caused him to fall in and out of consciousness so often that he thought he must have been there more than a week. He slept fitfully at best. He could not be sure, but he thought he remembered giving the surgeon permission to bleed him at one point.

A thirst burnt at Richard, and he rolled over to view the room for something to drink. He could see Marchadeus asleep in a chair; no one else seemed to be in the room. Noticing a goblet on the bedside table, Richard reached out for it. As he did, he caught site of his hand. Two of his fingers were missing their nails. *God's legs*! Horrified, he looked at his other hand. Three nails were gone. He thought of Philip as he reached up and felt his head. He could feel hair and was relieved, but only for a moment. When he withdrew his hand, a large clump of hair came with it.

Chapter Forty-five

Fear spread like a plague throughout the Christian camp.

Both the King of England and the King of France fell ill with a strange disease. Many feared all would be lost. Once Philip took to his bed, he remained there, frightened that he would meet God much sooner than he planned. On the other hand, it was hard to persuade Richard to remain at rest.

Just before he came down with his illness, Richard began a correspondence with Saladin. Richard impressed Saladin, and the Saracen sent Richard snow and fruit from the mountains to help aid in his recovery.

Throughout the illness, Andrew remained by Richard's side, and Baldwin conducted much of Richard's business. Joanna kept her distance but sent words of concern and encouragement. Berengaria, claiming that she feared falling ill and did not wish to endanger her chances of producing a healthy heir, kept to her own quarters. She spent most of her time crying, and at some points became hysterical, clinging to those around her in her hour of most heavy grief.

Philip recovered first. Still smarting from Richard's triumphant entry into Acre, Philip decided to take advantage of Richard's illness and once again gain the upper hand. His French forces would attack the city while Richard recuperated.

Philip sent the Count of Flanders, one of his most trusted and important knights, to Mategriffon to inform Richard of the impending attack. When Andrew showed the count into Richard's outer chamber, the sight that met Flanders shocked him; he could not help gaping at the form. Propped up in bed, Richard looked nothing like the king who captured so much attention less than a month ago when he entered the port dressed in gold atop the bow of his ship. This Richard looked much smaller; his face sallow, and his gray eyes seemed sunken. Despite the blue cap on Richard's head, the count could see that large chunks of the king's hair missing.

The count's expression was not lost on Richard. "I realize I must look a fright, but God's legs, man, I am not dead yet."

"Yes, of course, your highness." Flanders swallowed. "I just could not help but be concerned for my lord's health."

"Sire, I have been sent by my lord to inform you he loathes the delay in action and feels that the time for attack has come. He intends to send the criers out with orders for the army to move forward at daybreak." Flanders shifted his balance from one foot to the other.

"I see. Philip feels this is the best option?" Richard sat up taller.

"Yes, sire." The count looked down.

Richard let out a rough sigh. "Does your lord realize that he will have to undertake this operation without the aid of my armies? I am not in the position to partake in such a project, as you can clearly see. Also, I have more supplies and men coming within a fortnight. Once they arrive, we will be able to build more siege machines. The combined strength of the two armies would be more effective."

Choosing not to make a reply, Flanders just stood there waiting for dismissal.

Richard took a long look at the count. "It will not hurt to wait a few more days. The Saracens cannot receive any supplies or reinforcements from the sea, as we have blockaded them." Richard studied the count's face for a change, but it did not come. "Well then, commend me to your lord. Andrew, please show the count out."

The count gave Richard a long bow and then followed Andrew out of the room. In a moment, Andrew returned. "Do you think Philip will go through with it, my lord?" He helped Richard settle back down in the bed.

Looking up, Richard replied, "Of course he will. He is a fool bent on gaining glory. We can only hope that his stupidity does not set us back months."

Richard awoke to a clamor unlike any he heard before. He opened his eyes with a start. The scare caused a new found strength to course through him, and he managed to push himself out of bed. "What is that? What in the name of all that is holy?" He shouted out to Andrew nearby.

Andrew leapt to the window that overlooked the city. "My lord, Philip's siege machine is lined up, and they are about to strike."

"That is what is causing that horrible ruckus?" Richard made his way to the window to see for himself.

As he looked out, he discovered not the French causing the noise, but the Saracen defenders. Perhaps they recalled Joshua's army who conquered Jericho. Men pounding drums lined the walls, as trumpeters blared, and metal from pots and pans, not swords flashed in the sunlight as mens' arms moved rapidly back and forth, beating them. Those with nothing else raised their voices in a yell. The cacophony that resonated from the city sounded fantastic. It inspired something in Richard and a smile spread across his face. Puffs of smoke began to rise into the air from behind the city walls. "They must be signaling Saladin," Richard thought aloud.

Richard moved away from the window. "Well, this is not a day to be caught in bed. Send for my page."

"My lord, do you intend to fight?"

"No, hell no. Let Philip fight. He will not win." Richard plunged his hands into a water basin and splashing the cool water over his face. "I came here to end a siege, and end it I will. Today we will prepare for our own attack. When the French come limping back from their mess, the English will swoop in to save the day."

"I will assemble your advisors as well as your page." With an excited swoosh, Andrew left the chamber.

Philip and the Count of Flanders sat inside his cercleia, a little shed like structure built of latticework covered with leaves, twigs, and brush to conceal what was inside. Looking out he watched his siege tower move closer to the walls of Acre and noticed the many flags fluttering in the soft breeze blowing in from the Mediterranean on the already hot July morning. "Ah, a breeze to cool our men," Philip remarked to the Count of Flanders with a smile. "It is a good omen. It will cool their backs as they prepare to enter the city; they will be nice and fresh to meet the noise-makers."

In the distance, a cloud of dust billowed toward the city, and right away Philip knew that Saladin sent reinforcements. Meanwhile, a small group of French breeched one of the barricades into the city. At almost the same time, the Saracen relief party smashed into the French lines, and the fighting turned fierce. The French were driven back from the barricade and forced to combat the numbers of Saracen pouring outside the walls of the city.

Through the twisted mesh of leaves and green vines, the king watched in horror as his troops were cut down in front of him. Philip sent his orders for the troops with frightened criers who dashed off to the scene of the fight, and prepared to make a hasty retreat if necessary. With his finger, he cleared away some foliage to get a better view.

His blue eyes watched as the French overcame the Saracens, who ventured outside the city walls. Now the French turned their focus once again to the breech in the barricade. He licked his lips. "Flanders!" He shouted to the count. "Tell the criers to spread the word that I will pay three gold pieces for every stone brought to me from the walls of the city."

"With my lord's permission, I would like to bring you some of those stones myself," The count grinned.

"And so you shall, my friend!" Philip's face lit up with anticipation.

The Count of Flanders climbed out of the cercleia and mounted his horse, which seemed as anxious to fight as its master. He bolted off toward the battle, his steed leaping over obstacles with ease. Philip watched him go, and pressed himself against his screen of leaves. The count soon disappeared in the melee, and Philip returned his focus on the spot where his men now fought hand-to-hand, trying to break inside the city.

A myriad of thoughts raced through Philip's mind. Elated by the scene before him, he felt certain the French would triumph. Richard would be out shone, and he, Philip would be the hero of Acre. Perhaps in his humiliation Richard would slink home, and Philip would be able to go forth conquering the rest of the Holy Land. The pope would personally come to him  to bestow the title of *Savior of Jerusalem and the Holy Land*. Acre was only the beginning; no, Anne had been the beginning. When Anne left Richard, that was the moment Philip's fortunes began to turn. He knew it. Maybe Anne would become so disenchanted with Richard that there could now be a union between the two of them. Yes, if he could take Acre, he could take Jerusalem; and if he could take Jerusalem, he could have anything he wanted, even Normandy, Aquitaine, Pointu—and Anne.

Screams pierced the roar of battle interrupting Philip's musing. He looked to the city walls in horror. Greek Fire rained down upon his infantry, and he could no longer see his cavalry. Missiles and stone from ballistas accompanied the deadly fire. A cry of, "Retreat" sounded, and what remained of the infantry threw off their pikes, shields and axes and made a run for the sea.

Philip screeched orders for his men to turn around, but stopped as he looked again toward the wall. The siege engines and towers melted in Greek Fire. They burst info flame as though they were dry blades of grass. "God save them!"

Philip's dreams of victory crumbled into ashes like his men

and implements of war before him. As his army rushed back toward him seeking safety, Philip made a fast exit from his cercleia and stood behind it for a confused moment. He became aware that Norbert stood next to him. Philip looked at him and saw fear in Norbert's eyes. "Your highness," he puffed. "the Count of Flanders is among the fallen." Norbert led Philip's horse to him.

Philip could feel his body shaking and blood rushing to his head. His ears burnt and his chest felt constricted. Reaching out for Norbert, he gasped for air. "My lord!" Norbert caught his arm.

Philip steadied himself, but then began to walk around in circles as if trying to decide what to do next. When he had completed his third rotation, he stopped in front of his horse and tried without success to mount it. Norbert steadied him once again. "The king is ill! We must get him out of here!" he cried.

Within seconds his men led Philip away from the battle.

Richard observed what he could of the battle from his window. The physical rigor of merely standing proved too much, and forced him back into bed. He sent men to be his eyes, and they returned every minute with reports. Baldwin brought the news that Philip had been led from the battle.

Even though confined to his bed, Richard had no intention of waiting quietly between reports. His chamber became a busy hub of activity with men constantly coming and going. From his sick bed, Richard hoarsely barked orders. Luckily, the English reinforcements and supplies arrived early and Richard commanded that his own siege engines, towers, and all manner of war instruments be made ready. He knew that his turn would be coming, and he was determined not to repeat Philip's mistakes.

Chapter Forty-six

The next morning found Philip brooding in his tent

humiliated and shocked. To make matters worse, he lost one of his most able knights, the Count of Flanders. He stared deep into a goblet of wine when Norbert entered. "Your highness, Conrad of Montferrat is here to see you."

"I do not wish to see anybody right now." Philip grimaced as he sipped some wine.

Norbert spoke with conviction. "It would be well worth my lord's trouble to hear him out. It would seem he has had some communication from the city." Sniffing a little Norbert added, "He came to you first, not to King Richard."

Philip rolled his eyes. "Very well. Let him in."

Within half an hour, Philip sped toward Mategriffon with Conrad and Norbert. When they arrived, Baldwin was the first to greet the party. "Your highness." He gave Philip a low bow.

"Sir Baldwin, I must see Richard at once. There is a new development, and we must act." Philip beamed.

"I will tell him you are here." Baldwin sped off leaving Philip and the others to wait in the now empty great hall.

Philip glanced around remembering last Christmas and how they celebrated the season in that room. A noise sounded from the opposite end of the hall, and Joanna entered along with Berengaria. Philip gave the women a broad smile. "Your highness, what brings you to Mategriffon?" Berengaria extended her hand to him.

Taking her hand, he kissed it. "I have business with your husband."

"I expect he shall be with you mmentarily." Berengaria cocked her head to one side.

"It is pleasant to see you ladies." Philip looked at Joanna.

Joanna stuck her nose in the air and looked away from him. Her maneuver was not lost on Berengaria. "Your highness, I beg your forgiveness, but we were just going out to take a short ride."

"Do not let me detain you." Philip forged a smile.

The ladies gave him a short curtsy and left the room. Philip blamed Joanna's cold shoulder on the previous day's debacle. He thought to himself that she would see him in a different light by afternoon.

Baldwin reentered the room. "Your highness, my lords," he gave them a little bow again. "I apologize for the delay. The king is ready to see you now. If you would be so kind as to follow me." He indicated the direction.

With the assistance of his page, Richard slowly made his way to his outer chamber to prepare to meet Philip. He felt better than only two days before, but he still grimaced as he walked. *What on earth could make the King of France come to me the day after his humiliation, I wonder. Has he come to grovel for assistance?* Regardless of the answer, he would not let Philip know in the least how sick he still was, let alone see him in bed. He sat in his large chair behind his worktable. Without thinking he reached up and rubbed his bald head. He had it shaved the day before to hide the effects of his illness. His door opened again and Richard rose to his feet.

Philip swept into the room looking euphoric. "Richard, I bring good news." He turned and indicated Conrad. "You remember Conrad, I presume."

Richard nodded. "Have a seat, Philip." He pointed to a chair on the opposite side of the table.

"Oh, this is too good to sit, Richard. The defenders of the city are asking to surrender!" Philip's brilliant blue eyes sparkled. "We must both approve it, as well as the Duke of Austria. I have not yet informed him."

Richard sat back in his chair. "Surrender?"

"Yes, Richard, surrender. Do not tell me you do not know the meaning of the word. The representative of emirs inside the city came to Conrad. You see, they wish to use him to negotiate because of his reputation and their previous dealings with him in Tyre." Philip plopped down in the chair Richard offered him.

Richard leaned back and folded his arms, trying his best to make his slowness look like suspicion rather than pain. "And what are their terms?"

Philip leaned forward onto the table. "When my forces breached the wall, the infidel swine realized that it is futile to remain in the city. I believe it is safe to assume they have used their supply of Greek Fire. Saladin cannot, or is not, willing to help them. They only ask to be able to leave in peace. Naturally they want to take their women and children with them. The emirs have sworn that they will not damage the city in any way, but leave peacefully."

"What of their weapons?" Richard scowled at Philip.

Philip turned his head to Conrad, who said, "Nothing was said about weapons, your highness."

Richard pursed his lips and shook his head. "No, it is no good. Absolutely not."

"Richard! Are you daft, man? They are willing to give us the city—*the city of Acre, Richard!*"

"Yes, but at what cost, Philip? Think this through for a moment."

Philip interrupted him. "Think it through! I have thought it through! We came to Acre to end this siege, and now we have the opportunity. Let us take it!" Philip slammed his fist on the table.

"The terms are unacceptable." Richard remained calm.

Philip pointed a shaking finger at Richard. "Listen here, I know what you are about. You do not want to accept this surrender because it was not your troops who breeched the wall. You only want to keep this going so you can snatch the glory for having ended the siege at Acre."

"This is not about you or me, Philip," Richard raised his voice. "This is about strategy. If we allow those men to leave, they will only return to Saladin's army, and we will yet be fighting the

same men again. I am sure that the Duke of Austria would agree
with me."

"If you are such a brilliant strategist, what would you do
then? Slaughter them all?" Philip snapped at him.

"I would learn from the mistakes of others, Philip. The
terms they have proposed are almost the same that Saladin gave
the Christians when they left Jerusalem. Now he finds himself
fighting those same men he let go. We need to ransom those
people inside the walls of that city, especially the emirs. Not only
will that prevent them from returning to fight us again, it will help
raise funds to continue this war all the way to Jerusalem. In
addition, we can use them as leverage to get back some of our
Christian nobles still being held captive along with the True Cross
and other important holy relics." Richard threw up his hands. "And
then there is the whole issue of weapons. You cannot allow them
to leave with their weapons! If you do that, the place will turn into
a Christian slaughter pen within a fortnight because these same
men will lead Saladin back to reclaim Acre, and we will not have
time to plug all the holes and secret tunnels they leave behind."

Philip turned to Conrad looking at him for support. Conrad
shook his head. "It is possible what he says is true. I think that they
would need to have more pressure applied to them to convince
them to agree to those sort of terms." He looked down at the floor
as he spoke.

Richard closed his eyes, and with surprising sincerity
pleaded with Philip. "Philip, I implore you, whatever your feelings
are toward me, whatever our history is, listen to reason. Be patient,
and hold out a little longer."

Philip did not respond for a moment. He stood up and faced
away from Richard. At length a quiet "fine," issued from his lips.

Those in the room seemed to give a collective sigh. With a
twist expression on his face, Philip turned around to face Richard
again. "By the by, how is Lady Anne? I am sure you have heard
from her."

Richard sprung to his feet pushing the heavy table aside. "Leave us!" His command echoed throughout the room.

Richard's men flashed their swords, as did Conrad and Norbert. "Put your weapons away. The lion is only roaring to get attention. When all is said and done, he is nothing more than a large house cat." Philip smirked.

"I said leave us!" Richard had his head down, as if he were a bull about to charge, the grey of his eyes were stark against the red of his face, and he strained to keep in control.

The reluctant men emptied the room, leaving Philip and Richard alone. Philip faked a look of concern. "Do you mean to tell me that you do not know where she is?"

"Philip!" Richard growled.

"You disgust me!" Philip laughed. "I know where she is. From the moment she left Messina, I sent out men to track her, keep her safe, and I know exactly where she is." Philip did not pause but plunged on with his taunting. "You know for someone who professes to care about her so much I find it rather surprising that you have not done anything yourself to see that she is alright. You have not even troubled yourself enough to find out if her husband is still here. And yes, by the way, he is still in Acre, but I doubt will be for long. I have no doubt he will head straight for her."

Richard remained in place, and spoke through gritted teeth. "Philip, I am warning you…"

Philip bellowed at him, "Warn me all you like; she is gone!" Philip lowered his voice again. "You know, with the death of the Count of Flanders, I am left with a very pressing problem back home. You see, he left no heirs, and naturally there will be a scramble for his inheritance. I may need to leave Outremer much sooner than I expected. However, I believe that I shall make a stop along the way to personally see to Anne's welfare. I wonder how she will react when I tell her of how smoothly your marriage is coming along, how you lock yourself up in Mategriffon with your wife. At first it will be hard for her, I am sure. Then when she hears that her husband is looking for her, I will offer her the protection that you cannot—or will not—give her."

Richard slammed his fist into Philip's nose. It knocked Philip sideways, but he did not lose his footing. As sticky blood dripped down his face, he turned back to Richard. Richard prepared to strike again, but stopped himself. Philip wiped the blood from his nose and grinned at Richard. "Have a most pleasant day, Richard." With his head held high, he left the room.

Chapter Forty-seven

Anne rubbed her tired eyes as she sat at a desk covered with papers. All day long, she poured over accounts and books. The sun had long since set and a candle glowed in front of her. Fatigue began to take over, and Anne decided it best to end her labors for the night. Not wishing to blow wax all over her papers, she searched her desk for the candlesnuffer in vain. At length she gave up, licked her fingers and extinguished the flame with a quick pinch. As she stood, she stretched her tired arms above her head.

Going to the door, Anne called for Marguerite, but it was not Marguerite who came. Instead, Etienne knocked on her door. "Oh, Etienne. Here, I actually have some manifests that I would like you to look over for me." She gathered a stack of papers in her arms.

"My lady, a letter has come from Gustave."

"Have you read it then?" Anne tried to hide the unease in her voice.

Etienne took a deep breath before answering with a nod. Anne set the pile of papers down in the same spot. "Well, is it good news or bad news?"

"Oh, the news is good, but I am not sure how to tell you what is going on without saying the name you have *forbidden* us all to say or without speaking of matters you *forbid* us to speak of." Etienne rolled his eyes.

Anne leaned on the desk with her left hand, placing her right on her hip. "Just speak to the business, Etienne. I only need to know what effects Marseilles directly."

"That is just it." Etienne threw up his hands. "It all affects Marseilles. What happens to *him* has a bearing on what happens to us. I do not wish to be disrespectful, my lady, but…"

Etienne could not finish his sentence because Anne stormed from the room. He looked up at the ceiling. "God in heaven, when will she see reason?"

Richard went forward with his plans to attack the city even though he still felt unsettled by the incident with Philip. He decided it would be best to put his effort into the Crusade and move on. Toward evening, Andrew came to report on the progress. "My lord, the miners say that preparations will be complete before nightfall. The infantry, siege towers, cavalry, ballistae, and all others will be ready to begin a full attack before dawn, as you so desire."

Richard rested in bed. The events of the day took a toll on him, and he was not able to sit or stand. "Andrew. That is good news. Now, what of my cercleia?"

"It is ready for you, my lord. Much care has been put into its construction."

"Good, good. Have it taken to the trench outside the city wall just before dawn." Richard licked his lips.

"As you wish." Andrew looked down at the pale man before him. "My lord, you just shivered, and it is obvious to me that my king, my friend is in pain. I know full well that nothing I can say will prevent you from taking part in the battle, however…" Andrew scratched at his beard. "Please promise me you will look to your health. Conquering Acre will do us no good if you are not alive to lead us to Jerusalem."

Richard rolled his eyes at Andrew. "God's legs! You sound as bad as my mother."

Andrew just gave him a smile and shrugged.

"We will begin our assault an hour before dawn. Please do try not to oversleep. I would hate to take time to haul your sorry carcass out of bed." Even though sick, Richard's eye still held a twinkle.

An hour and a half before dawn, Richard's page still helped him dress. The act of dressing made his head swim, and he lay back down on his bed. Andrew and Baldwin entered his room. "My lord, do I have your permission to give the signal, or do you want me to wait until you are in position?" Andrew asked.

Still lightheaded, Richard struggled to his feet. "I am coming, Andrew. I will be there." He spoke with strong resolution despite his hoarse voice.

Baldwin looked down at Richard and shook his head. "Your highness, despite the danger of you having me disemboweled, I must beg you not to go. Unlike Andrew here, my motives are a bit more selfish." Baldwin grinned. "You see, should you go and something were to happen, for instance, your fever become worse, then I would have the task of delivering the news to Lady Anne. Quite frankly, I would rather be drawn and quartered than face her wrath after all the times I have promised to protect you. Clearly, it is my own neck I am protecting here, so do us," he pointed to Andrew and himself, "a favor and stay in bed."

At the mention of Anne's name, Andrew sucked in his breath. Richard looked up at both of them tipping his head to the side. "I give you my solemn word as an anointed King of England, that I will stay in bed."

"My lord?" Baldwin's eyes widened.

"Good heavens man! Are you deaf as well as thick?" Richard beamed at him. "I said I will be in bed, and I will be in bed."

"Then today will be a truly momentous day, your highness." Andrew raised his eyebrows.

"Well, it will not be momentous, as you say, if nothing happens, so do not just stand there like jesters with your mouths hanging open. Give the orders to get the men moving."

"Yes, your highness," they chorused.

The attack on the city was inevitable, and everyone within its walls knew it; only which king would command it? Would it be the French King whose progress they stopped, or would it be the much more feared English King? When the sun rose, the city had its answer as the English troops commenced their assault on the main tower.

As the sun erupted from the east, Baldwin relayed Richard's commands to the men, preparing to report back to Richard when a great cheer went up from the men. Knights carried Richard to his cercleia on a red silken litter. His white tunic with its red cross contrasted to the dull brown hues surrounding him; as the sun struck him, it looked like his litter-bearers carried an archangel. The red silk had its intended effect. Richard sought to inspire his men, and for the Saracens to see him—see that nothing could keep him from his prize. Understanding burst in Baldwin. Richard was indeed in bed, but he was still going to be part of the battle.

Andrew galloped up to Baldwin. "Well, do not ever say that the king does not keep his promises to you."

The men placed Richard in his cercleia and Baldwin and Andrew joined him. "Your highness." Baldwin handed Richard his cross bow. "I thought you might find this useful."

Richard took it from Baldwin, a gleam in his eye. "I am in bed."

"That you are! Aye, that you are, my lord." Baldwin laughed out loud.

Andrew laid a quiver next to Richard, who raised his
eyebrows, took a bolt and put it between his teeth. He slipped the
stirrup over his foot, leaned back, stretching the line to the catch,
and put the bolt in place. "Well boys, let us see what kind of a shot
I am lying down, shall we?"

Taking careful aim, Richard let an arrow fly, and it struck a
Saracen on top of the wall. The man staggered, but remained
standing, and pulled the bolt from his arm. Richard clicked his
tongue. "We can do better than that." He reloaded and shot again,
this time wounding another man in the side. "How are the miners
doing with the tunneling under the tower?"

"After all the weeks of work, they are through. They lit the
fires early this morning," Andrew answered.

Richard loaded a third bolt and shot it. "Good. I expect the
fire will quickly catch the timbers. Combine that with the constant
barrage of missiles, and I will give you each a castle if that tower is
not crumbling by nightfall."

"A castle, your highness?" Baldwin snickered. "Well then,
I should hope that you will not be too surprised to see me out there
building fortifications to keep that tower standing."

"Do not be too hasty Baldwin; he did not *specify* the
castle," Andrew chided.

Baldwin threw back his head as he laughed. "True, 'tis true.
I doubt King Philip would be as amused as I am when I march up
to his Parisian palace and tell him to hand it over on orders of King
Richard. Something tells me I would be leaving empty handed, if I
were allowed to leave at all."

Outside Richard's cercleia, the battle raged on. Richard
continued to direct the operations from his litter, and when
opportunity would allow, he let off shots at the enemy. Toward
evening, a loud rumble filled the air and the ground shook. The
great tower collapsed in upon itself. For a few minutes Richard
could see nothing but the dust surrounding it. As it settled, he
could see his men celebrating. The Saracens took refuge behind the

rubble and continued to shoot arrows at Richard's men.

"Spread the word that I will pay *four* pieces of gold to anyone who brings me stones from the wall next to the main tower, regardless if they are English, French, or German," Richard commanded.

Scores of men decided to take Richard at his word and braved the fire of arrows to relieve the city wall of stones. Many never made it back to claim their prize; some returned but were wounded, yet many carted the stones away from the wall near the tower. After darkness fell, Richard retired to Mategriffon to rest and gather strength for the next day.

The next morning, just as Richard prepared to set out on his litter again, Andrew burst into the room with the news. "Forgive me, your highness, but Conrad is here. The city is ready to surrender."

"Show him in then." Richard took a seat in his large chair.

Conrad entered the room and gave Richard a low bow. "Your highness, the city is asking for a surrender. The emirs are willing to submit to harsher demands than they offered previously. Saladin's trusted commander, Karakush himself is suing for the surrender."

"Have a seat, Sir Conrad." Richard signaled to his page to pull up another chair.

"Thank you, your highness." Conrad sat. "I feel it would be best to convene a meeting of the French King, the Duke of Austria, and yourself."

Richard just shook his head. "I am afraid you and your horse will be doing a bit of traveling today. It is best that Philip and I not be in the same room for the time being."

"Yes, my lord." Conrad looked down at his hands.

"Well," Richard continued, "you are familiar with the terms. Go and talk it over with Philip and the duke, then return, bring me word."

"As you wish." Conrad got up from his chair, gave the king

another bow, and left the room.

Saladin, or Al-Malik al-Nasir Saleh ed-Din Yusuf, as he was known in the Arab world, was a tall, thin man. His black hair and beard were peppered with grey, and he carried himself with an air of wisdom, both from study and experience. He came from a family of Kurdish soldiers, and began a successful military career at an early age. He united most of the Arab world, his great advantage over the Christians.

Sitting in front of his pavilion, Saladin stared down at the document before him. He had agreed to allow the men at Acre to surrender, but he would never have agreed to a settlement such as this. He wondered how bad the conditions must be in the city for his loyal commander to have agreed to such terms. Karakush was a strong man, and it would have taken a great amount of pressure from the Christians as well as the emirs to force him into this. Two thousand Christian nobles and five hundred lesser captives were to be returned, with two hundred thousand Saracen talents paid to the two kings, as well as restoration of the True Cross to the Christians, and all by the end of the month. Two thousand emirs and their families remained in Acre as hostages until payment was received.

Fury welled up inside Saladin as he picked up his quill and began to put it to parchment scratching out orders. He glanced up at the young runner, waiting there to take them from him when he finished, then returned back to his letter. Al-Adil, Saladin's brother, joined him. The two looked very much alike, only al-Adil was younger. He placed his hand on his brother shoulder causing Saladin to look up from his writing. Out in the distance, they could see the walls of Acre, and al-Adil pointed toward them. Saladin heaved a sigh. He could see the colourful banners of the Christians waving from the walls. Too late; the city was lost.

In anger, Saladin crumpled the parchment in his hands, and

in an unusually deep voice, al-Adil asked, "What will we do now?"

"We must honor the agreement." Saladin spoke in soft tones. "I am a man of my word, even if someone else speaks for me."

"It will be impossible to find all those Christian nobles and have the money together before the month is out. The Christians are spread nearly the length and breadth the kingdom, and the traveling time alone…"

"The English King is an intelligent warrior, al-Adil. He will give us the time we need," Saladin interrupted him.

"How can you be so sure?"

Saladin smiled to himself. "He did not accept the first terms offered to him for surrender. A lesser warrior would have accepted them, just to have the city. The English King sees beyond just the one battle; he is fighting to win the war."

Al-Adil nodded and both men returned back inside the pavilion. Had they been able to see the walls of the city more closely, they would have had an inkling of the internal struggle the Christians experienced.

When they entered the city, there was a scramble amongst the Christians. As the gates of the city flew open, men rode pell-mell in every direction. Once the Saracens abandoned it and the prisoners turned over to the Christians, the leaders of the Christian army each sought to gain the most they could from the city. The Templars dashed off to secure what had been the royal palace for Richard and his court. They laid claim to it just before the Hospitallers arrived to claim it for Philip. Philip took the second best lodgings in the city, quarters that once belonged to the Templars.

Richard recovered much in the last few days and could ride as well as walk. When he arrived at the gates to the palace, however, the scene shocked him. Had he not known that the men around him fought shoulder-to-shoulder just days before, he would have thought that the battle was continuing.

Sliding from his horse, Richard stomped to a couple of nearby men-at-arms wrestling brutally, for some unknown reason. Kicking one of them in the back, Richard growled, "The two of you quit acting like horses' asses. Is there not fortune enough for all?"

Before the two could rise, a rider came hard in, his horse billowing dust. As it stopped, its rider fell to the ground in a heap. "Andrew!" Baldwin cried out as he leapt from his own horse.

Richard forgot the two fraternal combatants and rushed to Andrew. As Baldwin removed Andrew's helmet, Andrew groaned, his face flushed and covered in sweat. Richard removed his gloves and felt Andrew's forehead with the back of his left hand. "Good Lord, he is on fire! Someone fetch my surgeon!"

Richard's page hurried off, and Richard turned back to a barely conscious Andrew. He and Baldwin worked to loosen Andrew's armor. Another group of Richard's knights came running up to him. The largest of the knights bowed. "Your highness, there is a situation."

"God's legs, I know there is a situation!" Richard snapped at him. "We are surrounded in chaos, man." Taking a second look at the man, Richard recognised him from London, but could not remember his name.

The knight continued. "Yes, sire, but I beg you to take a look at the wall there," he pointed forward, "Leopold of Austria has run up his standard next to yours and the French King's. He is a duke, not a royal. He has no right to do this."

Richard looked in the direction the knight pointed. Leopold's flag flapped back and forth in the breeze next to his own. Richard understood that the duke fought hard to take the city and since he was the German leader, felt he had a right. Still, the knight was correct; the duke was not an equal. Baldwin nudged the king. "Richard, look," he whispered, pointing behind him.

Richard turned around and saw standards rising all over the city. Men posted them to show they had taken possession of certain areas. He was about to turn back to Andrew when he saw it in the distance, the unmistakable flag of Marseilles with its blue cross on the white field. "Castile," Baldwin muttered.

Andrew groaned again and Richard turned his attention back to him. Richard yelled out, "Where is that damned surgeon?"

"My lord, what is to be done about the banner?" The knight hounded him.

"It is Castile, I know it," Baldwin murmured.

Andrew clutched at Richard's surcoats. "My lord," he croaked.

"God's legs! Take care of it!" Richard bellowed. "Baldwin, let us get him inside."

Chapter Forty-eight

Upon examining Andrew, Richard's surgeon, Marchedeus, gave the king a grim prognosis. Despite protests from his advisors, as well as Joanna and Berengaria, the loudest of all, Richard spent what time he could at Andrew's bedside.

Two days after the Christians entered the city, a messenger came bearing another letter from Philip. In the letter, Philip demanded half of all the spoils of Cyprus. Richard sent him a one-word reply, "No." There was no reason to give half of Cyprus' take to Philip since Philip was not there.

Early the next morning Norbert and two other French representatives sought an audience with Richard. They tearfully knelt before him to plead their case.

"Your highness, we come before you in supplication on behalf of our king," Norbert began.

"Let me stop you right there, Norbert. I know what Philip wants. I have heard the rumors floating through the city, and now they are confirmed. Philip wishes to be released from his Crusader's vow and return home. He wants my support."

"Your highness, please be aware that my king must resolve the inheritance question left by the Count of Flanders' death. He received word that his own son is ill. Also, my king's health is still very poor. He is afraid for his very life," Norbert continued recounting justifications.

Richard looked down at the man with scorn. "He is afraid for his very life? I have suffered from the same disease that he has, yet you do not find me attempting to escape the sacred oaths I have made because of it. It is a *fine* excuse for abandoning his fellow Christians."

"With all due respect, your highness, my king is willing to leave any of his army who wish to stay under your command. He will also leave money enough to pay them."

"And how am I to know that he is not heading back to France just to attack Aquitaine and Normandy while I toil here in the Holy Land?" Richard scowled.

"He will sign a treaty with all the terms I have mentioned and will also put to writing that he shall not attack your holdings. He would not do so until you have been home from crusade for seven months. He sends us to you as a courtesy to tell you of these things and ask that you assume the command of his men."

Richard remained quiet for a few moments, partly to let the men squirm a little. When he felt that enough time passed, he said, "Alright, if your lord can live with himself and the realization that he is not willing to give all for the Christian cause, then, by all means let him go. I am not his overlord. He does not need my permission, but if he will agree to set forth these terms in writing, I will give my support."

"Thank you, your highness." Norbert did not smile. "The Kingdom of France thanks you. It is in need of its king."

Richard dismissed the men with a wave of his hand. When they left, he exited the room in the opposite direction and returned to Andrew's room. There he found Andrew sleeping and Baldwin sitting in a chair close by. As Richard entered, Baldwin stood to join him. Richard stepped to a table and poured himself a goblet of wine. "Well, is Philip going home with his tail between his legs?" Baldwin whispered.

"More or less. He claims that France needs him, and his health is in dire peril." Richard took a mouthful. "I agreed to support him on certain conditions. I believe that Philip will leave before the week is out, and Conrad will accompany him as far as Tyre."

"With Leopold of Austria leaving last week, and now Philip going, it seems that many are abandoning this war." Baldwin still kept his voice low.

"I cannot blame Leopold for leaving; he was humiliated when my men tore down his banner and threw it in the mud. I hear he vowed vengeance on me for the whole affair." Richard turned around and looked at the figure in the bed. "How is Andrew?"

"About the same, I am afraid." Baldwin creased his brow.

"I see. For being Eden, this place is no paradise, is it? Well, go and get some rest; I could not bear it if both of you were to…" Richard could not finish his sentence, and instead gave a little cough.

"Yes, my lord." Baldwin obeyed him and left the room. As he did, he took a look back and to see Richard take his place in the chair beside Andrew's bed, and drop his head in his hands.

Although the palace at Acre was more lavish than Mategriffon, it was not as comfortable for the English King. The architecture reflected a mix of Arabic, Romanesque, and the more recent Gothic styles. The newer great hall sprouted with the vaulted ribbed arches so popular back home. The golden stones contrasted to the grayish rock familiar to Richard. The brown, sometimes almost red walls were decorated with colourful, intricate mosaic work. While the Saracans possessed the city, they changed many of the works to reflect Islamic themes. The Christians would change them back.

Richard tried his best to sleep, but tossed and turned. He knew it would not be long until morning. Shifting his pillows again, he heard a quiet knock on his door. His page jumped to his feet and answered it. Without waiting for permission to enter, Baldwin came bounding into the room. "Forgive the intrusion, sire."

"What is it? Is it Andrew?" Richard jumped out of bed and dressed.

Baldwin shook his head. "No, your highness. It happened after I left his room. A young knight came to me because he captured a man, and he wished to claim the reward you placed on his head. I went to see if he had the right man, and he did. Richard, he has captured Taillebourg."

"What?" Richard froze. "Is he alive? What of Castile?"

Baldwin led Richard out the door. "Castile is alive, and we have Taillebourg downstairs, but no, they did not find Castile. Taillebourg knows where he is; I am sure."

Richard and Baldwin bounded down the narrow circular steps and into the throne room. Once they entered, Richard commanded that Taillebourg be shown in.

The door at the opposite end opened, and two young knights dragged in a man who looked much thinner and older than the last time Richard saw him. "Taillebourg!" Richard barked.

The man lifted his head and glared at the king. At once Richard recognised Taillebourg, a changed Taillebourg, but the same man with the same old sour expression. "Ah, King Richard." Taillebourg sneered at him through a swollen eye and bruised lip.

"I must say, I am surprised to find you still here and alive." Richard walked around the prisoner, studying him.

"I am still here."

Richard stood in front of him. "Tell me, where is Raymond

of Castile?"

Taillebourg gave a snort. "Raymond of Castile?"

Baldwin hit him hard in the stomach and Taillebourg lurched forward. He looked up at Richard again. "You want to know where Castile is? The coward fled the moment he heard there was a price on his head."

"When, and where? When did he leave, and where is he going?" Richard snarled.

"Disguised as a wounded pilgrim, he left the same day as Leopold of Austria. To where I know not."

Richard gave Taillebourg another long look. "I will have this information confirmed." He turned to the two young knights. "Put him in chains and lock him away."

"I have given you the information you wanted, and you are going to lock me away?" Taillebourg narrowed his hate filled eyes.

"Why, yes. You have a debt to pay."

"Did you enjoy my castle, or did you give it to your wh…"

Richard did not let him finish. He grabbed Taillebourg by the shirt and shook him. Throwing the man sprawling to the ground, Richard put his foot on his neck. "House him with the Arab prisoners, and I do not mean the emirs. Put him with the unfortunate beggars and thieves."

The two young knights grabbed their prisoner by the arms, as Richard left them all.

As the end of the month came and went, Andrew hung on slipping in and out of lucid moments. Richard had not been able to be in the room when Andrew was coherent, and he regretted it. Late one afternoon, Andrew regained his senses, and Baldwin sent for Richard. Richard came as fast as he could. When he entered the room, he sent everyone away, so he could speak to his dear friend in private. The drawn drapes made it dark. Smoke from incense filled the room, but even the spicy smell could not mask the scent of death that hung in the air. Richard pulled a chair up next to the bed. Andrew turned to face him; his once full face now emaciated and grey. "Why did you not tell me you were ill?" Richard whispered.

Andrew's reply came in soft tones. "You had important things to attend to, my lord."

"That is rot, and you know it." Richard shook his head. "Andrew…"

Andrew raised his hand to stop him. "My lord, we all must die."

"You are not in the least bit nervous?"

"Well… yes. No one can be certain of what will happen, but I have come to terms with it."

"We have had a grand adventure, you and I."

"And Baldwin, let us not forget Baldwin. Promise me that you will always be patient with him. He would do anything for you." Andrew tried to smile.

"Yes, of course, but is there anything else I can do for you, any other wish?" Richard looked at him in earnest.

"I do have one regret, and it has been preying on my mind. I wish that I could see Marguerite one last time. There is much I would like to say to her. To be honest with you, we did not spend enough time talking." Andrew coughed brutally. When he recovered, he continued. "I have been thinking about it. Anne told me once she believed that when we die, we go to a place where we all know each other and can be together again. At the time I thought it a silly notion she clung to in her grief over her father. But now, I rather like the idea."

"I like the sound of it, too." Richard smiled.

"Do not let her go, Richard. Do not be like me, laying on your deathbed, thinking of all the things that you wish you had said and done. I cannot remember ever telling her that I love her." Andrew's eyes filled with tears.

Richard had never seen Andrew cry, and it made him even

more uncomfortable. "I am sure you did."

"You will tell her for me? She was more than just a good… good…" Andrew choked on the words.

"I will see to it that she is taken care of, my dear Andrew." Richard tried to reassure him. Richard no longer wanted to be alone with Andrew; it seemed too much for him, and he longed for Baldwin's humor. "Would you like me to send for Baldwin?"

Andrew nodded. Richard sent for him, and a subdued Baldwin entered the room. He joined Richard at the bedside. "Has he told you all his deep, dark secrets?" Baldwin attempted a joke.

"All I could get out of him was that you are an ass." Richard smiled, and Andrew weakly laughed.

"Well, all I have to say is it is too bad that I am already married, because your wife will soon be eligible." Baldwin continued, but a tear fell from his eye.

"Do not be concerned about my wife; Richard will have her married off to some other poor unsuspecting fool." Andrew's voice grew softer.

"Andrew, you cannot leave me here with Richard. That is just not fair. I cannot possibly keep him out of trouble all on my own. The two of us without your calming influence? Why, we are bound to end up in the most disastrous of circumstances."

"Oh, but think of the fun you will have getting there." Andrew grimaced. "You will manage."

Richard patted Andrew's shoulder. "Perhaps we should let you rest now, hum?"

"Promise me that you will stay here through the night, whatever it may bring," Andrew requested.

"Yes, my friend. We will be right here," Richard reassured him.

This seemed to give Andrew some relief, and he closed his eyes. Two hours later Andrew de Chauny was dead.

Chapter Forty-nine

Richard looked out the window of his outer chamber not paying attention to what was going on outside the window, instead lost in thought. Andrew was buried quickly, like all others to keep disease under control. Many of the dead were unceremoniously buried in large pits, some a hundred, some two hundred, some even five hundred at a time. At least Richard secured a private grave in the chapel for him. There was no real time for mourning, and Richard felt that somehow Andrew had been cheated. Richard wrote to Andrew's widow requesting that she observe tradition and display his hatchment to honor his valiant friend's memory.

"Are you not hungry?" Guy de Lusignan dined with him.

Aware of food in front of him, Richard poked at it with his knife but did not eat. Guy continued to drone on, and Richard became lost in his own thoughts again.

Once the funeral rites were over, Baldwin seemed to disappear. Richard did not begrudge him for it, since he knew that Baldwin only grieved. He understood; he too wanted to be left alone. Neither of the men dined in public. As king, it was Richard's duty to eat in front of others, and he did but closeted himself with either Blondel or Baldwin. Now Richard was compelled to dine with Guy.

"Would you not agree, Richard?" Guy asked him.

Richard just shrugged. He didn't want to answer either way because he did not know to what he agreed. "I shall have to think on it."

"Lady Anne is in Marseilles, so I am told." Guy stuffed another bite of bread into his mouth.

Richard snapped his attention back on Guy. "I beg your pardon?"

Guy waited until he had finished chewing and swallowed. "Lady Anne, Marseilles…" He now took a drink and made

Richard wait again. "Her man Gustave let it slip to me that she is in Marseilles. I began a correspondence with her. Now that we have taken Acre, Jerusalem will not be long in coming, and I can regain my throne. If she is anything like her mother, I know she would enjoy the palace in Jerusalem. Oh, by the by, the date has come and gone for Saladin to deliver on the promises made in the treaty. What do you think he is up to?"

"Saladin says he needs more time." No longer interested, Richard turned back to his plate, then looked down the table noticing a large variety of fruit, none of which looked appetizing.

"Well, that is what he says, but believe me, I have dealt with this man before, and he is the worst of the worst. He slaughtered one of my own barons right in front of me. I was lucky to escape with my life. He is like all other Saracens. They will tell you anything, say anything, to your face, but once you turn around, they stab you in the back at the first opportunity." Guy used his knife, jabbing it in the air to illustrate his point.

"I heard that your Reginald de Chatillon took a cup of water intended for a king." Richard raised his own cup and sipped.

"A heavy price to pay for a simple gaffe, if you ask me."

"If he reached for my cup, I'd have cut his bloody head off myself," Richard muttered under his breath.

"Trust me, Saladin has no intention of carrying through on his part of the treaty. These people don't think like we do. In fact, it could be argued that because he did not sign the document himself, he does not have to adhere to it. They have no sense of honor. They are animals, not capable of thinking of a high order with higher principles like you and me." Guy put the knife down and folded his hands together in front of his face. "Remember what he did to the Templars and the Hospitallers at Hattin. He killed them all! Slaughtered them like pigs!" He slammed his hand down on the table. Composing himself, Guy started again. "The man has no conscience. What is worse, he is making you look weak. The more time you give to him, the more the men will lose faith in you.

Do not forget that the Templars have stood beside you in everything. Besides, you did not come all this way to just take over one city. You came here to regain Outremer—*the Land of Christ*—for Christendom. Now you are saddled with almost three thousand hostages that you must feed and shelter every day." Guy observed Richard over the tips of his fingers. He waved one hand and pushed himself back from the table.

Desperate to have the English King's full attention, he changed the conversation. "Anyway, Lady Anne's man Gustave is planning on returning to Marseilles soon, and he has agreed to open marriage negotiations with her. I already sent men to take up the issue with the pope." Richard dropped his knife, and made a loud clank against his silver plate. He glowered at Guy. "Oh, come now. I know she was your mistress, but she left. It is over. Yes, she was lovely, but you can always find another woman. I can show you a dozen women just as pretty right here in Acre."

Richard said nothing, but picked his knife up again and grasped it so tightly that his knuckles whitened. Guy took in a sharp breath. "With your permission, your highness, I must take my leave, as I have dominated more than my share of your afternoon."

Richard gave him a slight nod, and Guy bowed himself out of the room. When he was gone, Baldwin entered and dropped down in the chair that Guy occupied, pushing away Guy's plate with disgust. "And *that* wants to be King of Jerusalem."

"He *was* King of Jerusalem." Richard pushed away his own plate. "He lost his kingdom, lost the Battle of Hattin, and was taken prisoner. That is what he will be remembered for. The more I consider it, the more I am assured that the barons could never see him as their king again. They will never respect him, they will never serve him, and they will never fight for him. They need someone who has demonstrated some strength against the Saracens, and Conrad has done that. He managed to keep Tyre when everything else around him fell to the enemy."

"Good hell, it is hot." Baldwin tugged at his collar.

"So, how much of the conversation did you hear?"

"The majority," Baldwin smirked. "The doors in this place are not as thick as they should be."

Finished with his meal, Richard rinsed his hands in a bowl of water and wiped them on a towel. "Guy does have a point about the prisoners though. I think Saladin is intentionally taking his time to let the prisoners drain our resources. While it is true that he has sent the first cash payment that he owed and five hundred prisoners, he failed to send not even one of those hundred specifically named Christian nobles. He has broken his oath. Also, he knows that there is, shall we say, a massive lack of harmony amongst the barons and the different armies here, and if he bides his time our shaky alliances will crumble to bits." Richard sighed. "We must solidify our force, and we need to act soon. We cannot stay here in Acre; we must continue on to Jerusalem. The sooner we take it, the sooner we can all go home."

"Humph. You cannot exactly drag thousands of prisoners with you on campaign now can you?"

Richard shook his head. Looking at Baldwin, he noticed that his blue eyes had lost some of their luster. It made Richard uneasy. "I am so tired." Richard expressed aloud.

"With all that has transpired, the heat, and your illness, it is no wonder."

"Do you think anyone would begrudge me a nap?" Richard asked him.

Baldwin shook his head. "I think it would be wise for you to get some rest. I doubt you have been sleeping very well."

Richard rose from his seat. "I think I shall retire then." He did not wait for Baldwin to reply but turned and entered his bedchamber.

The bed looked so inviting, and he lay down on top of it, letting the softness of the pillows and coverlets envelop him. With his eyes closed, he could feel the soothing breeze waft over him, and before long Richard drifted off to sleep.

Restful sleep eluded Richard. He experienced disorienting dreams. In them he saw Guy entering Jerusalem in triumph, then standing atop a balcony waving to his subjects below. Anne held Guy's right arm, and she looked happy and content. Will stood behind them. Guy put his arm around Anne's waist and pulled her close. He looked down at Richard and the crowd below with a twisted grin. "If only you had listened to me, you would have taken Jerusalem and been the hero, but instead I had to take action and," Guy looked hungrily at Anne, "do what you could not."

Anne gave Guy a tantalizing look, and led him inside. "Come, son." Guy called out to Will, who turned and obeyed. Richard shouted after them, but his voice faded in the crowd.

Then the crowd disappeared, and there stood Andrew in his burial shroud, his face uncovered and grotesque. Andrew opened his mouth and moths flew out of it. "My death was for naught. I died for nothing. I died in vain," The figure cried out to Richard in a hollow voice.

Richard sat up in bed dripping in sweat. "No! No, no, no, no!" He yelled out into the room.

It was dark now and the torches on the wall glowed in an eerie light. The startled page jumped to his feet. "Your highness?"

Richard did not respond. He flew out the door, speeding down the hall barking out orders.

The next morning, the sun shone down on the Saracen prisoners who huddled together in small groups of fifteen to twenty men, women, and children, on the low hill of Ayyadieh outside the city wall, Richard's men-at arms surrounded them with swords, spears and war-axes. Richard stood atop a platform overlooking the prisoners, watching as more were led to the field. Various representatives of the Christians were there with him: templars, hospitallers, priest, and clergy, as well as his own advisors,

Baldwin, and Guy. "Your highness, my Lord, please!" Blondel
pushed his way to where Richard stood. "My lord, I beg you, do
not do this. They are soldiers and innocents."

For a moment Richard's clenched jaw relaxed, but as the last
of the prisoners marched by in a line, he saw Taillebourg among
them, dressed in Muslim clothing. Only the men who followed
Richard's orders knew that he was a Christian. The sight of
Taillebourg made hatred well up in Richard, and he turned to the
frantic Blondel. "Blondel," he said coolly, squinting his eyes in the
bright sunlight. "This is a matter of state."

Blondel got up close enough so that he could whisper, "Your
highness, you cannot do this. There must be some other way. I
implore you!"

Richard's face turned red with rage. "Have I not already been
merciful? It is Saladin who has not kept the treaty! Not a single
one of the Christian knights has been released, and I have already
granted him nearly an extra fortnight! What mercy did Saladin
show at the Horns of Hattin? How many were spared?" He
grabbed Blondel by the shoulder, yanked him around, and pushed
him away. "You do not have to watch if you do not wish to!"

Terrified by the anger and sheer hate in Richard's eyes,
Blondel gave him a slight bow and stormed off. Richard watched
him go for a moment, swallowed hard, then shouted, "Do it!"

The ring of men around the prisoners began to close in. Some
looked eager while others hesitated. In the end their king's
command must be obeyed. As the knights drew their swords, a
general cry of panic went up from the group of prisoners. Women
screamed and dropped to their knees, children clung to their
parents, and men stood bound, helpless to resist the oncoming
slaughter.

From his vantage point Richard noticed the face of a man
about his age. The man seemed to be looking right at Richard, his
small black eyes focusing on the king, oblivious to the slaughter
that surrounded him. Then the man's lips moved and seemed to

repeat something over and over, as if in prayer. The man was run through, but his expression never changed. He fell to the ground with his lips still moving, still staring at the English King.

Richard looked away from the scene before him. The sight of blood never made him sick before, but now he felt weak in both body and spirit. He caught sight of Baldwin, who watched him not looking at the field of death. Baldwin seemed to understand something unspoken and turned to the gaggle of representatives. "The king should not be in this heat. He has not recovered completely from his illness."

"Gentlemen." Richard gave them a nod, and left the platform.

He remained composed all the way back to his bedchamber but once inside, he banished everyone from the room. Alone, he let loose his rage, anger and disappointment. Above all though, he had lost control, lost control of everything. Without even realizing it, he clutched at a bottle of wine. He took a long drink from it, and smashed it against the fireplace. The sound of it shattering made him feel better, so he hurled other objects towards the wall, not even aware of what he threw. When that did not seem enough, he clawed at the drapes, scraping his fingers and knuckles on the wall. He tore at the bedclothes and knocked furniture on its side. He threw a chair so hard, it splintered when it hit the wall, and he lost his balance. Falling to a knee, he looked around at the havoc he caused; this only added to his frustration. Then something red caught the corner of his eye and he turned to see Anne's token on the ground. His heart sank. "Damn." He picked it up, pressing it to his face. His tantrum did not make him feel any better; it only made the situation worse.

The door to his chamber flew open, and Berengaria strode in with Baldwin following. Baldwin's expression fell when he entered the room, and Berengaria looked down at Richard, her blue eyes wide. "My lord?"

The sight of her made him want to hit someone, and he rose

to his feet shouting, "It is a good thing you believe in Immaculate Conception, because that is the only way you shall ever produce an heir, Madame!"

Richard pushed past her and left before she could reply. He exited the palace and marched to the docks. Baldwin followed him, but kept his distance. Once he reached the docks, he turned south and strode onto the beach. As he did so, he realized he still clutched the handkerchief. This brought him to a halt. He pulled his knife, cut the strings of his boots, and walked out into the water, letting it splash up against his knees, hoping the water could wash something away from him. Fixing his eyes on the horizon, he stood motionless. The wash of the waves back and forth against his legs focused and relaxed him. The crashing tide broke the thoughts of the day, and he closed his eyes. When at long last he opened his eyes again, he looked out at the sea and took in deep breaths of the salty air. At length, he turned to go, and as he did, he looked down at his feet, almost stumbling in amazement. Tiny blossoms, like those from a peach tree, floated in the water.

Chapter Fifty

Fog rolled in from the sea and covered the city of Marseilles. It stretched up the narrow streets and wrapped itself around buildings. From the chateau, Anne could barely make out the lights of the harbor. It seemed to her that night came early, and she felt ill at ease. Moving closer to the small fire in her room made her feel better. A soft knock sounded on Anne's door. Guessing it was Etienne, she rolled her eyes and called out for him to enter. When the light from the fire caught his face, Anne could see his brow heavy with worry. "What is it, Etienne?"

"Lady Anne, there are some sailors downstairs who insist on seeing you."

"Sailors? Are they from one of our ships?" Anne did not move to rise out of her chair.

"No, they are not ours, but…" Etienne gave an overstated shrug, "they have a man with them in a stretcher, and they claim that he is the Viscount of Marseilles."

"What…what did you say?" Anne stammered.

"They say they have come from Acre."

Anne rose now. "The Viscount of Marseilles?" She repeated. "Surely they cannot mean Castile?"

"The man has dark curly hair, and I could not see much of his face, but he is very ill."

"What makes you so sure he is ill?" Wide eyed now, Anne's heart pumped faster.

"It is obvious he has a fever. I felt the man's head myself just to make sure that there was no deception."

"Where is Will?" Anne's panic grew.

Etienne reached out to steady his cousin. "He is safe, asleep in bed."

"How can you be sure? Good heavens, what am I do if it is him?"

Anne rushed to a little coffer on the table next to her bed. She popped it open and pulled out a dagger. Etienne spoke with a steady voice. "Anne, he is very ill indeed, and the sailors brought him here just to receive payment for the services they rendered. The way I see it, he is entirely at your mercy."

Anne put one hand on her head still clutching the dagger, and the other hand on her hip. "I cannot go down there and face him. I wish Richar…" she stopped herself, as if she couldn't say the name. "I wish *he* was here. I do not know what to do, Etienne."

"We cannot just leave him down there." Etienne motioned toward the door.

Anne tucked the dagger into her belt. "Alright, we shall go down then."

"You will not be alone. I am armed as well."

Anne gave a slight nod and deep breath, leaving the room to face Castile.

Two guards, with swords drawn, prevented the sailors from entering any further than the kitchen door. Anne could see a heap lying just beyond the feet of her guards. As she approached them, four other men, two more guards, her horse master and the cook, all wielding swords or knives joined her.

The sailors looked up at her with trepidation, and wonder. "Sailor, state your business here," she barked at the taller of the two.

The sailor gave her a bow. "My lady, we humbly beg your pardon for this intrusion, but we have the Viscount of Marseilles here, and he is very sick." His accent revealed the man was from Genoa or Pisa.

Anne looked down at the heap on the stretcher. The man writhed back and forth in pain, his black curly hair matted to his head with sweat, and his face flush with fever. "The Viscount of Marseilles is dead and buried. I am the Viscountess now," Anne snapped at the two sailors.

The form on the floor rolled over at the sound of her voice and opened his dark brown eyes, the fire from the hearth reflecting in them as he looked up at her, imploring her to help him. It was without a doubt Raymond. Despite the physical effects of his illness, she saw the scar on his cheek where she attacked him with the shard of glass all those years ago.

"Beggin' your pardon again, Viscountess, but he claimed that he is the Viscount of Marseilles and that all we had to do was bring him to the chateau, and you would pay us for our services." The sailor removed his cap and wrung it in his hands. As he spoke, he eyeballed the men behind Anne with their weapons at the ready.

Her instinct was to have Raymond run through. Perhaps these sailors would do it for a price, but then again, that seemed too quick. She thought of torture and especially liked the idea of thumbscrews. She didn't own any, but perhaps she could borrow some from the local priests. Regardless, she was not going to allow that man to stay in her house. Anne gripped at the dagger in her belt. "That man in not the Viscount of Marseilles." She drew in breath to say more as she was planning on passing her harsh sentence.

Raymond groaned in agony and stretched his hand out to her. "Anne, please, I beg you. Have mercy on me."

Instinctively she took a step back away from him, but something in his look made her stop herself from condemning him to death. As he reached out to her, he looked so like Will that it tugged at her.

"If these men are not paid, they will take it out of what little is left of my flesh."

Then an idea struck her. She crouched down close to Castile so he would be sure to hear her, no longer afraid of the weak man that lay before her. "You will not spend another minute in my house, Castile."

She addressed the sailors. "Gentlemen, Etienne will give you the name of a physician here in town. Take this man to him. You will be well paid for your services, and I will pay for the doctor. However, before you leave town, I ask that you deliver a message to a man named, Lugo in the Jewish section. Tell him where he can locate Raymond of Castile." Raymond's eyes went wide at the mention of the name Lugo. "You heard me right, Castile, Lugo. He is here in town and just last week came to me yet again, trying to collect on your considerable debt. I seem to remember the last fellow who did not pay that old man wound up not only dead, but it was… oh, what is the word I am looking for… messy perhaps?"

"Please, I beg you, Anne," Raymond tried again.

"Your problems with credit are of no concern of mine!" She found it hard to keep herself from shouting. "Now Etienne, gentlemen, get this piece of wretched filth out of my house."

She rose to her full height and marched back to her room.

Richard resolved to leave Acre and move on toward Jerusalem. For the most part, the Christian army needed convincing. Many did not want to leave the comfortable surroundings of Acre. The walls began to rise again and trade with the west reestablished. A boatload of women, ready to do their part for the cause, arrived. Little tempted the men to leave the city and face the Saracen army once again.

In a display of leadership, Richard pitched his tents outside the city once again and moved into them, leaving Joanna and Berengaria behind in the royal residence. Joanna did not seem to mind, but Berengaria acted as though given a death sentence. Despite her pleas, he was not persuaded, and Berengaria stayed behind in Acre. Eventually, the warrior spirit caught hold and the Christian armies marched out toward their destination.

Saladin split his army to defend the two most probable routes to Jerusalem. Richard took a different route, and marched south along the coast toward Ascalon. From there he could turn inland to Jerusalem. His fleet sailed down the coast in order to supply him and guard him from the rear.

The marching column of Crusaders created an impressive sight. The Templars led, sending scouts ahead of them. The French Crusaders and then Guy followed them with the barons of the kingdom and Richard's knights from Pointu. English and Norman knights came next, and they were hard to miss. They built a massive tower, as high as any minaret in the country. Atop the tower flew a flag proportionate in size to the structure, emblazoned with a cross. Behind them, the Hospitallers brought up the rear watching for stragglers. Richard appointed his nephew, Henry of Champagne, the job of commanding the pack and supply train, while he spent his time riding with either the Templars or his own men.

Richard sent scouts, many of the Templars, to do

reconnaissance. The rest of the army set out on yet another day of marching closer to Ascalon. Richard took a long drink from his flagon. Wiping his face with a wet cloth, he passed the flagon to Baldwin, riding on his right. Baldwin took a quick drink and passed it back to Richard. As he did, he smiled. "Do you think that this will count toward time in purgatory? It is certainly hot enough."

"Going on Crusade absolves one of the sins he has committed," Richard reminded him.

Baldwin grinned. "Perhaps, but I plan on committing more when I return home."

Richard laughed. "Baldwin, if you are interested in decreasing the number of hours you will spend paying for your sins, perhaps you ought to join the boys back in the infantry."

"No thank you, sire." Something in the distance distracted him. "What do you suppose that is all about?"

Richard looked to see a rider pounding towards them surrounded by a cloud of dust. When the rider got closer, Richard could tell it was one of his Norman knights who he sent out as a scout earlier that morning. The rider continued on past the Templars right to Richard who was riding with the English knights. Richard halted, and the man jumped from his horse to bow in front of the king. "Well, what is it?"

The young knight gasped for breath. "Your highness, we found the Saracens, but they were not a small group of cavalry. Our men have been attacked and cannot hold out much longer."

Richard's face flushed red. "How many cavalry are there?"

"Hundreds, but they are fighting so fiercely that it may as well be thousands, my lord."

Richard turned his horse to the right and to the left, as he called out orders to his men. The criers rushed off to pass along the orders, and before long a group of over three thousand knights sped away to rescue their Christian brothers.

In the evening, the Christians made camp. As Richard

walked to his tent, he passed a group of infantry men that had been marching near the rear of the column. They removed Saracen arrows from one another that stuck out of their thick, protective haerbacks, unable to penetrate the barrier. Many of these men marched all day, their backs covered with dozens of arrows. Consumed with their work, the men failed notice Richard as he passed. He took no offense.

Richard did not sleep that night. He remained awake waiting for news of the scouts. In the morning, the beleaguered warriors, at last, able to escape the onslaught of the Saracen cavalry, limped back to the main body of the Christian army. The casualties totaled over a thousand men wounded or killed, a great blow.

Saladin now prepared for an all out pitched battle with Richard. He had the advantage of being able to select the ground, and he chose a plain just north of the coastal city of Arsuf. Here Saladin could use his best weapon, his light cavalry. They already dealt the Christians one blow. Now Saladin felt confident they could repeat it.

Richard understood Saladin's tactic. This gave him pause for concern. For all his military experience, Richard never fought a pitched battle before. Sieges were his talent, not men marching over a field toward one another. Pitched battles were costly in both men and resources, and were to be avoided, but he knew that this one was inevitable.

His strategy began with him taking a defensive position on the plain. Saladin forced him to fight here, but *he* would force Saladin's men to come to him. It was a well-known tactic for the Saracens to fake retreat and lead armies away into a trap. Richard refused to let that happen. He lined up the Templars on the right flank and the Hospitallers on the left with the secular troops in the middle, taking his position with his knights in the middle.

Swooping down upon the Hospitallers, the Saracen cavalry hit with swift, deliberate, and deadly accuracy. As Richard sat a top the same Spanish charger he "rode" into the port of Acre, he could see some of the action on the right flank. He turned to Baldwin about to speak when a volley of arrows from the Saracen archers hit the centre. "Hold steady!" he cried out. "A few darts will not send us scurrying!"

Wave after wave of Saracens attacked the Christians. The Saracen cavalry inflicted the greatest amount of damage. Another surge of arrows rained down upon the middle and Richard put up his shield to protect himself. Baldwin and half a dozen other knights next to him also put up their shields to protect the king. A crier entered the protected huddle of shields. "Your highness!" he yelled. "I come from the Hospitallers; their Marshal de Carron sent me."

The men all sat back up, Richard's guards scanning the sky for the next incoming barrage.

"Well, what is it?" Richard shouted to be heard over the din of battle.

Finding it difficult to address the king in person, the boy swallowed hard as he looked up at Richard. "My lord, de Carron says that the left flank is suffering heavy losses. Their horses are being shot out from right underneath them. He says that if he does not receive help soon, he is afraid they will be lost," the boy squeaked out.

"The Hospitallers will not yield; they will fight to the last man if necessary." Richard spoke his thoughts aloud as he quickly worked out the situation in his mind. "If the Hospitallers are in that thick of a fight that all will be lost..." He turned to the boy. "Tell de Carron help is on the way."

The boy gave a bow then bolted off toward the left flank. Another flock of arrows headed down upon the king's position, so he and the others sought safety behind their shields again. The thunk of metal hitting the wood echoed inside their makeshift shell. The horse of the man farthest left was shot, and the animal screamed as it fell to the ground.

Under the shields, Richard spoke to Baldwin. "Send some of the Poitevins to relieve the Hospitallers and fortify the left."

Baldwin lowered his shield at another break in the firing of arrows. "Yes, my ord." He began to turn his horse around, but stopped. "What the hell?"

Richard turned to see what grabbed Baldwin's attention. To his astonishment, de Carron bounded across the field in a crazed rage toward the enemy, his standard bearer trying hard to keep up. A movement on his right caught Richard's attention. One of his Norman knights followed the Hosptailler's example. "Damnit! Did I or did I not give orders that the signal was to be six trumpets blowing in three different places. Now we will lose the defensive!"

With the two rogue knights rushing forward, the rest of the Christian army was compelled to action and a great wave of men rolled forward at the enemy. Without warning, Richard spurred his horse and galloped into the crowd, overtaking and passing the running infantry, his sword drawn. "Lord in heaven, there he goes." Baldwin took off after him.

The two armies slammed into one another, becoming a tangled mess of men and animals. Richard was right in the middle of the action, slashing away at the enemy with his sword. Dirt, sweat, and blood flew in every direction as the screeching of wounded men and beasts punctured the air.

"He hit me. The man actually hit me right on the nose!" Philip pointed to his nose to illustrate the point. "I have witnesses. He hit me so hard it bled!"

In audience with the pope, Philip tried to convince the Holy Father of Richard's villainy. Philip almost toppled his wine goblet as he rose from the chair at the table to pace back and forth. He barely touched any of the lavish meal the pope provided for a returning warrior of God. "I always knew that Richard had an uneven temperament; he takes after his father in that respect. But now, now he is completely volatile. You never know what he is going to do."

"And you are telling me that this is why you left?" The pope's demeanor looked calm next to Philip's.

Philip nodded. "I am afraid for my life. While it is true that I was ill, that was the least of my worries. I was forced, and am still forced to remain armed at all times. Do you know that he sent no less than four ships after me, when I left Acre?"

"My son, I heard that those ships carried messengers to Richard's territories to inform them that you were coming home and to be ready for an attack. Perhaps he is as leery of you as you are of him."

Pope Celestine III was an old man when elected to office the previous March. So far, he found the bickering of kings and princes a constant irritant. His dark eyes followed Philip as he stormed back and forth in front of the table. Celestine's years of living and dealing with human nature taught him the truth to this conflict probably lay somewhere in the middle ground, with neither man completely innocent. If at all possible, Celestine wanted to remain neutral in the matter.

Philip turned and looked in the pope's large brown eyes. "Richard has men everywhere that are loyal to him beyond all reason. I have intercepted plans for my own assassination. I am sure you can imagine my shock when I read the letter for myself... a man whom I have fought alongside, protected, and aided, a man who I regarded as my friend... That was a blow like no other I have ever felt." Philip let a few tears drop down his cheek.

Celestine studied Philip and when he began to cry, the pope felt sorry for Philip. "I cannot promise anything." The old man shook his head. "I will however, send an envoy to Richard to discuss this matter. In the meantime, I expect you to keep your word and not give him any reason for provocation. He is still on Crusade, and his lands are off limits. You will not invade them, my son." The pope wagged a long finger at Philip.

"I would not dream of it." Philip took his seat at the table again.

Chapter Fifty-one

"The Christians won a major victory at Arsuf, and Richard received credit for it. It was the first battle in open warfare since Hattin that the Christians won. The Saracens were beaten down and scattered. Due to the Saracen record of luring armies into a trap, the Christians did not pursue the retreating Turks. Despite his great victory, Richard could not feel joy; he only felt hollow." Father Breton looked about at the group of knights at his feet.

"With the dead and wounded collected, and the prisoners secured, Richard moved the army further south to what was left of Jaffa and Ascalon. They found both destroyed and abandoned. Richard set men to work restoring the coastal towns and went to work planning his next move."

"Isn't this when Richard refused to listen to the advice of the barons and Templars who lived there and insisted on marching ahead to Jerusalem?" Bogis asked Breton.

"Yes, it is." Breton nodded. "They tried to tell him that the winter would bring torrential rains, but he was so focused on his ultimate goal that he went forward with the campaign anyway. His whole army ended up wallowing in the mud. The wind was so strong that they couldn't even pitch their tents; their bread, and the rest of the food for that matter, all ruined. Finally, Richard saw reason and returned to Ascalon."

A sly smile spread across Breton's face. "Ascalon was so close to Egypt, it made Saladin nervous that Richard was preparing to invade Egypt. With Saladin's troops down to a skeleton, as most of the men returned home for the winter, Saladin could not hope to fend off an attack."

"I have a question then." Bogis wrinkled his brow. "I heard

that Richard and Saladin, when it came time to negotiate, ended up in a tournament with Richard knocking Saladin from his horse."

Breton chuckled in spite of himself. He remembered hearing the rumor about the tournament. "No, I am afraid they never met. Richard did all the face-to-face negotiations with Saladin's brother al-Adil. Do you know, at one point, he even proposed that al-Adil marry Joanna and they rule Jerusalem as Christian and Muslim?" This made Breton laugh out loud. "What's more is that Saladin thought Richard was bluffing, so he agreed. In the end, both the prospective bride and groom refused; well, al-Adil politely declined, but Joanna, I can only imagine her reaction. Richard is lucky he didn't end up with a dagger in his breast compliments of his sister. I shall never know what possessed the man to conceive such a ridiculous notion."

Bogis did not laugh. "I fail to find it such a ridiculous idea. Think about it for a moment. It could have brought about an end to a war through a compromise."

The smile faded from Breton's face. "Bogis, do you realize what you are saying? One or the other would have had to convert to the different religion. It would never have worked. Think of all that the Muslims have done to the Christians, those deeds cannot go unpunished. Consider it one of Richard's practical jokes; he never would have gone through with it. To have gone through with it would have been borderline heretical!" Breton stopped, his face flushed.

"Well, what about Anne? Did the money lender take his revenge on Raymond?" Another knight interrupted the argument.

Breton turned away from Bogis and spoke to the knight. "Well now, have patience. I am getting to that."

Anne walked along in the market place. Winter arrived in Marseilles, and the temperature dropped. Although not as cold as

London in winter, Anne still found she needed a cloak. As she walked, she noticed the stalls and the different guilds of the city represented. She wondered if it really was proper for the Viscountess of Marseilles to be walking in the market place; after all, she had never known her mother to do it. Then again, she knew her father did on occasion to help foster good relations. Even in the chilly weather, the vendors turned out to ply their wares, and it made Anne glad of heart.

A familiar figure sauntered up the narrow street toward her, bundled in a cloak himself. His hawk nose stuck out, and she recognised Captain Vasser. He called out to her, "Lady Anne."

She stopped to wait for him, giving him a nod. "Captain Vasser."

He smiled at her showing his mouth was missing a tooth here and there. "I was just on my way to the chateau to see you."

"I am surprised to see you here. When last I saw you, you were heading back to Cyprus. All the ports are closed for the season, and I thought surely we would not see you in Marseilles again until spring." Her breath showed in the frosty air.

"We only went to Sicily, m'lady, and we had a bit of a rough journey back. We arrived yesterday."

"Well, I am glad to see that you are home safe." She smiled at him, but wondered why he would want to come to the chateau to tell her this.

He seemed to sense her question. "M'lady, I have a letter for you." He reached under his cloak to fish it out. "It was rather odd, really. We met a crew from an English ship, on their way home. They saw our flag and their captain approached me. He said he was to deliver this letter to you in Marseilles, but seeing as we were from Marseilles, would we mind delivering it?" Vasser searched for it.

Anne bristled at the mention of an English ship, but did not wish to appear rude. "That is a rather roundabout way of sending someone a letter, would you not agree Captain Vasser?"

"Ah! Here it is." He produced it. "I am sorry. The captain was most adamant that it be delivered only to you personally, and I am afraid I tucked in here for safe keeping, and it got a little…wrinkled." He held it out to her.

"I thank you I…" She took the letter and slipped it under her own cloak without looking to see who it was from, not wanting to lose her composure in front of Vasser. "I beg your pardon; it sounds as if this letter has come a long way, and I had better see what is so urgent."

"Of course, viscountess. It has been a pleasure to see you again." Vasser gave her a bow.

Anne waved goodbye as she turned to walk back to the chateau. She started up the hill before she took the letter out because it felt as if it were burning a hole in her side. Immediately, she could tell it was not from Richard. Her name was scrawled across the front in Baldwin's sloppy handwriting. She stared down at the letter afraid to open it. Wrapped up in the letter, Anne didn't even realize she had come to a complete stop in the middle of the street and people walked around her. The sound of small carts bumping along on the stones made her jump, and she started walking again.

Turning up another less crowded street, Anne stopped in front of a doorway. Again she stared at the letter, her fingers trembling. A million raced through her head; the worst that Baldwin wrote to tell her that Richard was dead. She tried to comfort herself with the thought that if he died, she would have heard it by now. Then again, she forbade anyone to speak his name. Still, she gleaned bits and pieces of news here and there. Anne wanted to rip open the letter, but she hesitated. She didn't want to wait until she was back at the chateau because it would take too long to get there. With a gulp, she summoned her courage and pried open the seal.

Dear Lady Anne,

If you are reading this, I have scored a great victory in getting you to just open this letter.

Anne laughed. Baldwin began the letter with his usual good-natured tone.

Before you crumple this letter and toss it in the fire, I implore you to read on, for the sake of friendship. Let me start by saying that this is not about Richard, nor will I attempt to persuade you to return to him. Please relay the following message to Marguerite, as I know she cannot read. One more thing, please be so kind as to pray for us that we can all return home soon.

Your favourite "Silver Tongued Serpent",

Baldwin of Be Thune

Dear Lady,

It is with a heavy heart that I set my quill to parchment as I am writing to inform you of the loss of our great friend and companion, Andrew de Chauny.

Anne cupped her hand to her mouth as if to keep her

emotions inside.

He fell ill with a fever the day we captured Acre, and he never recovered, dying about a month later. I was at his side as well as the king, who is distraught over the death of such a noble comrade. Andrew's parting thoughts were of you, and I know that many times during his illness the image of your face brought him comfort. King Richard saw to it he was buried in the chapel here at the Royal Palace in Acre.

I am loathed to send you these sad tidings, but I know he would have wanted you to hear the news from a kind friend. I shall stop in Marseilles on my way home to deliver a token of his to you. God willing, we may see each other soon.

Your humble servant,

Baldwin of Bethune

Shocked, Anne didn't know which way to turn. Looking up she realized she stood in front of the side door to Saint Victor's. She opened the door and went inside.

In the dark interior, her eyes took a moment to adjust to the light. The chapel was empty, and she lit a candle for Andrew and one for Richard. Then she made her way down the nave and set out to find her father's grave. Her mother should have been buried next to her father, had she not died by her own hand. Kneeling down with tender care, she touched the carefully crafted letters of her father's name and wept.

A noise sounded behind her, and she jumped up with her back against the wall, dropping Baldwin's letter to the floor. A priest strode toward her. "Lady Anne de Marseilles, I expected you would find your way here, eventually."

At first Anne did not recognise the voice, but as the man moved closer, she sensed something familiar about him. "Pierre?"

"The very same." The priest's face brightened. "Only it is Abbot Mathias now."

"Abbot Mathias? Pierre? You became a priest? Not to mention you scared the soul out of me." Anne bent down and retrieved the letter, folding it and placing it under her cloak.

"Is that any way to greet an old friend?" He chided her.

Pierre, now Abbot Mathias, and Anne were friends in their youth. He was the son of her father's personal secretary, who often traveled with her father. Even though he was a couple years older, the two formed a friendship. As she looked at him now, Anne noticed that his light brown hair was gone but his thin pale brown eyes had not changed. "But you, the priesthood?"

He leaned in close and whispered to her, "I found it a bit more lucrative than the position of secretary."

She could not help herself and grinned at him. "That is frightening considering I know what my father paid his secretary." Absent-mindedly she wiped away some of the tears left on her face.

"You look like you could use a confession." He pulled two chairs over for them to sit.

"Confession to you? You forget I know many things about you that would make a priest blush." She took a seat.

"Ah, but here you are sitting down ready to tell me all." He took a seat himself. "Now, let us start with what has got you so upset."

Anne's expression fell. "I just received a letter informing me of the death of a friend. As if that weren't bad enough, I must now go home and tell a very dear friend that the love of her life is dead. I feel responsible, guilty even."

"How did he die?"

"Of a fever while in Acre."

"And how can you be responsible for a fever?"

"I cannot. It is that she came back to Marseilles because of me; otherwise, she could have been there with him, at least."

"I see." Abbot Mathis nodded his head. "Did you have her bound, gagged and tossed onto the boat?"

Anne shook her head.

"Then she came of her own free will." Mathis smiled down at her.

Anne choked as she teared up again. "He was a good man."

"Is the King of England a good man? Does he have a kind heart?" Mathis wiped her tears away.

"What do you mean?" Anne blinked.

"Anne, I have followed everything that happened to you since you left here. Things changed when you left." He grinned again. "Oh, speaking of change, did you ever hear what happened to our previous Abbot, the reason you left us in the first place?"

"No."

"He suddenly seized at his chest in the middle of a sermon, and fell over dead." Mathias raised his eyebrows. "But that's not the best of it. His sermon was about chastity."

"No! You are joking with me, Pierre." Anne laughed.

"Mathias, and no, I swear on the holy relics of Saint Victor that it is the truth. If I am lying, may God strike me dead just like he did that disgusting old man."

Anne scooted her chair away from him. "You must forgive me, Mathias, but I am just moving out of the way so as not to be hit when He rains down His wrath on you."

They both laughed out loud, and it felt good to Anne. She forgot how much she cared for Mathias. "I wondered why I never saw him with a delegation of priests. Well, I have avoided contact with the priests of Marseilles as much as possible."

"I know. I was with the Bishop when you came into the city with King Richard." Mathias rolled his eyes.

"Why did you not approach me?" She asked him.

"The last thing I wanted to do was approach you when the King of England was there. I was your first kiss after all. If he knew that, I doubt my head would stay on my shoulders long."

Anne looked out into the chapel. "He would not have done that; he is not a cruel man."

"I only know what I have heard." Mathias gave a shrug.

"Despite the rumors you may have heard, I have done nothing wrong, in the eyes of God or the eyes of the church." She looked up at Mathias.

"I am glad of it," he replied. "On a personal level too." His mischievous look returned.

In the corner of the chapel the pair continued to talk. Anne told Mathias all about her life since she left Marseilles, and Mathias told her about his life as a priest. They talked of Raymond and Will, of Richard and of her father. It comforted Anne to know Mathias administered to her father his last rights.

Even though it was only late afternoon, the sun began to fade. The warm glow of a winter sunset cast purple colours on the floor and Anne knew it was time to return home. "Mathias, I cannot tell you how glad I am to see you again. In all fairness though, I must go home and relay this unhappy information to Marguerite."

"Your lady Marguerite? She is the unfortunate woman then." Mathias shook his head. "I always liked Marguerite."

Anne stood to take her leave. "Well, good evening, Abbot. I hope I shall see you again soon."

"If you would attend Mass, you would." Mathias walked her to the door.

Once outside, he glanced around. "Do you mean to walk back to the chateau?"

"That is a viable means of transportation, Abbot Mathias."

"Do you really think that is wise, considering your husband is about?"

Anne laid her hand on his arm. "The money lender Lugo took care of him. Castile will be no threat."

"I am not so sure, Anne. I do not feel comfortable with you walking about by yourself. Stay right here," he ordered.

"What are you doing?" She stepped back in the doorway and called after him.

"I am going to get a cloak and accompany you home," he called out as he went to fetch one.

Mathias returned in a moment, and the two took a brisk walk back to the chateau.

"Marguerite?" Anne shut the door behind her.

Marguerite sat near the hearth in a room that once belonged to Anne's mother, but now served as a library of sorts. The light in here was good and Marguerite worked on some sewing. "M'lady." Marguerite looked up at Anne. "I was beginning to wonder if you were coming home. Will's been looking for you."

Anne took the sewing from Marguerite's hands and laid it aside. Kneeling in front of her lady-in-waiting, Anne took the woman's hand in her own. "Dearest, I need to talk with you. I received a letter today from Baldwin."

Shocked by Anne kneeling on the floor before her,

Marguerite squirmed. "Baldwin huh? What is that old rouge up to now?"

"There was some bad news in the letter." Anne's voice wavered. "Well, here. He wrote part to you, and I shall just read it."

"To me? Doesn't the fool know I can't read?"

Anne fished the letter out and ignored Marguerite's question. Carefully and clearly, she read the letter aloud to Marguerite. When she was finished, Anne looked back up at Marguerite whose face had become twisted. "Marguerite?" Anne whispered.

Suddenly, Marguerite pushed past Anne, knocking her on the ground, her fists clenched tight. She spun around to face Anne and pointed at the letter that now lay on the ground. "That is not true. There's been some sort of mistake. It's one of Baldwin's practical jokes, and it's not funny." Marguerite stamped her foot.

Anne blinked back tears. "No, how I wish to God it were a joke, but it is not. Oh, I am so sorry."

Marguerite screamed out, "I know it's not true. I could tell if Andrew was dead. I would know." She sank to her knees. "I would know."

Anne caught Marguerite before she hit the floor and wrapped her arms around her. "I would know. I would know." Marguerite sobbed as she rocked back and forth.

Chapter Fifty-two

Richard stared at the parchment that lay before him on the table. He ran his fingers through his hair, which had begun to fill in again. Baldwin stood nearby and waiting for his king to say something. Without looking at Baldwin, Richard shook his head and pointed to the message. "Well, something has got to be done. There are no two ways about it. God's legs, what an ass John is!"

Richard grabbed both sides of the table trying as if trying to hold in his temper. "I cannot believe he would…" He slammed the table on the floor and stood up. "Well, I guess I can believe he would betray me like this. After all, look what he did to his own father. But I gave that whining whelp more land and power than my father ever did. He owes me more than… than behavior such as this."

"My lord, Philip is behind this treachery. John didn't stand a chance when they matched wits," Baldwin observed.

Richard picked up the epistle again and read it over. It was from William Longchamp, Richard's appointed Justiciar of the southern portion of England. In his letter, Longchamp explained the disturbances occurring in Richard's kingdom and told how John and Philip became fast allies. The pair were trying to undermine Richard and having some success. If it weren't for Eleanor and her skills, the realm might already have been lost.

"John was raised in England. He cares nothing for Normandy or any of my other territories in France. He will certainly give them to Philip, if Philip helps him become king." Richard spoke to no one in particular. Then he turned to Baldwin. "We must finish up this Crusade and get home or I will not have a kingdom to return to. I know we are stuck here until spring, but there is one thing we can do in the meantime." Richard leaned his hands upon the table. "It is time that the matter of the King of Jerusalem be decided once and for all."

A day later, Guy de Lusignan stood before Richard, his anger so great that he shook violently. Richard prepared for this moment as soon as the barons selected Conrad of Montfort as their king. "Guy, I know you must be feeling betrayed right now, but you must understand that I acted in the best interest of the country, and yourself. Those men were not loyal to you. You would have spent years fighting them, and Jerusalem would never be recovered. The Christians need to be united if we hope to ever recapture and maintain the kingdom from the Turks."

"That is all good and fine, but where does that leave me?" Guy shouted at Richard. "I was crowned King of Jerusalem long before that usurper laid claim to it!"

Richard fought to keep himself from raising his voice. "You were not king by natural right, only because of your wife. She is dead now and succession falls to her sister, Conrad's wife."

"Yes, his wife that he kidnapped, so he could take my crown!" Guy did not let Richard finish his argument.

"Guy, have patience and just listen to me!" Richard thundered at him.

"Alright then." Guy folded his massive arms and plopped down in a chair.

Richard looked around. They were in his outer chamber again, and the constant winter rain fell outside. On his desk, Richard spotted a document that was curled up half way. He snatched it up and held it in front of Guy's face. "This document is your future. You are a king in need of a kingdom."

Guy let out a loud snort. "That is an understatement if ever I heard one."

"Hear me out." Richard shook the parchment. "Now as you know, I conquered the island kingdom of Cyprus. I sold the island to the Templars to help finance my operations here. In truth, the Templars are not in the business of governing. They are in the business of fighting, and now they wish to sell the island back to me." Richard gave long sigh. "I do not want Cyprus. There is no way I could govern it when it is so far from my lands."

"And just how am I going to afford buying it? I am the king with no kingdom, do you not remember?" Guy glowered at Richard.

Richard pointed at himself. "England will loan you the money, Guy."

Guy sat in silent contemplation for a moment looking away from Richard. The only sound was the rain dripping from the roof.

Guy pulled at his beard. "Cyprus, eh?"

"Yes." Richard nodded, "Cyprus." He laid the document in Guy's lap. "You will have a kingdom. You can remarry, and form your own dynasty there. Cyprus has endless possibilities."

The anger melted away from Guy's face as he made his decision. "Well then, it is to be Cyprus."

Anne just finished speaking with Master More regarding Will's lessons. Recently, Will was difficult and hard to manage during his studies. While Anne was gone and even when she first returned home, Will excelled, but now something changed in him.

As Anne sat warming herself by the fire in the kitchen, contemplating what to do with the child, she heard a soft voice behind her. "Lady Anne."

She turned. "Oh, Mathias. What are you doing here on such a cold afternoon?"

"Etienne said he thought you were here in the kitchen. May I sit?" The abbot drew a nearby chair next to her.

"You look troubled," he noted.

"Hum." She nodded. "Will—he's acting out."

"I see. Would you like me to talk to the boy?" Mathias offered.

"Thank you, no. I will handle it." Anne shook her head. "So, what brings you here today?"

Mathias visited the chateau almost on a daily basis. Anne enjoyed his company. He stretched his hands toward the fire and did not look at Anne as he answered her question. "Anne, Marguerite came to see me this morning."

"Oh?" Anne arched her eyebrows. Since Baldwin's letter arrived, Marguerite was quiet, withdrawn, and sullen. "She is barely speaking these days, and I am most worried about her."

"She wants to become a nun, Anne."

"Marguerite? A nun?" Anne stammered

Mathias simply nodded his head in silent affirmation.

"Well, that is something I never would have thought."

"Yes, she's quite adamant about the whole thing."

Anne shook her head. "Are you sure? Perhaps she is just not thinking clearly."

"Everyone experiences grief in their own way. However, I do believe that if she took the steps to join the sisterhood of the church, she would see her commitment through."

"Oh my, Marguerite a nun?" Anne sat up taller.

"Marguerite is still under an obligation of service to you," Mathias reminded Anne.

"I see." Anne stared into the fire. How could she spare Marguerite? But then, how could she forbid Marguerite? Anne knew the heartache she experienced. How could her heart ever heal other than devotion to God? "My wise friend, you have spoken to her, and she is of serious mind?"

"I have, my lady."

"Well, if it is what she wants, then I would never stop her, but I shall miss her."

Mathias leaned forward in his chair rubbing at his knees with his hands. "She will be glad to hear of your consent, I am sure."

"Where is she now? I would like to speak with her," Anne queried.

"At the abbey. She feared you would try to sway her from her resolve." One corner of Mathias' mouth went up in a quick smile.

Anne dropped her head into her hands. "Oh Mathias, I feel like I am losing everyone that I hold dear."

"Not everyone," he replied, stroking the top of her head.

Conrad of Montferrat made his way down the street in Tyre, weaving back and forth, lightheaded from the wine he consumed. He stopped and leaned against a large barrel outside of one of the houses but almost lost his balance. With caution, he repositioned himself on the barrel's edge, being wary not to fall in. Looking up at the sky he noticed the stars above and smiled to himself. He felt elated. He was going to be king. Balin of Ibelin brought him the news and right away preparations began for his coronation. The event had to be delayed until King Richard could come, but he, Conrad of Montferrat, would be king at last.

With his blue eyes still watching the stars above him, he gave a sigh and pushed some of his dark hair from his face. It had been an odd night for him. He meant to dine with his good friend, the Bishop of Beauvais, and Conrad's wife was to have joined him, but Isabella refused, saying she was bathing and did not wish to go. Conrad just attributed her prickliness to the fact that she was with child. Yet, when Conrad arrived for his dinner appointment, he found his host not at home. On his way back home now, his progress impeded by the fact that he drank copious amounts of wine and now felt the effects.

Conrad looked down the street and saw two men whom he recognised as Saracen converts to Christianity. Thinking they were coming to pay him homage as so many others had done on the street, Conrad stood up to greet them. "My lord, we have a message for you." One of the men said, and it sounded as if the voice came from far away.

Conrad reached out his hand to take the letter and the man who spoke suddenly seized Conrad's sword hand. In a flash the other thrust a dagger deep into Conrad's body. Grabbing at the first man's cloak with a bloody hand, Conrad slid to the ground, aware of screams floating around him, and laughter from a nearby house, when blackness closed in from everywhere.

The occupants of the nearby house, roused from the dwelling by Conrad's screams, found him lying of the pavement. Four men from the house pounced on Conrad's attackers. One fought so hard that in the scuffle, he knocked the knife out the assailant's hand. There was a scramble for it, and a man from the house clutched it, rolled back and stabbed the Muslim in the breast. The second man tried to flee, but the other men subdued him.

The master of the house rolled Conrad over and gasped when he recognised the man. It was too late. Conrad of Montferrat would never be crowned King of Jerusalem.

Chapter Fifty-three

"The people of Tyre dragged the murderer back to the palace, and under torture, he confessed to having killed Conrad on the orders of Sheikh Sinan, the *Old Man of the Mountain*," Breton recounted.

"Who on earth is this Old Man of the Mountain?" Bogis asked.

Breton explained to the men around him. "The Old Man of the Mountain was a ruler of a Shiite tribe of Assassins. You must understand, the Shiites hate the Kurds and Saladin was a Kurd. Kurds and Shiites hate each other like the French and the English."

Laughter rumbled amongst the men, and Breton continued. "The Shiite-Kurdish hatred goes back centuries. I would venture to say that the hatred is so deep that it will not be resolved, not even in a thousand years. But that is beside the point. The Shiites would have been happy to have Christians win the war, and they hoped that by having a Muslim kill Conrad, to strengthen the Christian resolve against their Kurdish enemies. Conrad was chosen to be sacrificed because earlier he captured an Assassin ship and took the cargo. But this incident played an important role later on. You see, some did not believe the tortured Assassin's story and claimed Richard had Conrad killed."

"I could see how they would think that." Bogis shook his head and he suddenly found it surprising that the more of the story

Breton told, the more sympathy he felt toward Richard.

"By the time all this happened, Guy was on his way to his new kingdom in Cyprus. Richard made hasty preparations to rush to Tyre, but word soon reached him that his nephew, Henry of Champagne, was already there. The dashing young man dazzled Tyre's citizens; a dispensation of the customary one-year mourning period of a widow was granted, and Champagne married the young Isabella only seven days after Conrad's death. He was quickly crowned King of Jerusalem and set up his headquarters at Acre."

"Nephew to both Richard and Philip. Well, either one would support him," Bogis spoke his thoughts aloud.

Breton nodded in agreement and then continued. "When Spring broke, Richard and his men campaigned to within twelve miles of Jerusalem."

"Why did Richard not take Jerusalem?" Bogis threw up his hands.

Breton tilted his head to one side. "Water, Bogis, water. You see water is the gold, the currency, the life-blood in the desert. Richard did not have water and his men died like flies as a result. He had no other choice but to retreat."

"While riding in the hills Richard caught a glimpse of Jerusalem, and he put his shield up to hide it from his eyes." Breton put up his hands in front of his eyes as if they were a shield. "Richard swore he would not lay eyes on the city until he came to conquer it."

In the pre-dawn hours Richard stirred in his bed. He lay awake all night as his thoughts raced. Messages poured in from Richard's realm, all begging him to return home as Philip and John gained more headway. The letter from his mother convinced Richard he must voice aloud what he had already known for months. The phrase his mother used echoed over in his head: "Son, you must return home to your kingdom, or you will lose it."

His brain worked on the problems of how to best end the war and return home. That led to thoughts of returning, to deal with John, England, Normandy, and Aquitaine. Then that always led to thinking about Anne. Richard did not want to think about Anne. He couldn't bear the thought of living without her, of returning to Poitiers, Normandy, or even London, and her not being with him. Desperately, he wished she were here right now to talk to. She would be able to help him sort out the options before him. She always did have a good head for politics.

Richard rolled onto his stomach and, with more force then necessary, fluffed his pillow. The noise startled the sleeping page on his pallet nearby. The youth rolled over onto his back and broke the quiet with a rattling snore. This annoyed Richard as he tried to drive Anne from his thoughts. He tried to focus on the reasons he should leave the Kingdom of Outremer and return to his own.

The first and foremost reason for leaving was that his own kingdom was threatened. He needed to return as soon as possible. But how could he just abandon Jerusalem? The more he thought about it, the more he realized that a treaty with Saladin was the best course of action. In truth, he could make a push and conquer Jerusalem, but then what? If he returned home, that would leave Jerusalem in the hands of a group of squabbling Christians. Richard knew once he left, Saladin would just recapture the city, and the cycle would start once again. No, it would serve Jerusalem better if he were to return home, set his affairs in order, then raise a larger army and come back again.

The page stopped snoring and mumbled something about boots in his sleep as he rolled onto his side. Richard picked up his pillow and tossed it at the boy who sat up startled and shaken from his slumber. "Shut up, will you!" Richard grumped at him.

"I am sorry, my lord," The youth squeaked back.

"Sorry, huh? Sorry? You shall be sorry when you find yourself sleeping out in the stables with the horses!" Richard shouted.

There came a knock on Richard's door. "Enter!" He thundered.

Baldwin strode into the room. "My lord, I am sorry to interrupt your sleep."

"Never mind that. The boy here has already done it for you."

"Yes, well, there is a messenger here from Jaffa. It would seem that the Saracens are attacking." Baldwin was ready for Richard to explode.

Shouting as he sprang from his bed, Richard did not disappoint. "God's legs! What are those fools doing down there? Did they just fling open the gates and say to the Saracens, 'Come on in and make yourself at home? May we fluff the cushions for you?'"

"The messenger did not give many details, sire. I am sorry." Baldwin hung close to the door, ready to use it as a shield if Richard started to throw things.

Richard threw on a tunic before the page could even reach one. Strapping on his sword, he turned to Baldwin and ordered, "Assemble the men and tell them to march directly to Jaffa. Roust them out of whorehouses or the chapels, wherever they may be, but they must be on the road no later than this afternoon."

Baldwin raised his eyebrows and tipped his head to the side. "Yes, my lord."

The page scurried around gathering clothing to dress the king. He grabbed Richard's boots from the hearth. "Why on earth are you bothering with boots, boy? We haven't time for any of that nonsense." Richard snatched the boots from him. "Go, tell them to saddle my horse."

The pageboy dashed off to complete his errand. Baldwin remained in the room. And Richard rounded on him. "Well, what on earth are you waiting for? Assemble the men, damnit!"

Baldwin remained calm. "I beg your pardon, my lord, but is your highness going to march with the men to Jaffa?"

"No, as a matter of fact, I am not. I will take the fleet and sail down the coast. It will be faster that way. In addition to the sailors, I want a contingent of Poitevins and Templars—about eighty should do nicely—on those ships. Four hundred bowman as well!" Richard headed out the door.

"My lord!" Baldwin stopped him. "I do not think it would befit a king to go off to battle barefoot."

Richard looked down at his feet and realized he still carried his boots. "Oh, yes. Thank you, Baldwin." Richard's tone softened toward his friend.

"I am only doing my duty, sire."

"You are loyal as always." Richard smiled at him.

"No, not really. It is just that I fear *her* wrath if I did not look after you, my lord."

Richard shook his head and his smile faded. "I see. My old friend is still afraid of a woman, even one who is thousands of miles away." Richard entered the room again and glanced around quickly. Spotting his slippers, he put them on his feet. "You can explain to Anne that I did not go barefooted into battle, but had no time to put on my boots- no time to spare." Richard left the room and Baldwin followed.

Will hid in the garden. He just endured a particularly boring lesson and fled as soon as Master More released him. Going directly to the garden, he lodged himself behind a row of bushes and plopped down on the ground. Picking up a twig, he snapped it in half and tossed it on the ground. He could hear his mother's laughter coming from the other side of the garden, and he peeked out from behind the bushes only to see her coming down the pathway with Abbot Mathias at her side. Will watched as his mother threw her head back and laughed at something the Abbot said. It made Will cringe. He hated the sight of that man.

Despite his effort to hide, Anne spotted Will's tunic. Upon

realizing his mother saw him, Will scrambled up a tree and into the branches. The smile faded from Anne's face, and Abbot Mathias whispered something in her ear. Anne put her hands on her hips and put called up to her son, "Will, come down here."

Placing himself flat on an outstretched branch, Will did not reply to his mother. "Perhaps if I spoke to the boy?" Mathias offered. He called up to Will, "Son, would you come down here for a moment?"

Will yelled out, "You are not my father!" He jumped from the tree landing in front of the Abbot and a bewildered Anne.

"Will!" Anne stamped her foot. "You will apologize to the Abbot this instant!"

Will turned and fled the garden as fast as he could. Anne started after him, but Mathias grabbed her arm. "Let him go. It is obvious the child is upset about something. Give him time to calm himself."

"No! This behavior is not to be tolerated."

Mathias gave her a wide smile as he released his grip. "If I may be frank, he reminds me very much of you, and I dare say, there were times when it was best to let your anger wane before approaching you."

Anne gave a long sigh. "Oh Mathias, what am I going to do with him?"

"Let me handle the boy. I will speak with him later, man-to-man." Mathias took her hand and gave it a gentle pat.

The coastal city of Jaffa brewed in chaos. Fighting broke out amongst the Kurds and the Turks in the Saracen army, and finally they turned their anger against the Christians at Jaffa. At least they could agree on one thing, that they hated the Christians. The Saracens attacked the loosely guarded city, and it was all the defenders inside could do to keep the enemy from bursting through the gates.

Camped five miles inland with his army, Saladin sent word to the Christians not to surrender until he arrived. If they did, Saladin could not guarantee their safety.

At last, the Christians felt they could hold out no longer, and the knights prepared to surrender to the Muslims. Just as they were ready to do so, a cry went up from a Saracen watchman. Something was coming on the horizon.

At first it was a small white square in distance, then four squares. Then even more appeared. As they drew nearer, the red crosses blazing on their sails burst forth against the blue sea and azure sky. The Christian knights took up their swords again and barricaded themselves behind the city gate. A desperate priest flung himself into the sea and swam out to meet the ships.

Richard didn't waste a moment but headed for the shore instead of taking time to dock. The bow of Richard's ship slammed into the beach, sending sand scattering before it. The other ships in the fleet soon landed alongside Richard's. Even if he wanted to hold back the men, it would have been impossible. Almost before the ship beached, Richard jumped from it, his sword drawn. The knights and bowmen followed, swinging on ropes, and jumping over the sides. They all rushed toward the city.

A great cry sounded from the men as they charged across the beach, and the defenders inside knew that help was coming. Watching from the ships, the sailors of Pisa and Genoa could not contain themselves. They too grabbed their weapons and poured out of the ships, following behind the army. The mass of warriors led on by the English King blazed across the beach to rescue the beleaguered city.

Saladin paced back and forth in his tent. Al-Adil stood behind him and off to the left. The Turkish commander Saladin put in charge of recapturing Jaffa was dead and his captain brought the news to Saladin. Saladin narrowed his eyes as he stopped and peered down at the man. "Well, what excuse do you have for me now?" Saladin's dark eyes pierced the poor man.

"Sire, I am truly sorry, but the English King stormed the beach, and…"

Saladin cut him off. "Not only did you lose the city, but you all fled like sheep from a dog."

The man had no answer; instead he looked down at the ground. Saladin went back to pacing. He did not shout at the man; that was not his way. Saladin showed his anger in a manner so calm it inspired fear and self-loathing in the recipient. Saladin did not need to shout and rant to express his consternation. It came through clearly without words.

The captain kneeling before Saladin trembled as the leader folded one arm across his chest, resting the other on it and gently stroked his beard. "We shall return to Jaffa. The city will be taken back from the Christians, even if their king is there." Saladin strode out of the tent.

Al-Adil stepped forward, yanked the beleaguered captain by the arm to his feet, and gave him a shove toward the door. "Get going! It is back to Jaffa for you."

The young Genoese sailor reached down, yet again, to pick up another crate. As he loaded it onto the waiting cart, it landed with a thud, and he leaned on it while wiping his brow. Now that Jaffa was rescued, supplies poured in from Acre, and the burden of unloading all the goods fell on every able bodied man on the docks.

Just as dawn broke, the young sailor found himself exhausted from working all night. Looking away from the port, the young man gazed up into the hills. Something seemed to flash. He dismissed it as a trick of his tired mind and turned to go back to his work. Lifting another crate to put onto the cart, pausing again, he gazed into the hills. This time there was no mistake; something had flashed in the distance. The flash repeated in quick successions, until it became clear to the sailor that an army marched in the distance. Without hesitation, the sailor dropped the crate he held and sped off toward the city to sound the tocsin and rouse the Christians.

Chapter Fifty-four

Saladin pushed his army to march on Jaffa before the Christian reinforcements could arrive. Now perched on a hill overlooking the city, his black eyes narrowed as he watched his men move closer.

Despite the fact that Richard numbered only two thousand men, it would be difficult to take Jaffa. In the distance, Saladin could see that Richard had enough warning of their advance to align his men for the defence of the city. Saladin could see a wall of shields awaiting his men.

Saladin sent his cavalry first. The horses and men advanced on the Christians. Then, without warning, the horses began to fall. The sound of the screaming animals pierced the air. "What is happening to them? I do not see arrows!" Al-Adil shouted.

Saladin's eyes still narrowed, and his face showed no emotion as he responded. "Tent stakes. See there, the dark line. The King of the English implanted tent stakes to trip our horses. That is an interesting tactic. Fear not, the cavalry will find a way through soon enough."

Saladin was right. The cavalry did discover what hindered them, how to avoid the stakes, and they proceeded to the wall of shields. Not only did the Christians make a wall of shields, each man behind the shields dug his spear into the ground with their points angled to impale any horse who tried to cross the line. Still, the Saracen cavalry moved forward. Just as they reached the wall, Saladin saw him; Richard, on his horse behind the troops, riding up and down the line, shouting out orders. It surprised Saladin that Richard remained so close to the fighting, and as he pondered this, the sound of the crash of his cavalry trying to breech the wall of spears reached him.

The Saracens met with fierce resistance at the shield wall, followed by a thick barrage of arrows. The speed at which the crossbowmen shot was astounding. The process of loading and firing a crossbow was infamously slow. Upon closer look, Saladin realized Richard split his bowmen into two groups. One group stood behind the shield wall, and the second directly behind the first. The second group loaded the weapons, while the first groups shot their bolts, then exchanged weapons. Saladin found himself marveling at the tactic.

Seven waves of Saracens hurled themselves at the Christians, and Muslim bodies and horses piled up in front of the shield wall. The cavalry weakened. Saladin studied Richard. He had no wish to admire this man, especially after all the innocents that he slaughtered at Ayyadieh, but Saladin could not help himself. There sat the English King atop his horse in the thick of the battle, never flinching as the arrows flew around him, leading his men as they attacked the Saracens.

Then, the knees of Richard's horse buckled and the animal fell to the ground. Richard tumbled along with the horse, and from where Saladin stood, it looked as though the animal crushed the man. Saladin held his breath, elation beginning to well up inside him with the possible death of the Christian leader.

Without the aid of his knights, Richard rose to his feet. Saladin closed his eyes and let out the breath he held. A surprising wave of relief wash over him. He could see Richard's golden beard in the distance, and despite his anger at the man, Saladin respected Richard as a warrior. "It is enough." He turned away.

"Enough?" Al-Adil furrowed his brow.

Saladin laid his hand on his brother's shoulder. "Enough. We shall withdraw from this place." He began to walk away but turned around to face his bewildered brother. "Send the English King two fresh horses."

"Will! Will!" Anne called for the boy as she entered his room. She looked all over for him and her patience wore thin. Will was not in his room. "For the love of…. Where is that child?" Anne stamped her foot.

"I sent the child out to the bluff." Nannette's voice came from a large chair in front of the fireplace.

Anne walked around the chair to see Nannette better. "I did not know you were here, Nannette."

Sitting in the large chair, Nannette looked smaller than normal. She hunched over and a blanket lay across her lap. Anne suspicioned that the old nurse was sleeping there, a new habit of hers. "Master William was rather upset this morning, so I sent him to the bluff where I used to send you when you had much on your mind."

Anne gave a heavy sigh as she sank down on a stool facing Nannette. "Honestly, I do not understand that boy. He has been in such a snit. Two days ago Mathias tried again to speak with him and Will refused. Etienne told me they found him asleep in the corner of the stable."

Pushing herself up taller in the chair, Nannette's feet did not reach the floor. "He is an angry child right now, my dear."

"What has he got to be angry for? He is only a boy, for heaven's sake."

Nannette took a long look at Anne before she answered. "You really do not see it?"

"No. I do not see what the matter is," Anne huffed.

"The child misses the only father he has known. He misses King Richard." Nannette did not hesitate to speak the forbidden name.

Anne's shoulder's dropped. "Oh, I see. Well, there is nothing

I can do about that."

Nannette explained further. "William spent most of his life being raised in Richard's household, and he sees the king like a father."

"I cannot help it if he got attached. We both got attached." Anne stood and walked to the fireplace. Taking a poker from its stand, she stoked the fire. "Yet another reason that I should have ended that relationship long ago."

"It is not only that he misses Richard; he is very concerned about Abbot Mathias."

"The abbot? Really now. What does Mathias have to do with anything?"

"William worries about the nature of your relationship with the abbot," Nannette's voice cracked.

Anne put the poker back in its place and turned around to face Nannette with both hands on her hips. "The nature of my relationship with the abbot? He said that?"

Nannette smiled back up at Anne, adding more wrinkles to her face. "Not in so many words, dear, but the time you are spending with Abbot Mathias makes more than just your son wonder."

"My relationship with the abbot is perfectly innocent!" Anne defended herself. "He is a leader among the clergy in the city, and I am just trying to foster good relations."

Nannette pushed herself out of the chair with the aid of her stick. "You must not forget that there is a history between you and Abbot Mathias."

"Nannette, we were children!"

"Did you know that he was inconsolable when you left for Poitiers? He sat on the docks for two solid days, and then without saying a word to his father, went straight to the church and took orders." Nannette raised her eyebrow and tipped her head.

Anne whispered, "Why did no one tell me this before?"

Before Nannette could answer her, Anne heard Will

bounding down the hall. "Mother! Mother!"

"Ah! I think I have located the child." Nannette turned and made her way to the door.

Before the nurse reached the door, Will flung it open and burst into the room. "Mother! Mother, you must come see."

"What? What is it, Will?"

A grin replaced the frown he wore so often."Downstairs, they have been sent to you." Will tugged at his mother to follow him. "You must come and see!"

"Alright, Will."

Will led his mother outside to a large cart parked in front of the chateau. Etienne spoke with the driver when Anne approached him. "My lady, it would seem that someone has sent you a present." Etienne threw back the cover on the cart, and two beautiful Mastiffs peered out at her from a cage.

"What on earth?"

Etienne motioned to the driver to open the cage. "This came with them." He handed Anne a letter.

As she opened it and read, the dogs bounded out of the cart and pranced around a delighted Will.

My Dearest Cousin,

I regret that my business made it impossible for me to bring you these two dogs personally, but I had to make my way to Paris as quickly as I could. I know you will understand.

I am sending you these two mastiffs to protect you. They are of the best breeding and quality. The male is the one that took such a shine to you in Messina.

Anne, I know that Castile is in Marseilles and I worry constantly for your safety, as well as Will's. Please accept them as a token of my esteem. I call them Sigurd and Nanna.

I am sure that you are aware that...

"Mother, can we keep them?" Will tugged at her sleeve.

"Just a moment, Will." Anne tried to continue reading the letter.

Will interrupted her again. "Did Uncle send them?"

"No, dearest. King Philip sent them." She watched as the two massive dogs bounded around in circles after Will.

Etienne put his hand on top of the crate and blocked her view of Will. "The King of France is sending you gifts, the King of England wants you for his mistress, Guy de Lusignan is sending you letters, trying to negotiate a marriage, *and* you are already married." Etienne shook his head and laughed. "No one told me my cousin was going to be such trouble!"

"Etienne!" She grinned up at him.

"Oh, look, Captain Vasser is coming. I shall have to tell him he is going to have to wait in a rather long line." Etienne pointed behind her.

Anne turned as Vasser approached her. "Good day, Lady Anne." He gave her a deep bow.

"Captain Vasser, what brings you here? Do not tell me you are the poor soul who had to transport these beasts. I am told they are dogs, but to me they look more like miniature horses." Anne extended her hand to him.

"No, not me." Vasser pursed his lips. "M'lady, I must speak

with you at once." He looked at Etienne.

"Anything you have to say to me can be said in front of my steward." Anne folded the letter back up.

Vasser moved in closer and lowered his voice. "M'lady I have news of the money lender Lugo. He took his household to Aix en Provence and thieves attacked him on the road. Lugo was killed."

"I see." Anne nodded.

"His servants all fled, but have since been rounded up, all but Raymond of Castile," Vasser continued. "Castile was working off his debt to the money lender I suppose."

"We will keep the dogs, Etienne," Anne commanded. She looked beyond her steward and could not see Will. "Will? Where is my son? Will!" She shouted.

Will ran to her and skidded to a halt, the dogs following close behind. "Here I am, Mother."

Anne tried not to let her panic show to the boy. "Will, take the dogs in the house and stay there."

Will looked up at her in confusion, but decided to obey. "Yes, Mother." He turned and entered the house with the dogs trailing him.

Once Will was gone, Anne turned back to Vasser. "Are you certain? Are you absolutely certain Castile was still alive and with Lugo when he left the city?"

"In truth, I have known that he became a servant in Lugo's household. I did not wish to worry you, so I said nothing," Etienne confessed.

Anne remained quiet as thoughts swirled in her head, and she tried to decide on the best course of action without giving way to full blown panic. At length she said to Vasser, "Thank you, Captain, for being so kind as to bring me this information. I must take my leave now, as there is much to do."

Vasser gave her another bow and left. Anne took Etienne by the arm and led him back up the stairs into the chateau. "I want you to double the guard. Hire more if you have to. Put men outside Will's room. He is not to go outside the chateau without an armed escort. I do not care how much he protests."

"Yes, my lady." Etienne hung his head.

Anne stopped at the door. "I will write to the Count of Provence, and ask him to put a price on Castile's head."

"For what?" Etienne asked.

"For murder. He fled the scene did he not? It does not really matter if Castile did it; the moment there is a price on his head, he will flee the region."

Chapter Fifty-five

Richard entered his room, his head throbbing. He made straight for the bottle of wine on the table and poured himself a glass. He set the goblet down on the table and stopped up the bottle. Hearing a slight noise behind him, he instinctively drew his sword as he turned. "Your highness." Berengaria gave him a deep curtsy.

"Oh, it is you." He sighed and sheathed his weapon. "You should not be sneaking around like that." He downed the glass of wine.

"I apologize, my lord. I have been waiting for you." She spoke with an air of humility foreign to her nature.

"Well, what is it? What do you want? I am in no mood to quibble with you," Richard grumbled.

Berengaria took the cup from his hands and filled it again. Handing it back to him, she said, "How are the peace negotiations with Saladin coming, my lord?"

Richard tipped his head to the side. "They… are… coming. I have not been able to negotiate face to face, as I would have hoped, only with al-Adil."

"May I?" She motioned to a chair by the table. Richard nodded and Berengaria carefully placed herself in the chair, smoothing out the fabric of her dress. "Is it safe to assume we will be going home soon?"

Richard plunked down in a chair next to her. "We will be returning to England soon, if that is what you mean."

"It is."

"Well, you and Joanna will be leaving sooner than I will."

"I see. It is to be separate ships then." Berengaria looked down.

Richard set his goblet of wine on the table. "I know you may find this hard to believe, but it will be safer for you." He glanced at her and she looked back at him with unquestioning submission. He continued, "Philip has been telling anyone who would listen that he fears for his life and that I sent men to kill him. John is conspiring with Philip. Leopold of Austria swears vengeance for the insult he received when his flag was torn from its standard and tossed into the mud. Not to mention the fact that I am concluding a peace treaty with the enemy and leaving without having won Jerusalem. I am a target all over the Mediterranean Sea. At every port, there are men laying in wait for me. There are many who do not wish to see me return to my kingdom." Richard stood up and took off his belt and sword, laying them on the table.

"I understand," Berengaria's voice quivered.

"I shall send you via Rome. The pope will protect you."

"Traveling without you and with Lady Anne in Chartres, I know that I will be safe. I mean no disrespect, my lord." She attempted a smile at him. "That is to say, if they could not get to you, the next natural target would be Lady Anne. It is obvious to everyone that your wife falls far behind her in your lists of priorities. I have accepted that."

Surprised by her candor Richard felt pity for his wife. It was not her fault that she was thrust into these circumstances. Still, he knew he could never love her. "Madame, I am sorry that you find yourself in such a situation. Something I learnt long ago is that love does not equal marriage."

"Unfortunately for me, no, it does not, but you cannot blame me for trying."

"Hum." Richard shrugged.

Berengaria gave him a genuine smile now. "I remember the first time I saw you when you visited the court in Navarre all those years ago. Anyway, you were sitting on top of your horse; you just came back from a hunt. I remember thinking to myself that if I could choose any man to marry, it would be that man there, Richard." She shifted in her seat. "When Sancho told me that he was in negotiations with you for my hand in marriage, it was as if all my prayers were answered."

"Berengaria I…"

She did not let him finish. "It is alright. You needn't say it. I know why you married me. Richard, I know you cannot say to me with honesty what I long to hear."

"You are known to be a beautiful woman, and I know that there are many who think me a fool, who envy me."

"As well they should." She laughed.

Richard smiled back at her. Her joke made him laugh. For the first time he noticed her sense of humor.

Berengaria placed both her graceful hands neatly in her lap and continued. "Richard, I have been trying to understand, and perhaps I never will completely, but now, I know you a little better than you think. You see I read Capellanus' *Treatise on Love and its Cures*, the book that your sister, Countess Marie commissioned in Poitiers all those years ago. Those Courts of Love are legend now. Let me see if I remember the tenants set forth in that book.

"Yes, there is the one about marriage and that it cannot be pleaded as an excuse for refusing love. Also, no one can love two people at the same time. Love never stands still; it always increases or diminishes. Favors, if unwillingly yielded, are tasteless. It is not becoming to love those ladies who only love with a view to marriage. I suppose that rules me out does it not?" She shrugged and then continued on in her recitation. "Too easy possession renders love contemptible. Possession that is attended with difficulties makes love, I believe he termed it, 'of great price'. Let us not forget that love invariably increases under the influence of jealousy. A person who is the prey of love eats little and sleeps little. Well, that certainly pertains to you. Lastly, love can deny nothing to love."

Richard looked down at his hands. "You have forgotten one. If love once begins to diminish, it fades and rarely recovers."

"Richard, your love for her never diminished."

Richard coughed and tried to change the subject. "Well, before you know it you shall be in London, and you will miss all this sunshine and heat."

Berengaria got up, went to the bed, and picked up a package that lay there. She returned and stood in front of Richard. "We shall return to your kingdom, you and I. You are the King of England, and I am your wife. I will play my part and do my duty. You will be the knight that you so strive to be, the new King Arthur of our time." She sighed. "I fear that Anne may have left you, but the lady in Chartres will never be gone, not for you, and not for me."

She gazed above him as if thinking of something far away but only for a moment. "If I am to be as a nun, then I shall play my part well. I think it best that I see to those in your realm who are less fortunate, the poor, the widowed, the orphaned."

"They will benefit greatly from your patronage." Richard was sincere.

She handed him the package. "God only knows when we shall have an opportunity to speak like this again to one another. Please take this. I brought it with me with every intention to give it to you on our wedding day, but..." Berengaria did not finish.

Richard took the package from her and held it in his hands. Berengaria went to the door to leave, but suddenly turned around.

"You need not worry, my lord. I shall always remain your loyal and faithful wife." She left the room before he could respond.

When she was gone, Richard unwrapped the package and found in it a beautiful belt, an intimate gift meant for a lover. He laid it on the table in front of him, leaned back his head, closed his eyes, and rested his head on the top of the chair. Soon he found himself wondering if he would ever see Anne again, if she was in Chartres. It was true; she left him, and she did not return or communicate with him in anyway. He even heard rumors that she had taken Will and gone to Chartres after all, or that Castile was dead from a fever, and now Anne would consider marriage to Guy or worse. While these were only rumors, Richard knew one thing for certain; *she was not with him.*

Anne couldn't return to the letter from Philip until late that night. After the hustle of the day finished, she bid Will goodnight and went alone to her room. Ines, her new lady proved to be anything but adept at her task, and on more than one occasion Anne missed Marguerite. Tonight, she dismissed the girl just as soon as she could, and now she sat alone in her room reading the letter once again.

I am sure you are aware that France is still in need of a queen. I am finding it most difficult to pursue a marriage when there are so many issues of unrest in my kingdom and when my personal safety is so in question.

Dear Lady, I have resolved to put aside my search for a new queen for the time being. However, I shall always be ready to take up the quest again should you decide that Paris would make a good home.

No matter where you choose to make your home, you are ever in my thoughts and prayers, and I stand ready should you ever need me.

Your Most Humble Ally,
Philip

Anne gave a long sigh as she set down the letter. She found herself tempted to write back to Philip and accept his offer. Snatching a piece of parchment and a quill, she began to write.

My Most humble Ally,

Her thoughts raced. If she accepted Philip's offer, she knew that she and Will would be protected. She could go to Paris and be safe there. She could hide from Castile, from Mathias, from Guy, and she could even hide from Richard. She reasoned that if she were with Philip, then she would never have to see Richard again and she could be protected from the pain that meeting would bring. Seeing Richard again was what she feared. Or was it? Feeling the weight of confusion and frustration grip her, she continued to write.

Proceed to take up the matter with the pope.
Your humble Servant,
Anne Viscountess de Marseilles

It hardly seemed worth the parchment, for so few words, but

Anne did not know what else to say. She trimmed the parchment, sprinkled the pounce to prevent the ink running, folded the letter, and put her seal to it. Once finished, she looked at it a long time debating with herself whether or not to send it. Finally, she reached the conclusion that tonight she felt emotional and needed more time to think. This was an enormous choice with far reaching consequences. She needed to sleep on it rather than act rashly. Placing the letter securely in the small chest next to her bed, she blew out her candle.

Chapter Fifty-six

Anne fell asleep much faster than she anticipated, but her sleep was not restful. Soon she dreamt something she had dreamt before. Richard was atop his horse, ill and shaking from the fever. Snow fell, blanketing his form. Just as before, he headed into the black woods and others tried to stop him. Anne shouted his name as he passed. Turning, he looked at her, his face ashen and pale. Desperately, she tried to call out to him again, but her lips felt like lead, and she could not form the words. Richard rode into the woods and disappeared from view.

This time, Anne tried to go after him, but as she stepped into the wood darkness surrounded her. It enveloped her like the thick folds of a heavy cloak tightening around her. Gasping for breath, she struggled against the constriction, but to no avail.

Just as she was ready to give in, she heard a voice. She recognised it at once. Will yelled for her. With all her might, she screamed his name.

In the distance, she caught sight of Richard lying in a heap on the forest floor. He looked dead; his crown abandoned in front of him. Alternating, she called for Richard, then for Will as she thrashed about fighting against the darkness.

Someone shook. "Anne! Anne! Wake up!"

In confusion and trembling, Anne opened her eyes. Etienne stood above her. It took Anne a moment to get her bearings. While she looked around widely, Etienne gently wiped tears from her cheeks. "I was headed back from looking in on Will and could hear you screaming. I feared that somehow Castile had…"

"Will! Where is Will?" Anne grabbed at him.

"He is in his room sound asleep." Etienne reassured her.

Throwing back the covers, Anne leapt out of bed and rushed down the hall.

Etienne followed her but almost knocked Nanette to the floor. "What is all this commotion?" The nurse demanded.

Etienne gave the old woman a concerned look. "She was calling out for Richard in her sleep."

Nanette closed her eyes and nodded.

Anne opened the door to Will's room with care so as not to wake him. The two guards snapped to attention, but she silenced them with a finger to her lips. Lying on the floor, Sigurd and Nanna lifted their heads to investigate, but promptly laid them back down.

On the bed stand a night candle glowed. Nanette insisted one be left burning to ward off evil spirits. The illumination from the candle allowed Anne to see her son. The boy slept on his back, his arms and legs spread out. Will often slept this way, all sprawled out. As she approached him, Anne noticed his face looked so peaceful. With the tenderness of a mother, she gently pushed some of his dark curly hair away from his eyes. Will stirred a little, and Anne tucked the covers closer around him.

When she finished, she sat down in a chair next to the bed. Sigurd made his way over to her and placed his massive head on her knee. Stroking behind the dog's ears, she watched her son sleep.

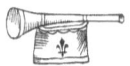

"Did you know that when Richard made the treaty with Saladin, he was deathly ill again?" Breton asked Bogis.

Bogis shook his head. "No. No one ever told me that."

"Yes, seriously ill. So ill in fact that they moved him across the bay to Haifa where he was under the care of the Hospitallers." Breton wanted them to appreciate the conditions in which Richard was forced to make the treaty. "Gentlemen, you must understand, Richard had very little choice. The contentions amongst the Christian factions made it impossible to win against the more united Saracens, his kingdom was in peril, and twice he took dangerously ill while in the Holy Land. He needed to go back to England, set his affairs in order. Only then he could return with a strong army." His throat dry from all the talking, Breton began to cough. "Later... later there would be others who would conveniently forget these facts."

"Here." One of the knights handed him the flask.

"Ah, thank you." Breton drank and then continued, "Jaffa was to go to Christian hands, but the town of Ascalon was to be destroyed and neither army would try to rebuild or occupy it for three years. Christians were allowed free passage and access to the Holy Sepulcher and would be allowed to exercise free commerce in the land. Richard agreed to the treaty, but he could not take an oath to uphold the terms. He was leaving and would be thousands of miles away. If the Christians remaining there chose to break the terms, he would not be held responsible. Henry of Champagne, now King of Jerusalem, Grand Master de Sable of the Templars, and the grand master of the Hospitallers swore to uphold the terms, and Saladin accepted this. Richard was anxious than ever to return home.

"And Anne had nothing to do with that?" Bogis smirked.

"Well, yes, Richard desired a reconciliation, but he wasn't even sure where she was. Every time he spoke with Gustave, her secretary swore that she had gone to Chartres."

"What I want to know is, did she ever send that letter to

Philip?" Bogis demanded.

Breton enjoyed the power he held over the eager men listening to the story. "Patience, my son. I will tell all." A wide smile spread across his face. "Now let me see. Where was I? Oh yes, the treaty was concluded in early September, and Richard did begin to recover. He sent the women on ahead at the end of the month with his knights accompanying them. Just as he promised Berengaria, they travelled straight to Rome. He followed ten days later.

It was dark, and for the most part, the city of Acre slept. A few shady individuals ventured out and about, the dregs of Acre society, the women of the night ready to do their part for the crusaders. In the harbor, a ship set out. As it passed by the Tower of Flies and slipped out to sea, a lone figure stood at the stern, wrapped in a cloak watching the city of Acre disappear. Richard was going home.

Baldwin joined him at the stern. Without Richard saying anything, Baldwin knew he thought about how different his departure was compared to his arrival. "My lord," Baldwin spoke to him. "I think it was wise of you to sail on a bus instead of a large galley."

"My enemies will be more likely to look for me on a galley." Richard leaned on the rail. "I am sure that the Templars below find it cramped, but it will have to do."

"If you ask me, I think they are concerned about traveling on the sea so late in the year. Sailing in October, even early October, has got them nervous." Baldwin wrapped his own cloak more tightly around himself.

"I have my reasons. I am trying to avoid those who are laying in wait for me, and since most ports will be closing soon, many of my enemies will not expect me until spring."

"You need not explain your reasons to me. I would not mind being in London by Christmas." Baldwin tried to smile, but the cool wind made it hard.

The last sight of Acre disappeared over the horizon, and as Richard watched it go he muttered, "Oh, Holy Land, I commend you to God. In His loving grace, may He grant me such a length of life that I May give you help as He wills. I certainly hope some time in the future to bring you the aid that I intend."

Baldwin laughed. "Will you just look at us?" He opened his cloak and showed the Templar costume he wore.

Richard opened his own cloak revealing his own Templar costume. "Who would have thought that the King of England would have to slink away disguised as a Templar?"

"Well, the warrior part of the Templar, that's understandable but..."

"...either one of us joining any kind of holy order." Laughing himself, Richard finished the sentence for Baldwin.

"Guess one could call it the perfect disguise then." Baldwin shut his cloak.

"Precisely." Richard agreed. "It was kind of Grand Master de Sable to suit us up with the proper gear and send a dozen Templars to accompany me." Richard tightened his cloak again and leaned on the rail looking down at the dark water below.

Baldwin leaned over. "My lord, you have been most secretive about our course, but now that we have departed, may I ask where we are going to put into port?"

"Baldwin, there are so few that I can trust, but you, you have always been one of them, and I thank you for that." Richard did not look away from the water.

"I would give my life for you if necessary." Baldwin sounded unusually serious.

Richard smirked at him. "Either that is rather telling of our friendship or the quality of your life. I am not sure which."

Baldwin remained serious. "My Lord, you have always been

a true, loyal, and might I say, generous friend."

"Well, to answer your question," Richard stood up straight, "after mulling it over for quite a while, I have come to the decision that we are headed to Marseilles."

Baldwin grinned. "Trading one war for another are we?"

Richard's jaw tightened. "Marseilles is the best option. Even if Anne is there, it is likely that she will refuse to see me. At least I know she will not try to slit my throat. Yes, the port of Marseilles is the safest option."

"Yes, sire."

Anne stayed mostly within the confines of the chateau. At first Will resisted, but once he saw that it was no use, he accepted his new boundaries and spent much of his time running with the dogs.

On a blustery afternoon, Abbot Mathias made his way to the chateau, troubled by the rumors of Castile and the fact that Anne hadn't attended Mass in weeks. Several times he attempted to see her, but Etienne informed him that she was occupied with business and could see no one. Today Mathias would try again. It wouldn't do for the Viscountess of Marseilles to hide herself away, even from the likes of Castile. A reward was posted for Castile, and he had not been seen or heard from since.

As Mathias rounded a corner and began to make his way uphill to the chateau, he noticed a group of returning crusaders. Pilgrims and Crusaders coming from the Holy Land became more prevalent in the city as of late. They brought with them news of the treaty.

Walking on, Mathias wondered how much of the news Anne knew. After all, she forbid Richard's name even to be spoken around her. Would Richard make for Marseilles, or would he leave Anne in peace? For a moment a thought entered his head. If Richard came, would Anne go with him? Mathias dismissed the thought, reassuring himself that she left Richard, and once Anne resolved to do something, she stuck to it.

A servant showed Mathias into the chateau and Etienne soon greeted him in the Great Hall. "Abbot, the Lady Anne is here at the moment, but I am not sure if she is able to see you. Would you be so kind as to wait here?" Etienne pointed to one of the large chairs sitting before the fireplace.

"Thank you." Mathias acknowledged Etienne but chose not to sit.

Etienne left the room and Mathias looked around unsure of just how persistent he was going to have to be if he wanted to see Anne today.

Lost in thought about Anne, Castile, and Richard, the sound of a low snarl caught Mathias off guard. Looking down, he saw a large mastiff growling. The animal moved closer and leaned up against the abbot. "Sigurd, here boy!" Will entered the room, and the dog bounded over to him.

"Good afternoon, Master Will. I have come to see your mother."

Will glared back at the abbot and Sigurd planted himself in front of the boy. Despite feeling awkward, Mathias decided to try to be polite with Will. "You have a new addition, I see."

"Two." Will answered him tersely.

"Oh, there are two of them?"

Narrowing his eyes, Will spoke again. "Yes, they were a gift to my mother from the King of France."

Mathias blinked rapidly. "I see. Yes, well, it is most important that I see your mother, Master Will."

Will folded his arms and puffed out his chest. "Sigurd does not like you, Abbot Mathias."

"I am sorry to hear that, especially as I have done nothing to cause Sigurd to dislike me."

Will did not change his stance. "Uncle loves my mother very much, and she loves him. He *will* return soon; have no doubt of that."

Mathias stepped back. "I… um… I am a man of the cloth, my boy."

"I am not your boy, nor am I your son!" Will did not shout but spoke through gritted teeth as Sigurd growled again.

"Sigurd!" Anne snapped from the doorway. She turned to Mathias. "I apologize. Mastiffs are lovely creatures but can be so loyal that it is hard to have company."

Mathias wondered how much of the conversation if any she heard. If she heard anything, she wasn't letting on that she did. "My Lady." He gave her a graceful bow. "I am glad to see you."

Anne joined Mathias by the fireplace and a second massive dog followed her. "Will, why don't you take Sigurd and Nanna somewhere to play, dear."

Will whirled around, whistled, and the two dogs followed him. Once he was out of the room, Anne turned to Mathias again. "He has become so attached to those dogs, and they to him."

The light from the fire caught the auburn highlights in Anne's hair just right, and it made her glow. Mathias took a deep breath. "I do not think your son cares for me."

"Will is… he is… well, I fear he feels that he must protect me." Anne rubbed at her left thumb with her right. "Circumstances have been confusing for him."

"I have come to see you because I am concerned about you." Mathias changed the subject to Anne.

"Me? Oh, I am fine, busy, but just fine."

"You have not come to Mass for weeks." Mathias reached out to touch her.

Anne moved away from him and sat in one of the chairs by the fire. "With Castile's whereabouts unaccounted for, I felt it best that Will and I remain close to the chateau."

Mathias sat down next to her. "I bring you news of Castile. They say he fled the region, and that he dare not show himself especially with the possibility of Ri…" Mathias stopped himself from saying the name. "… with so many returning from Crusade."

"Castile is a desperate man. He has nowhere to go, and I am afraid he will take desperate measures. I should have killed him when I had the chance, but I could not do it. I could only think about Will."

Mathias knew that despite what she said, Anne never would have actually killed Raymond of Castile. It was not in her to take another human's life. Still he felt uncomfortable to hear her talk about it. After a moment he asked, "Anne, why does Will dislike me so?"

"Do not be offended, Mathias. He is just very loyal to… Richard," she whispered the name. "He is the closest Will has had to a father."

"How much of our conversation did you hear?" Mathias looked Anne straight in the eyes.

"Enough."

"And do you harbor the same accusations as your son?"

She decided to be honest. "Nanette told me what you did when I left for Poitiers."

"I see."

"Why did you not tell me yourself?"

Mathias leaned forward his elbows on his knees and his head in his hands. "I was embarrassed." He took a deep breath. " I knew you would come back some day, that when you did you would be married, and so I thought that taking vows was the answer."

"Was it?"

He turned his head to look at her again. "Anne, I just want to see you happy and safe."

"Well, I am safe.

"But not happy."

Anne opened her mouth to answer him, but Mathias held out his hand to stop her. "Do not answer, Anne, my dearest, Anne." He took a long breath and looked around the room, "That night you held the feast in his honor here in this room, I studied the two of you, especially the king."

"Mathias, please," she begged.

He rose out of his chair and gestured to where Anne and Richard sat that night. "Clearly he loves you, Anne. He loves you, and I hate him for it."

Anne stood up and gently placed her hand on Mathias' extended arm, and he dropped it limply at his side. "I am sorry, Mathias."

Smiling at her, Mathias sighed. "Wishing cannot make a thing happen; sometimes even praying is futile."

Tears formed in Anne's eyes. "Time changes people." A tear rolled down her cheek.

Mathias cradled her face in his hands, wiping away the tears with his thumbs. "Anne, when you returned from Cyprus, you were broken. I cannot fix you. I cannot tell you what course to follow. I only know that we were not meant to travel the same path, you and I."

"You have always been a true friend. Thank you for that," she whispered.

"I am a friend that can help patch you up, but I cannot give you what you need. I will always be there to offer aid should you need it." He kissed her lightly on the forehead and turned to leave but stopped. "Something for you to think about… why is it that you still wear what you wear around your neck?" Mathias did not wait for her to answer; he took his leave.

Anne felt for the ribbon on her neck and pulled at it. In truth she had worn it for so many years that it became second nature to her. Now she thought about the ribbon and wondered that she had not felt the weight of it or the ring that dangled from it.

Chapter Fifty-seven

When Anne entered her room, Will and the dogs startled

her. Just as she opened the door, Will scooped up a piece of parchment from the floor. "Mother!" He jumped.

Anne noticed he tears in his eyes and saw that many items from the table lay scattered on the floor, including her casket where she kept her correspondences. The casket lay on its side and the letters scattered about. "Will?"

"I am sorry, Mother. I did not mean to. I waited here for you, and we got a little rambunctious." Will pointed to the dogs. "Sigurd knocked the table and now everything is all over the floor. I am sorry."

"'It's alright. It was an accident." Anne bent down. "Here, let me help you." She began to gather to letters together.

Will began to cry. "I am sorry, Mother."

"It is alright, Will." She tried to reassure him. She studied him for a moment and could tell he was not upset about spilling the letters.

"I know that I should not have been in here without your permission." Will tried to stuff a handful of letters back into the casket.

"Just a moment." She took the letters from him. "Now, how about you telling me what is really troubling you, son."

Will hesitated, then, to her surprise, he pulled out the letter from Philip where he hid it in his sleeve. Handing it to his mother, he apologized. "I am sorry it is so wrinkled now."

Sitting down on the floor, Anne took it from him and smoothed it out. "Did you read the letter Will?"

Will nodded. "Yes."

"Why?"

"I was curious." The boy shrugged.

Anne kept her temper. "Why did you try to hide the letter from me, Will?"

"Mother, why did you leave Uncle in the Holy Land? Are you going to marry King Philip?" Will blurted out as Sigurd and Nanna lay down beside them.

"Will, it is complicated, dearest. There really is not a simple answer, but you needn't worry yourself about such things." Anne reached out to pat his hand, but Will grabbed it away from her.

"Mother, I have the right to know! Stop treating me like a baby! I know what goes on between a man and a woman behind closed doors!" Will shouted at her.

Instinct made Anne want to punish the boy for his impudence, but she knew he was spoke out of frustration. "Will, how do you know what goes on behind closed doors, between a man and a woman that is?"

"Germaine told me." Will looked down at the ground.

"Germaine? The stable boy?"

"Yes."

"And what did Germaine tell you?"

"Well, actually, I saw Sigurd and Nanna doing something. We were in the stable and Germaine was there. He explained it to me." Will could not look at his mother, his face now red up to his ears.

"I see." Anne let out a sigh.

Will whispered, "To be honest, I was a little revolted by the whole thing."

Unable to help herself, Anne laughed. "Sorry, Will. I am not laughing at you, dear." She took a deep breath. "I am sorry you learnt about it in such a way."

"I did not believe Germaine, so I asked Etienne, and it turned out Germaine was right." Will rolled his eyes.

"Well, I see that you are becoming a young man, and I should be more honest with you." Anne touched his cheek. "I just did not want you to burden yourself."

"Mother, can I ask you some questions? I want you to be truthful with me." Will looked at his mother with searching eyes.

Looking into her son's eyes, Anne knew that he had left an era of innocence behind. She questioned her decision to withhold so much information from him. Something inside told her that he would grow up, and she needed to prepare him for whatever may come. "Alright, Will."

"That thing that people do behind closed doors, what happened with my father?"

The question surprised Anne, and she tried to deflect it with some humor. "Well, considering the Virgin Mary is the only one to conceive immaculately..."

One look at Will's face told her the joke did not work. Serious now, she spoke softly. "Will, I was staying at Poitiers with Richard. Richard went to deal with a rebellious vassal, and Raymond of Castile kidnapped me, married me, and forced himself on me."

Will let it all sink in for a moment. "Mother," he said, "I have another confession to make. I snuck out to see Raymond of Castile, but don't worry, he never saw me."

"Will!" Anne gasped.

"Let me explain. From a doorway I saw what happened the night he came to the chateau. I snuck into the Jewish quarter one night after dark and looked into Lugo's window. I knew it was him, because he looked so much like me." Will looked at his mother with trepidation. "I had to see him, I just had to. Please don't be angry with me Mother. I needed to see who my father was." Will began to cry.

"Oh, my dear son, come here." Anne took Will in her arms. "You could have been... that was dangerous. You mustn't do things like that. I could not bear to lose you."

Will pulled away from his mother. "Before Uncle Richard left, I begged him to let me be his son. I even promised to not want to become king. Now I know why he wouldn't, couldn't let me be his son."

Anne cried now. "Will, you are my son and the grandson of William Viscount of Marseilles. You come from a long line of a proud and noble family."

"But what of my father? Perhaps it would have been better

for you to have the marriage annulled and then I would truly be a bastard. Now I just feel like one."

"Do not ever say that, Will!" Anne took hold of his shoulders. "I have stay married to your father so that you could inherit Marseilles. You are not a bastard. The house of Castile is just as noble and proud as the house of Baux! Your grandsire was the King of Castile. He was a good man. He would be proud to call you his grandson; I know he would. It is not your fault your father is what he is. Neither one of us is to blame, and believe me, Richard loves you like a son, even more than some men love their real sons."

Will slid next to his mother. "Will I ever see Uncle Richard again? Will he come back?"

"I do not know." Anne put her arm around Will. "I left Richard because he married the Princess of Navarre, Berengaria, while we were in Cyprus. He has other obligations that he must meet now. I could not stay. By the way, I do not think you will be seeing as much of Abbot Mathias around either."

"What about King Philip?" Will pointed to the letter that now lay on the ground where Anne dropped it.

"Cousins." Anne smiled and shrugged. "Besides, I have other obligations, to you for example."

Contemplating their conversation, they both sat there. At length, Will turned back to his mother, "I am sorry I upset your desk."

"That is no matter." Anne got to her feet. Looking at the dogs she commented, "Well, perhaps Sigurd is going to be a father."

At the mention of his name, the dog took to his feet, and Nanna followed. Will patted one after another on the head. "I did promise Master More I would do some more Latin exercises if he let me take a rest from them for an hour. I think my hour is long up."

"Then, you better hurry back. I know neither one of us wants to face Master More when he's flustered." Anne winked at Will.

"Thank you, Mother." Will scooped up the pile of letters and set them on the table.

Anne spoke before her son could leave. "Will, I love you. Remember that."

"I will, Mother, and I love you too."

Once Will was gone, Anne placed the letters back in the casket. She found the letter that she hastily wrote to Philip. With a sense of relief, she tossed it into the fire and watched the flames consume her moment of weakness.

It was one of those days on the sea where the sky becomes so dark that it almost seems to be night. The little ship rolled back and forth on the waves as if it were nothing more than a large branch. While the storm raged outside, Baldwin, Blondel, and the Templars remained below deck trying to ride it out. "Have I ever told you how much I loathe sea travel?" Blondel was so nauseated, his face looked gray.

"No, I do not believe you have." Clenching his teeth, Baldwin continued, "Please do tell me once more."

Next to Baldwin, Gerard, the Templar in command, let out a snicker. "I take it you two have traveled together on more than one occasion."

Blondel looked up at Gerard. "Have you been on many sea voyages before, sir?"

Gerard nodded. "I must confess, it's not my favourite mode of travel either."

The ship shuddered violently as a large wave smacked it. "We cannot stay this course much longer." Baldwin mumbled to himself.

"The king chose it." Gerard shrugged.

"Well, I do not know about you, but I have been shipwrecked before, and it is an experience that I do not care to repeat." Baldwin stood up. "Someone must talk some sense into him. He will do no one good for anyone if he is dead." Baldwin headed above deck to find Richard.

Gerard stood and followed him. He was so tall that he was forced to crouch down to make his way around below deck.

Richard stood on deck close to the bow, his gray eyes scanning the horizon for any sign of hope the storm would relent. Clinging to a rope from the nearby rigging, Richard was drenched head to foot from a combination of rain and sea spray. His long hair matted to his head, and water dripped from his beard. He pushed hair out of his eyes as Baldwin approached him and took a firm hold of a rope. "Sire!" He shouted to be heard.

Wearing an odd expression, Richard turned and looked at Baldwin. He also nodded to Gerard as the Templar made his way on deck. "They say that Saint Anne is the patron saint of seafarers," Richard commented.

Baldwin took a deep breath. "I do not think Saint Anne favors us." He waited for Richard to reply, but he did not, so Baldwin continued, " My lord, we have no choice. We must turn back. We cannot reach Marseilles in this. If we do not turn back we will surely be shipwrecked and prey to any who wish to do your highness harm!"

Richard shook his head. "We are but five days, a week at the very most from Marseilles."

Gerard, added, "Yes, my lord, but we know that every port between here and Marseilles is packed full of men who either want you dead or wish to capture you. If we should be shipwrecked, we will be at their mercy. We should steer away from the storm, then, once it passes, continue on to Marseilles."

"I have been in worse storms than this!" Richard set his jaw.

Baldwin shouted. "When? When have you, my lord?" Baldwin quickly regained control of his temper but remained adamant. "Sire, we must turn around and steer clear of this storm."

An eerie smile spread across Richard's face. "At last you have reached your limit, eh Baldwin?"

"No! You know I would give my life for you if necessary, but here, now, it is not necessary!" Baldwin pleaded.

"Sire, it is my duty to keep you safe, and I believe that we must turn back." Gerard agreed with Baldwin.

The ship shuddered as another wave smacked it sideways, and the men held fast to their ropes until they regained their footing.

"Richard!" Baldwin dared address the king by his first name, even with Richard's cantankerous mood. "Richard, if you are going to Marseilles for a reconciliation, if you want to win Anne back, it would be a mite easier if you were alive."

Richard looked as though he would to strike Baldwin at any moment. Instead, he dropped his head in despair. Turning away from the men he looked back out at the sea again. Letting go of his rope, Richard looked heavenward. "Why? Why do you hate me? Why do you curse me so? What do you want of me?"

Baldwin was at a loss for words. In all the years, he had never see such a wild look in Richard's eye. Gerard stepped forward. "Sire, I believe the Lord wants you live and return to your suffering kingdom."

Richard looked at both men; his crazed expression faded. "Take us out of the storm," he commanded. Grasping the rope again, he murmured, "I hope you are right, Baldwin. I hope you are right."

Chapter Fifty-eight

"I'll tell you what happened." A voice groused from the back of the group listening to Breton. The men all turned to see who spoke. It was one de Mello, Philip's constable. Everyone was listening intently to the story, and no one noticed his arrival. "Richard shipwrecked anyway," he continued. "That's what happened. Now, where is the king?"

Breton stood up, placing himself in front of the door to the chapel. "The king is unavailable at the moment, sir."

"Unavailable, huh?" de Mello looked sour. "The castellan, Roger de Lacey, is wanting to speak to his highness. It seems he will not turn over the keys to the castle until he speaks with the king."

"The king will meet with the castellan as soon as he is available." Bogis now stood up to face the advisor.

Glaring at them, de Mello growled, "It is only matters of state, nothing important." He turned and walked away, adding as he left, "It's not like listening to a silly love story."

Breton watched the man go, and once he was gone, sat down in his chair again. "Well then, shall we not continue with the silly love story?"

"He is a disagreeable man," Bogis observed. "I should like you to continue, Father Breton." Bogis sat down as well, and the others around him seconded the sentiment.

"Regardless, de Mello was only partly correct. It is true Richard shipwrecked, yet it happened not once, but twice." Breton rubbed his forehead and then continued with his explanation. "The first time they shipwrecked near Communitas Ragusina. Richard purchased the favor of the locals with a sizeable donation to build a cathedral. Then, he hired a new boat from the town fathers and set out again. This time, he hoped to land on the coast of Hungary where he hoped to negotiate with the king. Alas, he was thwarted in this effort as well."

Baldwin stood next to Richard as he watched the sinking ship. They salvaged what they could, but now the group found themselves stranded on a coastline of muddy swamps and forest. At length Richard spoke. "Gerard, have you any idea where we are?"

Gerard stood ankle deep in the muck next to the king and Baldwin. "Not entirely, your highness." He looked around him sizing up the situation. "However, I do think we have overshot the coast of Hungary."

"I agree." Richard scratched at his beard. "Something tells me we are in the Holy Roman Emperor's territories, and that is not good for us."

"No indeed, my lord, it is not." Baldwin wrenched his foot and boot from the mud.

"Well, we cannot stay here." Richard sighed. "We shall have to find a way through this swamp. I do not see any other choice."

"Before we leave, what is our story? By now word may have spread that you are traveling as a Templar." Gerard shrugged.

"That is a good point, Gerard." Richard took a look at Baldwin and Blondel. All three of them let their hair grow long as well as their beards, hardly the look of the infamously clean-shaven Templars, more along the lines of a pilgrim returning from Crusade. This gave him inspiration. "Gerard, we *are* going to need to assume new identities. I am now a merchant named..." He snapped his fingers.

"Hugo," Blondel mumbled.

"Yes, Hugo. That will do. I am Hugo of Marseilles, and you are pilgrims and servants returning from the Holy Land. I just finished a large business transaction there, and I am on my way to Flanders to conclude another," Richard thought aloud.

Gathering what supplies they could, they shed their Templar costumes and began to pick their way through the swampy forest. They were fortunate enough to find a hermit to guide them. At last, they made their way to the village of Aquileia on the coast.

Aquileia, an ancient Roman town, sat at a crossroads from the coast to the Alps. Once there, Richard purchased horses and supplies for the journey north. He concluded that the best option would be to travel as swiftly as possible and head north to his brother-in-law, the Duke of Saxony's lands. If he could only reach Saxony, Richard knew he could obtain safe passage back to England.

The group reached a consensus as to who would travel with the king. They were well aware that by now news had spread of the number in their party, so they decided to split the large group into an increasingly smaller number as they traveled north. Each time the group split, the decoy group headed south or eastward in the opposite direction with someone dressed as the king. That person would spend large amounts of money in order to draw the attention to the decoy group and let Richard continue his journey.

Another problem they faced was the language barrier. Gerard went to the church and asked for help with this. The local monastery lent them a boy, Ioldan de la Pumerai, who could speak German.

The first decoy group set out for Venice while the rest headed north. The journey proved to be harsh as they made their way through the Alps in December. They stopped only to hire a guide to get them through the next leg of the journey or to spend the occasional night at an inn.

When they reached the mountain town of Villach, Gerard received word that the Duke of Austria now knew that Richard traveled in his territories and vowed to arrest him in retaliation for the flag incident at Acre. The duke sent bounty hunters after them. Gerard was now to leave Richard, Baldwin, Blondel, and the boy Ioldan. As the king's group prepared to leave town, Gerard spoke to Baldwin. "I did not expect to have to split the group so many times. There is still so much territory to cover before the king is safe."

"I find myself wishing we rode out the storm in the first place. We would be safely in Poitiers by now. So much for being in London for Christmas," Baldwin murmured.

"Take care to watch the King. I do not like the colour in his cheeks. He seems to be taking ill again," Gerard instructed him.

Baldwin nodded. "I too have noticed it. I am afraid he never fully recovered from the illness he suffered in Outremer."

Gerard slapped him on the shoulder. "Well, God's speed be with you."

"And you as well," Baldwin replied.

Richard and his small group made it only as far as Friesach before they encountered another threat from the Duke of Austria. The duke's men knew that Richard was in Friesach and were coming to arrest him. As an exhausted Richard and company saddled up instead of resting at the inn, as they so desperately wanted to do, Baldwin approached Richard. "My lord."

"Do not say it, Baldwin. I do not want you to do it." Richard shook his head.

Baldwin looked at his friend. There were dark circles around Richard's eyes, and underneath his bushy beard his face looked pale. "There is no other way."

"No."

Blondel joined them now. Baldwin continued. "Please listen to me, your highness. No one is going to be looking for a man traveling with a scribe-minstrel," he pointed to Blondel, "and a boy. They will be looking for a king and his knights."

Richard lowered his voice. "When they arrest you and find out that you are not me, they may torture you. The Duke of Austria will be furious. I am afraid of what he will do to you in retaliation."

Baldwin threw back his head and laughed heartily. "I mean no disrespect, but this coming from the man who insisted that I accompany the royal ladies and Anne on the same boat. No, the Duke of Austria does not scare me!"

Richard did not laugh with him. "Baldwin, I am being serious. You could be in real danger. If you were with me, then there is a chance that you would come out of this adventure unscathed."

Baldwin still smiled. "That is why it must be Blondel who accompanies you and not me. Besides, there is no certainty that I will be captured. I am appalled you have such little faith in me." He handed the reigns of Richard's horse to him. "Before you know it, we shall be in London, sitting by a roaring fire and laughing about how we duped the Duke of Austria."

Reluctantly, Richard took the reins. "Promise me that you will be careful, Baldwin."

"I am the epitome of chary." Baldwin gave a sweeping bow.

Richard mounted his horse, and behind him Blondel and Ioldan mounted theirs. Richard motioned for Baldwin to come closer and leaned down to him. "Baldwin, if I should not return… Anne…"

Shaking his head, Baldwin interrupted Richard. "*Now* you are asking me to do something dangerous. I already promised Andrew I would go to Marseilles and give Marguerite a token, and now you are asking me to face Anne as well. So much for concern for my safety."

Knowing Baldwin would only continued to jest, Richard decided he said enough, and instead of refuting, he sighed. "Baldwin, Baldwin. I shall see you in London then."

With that, Richard set out with the other two following him. Baldwin watched them ride off and take to the road that led to a dark forest beyond.

Chapter Fifty-nine

They rode hard, covering over three hundred miles since leaving Aquileia. By the time they reached the outskirts of Vienna, they had traveled over two hundred miles from Friesach in a little more than three days.

The frigid weather made the roads miserable, covered with

ice, snow, and mud. The fact that they traveled at all in the winter
would draw attention to them. Most people now huddled up close
to a fire, preparing for the Yule season.

As the snow started to fall harder, Richard kept one hand on
the reins. With his free hand, he pulled his cloak tighter around his
neck. He heard the sound of Iolan's horse snorting behind him, and
he thought about the boy, not much older than Will. To Richard's
surprise, the boy never complained about their state.

Richard's horse stumbled on an icy patch, but regain its
footing. The jarring motion caused a wave of pain to shot through
his body. Richard's knew the fever was back. It became hard to
even hold onto the reins because his fingers and body ached so.
For the past several miles, Richard tried to find a less painful
riding position. Right now he found it difficult to even sit up
straight, so he leaned forward a little onto the neck of his horse as
they continued toward Vienna.

They planned to skirt Vienna and travel onward toward
Moravia and safety, but by the time they reached Erdberg, just
outside Vienna, Blondel knew Richard was too sick to travel. At
the first inn they came to that looked decent, Blondel stopped.
Quickly he dismounted and went to Richard who seemed to roll off
his horse rather than dismount. The innkeeper met them in the
courtyard. "We seek food, and lodging," Blondel spoke up and
Ioldan translated.

Ioldan added, "This is my master, Hugo of Marseilles, and
his scribe. We are on our way to Cologne."

The innkeeper, stunned that anyone should be traveling in
this weather, nodded and motioned for the trio to follow him. He
led them up a flight of stairs to a room where several straw pallets
were stacked against a far wall. There was a small table with a
bench on each side and a fireplace opposite the pallets. Not
expecting anyone, the innkeeper had not lit a fire and the room felt
chilly. On the wall opposite from the door, a little window whistled
as the wind whipped through it. This was hardly the place to

accommodate a king.

As the innkeeper eyed them, Blondel helped Richard to one of the benches. Richard reached under the cloak and pulled a pouch of money out, handing it to Blondel who then tossed it to the innkeeper. The innkeeper caught the pouch. "You shall be well paid," Blondel said to the man.

The man opened the pouch and looked at Blondel with suspicion. He spoke to Ioldan who replied in German. They exchanged words for a moment, then the inn keeper nodded and spoke what Blondel knew to mean, "Yes, yes, naturally."

When the innkeeper left the room, Ioldan translated to his companions as they both helped Richard onto a pallet. "He said he never saw coin like that before, and I told him that my master just finished a large business transaction in Messina, and that we were headed to Cologne to complete another. I also, told him that my master needed rest and quiet. He is coming back to light the fire."

As if it were planned, there came a knock on the door and Ioldan opened it to let in the innkeeper in. The man eyed the trio then lit the fire. When he finished, he turned to Ioldan pointed at Richard and spoke gruffly. Then left the room.

"What did he say?" Blondel questioned the boy.

"Your master better not die." Ioldan responded.

Ioldan approached a butcher's stall in the market. The proprietor, a veteran of Crusade, waited for him. For several days now the boy had come and purchased food. The fact that the boy was a stranger did not attract the man's attention; it was the fact that the boy paid in strange gold and made unusual requests for food, like two entire chickens in one day. Granted, it was Christmas time, but only a nobleman would be eating such a feast, not a trio of travelers. He harbored suspicions about the boy and the story he told. The butcher greeted Ioldan. "Well boy, have you come to spend more of that lovely gold of yours this morning?"

Ioldan confidently smiled at the man. "Why, yes. I have."

"Good. Let me see. Dare I hope you would like the same thing as yesterday?"

"No, my master is only in need of one bird today."

The butcher looked disappointed, but set to work preparing the boy's order. "I see. And how is your master?" He handed the bird to the boy.

"My master is doing much better. He should be able to ride again within a few days and we will be off to Cologne," the boy replied.

"Traveling at this time of year and so close to Christmas?" The butcher clicked his tongue.

"My master has important business." The boy handed the butcher the payment of gold.

"I shall miss you master's gold very…" The butcher stopped abruptly as something caught his eye, a pair of gloves dangling from the boy's belt. The gloves bore a crest on them, a crest that the butcher recognised. He saw that crest when he served Duke Leopold in Acre. He began to speak again rather briskly, "…much. Well, good day to you then."

Once the boy left, the butcher hastened off in the opposite direction.

Richard lay on his pallet. The days of rest did him good and strength returned to his body. He was alone in the room, as no other travelers came to the inn, Blondel sat down stairs at the hearth, and Ioldan at the market.

Thinking if he could get just a little more sleep he could be well enough to ride in the morning, he closed his eyes. Only about fifty miles remained before Moravia where there would be allies who would help him get to his brother-in-law. Only fifty miles to safety, surely he could make that ride.

Just as Richard drifted off to sleep, a noise woke him. Slowly he realized that there were raised voices outside the inn. He sat up. The voices came again only louder. Peering out of the little window, he saw that around two-dozen armed men gathered outside.

Richard sprang to his feet and rummaged through what baggage there was in the room. Luckily, they still possessed a pilgrim's cloak, and Richard threw it round his shoulders and made for the main floor.

Once he reached the kitchen, he looked around to assess the situation. The men were still outside. They seemed to be hesitant to come in and this bought him time. Looking around, he noticed a bird on the spit over the fire, so Richard ran to it, turned it like he was a mere scullery boy. "My lord!" Blondel hissed at Richard from a far dimly lit corner of the room.

Richard shook his head. "Stay out of sight, Blondel!"

The door burst open as the armed men pushed their way past the innkeeper. The lead knight, dressed in a yellow and black tunic, shouted at the innkeeper. The innkeeper just shook his head and replied firmly. Richard could understand the words, *templar* and *merchant* being used by both men.

With sword drawn, the knight strode to Richard at the fire and shouted at him. Richard feigned deafness and continued to turn the spit. With all his might, the knight shoved Richard, knocking him to the ground. Richard stood and dusted himself off as the man continued to screech German at him. Pointing to his ears and shaking his head, Richard still tried to convince them he was deaf.

The knight turned and shouted something to his companions, then one of them brought forward Ioldan. Two men dragged the boy to the fireplace while the knight grabbed a poker from it. He stuck it into the flames, and as he did so he spoke to the boy with a sickening tone that made it possible for Richard to understand.

Slowly the knight withdrew the poker with a red hot tip. He motioned for the men to bring the boy closer. Putting the poker right up next to the boy's face only inches from his eyes, he spoke again, but this time he spoke in Latin and Richard could understand him clearly. "Now boy, where is the merchant you call Hugo of Marseilles?"

Richard could stand it no longer. "Leave the boy alone!" He snapped.

As the man dropped the poker back into the fire, several men rushed forward to grab Richard, but he eluded their grasp, partly because of fierce reputation. Richard drew his sword, and the leader drew his again as the men froze in place. "We know who you are, and you are to be arrested."

"On whose authority?" Richard demanded.

"Duke Leopold of Austria. You are trespassing on his lands, and therefore you will surrender yourself!"

"I will not!"

"In England you may be considered a hero, but here you have many crimes to answer for." The leader still stood ready to thrust his sword if necessary.

Richard thundered at him, "Crimes? You impudent whelp! What crimes do I have to answer for to the likes of you?"

"The duke commands that you be arrested and…"

Richard cut him off. "I will not surrender myself to such as lowly man as you. Despite my alleged crimes I am a king, and as such, I will only surrender to the duke himself!"

"I am to bring you to the duke. These are his orders and *you* are not *my lord*," The knight sneered.

"Mark me, my patience is wearing thin. Now, I have hidden on my person some poison of the most powerful nature. You and I both know that I am more valuable to your master alive than am I dead. The moment you or your men try to remove me, I will take it and you will have nothing but a dead body to deliver to the duke." Richard slyly grinned.

"This is a ruse."

Richard gave a fake sigh. "Perhaps, but is it worth the risk to you personally?"

The solider hesitated for a moment then relaxed his stance slightly. Without taking his eyes off Richard, he commanded, "Send for the duke and hurry!"

Richard sheathed his sword. "You have my word as a sovereign and a solider for Christ that I will not try to escape." He sat down at one end of the table in the main room.

In the dark far corner of the room, the Austrians did not see the man hidden in the shadows.

At length, word came that the Duke of Austria was coming down the street. "Well," Richard rose from his seat. "Let us go to your master. Lead the way."

Richard followed the men outside, through the courtyard, and up the street. He walked with his head held high and enjoyed the palpable sense of fear the Austrians had. In the distance, he saw the duke coming on horseback. When the duke saw Richard, he too dismounted and strode toward his prisoner.

They met and the King of England surrendered his sword to the Duke of Austria.

Part Five:

Lord of All

Chapter Sixty

"Richard spent the night at the duke's palace in Vienna under heavy guard. The next morning Leopold began writing a flurry of letters to the Holy Roman Emperor, and sent Richard to his stronghold at Durnstein. Built of dry stone above the Danube River, it is indeed properly named, " Breton explained. He gave the group another of his knowing looks. "The soldiers sent to escort Richard were not told his identity. It would seem that his reputation frightened those who were sent to arrest him, and they almost did not do their job."

Bogis smirked and could not help but think to himself that he understood how those men felt. Just look how long it took them to capture Richard's castle, and the man had been dead for several years now.

"I can just see it in my mind's eye," Breton interrupted Bogis' musings. "Richard traveling to that castle in the middle of winter, the snow laying a blanket of white on them as they climbed higher and higher, and him still sick with fever. He arrived at Durnstein on Christmas Day, the very day he meant to be in London. In London a spectacular display of God, lights of all colours flashed in the northern sky, and many took it to mean an ill omen for the King."

Berengaria and Joanna remained in Rome. They took up residence in some apartments there and waited for word from Richard. Christmas came and went. Joanna did not know whether to be worried that something happened or to be annoyed that he did not sent for them.

The royal ladies rarely ventured out. They were under the protection of the pope, but still they feared for their safety. On occasion, an old peddler broke the monotony when he brought his goods to them for their perusal. Today he visited the royal ladies again.

Joanna and Berengaria entered the room where the old peddler laid out his wares on a table. At first nothing seemed to catch the eyes of the royal ladies. Joanna ran her finger over some yardage of silesian cloth. Behind her Berengaria gasped, and Joanna turned to see what treasure she found. "What is it, dear?"

Berengaria wore a twisted expression on her face. "Where did you get this?" she demanded of the peddler.

"Your highness has impeccable taste." He smiled at her.

Berengaria repeated herself, "Where did you get this?"

"Let me see. Ah yes, this belt just came in from the north, your highness." The peddler replied with a little bow.

As she sank to the floor, Berengaria cried out, "This belt belongs to my husband, and I made it."

After Richard's capture, Blondel searched the items left in their room. The Austrians carried off most anything of value. They stole the money and even took the great seal of England. Much to his relief, Blondel found his lute only slightly scratched under one of the straw pallets. Also Blondel carried some gold in his own pouch. He looked for the boy, Ioldan but never found him.

Blondel was always favored by Richard's patronage. He was never forced to travel from place to place singing to earn his keep. Now he was on his own, so he made his way into Vienna where he was sure that Leopold took Richard. Blondel decided to use the story that he was a traveling troubadour who had come to this part of the world to learn from the great minnesingers.

Once in Vienna, Blondel struck a bargain with an innkeeper to entertain the guests in exchange for lodging. He used this time to study the language and listened to the gossip of the travelers. At last he learnt a great lord was held prisoner at Durnstein Castle, and he set out to find Richard.

Philip's nerves were fraying, so he decided to spend the day hunting. He needed a diversion from the constant worry Richard would appear any day now. Careful to let everyone know that no matter where he went, he went armed, Philip increased the number of sergant-at-arms, who accompanied him. In his heart Philip knew that he was in no real danger from Richard, but his charade became so convincing that at times he believed it himself.

The hunting that day was successful. After stalking it for two hours, Philip killed a large stag. Even the weather seemed to smile down on them with a touch of spring in the air.

Around midday they stopped to eat. Norbert had stayed at the palace, but now came to join the king's party. At the commotion Philip's bodyguards sprang into action. "It is only Norbert, you fools." Philip laughed at them.

"Your highness, this message, and this casket came for you. It is most urgent." Norbert handed Philip a letter.

"Urgent enough to interrupt my dinner and my sport?" Philip snatched it from him. "It is from the Holy Roman Emperor. What in heaven's name could he want with me?" Philip opened the letter and walked away, so he could read it in private.

Henry by the Grace of God, Emperor of the Romans and ever august to his beloved and special friend Philip, the illustrious King of the Franks, We have thought it proper to inform your

nobleness by means of these presents that while the
enemy of our empire and the disturber of your
kingdom, Richard King of England, was crossing the
sea for the purpose of returning to his dominions, it so
happened that the winds brought him into our hands.

Philip put one hand on top of his head, let out a hoot, and danced a jig. "The king has gone mad!" one of his confounded bodyguards whispered a bit too loudly.

Philip turned around to the astounded group. "He is captured! He is captured!" He kissed the letter and dropped to one knee, shouting to the heavens, "Thank you, God, thank you!"

"My lord?" Norbert questioned.

"See here, Norbert." Philip pointed to the letter. "The Emperor has captured Richard, and there is more! He goes on to tell all about how he was captured." Philip skimmed the letter. "Oh, oh! Listen to this! He was discovered at an inn—an inn of all places—an inn next to the stable where Leopold keeps his hounds! Oh Norbert, can you imagine the humiliation? What I would have given to have seen Richard's face!"

"Your elation shows," Norbert raised his eyebrows.

"Of course it does, you silly old fool. Now, there is so much to be done. I must write the Emperor back—oh, and John! Oh, he will be thrilled to hear this news." Philip mounted his horse then turned back as if he were speaking to someone in particular, but no one could tell who for certain. "I will write to Richard. Yes, I believe I will even write Richard—I will denounce him and declare war on him." He turned his horse and rode off.

Norbert scooped up the small casket, and one of the sergant-at-arms commented to him, "I wonder what's in there."

"Nothing that could be better than the gift the king was just given," Norbert replied.

Richard looked out from his window over a cliff and the river below. He knew that he was given this room in Durnstein to make an impression. There was no better room in all Austria to show the hopelessness of his condition and break his spirit. However, he resolved to never let his captors see him as anything other than calm, optimistic, jovial, and the epitome of chivalry. Just as the castle holding him was meant to make an impression, Richard would make an impression on those who held him.

From the moment he sat down and waited for Leopold at the inn, Richard began planning. He would not try to escape. There was no honor in it. He would, however, use diplomacy and manipulation to get himself out of this mess. Richard also resolved that once free he would do whatever it took to reconcile with Anne.

A noise outside interrupted his thoughts and desiring to see the source, he knocked on his door until one of his guards threw it open. Richard stepped outside barred from going further. Guards led a group of three men down the corridor. The first two were templars followed by Baldwin. Richard grinned. "It is about time you ladies got here!"

Baldwin looked up at the sound of Richard's voice. His badly beaten face twisted into a smile. "Ah, yes! I was trying out a new visor. Do you like it?"

"I think it suits you!" Richard laughed.

"Well, if you think this is good, you should see what I gave to the other man." Baldwin passed Richard now straining against his guards to turn around and continue the conversation.

"When you get a moment, you must come by my room and try some of this Austrian wine. It is like nothing I have ever tasted," Richard called after him.

"Count on it!" Baldwin's voice echoed down the hall as he went out of sight.

Richard just chuckled to himself, gave the guards a friendly wave, and retreated back into his room, closing the door behind him.

The sight of Baldwin, no matter how badly he looked, gave Richard some peace. At least he knew Baldwin was alive, and the fact that Baldwin was a noble meant that he was worth a ransom. He would be taken care of to a point. As for the two templars, once it was sorted out that they were templars, they would be freed. It would not do for anyone to keep a templar hostage. Richard was certain with some clever talk, he could see to Baldwin's release very soon.

The door to the royal ladies' apartment burst open and in stepped a brightly dressed young man who announced, "His Holiness, Pope Celestine."

With a stiff gait, the pope entered. "My dears, I came as soon as soon as I could. How may I, a lowly servant of Christ, be of assistance?" The words were full of humility, but not the voice.

"Thank you, holy father." Joanna curtsied and kissed his outstretched ring. "You have no idea how much your kindness means to us at this time."

Berengaria sat in a chair weeping, but somehow made it to her feet and greeted His Eminence likewise.

"Yes, I am sure. I came to you because I feared it was not safe for you to leave your abode." He put his arm around Berengaria and guided her back to the chair where she buried her face in a kerchief.

"Poor thing." He turned back to Joanna. "I have excommunicated both Leopold of Austria and the Holy Roman Emperor, Henry Hohenstaufen. It seems they have reached an agreement. King Richard is to be turned over to Hohenstaufen, and in exchange Leopold is to receive half of whatever ransom is raised." The pope's face flushed red with anger. "There is no justification for any man to interfere with a solider of God returning from Crusade. It is truly deplorable!"

"We are in shock, as your holiness can see." Joanna motioned toward Berengaria. "Please excuse my sister-in-law. I am sure that your holiness understands she is beside herself."

"Naturally, naturally."

"Would you care to have a seat, holy father?" Joanna asked.

The pope shook his head. "No, my dear, I am afraid I cannot stay long. I just wanted to check in on your highnesses, and to let you know that I have made arrangements for you."

Joanna raised her eyebrows. "Arrangements?"

"Yes. A contingent of my men will take you to Marseilles, where ..."

"Marseilles?" Berengaria whined as she looked up at him, then broke into a fresh burst of sobs.

"Marseilles is the safest port, you must understand that my child. It would not do to have you two captured as well as your husband."

"You are most generous, holy father. Marseilles will do. Pray, continue," Joanna intervened.

"The King of Aragon is to meet you in Marseilles. He will escort you to the Count of Toulouse who will then get you safely to Poitiers."

"My family has a rocky history with the Counts of Toulouse," Joanna whispered.

"Yes, child, but things are being managed. Count Raymond of Toulouse will receive his long desired annulment if he will see you safely to Poitiers. He will not receive that annulment until I am assured you are in Poitiers."

"Yes, your holiness." Joanna nodded. She despised the thought of having to go through Marseilles but understood that it was the best option.

"Now, my dears, I must leave you. I still have some final arrangements to make before you can leave. You will not be leaving until the ports are open, and I am sure that the King of Aragon is underway." He excused himself.

"Thank you again for your kindness, holy father. We shall never forget it." Joanna kissed his ring.

"Fear not, God will be with you." He gave her a parting smile and left.

Chapter Sixty-one

Nanette hobbled past the doorway. As she did, she gave a sideways look at the figure in the room. Etienne sat at his desk bent over a letter. Nanette stopped, turned back, and entered the room without waiting to be asked. "You look troubled."

Etienne nodded. He motioned for Nanette to take a seat as he got up and shut the door behind her. "I have troubling news, Nanette."

"It must be troubling if you are shutting the door." Nanette settled herself in a chair.

Etienne resumed his position at the desk. "This message is from the pope himself. He asks that the King of England's wife and sister be given safe harbor in Marseilles. Their stay is not intended to be long, for the King of Aragon is to meet them here and escort them to Toulouse."

"Surely Anne would not turn them away," Nanette scoffed.

"No, no indeed she has not. She instructed me to assure the pope that they will be welcome here. It did not make her too happy though." Etienne sighed.

"Do not fear, I will have a talk with our Anne and make sure that she is not sullen and irritable." Nanette smiled at him.

"It is not that." Etienne shook his head. "There is more in the letter, more that I did not tell her."

"Is there now? Are you going to keep the secret from me as

well, or am I to be your confidant?" Nanette winked.

"Nanette, King Richard was shipwrecked and captured by either the Duke of Austria or the Holy Roman Emperor. I am not sure which."

"I see." Nanette furrowed her already wrinkled brow. "This is troubling news indeed. What made you decide not to tell her?"

"I began to, but I barely got out the first part of his name before she turned on me and drove me from the room." Etienne shrugged.

"Pooh-pooh. I shall tell her then. She shan't behave that way with me!" Nanette made to get up.

Etienne stopped her. "Wait, Nanette. I have been thinking about it. I am not certain that she really needs to know what was in this letter. You see, the ports are all still closed for the winter and then there's the fact that the King of Aragon must be underway before the pope will send the women. It could be months before the royal ladies are to arrive here. Who knows? Perhaps the pope does not have correct information. There are rumors swirling all over regarding the King of England whereabouts." Etienne folded the letter back up as he spoke. "Even if he was captured, he is worth more alive than dead, and by then I am sure there will have been some sort of ransom agreement reached, and he will be free."

"I am afraid Anne is still very much in love with King Richard. She should…"

"… That is exactly why we should not worry her yet," Etienne interrupted. "Let us wait and see how this plays out. Then, if necessary, we will break the news to her as gently as possible. I do not want any of the servants gossiping about this; Will does not need to overhear it."

"Very well, Etienne. It shall be so for William," Nanette agreed.

Over the next week, Blondel made his way to Durnstein

Castle and was accepted into the court there as a minnesinger. At first the castellan thought having him there would be a nice way to entertain the prisoners, but after a solid tongue lashing from his wife, he decided to keep the Blondel as his—or rather his wife's—personal entertainer. As a minnesinger Blondel enjoyed a certain amount of freedom in Durnstein, yet he was always careful when exploring not to get caught in a questionable area. It did not take him long to learn where the secret great lord was kept. He also learnt that two templars were released and that another noble was held hostage in the castle.

Blondel determined to discover if Richard was there. He studied the guards, learning who was stationed where, when, and which of them would be the easiest to befriend. Fortunately the guard, Franz, who Blondel pegged for the easiest to get information from, showed a fondness for music. Blondel waited for a night that the castellan retired early and Franz was on duty. Arming himself with his lute and plenty of wine, Blondel made his way to the hall outside the room.

"Here you are, good fellows." Blondel handed the guards the bottle. "Have a drink on me, or two, or three if you like." After having now spent several months in Austria, Blondel had a good command of the language.

Franz grinned as he took the bottle from Blondel. He was older and thinner than his counterparts, but even still, Blondel noticed that he knew how to carry himself with smooth determined movements. This man could separate his head from his shoulders just as easily as he took the bottle. In watching the man for a moment, Blondel noticed that the sword of the old guard hung on his left side, but he always held the bottle, and for that matter anything that he had ever seen him hold, with his left hand. He remembered seeing Marshal do the same thing. It dawned on Blondel—he kept his sword-hand free. While friendly, this man was truly not one to take lightly. *I must be cautious*, Blondel admonished himself.

Blondel sat himself down on a bench in the hallway, and let out a long and loud belch. They all chuckled. "This evening's supper decided not to allow me to sleep, so I thought I would come keep you gentlemen company."

"It is just another long night in front of this door," Franz grumbled and took a swig of wine. After swallowing he continued, "Honestly, he is sleeping in there, I don't know why it takes three of us to guard the door. He is not going anywhere. Here," he passed the bottle to his partner Rolf.

"Who?" Blondel picked at the strings on his lute.

"The prisoner." Rolf was gruffer than Franz and his hands were wrapped in mitts even though it was not cold in the corridor.

"Oh, well yes, that would make sense." Blondel returned to the notes on his lute.

"Well, I for one am glad you are here, minnesinger It gets dull just sitting here night after night. I welcome a song." Franz disregarded his partner's sour tone.

"I would be happy to oblige." Blondel played them a couple of lively tunes that he found popular with this court.

When he was finished with his second tune, the youngest guard they called Peter reached for the bottle and took a long drink while Rolf snorted for another song.

Feeling that he was gaining their trust, Blondel played a tune that was on the randy side and sang along. Even Rolf found it funny enough to laugh. Upon finishing this tune, Blondel went back to picking at his instrument and attempting conversation. "You do not think that we are keeping the prisoner awake in there, do you?"

"Aw, who cares?" Peter finally spoke. "Do you know who is in there, minnesinger?" The man's faced was flushed from the wine.

"No, only that he is supposed to be a great lord." Blondel did not look up from his lute.

"It doesn't matter who is in there. We are out here and it is our duty to guard who is in there." Rolf made it clear to the others not to say the name.

"Oh, what does it matter? By now…" Franz started.

"Enough!" Rolf shouted.

Blondel chuckled.

"What do you find so funny?" Rolf demanded.

"Oh, I am sorry, gentlemen. I just find it rather funny that you would think that I…" He laughed again, pretending to be drunk from the wine. "Really, I am just a wandering minstrel who goes from place to place singing for my supper. I could care less who you have behind that door. It does not affect me."

"Well, just down the hall there," Peter pointed, "the King of England's right hand mate is rotting away. There's another trio of guards down there and they don't have anyone playing 'em music to pass the time."

"Enough, enough." Franz gulped more wine from the bottle. "Play on man. They can find themselves a minnesinger. We got us one here."

Blondel's mind was racing, and he hardly knew what he was playing. "Let me see," he said aloud. "What would you boys like to hear?"

"Anything, just play." Peter took the bottle from Franz.

Blondel strummed a few chords and thought hard. He kept muttering about songs, while trying to think. He knew that as long as Rolf remained there, he would not get any more information from the other two. However, he now knew that Baldwin was there. Perhaps Richard was not the one behind that door; it was Gerard or another templar. He needed to know for sure. Then an idea struck him. "Ah, yes, I think I have the perfect song for you gentleman. This is one I have not played for a long time." He took up his lute fully and played a verse before he began to sing.

> *Your beauty, lady fair,*
> *None view without delight;*

But still so cold an air
No passion can excite;
Yet this I patient see
While all are shunn'd like me.

Blondel stopped singing but played more on his lute. It was the song that Richard wrote to Anne at Vezelay when they fought. Blondel contributed to the writing, and he knew this song very well. He also knew that Richard would know this song, and if he was on the other side of the door and could hear it, then the king would know he was there.

Blondel brought the song to an end instead of singing the next verse. "Sorry gentleman, I do not feel much like playing the next verse. It reminds me too much of a woman I know—or knew."

"Minnesinger, why'd you have to go and play something like that for? I enjoyed your others much more." Franz frowned. "Can't you play something' a little more . . . Well, you know."

"I will do so." Blondel almost began another song when a piece of parchment shot out from underneath the door.

"What's this?" Rolf grabbed it.

"He's never done that before." Peter's sleepy eyes snapped back to life.

"Let us see it." Franz snatched it from Rolf. "I can't read it."

"May I?" Blondel questioned.

"You read?" Rolf looked him up and down.

"I can." Peter took it from Franz. He looked at it. "It's in French or something."

"Gentleman. I *am* from France." Blondel sighed.

"Alright, but no tricks now," Rolf agreed.

"You have my word." Blondel took the parchment and read it aloud.

No nymph my heart can wound

If favor she divide,

And smiles on all around

Unwilling to decide;

I'd rather hatred bear

Than love with other's share.

It was the second verse of the song, the one that Blondel did not sing. Only Richard knew the second verse, and now Blondel knew for certain that Richard was behind that door. "It appears your prisoner has suggested some song lyrics for me," He pronounced to the waiting guards.

"Well, I for one can't stand another song whining about a woman." Peter sat back down.

"In truth, I think the wine has worked its magic on me, and I find that I am now sleepy, gentlemen." Blondel tried to make an excuse and hoped they would not catch on to his ruse.

"We have kept you here long enough, minnesinger." Franz clapped Blondel so hard on the shoulder that he almost tripped.

"Then I shall leave you with a parting song." Blondel took up his instrument one last time and repeated the song the to let the King know that his message was received. This time though, Blondel did not sing the words; he strolled away playing the last of the chords.

Early the next morning, Blondel made his excuses to the castellan and bid farewell to Durnstein, but not before he overheard some important information. As he waited to take his leave of the castellan, he listened in on a conversation where the castellan and a sergeant-at-arms discussed the fact that Leopold and Hohenstaufen reached an agreement, and the prisoner was to be taken to Speyer to meet with the Emperor.

As soon as he could, Blondel set out to find Richard's brother-in-law, the Duke of Saxony.

Chapter Sixty-two

Eleanor did not felt right all day. Something seemed to gnaw at her, but she was unsure what. Sullenly she sat looking out her window down at the courtyard below, wondering why she felt so off. She did have a great deal on her mind. Trying to stay one step ahead of John and Philip proved strenuous— and then the constant worry about Richard. She told herself it was no wonder she felt ill at ease with all the stress. Marshal burst into the room, quite uncharacteristic of him. "Your highness, there is a messenger here from the Bishop of Rouen."

"The Bishop of Rouen?" Eleanor tilted her head. "Well, show him in then. Show him in."

The messenger burst through the door almost before she got the words out. "Your most gracious highness." He knelt before her. "I come from the Bishop of Rouen, and I bring news." His eyes were wide as he paused to catch his breath. "The Bishop *intercepted* some letters meant for the King of France. These letters told of the whereabouts of the king, your son."

Afraid of hearing the worst, Eleanor braced herself, determined to keep her composure no matter how devastating the news. "Go on."

"My lady, King Richard was taken captive by the Holy Roman Emperor and Leopold, Duke of Austria."

"Captured?" Eleanor repeated the word.

"I am afraid it is true. The Bishop is certain it is true."

"They captured him? How? Where?" Eleanor sputtered

The messenger produced a letter and handed it to the queen. "My lord Bishop sent this for you. It is a letter explaining everything he knows, along with a copy of the letter which he intercepted from the Holy Roman Emperor to King Philip. William Longchamp, King Richard's co-justiciar, as you know, was already in Normandy and has set out to Austria to negotiate for the release of the king."

"Does he know where Richard is?" Eleanor demanded.

The messenger shook his head. "I am afraid not for certain, your highness. He reasoned that it best to head straight for the emperor's court."

"Yes, yes. I suppose that is the best option, for the time being." Eleanor nodded. "I will need time to review these letters, and then I shall need you to carry my response back to the bishop."

"Yes, your highness." The messenger rose and gave her a bow. Marshal escorted him from the room.

Eleanor read the letters from the Bishop of Rouen, and took a moment to think the situation through before composing a response. Once she wrote her response, her next move would be to begin raising funds for a ransom. At first she thought it might be prudent to keep this a secret, but she knew that John must know by now. He would be gathering his supporters. It would be best to rouse the English people to come to the aid of their king and not to delay a moment. The sooner the people had their hearts into the cause of rescuing their king, the less likely they were to support John.

Thanks to Blondel, Henry of Saxony got word to England and Richard's co-justicar, William Longchamp as to where to find Richard. Longchamp made his way to the Emperor's court at Speyer. Leopold's men took Richard to Hohenstaufen's to be turned over to Emperor's custody. It was the twentieth of March. Richard kept meticulous track of the dates in his head. His hair and beard were long as he had not shaved since leaving Acre. He wished to trim his beard, but he wasn't allowed the proper implements. It was ragged. The fact that he was being moved gave Richard hope. The more they moved him the better. After a sparse breakfast, Richard had an audience with Hohenstaufen.

The Emperor sat in a hall decorated with golden ornaments, and intricate tapestries on a throne atop a raised dais so that he would be looking down on those before him. The fickle spring weather compelled Hohenstaufen to wear fur-lined robes. His icy blue eyes studied the prisoner brought before him.

As Richard entered, Hohenstaufen dismissed all those around him except the two armed guards who stood on either side of Richard. Hohenstaufen looked down on Richard. "So this is Richard, by the grace of God, Duke of the Normans and Aquitanians, Count of the Angevins, Lord of Ireland, and King of England."

Richard gave him a polite bow. "At last, I am able to meet, Henry of Hohenstaufen, by the grace of God, Duke of Swabia, King of Burgundy, King of the Romans, King of Germany and Holy Roman Emperor."

Recognizing his own tactic being used against him, Hohenstaufen smiled at Richard. "Well, then, I would say it is safe to assume that we both know who the other is."

"Allow me to extend my deepest condolences on the loss of you father," Richard offered with sincerity. "He was a great warrior and would have been a valuable asset to us in Outremer."

"Yes, my father's death was tragic, and I know that you would never have dared to throw his standard in the mud." Hohenstaufen smirked.

"Indeed no. What happened to slight the Duke of Austria was a regrettable misunderstanding." Richard sighed then added, "Just as your current trouble with the princes of your realm is, I am sure a regrettable misunderstanding."

Hohenstaufen shifted in his seat. The office of Holy Roman Emperor was an elected one. The princes of the empire elected their leader. It did not always pass to the Emperor's son. Hohenstaufen gained the title when his father Frederick I died on his way to crusade. As of late, there was much unrest amongst the princes and a faction, led by none other than Henry of Saxony, Richard's brother-in-law, sought to overthrow Hohenstaufen. With the delicate political situation, Hohenstaufen knew he must play the game with supreme care and cunning. "I see you have been studying the political climate in my kingdom during your stay in Durnstein."

Richard gave a little nod. "I find it prudent to know what is going on around oneself and who is involved, especially when one is being held against one's will."

Tilting his head to one side and narrowing his icy blue eyes, Hohenstaufen raised one hand in the air to stop Richard from speaking. He clicked his tongue. "Richard, Richard, Richard. I heard you were bold but…"

"But I have an entire kingdom depending on my safe return." Richard looked Hohenstaufen in the eye. "My people need me."

Hohenstaufen's expression changed to one of anger. "My people!" He began. "My people have been wronged. You allied yourself with Tancred, and the throne of Sicily rightfully belongs to my wife. Now I must take it by force. *My* kingdom has been wronged, and that wrong must be redressed."

"Then I must ask, what are your terms?"

The flash of anger disappeared from Hohenstaufen's face.

"The Duke of Austria and I have worked out the terms for your release. Do not forget the wrong you have done him and his family. He is related to Isaac Commenus. I admit, he was reluctant to give you up, but we have come to an understanding. You will be ransomed for 100,000 silver marks." He paused for effect. "I will release you when the down payment has been made and 200 hostages arrive as collateral for the remainder. In addition, Isaac Commenus must be released."

"Just how do you propose to pull that off? I am a returning crusader, and if you are seen to benefit too much from this transaction, it will ruin your reputation as well as give your princes justification to rebel against you. Worst of all, you could face excommunication." Richard grinned. "I am only thinking of you naturally."

"Naturally." Hohenstaufen smiled right back at Richard. "I have already solved this dilemma. Half of the money will go to Leopold. Also, we shall not call this a ransom; instead, we will call it a dowry payment."

"A dowry, wonderful! And the happy couple?"

"Your niece Eleanor of Brittany and Leopold's son."

Richard shook his head. "Despite your fancy title, all will see it for what it really is, ransom money."

"Those are the terms." Hohenstaufen shrugged.

"What if I do not agree to your terms?" Richard countered.

"Those are my terms," Hohenstaufen repeated only this time he spoke each word slowly.

"Ah, I see." Richard gave a nod and gazed at something above the emperor. Then he looked back at the emperor and without trepidation replied, "I do not accept your terms."

"You have little choice here. You *are* my prisoner." Hohenstaufen raised his voice.

"I do not accept your terms," Richard mimicked the emperor, repeating himself as Hohenstaufen had done.

Hohenstaufen slammed his hands onto the arms of his chair and rose to his feet in an instant. With a finger pointed in Richard's face he shouted, "See here, Richard. You are in no position to bargain. It is either you agree to those terms, or I take your life. You have already caused me plenty of trouble, and I am not afraid to do it. It would be nothing, do you hear me? Nothing! I can kill you just as I can any common criminal."

At first Richard looked at Hohenstaufen, then a smile slowly spread across his face and his low laugh echoed in the chamber. "You will not kill me. No, I am worth more to you alive than dead. You have too much to lose should I not survive. Despite your posturing, you will not kill me."

"Your arrogance will be your undoing, Richard. I promise you that. My princes have been summoned and tomorrow you will go on trial for you life." He spoke to the guards, "Get him out of my sight."

Richard seemed to lead the two guards out of the room rather than the other way around. "It was a pleasure to meet you, Emperor," he called out as he left.

Richard alluded to Hohenstaufen's posturing, but he was doing some of his own. Once back in his chamber with the door closed and alone, Richard felt tired and weak. For fear that somehow he was being watched, he hid his fatigue. He looked around the room for something to do to ease his mind. There was a little secretary in the corner with parchment, quills, and ink at the ready. Richard sat down in the chair and began to think of the one person he wished to see most. For this person, he would do whatever it took to free himself from the emperor. After a long cleansing sigh, he began to write.

Chapter Sixty-three

As Richard was trying to dress and prepare himself the next morning, a knock sounded at his door. He found this unusual as few of the guards bothered to knock, only enter and exit as they pleased. "Come," he called out as he sat down to lace his own boots. Last night, the guards allowed him to bathe, but not trim his beard. Richard suspected the guards were afraid of him being near anything sharp. The door opened and Richard looked up to see William Longchamp standing before him. "Your highness."

"Longchamp?" Richard stood up. "I am surprised they let you see me."

Longchamp explained, "Blondel was able to get information to me as to your whereabouts, sire. I am here to aid in the negotiations."

"I am glad to see you, Longchamp." Richard went back to lacing his boots. He spoke in Occitan, the language of Southern France, his native tongue, and the language least likely for the guards to understand.

Longchamp also spoke in Occitan, "Right now England is a bloody mess, my lord. If it weren't for your mother, the whole place would have succumbed to John and his scheming, and your lands in France as well." He did not address the fact that he fled the country in fear of his life due to political infighting.

Richard finished with his boots and motioned for Longchamp to take a seat on the bed, the only other spot besides the chair at the writing desk where he sat. "I am sorry that I have nothing other than my company to offer you at the moment, not even a drop of wine."

"Your highness, I am not the only one here. I am leading a delegation from England. The German barons have gathered and are here to see you put on trial for these supposed crimes," Longchamp explained.

"And Saxony, is he here? Or did Hohenstaufen only invite those who are loyal to him?" Richard questioned.

"Saxony is here, and Blondel came with him. Your troubadour is much distressed and vowing that he will not leave Germany without you."

"I owe much to Blondel." Richard leaned back in the chair. "I do not even know for certain what charges are being leveled against me. I have some idea, but have been told nothing."

Longchamp scowled. "Regrettably, I do not know the specifics either. The emperor has been—how shall I put it—cryptic when he speaks of you. The Bishop of Beauvais is here, and as Philip's bishop is doing his best to stir up feelings against you. Also, Conrad of Montferrat's brother, Boniface is here. He is convinced that you are responsible for his brother's death."

"I had nothing to do with Conrad's death!" Richard groaned, then regained his composure. "However, I do know that Hohenstaufen has just as much riding on this trial as I do. Those men gathered here are the very men who vote the emperors to their throne. Not all of them are supportive of him. The Bishop of Liege, one of his very own bishops, was assassinated not too long ago and there are those who believe Hohenstaufen orchestrated it. He told me that this trial was for my life." Richard shook his head. "It is more than that; this trial is also to solidify his title as emperor."

Longchamp nodded in understanding. "I overheard some of the barons whispering about the crown jewels used in your coronation."

Richard chuckled. "My grandmother Matilda was, as you know, at one time the Holy Roman Empress, but upon the death of her husband, she returned to her native Normandy, married my grandsire, and asserted her right to the English throne. When Grandmother left Germany she took the crown jewels with her, something never forgiven. These very jewels were put to better use in the crown jewels of England, and I was crowned King of England using the crown that once belonged to the Holy Roman

Emperor. Some might say this gives me a claim, although tenuous, to the Emperor's throne."

They were both quiet for a moment neither knowing what to say as the seriousness of the situation pressed in on them. Richard broke the silence. "Longchamp, I need you to promise me something."

"Yes, sire."

"No matter what happens today, you must do your best to convince Hohenstaufen that Baldwin must be allowed to return to England to negotiate with my mother. Tell him that she will only trust Baldwin."

"I understand, sire. Oh! I thought you might want to know that your sister Marie has written to the queen and told her that she expects a visit in Chartres from a certain old friend of hers and yours as well."

Richard nodded. "I see. Please be so kind as to relay a message to my sister's friend that…"

Just then the door opened and the two guards from the previous day entered. "The prisoner is to come with us," the taller of them spoke.

Richard rose to his feet and without saying a word followed the men from the room. Longchamp hurried after them.

The great hall of Speyer was long and narrow. It lacked the windows and light of the great hall of Poitiers. There was the raised dais where Hohenstaufen sat the previous day, and behind that was a large fireplace. What windows there were, were long and narrow like the room. Today it was bursting full of princes, barons, bishops, the English delegation, and spectators hoping to catch a glimpse of the famous warrior of Christendom. If any more nobles were to fit in the hall, they would have to start climbing the towering walls or columns. The assembled parted to make way for Richard as his guards led him before the Emperor. He stood in approximately the same spot as the previous day, but with the crowd in the room, it seemed smaller.

Hohenstaufen sat on his throne again, and at a wave of his hand, the onlookers became hushed. A gangly man stepped forward, and Richard assumed it was Hohenstaufen's chancellor. The man turned to the spectators and spoke in Latin, "The prisoner has been brought here today to hear the charges against him read before this assembly. The charges are as follows: The prisoner betrayed the Holy Land by making peace with Saladin, the enemy of all Christendom. He exchanged gifts with Saladin. He plotted the assassination of Conrad of Montferrat on the eve of the latter's coronation. Under his direction, the defences of Ascalon were demolished. The prisoner broke agreements with our Emperor and put the life of Philip, King of France, in peril." To the right and behind the chancellor, the Bishop of Beauvais sniffed at the mention of Philip. Now the chancellor turned to Richard. "How does the prisoner answer to these charges?"

All eyes turned to Richard, waiting to hear his response. "Your imperial highness, kind bishops, my lords, and all others of title to whom I may have missed because I could not see for the press, I humbly beg your pardon and that you give me leave to address each of these charges."

Hohenstaufen gave Richard a condescending nod. Composed as if he were speaking to a group of allies and not men who held his fate in the balance, Richard began, "Whatever else any man may think of me, I am a man of honor and hold it most dear. It is my inspiration that carries me at all times. As a man of honor, I wish to address the charges placed before me and defend my honor.

"I will address the last charge first. I will say that I do not now, nor have I at any time sought to harm King Philip. I consider that man a brother. We have fought side by side, and he took me in when even my own father would not. I would be ungrateful indeed if I were to do anything other than honor my lord and my friend. I know nothing that ought to have brought on me this ill humor except for my having been more successful than he. It wounds me to my very core that anyone would think me capable of doing harm to my brother king, a man whom God anointed and placed to rule and reign over the Kingdom of France."

Beauvais coughed, but there came no other sound from the crowd. "As to Sicily, it was a matter of family honor, and no true man would have done any less. My widowed sister was being held as prisoner, and I determined to free her. However, her freedom came with a price, a compromise, which forced me to make an alliance with Tancred. I did not make the treaty with the intention of offending the emperor; I thought only of my sister's welfare. Is there a knight that would do less? If so, he is no knight, and not a man even, but a coward, who should be branded with a mark and driven."

Richard looked around at the assembled and tried to make quick eye contact with as many as possible. He turned back to Hohenstaufen. "The murder of Conrad of Montferrat is a tragedy."

A red-faced, angry man seated to the left of Hohenstaufen began to stand, but the emperor raised his hand, and the man remained in his seat. Richard continued, "Montferrat was the man who had the support of the barons of Jerusalem. Without that support they and Jerusalem are difficult to unite. Jerusalem needed Conrad for their king.

"Furthermore, the murder of which I am accused of orchestrating is foreign to my nature. I think my reputation speaks well enough that any man here would know that I am not capable of attacking anyone's life otherwise than with sword in hand, and not in such a dishonorable manner as was done to that noble man."

Richard shifted his weight and moved to the right. He expected the guards to jump at him, but they remained still. His passionate voice continued to fill the room, "I find it nearly humorous that I am charged with exchanging gifts with another monarch. Were gifts exchanged with Saladin? Yes, of which the

King of France received as generously as myself. These are civilities, and if I had not been brought before the emperor under such circumstances, we should have exchanged gifts as well. These civilities extend not only among allies, but a host must always honor his guest and likewise a guest his host, even an enemy in time of war. These exchanges of gifts are merely things which brave men during war give one another without ill consequences.

"I regret that amongst the exchanging of gifts, I did not receive Jerusalem. Indeed, my heart tore when I knew that I would not take Jerusalem. It has been said by some, who did not take the Cross, that I should have taken the most important, most holy of cities. Had I been given the time, I would have done so; this is the fault of my enemies, and not of mine, and I believe no just man could blame me for having deferred this enterprise. I will gladly undertake it again but only after I have afforded my own people the succor for which they could no longer wait. I am not the King of Jerusalem, noble ones, but I am the King of England, having duties and responsibilities to my people."

Richard took a step toward Hohenstaufen and knelt before him. "There, sire; these are my crimes laid bare."

Taking a deep breath, Hohenstaufen rose to his feet. With tears streaming down his own face, playing to the crowd, he approached Richard's kneeling figure and lifted him up. Looking into Richard's grey eyes only for a moment, he searched for the slightest hint of deception, but found none. Hohenstaufen gave Richard the kiss of peace, and the crowd applauded their approval.

As the guards led Richard back to his room, he noticed that Beauvais and Conrad's brother were huddled together deep in a whispered conversation.

When Richard returned to his room, he felt optimistic. Hohenstaufen's kiss of peace surely meant that the charges were forgotten. Still, Hohenstaufen was no fool, and neither was Richard. He knew there would still be a ransom and there were still many details to negotiate. Many of his enemies at court would do their best to prevent his freedom. Once again, Richard sat down and began to write.

Over the next few days, the terms of ransom were hammered out with the English delegation. Hohenstaufen allowed Longchamp to see Richard and explain the outcome. "The terms are one hundred thousand marks, a loan of fifty galleys, and two hundred knights a year, your highness." Once again Longchamp sat on the bed in Richard's room and Richard sat in the little chair at the writing desk.

Richard gave a low whistle. "One hundred thousand marks? The emperor still aims high." He could not comprehend how they would raise the money.

"Yes, sire." Longchamp looked down.

"And Baldwin?" Richard questioned.

"I was able to persuade the emperor that the only person your mother would believe would be Baldwin. I said he needed to be sent back to England as proof that you were alive and well and as a token of good faith." Longchamp rubbed his hands together even though it was not cold.

"Good man, good man." Richard turned to a pile of letters at his desk. "Here, send these to England. They are all letters of great import. You will see that each one is addressed to someone specific." Richard handed Longchamp the stack.

"As you wish, my lord." Longchamp took them.

"As you know, they have taken my seal, so I cannot even seal the letters properly." Richard rose and went to the window to look out. "I guess it is really no matter, as I would like you to copy them anyway." He turned around and looked back at Longchamp. "Have you got good messengers for me?"

Longchamp nodded. "The best. There is Hamelin, and Lucas, also Walwan, as well as Roger le Tort."

"Oh, yes, I remember him from London."

"And, of course, Baldwin will be heading straight for London, my lord." Longchamp nodded.

"Longchamp, we must raise this money and do it quickly." Richard's voice grew impassioned, "I have got to return to my kingdom soon, or there will not be much left of it."

"I assure your highness that we are doing everything within our power..."

Richard cut him off. "Yes, yes. But is it enough?" Richard looked Longchamp over. He could see dark circles under the man's eyes. His wrinkled face seemed even more so this evening, and his exhausted shoulders slumped forward. "Tonight I am tired, and there is nothing more that can be done. I think we both could do with rest."

"As you wish, your highness." Longchamp understood and took his leave of the king.

After he was gone, Richard tucked away the few pieces of parchment that still remained on the desk, the letters that he did not send—that he was not ready to send.

Lying on the bed, he closed his eyes and tried to sleep, but his mind refused to stop running through the terms, making sleep seem as far away as Marseilles.

Early morning came, and Richard could sense it without opening his eyes. Smoldering embers were all that remained of what was a small fire to begin with, and the room grew cold. Wishing to recapture that elusive sleep, Richard pulled the bed quilts tighter about his chin.

Just as he drifted off again, the door slammed open. Richard sprang out of bed. The rush of cold struck him hard, making him furious. The two guards assigned to him came bursting into the room, followed by several others. "I demand to know the meaning of this!" Richard shouted.

Hohenstaufen's chancellor stepped forward from behind the guards. "Due to information that reached the Emperor, he ordered that you be moved to the castle at Trifels, for your safety."

"What? Why the reinforced guard? This is outrageous!" Richard protested.

"As I said, it is for your own safety, sir." The chancellor looked down his crocked nose at Richard.

Richard made a quick glance at the desk and wondered if the guards would allow him to strike this chancellor to the ground with the chair before restraining him. But that might make things difficult for Baldwin, so he did nothing. "When?"

"Immediately," the chancellor growled. He pointed to Richard's trunk in the corner. "You need not worry for your personal effects, they will be sent to you hereafter, but your safety is of the utmost importance."

One of the guards motioned for Richard to follow him. Richard remained where he was. The chancellor spoke again. "It would be very unbecoming to carry the King of England from here in chains, sir."

"I believe what you mean to say is that it would do *you* no good to have the emperor's barons, who are supportive of the King of England, watch as he is dragged away in chains," Richard snapped at him.

"Unfortunately, the princes have returned home," the chancellor returned.

At that, Richard knew he had no choice but to follow the guards.

Chapter Sixty-four

The mere remembrance of you cuts me to pieces.

You are my most valued treasure.

Without you bliss is vanished.

When I cannot see you, I lament and cry because

I remain alone, bereft of soul,

Obtaining no repose

Until your restoration to me.

I pray to God in heaven that day will come

When my misery shall be at an end.

Until then I will wait.

As I told you long ago,

I will wait.

"What the devil do you suppose this is all about, your highness?" Hohenstaufen's chancellor handed him the piece of parchment.

"It's not a question of *what* it is about; it is a matter of *who* it is about, Martin." Hohenstaufen addressed his chancellor by his first name. "You say you found these after Richard left?"

"Yes, my lord." Chancellor Martin affirmed.

"So, let me see if I have this correct," Hohenstaufen spoke his thoughts aloud. "Richard is imprisoned, and while he is alone he writes love poetry?"

"Well, perhaps it is meant to be a song. See here." Chancellor Martin handed Hohenstaufen another piece of parchment, this one with musical notations scribbled on it.

Hohenstaufen examined it. He was an adept musician himself. At the very least he and Richard shared a love of poetry, language, and music. He sounded the notes in his head then examined the poem before him.

While the emperor looked at the parchments, Chancellor Martin glanced around the room. The emperor's love of the colour red filled the room, and the thriving fire in the grate made the vivid colour splash about the room even more.

"I think this music goes with this one." Hohenstaufen spoke at last pointing from the music to another shorter poem. Setting the papers down he continued, "I just find it rather interesting that he is spending his time writing something like this instead of the obvious letters to supporters. I wonder who these could be about."

"If I may, sire, I overheard the Bishop of Beauvais whisper of a mistress of his; although, I have not heard mention of her name."

"I find this so intriguing Martin. I wonder, could it be a code? A plea of some sort for rescue, or perhaps an order to retain the crown jewels at all costs?" Hohenstaufen refolded the parchment and set it down on his own desk.

"Oh, by the way, Longchamp is desperate to have an audience with your highness."

A broad grin spread across Hohenstaufen's face, "I wager he is. He would not be a very good servant if he were not." By sending Richard to Trifels, Hohenstaufen scored a victory. "I can only imagine what Richard is thinking right now." He turned back and looked at the letters on his desk. "Find out who she is or what these are about, Chancellor. Something tells me Beauvais would be an excellent source."

At once, Richard understood why Hohenstaufen chose Trifels Castle, the stronghold of the Holy Roman Emperors. The crown jewels were housed there along with prisoners condemned for treason. Sending him there was meant to send a clear message. He was not to be housed in a room like a guest, but shut away in the dungeon like a murderer or a traitor. Humiliation became Hohenstaufen's strongest weapon.

Richard sat on a little stool in the middle of his cell. Not only was he locked up, but guards with drawn swords surrounded him. Trying to make the best of the situation he attempted to put the guards at ease. "I do appreciate all your little attentions, gentlemen, but I assure you it is not necessary."

None of them replied, but remained stone faced. Richard wondered if they did not speak Latin and therefore didn't understand him. His German was getting better, but it was by no means fluent. He tried again but in German, "Has anyone seen the weather outside? I noticed you have a bit of a leak there." He pointed to the corner where some water trickled down the wall. "I thought perhaps it is raining out?" Still there was no response. "No, then?"

He stood to stretch. Instantly pointed blades surrounded him. "God's legs! I only need to visit the bucket in the corner. I may be a king but I still have to visit the jakes, same as everyone else." He made a gesture toward the waste bucket in the corner.

After a moment, the guard in command nodded his head and allowed Richard to pass by and take care of his need. When finished, he turned around smiling at the men. "You know, you are all welcome to use my pot should the need arise. How many people can say they have shared a garderobe with a king, eh?" Richard amused himself.

"I think that I shall sit on the bed now, if you don't mind." He crossed the cell and sat down on the straw pallet, which lay on the floor, serving as his bed. "Do you mind if I sing?"

Richard didn't wait for a reply. He launched into a bawdy siventes in Occitan, changing the lyrics to poke fun at his guards who still stood facing him with drawn swords. This lifted his spirits, so he continued singing until the guard changed. With the new guard firmly in place, he started over, talking and singing and even occasionally laughing, confusing the guards with his behavior. Richard determined he would not show the despair he felt in his heart.

In late evening, his meal came. "What is for banquet?" he called out cheerily.

The boy who brought the food approached Richard with caution, laid the trencher down on the little stool, and scurried off. Richard picked up the trencher and sat down on the stool. "Ah gruel. Morning, noon, and night, it is gruel." He grinned at the men around him. "Your cook is a smart one. If you plan gruel for every meal, then no one will ever be disappointed." He took the piece of stale bread that lay on the plate and dug in with enthusiasm, grateful that it was not moldy. He swallowed. "You know for gruel, this is not all that bad. Do give my compliments to your cook."

Picking up the cup he swallowed a swig. "Mead?" He observed. "Come now, please tell me they feed you better than this, Gentlemen. If they do not, then I think you should come with me when we get out of here, and I shall show you what real drink there is to be had!"

Richard finished his meal, and thanked the guards again. By now he felt sleepy, no longer sure if it was night or day. He crawled onto his bed and laid down rolling on his side with his back to the guards to show he had no fear of them.

Closing his eyes he tried to sleep, but in truth he was afraid of one thing, that in his sleep he would call out that name, her name. As a result he only slept lightly. He knew that when he woke it would all start over again.

Pope Celestine looked at the letters before him. He read them through three times, but still he did not know how to answer. The letters were from Queen Eleanor, and she was enraged, as she had a right to be. He now had a bit of an insight into Richard's famous temper. Now that a second letter arrived, he knew that he must send some sort of answer. Ready with quill in hand to answer the letter, he skimmed the first one again and several passages stuck out to him.

> ...I am all defiled with torment, my flesh is wasted away, and my bones cleave to my skin. My years pass away full of groans, and I wish they were altogether passed away. O that the whole blood of my body would now die, that the brain in my head and the marrow of my bones were so dissolved into tears that I might melt away in weeping. My very bowels are torn away from me. I have lost the staff of my old age, the light of my eyes, and would God accede to my prayers He would condemn my ill-fated eyes to perpetual blindness that they no longer saw the woes of my people...

> ...King Richard is detained in bonds, and his brother John depopulates the captive's kingdom with the sword and lays it waste with fire. In all things the Lord has become cruel towards me, turning His heavy hand against me. His anger is so against me that even my sons fight against each other, if indeed it can be

called a fight in which one anguishes in bonds and the other, adding grief upon grief, tries by cruel tyranny to usurp the exile's kingdom...

...What do I do? Why do I yet live? Why do I, a wretched creature, delay? Why do I not go, that I may see Him who my soul loves, bound in beggary and irons? At such a time as this, how could a mother forget the son of her womb? Affection for their young appeases tigers, nay, even the fiercer witches...

...Is your authority derived from God or from men...

...The kings and princes of the Earth have conspired against my son, the Lord's Anointed. One tortures him in chains, another ravages his lands with a cruel enmity. The Supreme Pontiff sees all this, yet keeps the sword of Peter sheathed, and thus gives the sinner added boldness, his silence being presumed to indicate consent.

"Is my authority derived from God or men, indeed," Celestine grumbled. "Is there more that a pope can do than to excommunicate the Holy Roman Emperor, and the Duke of Austria, as well?" Philip he threatened with an interdict over the whole of France if he invaded Richard's lands, and he even threatened England with an interdict if the people failed to raise the ransom money. He hoped the latter would help stir any reluctant persons to action.

He laid the first one on his desk and took up the second one that she signed, "Eleanor by wrath of God, Queen of England, Duchess of Normandy, and Countess of Anjou..."

The pope rubbed his aged hands to fight off the rheumatism that settled there. He was not a young man; far from it, and to add to the complications imperial troops were already in his territories preparing to win back Sicily. Should he anger Hohenstaufen enough, it would not take much for the Emperor to turn his troops on Rome. At his age, Celestine knew that going to war would be too much.

On the other hand, here was a mother, clearly in pain, and Celestine felt that he had an obligation to offer her comfort. The royal ladies should be leaving for the safety of Marseilles anytime now, thanks to him. Perhaps that would serve as some comfort to Eleanor.

Anne went over the latest letter from Gustave. Currently, in Cyprus he would now make his way westward back to Marseilles. "My lady?" Etienne tapped on the door as he opened it.

"Etienne, come in." She smiled at him as she put down the letter. "Are you sure this is all the letter that Gustave sent? It seems to end abruptly."

"Yes that is all that was there," Etienne lied. In fact, he hid the second page because it contained information about Richard. "But there is another matter. The abbot is downstairs, and I think you should meet with him."

"Oh, is there trouble?" Anne folded Gustave's letter and put it into her coffer.

"I am afraid so."

"Take me to him." Anne followed Etienne to the hall where Mathias waited.

The Abbot paced back and forth obviously upset about something. Upon seeing Anne, he rushed to her and took her by the hands. "Anne, I am so sorry to come here like this."

She shook her head. "What is it?"

"One of our priests just returned from *O Camiño de Santiago, Compostela*, seeking absolution through pilgrimage. He passed through Castile on the way home, and it would seem that King Alfonso took his brother back into his good graces."

"You mean Raymond's brother allowed him to return home?" Anne gasped.

"He decided to reconcile with his brother, has paid Raymond's debts, and is sending a delegation to Marseilles headed by Castile." Mathias released Anne's hands, and balled his own into fists.

"He will need an army to get in. I will never let him have any part of this city." Anne held her head high.

"Do not worry. Even though Castile is sending the delegation to the priests, I can persuade them to not allow him refuge." Mathias gave her a weak smile.

"The Bishop, though, has never been fond of my family. It would be quite easy for him to support Castile in his efforts," Anne thought aloud.

"I will not let that happen," Mathias stated firmly. "However, I think it would be wise if you and Will were to leave for safer territory."

"Where? There is nowhere that is truly safe. Besides, it is out of the question." Anne shrugged.

"Even though King…" Mathias begun, but Etienne cut him off.

"Paris would be a good option. King Philip would certainly give you a safe place to stay until this whole matter is resolved."

Mathias glared at Etienne. He did not agree that Anne should not know about Richard, but held his tongue all the same, because he did not want to be the one to tell her. Now he felt she must know. "Anne…"

"Mother! Mother!" Will burst into the room; his face filled with fear.

Anne turned to the boy, "What is it, dear?"

"You must come quickly. It is Nanna. Her puppies are coming."

"I will be right there, Will." Anne tried to calm him.

"Please, Mother! Please!"

Anne knew how much the dogs meant to Will. As his activities were more and more restricted, they had become his constant companions. "Alright." She turned back to Etienne and Mathias. "Thank you for this information, Mathias. I am grateful for your friendship."

"Shall I start to make the necessary arrangements for you to travel to Paris, Cousin? I am sure Philip would be happy to send an escort." Etienne looked hopeful.

"Thank you, but that will not be necessary. I will stay here in Marseilles, my city, and so will my son. Now, if you will please excuse me, gentlemen." Anne hurried off behind Will.

Chapter Sixty-five

Lying on his straw pallet, Richard could no longer tell if it day from night, even unsure of how long he had been in Trifels. The door creaked opened and Richard placed his arm across his eyes to block the light. "What is it with you Germans and your obsession with disturbing a man who is trying to get himself a restful night's sleep?"

"King Richard," The voice spoke in Latin.

Richard bolted up. No one had spoken Latin since he arrived at Trifels. Getting to his feet he could see Hohenstaufen's Chancellor Martin standing there in front of him. Richard folded his arms across his chest. "Chancellor."

"It is my duty to inform you that the danger to your person has passed, and you will be returning to court this morning." Chancellor Martin's glared at him.

Richard tipped his head to the side and smiled. "But I was just beginning to feel so at home here."

Chancellor Martin ignored the snide remark. "Once you return to court you will be allowed to conduct state business through your delegation and messengers. A member of the Emperor's court will naturally be there to aid you. Oh, and your escort will come to fetch you within the hour."

With great suspicion, Richard watched the chancellor leave his cell. Was he really going to court, or would his escort be an assassin?

"Your highness, here is a letter from the king. This is the one that he wishes to be circulated amongst the people. Furthermore, he addressed the last part to your daughter, Countess Marie." Marshal handed Eleanor the parchment.

"Interesting," Eleanor observed.

Marshal added, "It would seem he put his letter to music."

Eleanor took the letter and grinned. "Of course he did. It is easier to remember words when they are in song. He means for this to spread across his realm."

She read the song to herself.

No one who is in prison sees his fate

With honesty; for all he feels is sad—

But he can still compose a hopeful song.

I am so rich in friends, but poor in help

They should be ashamed if, for my ransom,

I lie here one more year.

They know this all to well, my home. My Lords.

The English, Norman, Poitevin, Gascon:

I never had a friend who was so poor

That I would leave them in their prison cell.

I do not sing these words to criticise—

Yet I am still in prison here.

The ancient saying I now know too well:

In prison, death: no family nor friends.

Because they leave me here for lack of wealth.

I grieve my fate, but grieve for them still

more—

When I am dead, they will have their

remorse

If I am too long here.

It's no wonder that my heart is sad

When my own overlord torments my lands.

If he remembered what we both agreed

And held back knowing what he swore,

You would not see me held in chains so long,

Nor stay in prison here.

They know this well, Tourains and Angevins—

Those youthful gentlemen so strong and

rich—

That I am far away, in hostile lands.

They loved me so, but have not loved

enough—

There'll be no tournaments held on their

fields

While I'm in prison here.

Comrades I loved, and those I still do love,

My Lords of Perche and also Caieux:

Tell them, song, that they have not proven

friends.

My heart was never false or vain to them.

But they'll be criminals if they still fight

me

While I am lying here.

Eleanor paused when she saw the last lines.

Sister, Countess, your sovereign right

May God preserve, and guard the one I

claim

For whom I suffer here.

I do not speak of the lady of Chartres,

The mother of Louis.

Putting two fingers over her mouth, Eleanor whispered, "Anne." She looked at the paper that so recently was in her son's hands, then turned to Marshal and asked, "Where is Sir Baldwin? I need to speak with him."

"I shall bring him to you, your highness." Marshal gave her a bow and left the room.

Eleanor turned back to the song. She understood the majority of Richard's message, but the last lines were puzzling. If she was correct, those last lines regarded Anne, who was rumored to have gone to Chartres.

Eleanor sat down in a chair and waited for Baldwin. "Richard, what are you trying to say?" She set the song down in her lap.

Father Breton thought he heard some noise coming from the chapel and put his ear to the door. After waiting, he could hear nothing and dismissed it. He turned back to the men and returned to his story.

"King Philip was livid when he heard that Richard was let out of Trifels, he arranged a meeting with the Emperor in June at Valcouleur. Alas, that meeting never came about."

"Why not?" Bogis wrinkled his brow.

"Richard got wind of the arrangement, and he knew he could not allow that meeting to take place. To prevent the meeting, Richard arranged a summit of those princes who were in opposition to Hohenstaufen. Richard invited the emperor to attend with the promise he would use his influence with his brother-in-law to come to a new treaty. Well, the emperor couldn't pass up such an important event that dealt with his own affairs of state, so he accepted. Oh, and Richard made sure that the only time the princes could all meet together was the same time Philip had scheduled the parlay, and of course it was too late to change the date because many of the princes were already on the road."

"Hohenstaufen did not see through it?" Bogis clicked his tongue.

"If he did, Richard arranged it so he would have little choice but to attend to the princes. That is the beauty of politics, gentlemen." Father Breton gave an exaggerated shrug.

"Over the summer and into the fall the ramblings went back and forth. Richard reconciled the Emperor with his princes, and worked as hard as he could from his end to raise the ransom. He could have written to Anne for money, but he still refused to let anyone so much as mention her name. He did not want her involved in any way."

One of the gathered knights interrupted, "Come now, King

Philip just sat there and did nothing?"

"No, no, actually, he and John sent a counter offer to the emperor of eighty thousand pounds to keep Richard until the following fall. The Emperor considered it, and the English had no time to waste.

"In England the down payment was gathered, along with many hostages meant as collateral. Many a noble family had to send members to Germany. In December, Eleanor and the English delegation set out to deliver their captive King. Before Eleanor left, Baldwin left London, and headed south for Marseilles. He had a mission to fulfil."

The many years of benevolent works, the charity, and the prosperity cultivated by Anne and her father paid off. No army needed to defend Marseilles. When Raymond of Castile arrived, the people of Marseilles were at the gates and greeted him, not with a cascade of flowers, but of eggs, rotting fruit, and a chorus of, "Usurper go home." One well-thrown egg exploded on the head of his steward's horse, causing it to throw the steward to the ground. That made the crowd roar with delight, and the fusillade commenced again heavier than before. "If you wish to raise an army, you will have to do it with those bastards in Castile, not Marseilles," shouted a particularly rough-looking man with a beard.

Two men helped the steward back onto his mount, and found themselves to be targets as well. Without a word, Raymond wheeled his horse and charged away.

When word of the greeting reached Anne, she breathed a sigh of relief. However, she refused to become too complacent and kept her guard up in case Castile found a way to bribe himself into the city. There was always the possibility that he would seek an alliance with the bishop. Fortunately, Abbot Mathias would always hold out against Castile and could most likely sway the clergy.

On a gray winter morning, Anne finally relented to Will's pleas to take a ride insisting that she come too. Under heavy guard, they rode out to Anne's spot on the bluff. Once there, she took the time to tell Will stories of his grandsire, as they looked out over the sea.

Not too deep into an anecdote, Anne noticed Will looking off in the direction they came. "Will, dear, I am trying to tell you something."

"I understand." Will nodded with his attention still focused away from his mother. "But I think there are men riding this way."

"What?" Anne turned to look, cursing herself for not having seen them first. In the distance, she could see three riders headed toward them. She grasped Will by the arm. "Will, I want you to do exactly as I say. If I tell you to ride, you ride hard. Do not look back, just ride. Double back and get to the chateau. If you cannot go there, go to Saint Victor's and the abbot. Do you understand me?"

"Yes, Mother, but I think it is Etienne." Will pointed to the trio. "Look how the one in the lead leans to the left, just the way Etienne rides in his saddle."

Looking more closely, Anne could not only tell that Will was correct, but that he had better eyesight than she. The rider on Etienne's right flank was one of her guards, but the third man hung back. She wondered who rode with her cousin.

The riders were almost to them when Anne recognised the blonde hair peeking out from underneath his cap. Surprised, she drew in a sharp breath. "Is that Sir Baldwin?" Will spoke behind her.

The three men stopped and dismounted. Graceful as ever, Baldwin strode over to her, and she extended her hand to him. He took it. "My dear, Lady Anne."

Immediately she noticed a scar on his cheek. "Baldwin of Be'Thune?" She found it hard to speak.

"Master Will?" Baldwin looked at Will. "That cannot be Master Will. Why, you must have grown at least two feet."

Will gave him a polite bow. Etienne spoke up, "My lady, I think I should like to take Will back to the chateau."

"Yes, that would be best." She gave Will a look that centreed somewhere between stern and pleading.

Will did not argue. He mounted his horse, and rode off with Etienne and all but four guards. The remaining guards did not need to be told, and they positioned themselves in the distance.

Baldwin still said nothing to Anne, so she spoke, "I must say, I am surprised to see you here in Marseilles, Baldwin."

"This is a bit more awkward than I had imagined it." Baldwin peered over the edge of the bluff at the sea below.

Anne's heart beat so rapidly, she was sure that Baldwin could hear it. Trying to speak, she found herself unable. Baldwin put one foot up on a sizeable rock and took a deep breath. "I talked with your man Etienne, and he apprised me that you refuse to even hear Richard's name, so you do not know what has happened." He turned to look at her.

Anne turned to him in shock, and seeing him looking back at her, she turned back out to the sea. When she spoke it was as though the voice she heard was not her own. "Baldwin, I beg you, if you have come to tell me that Richard is dead, be merciful, and tell me quickly. I cannot bear it otherwise."

"In one respect, I bring you good news. The king is not dead." He stopped.

"But you have more to tell me." She looked at him.

He nodded. "Anne," he spoke addressing her as a friend, "Richard is not dead, but he a hostage of the Holy Roman Emperor."

"What? How?" Anne sputtered.

"We were caught in a storm a few days from here," Baldwin began to explain.

"He was coming to Marseilles?"

"Yes. Richard reasoned that it was the safest port, but I think we both know why he chose Marseilles."

"I knew of his treaty with Saladin. People do talk, but the gossip stopped." Anne spoke aloud to make sense of it all.

"That is probably because when Etienne found out about Richard, he silenced them all to protect you and Will."

"I always wondered if Richard would make for Marseilles, but so much time passed." She shook her head as if to bring herself back into focus. "Forgive me. You were headed for Marseilles and caught in a storm?"

"Yes, and Richard tried to sail right through the tempest, but I was so afraid of being shipwrecked again—"

"I cannot blame you there."

"You of all people would understand. Well, because of my pleading, Richard agreed to sail out of the storm, but we were shipwrecked anyway, and not once, but twice." Baldwin stood up straight.

"Oh, Baldwin."

"To make a long story short, we tried to make our way north to the Duke of Saxony. Richard was captured just outside Vienna, only a hard day's ride from safety."

"The Duke of Austria? The one whose banner was thrown in the mud?"

"More you learnt from the gossips?"

She nodded. "Then I assume that the Duke turned him over to the Emperor." She paused. "Did Richard send you here?"

"No, actually he does not even know that I am here. You see I was also taken captive, but Richard and William Longchamp won my release by convincing the Emperor that Queen Eleanor would trust only me. I went to London to aid in raising the ransom, and now I am here." He unlatched his cloak and folded the garment over his arm.

"I can guess your reason for coming then." Anne let out a loud breath.

"I did promise Andrew, and I have something for Marguerite."

"Andrew's death fell hard upon us, gentle Andrew." she looked back out at the sea.

"I did not see Marguerite at the chateau. I though perhaps she'd be here with you." Baldwin shrugged.

"Our Marguerite has become a nun, Baldwin."

Baldwin almost choked. "A nun?"

Anne smiled at the thought of it herself. "I am not in jest, Baldwin. She left my household and became a nun."

"A nun? Well, I'll be damned."

"Undoubtedly," she teased. "But in the meantime, I shall help you get in contact with her, if you like. However, I deduce that since Richard is being held captive, he is in need of funds for a ransom."

"The queen," Baldwin meant Eleanor for no one referred to Berengaria as the queen, "and others have been working diligently to raise the ransom. Philip and John have been scheming the entire time, and if Richard is not released soon, the entire kingdom may come apart at the seams."

"And what are the terms?"

"One hundred thousand marks, a loan of fifty galleys, two hundred knights a year, and he is to be released on payment of seventy thousand marks, and two hundred hostages as collateral," Baldwin answered. "Queen Eleanor and her delegation are on the way with the money and hostages as we speak." Baldwin laid his cloak down on the considerable rock in front of him, and rubbed his face with his hands.

"A heavy price indeed." Anne's eyes widened at the amount.

"Anne, there were some hostages that were on the list that were very specific. I am to be one of them. Once I am done here, I will be leaving for the Emperor's court."

"Oh, Baldwin, how long do you expect to be there?"

Anne's face went a shade paler.

"I am sure Richard will have me out of there in no time at all."

"I will help. What do you need for your ransom?" Anne offered.

"No." Baldwin set his jaw. "Richard does not want you involved in any way. He tried very hard to keep even your name from Hohenstaufen, but…" Baldwin did not finish his sentence. "As I said before, he does not even know I am here."

"Baldwin?" His demeanor frightened Anne.

Baldwin drew in a long breath, and then let it out. "The French delegation assigned to the Emperor's court, most likely the Bishop of Beauvais, let slip your name. Anne, you were named as a hostage. You and I are the last two. All the others are on their way, and once we arrive in Speyer, Richard will be freed."

Anne clutched at her stomach and reeled.

"Here," Baldwin reached out to steady her, "let us have a seat." He helped her to the rock.

"Me?" She croaked.

"Listen to me, Anne. You do not have to do this if you don't want to. The queen was dead set against this; Richard doesn't even know. He would not hesitate to strike me dead if he knew why I was here." He knelt in front of her. "At length the queen and the her counselor's reasoned that if you come with me to pay for your own ransom, then Hohenstaufen will not keep you. He needs this money for a campaign against Sicily. We can convince him."

Anne opened her mouth to speak but found that she could not. Baldwin stood back up and continued, "We have a solemn promise from Hohenstaufen no harm of any kind will come to you. You will be treated like a guest. The rationale is if you actually come, it will be a show of good faith, and we can negotiate with the Emperor. I will be there with you."

Anne dropped her head in her lap. Baldwin stood, walked a few paces, and cried, "Oh, God! Will you not have mercy upon us?" He stood looking away from Anne with his hands on his hips regaining control of himself. "Oh, Anne, I don't know what to do. I am torn. He is not just my king—he is my friend. God and the angels only know what you must have suffered when Henry imprisoned you. There has got to be some other way, but I cannot seem to work it out. Even if you go with me, there is no guarantee that the emperor with take the money in exchange for your ransom."

Anne looked up at Baldwin. "Can you guarantee that if I go, Richard will be released?"

"That is Hohenstaufen's promise."

Anne put her hands on her thighs and pushed herself up. Raising an arm aloft, she shouted, "My horse!"

Baldwin caught her by the arm. She turned to him and with a determined voice, said, "Baldwin, I am going to make arrangements for my son." She did not flinch. "Come with me to Saint Victor's. The Abbot there will help arrange a visit with Marguerite."

Chapter Sixty-six

"I do not like it." Abbot Mathias glared at Anne and Baldwin. It was evident from the décor of rich tapestries, and velvet curtains that the church proved a lucrative profession for the abbot. While Anne explained the situation, Baldwin mostly sat still and looked down at his feet. Mathias remembered the knight from Richard's visit. "You simply cannot go, Anne."

Anne stood facing Mathias. "I did not come here to ask for your permission, only to ask for your help."

"This is ridiculous! King or not, he has no right to ask this of you!" Mathias shouted.

"The king does not know about this," Baldwin offered.

"Yet, you come here to fetch her to the emperor." Mathias threw him a disgusted look.

Anne stepped in front of Baldwin. "Please, try to understand. If I go, he will be released from prison."

Mathias shot back, "You are willing to sell yourself to free him? Not to mention, you are talking about starting an arduous journey in the heart of winter!"

"Listen to me, Mathias." Anne tried to reason with him. "This is not about you or me, or just Richard. He is a king and his people need him. They are suffering at the hands of those who are starting a civil war in his realm. Think how many of them are going to die if Philip attacks Richard's lands, and I shudder to think what would become of England if John were allowed to do as he pleases. Why, there wouldn't be anything left of a crown to defend by the time he got done with it. John would sign away the powers of the crown to the first noble who could dupe him out it. Then what would happen to our trade with the north, wool, tin, all gone?"

"That is England's problem, not ours. Your father would never have approved of this, God rest his soul," Mathias growled.

"My father is not here."

"You should have come home the moment King Henry freed you. Instead you dallied with *him*. If you had come home, we would not have Raymond of Castile knocking on the gates of the city. What about the people of Marseilles Anne? What about your duty to them?" Mathias argued.

"Marseilles is strong. She will always withstand anyone who tries to oppress her." Anne narrowed her eyes at him.

Mathias waved his hand in front of his face. "Putting all of that aside, your plan has too many variables."

"I will leave here with Baldwin for Speyer. Because you are the only one I trust, I need you to take Will to London, and wait for Richard and myself to come." She could tell Mathias was about to speak, so she raised her voice and didn't give him a chance. "I know what you are going to say, that Castile could go after Will, but you can disguise Will as a young oblate traveling with you on pilgrimage to Canterbury. In the meantime, Baldwin will arrange a decoy, and we will spread word I am going to Rome to persuade His Holiness to intervene on Richard's behalf. Castile will go after me."

"So, on top of everything else, you are to be bait as well?" Mathias rolled his eyes.

"Abbot, I assure you Lady Anne will be well protected. She will be disguised as my wife." Baldwin rose from his chair.

A vein in the abbot's forehead bulged. "Oh, I do not think so!"

"Mathias! Baldwin is a longtime friend of mine, as well as the king's. He would never do anything so base as to…"

Mathias threw his arm out in a wide gesture. "Anne, you are headed down the same path as your mother, and we both know how that ended for her. She was a whore!"

"My mother was no whore!" Anne's shout resonated throughout the room.

Everything fell quiet. Mathias remained silent, and Baldwin took up a threatening stance behind Anne. Anne put one hand on her hip balled into a fist, and pressed the heel of the other on her forehead. She spoke delicately repeating herself, "My mother was no whore." Then she groaned. "Maybe she was. Maybe I am; I do not know."

"Anne!" Baldwin made a step forward.

Anne shot out her arm and blocked him. "I do not know. But, I do know that she did not love her husband, and that she cared so for her lover, that she would have rather died than to live without him. I use to hate her for the way she betrayed my father, but now that I am older, I think I understand her better than I did before." She looked directly at Mathias. "Why does God make it so we fall in love with those people that we are not suppose to?

Oh, I am weak!" She bit her quivering lip.

"Anne, I am sorry," Mathias whispered.

She turned back to Mathias with an overwhelming passionate look and continued, "I love him. God in heaven, help me. I love him. I never intended to love him, and I fought it for so long. I am sorry if I hurt you Mathias. I am uncertain of the future, and I do not even know if I am making the right choice. Yet, I know what it is like to be held prisoner. I have it within my power to free him from that torment, and I am going to do it."

Mathias stared at the ground while Anne pleaded with him. Baldwin studied the two of them and could tell that something passed between them. "When you will leave?" Mathias' voice cracked as he spoke.

"As soon as possible, within two or three days, I hope." Anne couldn't look at Mathias.

"I will need more time than that to arrange for pilgrimage to Canterbury." He explained. "It wouldn't be prudent, and it would look suspicious for me to leave in winter."

Anne nodded. "I understand. Etienne will watch over Will until the time comes for you to leave."

Mathias turned away from her and faced Baldwin. "If you will come tomorrow morning, sir, I think I can arrange a visit with Marguerite."

"Thank you, Abbot." Baldwin replied.

"I shall see you tomorrow then." Mathias turned, walked to his table, and sat down, as if wanting to be rid of their company.

Anne said nothing else as she left. As she and Baldwin left the room, Anne turned back to catch one last glimpse of the abbot. He sunk down into his chair and stared at the opposite wall.

When Will entered his mother's room she knelt before her massive trunk. "Mother, Nanette said you wished to see me?"

"Yes." Anne turned. "Yes, have a seat."

Will obeyed, and his long skinny legs now comfortably reached the floor. Still, sitting there in the chair, he looked so young to Anne as the weight of choice pressed in on her. "Why are you packing?" He asked.

She replied, "Will, I have something I want to tell you. It is about Uncle Richard."

Will noted that this was the first time she spoke his name, and he could tell something was wrong. "What?"

"Dearest, the Holy Roman Emperor took Richard prisoner. They have reached an agreement, and the good news is Richard will be freed. However, part of the treaty is that certain hostages are to be turned over to the emperor as collateral." Anne remained on her knees.

"What is collateral?" Will furrowed his brow.

"Well, when one owes another a debt, then sometimes something of value is given to the person who is owed, as a promise that the debt will be paid."

"Is Uncle giving you to the emperor?" Will grumped.

Anne shook her head. "No, no. The emperor named me as a prisoner, and Uncle does not yet know."

Will let out a long sigh. "Well, what is he going to do about it? How long will we be collateral?"

"Will, there is more to it. You see, I have collected the money to pay the emperor for my part of the ransom, but I have to take it there to him myself. Also, I cannot take you with me—not this time."

"Not going! You said that the—"

"Will!" Anne snapped back.

"But you said—"

Anne slammed the trunk lid closed.

After a brief moment of silence, Will apologized. "I am sorry, Mother."

"You must understand, Son. The situation is too uncertain for me to take you along. In truth, I do not know if the emperor will even accept the money in exchange for my part of the ransom. It is not certain." A look of trepidation spread over Will's face. "I am sorry Will, I feel that I really must go, but I am worried about leaving you. I did make some arrangements for you that I think you will like. You will go with Abbot Mathias to London, disguised as an oblate. It will be an adventure, a quest!"

"Ugh!" Will stuck out his tongue. "Not with the abbot. I would much rather just stay here."

"It is the best option for you." Anne remained firm. "With Castile out there, I do not want you left here in Marseilles. Baldwin arranged for a decoy to convince Castile that I have gone to Rome, but I am not willing to take any chances with you. I will meet you in London. While you are there, you may visit with some of my friends, and as the tournament season will soon begin, you can attend a few." Anne looked at Will, but he said nothing. "Well?"

Will looked pensive, taking a long time to respond. When he did, he straightened himself up in the chair. "May I ask you a question?"

"Yes, my dearest."

"When my father...I mean Raymond of Castile took you, how long did Uncle Richard wait before he came for you?"

"I understand he received the news in the morning while in a long siege of Bordeaux. He immediately assaulted, and took the castle that afternoon, and by nightfall was on the road to Taillebourg," Anne recalled.

"Then I don't think you shouldn't wait any longer. I think you should leave as soon as possible," Will pronounced. "If he would do that for you, you should do the same for him."

"Thank you, Will, that makes me feel better." She reached out and took his hand. Although normally he would have protested at the show of affection, he didn't resist. "I think you should take Sigurd and Nanna with you, Will."

Will grinned. "What about the puppies?"

Anne raised her eyebrows. "I was thinking of sending one

to King Philip as a gift."

"And what about the other one?"

"Well," Anne picked up a dress to fold. "Perhaps you could take her with you to London and present it to Uncle Richard when he is released."

Will nodded. "That would be fine. You don't think the abbot will mind though do you? What I mean is, it is obvious the dogs don't really like him, either."

"I will see to it that the abbot understands how important the dogs are to you." Anne gave him a warm smile.

"May I stay here with you while you pack?" Will didn't wait for an answer but got down on his knees next to his mother and helped her.

When the royal ladies arrived in Marseilles, Etienne met them at the dock along with the King of Aragon, Alfonso "the Troubadour". Tall and slim with long black hair, King Alfonso stood out in the crowd. With his large dark brown eyes, he watched as the women disembarked from their ship. Berengaria was a princess of Navarre, a country he fought with many times, but now he must time put those differences aside. In an instant, he could tell which lady was which, and he approached them. "Ladies, welcome to Marseilles."

Joanna took the lead and gave him a curtsy. "Your highness."

"Thank you so very much for your gallantry." Berengaria followed Joanna's example.

"You must be exhausted." He motioned to Etienne who stood behind him, "May I present Etienne, the steward of the Viscountess of Marseilles, who generously welcomes us into her house."

"Where is the viscountess?" Joanna narrowed her eyes at the breach of decorum.

Etienne stepped forward and gave the ladies a deep bow. "Your highnesses, I bring you the tidings of my mistress, the Viscountess of Marseilles, who sends her regrets that she is not in Marseilles to greet you. However, she does offer her chateau for your pleasure."

Joanna sniffed and lifted her chin. "I see."

"Come, we have litters waiting to take you to the chateau." Alfonso guided them.

Once the women settled in the litters, Alfonso mounted his horse and rode beside them. "I do not think we shall stay long. I trust you ladies are anxious to get to Poitiers."

"I have no wish to stay in Marseilles any longer than necessary." Berengaria pouted.

"As soon as you shake off your sea legs, we shall be underway to Toulouse," Alfonso reassured her.

Upon their arrival at the chateau, the servants lined up to greet the guests. Etienne and Alfonso helped the ladies from their litters, and Etienne made introductions. They made their way into the chateau, and the ladies were shown to their rooms. They were afforded all the niceties that were appropriate to their stations.

As servants placed Berengaria's trunks in her room, Etienne extended an invitation. "Your highnesses, a banquet has been prepared in your honor."

"Oh, I am much too tired to attend a banquet." Berengaria sighed.

Embarrassed, Alfonso tried to recover the situation. After all it would not do to slight Marseilles, much less the riches she held. "Thank you, sir. We will all be happy to attend. I am sure once the ladies have a chance to refresh themselves, we will all be in better humor. After all, a safe arrival does call for celebration."

"As you wish, my lord." Etienne gave Alfonso a gracious bow and left the room.

When the royals finally did come down to banquet, the assembled had been waiting for hours. It was a challenge for the scullery servants to keep the food hot, but not burnt. The three royals were seated as honored guests, and many of the important men of the town came to pay their respects.

At last the meal was served and entertainment soon followed. Alfonso, Berengaria, and Joanna greeted their callers coldly and huddled together, speaking in hushed tones. Berengaria put her hand in front of her mouth and whispered to Joanna, "How long do we have to stay down here? Can we not just go back upstairs and cordon ourselves off from these people. My nerves cannot take much more."

"I know, dear. Just bear it a little longer." Joanna gave a big sigh. "I wonder what urgent business called Lady Anne away? Did not wish to meet us is more likely. I find it insulting." Joanna took a sip of wine and to her surprise it was surpassingly good.

"They are telling everyone Lady Anne went to Rome to appeal to the pope on Richard's behalf, but something tells me that is far from the truth." Alfonso spoke only loud enough to be audible to the two women.

"Could she be going to Richard?" Berengaria rolled her eyes.

"Her son remains in Marseilles," Alfonso continued. "Her husband is my brother-in-law you know."

"That is right. I had not thought of that. And where is her husband?" Berengaria asked.

Alfonso only smiled in response to her question. After taking a drink from his own goblet he said, "You know, all of these people in this region who speak Occitan should come together as one country. Just think how powerful we could be. Raymond of Castile ruling Marseilles would be such a boon."

Berengaria bristled because she knew Alfonso included Navarre in his ambitions. Joanna tried to steer the conversation elsewhere. "Where is Anne's son if he is in Marseilles? All the rest of the town has seemed to turn out."

"Oh, he is upstairs, heavily guarded. They are pretending he is not here as well, but I heard his old nurse over there," he tossed a thumb in the direction of Nannette, "talking about him to Etienne."

Berengaria felt a severe curiosity to see Anne's son. "I want to see him," she demanded.

Alfonso beckoned Etienne over to them, and talked so quietly that the steward leaned in close just to hear him. "The ladies and I would like to retire now."

Etienne nodded. Alfonso added, "But before we do, we would like to meet the heir of Marseilles."

Etienne swallowed hard. "If you mean Lady Anne's son, he is also not here."

Smiling like a minx, Alfonso protested, "I know he is here in the chateau because I overheard his nurse."

"I am afraid it is impossible, your highness." Etienne remained firm.

"I am a king and you are a steward. It is not impossible, sir. Simply take us up to my nephew. After all, at a time like this with his mother gone to the *north*, he needs family."

"I am kin to the Lady Anne, so the boy has family."

As if out of nowhere Nannette appeared. "Etienne, I think it would not hurt to let our guests meet Master William."

"See, his nurse does not object." Alfonso held his hand out to her.

"Your highnesses may follow me if you like." Nannette turned. "Oh, of course you should probably bid farewell to the assembled first," she added.

Once out of earshot, Etienne caught her by the arm. "What are you doing?"

"I have no fear that William can hold his own against the likes of them. Besides, as soon as they are gone, we will take William to the Abbot. Alfonso will most likely tell Castile where his son is, but Castile will look for him here first and have no idea about the abbey. By the time he figures it out, Master William will be well on his way. I like to call it a ruse, Etienne." Nannette nodded her head once.

By now, the three royal persons finished bidding the crowd farewell, and they turned to follow the nurse and the steward.

As they climbed the stairs, Berengaria whispered to Joanna, "That nurse is a little…"

"Odd?" Joanna offered.

"Frightening, I believe is better. She makes me feel uncomfortable."

They arrived at the door to Will's heavily guarded chamber. The guards let Etienne and the group pass by without a challenge.

Will was inside with Master Moore. When they all came in, the two stood, and Will looked at Etienne tentatively. "Your highnesses, the King of Aragon, the Queen of England, and the Dowager Queen of Sicily, may I present Master William de Marseilles?"

Will gave them all a courtly bow. "Welcome to Marseilles, your highnesses. May you find it a haven of rest on your journey."

Nannette smiled as Will played his part flawlessly. He was his mother's son.

"We are so pleased to make the acquaintance of our gracious host." Joanna gave him a polite nod.

"I am most pleased meet you, young Master William." Alfonso stepped forward. "I am married to your aunt Sancha of Castile, and am thus your uncle."

Uncomfortable with the reference to his father's family, Will only repeated a greeting. "You are most welcome here, my lord. How may I be of assistance to you?"

"We would like a seat, if that is alright with you." Alfonso spoke to the boy kindly. He remembered what was like to be young and dealing with matters of diplomacy that were meant for adults.

"Oh, yes, but of course. Forgive me." Will nodded and the servants brought chairs. "Do have a seat please." Will waited until the others were seated, and then took a seat himself.

Berengaria said nothing; she could not take her eyes off the boy. She studied him. His dark curly hair assuaged the suspicion she harbored that Will was Richard's son. Will looked nothing like Richard. In fact the only resemblance to Anne was his soulful hazel eyes. The sound of Alfonso's voice broke her train of thought.

"I think it very prudent of you to stay here while your mother is away. There is no better way to learn to govern than by doing. I was just a little younger than you when I myself became king."

Will answered, "Thank you, my lord."

"I can see the family resemblance." Alfonso referred to Will's father.

Will jutted out his chin. "Yes, I am told I have my mother's eyes."

"Does your mother go off and leave you often?" Berengaria spoke. "What I mean is, I know she did not take you to Sicily or Cyprus with her, and now it would seem that she is gone again." She tilted her head with a slight smirk as if she were speaking to a dog.

"Regrettably my mother was not able to be here for your arrival." Will bristled at the company in his room.

"Yes, but I understand she has gone north. It must have been hard for her to leave her child here all alone." Berengaria continued to push.

Will lost the patience that his mother possessed and the temper of his father flared. "With respect to your highness, my mother has gone north to help free the King of England, and as you can see I am not alone."

Berengaria made a funny little noise. "Free him. She is a

woman. She can no more free him than I can."

Will's tone was short. "The emperor named my mother as a hostage. When she arrives in Speyer he promised to release the king." Etienne closed his eyes, and Will knew that he said too much.

This was news to all three of them. "You mean she is to be a prisoner in exchange for the king's freedom?" Alfonso asked for clarification.

"She took her share of the ransom money to the emperor, and God willing he will accept that." Will fought the desire to shout at the woman before him. He knew he was ruining his mother's plan, but he could not bear the insult to her.

"May God grant it," Alfonso said.

Neither of the women spoke, too taken aback by the news they just heard. Alfonso pitied the boy. He got up from his chair. "We did not wish to keep you long, Master William. We only came to thank you and your mother for your hospitality."

"Again, you are most welcome," Will responded coolly.

The ladies took a cue from this and rose from their seats.

Once they were outside and the door closed behind them, Alfonso took Etienne aside. "Sir, I have dealt with the Holy Roman Emperor before, and I doubt that he will take the money instead. Hohenstaufen is a shrewd man. In all likelihood, he will keep Lady Anne as a bargaining tool."

Etienne nodded his head in understanding. "Yes, sire." He looked into Alfonso's eyes. He would keep him from Will at all costs now.

"What can I do to help the boy?" Alfonso queried.

"I think all anyone can do at this point is pray."

Chapter Sixty-seven

Philip sat in his chamber answering letters and completing his morning briefing. As of late, he found himself busy, preparing to march upon Richard's lands. Philip determined to regain the Vexin, as well as everything and anything around it that he could possibly take. Norbert entered the room with a mastiff puppy trailing behind him. "What is this?" Philip looked up from his papers.

"It is from the Lady Anne, your highness," Norbert explained.

"Really?" He made a kissing sound to call the dog, and to Philip's delight it came.

"Yes." Norbert nodded.

"Sit." Philip commanded the dog, and again it obeyed. "This is a good dog. He, she whatever it is, must be from those dogs I sent her."

"She is a female, sire."

"Even better." Philip laughed.

"This is also from Lady Anne." Norbert handed Philip a letter.

Philip opened it and read:

To My Most humble Ally and Dear Cousin, his highness, King Philip,

I am sending you this dog as a token of my esteem and gratitude for the kindness you have shown to my son and me. I regret that it is a poor substitute for a queen. however, this female is of good stock and breeding. You will find, I think, that she will be a most loyal companion.

By now I am sure you are aware of the troubles that have befallen our dear friend, King

Richard. As you read this letter, I am on my way to the emperor's court at Speyer. It would seem that someone in your delegation told the emperor about me; he took a notion, and I was named as a hostage. I am sure that the emperor is a reasonable man, and we can come to an accord, as I am prepared to pay for my ransom, and am confident that he will see my willingness to deliver it in person as payment enough.

Perhaps someday in the future we can enjoy another afternoon together, you, Richard, and myself. Until then, please accept my gift as a sign of friendship. I pray you keep my son and me in your prayers, as you are ever in ours.

Your humble Servant,
Lady Anne de Marseilles

When Philip finished reading the letter, he crumpled it; his face twisted in anger. With a loud cry, he upset his table scattering the paper, ink, and quills about the room. The puppy ran for the door behind Norbert and pushed up against it. "My lord!"

Philip shook as he spoke through gritted teeth. "Recall him! Recall them!"

"Yes, my lord, but who? Who shall I recall?"

"That bastard Beauvais in the Emperor's court who claims to serve me!" Philip bellowed.

Norbert was wide eyed. "As you wish, your highness."

Philip marched about the room now. "In fact, it would be better for him to meet with some unfortunate accident on their way home than to see my face again!"

"What happened, my lord? Is King Richard freed?" Norbert placed a cloth on the spilled ink in an attempt to stop it from ruining anything else.

"No, Richard is still imprisoned, for the time being. I do not think those so-called ambassadors of mine are doing a damn thing to keep him that way. But no, that's not the worst. It seems that in Beauvais' arrogance he got Anne involved. She is going to be made a prisoner for Richard's sake. Oh, may they rot in hell for their efforts!" It was unusual for Philip to curse, but his outrage got the best of him.

"Can anything be done, my lord? Surely you can send someone else to the emperor," Norbert offered.

Philip stopped walking and rubbed his temples as he tried to think about what to do. "I will go to Germany myself."

"My lord!" Norbert dropped the papers that he gathered up. "What about the matter concerning your...uh..."

"My uh...?" Philip balanced his hands. There was fire in his eyes.

"Marital affairs?"

Philip groaned. "Ah!"

In a haste to gain allies against Richard, Philip married Ingeborg the reasonably nice looking, princess of Denmark. The morning after their wedding Philip, ordered that his new bride be sent away to a convent. When pressed about it, Philip explained that just before their wedding night, news reached him that there was an issue of consanguinity. He was vehement he never consummated the marriage, and petitioned the pope for an annulment. Ingeborg fought tooth and nail. She was just as passionate that the marriage had been consummated as he was that it had not. Next, Philip reached an agreement with the Count of Geneva to marry the count's daughter, but on her journey to Paris, Thomas of Savoy kidnapped her, and married her instead.

Philip knew he could not leave France at a time like this and that he needed Beauvais to annul the marriage. In addition, he was poised to invade Richard's lands. Philip sank down into a chair before his fire. "We must sort this out somehow, Norbert. I may not be able to go, but I am not about to let Anne be sacrificed for *him*."

Anne and Baldwin traveled North to Lyon and onward toward Beaune. There they turned northwest to Strausborg skirting the Scharzwald region. To Baldwin it seemed as though he was just there, traversing the mountains in the same conditions. The weather slowed their progress, but they pressed on as fast as they could. Much of the time, they traveled by horse as it was difficult to pull a cart or wain over the snowy ground. Eventually they followed the partially frozen Rhine River northward. At first, Baldwin joked and tried to keep everyone's spirits up. Those servants with them seemed to only know words of complaint. Anne hid her anxiety from Baldwin and joined in to rally the travelers. Richard or their destination were rarely mentioned.

One afternoon as they were traveling through the dense forests of the Schwarzwald region, Baldwin steered his horse close to a particularly meditative Anne. "Our guide says that we are nearing Strasbourg."

"Hum. That is good," Anne replied. The forest around her reminded her of the forest she visited so often in her dreams.

"Well, I do not know about you, but my posterior could use a day's rest." He winked.

"I never asked you, what was it that you brought to Marguerite?" Anne questioned out of the blue.

"It is almost funny to think of it now, but Andrew bought a cross for her when we were in Cyprus, just after you left. It is about the length of my palm, and is exquisitely carved olive wood from the Mount of Olives." A smile spread across Baldwin's face. "I gave him no end of ribbing when he bought it. I teased him she would never have use for such a thing, and it was a waste. Who would have thought?"

"Who would have thought?" Anne repeated, her far away look returning.

"It nearly killed *him* when you left." Baldwin looked at the road ahead. "He was very much a changed man."

"Andrew?"

"No, Richard," Baldwin clarified.

"Richard had a wife to think about then."

"He will kill me when he finds out I have brought you into this mess." Baldwin tried to laugh.

"Richard will not kill you—maim you perhaps. But kill you? No. He will box your ears one moment, bargain for your freedom the next," Anne reassured him.

"I am going to be a father," Baldwin softly announced. "I spent some time with my wife in London. Not too long after I crossed the channel, I received the joyful tidings from her."

"Congratulations are in order then," Anne genuinely smiled.

"I will not be able to be there for the birth of my, and I say this with confidence, son. That I do regret." There was sadness in his eyes.

Anne tried to cheer him. "I hear that most men would prefer to be as far away as possible from a woman in confinement."

Baldwin chuckled at a memory. "I think if the midwife would have let him in, Richard would have preferred to be with you. We tried to tell him he was better off where he was."

"All will be well." Anne reached over and gave his arm a pat. "I think it wonderful, Baldwin, you being a father. May you have a son just like you."

"That's not a congratulations; that's a curse."

"I do not think so." She gave him a stern look.

Baldwin remianed quiet for a moment, then spoke again. "I find it funny, really. Unlike Andrew, I do not mind my wife. In fact, I am rather fond of her. She is witty, charming, pleasant company, and even fair to look at."

Anne responded, "She is a lucky woman, Baldwin."

Moments like this where Baldwin talked seriously were rare. They rode on in silence.

Count Raymond VI of Toulouse, a complex man, with a web of alliances built on family and treaties, rode out to meet Alfonso, Berengaria, and Joanna and escort them into his city. To begin with, he was first cousin to King Philip. In addition, Toulouse was on his third marriage. His first wife died only four years after they were married, and that union failed to produce an heir. His second wife became a heretic Cathar, and the pope readily gave his blessing for annulment.

Toulouse's third wife was the niece of Balin of Ibelin, the powerful baron of Outremer, and Toulouse hated her, was desperate to be rid of her.

The pope personally wrote and asked Toulouse to escort King Richard's sister and wife to Poitiers. Normally he would have balked at such a request. The Counts of Toulouse and the Dukes of Aquitaine were known to war over the claim Aquitaine asserted to Toulouse. Queen Eleanor's first husband, Louis VII, even tried to invade Toulouse based on her claim, but it proved disastrous for the French crown. If the pope had not dangled the promise of an annulment in front of him, Toulouse would never have agreed to escort the ladies.

As he approached, Joanna could see the count in the distance. Toulouse waited for them atop a chestnut horse, wearing a bright blue coloured tunic and matching cap that made him stand out.

Alfonso and Toulouse greeted one another while Joanna studied the count. Even though he was in the saddle, she could tell he was tall. The image of the man before her excited her. He had fine strong legs and arms, and he gripped his reins with a commanding authority. Underneath his cap, dark hair peeked out, and even without touching it, Joanna could tell it was soft and thick. Toulouse's face looked as though it had been crafted to perfection, not fashioned by fortune.

While Joanna perused the specimen before her, Toulouse greeted Berengaria with gallantry. "And you, your highness, will be most welcomed to Toulouse." Toulouse's deep voice resonated, and Joanna found she could not think.

Without knowing it, she extended her hand to him and his lips brushed it lightly with a kiss. Joanna's heart was lost.

Toulouse led them into the city, and they lodged in the castle. Just as in Marseilles, a feast was held in honor of the royal visit. This time however, Joanna did not shy away with her sister-in-law, but spent her time making sure the count took notice of her.

Berengaria felt abandoned with Joanna off flirting and King Alfonso beset by many wishing to pay their respects. One particular man hung close to Alfonso, and he caught Berengaria's attention.

After dinner alone in her room, she pondered the mysterious man. If Joanna could find someone charming to cling to, why couldn't she?

Not even her lady was present when a knock sounded on Berengaria's door. Berengaria sent her on an errand, it seemed like hours ago, and her lady had not yet returned. Assuming it was her lady, she called out with irritation, "Enter."

To her surprise, a pageboy stepped inside followed by the man she noticed with King Alfonso. "Your highness, may I present Raymond of Castile?"

Chapter Sixty-eight

Berengaria noted the man's dark curls and features. She could not help but see the scar on his cheek. Without a doubt, she knew he was Castile. The idea of a conversation with this man intrigued her. "Sir," she nodded her head.

"Your highness." Castile gave her a deep courtly bow. "I came to pay my respects."

"Please, come in and have a seat." She beckoned him.

Castile followed her to two chairs at a table. Helping her into the one at the head, he took a seat next to her. She looked at him with curiosity. "So, you are Raymond of Castile, husband to Lady Anne."

"And you are the fair Berengaria, Queen of King Richard." He smiled. "I think we have much in common."

Berengaria nodded her head again. She thought to herself Richard would not approve of this. Yet, at the same time, she longed to talk with Castile, feeling a certain kinship with him. Castile could understand her in a way no one else could. She glanced at the pageboy standing in the corner. "Bring us some wine," she ordered.

"Word of the beauty of the Queen of England has been greatly maligned. Those words are but mere shadows of your true splendor. Why, if I had a wife as lovely as you, I should think I would never leave her side." Raymond's smile charmed her.

"You flatter me, sir," Berengaria protested.

"Please understand, I do not jest. I am genuine in what I say. After all, what good would it do me to make you a fool, you who are possibly the one person in this world who can understand how I feel."

The pageboy entered with the wine, and placed it on the table. Berengaria sent him away again, reasoning that her lady would return any moment. She did not want the pageboy listening in or spreading gossip.

"What brings you to Toulouse?" Berengaria went to pour the wine, but Castile beat her to it.

"My lady."

"Thank you." She took a sip.

"To answer your question, I came to meet my brother-in-law, to seek his advice. You see, I want to recover my family."

"You mean Anne?"

"Yes, but not just my wife." He paused and tilted his head. "I am sure that you have heard horror stories about me. No doubt, your husband and my wife make me out to be a monster."

"It has been rumored." She winked.

"May I tell you my sad tale?"

"Please do, but do not make it too sad." She took another drink.

"It started in my home country of Castile. I am the youngest of six brothers, and early on it became evident that I must seek my fortune elsewhere. I knew of an eligible young lady, Anne de Marseilles, and I set out to meet her. On my way to Marseilles, I received word she was in Poitiers, so I turned north. I am not going to lie. In the beginning, I sought her wealth, but then…" He let out a long slow sad sigh. "Anne was one of the most beautiful women I had ever seen, present company excluded."

"Naturally."

"At Poitiers, I paid court to her and tried to win her love. Then, she met Richard, and all my hopes were dashed. She would no longer even so much as look at me. My devastation was utter and complete. I challenged Richard; honor demanded it. We dueled and I won, b—"

"Ho! You won!" Berengaria rapidly blinked.

"Yes, my lady, but still Anne would not have me. I felt as though my body would cave in on my spirit crushing me."

"You were infected with your love of her," Berengaria observed. "I can understand that. It was as though you would give anything to be with her. You would gladly die if necessary. All you wanted was to know that she was yours."

"Precisely! That is exactly it. Well said. I have never been able to put it so eloquently." Castile reached for her goblet. "Here, more wine?"

Out of boredom, Berengaria drank more than usual at dinner because she found she had nothing to do and the wine was right there in front of her. Now she held up her goblet for Castile to fill it. "This wine is impeccable." The effects of the drink coursed through her body as she felt the warmth reaching her extremities.

"It is one of my favourites. Fortunately they make it in Toulouse." Raymond topped off his own goblet and put it to his lips, pretending to drink.

Berengaria's glassy eyes reflected the intoxication taking hold of her. "Pray, continue with your story."

"Ah, yes, let us see. After Poitiers, Anne was imprisoned. I wrote King Henry on a regular basis, pleading for her release. Then he let her go, but only for a moment. I do not think he truly intended to free her, but just wanted to control Richard. Richard double crossed his father and took Anne south. King Henry reached out to me for help. Well, who am I to deny a king? I did as I was bid. King Henry ordered me to marry her."

"Are you trying to tell me that you objected to the marriage?" Berengaria gave him a sly look.

Castile returned with a look of his own that radiated sincerity. "All the time she was imprisoned, I tried, honest to God I did, but I could only think of her. I will confess, when Henry bade me marry Anne, it was as though everything I dreamt of was coming true."

Berengaria's gaze was transfixed on the man before her. "I understand."

Castile continued, "We were married, and I was in the midst of arranging to take her back to her beloved Marseilles when Richard came and stole her. He kidnapped my wife from me. I barely had time to escape with my life. King Henry's attentions became fickle. Richard threatened my life. Now I had no choice. I took up the cross." Castile's eyes filled with tears as he continued, "I did not even know I had a son until Richard arrived in Acre."

"I met your son. He looks very much like you. He is a beautiful boy." Berengaria reached out and touched Castile's hand to comfort him.

Castile looked straight at Berengaria and let the tears roll down his cheeks. "Everything has been taken from me. I was even forced to work for a Jew just to repay my debts on top of everything else. I daily thank heaven for my brother's generosity in saving me from that hell. Still the humiliation is… is…" He choked up and did not finish his sentence.

Pity welled up inside Berengaria. Feeling as though they were one in emotion, and experience at the moment, she wanted Castile to know that he was not alone. She wanted to know she was not alone. Leaning closer to him, she gently wiped his tears away, touching his scar with extreme sensitivity.

"Thank you," he whispered.

Silently they looked at each other and an understanding passed between them. Castile leaned closer to her and in a tender voice whispered, "Have you ever wondered what it would be like to be kissed by a man who was kissing you, really kissing you, and not thinking of another woman?"

They were so close now that their noses were beside each other. Berengaria opened her mouth slightly.

"Don't you want that?" Castile whispered.

"Yes, I do." She could hardly form the words.

"So do I," Castile replied. Then he moved back away from her. "I mean everything but the man part." He laughed at the implication.

Berengaria couldn't help it; she laughed too. Her goblet was empty again and she made to fill it, but Castile took care of it first. Taking up the refilled goblet, she declared, "I wish to make a toast."

Castile held his up in response. "Then by all means, make your toast, my lady."

"Here is to the most amiable cuckolded husband I ever met." They drank.

Castile raised his glass. "And here is to those who have

been wronged by love. May they find solace in friends who truly understand their plight."

Even before she opened her eyes, Berengaria felt the pounding in her head. Aware that she was lying on her stomach, a position she did not normally sleep in, she pushed herself up. Her unbound hair fell in her face and she used her forearm to shove it back. In a daze, she looked around the room, blinking her eyes, trying to remember where she was. As she rubbed the sleep from her eyes, flashing memories of the previous night came to her. "Castile!" She whipped around to see if he was in the bed behind her.

No one was there. Not even her lady was in the room. The bed was mussed, but that was normal for Berengaria. Looking down, she saw that her clothes were still on but in much disarray.

The sudden movement made her head swirl, and she collapsed back down. A horrible thought came to her. *What if? No! I would never! I was so full of wine—oh, why can I not remember?*

Berengaria slowly got up from the bed. On the table she could see wine goblets. "Lucinda!" She called out for her lady, holding her head between her palms.

Almost instantly, the servant appeared through the door. "Good morning, your highness."

"Where have you been?" Berengaria snapped.

"Last night when I returned to the room, you sent for more wine, which I brought, then you told me to wait outside the door, you wished to speak to the gentleman in private," the lady responded.

"How long did the viscount stay?"

"I believe it was early morning when he took his leave, m'lady."

"Did he speak to you? Is he still here."

"No, your highness." Lucinda shook her head." He said

nothing to me. I believe he and the King of Aragon left the castle just a little while ago." She paused. "Thinking a bit more of it, m'lady, the gentleman did have an odd sort of smile on his face. You both were making rather merry last night."

Berengaria let loose and fiercely slapped her lady on the cheek. Standing there seething with rage, she grabbed the shocked lady by the arm. "Oh, how you insult your queen! I will have you boiled if your tongue ever lets loose!"

The lady clutched at her cheek. "Yes, your highness."

"Now, I wish to bathe in hot water. Make it so, and do not be all day about it!" Berengaria pushed the lady away from her. She grabbed the table and fell into a chair, squinting in pain as her lady closed the door. Berengaria muttered, "This is what it feels like to be a cathedral bell."

When Baldwin and Anne reached Speyer, they learnt not all had gone as hoped. It was late and Queen Eleanor had already retired. Anne did not wish to disturb her, but Longchamp came to the little inn where they lodged and explained what transpired. They huddled together in the corner of the tiny room that served as kitchen, and common room. "Sir Baldwin," Longchamp shook his head. "King Philip tried his very best to prevent the release of our king. The emperor's mind seems to change as easily as a stormy wind can change direction."

"But has the emperor kept his word? Will the king be released when we arrive at court tomorrow?" Baldwin gritted his teeth.

"Yes." Longchamp nodded. "The emperor will keep his word and King Richard will be released tomorrow. It hasn't been easy though. Beauvais has the emperor's ear, and continually turns him against King Richard. When Queen Eleanor arrived, the Emperor was reluctant to release the king, and he actually went on trial again. Such disgrace." Longchamp screwed his face in disgust. "However, the princes, once again swayed to support King Richard, and with that weight upon him Hohenstaufen will have to release him."

"Have you heard if the emperor reached a decision regarding Lady Anne's offer?" Baldwin asked the question, while Anne sat silently next to him.

Longchamp looked at Anne with pity. "Your letter was delivered last night my lady, but there has been no response."

"Thank you, sir," Anne whispered. She looked at Baldwin and gave him a weak smile. "I believe I shall retire for the evening."

The two men arose as she took her leave. They watched her ascend the stairs and go out of sight. Baldwin spotted Anne's lady Ines, sitting comfortably close to the fire, and he hissed at her, "Go girl! Attend to your mistress."

The girl scrambled up the stairs after Anne. Baldwin grumbled to himself, "Bloody girl. Anne would be better off without her. Anne would be better off without many people she knows."

Chapter Sixty-nine

Accompanied by members of the English delegation, Baldwin and Anne mounted their waiting horses outside the inn. Baldwin took Anne's arm. "The Emperor knows we are coming this morning, and Longchamp is already at court beginning negotiations for the exchange."

"I understand." Anne looked straight ahead.

Baldwin continued, "The queen is in her lodgings and wishes to see you." He paused slightly. "But I leave it up to you."

"Baldwin…" Anne's voice faltered.

"Perhaps it is best that we should go straight to court. At

any rate, God willing, you shall see the queen within a few hours. Shall we?" He asked

She only nodded.

They rode slowly toward the castle, their horses' hooves echoing on the cobblestone. The narrow winding streets seemed to stretch for miles, and Anne thought to herself how often the journey seems longer than it really is when one is in new territory, anticipating the destination. With each clop of the horse hooves, she drew closer to Richard.

When the party reached the gates, imperial guards armed with swords and pikes instantly surrounded them. Even though this was expected, it still made Anne nervous, and she exchanged glances with Baldwin. They came to a halt before the main entrance of the castle. Looking up, Anne failed to notice that more guards surrounded them. Two beside her horse caught her attention as they each raised a hand to help her down. She allowed them to do so.

Once she was on the ground, the situation changed rapidly. Suddenly, Baldwin shouted something she couldn't understand, and instinctively Anne turned to see the reason. Before she could completely turn, she felt someone grab her hands. The guards who helped her down tied her wrists together. "Stop!" Trying to resist, she managed to catch a glimpse of Baldwin bound, but with his hands behind his back. The unarmed English delegation yelled at the Germans, and they bellowed back.

Anne could hear Baldwin's voice booming. "We came of our own volition as hostages, not as prisoners or criminals. This is an insult, an outrage! Leave the lady alone, or I swear to God..." One of the guards struck Baldwin squarely in the jaw before he could finish his sentence. He managed to stay on his feet, but the clamor continued. Anne could not understand what the emperor's men said, and it was hard to make out the words of the furious English. Baldwin still struggled against his captors, and she called out to him, "Baldwin!"

The two guards put their arms under hers and nearly lifted her off the ground. The cording bit into her wrists, as they walked her to the castle. Behind her, Baldwin loudly cursed.

Upstairs in his room with Longchamp, Richard just finished packing the last trunk and was in high spirits, counting on being released. Suddenly, they heard a swelling commotion coming from the courtyard below. "What is it now?" Longchamp complained.

"You had better see." Richard sighed.

Leaving the room, Longchamp disappeared down the hall to a window over looking the courtyard. Richard could tell the fracas was moving inside. When Longchamp returned his face flushed. "Your highness, you had better come—it's Baldwin!"

Richard didn't hesitate. He shot through the door and passed the distracted guards. "Halt there!" One of them shouted, but it did no good.

Once on the stairs, Richard heard angry voices resounding from the great hall, and with the guards close on his heels, he made for it.

When he burst through the doorway, what he saw sucked the breath from his chest. Baldwin screaming, bound, and mad as hell. Beside him stood Anne, bound as well, and wide eyed as she clung to Baldwin's elbow. Just then, another round of yelling erupted, and a scuffle ensued. In the melee, Anne fell to the floor. Crying out, Richard charged into the crowd.

Awkwardly Anne tried to get up, but the toe of her shoe caught on her hem. With her hands tied so tightly she could not unhook the shoe from the hem or gain the leverage she needed to rise to her feet. Helpless, Baldwin could only stand over her.

Richard continued to push his way through, when suddenly something caught his shoulder and spun him. Before he fully understood what happened, a guard pinned him against the wall while two more stepped up quickly. One of them pulled a knife and thrust it in front of him, poised to slit his throat. "Take one more step, highness, and I'll cut your wind!"

"Let me be, man!" Richard pushed against him.

"Your highness, I don't wish to harm you, but if you force me to, I will. Now, turn around and return to your room." The guard snarled.

Anne still struggled to get up. "Is this how you make yourselves feel like men?" Richard gestured toward Anne as he shouted, "God's legs! Let me help her!"

Abruptly the room hushed. The sounds of footsteps echoed through the hall, as the crowd parted to make way for the emperor. Walking directly to Anne, he stooped down and helped her to her feet.

"My sincerest apologies, Lady Anne. This is not how my people treat a lady." His voice rang out angrily on the last sentence.

Anne stepped away from him and grabbed Baldwin's arm, which he angled toward her as best he could.

"Hohenstaufen!" Richard's voice erupted from behind his guard.

The emperor signaled for him to be allowed to come forward, and Richard shoved passed his guards. "I demand to know the meaning of this!"

Hohenstaufen shrugged. "Your last two hostages are here, Richard, and you are to be given over to your mother's custody this morning."

Richard lowered his voice, "Damn you, what are you playing at?"

"Perhaps you would like a moment in private with the lady?" Hohenstaufen didn't wait for an answer. He made a motion with his fingers and the guards seized Anne again.

They followed Hohenstaufen down the hall with Richard close behind. Hohenstaufen stopped at a door of a small room belonging to his chancellor. "This will do."

Anne entered first, and Richard followed her. Hohenstaufen and two imperial guards entered next. Without hesitation, Richard took Anne's hands. "Let us get these bloody things off you," he spoke softly to her.

Tugging at them would do no good. In desperation, Richard began to pick at them with his teeth. Coming forward, Hohenstaufen held out a knife to Richard. "I can do it," Richard snapped.

"Richard, do not be a fool, take the knife." Hohenstaufen rolled his eyes.

Grasping the handle end, Richard took it from Hohenstaufen and made quick work of the ropes. When he finished, he dropped the knife on the ground and kicked it toward Hohenstaufen without taking his eyes off Anne. Tenderly, he examined Anne's wrists where the ropes left burns or cut into the skin. "This is inexcusable!" Richard choked on the last word.

"I could not agree more." Hohenstaufen moved next to Richard. "May I?" He reached out for Anne.

"Do not touch her!" The façade of composure that Richard so carefully constructed came crashing down.

"Richard, I swear to you those guards will be punished. I am truly appalled."

Anne spoke for the first time but not to Richard. "Your highness, am I to understand from this you have declined my offer?"

"What offer? I demand to know what is going on, and I demand to know now!" Richard released Anne.

"It is simple really. Lady Anne here has agreed to be a hostage to secure your freedom," Hohenstaufen explained.

"What? This was nothing we discussed!"

"Your delegation, acting on your behalf agreed to this. Are you going to go back on our treaty that we have work so hard for?" Hohenstaufen picked up the knife from the floor and tucked it into his belt.

"Richard," Anne whispered.

"You are not going to do this, Anne, no." Richard instinctively put himself between Anne and Hohenstaufen. "Since when are women hostages?"

Anne gently touched him on the arm, and Richard spun around. "Think of your kingdom."

"I will not allow it!" Richard shook his head. Anne looked into his eyes, and Richard repeated more empathically, "I will not allow it. You will not remain here."

They stood silent for a moment. "The treaty has already been made." Hohenstaufen's voice sounded behind Richard. "So long as you keep your end of the bargain, I swear before God and his angels no harm will come to Lady Anne."

"Just as no harm has come to me? Will she be getting the kind of hospitality that you show to kings?"

"When I am certain that you are not double crossing me," Hohenstaufen continued undeterred, "I will accept her ransom, and she will be returned to you."

Richard fiercely shook his head. "I have been tricked by this ruse before! No!"

"It should be no more than a year."

"By God's right arm, I damn you! I will not leave without her."

Hohenstaufen moved away from Richard and Anne and took a seat in a chair across the room. "You will be free to go as soon as we have concluded our business. By that same token you are free to stay. The choice *is* yours, but the lady is going to remain here."

As Richard looked at Anne the horrible realization began to crush him. Hohenstaufen had the upper hand. He had been outwitted. He had to choose between Anne and his kingdom.

"Will is…" Anne's voice trailed off.

"Where is Will?" Richard wanted to gather her into his

arms, but something prevented him.

"The Abbot of Marseilles is a childhood friend. He is bringing Will to meet you in London." Anne looked away from Richard.

"No, no, you are not staying here. I cannot leave you here, Anne." Richard tried to reach out to her, but she drew back.

"You are the King of England," she pleaded, still not looking at him.

"And you the Viscountess of Marseilles," he retorted.

"Etienne has Marseilles well under hand, and Will will be of age soon enough."

He took a moment before he replied, trying carefully to form his words. "Anne, when you left Cyprus... I swore if I ever got the chance, I would... Anne, I was coming for you."

"Please do not make this any harder than it is," Anne whispered.

Richard still fumbled for words, "I am not going to..." He suddenly seized on what to say. "England—the kingdom—be damned. I cannot trade you for a crown."

Anne put her arms around his neck. Placing her right hand in his hair, she pressed his ear close to her lips. "You could never give up your kingdom. It is a part of you just as your hands or feet. You need her, and she needs you. Think. Where would we go, Richard? Marseilles? You would never be content to let John and Philip tear apart your realm. It would wound you to your very core. If you lost England, you would lose yourself, and then I would lose you. This is the only way. All I ask is that you take care of Will." Her left hand tightened around a bunch of his tunic, and she whispered, "Do your duty, Richard."

She released him and walked over to Hohenstaufen giving the emperor a curtsy. "Your highness, I know it is yet still early in the day, but I humbly ask to be shown to my lodging. I need to make arrangements to have my things sent up from the inn."

"Of course. My chancellor is just outside, and he will show

you." Hohenstaufen rose to his feet and opened the door for her.

Anne did not look back at Richard. She simply left the room.

Chancellor Martin took her down another hall as he inquired about her belongings. "Up here," he motioned to a staircase. "We will be going all the way to the top."

The significance was not lost on Anne. No matter the kingdom, servants lodged in the highest rooms; still, she followed without protest.

The staircase twisted around in the usual manner, built for defence so anyone coming up would find it hard to slash with his sword arm, while those coming down had room to do so. At intervals, there were arrow slits, and Anne paused at one. She could see through it down to the courtyard where Richard mounted a walnut coloured horse. Longchamp and the English delegation joined him there. Two German bishops on their horses would facilitate the exchange. The bishops began to move, but Richard hesitated.

"Lady Anne, if you will…" Chancellor Martin tried to steer her by the shoulders away from the slit.

Anne shook him off. She watched as Longchamp said something to Richard, and finally Richard gave his horse a soft spur and followed the bishops. Anne remained in place until he passed out of her sight beyond the gate.

Chapter Seventy

While in Speyer, Eleanor chose to lodge not with the emperor's court, but as a guest of the bishop just in case the emperor proved fickle. This morning the long months of waiting were to be over. She rose early in anticipation. As she and her entourage waited outside the cathedral, Eleanor looked around, her emotions wild. The return of her beloved son should have been a happy occasion, but the fact that many she personally cared about served as hostages, marred it. Worst of all, Anne as a hostage bought Richard's freedom. Two men returned from court to report what happened when Anne and Baldwin arrived. The news deeply grieved Eleanor. She felt forced to choose between two children. She cared for Anne as though she were her own, and Anne already spent too much time imprisoned because of her connection to Eleanor's family. In the end though, the good of the realm weighed more heavily than personal feelings.

The sound of horses in the distance drew her attention. Looking up she could see the bishops approaching, one being the Bishop of Speyer. Just then, a burst of sunlight came through the clouds. Eleanor thought to herself that it could not have been more poetic if she wrote it herself. The banners of the King of England snapped in the wind. Behind them rode the English delegation and, much to her relief, Richard. She said a silent prayer of thanks to God for his deliverance.

As they approached, Eleanor descended the steps of the cathedral. He dismounted and knelt before her. "Mother."

Finding it difficult to control her conflicting emotions, Eleanor rushed into his arms, weeping and shaking. She looked much more frail and thin than ever, little more than skin and bones. Fifteen months ago he was supposed to have arrived in London. Clearly the pressure took its toll on Eleanor. Several of the company shed tears at the sight.

"I am free," he whispered in her ear.

Eleanor composed herself. "We have a barge waiting on the river. We must be on our way."

Richard noticed their horses and carts already packed for the voyage, but hesitated to make a move towards them. "The sooner we get you out of Germany, the sooner we can get Anne out," Eleanor spoke discreetly to him.

Richard's eyes flashed. "Did Philip have anything to do with this?"

"No," Eleanor answered swiftly. "His delegation let her name slip, and as soon as he found out, he recalled them, all except the Bishop of Beauvais who somehow convinced Philip it was not him who let her name be spilt." Eleanor narrowed her eyes. She knew that it must have been the vindictive manipulator Beauvais. "Of those that were sent home, not one of them arrived at the border alive, if rumors are to be believed."

Still, Richard did not make a move to leave. Eleanor prodded him, "Richard we must both get on that barge. The sooner we get out of this God-forsaken territory, the better."

Richard closed his eyes and gave a slight nod.

Philip wrote John a letter containing the words of warning: *"Beware, the devil is loosed."* As soon as John received this letter, he fled England and made for Paris, because he wanted to consult Philip.

Philip received John in his throne room. He knew that John brought him a gift. Philip watched as John marched up to his throne and knelt before him. "My lord, here are the keys to the fortress at Touraine." John thrust them forward tied to a parchment. John sought a haven from the storm that would rage when his brother returned.

Philip rose from his throne and slowly descended the steps. He studied John. John did not have the same build as his brother. He lacked not only the barrel chest, but also the commanding regal air that surrounded Richard. John exuded only arrogance. "You are giving me the fortress of Touraine, a very strategic key to your brother's realm, just like that?"

"For you, your highness." John held the keys out further.

Philip narrowed his eyes. His brothers were hard to win

over, but John seemed to jump at the first hint of opportunity in the wind. Remembering how John turned on his own father, the man who championed him for so long, made Philip's stomach churn.

As he reached out and took the parchment, Philip felt nothing but disgust toward the man kneeling in front of him. John moved too quickly to betrayal. He had neither principles nor backbone. But John was handing over an important castle to him— Richard's fortress, his enemy's fortress, his *friend's* fortress.

Next to him a great mastiff, now named Beatrice gave a low gruff as if speaking her master's thoughts. Philip closed his fingers around the parchment as he looked down at John. "France thanks you for your gift." He dismissed John with a wave of his hand, without offering a gift in return.

Anne explored her new lodgings. In the bleak room several straw pallets were stacked up against the wall. She would be sharing this room with others, but how many was uncertain. Above her something fluttered, and looking up, Anne could see a slight hole in roof letting in a cold breeze. Visions of her time imprisoned with Eleanor flashed in her head, and a shudder ran through her. Perhaps it was the cold, the memories, or both.

"Cousin Anne." A voice came from behind her, and she spun around.

To her disappointment, the Bishop of Beauvais, her other cousin Philip, stood before her. "Bishop," she whispered a weary greeting.

Built like Philip, Beauvais had the same blonde hair, but the Bishop's eyes were darker, and narrower. "I heard you were here, my child." He moved closer to her.

Immediately Anne did not trust him. Something deep inside her sounded a warning. She decided it was he who let her name slip to the emperor. "Indeed, I am here."

"I sense that you do not like me." Beauvais gave her a

mocking look of concern. "Come now, we are family, after all."

Anne snickered. "That does not mean much to some."

"I wonder if it means anything at all to you." Beauvais scolded her like a child. "But here I am come to minister to you, comfort you, in your present… situation."

"I am not in need of your services, at present."

"Oh, but you are. Your life is in danger; your soul is in danger." Beauvais became animated and threw his arms out as he spoke.

Anne bit the inside of her lip trying not to lose her temper with the overly dramatic man. "We are human, therefore, our lives and souls are constantly in danger, even yours."

"Clearly you do not appreciate your particular peril." Beauvais moved himself directly in front of Anne. "Let me elucidate it for you."

"Bishop…" Anne put up her hands to stop him, but he continued on.   "You see, cousin, you have disgraced your family by falling prey to that lecherous man England calls their king."

"I have disgraced no one!" Anne straightened herself up. "You have no idea what you are talking about. You do not know me, and you obviously know nothing about Richard."

"Aye, but King Philip knows you, and you have betrayed him. How could you after all he has done for you?" Beauvais eyes turned darker as he narrowed them even more.

"This is ridiculous," Anne scoffed.

"Perhaps you are thinking that you can use Richard to somehow further your position in life? You are delusional, cousin."

"You certainly know about delusions." Anne didn't censure her thoughts.

"Let me tell you what I know!" Beauvais raised his voice. Anne tried to duck passed him, but he caught both of her sore wrists in his hands. "I know that you have taken up with Richard like harlot. He commits sodomy, Lady Anne, sodomy!"

"How would you know which sexual positions he prefers if you are not in his bed?" Anne wanted to scratch at him, but could only struggle against him.

In a rage he slammed her back against the wall. "Do you dare accuse a servant of God of such vile acts?"

"You are accusing a king, who also serves God, and you are accusing me," she shouted.

Pinning her against the wall with his forearm, he fished out a crude wooden cross from under his robe. He took it off and placed it in her hand. "Take hold of the sign of Christ, Lady Anne!"

Anne would not wrap her fingers around it. She wanted to ram the symbol of Christianity down his throat. "You cannot convince me that just because you call yourself a bishop that you are above carnal lusts."

"Take hold of it!" He screamed as he forced her fingers closed, his nails digging into her flesh. "You have been shown the grace of God, Anne. He has seen fit to remove you from your temptation, and place you here where you are safe from that monster." Anne sank towards the floor in pain, but Beauvais pulled her back up. "You have been given the chance to repent your sins and save yourself from the eternal fires of hell." He pinned her again, but this time he slipped the cross around her neck and lifted it up to her eyes. His breath reeked of spoiled cabbage. "Pray, Lady Anne. Pray to God. Embrace the gift you have been given. The Counts of Anjou were spawned by the devil himself, and God in his mercy sees fit to liberate you. Do not spit in his face." He forced Anne to her knees.

Beauvais' fanatical fervor made her fear he would cut her throat as a sacrifice. Beauvais took her hands and placed them together if to pray. "Please," she begged. "Let me go. You are hurting me."

"Pray, Lady Anne." He shook her roughly. "This pain is

nothing compared to eternal damnation. Pray!" In one swift move he released her, moved away from her, and Anne fell on her hands and knees.

Anne lifted her head to see what Beauvais would do next. She expected him to be holding a dagger over her, but he wasn't. The bishop slowly backed away toward the door. "Pray," he whispered over and over until he was gone from the room.

Rising to her feet, Anne found herself alone again. The bishop was raving mad. How long would he stay in Speyer? The thought terrified her. She wanted more than anything to raise her voice and have Richard return to her, but she knew he was long gone by now. It was too late.

In the scuffle several of the straw pallets tumbled from their stack. Anne took one and shoved it in the corner, then lay upon it. At last, she allowed herself to cry.

Long before dawn a husky woman's voice barked at Anne, "Time to get up!"

Anne remained in the realm of sleep between dreaming and waking. "I haven't got all day! Get up!" The woman kicked at the straw tick Anne slept on.

Slowly Anne opened her eyes, and before her stood a large woman as round as she was tall. "You speak French?" Anne slowly rose to her feet.

"Yes! That is why I'm saddled with the unpleasant task of watching after you," the woman gruffed.

"I am sorry to be any trouble," Anne offered.

The woman huffed at Anne. "You might not want to wear that dress to start the empress' fire."

"I am sorry, start her fire?"

"Come now, don't tell me you thought they started themselves. The fires have been out since last night, and in case you haven't noticed, it's cold in this castle."

"Although I was promised to be treated as a guest, I do not mind serving her highness, but to be assigned fire duty," Anne protested.

"Well now, just who do you think you are? You may be the mistress of a king, but here in this court, you are nothing more than a servant to her highness. You're not to be seen or heard; just do as you're told." The woman looked more like a troll than a person.

"Fine," Anne grouched. "Where is my lady, and where are my belongings?"

"Your lady?" The woman cackled. "The emperor sent her on her way with the English. You've no need of her here. As for your enormous trunk, it has been stored away for you. As you can see, there is no room up here. Now, get going. Her highness's chamber is on the third floor, second on the left." She turned and left the room. Anne could hear the woman's gabble, "Where is my lady?" trail off behind her.

Looking around, Anne noticed everyone else who slept in this room left to perform their duties already. She let out a long groan. How could she change her dress without her trunk? Then the thought occurred to her that it had probably been plundered. It seemed that the emperor would not keep his promise, and she must be constantly on guard for her safety. To begin with, Anne knew she must obey the troll-woman. It would be best to not be seen or heard.

"Surely Anne did not stay there long. Richard or even King Philip must have done something!" Bogis interrupted Breton.

"Philip did what he could, but I will get to that later." Breton waved his hand. "Sadly, there was very little Richard could do for the moment. Eleanor was wise to leave Speyer at once. Just as Pharaoh of old, Hohenstaufen changed his mind and sent men after Richard, but he arrived safely in Cologne where the emperor had little influence."

"Do not tell me Richard parted the English Channel," Bogis snickered.

Breton smiled at the joke. "No, no parting of waters, but he did arrive safely back in England, welcomed as the returning hero."

"Wait, didn't he have some kind of a second coronation or something?" Bogis furrowed his brow.

"Nice, Bogis. You were young, but I see you remember. Richard did have a second coronation. He needed to make it clear that he was still King of England, not only because of the trouble John caused or to dispel the rumors that he was dead, but because of what Hohenstaufen made him do. After the third trial, Hohenstaufen forced Richard to swear fealty to him for his lands in France. Richard wanted it perfectly clear that England was his and no one else's."

Bogis clicked his tongue. "King Philip must have been furious. Richard owed his fealty to him."

"It certainly did not make them allies again." Breton smirked. "There was another part of the agreement—Richard was to be crowned King of Provence. That coronation never did take place though. I personally think he wanted to wait until he had Anne back. She would have owed her fealty to him, had he actually been crowned." Breton shrugged. "Regardless, Richard did have a second coronation-like ceremony. After that, he went on progress to let the people of his kingdom know their king had returned. I doubt his heart was really in it though. Oh, to be sure, he put on a façade and performed like the most accomplished of players. With Eleanor at his side, he ordered Berengaria to remain at Poitiers until further notice."

Anne's duties fell far beneath a lady in waiting, but she performed them just as well. Early one morning as she cleaned cinders from the grate in the empress' outer chamber, the door to the inner chamber opened. The emperor emerged wearing a dressing robe and looking cross. As quickly as she could, Anne rose from her knees to a curtsy. The emperor looked right at her and swore, "Damnable cantankerous woman."

Squinting his eyes, Hohenstaufen stepped toward her. "Lady Anne?"

Anne's head shot up in surprise. "Yes, your highness," Anne lowered her head again.

"What on earth are you doing playing in the fireplace?"

"I was told to clean it, my lord."

"You are supposed to be at Trifels." He shook his head in confusion. "How long have you been here?"

"I have not left your court," Anne spoke quietly.

"You look… what are you wearing? I hardly recognised you." Hohenstaufen wrinkled his nose.

Anne looked down at her outfit. She traded her dress for a linen cote, and her hair was pulled back under a long blue kerchief. She felt her cheeks flush with embarrassment. "The tr—" Anne coughed on what she almost said. "Berta, the one who speaks French, told me to serve the empress."

Before Hohenstaufen could speak again, the door to the inner chamber flew open, and Empress Constance stepped out. "Oh," she turned her nose up at Hohenstaufen. "I did not think you would still be here."

"Still here, my queen." He gave her a sarcastic smile.

"You woman, if you are not too busy being seduced by my husband, I would like my breakfast brought up as soon as possible. And find someone who can play a decent lute." She narrowed her eyes at her husband. "I need to hear something pleasant sounding to restore my spirits." Empress Constance returned to her bedchamber, slamming the door behind her.

Swiftly, Anne gave the emperor another curtsy and left the room for the kitchens.

"Joanna wrote me a letter," Richard informed his mother.

They were staying at the royal hunting lodge at Clipstone in Sherwood Forest, taking a break from progress. Richard spent only as much time with others as absolutely necessary. Tonight, as with many nights, he retired to his room early. Eleanor frequently followed him, and the two kept each other company. Often saying nothing for long stretches of time, they sat together, Eleanor sewing next to a fire and Richard responding to letters. Members of Richard's council would come and go only as needed. At Richard's speaking, Eleanor put down her sewing. "What does Joanna say?"

"She wants to know what I am going to say about the suit that Count of Toulouse proposes." Richard sat back in his chair and folded his arms across his chest.

"Impertinent girl, matchmaking for herself," Eleanor mumbled.

Richard could not help but chuckle. "Like mother, like daughter."

"Oh, my son! If I were not so old, I should pretend to be offended."

"In some ways the match makes sense. It would form an alliance with Toulouse, which has always been a problem area." Richard thought aloud.

"Yes, but she would be his what, fourth wife?" Eleanor added. "That man goes through wives as an archer goes through arrows."

Richard held a far away look in his eye. "And Joanna longs to be added to his quiver. She is pleading with me like I never heard her do before. I think she really is in love with him."

"Be that as it may, you of all people know that one does not marry for love."

Giving a long sigh, Richard continued, "Joanna said

494

something to me while we were in Sicily, '*Is it so hard to believe that someone could fall in love with me and I with him?*'" He looked at his mother. "I believe you loved our father when the two of you married. You may have even loved him until the day he died."

Eleanor looked at her son. The frustration, anguish, loyalty, love of his realm, sense of duty and honor, depression, and regret in him seemed to be balled up into a tangible form around him. "You should do what you feel is best."

Richard slowly nodded. "I think I shall give Toulouse permission to marry Joanna when his annulment is finalized." He let out a long breath as though cleansing himself of guilt.

Eleanor smiled at him. Instinctively she knew what he hoped by giving his consent to the marriage, he would somehow feel better. She went back to her sewing.

While she worked, her thoughts wandered. She knew Richard had not heard from Baldwin or the delegation he ordered to stay to negotiate Anne's release. Eleanor knew what it felt like to be a prisoner, and now, so did Richard. That made bearing the silent wait even worse.

Midmorning the next day, a small group of clergy arrived at the lodge. Richard was hunting with Longchamp, Blondel, and Marshal, who joined him from London. Marshal's page brought the news of the clergy to them, just as they were about to flush out a doe. "Your highness, my lords, there is a group of clergy at the lodge. They say they are returning from a pilgrimage to Canterbury."

"They are a long way from Canterbury," Marshal observed.

The page continued, "They say that they have come all the way from Marseilles."

Richard did not reply. He turned his horse and sped toward the lodge.

Reaching the lodge before the others, he demanded of the stable boy, "Where are the men from Marseilles?"

"I believe they are in the hall, your highness." The boy bowed.

Hardly pausing to listen, Richard bounded up the steps and into the building. Rounding the corner, he could hear Occitan coming from the hall. He entered and there saw a group of half a dozen clergy. One, he could tell, was an abbot. They all bowed to the king. Without being told, Richard knew the oblate. "Will!"

"Your highness." Will bowed gracefully before him.

"God's legs!" Richard exclaimed. "You must be as tall as your mother…" Richard's voice trailed off on the last word.

"Your highness, may I present Abbot Mathias, Fathers Bartholomew, Clemens, Johan, and Vincent."

"Welcome to England," Richard grinned at the polish of Will's manners. "I humbly thank you for escorting my godson to me, Abbot Mathias."

"I regret that we were unable to meet you in London. We were detained in our crossing of the channel," Mathias apologized.

"My lord, where is my mother?" Will turned his hazel eyes up to Richard.

Cautiously Richard put his hand on Will's shoulder. "Will, I am afraid that she is still in Germany." Next to Will, Abbot Mathias flushed a shade of scarlet. "Here, come with me, and I shall explain."

Richard motioned for Will to follow him and Will began, but as if from nowhere came three mastiffs, two adults and a puppy. Richard gave Will a quizzical look.

"King Philip sent the two to my mother as a present, for protection. I hope you do not mind." Will was sheepish.

"No, son, I do not mind."

"The pup is a gift from me to you to celebrate your release," Will added.

"Thank you, Will. Perhaps we can all go hunting together later. Would you like that?" Richard tried to smile, but his guilt about Anne gnawed at him.

"Yes, sire."

"Good. Well, first come with me to the garden. We must speak."

"Yes, your highness."

"I am still Uncle Richard, Will," Richard reminded his godson.

Chapter Seventy-one

Richard spoke to Will in frank tones. Instinct told him that the boy was growing into a young man, and being anything less than direct would be insulting. Will seemed to take the news well and remained stoic as Richard explained the events of Speyer. The last thing Richard said to Will as they sat side-by-side on a bench in the rustic garden, was, "I will get her back, Will. I promise you."

Will only nodded. Behind them Marshal entered the garden. "Your highness, I am sorry to disturb you, but the clergy are preparing to leave."

"Leaving?" Richard wrinkled his brow.

"Yes, I tried to persuade them to stay, but the abbot is bent on going." Marshal shrugged.

"I think I know why; they must be anxious about the return of their viscountess." Richard breathed a long sigh. "I will go to them."

"They are in the stables, my lord."

"Thank you, Marshal. Would you be so good as to show Will to his room?" He called over his shoulder as he left the garden, "I still want to hunt with you this afternoon, Will."

t

The five men were in the stables just as Marshal said. "Abbot," Richard called out. "I have been searching for you."

Mathias stopped what he was doing and turned around. "Pray, forgive me, your highness, but we must be on our way." Mathias tried to be civil. He turned to his companions. "Go on, I will be with you shortly."

Richard watched the other priests leave, then turned back to the abbot. "I wanted to thank you again for bringing Will safely here to me."

"I did it for the boy's mother. Castile is on the prowl again, so it will be a great comfort for her to know that her son is safe." Mathias wanted nothing more than to leave the presence of the king.

"Are you returning to Marseilles then?"

Mathias let out a long breath. He did not wish the conversation to continue. "No, not just yet. My lord, I pray you allow me to take my leave now."

Richard declared, "Abbot, I will get her back."

Abbot Mathias placed one hand on his saddle and took in a deep breath, trying to calm himself. It failed. "With all due respect, your highness, I cannot delay any longer. I am going to do what you cannot."

Richard began, "You must believe me when I say…"

Mathias lost his temper and balled up his right fist. "I cannot believe you would leave her there. I mean really, who uses a woman like that?"

Richard waved a finger at him. "Watch that tongue, Abbot Mathias. I had no knowledge of any of this. Had I known what was in motion, I would have put a stop to it. Hohenstaufen took her hostage. If I stayed, then we both would have been prisoners with no hope of freedom. Now that I am free, I can work to free her."

"And what have you done to that end, my lord?" Mathias glared at Richard.

"I am doing all that I can. The money is there for her ransom, and I left men to negotiate the terms, including my man, Sir Baldwin."

"Your man, the one that convinced her to go in the first place? That is comforting." Mathias scowled.

Richard's body tensed. "I understand your anger, Abbott, and I understand the people of Marseilles are anxious to have their lady back but…"

"I am a man of the cloth, and I can tell when people are only trying to ease their own conscience," Mathias sneered.

Richard growled. "I love her with my whole soul."

"Love her?" Mathias let out an odd laugh. "Love her? I loved her long before you even knew she existed. I would never have left her in Hohenstaufen's court! Nothing in this world or even the next could have compelled me to leave her there."

"If that is they way you feel, then you do not really know Anne."

Before he was conscious of his actions, with his balled up fist, Mathias hit Richard in the jaw. It felt good and Mathias did not care what consequence it might bring. As quick as thought, Richard's forearm pinned Mathias by the throat, throwing his back against the stable door. "I have done it," Mathias choked out. "Run me through, if it be your will."

Richard regarded Mathias for a moment. "For her sake, you will live today." Richard released him and rubbed at the spot where Mathias made contact. "I never thought a priest could have such a powerful fist."

Mathias held his head high. "I am not just a priest. I am an abbot."

"Then, Abbot Mathias, you do what you feel you must, and

I will do what I must." Richard slightly nodded toward Mathias and left him standing there in the stables.

Mathias felt stunned, not only at himself, but that he was free to go. He expected after he struck a king that he would die.

t

The Empress took a shine to Anne, and Anne's situation improved after that morning by the fire. She brought the empress' breakfast personally and luckily secured a lute, which she played for the empress. After that, the empress called for Anne to wait upon her more often.

As the days turned into weeks, Anne continued to attempt to make the best of her circumstances. One evening Empress Constance prepared for bed after soaking her feet in rosewater and Anne dried them for her. Constance sighed. "The emperor will be here any moment now." Anne only nodded.

Constance continued, "If I do not conceive soon, I fear I shall go mad. The less time I spend with my...*husband*... the better." Constance leaned her head back against the chair and closed her eyes. "How I miss those blissfully ignorant days before marriage. Lady Anne, play us something so that we may pass the time pleasantly."

"Yes, your highness." Anne picked up the lute propped up against the cushioned window seat and played several soft songs to soothe the empress. She played them by instinct, not reason, as if her fingers were doing the playing while Anne was lost in thought. From her chair, Constance continued reciting her inventory of the emperor's faults. Anne paid no attention, as she felt particularly lonesome for Marseilles, Will, and Richard.

As if waking from a dream, Anne became aware of the song she was playing, the song she played the night she first met Richard. Abruptly she stopped. Constance halted her complaining. "Do not stop, Lady Anne. I like that one. Does it have words?"

Tears welled up in her eyes. "Yes," she managed, "but they

are in Occitan and hard to translate."

Constance waved her hand and commanded, "Sing them anyway."

Anne looked down at the instrument. Her fingers were as heavy as lead and would not rise to touch the strings. "I cannot," she whispered.

Constance turned around to chastise, but saw Anne sitting there limply holding the instrument, tears filling her eyes. The empress knew who Anne was but never breeched the subject with her. The sight of Anne now made her feel sorry for the lady. In her younger days, Constance longed to love and be loved. Now dreadfully unhappy in her marriage, she desperately missed her native Sicily. Constance knew what it was like to be so far from the people and places that one loved. "Lady Anne, what did you do to deserve this fate?" It was almost as if she were asking the question of herself.

Anne looked up from the instrument and a tear rolled down her cheek. "I dared to love a king."

Hereafter, Empress Constance adopted a stance of compassion towards Anne. Constance even let Anne know that Baldwin was at Trifels, and by all accounts doing well there. Even better, soon the court would be moving there. Much to Anne's disappointment, when they arrived, she learnt that Baldwin was sent to Speyer. Hohenstaufen did not want to take a chance that Baldwin would get a gallant idea and try to rescue Anne.

Shortly after the court moved to Trifles, the physicians confirmed Constance was with child, and the entire court seemed to give a collective sigh of relief. Hohenstaufen called for a celebration. The festivities began at midday and lasted until well into the night. At last, the empress rose to go to bed. Along with the other ladies, Anne followed, but Hohenstaufen stopped her. "Walk with me, Lady Anne."

The emperor started up the staircase with Anne behind him. They climbed to the arched balcony that overlooked the great hall below. There he stopped.

Laughter crescendoed from below as the assembled seemed to take the leaving of their sovereigns as a cue to relax their behavior. Hohenstaufen stood looking down upon them with a slight air of disdain. He took a sip of wine from his goblet. Trying to discern what the emperor watched so intently, Anne looked over the edge. Below many people moved about, and a couple of musicians prepared to play. Then one man caught her attention. His dark soft hair and mannerisms were unmistakable. "Why, Lady Anne, you look as though you have seen a ghost," Hohenstaufen observed. "Here," he handed her his goblet, "have a sip."

Taking only a taste, Anne obeyed but said nothing. Handing the goblet back to Hohenstaufen, she continued to watch Castile below. "I can tell who you spotted below. It would seem your husband has come to court, Lady Anne. His brother-in-law, the King of Aragon, told him where to find you."

"Your highness," she managed to whisper.

"Oh, you need not fear, my dear. Why do you think I brought you up here?" He didn't wait for her to answer but continued on. "He says he came to pay your ransom."

"With what money? Mine?" Anne blurted out.

Hohenstaufen smiled at her spirit. "He claims to have the entire amount and more."

Anne scowled. "Raymond of Castile has no money of his own. He borrows from someone with nothing but promises for collateral. Then borrows from another to pay the first."

"That is a rather interesting way to do business." Hohenstaufen took another sip.

Anne shook her head. "I beg your pardon, sire, but the bill must always be paid. In the end, the money comes due."

"Lady Anne, have a care with my castle, clawing at it will do you no good. I assure you, if it can withstand Richard, it can withstand your clutches."

With the Emperor's comment, Anne became aware that she

was digging her fingers into the lip on the balcony before her. Her knuckles turned white, and her fingers scratched from the rough stone. Embarrassed, she released her grip.

"I assure you, I am not going to take his offer. You are worth more than his promises. You will bring a good price, and Richard will keep to his bargain if you are here." Hohenstaufen spoke into his nearly empty goblet, "Not to mention the fact that by some miracle of God, you are able to placate my wife."

"Most humbly, I thank you, your highness."

"Well then, Lady Anne, I believe I shall retire. Do us both a charm and stay close to the empress, will you? It will make it easier to keep track of you, and make her easier to live with." He bid her goodnight and left for his apartments.

Anne took one last look at Castile. He had a serving girl on his lap with one hand clutching a turkey leg and the other her breast. Anne grumbled to herself, "At least if he is milking the maid, he is nowhere near my son."

Chapter Seventy-two

Will trudged to a clearing in the woods behind the hunting lodge, the dogs trailing after him. He followed the sounds of wood knocking together and found Richard sparring with another knight. Leaning against a tree, he watched as Richard and the knight used wooden swords to practice their technique. Even from a distance he could tell that these wasters were not the kind of wooden weapons given to children. These were carefully

crafted and balanced to simulate a real sword. Naturally, a knight would not use his real sword to spar with; that could inflict too much damage on a valuable piece of weaponry.

"They say your father is very good with a sword." Marshal's voice sounded behind Will.

At the mention of his father, Will wrinkled his nose. "My mother says diplomacy is important." He noticed Marshall a few feet away on the other side of the tree and wondered if he had been there the whole time.

Marshal stepped past the tree, his hands resting on his hip and pommel. "Yes, diplomacy has its place, but sometimes the sword must be unsheathed."

"Yes, sir," Will spoke softly.

Will knew Marshal studied him for a moment. "Master Will," Marshal continued, nodding at Richard. "Do you know why a knight does what he does?"

Will watched Richard take a solid stance, preparing for his opponent to come at him again. "I suppose it is because that is what people expect him to do. It is what he must do."

"My boy, you should not become a knight just because it is expected of you." Marshal shook his head. "See, Will, a knight must decide the best weapon to use in a fight, be it diplomacy or the sword."

"Yes, but must a knight always fight?"

"He does not always fight, but he must fight when needed, or he is no knight," Marshal explained. "A good knight must always have a just reason to fight."

"And what about a king? He has plenty of knights to do the fighting for him." The boy paused for a moment, realizing that he was irritated not by the topic, but because his father was mentioned. Marshal remained silent, allowing Will to work it out on his own. Finally Will answered himself, "Yes, Sir Marshal, I understand that it is his duty to do so, and to inspire his men."

"That is not all, boy. Just as any other knight, be he a king or not, he fights for God. He fights for his kingdom. He fights to protect those weaker than himself. He fights for his honor." Marshal paused and looked out at Richard. "He fights for her."

"Her?"

Marshal's firm hand softly patted Will on top of his right shoulder. "Your mother, boy. The woman he loves." He turned around and left Will to his thoughts.

As Hohenstaufen continued with his celebrations, the thought occurred to Anne that part of his joy stemmed from the fact that he did not have to spend as much time with Constance now that she was with child. The emperor was so giddy that he even performed some of his own compositions for the court. Although many of the songs were in German, Anne was surprised to find them interesting, the carefully crafted melodies pleasing to the ear.

After one evening of watching her husband perform, Empress Constance decided to retire early and called on Anne to help her prepare for bed. As Anne brushed Constance's hair, the empress queried, "As a musician, what did you think of that last song of the emperor's?"

Anne had a mouth full of hairpins, which she removed and laid gently on the dressing table before Constance. She knew she must carefully weigh her answer because too much praise of the emperor would put Constance in a foul mood, but too little praise would be an insult. "I found the melody to have a slight lilting quality, but as the lyrics were in German, I do not think I can truly weigh the quality of the song."

Constance replied slyly, "I found the lyrics exceptionally interesting. You did not understand them then?"

"I am afraid not, my lady."

"*ê ich mich ir verzige, ich verzige mich ê der krône.*" Constance repeated the lines in German, and then translated them for Anne, "Before I give her up, I'd rather give up the crown."

Caught off guard, Anne nearly dropped the brush. She grabbed it and mumbled, "I beg your pardon, your highness. That was clumsy of me."

"Clearly, the emperor had some inspiration for his song, obviously not me." Constance put her hand up to stop Anne. "I think that will do for tonight. I should like to sleep with my hair unbound."

"Yes, Empress." Anne placed the brush on the table next to the hairpins.

"Play me something while I fall asleep," Constance ordered Anne as she climbed into bed.

Anne obeyed, and at length the empress fell asleep. When Anne was sure of this, she silently slipped out of the bedchamber and into the outer chamber where she met the troll, Berta. "And just what do you think you're doing?" Berta demanded.

"The empress is asleep." Anne shrugged.

Just then a soft knock sounded at the door. Anne went to open it, but Berta shoved her out of the way. "Whoever it is had best not be waking the empress," Berta gruffed.

When Berta opened the door, Anne saw Chancellor Martin. "Good evening, Chancellor." Berta greeted him so sweetly, that Anne simply rolled her eyes.

"Ah, Lady Anne." Chancellor Martin spied Anne standing behind Berta.

"Chancellor." Anne gave him a polite curtsy.

Berta pouted that the chancellor came seeking Anne, and she firmly planted her large body next to Anne. Chancellor Martin looked at Berta standing there. "Um… yes… pray, excuse us. This is a private matter."

Anne was certain she heard the woman beside her growl, as she walked away. Once Berta was gone, Chancellor Martin produced two pieces of parchment and held them out to Anne. "Lady Anne, these were written by your King Richard during his stay with the emperor. The emperor now wishes that I give them to you." Martin gave a crooked smile. "These papers intrigued his highness, and I think perhaps he hopes you can shed some light on them."

Also curious about what was written on that parchment, Anne first thought it was something that Hohenstaufen wanted to use against Richard, but she remained polite to the chancellor. "I thank you, sir, and the emperor as well." She took the papers from him.

"Yes, well, give them a good read tonight because the emperor wishes to see you tomorrow morning before breakfast in his throne room."

After he left, Anne quickly thought of a place she could read the parchment without interruption. Knowing that Berta was close by and undoubtedly planning to bully her, Anne slipped out of the room to the back stairs. "Just where do you think you are going?" Berta boomed after her, but Anne ignored the troll.

Anne made her way to the kitchens, where Berta was unlikely to follow because there were stairs involved. Also Castile would not likely be there, as he would never lower himself to be seen in a kitchen. The massive spits were empty, the fires waning. Only a few souls remained there to finish cleaning the kitchen, and the next crew for the morning meal had not yet arrived. The smell of spices and herbs tickled her nose as she made her way to a stool, usually reserved for a spit boy, by one of the fires.

Turning her back on those in the kitchen, she opened the first parchment. Musical notations were written on it, and it was indeed in Richard's handwriting. That was certainly not what she had expected to see. She opened the second piece, containing lyrics.

I want to stay constant, defend your virtue

For I love you so deeply

That even the limitless sea could not my

heart hold.

I cannot coerce myself from loving you.

My memories, my pleasure, and my desires

are all eternally of you.

Why would the emperor possibly want to discuss this with her? Anne felt uneasy with the thought that Hohenstaufen read these poems, clearly about her. She felt he invaded a private garden or sanctuary of Richard and hers.

Trying to forget Hohenstaufen, she focused on the wording of the poem. It was as if Richard spoke to her, and his words held her tight. By reading his words, she thought she could somehow repair the imaginary garden wall that Hohenstaufen invaded. She read the next poem.

Not capture, nor malady

Nor what others tell me

Can compel my soul to forget you.

So significant is my longing to see you I

can think of nothing   else.

My paramour, my queen, my beloved,

It is you and only you who keeps me alive.

Images of Richard held captive in this place, alone, bereft of all friends, and humiliated, tormented her. The thought of his pain made Anne ache inside. She could empathize very well with his feelings when he wrote these words. The misery spilled out from her soul until her body felt the physical longing to be near Richard, hear his voice, or even touch his hand that wrote these words. For now, his writings would act as a balm.

Before breakfast, Anne entered the throne room as instructed. The house was just beginning to stir, and not many walked the corridors. When Chancellor Martin showed her in, she immediately noticed there were only four men in the room. The emperor sat on the throne, and to his left stood three men dressed for travel. There was also a young woman in the shadows behind the throne.

Even as Anne approached the throne, the emperor and the tallest of the three strangers were immersed in a whispered conversation. At the foot of the throne, Anne gave the emperor a curtsy and waited until he acknowledged her before standing completely upright. "Lady Anne," Hohenstaufen said, abruptly ending his conversation with the tall man.

"Good morning, your highness," Anne greeted him pleasantly, but wary as his tone toward her was short and stiff.

Hohenstaufen sat taller in the throne. "Lady Anne, I find

the time has come for you to leave our court."

Anne drew in a sharp breath. This was the thing she prayed for, but the presence of the three strangers made it seem unpropitious. Hohenstaufen motioned the three men forward. "These men have bought you. Well, they have bought you at the behest of someone else, and their task is to deliver you."

"My lady, you will come with us." The tall, unusually clean-shaven man stepped forward, his height even more apparent.

Ignoring decorum, Anne began to rapidly fire questions at Hohenstaufen. "I do not understand. You say they have bought me? What does that mean? Am I a slave? And who is it that shall be my new master? Where am I going? Who are these men?"

Perhaps because of her impudence, perhaps not entirely satisfied with the situation, Hohenstaufen stiffened even more, and replied sternly, "Lady Anne, I cannot answer these questions." He tilted his head. "You will find that your trunk restored to you, not meddled with. Also, as a thank you for the service you have shown our empress, I am sending you this girl to serve you. She is called Greta."

The young woman about ten years Anne's junior stepped forward from the shadows and curtsied to Anne. The tall man spoke again, "My lady, our departure now is vital."

Hohenstaufen exchanged looks with the man. "God's speed on your journey, madame." He dismissed Anne.

"Come." The tall man took her by the arm and led her out of the throne room, through the castle and down to the courtyard.

To Anne's amazement, horses waited for them and a cart packed with her belongings. When the tall man steered her toward a horse, she dug in her heels. "No, I am not going anywhere. I want some answers. Who are you? Where are you taking me? Where is Baldwin?"

The tall man spoke firmly, "Lady Anne, there will be a time for answers, but it is not now. We cannot delay another moment."

"I refuse to go." Anne scowled at him.

"Lady Anne." The tall man's accent was not German, perhaps French, or even Spanish, with a hint of Sicilian. "It would be in your best interest not to cause a scene or attract attention to yourself. However, if you refuse to go, you leave me no choice. I shall throw you over my saddle if I have to. Now, kindly get on the horse."

Anne decided to negotiate. "Answer me one question, and I shall get on the horse."

"No matter the answer?"

"No matter the answer," she promised.

The man nodded. "Quickly then."

"Does King Richard, or King Philip for that matter, know about this?"

"Get on the horse, and I shall answer your question." The tall man was accustomed to negotiation as well.

Anne looked around at the two other men and the bewildered young woman, Greta. Finally, she put out her hand, and the tall man helped her onto her horse. He mounted his own horse and came close to her.

"Gerard!" One of his companions took off his own cape, balled it up, and tossed it to the tall man.

Gerard caught it. "Good idea." Careful not to spook the horses, he put the cape around Anne's shoulders, and then pulled the hood up over her head. "Lady Anne, neither king has any knowledge of my errand here."

Chapter Seventy-three

They traveled to the river where a large commercial barge waited. As Gerard helped her from her horse, Anne thought she saw a flash of a scarlet cross on his white tunic under his cloak. "Kindly put your hood on, and keep it on," he reminded her.

Anne tried pleading with him. "Please, I beg you, tell me where you are taking me."

Gerard did not answer her question. As he took her by the elbow and ushered her toward the barge, he whispered, "Come, your ladyship will follow."

Anne did as she was told and embarked on the vessel. Gerard led her below deck to an especially cramped area. He had to bend practically in half just to walk. To the right of the stairs a section was cordoned off from the rest of the ship with a makeshift wall of crates and canvas. Behind the crates a little pallet of straw served as a bed. The area was only slightly wider than the pallet, extending about four feet past the end of the little bed. It was not well lit and lacked the window a galley might have.

"You must remain here. Your lady can attend you, but you must remain in here." Gerard pointed at the bed. "Do not speak to anyone other than the three of us or your lady. Do you understand?"

Anne nodded. Two sailors brought her trunk and placed it in front of the opening to her makeshift chamber. Gerard stepped beside Anne to block the sailors' view. When the sailors left, Gerard turned back to Anne. She determined not to show fear. Gently, he took her arm again and drew her very close to him. He pushed the hood of the cloak back to whisper in her ear. "All I can tell you at present is that we are Knights of the Temple of Jerusalem. We are in the business of transporting valuables for clients, and we have been employed to deliver you to the man who bought you from the Holy Roman Emperor. There are those who would try to steal you from us. It would seem that you have some value to many who seek to use you against either King Richard or King Philip, and that is the reason for our secrecy."

"Where are you taking me?" She looked directly into Gerard's brown deep-set eyes.

"I cannot tell you." He eyes were earnest and sad looking. "Let me reiterate that neither King Richard nor King Philip knows of your whereabouts, so you must do as I say for your own safety. Do not try to do anything rash, my lady. One of the three of us will be posted as a guard at all times. Now, I shall send your lady to you as I need to see to matters above deck."

The moment Gerard took his leave, the man who threw his cloak, pulled a crate over and set it at the opening next to her trunk. He took a seat on the crate, and quietly unsheathed his sword, keeping it in his hand furthest from the crew to hide it from their view.

The time came for Richard to turn his attention southward to Normandy and his lands beyond. John of Alencon, the Archdeacon of Lisieux, the man Richard left in charge of Normandy, arrived in England to raise the alarm that Philip attacked and successfully captured some of Richard's lands. With all haste, Richard raised his army and assembled every available boat, be it ancient longship, barge, merchant ship, or fishing vessel, and prepared to cross the channel. It was the greatest assemblage since William the Conqueror crossed the Channel more than a century before.

Eleanor remained with her son. Now that Richard was back, she wanted to stay close to him, her glory and her protection. As Berengaria was not wily enough to negotiate dung from a cow, Eleanor knew she must continue her old role when needed. After a delay of a fortnight due to bad weather, Richard, Eleanor, and the army set sail, not knowing if they should ever see England again.

Anne and the Templars traveled for days on the barge. Being down below, Anne lost track of how many passed. When the barge stopped, Gerard forbade her from leaving her hole, as she called it. Occasionally, she tried to glean information from Greta, but this was the first time the young woman traveled anywhere. Greta only said they were still on the river. Even if Anne asked Greta to describe the towns, it did no good, as she was unfamiliar with the towns herself.

Eventually, Anne gave up this line of questioning, and asked Greta about herself. Greta was the youngest of four daughters of a nobleman. The nobleman served Hohenstaufen, so when her father died, Greta and her sisters became wards of the emperor. Hohenstaufen found suitable situations for her sisters, but not for Greta, who remained serving in his household. She was a pleasant, smart girl, and although she could not read or write, she understood Latin as well as her native German. She seemed glad to finally be having adventure in her life. In turn, Anne enjoyed her company. Every time she saw Greta's rosy cheeks framed by her golden hair, accented by her bulbous blue eyes, Anne felt at least there was someone with her who was genial. Still, the longer they traveled, the more Anne fought despair and fear.

One day in the early afternoon, a particular scent crossed Anne's nose, a scent so familiar to her she almost climbed over her guard, but thought better of it. "Sir," she got his attention. "Sir, can you kindly tell me, is that the sea I smell?"

"Perhaps." The guard looked away from her.

Certain she smelled the sea in the air, Anne turned away from her guard and concentrated on the smell that reminded her of Marseilles. The thought occurred to her before—she certainly had plenty of time to think—was she going to Marseilles? Could she dare to hope? Had Etienne and Mathias arranged this? What if Castile brokered the transaction and was going to march her back to Marseilles as his captive?

Trying to banish these thoughts from her mind, Anne pulled out the poems that Richard wrote. In the dim light she couldn't see the writing, but she knew them by heart. For now, it would have to be enough to just touch them.

The following day, the barge stopped again, but this time Gerard informed Anne that she would transfer to another ship. "Your things will be loaded onto the new boat, but you must come with me now. Here." He handed Anne what appeared as a pile of rags. "You and your lady will wear these."

Greta appeared behind him, and Gerard turned his back as the two women dressed themselves in the garb of pilgrims, not of a noblewoman and her lady.

When they emerged on deck into the chilly night air, Gerard and the other two Templars led the women from the barge to the dock. From there, they walked to another area where the larger sea going vessels moored. Although Anne was right about the sea, this was not Marseilles. She did not know for certain where they were, and the buildings looked nothing like those anywhere on the Mediterranean. She surmised it was on a northern sea because of the colder climate.

Gerard escorted them to a galley, and they boarded it without delay. He took Anne below deck and assigned her to another makeshift quarter, this time with more room. Again, he posted one of the men to guard them at all times.

They traveled for many days before stopping. This time Gerard went ashore alone and returned in a foul mood. Sitting on a crate in her new slightly larger "hole," Anne could tell Gerard was on deck directly above her. She snatched bits and pieces of the conversation taking place overhead as Gerard spoke to the captain. "Our destination has changed," he said.

The captain said something that Anne could not make out; the words were too mumbled. By the inflection in his voice, Anne could tell the captain asked Gerard a question. "No," she heard Gerard say, his deeper voice carrying through the deck better than the captain's. "He will follow behind us on another ship."

Above her, the timbers creaked as the two men moved slightly to the left. Anne climbed on top of the crate in order to press her ear against the ceiling to hear better. The captain just finished saying something and now Gerard spoke again. "Yes, Castile is not far behind us." Then came a pause. "I do not like it either. This is too risky, too dangerous for the lady. It is not right to treat a lady this way if you…" Gerard's voice trailed off.

The captain spoke again, but all Anne could understand was, "when?"

"You will get paid when we get paid!" Gerard's voice carried.

The Templar's heavy footfalls echoed across the deck and toward the stairs. Anne knew he was coming down below deck, and she scrambled off her perch. Gerard came around the corner and relieved the guard on watch. As he took his post, he refused to even look at Anne.

Anne estimated that they traveled for just over a month. The traveling and stress of not knowing her destination was beginning to wear on her. She ate little, and slept even less, always afraid of what might happen when she closed her eyes. At night alone in the darkness when she was sure no one could see, Anne wept.

When the boat stopped again, Gerard informed her it was time to travel by another means of transportation. Just as they were about to go above deck, he turned to her. "It is chilly outside, you had better wear this." Taking his off own cape, he draped it over Anne's shoulders and pulled up the hood to hide her face.

As they disembarked, it took a moment for Anne's eyes to adjust to light, but once they did, she could tell they arrived in Caen. She recognised the palace from that winter visit years ago when Henry gave her to Richard's keeping. Caen was in Normandy, and this gave her some hope, but that soon faded. As she looked about, no familiar face other than their traveling party waited for her. She was disappointed by the lack of horses. As if he read her mind, Gerard remarked, "You are pilgrims; we will walk."

They traveled through the city to a small village beyond, staying the night at an inn. Gerard told the innkeeper's wife the two women were pilgrims returning from Canterbury. Their boat blew off course and both their husbands lost at sea. Widowed, they now traveled to Chartres to retire to the convent there. He and the other Templars were their escorts. "Poor lambs," the large woman commented, and she approached the women.

Gerard stopped her. "They have both taken a vow of silence."

The proprietress simply gave Anne and Greta sympathetic looks and showed them where to sleep.

The three templars and the two women traveled on foot for three days. Everywhere they stopped, Gerard repeated same story. Until now, Greta had not shown any trepidation about their journey, but that changed. The two women walked behind a cart that carried Anne's trunk, hidden underneath canvas. As they walked along, Greta hopped back and forth to keep from walking in any of the donkey droppings, but on the morning of the third day, she gave up the practice and simply seemed to forget they were there.

Anne glanced sideways at Greta and noticed a tear or two. Instantly, Anne felt pity for the poor young lady. Greta was mixed up in all of this through no fault of her own. Wrapping her arm around Greta's, Anne pulled her closer. "These shoes were not made to walk long distances."

Greta shook her head. "Nor were mine."

"We should be stopping soon." Anne tried to sound cheerful for Greta's sake.

Greta leaned closer to Anne. "I would feel much better if I knew our destination."

"Gerard has assured me that you will be safe." Anne fibbed

to make Greta feel better, even if for a moment. She also resolved to do whatever possible to keep Greta safe.

Greta glanced up at Gerard leading the donkey pulling the cart. She looked back at Anne and seemed to study her for a moment. "Forgive me, my lady, but at this point I think my fate is closely tied to yours, and since you do not know what your fate is, then I do not see how I can know mine."

Anne liked Greta. She began to feel a bond with her. "Then we shall face fortune together."

The travelers stopped for a quick bite to eat of stale bread and ale; something a peasant would take to the fields. Then they continued on their way. By early afternoon, they reached the town of Lisieux. Anne watched the spires of the cathedral grow larger as they drew closer. She assumed that they would stop at the cathedral, but to her surprise, when they entered the town, they passed by the cathedral and continued to a smaller village outside of town.

They came to a house, slightly larger than many of the others around; still, its squat structure, thatched roof, and mud walls showed it belonged to a peasant. "Stay here," Gerard commanded her as he disappeared inside the house.

A few moments later, Gerard emerged again with a man and his wife. "Ladies, this is Pierre, the reeve of this village." Turning back to Pierre, he said, "These are the pilgrims I told you about."

The sudden appearance of this group of travelers at his home befuddled the reeve. He wrinkled his brow, and when he unfurrowed it, the lines remained in dirt. "Yes, my lord," the reeve spoke, and his voice wavered with trepidation.

"Do you understand all that I have told you?" Gerard glared at the reeve.

"Yes, my lord."

"Good." Gerard turned to Anne. "Follow me please."

When Greta stepped forward, Gerard stopped her. "You

will remain here."

Gerard and Anne entered the reeve's house. A fire attempted to thrive in a pit in the centre of the one room cramped, foul smelling dwelling. Gerard shut the door behind them, and the darkness enveloped them, making Anne feel blind.

"Lady Anne," Gerard's voice sounded barely above a whisper. "You will stay here."

Her thin nerves made it hard to keep her emotions in check. "Gerard, please tell me exactly where here is and what is happening."

"Soon, my lady. There will be a time for answers, but not yet." Gerard pushed the hood of her cloak back from her face. "Now, I need the ring from around your neck."

"No!" Anne stepped back.

"I must deliver the ring to prove that I have brought you," Gerard explained.

"You shall not have this ring." She fervently shook her head. "I demand to know who wants it."

"You know I am sworn to secrecy until you are delivered. All will be revealed soon. He will be here to claim you shortly." Gerard's tone turned compassionate.

"Who? Who is coming to claim me? Tell me!" Ann resorted to threats. "Tell me, or I shall raise such a stir that you will have half the village running to this hovel."

"I told you before, my lady, that would be very unwise. There are many who would love to take you hostage. King Richard may be free, but he still has many, many enemies, and your cousin, King Philip, angered his share of people as well." Gerard stepped toward her.

Anne backed up further to get away and smacked into the wall. "Not the ring!" She fiercely shook her head and grasped the ring with one hand, holding the other against her oncoming foe.

Gerard placed and arm on each side of her and leaned in to block any escape, looking her squarely in the eyes. "I was with

King Richard when his ship wrecked. I traveled across the Holy Roman Empire and was one of the decoys. He loves you very much, Lady Anne. For his sake, do as I ask. I am trying to protect you."

Anne turned her head to the side and closed her eyes. As she held her breath, Gerard slipped the ribbon over her head. When he had it in his grasp, Anne opened her eyes, and stared into the darkness. "Thank you," he whispered.

Gerard turned away from her and opened the door. The light from outside flashed, but was gone in an instant as he closed the door behind him.

Slowly Anne slid down the wall until she sat on the dirt floor, too numb to cry, too frightened to speak, too shocked to move

Chapter Seventy-four

Hours seemed to pass as Anne remained on the floor. At one point she became aware that she was wringing her hands, but did not stop. The neighing of horses sounded outside, and Anne got to her feet. No matter who came through that door, she would face him standing. She stepped over to the table to see if there was a knife with which to defend herself, but before she reached it, the door opened and light flooded in. The contrast between the dark hovel and the bright outside was too much for her eyes to take in, and all she could see was the dark figure of a man in the doorway.

The door shut behind the man, and he hesitated as his eyes adjusted to the change in light. At first the figure did not move, and Anne's heart pounded so hard she was sure it would reveal her position. She moved quickly for the table. Then the figure let out an audible gasp, and a voice faltered, "Anne?" She felt a surge run through her body and tried not to lose consciousness.

Richard could not believe his eyes. Afraid the light tricked him, he moved closer. He reached out to touch her to assure himself it was not a dream. The moment his fingers brushed her soft familiar cheek, he knew for certain that his Anne stood right there with him. She did not speak but looked up with wild frightened eyes. Pulling her close to him, he tenderly kissed her on the forehead. He wanted to assure her she was not dreaming, to help her realize what he discovered an instant before. Leaning close, he kissed her mouth and the rigidity in her body seemed to melt away, replaced by a tremble.

Anne gave a strong shudder and buried her head in Richard's shoulder. "How did you get here?" Richard asked.

"I do not understand," Anne whispered. "Gerard told me you were not the one who bought me."

"Bought you? I did not even know that Hohenstaufen released you." Richard brushed the top of her head with his lips. "Gerard handed me the ring, then brought me here."

The door opened again and while still holding tightly to Anne, Richard turned to see who was there. "Your highness, shall we get the lady to a more comfortable place?" Gerard stepped in.

Richard looked back down at Anne. Even in this dim light, she did not look well. "Gerard, how did this happen?"

"I will explain everything, but I would feel better if both you and the lady were safely back at the Archdeacon's. Castile trailed us from Speyer."

Richard's experience with Gerard taught him to trust the Templar and respect the man's instincts. "Let us get you out of that uncomfortable pilgrim garb," Richard whispered to Anne.

Outside several of Richard's men gathered, including Blondel, along with the two other Templars, Greta, the reeve, his wife, and a few curious villagers. When Richard and Anne exited the hovel, the bright light hurt Anne's eyes, so she buried her head in Richard's shoulder again. Blondel came toward Richard and Anne, offering his own horse. Sensing Anne was still in shock,

Richard gave a slight shake of his head and motioned for his own horse. He put Anne on it and mounted the animal behind her.

By now the others mounted their own horses, and Richard gave his a soft spur to urge it forward. When the animal moved, Anne swayed, so Richard wrapped his left arm around her shoulders to steady her. Taking the reins in his right hand, he moved his horse again. This time Anne leaned back against him. She trembled so violently that Richard worried she would tumble from the horse if he did not hold fast to her.

As they slowly made their way to the Archdeacon's, Gerard rode next to the king. "I am utterly amazed," Richard spoke to the knight.

"To be quite honest, so am I," Gerard returned.

"How? How did this happen?"

"Your brother John, my lord, he sought my services. When he told me of the errand, I was surprised, to be sure. He sent me to Hohenstaufen with a large sum of money to buy Lady Anne's release. Normally I would never have even considered any task for one so traitorous as John, but because your Lady Anne was involved, I determined to go. I thought that if I refused, John would seek another, perhaps someone less friendly."

"I cannot thank you enough, Gerard." Richard pulled Anne closer to him. "So, I take it you double crossed John then."

"Actually, no. I planned to all along, but much to my amazement John met us in Dieppe, and he ordered to me to deliver Anne to you. I think she is meant to be a peace token."

"Well, perhaps John is smarter than I gave him credit," Richard mumbled.

Gerard continued, "Unfortunately Raymond of Castile was also in Speyer. Regrettably I could not chance even the slightest hint of who we transported to escape. I am afraid the lady's journey was not the most enjoyable, but I did what I had to do to keep her safe."

Richard nodded his understanding. Then another thought

occurred to Richard. "How on earth did you convince Hohenstaufen to release her?"

"The emperor is preparing to invade Sicily to push his wife's claim to the throne. The money John gave, coupled with Anne's ransom proved too tempting for him."

"And where is my dear brother now?"

"He followed us from Dieppe, and I am confident that you will be hearing from him shortly."

Anne stared straight ahead as the two men conversed. Ahead stood the chateau of Sir John Alencon, the Archdeacon of Lisieux and the vice chancellor of Normandy, staging ground for Richard's operations. All around it, a city of tents sprung up, populated with the king's army.

As Richard wove his way through the tents, he could see Alencon outside waiting in the courtyard. A slight man whose appearance fooled many, he was as fierce a fighter as any larger man and as loyal a vassal as any lord could hope for.

Just as criers announced the king's arrival, Eleanor rushed from the doorway anxious for news. In her hand she held the ring, Richard's token to Anne, on its green silk ribbon. Richard stopped his horse before his mother and dismounted. Then he helped Anne down, but she still seemed so weak that he put his arm around her waist, wanting nothing more than to get her into the shelter of the house.

Half walking on her own, half steered by Richard, Anne came to an abrupt halt in front of Eleanor. "Oh, my dear child," Eleanor cried.

Anne rushed to the queen, and Eleanor tried to gather her up in an embrace, but Anne sank to the ground in a heap, sobs wracking her body, clutching the queen's legs. Kneeling down, Eleanor patted Anne's back. The queen said nothing; she did not need to. What passed between the two women was unspoken, yet understood. They shared the experience of imprisonment before.

Awkwardly, Richard stood by, not knowing what to do.

Anne never behaved like this, and he sensed that the two women were somehow sharing a moment that he was not meant to share.

"My lord," Blondel spoke from behind Richard. "I sent for Master Will."

Richard nodded his acknowledgement.

Eleanor looked up at Richard, closing her eyes and giving him a nod, as if to say 'thank you.' "Come, my dear child," she spoke to Anne. Looking to her attendants, she ordered, "Help me get her to my room."

Richard bent down and helped Anne to her feet. Around them Eleanor's attendants scurried off. "Let me see to her, Richard." Firmly Eleanor placed her arm around Anne and led her away.

Eleanor's ladies had prepared a bath for her, but before she could undress, a wide-eyed Richard burst into the room. He gave his mother the ring Gerard brought him, then hurried off to follow Gerard.

Now Eleanor aided her ladies as they undressed Anne and placed her into the large tub of water. Anne sank down, the water surrounding her body.

"Your highness, the king is here," one of Eleanor's ladies informed her.

Eleanor took a quick look behind her, and Richard stood there looking lost. She glanced back at Anne sitting silent in the tub with a blank stare. "Watch her," Eleanor commanded one of her ladies. "Richard." she took him by the arm and ushered him out into the hallway.

"What can I do?" Richard fumbled with his cap in his hands.

Eleanor closed the door behind her, and even though she faced Richard, she still kept her hand on the latch. "I suspect Anne is in distress. No doubt she has been on a knife's blade ever since she left Marseilles."

"She barely spoke to me." Richard tugged on his cap with

both hands in different directions. "She must blame me for all of this."

"Give it time, my son. Leave it to me." Eleanor assured him with a soft pat on his chest. "Just keep Will away until she is more herself. She would not want her son to see her like this."

Just then, Greta appeared. Stopping short she gave them a deep curtsy. "Your highnesses."

"Who are you, girl?" Eleanor prickled at the sound of Greta's German accent.

"I am Greta, sent by the Holy Roman Emperor to serve Lady Anne." Greta kept her head low not daring to look at the royal mother and son.

"Then attend your mistress." Eleanor opened the door and shooed Greta inside. Before she followed, she turned back to Richard. "Give it time, dear." Eleanor closed the door behind her.

In the bath Anne sat with her knees pulled into her chest, her face buried into them. "Your highness, " Greta whispered. "My mistress will not say a word."

Eleanor pushed back her sleeves and went to the side of the tub. With effort the queen knelt down. "Anne, dear." Gently she placed her hand on Anne's back.

At Eleanor's touch, Anne looked up, her eyes red and sunken. Curiously Anne put her hands in front of her and seemed to study them. When she finished, she dipped her fingers into the water. "I believe that there is nothing in the world so soft as water." Anne burst into tears and buried her face in her hands again.

"It is alright. I understand, dear." Eleanor picked up a cloth, wet it, and used it to draw water up over Anne's back.

"I am sorry." Anne tried to wipe away the tears from her face, but her wet hands, just added more moisture. "I just cannot seem to stop crying."

Eleanor took this as a sign that Anne was thinking more rationally. "'Tis no wonder, child. I understand, really I do."

Eleanor smiled warmly at her. "Will is on his way. He is out tilting with Marshal."

"Oh, my Will!" The thought seemed to help break her out. A moment later she muttered, "Tilting? Marshal?"

"There will be time for him to explain, but first thing is first. We must get you cleaned up and ready to greet your son. You would not want him to see you like this, would you?"

Anne nodded. "Will."

"Alright then, let us get your hair washed." Eleanor motioned to Greta who brought over a pitcher.

After Eleanor and Greta finished washing Anne, she dressed in a gown that Greta found in her trunk. "Here, dear," Eleanor directed Anne over to a chair in front of her dressing table.

Anne sat down and picked up the mirror that lay on the table. The face staring back at her seemed foreign. It did not seem possible that was her reflection. The face was thinner than she thought it should be. Even against the white fabric of her brane, her skin looked pale. Alarmed, she set the mirror back down.

Eleanor picked up the brush from the table, and ever so gently began to brush Anne's hair. Anne performed this service hundreds of times for the queen. Now it was Eleanor's turn. Lovingly, and with the tenderness only a mother can possess, she brushed and stroked Anne's hair.

When she finished with Anne's hair, she put her arms around Anne and produced the ring. "I was preparing for a bath when Richard came bursting in. He said nothing to me, but just handed me this and then dashed off."

Eleanor slipped the ribbon back over Anne's head, and Anne felt the thump of the ring against her breast bone. It vitalized her. "Will is coming."

"Yes, dear. He should be here any moment."

"I should dress properly then." Anne pushed herself away

from the desk and stood.

Eleanor smiled. "Perhaps you would like some time alone with your son. Use my room, Anne. Use it as long as you like."

Grateful for Eleanor and her understanding, Anne embraced the queen again. "Thank you, my lady. This will make it a good reunion for us."

Now tears filled Eleanor's eyes. "No, no it is you who I must thank."

Embarrassed by the sentiment, Anne let go of Eleanor. "Greta, there should be a green gown near the top of that trunk there." Anne pointed. "I would like that one."

"Yes, my lady." Greta looked for it quickly.

"I must go and see to my own son." Eleanor patted Anne on the cheek. "He is anxious about you, but I think you need this time with Will."

Greta found the green dress and brought it to Anne. It was wrinkled from being in the trunk, but there was no time to worry about that. Both Greta and Eleanor helped Anne into it. As Greta tightened the laces, Eleanor took her leave. "I will send Will in." She smiled at Anne, but her aged eyes filled with tears again.

The door closed behind Eleanor, and Anne took in a deep breath.

Chapter Seventy-five

Richard met Will as soon as he entered the house and hurried the boy away to his private chamber, Marshal accompanying them. "They said my mother is here. Sire, is that true?" Will looked at Richard with searching eyes.

Richard removed his riding gloves and laid them on the table. "Your mother is here, Will, but she needs a moment. You know her as well as I do, and we both know she wants to look her best to greet her son."

"My lord, I do not care how she looks. I want to see my mother." Will folded his arms.

"Squire Will, remember patience is a virtue that all knights should strive to embrace," Marshal admonished him. Will now served as Marshal's squire, training for knighthood.

"Yes, Sir Marshal," Will replied.

"Let us have a seat, shall we?" Richard suggested. "Your mother will send word when she is ready." Richard, just as keen as Will, hid it better.

Will could hardly sit still. "Master Will is becoming rather skilled at tilting, your highness," Marshal tried to distract both Will and Richard.

"I always thought he would be natural for it." Richard raised his eyebrows.

"That he is."

Just then Richard's page announced, "Sire, your mother's lady is here."

Both Richard and Will sprang to their feet, and Marshal followed their example. Eleanor's lady gave the king a curtsy as she spoke timidly, "Sire, the queen sends for Squire Will. My mistress respectfully asks that you remain here, as she is coming to you."

Will looked at Richard, and Richard gave his godson a nod. The boy shot off like an arrow, and the lady followed after him to avoid any outburst from the king.

Disappointed, Richard sank back down into his chair. "Oh, for God's sake! Why will she not see me?"

Marshal didn't answer Richard's question. "My lord, there is something you should know about Will."

"Oh?"

"Will feels guilty, as if he is somehow to blame for his mother's misfortunes."

"And how is that?"

"It was Will who let slip to King Alfonso his mother's location." Richard sat up attentively as Marshal sprang to Will's defence. "When your wife and sister were in Marseilles, they goaded him, insulting his mother, and the boy lost his temper."

"He is very protective of his mother." Richard understood, but at the same time felt relieved. Will acted standoffish with him, and Richard thought it was because Will blamed him for the mess his mother was in.

"Will is terrified that he put his mother in more danger and that Castile might hunt her again."

Looking weary, Eleanor entered the room. Richard leapt to his feet, and Marshal again followed suit. Eleanor signaled them to sit down, but Richard remained standing. "Lady Anne will recover," Eleanor announced.

Marshal looked back and forth between mother and son. "Your highnesses, I pray you will excuse me, I must see to some neglected correspondences."

Richard answered, "I understand, Marshal. Will keeps you rather busy as of late."

"Yes, my lord."

"I shall see you later then." Richard excused him, and Marshal left.

Once alone, Eleanor turned to her son. "Richard, sit. You will wear yourself out."

"Is she asking for me? Why can I not see her?"

Eleanor gingerly placed herself in the chair Marshal vacated. "Richard, your brother is downstairs."

"John?" Richard expected to hear from John, but not this soon.

"Yes, John. You thought perhaps Geoffrey rose from the grave?" Eleanor quipped.

"I guess you have spoken with him then." Richard eyed his mother with suspicion.

"Of course, I spoke to him. After everything, he is still my son." Eleanor pushed a wisp of gray hair back under her wimple.

Richard ran his hands swiftly back and forth through his hair. "I am not in the mood to deal with him at the moment."

"Well, you must eventually." Eleanor quickly added, "I did not promise him anything."

Richard returned to his own chair, slumped over, and gave a long sigh. Eleanor reached over and patted his knee. "Son, what your brother did is beyond the pale, but we can ill afford for him to entangle himself with Philip again. It will be much easier to fight just one of them than both at the same time."

Richard grouched, "Of course I am going to receive him. After all, he is the one who made it possible for Anne to be here." With more decisiveness he continued, "I am, however, going to make him wait for a while. He deserves to worry a little more."

"Such a wise king," Eleanor chuckled. "I will see to it he is told to wait then." She pushed herself from the chair.

"Thank you, Mother." Richard's voice grew quiet again as he seemed lost in his own thoughts. "Please tell them I shall have supper in my chamber tonight. In truth, I am not very hungry."

"I shall do so." Eleanor gave him a reassuring look.

When his mother left, the room fell silent. To Richard it seemed like a dark empty cave. A chill shot through his body and he shivered. It was mid-May, but still he felt cold. On his bed lay a blanket, and Richard reached for it almost tipping his chair over. His fingertips brushed the gray wool, but he was unable to fully grasp it. With a groan, he stood up and snatched the blanket from the bed. He laid the blanket in his lap, and closed his eyes.

Before him scenes flashed in his mind, scenes of the last time he saw Anne in Cyprus, of Andrew ill and falling from his horse, of leaving Acre, traveling on the sea, and then traveling in the dark winter forests. The memory of the pain of his illness pricked his fingers and he rubbed them together. Next, he saw himself walking down the street in Erdberg to relinquish his sword; he remembered meeting Hohenstaufen, and that horrible moment when he saw Anne struggling to gain her feet in the great hall of Speyer.

At last, the scene changed to this afternoon when he entered the reeve's home to find Anne, *his Anne*, there. His mind followed the events as he brought her here to the archdeacon's chateau. These last two scenes pained his heart. This was not the way he imagined he would reunite with Anne—and he had imagined the scene over and over, a pleasant fantasy that kept him from going mad in moments of despair and loneliness. He carefully choreographed their reunion in his mind, but now that the event actually happened, and not in a way he imagined, he felt crestfallen.

Anne barely noticed him. In his version, Anne ran directly into his arms, and they enjoyed a passionate embrace. Yet Anne said but a few words to him. When they reached the archdeacon's, it was into his mother's arms that Anne fell, not his. Also, Anne seemed so weak. All his life, strong women—his mother, his grandmother Matilda, Anne—surrounded Richard. The Anne he brought back here with him was… frail, like the last leaf on an oak.

Quickly he drove that thought from his mind. He comforted himself with the fact that Anne had not lived an easy life, but she always overcame her tribulations. Even when she returned from Taillebourg, one of the most horrific experiences for her, she remained, well, Anne. But what of *them*? What of their relationship? She left him in Cyprus. It was Anne who walked away in Speyer.

The more he now thought on Anne, the more angry he became. There was nothing he could do at the moment; however, he could take care of his little brother. Richard sat up straight and threw the blanket back onto his bed. "Boy," he called out to his page. When a young man appeared, Richard shouted, "Send my brother to me." The page bowed and turned to go. "And for heaven's sake," the page turned back to Richard, still bowed, as the king continued to shout, "Bring more light into this damned tomb!"

The door creaked open and John's pale face appeared in the light. Almost instantly, he fell to the floor in front of Richard, who sat tall in his chair surrounded by dignitaries. John did an odd sort of crawl and landed prostrate before his brother, blubbering unintelligible words of regret and repentance.

Slowly and deliberately, Richard rose to his feet. Reaching down, he took his younger brother by the shoulders and guided him to his feet. Taking John's face in his hands, Richard gave his mother's youngest son the kiss of peace. John cried aloud, "Oh, God in heaven, I am sorry beyond anything that can be put into words."

With his hands still firmly holding John's face, Richard spoke, "Think nothing of it, John. You are but a child and were left to evil counselors. Your advisers shall pay for this."

Around them the crowd applauded with reserve. To Richard's right, while moving his unenthusiastic hands, Marshal narrowed his eyes. Richard still had a plan for John. The only reason the twenty-six year old "child" stood before them was because Anne lodged in a room on the floor above them.

"Thank you, brother. I do not deserve your kindness." John grasped Richard's hand and kissed it.

Richard withdrew his hand from John's fervent grasp. Putting one arm around his brother, Richard made a motion with the other toward his table. "Now, come and have something to eat."

Questioning, John looked up at Richard. "But that salmon is obviously meant for you, my lord, a king."

"You are still a prince," Richard chided him. "God's legs! Strike up some music in here, Blondel."

With a look of sheer gratitude, John took a seat and ate the meal of fresh salmon, a gift for the king. And now, the king lured John in, just as the fisherman snared that pink fish lying there on the plate.

Chapter Seventy-six

John leaned back in his chair, his stomach full, the wine lulling him into a state of ease. Richard sat in a chair across from his brother regarding him with his gray eyes. He waited for the moment when John relaxed.

By now the crowd in Richard's chamber thinned to Blondel, who gently strummed on his instrument, Marshal, who carefully noted every movement and gesture, no matter how slight, and Richard's page. John addressed Richard, "Thank you for the meal, brother. You've no idea what your kindness has meant."

Richard leaned one elbow on the armrest. "Tell me, John. How did you manage the whole arrangement with Lady Anne?"

"Well, it wasn't easy." John took this opportunity to show off and play up his part.

"Of that I have no doubt." Richard restrained himself from rolling his eyes.

"I was at Philip's court, and I began to get the distinct impression that Philip had been manipulating me, that my term of…usefulness… was about to expire. Then, the Abbot of Marseilles showed up. He sought Philip's help to free your Anne. That's when the idea hatched."

Richard poured his brother another glass of wine, hoping to loosen his tongue even more. "Pray, go on."

John took a long swig. "Philip and the abbot struck an agreement. Some of the money Philip wanted to use to bribe Hohenstaufen to keep you was just lying there. They decided to use it to buy your lady's freedom, and the abbot was to take the money to Hohenstaufen. He only made it as far as Dieppe."

"Abbot Mathias is not dead, is he?" Richard raised his

eyebrows.

"No, at least not the last time I saw him. He took ill and could not travel." John shook his head. "I followed him to Dieppe, thinking I would somehow persuade him to let me turn Anne over to you, or if necessary, use stronger persuasion." John placed his hand on his heart. "When he became sick, I learnt Gerard was in also in Dieppe, and I hired him to bring Anne to me at Dieppe. Mathias agreed because of Gerard's connection with the Templars. I think he felt he could trust Anne with Gerard." John gave a satisfied smile.

"I see. What of Philip?"

"Philip intended to take to Anne to Paris with him." John shrugged.

Richard scratched at his right eyebrow. "Yes, but does he know you delivered Anne to me instead?"

John laughed. "He shall find out soon enough; although, Gerard was very good at his job of keeping everything a secret."

Richard realized John's vulnerable position since he betrayed both kings. It wouldn't take much to turn him over to Philip for retribution. If Philip got his hands on John, drawn and quartered would be a blessing. Keeping that realization quiet, Richard continued. "So, where is the abbot now?"

"Still in Dieppe when I left, waiting for Castile." John ran his finger back and forth over the edge of the table as he spoke.

"Right, Gerard said that Castile followed them."

"Yes, he did; saw the man myself." John interrupted Richard's musing.

Richard snapped into a more attentive mood. "Well, now, John, I will be completely forthright with you. Your present to me is gratefully appreciated. Thank you for seeing Lady Anne released and brought here to me."

"I remembered how much Father seemed to love your Alice. There were days his mood depended on hers. When she was not with him, he was unbearable." John spoke with reservation regarding their father, a subject the two brothers had never breeched since the man's death.

Hiding his discomfort, Richard stood up and motioned to John. "Come. Marshal will show you where to rest your weary head tonight, and soon you will be off."

John rose and took his cap off the chair back. "Where are you sending me, my lord?"

"To battle, John. For the time being, you are going to help me regain those lands Philip stole. You can start by retaking Evreux, the town Philip put under your charge." Richard studied John's face to see if his predicament registered.

"I see that I am to serve you faithfully, and if not, Philip and his vengeance await," John told Richard.

Richard said nothing in reply. Instead he laid his hand on his brother's shoulder and gave him a grin. From behind Richard, Marshal spoke to John. "My lord, if you will follow me."

John looked back at his older brother, and Richard gave him a little nod. John followed Marshal.

Night arrived long ago, and would soon give way to the first rays of dawn. Marshal stayed outside Richard's door. At length, the figure he waited for glided down the hall. "Sir Marshal," Anne whispered.

"My lady." His manner was much more civil than the last time he met her when posted outside the king's door.

"I know the king has probably long since gone to bed, but I felt I should at least come to see." She looked exhausted, and the pair continued to speak in hushed tones.

"The king requested that I send all away tonight." Marshall paused for emphasis. "Except you."

"He is expecting me then?" Anne raised her eyebrows.

Marshal shifted his weight. "I do not think that expect is quite the right word. Perhaps *hope* is more appropriate."

Anne took a deep breath, nervous to enter that room. There were too many uncertainties still between them. "Sir Marshal, thank you for the attentions that you have shown my son."

"Will is an exceptional young man, my lady." Marshal shifted his weight.

"Forgive me, but I was under the impression that you rather disliked me, so naturally, it surprised me that you took Will under you wing," Anne continued.

"Forgive me, Lady Anne, but I think perhaps you are stalling. You cannot avoid going in that room forever," Marshal gently scolded her.

Anne did not have a chance to respond because Marshal moved the latch and opened the door for her.

Richard lay on his back, his hands underneath his head, staring up at the canopy roof. He had not fallen asleep. Instead, he waited there just as Marshal said, hoping that Anne would come to him.

When the door opened, he did not move. He suspected it might be Anne, but didn't look for fear of disappointment. Hearing the padding of Anne's bare feet on the wooden floor as she entered, he knew it was his Anne.

Anne stopped at the end of the bed, wrapping her arm around the bedpost. The only sound was the popping wood in the fireplace. Neither of them heard Marshal shut and latch the door behind her.

"Are you feeling better?" Richard still did not look at her.

Anne responded shyly, "Yes, thank you, my lord."

It took another moment for Richard to say anything. "Tell me, did you ever go to Chartres then?"

Anne furrowed her brow. "At first I had every intention of going, but I could not bear to leave Marseilles." She looked down at Richard lying there, gazing up at the canopy above him, and before she was conscious of it, she blurted out, "You mean to tell me, after three years and six days, all you can ask me is if I ever went to Chartres?" As she said it she realized that Chartres was in Philip's territory and therefore, Richard might be implying something about Philip. She quickly added, "But who's counting."

Richard grinned. "Indeed, who is counting? By my estimation it is has been one-thousand, one-hundred and one days."

"Richard," Anne gave a weak protest.

Richard propped himself up against the headboard. "You are looking much better than when you arrived." He patted the bed next to him.

Anne walked around to the other side of the bed and sat down, facing him. "I was so taken by surprise. When you walked through the door, the light momentarily blinded me. Then you slowly came into focus almost as if you were a ghost. For an instant, I thought perhaps I was dead. My senses simply could not comprehend."

"In truth, I was stunned myself." Richard wanted to reach out and touch her, but felt unsure.

"I still do not understand how I came to be here." Anne looked at him, her eyes still red.

Richard related what Gerard and John told him, recounting only what he thought necessary. Anne folded her hands and looked down at them as he spoke. When he finished, she said nothing as her thoughts raced wildly. Philip would have taken her to Paris, but would he have renewed his offer of marriage amid all the scandals, or would she simply have become his prisoner? Was Mathias doing whatever he could to gain her freedom, but handing her over to anyone other than Richard? Castile was also on her trail. He had come close at Trifels and hadn't given up yet. To take it all in made her head swim.

"Anne?" Richard's voice brought her back. "Say something, please."

Anne did not wish to talk about Mathias, Castile, or Philip.

"Thank you for all you have done for my son and me."

"There was never any question." Richard finally gathered the courage to reach out and touch her face.

Anne's unbound hair fell over her shoulder and partially covered her left eye. As Richard tucked it back behind her ear, he noted again how thin Anne had become.

"It comforted me to know he was with you." Anne took his wrist in both her hands and rubbed her cheek against his palm.

Looking at her with longing, Richard said what he was most frightened to say. "Anne, I need to know. Will you be here when I wake? Tell me now if you do not plan to stay, and I do not mean just tonight. I cannot bear to wake and find you gone again." He moved closer. "Be merciful. Tell me now."

Anne looked into Richard's gray eyes. "At the time, I did what I thought was best."

"Yes, but at some future point, will you decide that it is the best thing to do again?" Instantly he felt badly for having snapped at her. "Without you, I did things that I am not proud of."

"Richard, I thought I kept you from your duty, and you kept me from mine. Perhaps I misunderstood my duty."

He reached out and took her by the hand, pulling her close to him. "You make it easier to do my duty."

"Then I am obliged to inform your highness that you are stuck with me, may heaven help you. You will never wake to find me gone."

Richard pulled her closer still and gave her a tender kiss on the lips. She kissed him back. As he ran his hands up her arms, his brow furrowed and he stopped kissing her. "You are positively freezing, Anne. Why did you not say something?"

"I was not really thinking about that." Anne shrugged.

"Here," Richard threw back the bed covers, "get in."

Anne raised her left eyebrow, as she looked at him. "Sire?"

Richard gave an exaggerated sigh. "Now I am getting cold. Will you hurry please?"

As Anne got under the covers, Richard laid back down flat on his back stretching his arm out to her. She snuggled up next to him, and laid her head on his shoulder. Richard wrapped his arm around her and felt at peace. "Thank you," she whispered.

"Tell me, how did you find our Will?" Richard continued their conversation.

"I finally made him go to bed; the poor child could hardly sit up he was so tired." Anne laid her hand on Richard's chest, and she could tell he was smiling even though she could not see it.

"He works so hard. Both Marshal and I thought it high time he became a squire. Well, it was Marshal's idea really, but I agreed whole heartedly." Richard's chest vibrated as he spoke.

"I confess I was rather surprised that Marshal would take such an interest in Will. Marshal made no secret of what he thought of me."

"I believe it had to do more with Will's father than anything." "Castile?"

Richard explained, "Well, you must understand that Marshal's own father, a loyal supporter of my grandmother Matilda's fight to claim her throne, was a horse's ass. When Marshal was only six, the forces of King Stephen laid siege to the Marshal family castle. Stephen captured Marshal and threatened to hang him if Marshal's father did not surrender. His father replied that he, 'had the anvil and the hammer with which to forge more and better sons.'"

"That is awful!"

"Yes, but luckily for Marshal, Stephen did not have the heart to kill him." Richard stopped for an instant and then continued, "Perhaps that is why he loved my father so. Henry and he seemed to have such a strong relationship. It grieved the old man when there was the whole scandal about Young Henry's wife and Marshal. To be honest, I think he would have preferred to banish Young Henry instead of Marshal." Anne did not reply, so Richard kept on talking. "Marshal was the one who knighted

Young Henry, you know. He is the best. He could knight Will, or I could. Who would you prefer? Or would you rather Will chose?"

Anne responded sleepily, "You."

Richard felt obligated to say something to Anne about her imprisonment. Desperately he wanted to know if she had been harmed, a concern that haunted him since he left Speyer. "Anne, what you did for me… I cannot put into words... Were you mistreated in any way? If any man touched you, I will see to it that he suffers the most horrific death."

Anne's breathing had fallen into an easy regular pattern, and her head became heavier on his shoulder. Richard knew she was asleep. Gently he kissed the top of her head and watched as the light from the fire danced across her hair, sparking the red tones. Richard eventually closed his eyes and drifted off to sleep too. Neither of them could know that, in the coastal town of Dieppe, Mathias had found Castile.

Abbot Mathias raised his glass in a toast. "To Marseilles."

"Marseilles," the man across from him repeated.

The men both drank and regarded each other at the same time. Abbot Mathias set his goblet down and smirked. "Well, well, Castile, *the* Raymond of Castile, who I have so often heard about."

Looking around him, Castile took in his surroundings. The abbot set up quarters in a house in the city of Dieppe, not the austere apartment of a devoted clergy, rather one who used his title for profit. The abbot supplied Castile with one of the most sumptuous meals he had eaten in months. "Abbot, I must say, I was surprised at your invitation here tonight," Castile replied.

"While we may have many differences, we have a common enemy, and I have found that can form a most powerful bond between men." Mathias cocked his head to the side. "I would like to propose another toast, but this time to a new era in Marseilles, one that is free of any, shall we say, *Northern* influences?"

"How do you mean, Abbot?" The veiled reference to Richard intrigued Castile. He didn't wait for Abbot Mathias to finish his toast but took another drink of the wine.

"Sir, I am in a unique position. I have the trust of Lady Anne. I delivered her… your son to Richard. Now before you grow angry, let me tell you, I had my reasons. You see, I needed to get close to King Richard to earn his trust. The best way to do that was to bring the boy to him."

"I'm listening." Castile felt beads of sweat breaking out on his forehead. His stomach tightened, and he regretted that he ate so freely of the rich food that the abbot served.

"Once King Richard is dead, our Lady Anne and your son will need someone to turn to. I will be close by when the event occurs, and she will turn to her old friend for counsel. Going home to Marseilles will be the most logical step for her."

"Yes, Abbot, and what is it you are driving at?" Castile interrupted him. Now he felt tired and wanted to get all the information he could quickly, then retire for the night.

"I shall bring your family back to Marseilles for you." The abbot turned to a monk standing behind him, "Brother Bartholomew, I believe the viscount is feeling uncomfortable. Douse the fire for us."

The monk nodded his head and did as he was told. Castile cleared his throat. "Just like that? You want me to believe that you will just hand me Marseilles? Nothing in life comes without a price."

"My son, you will have a part in this passion play. It will be your responsibility to leave here at once for Marseilles. You will remove Etienne and others that rule in Anne's name. The sooner you leave the better. If you are seen anywhere near Anne, it will make Richard skittish, and that would be no good for our plan." Mathias produced a sealed parchment and placed it before Castile. "This is a letter of introduction to the Bishop of Marseilles. As you know, he is no friend to Anne's family. He will happily aid you."

Castile looked at the letter before him. "How do I know I can trust you? How do I know that letter isn't meant to send me to my death? I do not recall you there at the gates of Marseilles ready to welcome me in."

"That was before Anne left Marseilles to be a prisoner for Richard, the final act that sealed my contempt for the man. While it is true that Anne and I have been friends since childhood, I have seen her put that… that demon before anything else, even Marseilles. Did you know that my father was Anne's father's secretary. He was devoted to that man, and when he died, what kind of thanks was shown to my family? None! After all the years of loyalty my family showed the viscounts, they gave a pat on the head and an *off you go*."

"Interesting," Castile blinked quickly, trying to take in the extent of what the abbot said.

"What is best for Marseilles is best for me, and best for you. She needs a strong hand to rule her. If the church and the viscount can come together, Marseilles will be the strongest city on the Mediterranean. She will eclipse Genoa. Pisa will look like a run down fishing village compared to her." Mathias motioned at the room around him. "As you can see, I like to live comfortably. I have a monetary interest in Marseilles, as well as a deep and abiding love for my city. As for the letter, open it if you like. See what is written."

Castile narrowed his eyes. With his pointer finger, he dragged the letter closer. "I will read the letter, but not right now." He picked it up and tucked it into a pouch that hung around his waist. Taking another gulp of wine, he swallowed hard. He felt extremely thirsty but the drink did nothing to quench it. Castile tugged at his tunic. "So tell me, just how do you plan to do Richard in? I would love to see him die in agony," Castile sneered.

"Oh, it is an excruciating death to be sure." Mathias licked his lips. "You see, in my abbey, we have a particular monk who is very skilled in the use of herbs. He developed and perfected a poison that punishes as it kills. Shall I describe what happens to the victim for you?"

Castile barely nodded his head.

"First one feels hot and begins to sweat. Then his head swims, and his vision blurs. He blinks rapidly trying to restore his eyesight, but it is no use. Deep within his bowls a raging torrent begins, as pain shoots through them. At the same time, he experiences an unquenchable thirst."

Abbot Mathias' description snarled at Castile. He was a cunning man with a quick mind, and it did not take long for the abbot's words to take root in his brain. "Poison?" Castile could barely form the words.

"Oh, but we are not done," Mathias rose from his chair, speaking rapidly now. "Next his limbs begin to shake, and then he looses control of them."

Castile became aware that his limbs were trembling, and he slumped in his chair. Mathias made his way around the table and kicked at Castile's chair. The helpless man fell into a convulsing heap. Mathias rolled Castile onto his back and plucked the letter from the pouch. "Had you not been such an arrogant fool, you would have opened this letter." Mathias broke the seal and unfolded the parchment as he spoke. "You would have seen that it is nothing more than a blank sheet of parchment." He grabbed Castile by his hair. "No one, absolutely no one, will take Marseilles. She is not yours to have. She does not belong to you."

Castile hit the floor with a loud thud. With his foot, Mathias flipped Castile over. Violently Castile vomited. "Ugh!" Mathias cried. "A disgusting way for a disgusting creature to die." He turned to Brother Bartholomew. "Get him out of here before he expels his bowels on the rug, too."

Three other monks appeared to help. "Cast him to the sea," the Abbot ordered. "I do not want this wicked man's bones ever to lie in holy ground." They picked up Castile to carry him from the room. "Yes, do it and be done with it. When you are finished we

will be leaving." Mathias grew pale at the sight before him.
"Brother Johan, kindly help me with this mess." Mathias pointed to
the rug.

Once the monks left with Castile, Brother Johan and Abbot
Mathias began to clean the rug. Mathias stopped abruptly and
crossed himself. Johan looked up at him. "You had to do it. We all
agreed. It had to be done."

Mathias shook. "I do not think this rug can be saved,
brother. Would you be so kind as to dispose of it? I cannot bear the
smell. Trim it down if you can, but get it out of here one way or
another."

"Yes, Abbot," The monk replied.

Mathias watched him place a cloth over the mess, roll up
the carpet, and haul it from the room. When he was finally alone,
the abbot went to a basin of water and washed his hands. He
scrubbed hard at them even though there was no blood. Which was
worse? The fact that he committed murder, or that he did it for a
woman who would never love him. He tried to tell himself he did it
for God and Marseilles, a lie, and God would know it. Taking his
hands from the basin, he dried them and then leaned against the
table. The deed was done. What could he do now as recompense?
He thought about Anne and silently cursed her, but just as quickly
took it back again. He wondered if she had reached Paris yet. What
would she think of him now? Suddenly, the plate from which
Castile had eaten seemed to leer at him from the table.
Before he was conscious of himself, Mathias crossed the room and
gorged himself on the leftovers. He drank from the poisoned goblet
and stuffed the food into his mouth as fast as his fingers would
allow. When the food and wine were gone, he went to his own
satchel tossing it open and dumped the contents on the floor. A
small vile rolled out, and Mathias grasped it opening the lid. Only
a drop or two remained, and desperately he tried to get at it. Then it
began, the sweat on his brow, the pain in his bowls. Mathias fell to
the floor and waited for death.

Chapter Seventy-seven

Sometime during the night Anne rolled onto her side, and Richard followed her. With his chest pressed against her back and his arm around her waist, they curled up together.

Slowly Richard's senses were aroused to the arrival of morning. The fire in the grate had died down and the quiet shuffling of others outside the door sounded. As he opened his eyes, light filled the room that last night seemed such a dark and dismal space. Richard could smell the scent of Anne, so familiar to him. Her hair smelled of spices found in far away places, and the sweet smell of cinnamon tickled his nose. In front of him he could see Anne's shoulders rise and fall to the rhythm of her breathing.

Careful not to wake her, Richard moved so that his hand lay on top of hers. He was surprised as she entwined her fingers with his, but remained asleep. He was sure she still slept because her breathing pattern did not vary.

As Richard lay there, he let his senses take in everything. Concentrating on the feeling in his fingers as he touched hers, he had a strange sensation, that he no longer knew where his sense of touch ended and Anne's began.

They remained there together for about a quarter of an hour. Then Anne began to stir. She did not wake with a start as she had done regularly for so many months. Her waking was slow, gradual, and pleasant because her sleep was restorative, not hampered by nightmares or feelings of dread.

When Richard could tell Anne was awake, he pulled her closer and tenderly kissed her ear. Anne spoke first, "I must have fallen asleep; I am sorry." She yawned. "Oh, I have not really slept for such a long time."

Richard closed his eyes as if he were relishing some wonderful dish. "That is possibly my first decent night's sleep since Cyprus."

"Have you any idea what time it is?" Anne rolled onto her back.

Richard propped himself up on one elbow. "None whatsoever, nor do I care."

Anne smiled. "Surely the house is awake and stirring."

"Do not care." He shrugged.

Just then Anne's stomach awoke with a growl. Chuckling Richard laid his hand on her stomach. "Let us hope that the cook is up. It sounds as though you need to eat."

Before Anne could protest, Richard bounded out of bed and opened the door. "Bring up some breakfast," he ordered the page on the other side.

Just as quickly as he left, he jumped back on the bed, eyes shining with the excitement of a child. "Richard." Anne giggled at him as she sat up.

"Well, now what do you want to do today?" The bed still jiggled.

"Certainly you have got a full day ahead of you. From the looks of it," she motioned to the window, "you have a war with Philip on your hands."

"Not today." Richard emphatically shook his head.

Anne chided, "Dear, you are at war with Philip everyday."

"Exactly! I will still be at war with him tomorrow. So, how about you, Will, and I go hunting?" He exuded an energy he hadn't felt in years.

Anne didn't get a chance to answer him because the page returned with breakfast followed by a female mastiff. As the boy began to lay out the meal, Anne started to gather the papers. Richard stopped her, "No. Let others do the work today."

Reluctantly, Anne set the papers back down, and Richard offered her the chair by the table. She sat and waited while Richard grabbed another chair from the corner of the room. He set it across from Anne took his seat, and the mastiff plopped down beside him. "Is that the pup that Will brought to you?"

"Yes, and a fine dog she is too, wonderful hunter. I named her Ursula." Richard stroked the dog's head.

"Ursula?" Anne raised an eyebrow.

"I am told it means little bear."

"That is fitting." Anne tucked some hair behind her ears.

When the pageboy finished laying out the meal, he took up his place behind Richard. "That will be all for now." Richard dismissed him.

Now alone, Richard poured Anne a drink. "I remember you do not like to take meat in the morning." He smiled at her.

Wrong. Anne did not like to eat meat in the evening. She felt it too hard to digest at that time of the day. She couldn't help thinking Philip remembered that fact the last time they shared a meal, but chose not to say anything—it wasn't worth either the energy or making him feel ashamed. Instead she politely thanked the king.

Richard sliced off the top crust of the loaf of bread, but instead of eating it himself, he handed it to Anne.

"Richard," Anne said aghast. "Surely, I am not above a king," she protested the breech of decorum.

"Good hell! It is my crust of bread, and I shall give it to whomever I damn well please. Besides you look as though you need the nourishment."

Without further argument, Anne took a bite of the bread and recognised the gesture as another sign of Richard trying to make amends. "It is not your fault, you know."

"Something wrong with the bread, dear?"

"Richard, I agreed to go to Speyer."

"That is the second time you were imprisoned for my sake." Richard's voiced wavered.

"I am home now." Anne split the piece of bread and handed the other half to Richard.

Hesitatingly he took it. "I love you, Anne."

"And I you." Anne put another chunk of bread in her

mouth.

Upon beginning to eat, Anne realized the depth of her hunger. Across the table Richard ate heartily himself, but he never took his eyes off Anne. "Richard dear, you are staring."

He swallowed, "Cannot help it."

"It makes me uneasy," she whispered playfully. The days of youth seemed to be returning to the couple.

"Not me. I could look at you all day." He grinned again.

Marshal softly entered the room, and Richard greeted him with a gripe, "Not now, Marshal!"

Anne looked up at Marshal who looked as though he slept comfortably the entire night through. "Forgive me, your highness."

"No!" Richard shot back.

But Marshal was undeterred. "I have news of the Count of Aumale."

"Sir Baldwin? How is he? Is he here?" Anne questioned.

"Depending on the news, I may spare you yet," Richard emptily threatened.

"I am pleased to say," Marshal reported confidently, "word reached us this morning the count has been released and is on his way here to meet with your highness."

Richard thumped his fist on the table. "Well, it is about damn time."

"Hohenstaufen really must be desperate for funds. How much did Baldwin have to pay to gain his freedom?" Anne wondered aloud.

Richard and Marshal exchanged glances. "His ransom was paid, Baldwin was free to go with me. He only stayed on as a favor to me, to watch over you," Richard explained.

Anne took it in. "I see, but we were separated the whole time." She panicked. "Richard, his wife was with child."

Trying to cheer her, Richard reached out and took her hand. "Well, she is no longer with child. He has a fine healthy son, Anne."

"Speaking of sons," Marshal interjected. "Lady Anne, your son is already hard at work this morning. I know he would love to show off his new skills."

"And I really would dearly love to see them," Anne spoke to Richard.

"I agree; we should." Richard pushed away from the table. Helping Anne from her chair, he continued, "Marshal can take us to him."

"I beg your pardon, sire, but a messenger also arrived from Verneuil." Marshal needed Richard to stay focused.

"Verneuil? Is that not the castle Philip has under siege? Will said something about it last night." Anne steered Richard back to the priorities at hand.

Richard saw through their tactics. "I sense a conspiracy against the throne by the two of you." He playfully wagged a finger.

Anne took Richard's arm. "Today is only the beginning. Remember, you are stuck with me whether it be in a castle or on the field." She looked up at him with her hazel eyes.

Richard could not resist her. "Very well. Go—get yourself ready. In the meantime, I will *allow* Marshal to present the messenger to me." Then he kissed her.

Anne blushed. "Richard, Marshal is right there," she whispered.

"The good earl has seen a kiss before. Am I right, Marshal?"

"Ah, … quite right, sire." Marshal coughed.

"I shall see you later then." Anne waved goodbye to the men and headed back to Eleanor's room to change.

Will readjusted his footing and looked across at his opponent. Silently he admonished himself that his eyes must show no fear. His opponent, a squire of four or five years his senior, glared back at him. They both waited for the signal to begin. Will gripped his waster tighter as the older squire curled back his lips in a sneer. "Your mama is watching, boy. Don't let her down now."

Will did not know if his mother was really there or not, but he refused to let the comment throw him off guard. "Oh, Abram," he fired back, "you must not be sore just because I out-rode you this morning."

Abram mumbled, "What a joke. I'm to be used as the spoiled little godson's quintain."

"Gentlemen," Marshal called the two squires to attention. "Begin."

Will hardly had time to reposition himself before Abram moved. As the older squire circled him kicking up little puffs of dust, Will methodically sized up the little twitches and nuances of his opponent. Abram switched direction and, at the same instant thrust his waster forward. Will deflected the blade with his shield. Abram came at him again, and this time Will used his own waster to parry the blow and attempt a return. Will's waster caught Abram's shield just on the top edge and the force caused Abram's footing to falter, yet he did not fall. In one swift move, he caught himself and came at Will with a flurry of thrusts. Instantly, Will raised his shield again, and the blows continued to come.

Using his shield as defence, Will remained steady until Abram's blows slacken ever so slightly. He assumed that Abram exerted too much into the blows and began to tire. With the grace of one performing the steps of a dance, Will rammed his shield edge-into Abram's open chest, driving his opponent to the ground. Before Abram could regain his wits, Will stood on Abram's sword hand and pinned his waster against the squire's chest. "Nicely done, Master Will," Marshal called out, thus stopping the match from continuing any farther.

At the sound of Marshal's voice Will withdrew his sword and foot and extended his hand to Abram. Begrudgingly Abram took Will's hand but pulled himself upright. "I do hope that was a good enough show for your mama." Abram flipped his head in the direction behind Will.

Will turned to see and his mother standing there, white faced with her jaw set. She watched him spar after all. "Abram, Will, a word." Marshall beckoned the two squires to him.

Anne stood still and watched as Marshal demonstrated a move to the two squires. Aware of someone behind her, she could sense Richard. He put his arms around her. "So, how is our young squire doing today?"

"Well." Anne forced a smile.

Richard chuckled. "He may be doing well, yet something tells me you are not enjoying this."

"Oh, he is skilled to be sure, but that other squire is so much bigger than he is." Anne leaned back against Richard.

"Yes, he is older, and he is not taking it easy on Will either. Will is talented."

"If this squire is older than Will, why is he not a knight?" Anne wrestled with the fact that her son was growing up.

"I believe he comes from a lesser noble family, and Marshal tells me that he has too quick a temper."

"So Marshal puts that squire up against my son." Anne folded her arms.

"What better way for Will to learn self control?" Richard offered. He could feel the tense muscles of her arms. "Anne…" He leaned his chin on the top of her head. "Our little Will is becoming a man. By the time I was his age, I was already invested as the Duke of Aquitaine. I was knighted when I was only fifteen."

Anne softened slightly. "Watching this makes me miss that song about the crocodile and the monkey."

Richard chuckled. "Me too."

Suddenly he released Anne and turned around snapping his fingers. The abrupt movement startled Anne. "Richard?"

"Sir Marshal, may I interrupt and speak with Master Will for a moment?" Richard called out.

"Yes, my lord?" Marshal gave the king a bow and sent Will over.

Will jogged to the king and his mother, then bowed. "Your highness, my lady."

"Come, Will. I have something for you." Richard held up his hand and made a motion behind him without taking his eyes from Will.

A stable boy brought forward a black horse with a white blaze on its face, a destrier, one of the most expensive and highly trained horses available. Will's eyes grew large. The stable boy handed the reins to Richard, and he held them out to Will. "Sire?" Will choked.

Richard's grin was almost as wide as his face. "Here, take her. She is a fine animal."

Will looked to his mother for guidance, but she looked away in the direction of Marshal and Abram. It seemed she could not look at him. Will turned back to Richard. "With all due respect, my lord, I cannot accept this gift. This type of a horse is meant for a knight, a rank I do not hold."

Richard reached out and slapped Will's shoulder. "That shall soon be remedied."

At this Will beamed, reaching out to take the reins from Richard. "Your generosity is overwhelming, your highness."

Anne stood behind Richard, silently observing the scene. Richard reached out to her and she took his arm. "Well, what are you waiting for? Take her for a ride, son!"

Will obeyed and mounted his new steed. In a flash, he took off. As he rode away, Anne looked up at Richard. Teasing her, he began to sing the song of the monkey and the crocodile. She laid her head on his shoulder, and they walked to the chateau, Richard singing all the while.

Far away in Dieppe, a sailor on the busy docks heard a strange sound. At first, he shrugged it off as the docks were crowded. Then he heard it again, only this time louder. The sailor stopped and listened. Again he heard it, and it sounded as though it came from beneath him. Looking down through the cracks in the wooden planks, he thought he saw something moving and the sound came again.

Cautiously the sailor jumped from the dock and peered under it. There seemed to be a pile of expensive clothing lying there. The sailor panicked, and fumbling pulled a talisman out of his shirt and kissed it, muttering, "They that trust in the Lord shall be as Mount Zion, which cannot be removed, but abideth forever. They that trust in the Lord shall be as Mount Zion, which cannot be removed, but abideth forever. They that trust . . ."

Then the pile groaned again; the sailor gasped, and drew his dagger. In horror, the sailor watched as the pile rolled over to reveal a man with dark matted hair. The man stretched a hand out to the befuddled sailor and moaned, "Help me."

Chapter Seventy-eight

Even though Richard and Anne reunited, they soon found themselves parting with someone else. As Richard campaigned against Philip, Anne and Eleanor accompanied him, traveling with the pack train. Richard proved difficult to keep up with. Sometimes he possessed a demonic vigor that propelled him onward toward revenge.

Baldwin joined them from his sojourn in the Holy Roman Empire. Much to his surprise, instead of commanding Baldwin to aid in the fight, Richard told him to go home and spend time with his family. Richard felt Baldwin more than deserved this respite.

The task of guarding Eleanor and Anne fell to the mercenary Mercadier who faithfully served Richard long ago and proved his loyalty while Richard was on Crusade by defending the king's lands from John and Philip. Mercadier also had the monumental task of seeing to it Richard was supplied with a fresh horse whenever he needed it, and at the pace Richard rode, he needed many a fresh mount.

A farewell came early one morning as the men struck camp. Eleanor and Anne were in the queen's tent. Anne just finished plaiting Eleanor's hair, pinning it up, and putting it under a wimple. Slowly, Eleanor rose from her chair and took Anne's arm. She was not as tall as she used to be, and Anne could feel the soft crush of the now excess skin hanging from the queen's arm as she supported her. "I shall miss you dearly," Eleanor said, in a strong voice, but one muffled by age. "Not one of my ladies can fix my hair as well as you can."

"My lady, whatever do you mean, miss me?"

With her arm still entwined around Anne's, Eleanor left the tent and began walking toward her litter. Anne noted that more guards waited around the vehicle than usual. "Anne, I am not coming with you this morning."

"My lady?"

Eleanor patted Anne's arm. "You see, Anne, I am over seventy years old but not by much, yet I have grown accustomed to certain comforts an army camp cannot provide."

Anne nodded in agreement. "I know what you mean."

Eleanor laughed. "You are young still, my dear. On the other hand, I have spent a great deal of time, especially of late, traipsing back and forth all over Christendom and beyond. I want to know my bed will be in the same place every night."

"We have been lucky on those rare occasions when we have not had to sit about and wait while your tent is erected," Anne added.

"Yes, those times have been few and far between." Eleanor laughed. Hearing a great stir around them, she said, "Ah, the king is coming."

As Richard approached, Anne took another look at Eleanor. She thought it remarkable that the queen did not show her true age on her face. She still seemed so vibrant, and it was easy to forget Elenor's true age.

Richard rode to his mother's litter and dismounted. He made it a habit to see the women at the beginning and end of each day. "Good morning, ladies." His face forced a look of congeniality.

"Your highness, your mother just told me that she is leaving." Anne gave Richard a questioning look.

Richard shyly opened his mouth, but Eleanor spoke before he had a chance to answer. "Richard thought we should tell you, but I wanted to tell you myself, and I confess that I kept putting it off until there was no other option."

Richard nodded in affirmation. "She will be missed."

Anne felt a tinge of panic at the thought of being separated from the woman she had come to love as a mother. She relished the fact that even though they were on campaign, they were together again. "But, my lady, where are you to go?"

"I shall retire to Fontevrault. The sisters there will see to my needs, especially after I made such substantial donations to Abbey…" Eleanor winked. "For the welfare of my departed husband's soul." Eleanor straightened up. "Well, I do not care for long goodbyes—they can ruin a perfectly good morning." She turned to Richard. "Help your poor old mother into the litter, dear. I know you are terribly busy—battles to fight—people to kill and maim."

"Yes, mother. I promise you, I will become lord of all."
He waved his hand to indicate the surrounding countryside.

Eleanor pulled him close to her side. "Pish posh," Eleanor
said with a twinkle in her eye. "Lord of all… lord of all… Such
nonsense."

Richard felt both confused and irritated at his mother's quick
dismissal of his grand design, but he was smart enough to hold his
tongue.

"My dear son," she said, caressing his face with her wrinkled
and spotted hand. "My dear, brilliant, stupid son. Here I am at my
end, and I shall teach you this one last thing. These lands and fame
are the wonders of the world, and there is none greater than the
Aquitaine. But there is only one lord of all, and that is love. Love
is the thing that breaks down castle walls. Love rules the hearts of
men. In all the years that your father locked me away, what kept
me going? The love of my children. What kept you going in your
imprisonment? Why, it was love. Love, child of my heart, is the
Seeking Absolution." She drew back the curtain of the litter. "The
time has come, and I must go."

Richard helped his mother into the litter. Anne reached in
and adjusted the cushions for the queen. As Anne spread a blanket
across Eleanor's lap, Eleanor reached out and took her hand. She
looked into Anne's eye and her own filled with tears. "Anne, I
chose Fontevrault because that is where my beloved lord lies. It
was not easy to make this decision; I worry so about my son and
about you." Eleanor lowered her voice so that only Richard and
Anne could hear her. "Just as I did at that banquet on an autumn
day long ago, I am leaving my son in your capable care. That day
you two met was not a happenstance, but a gift from Fortune
herself. But remember, my children, Fortune can only take you so
far; you determine the end of the journey."

"Your highness," Anne said with tears streaming from her
eyes. "I do not know what to say."

Eleanor took Anne's face in her aged hands. "Anne, the

languages of men often cannot contain the words that need to be said. Not even a poet can speak justice to some circumstances." Eleanor kissed Anne on her wet cheek. When she withdrew, a look a pain flashed across Eleanor's face. "And you, Richard, take care of Anne. She may not be blood, but she is my daughter nonetheless, and I do not want my peaceful repose interrupted."

"You know I will, mother." Richard kissed her cheek.

"Good. All is settled." She turned her attention to her teamster. "Listen here you! We have got a long journey ahead, and if you jostle this contraption like you have been doing, I will have you carry me on your back until you learn to hold a steady pace! Now, let us get a move on then."

The driver looked to Richard who gave him a nod, and closed the curtains. The litter started forwarded, and Eleanor poked her head out of the curtains, calling out to Richard and Anne, "Do come and visit when you can, dears."

Richard and Anne watched Eleanor's train leave on a course for the southwest. Once she was a significant distance away, Richard kissed Anne goodbye, and he set out to lead his army against Philip.

Breton coughed. His throat was dry, and he needed something to drink again. He tried to take another sip from the flask, but it was all gone. One of the knights standing at the back of the group reached out and took the flask from Breton. "I shall fill that for you." He turned and headed down the hallway.

"Thank you, my son," Breton called after him. He looked back at the group. "Let us see, where was I now? Oh yes, I remember. Well, I do not need to tell you what happened next. Many of you lived through it." He eyed Bogis.

Bogis nodded. Many of the knights gathered there fought, or had fathers and brothers who fought this war. The sympathy that many felt toward Richard melted as memories flashed before them. Land and villages changed hands, and some even changed back again as the two kings wrestled to gain the upper hand. Richard fought to regain his stolen lands, and Philip fought to keep them.

Breton continued. "Richard made peace with many who betrayed him while he was away. With Philip though… with Philip, Richard would not—could not—forgive and make a lasting peace. Perhaps because of their former friendship, the kings harbored such deep rancor. Perhaps that friendship made the sting of betrayal worse, or maybe it was because Philip tried to take the one thing that meant the most from Richard: Anne.

"As the kings battled back and forth, they met many times, but I think the most interesting was at Vaudreuil, eh?" Breton sensed that the men knew to what he alluded. Around him laughter erupted. "Of all the castles and land that exchanged hands, Vaudreuil was amongst the more interesting. When Richard went to war this time, Will went with him."

The knight returned with the flask and handed it back to Breton, interrupting his narrative. "I was at Vaudreuil," he said to the priest. "I remember seeing the young squire on a dark destrier riding away from the kings. I thought it strange for a squire to have such a fine animal. That was Anne's son Will then? Interesting. That was quite the day." The knight grinned at the memory.

"You may have been there, but what you do not know about is the letter, and the part it played in the accord that day." Breton took a long swig from the flask.

"The letter?" The knight took up his place again.

Both kings and their armies met at Vaudreuil when it became apparent that Philip would lose the castle. He needed time to rest and regroup, but that did not mean that he would make this easy for Richard. They met on the shore across from the motte and bailey castle. The castle itself, situated on an island in the River Eure, was by many standards, not a large castle, but that day it became an important object that each king wanted to control.

Richard's armies came down from the north, and he positioned them along the river to his left. As Richard watched, Philip approached from the south on the same side of the river. He remained on his horse.

"This is not a very civilized way to strike an accord," Philip said, trying his very best to look down his nose at Richard.

"I think you and I have long since left civilization behind."

"Still, you have come here to accept my surrender of this edifice." Philip's restless horse turned in different directions fighting the bit in its mouth.

"Yes, I have. You appear to have just as much trouble maintaining your lands as you do your mount," Richard taunted.

Philip shrugged. "Perhaps he does not care for the company."

"Perhaps he doesn't care for his rider." Richard knew that this stung Philip's pride and almost smiled at his opponent's pain. "We should conclude our business quickly then, before you are thrown to the mud and that fine horse is someone's dinner. Now…"

"Not so fast." Philip interrupted. "You have not met my demands."

"Your demands?" Richard raised his eyebrows.

"Yes my demands! Have you lost your hearing in your old age? Where is Lady Anne? I distinctly said that I would not discuss any terms unless my cousin was present." At last, Philip gained control of his horse.

"Oh, she is here. If you will direct your eye to that rise there, you can see her flag being flown from my camp." Richard motioned over his right shoulder.

"Your eye sight lost as well, 'tis a pity." Philip leaned closer and continued in a mock whisper, "Richard, a woman and a flag are two very different things." He sat back up in his saddle. "Then again, that may be the reason why your wife has never . . ." Philip knew immediately that he had gone too far, so he gently pulled on the reins to make his horse turn a circle.

"Just you say it, Philip. I am in no mood for games. I have come here as a courtesy for you to surrender a castle to me," Richard huffed.

"You have not met my demands." Philip shook his head.

"What can you possibly demand? You are fallen! The castle will be mine before nightfall with or without your surrender!"

"Yes, Richard." Philip tried to slow the pace down. "The castle will be yours before nightfall, but I do have a demand."

"What kind of a fool do you take me for? I am not about to let you anywhere near Anne."

"What are you afraid of, Richard?"

"Oh, you pitiful fool. You always did have a hard time seeing when you were bested."

"Bested or not, I have made a demand."

"Demand away all you like," Richard retorted. "Much good may it do you."

Philip sighed. "I suspected that you would behave as such, so I came prepared." Philip withdrew a letter from an ornamented pouch on his belt. "If indeed Anne is here, I want this letter delivered to her. I will not discuss any negotiations until it is in my cousin's hands."

"You accuse me of pettiness, yet this is beyond ridiculous! Come, give me the letter, and I will deliver it to her when I return to camp," Richard scoffed.

Philip smiled like a wicked child. "You will have brought your army an awful long way for nothing, Richard. Do not make this a wasteful campaign."

"Why? What does Anne have to do with any of this?" Richard flung his left arm out toward the castle.

"Richard, she is my cousin, and believe it or not, I care deeply about her." Philip's manner was sincere. "There is something that I must say to her, especially after all that occurred."

Richard wasn't sure whether he was convinced of Philip's plea or had grown tired of the game, but he slowly gave Philip a nod. "Alright, I will send the letter to her." He turned to Marshal. "Send for your squire."

Marshal did so. Swiftly, Will emerged on his horse. He made a bow to the two kings and Marshal. "Yes, your highness?"

"Philip, kindly give Squire Will the letter. I believe you can trust him to deliver it." Richard gestured to Will.

Philip gave the letter to Will. "Thank you for the dog, Master Will. She is one of my most prized possessions."

"She comes from good breeding, your highness," Will replied as he took the letter.

"Take this to your mother, Will and once you return, our negotiations can continue." Philip glared at Richard as he instructed Will.

"Yes, sire." Will wheeled his horse and made his way to the camp.

As Will sped away, Philip commented, "That cannot be our little Master Will."

"He is a squire now." Richard proudly puffed out his chest.

Philip clicked his tongue at Richard. "A destrier? Really, Richard? You shall spoil that boy."

"I intend to knight him by next spring." Richard narrowed his eyes at Philip, suddenly wary of a trap.

"He is young." Philip disapproved.

"You were not exactly an old man when you were knighted." Richard defended himself. "I was fifteen when your father knighted me. He knew my time had come, just as I know Will's has. He is fifteen now." Richard realized he was justifying his actions to Philip. "God's legs, why am I explaining this to you? You are not his father."

Philip laughed and shook his head. "Nor are you, Richard. He is not, nor will he ever be *your* son."

Knowing his king's temper wore thin, Marshal moved his horse forward to distract the two kings. "Your majesties, it is rather dusty today; would either of your care for a drink?" he asked as he withdrew a flask from his saddlebag.

Philip regarded Richard with suspicion. "What kind of drink?"

"Hopefully arsenic." Richard quipped knowing Philip worried about any secret ingredients that might be lurking in the flask, so he took a swig himself, then held the flask out to Philip.

Philip took it and drank. "Thank you," he said giving it back to Richard.

An awkward silence fell on them. Finally, Richard broke it, "About the castle…"

"When Will returns from his errand, Richard," Philip scolded.

"If that is what the child in you insists upon." Richard shrugged.

Philip did not respond. Things were going as he planned. He needed to stall, and that was exactly what was happening. The kings waited in silence for Will's return.

Chapter Seventy-nine

A confounded Anne held the letter from Philip as she stood watching Will until he became lost in the maze of men and beasts as he sped away to take up his post. She preferred Will remain with her, but she trusted that Richard and Marshal would keep him safe.

A slight slope dropped down to the river's edge, and Anne was positioned at such an angle that she could see much of the army in front of her. In the distance, she spied the two kings. Mercadier stood next to her, too close for her comfort, his smell drifting her direction on the wind. She turned her shoulder away so he could not see the letter.

Turning the letter over, she broke the seal, and unfolded the parchment. There, in Philip's now familiar script was written:

To my much beloved cousin, Lady Anne de Marseilles,

I hope that this letter finds you in good health and happy. First let me thank you for the gracious present. I cherish the dog. Even as you read this, she is here at Vaudreuil with me. I know you are reading this at Vaudreuil because that is exactly when I mean you to read it.

Remember, my dearest Anne, what I said to you in Sicily. Should you ever need me, all you have to do is ask, and I shall come for you.

I understand that you made your choice long ago. Still, I feel a deep sense of loss. My heart has grown heavy. If you are still, you shall hear it tremble. The earth will quake to show

you the anguish that is in my soul.
Humbly yours,
Philip by the grace of God, King
of the Franks, Count of Artois, and
your cousin

Anne looked up from the abstruse letter and across the valley. Could Philip truly be pining for her? It was nothing short of odd. Why would the surrender of a castle be held up for this sad sort of love letter about trembling and quaking? As she pondered it, she looked down to the river at the two kings below. Beyond them the castle rose up from the island in the water. Realization came to her, and she turned around at a run nearly knocking Mercadier over. "Mercadier, I need a horse!"

"Lady Anne, what on earth is the matter?" His low, gravely voice matched his bristled face.

"Mercadier, I need a horse!"

"Yes, you have already said that, but why? Why do you suddenly need a horse? You are in no danger here." Mercadier spoke as though she were a child.

"Richard will kill him. Philip will not let him have that castle." Anne tried to push her way past him.

Mercadier caught her by the wrist. "Lady Anne you are not making any sense."

"Mercadier," Anne snapped at him, jerking her arm away. "I do not have time to explain all this to you. Either you give me a horse or your dagger to spill you with. I need to get down there before…"

"…With all due respect, Lady Anne, my job is to protect you and I cannot allow you to go trotting off riding a horse through an army."

"Then come with me, you fool! Listen to me! You do not understand. Philip is going to…"

Mercadier snapped, "King Philip is not going to harm King Richard. The king is surrounded by armed guards and…"

A noise interrupted him. Both Anne and Mercadier turned toward its source. In the distance, Anne could see the kings, and both were more animated now. Then the ground began to shake and another loud rumble rolled outward from the castle.

The English watched in astonishment as the castle crumpled to the ground in a cloud of dust and smoke. While Philip delayed, his men frantically fanned fires beneath the castle in newly mined tunnels. The structure collapsed just as Philip planned.

"Arm yourself, you vile, dishonorable, coward!" Richard roared at Philip, spurring and rearing his horse.

"Do not tell me you thought you could have everything, you greedy devil!" Philip's countenance turned sinister. Better than a half-dozen Frenchmen took a defensive position around their king. "Richard!" Philip shouted through the dust, "I swear by all that is holy, if you ever again allow my cousin to suffer for your sins, a castle is not all that you will lose!" He swung his horse around.

"You are the ass that was mute! What did you do to prevent it?"

Philip yelled back, "Vaudreuil is yours, Richard! Do with it as you will!" He turned his horse and rode away, leaving his guards to protect his withdrawal.

"Shall we pursue, my lord?" Marshal was at Richard's side.

Richard spoke through gritted teeth. "I swear by God's legs that I shall see to it that French saddles will be emptied!" He swung his sword with a mont joie then charged after Philip and his retreating army.

Behind him, Richard's army bolted into action. It was a true melee with the French fleeing south and Richard's army in hot pursuit. Richard and his men were getting too close, so the full French rear guard turned to allow their king time to escape.

Marshal reached the first of them, slashing at a French knight who lost his balance and tumbled from his horse. The man hit the ground hard enough for a thud to be heard, and in that time, the remainder of the French were almost upon Marshal. Turning his attention to the new threats, Marshal raised his sword over his head, ready to jab the face of the next Frenchman. Unexpectedly, a loud cry came from behind him, and to Marshal's astonishment, the first knight was back on his feet, his sword raised and already swinging for his leg. There was no time for Marshal to move out of the way or properly deflect the blow. "Shit!"

As if out of nowhere someone struck the French knight on the top of the head with the hilt of a sword. The knight reeled and his sword missed Marshal's leg leaving a gash in the flesh of his horse instead. The animal leapt and squealed as Marshal fought to stay mounted. After a moment or two, his animal settled but still pranced about in pain.

When he was able, Marshal turned to see who aided him. There was Will, thrown from his own horse, and fighting with the knight. Marshal went to Will's aid, but Will timed his attack and stepped in under the knight's raised arms, jamming a dagger in the armpit of his left arm. The knight raised his head to shout, and as he did, Will put the blade into his throat. Blood burst in both a mist and stream, spraying Will in the face, and the French knight fell on top of him, both tumbling to the ground.

Marshal leapt from his horse and ran to his squire, rolling the now jerking and groaning man off Will. The boy was dazed and covered in blood. "Will! Are you injured? For God's sake, say something, son!"

Around them the French rear guard was either going down or retreating toward their king. Will looked around stunned, blinking at his surroundings. He sat up slowly but in time to see the life pass away from the French knight who lay next to him. "I killed him?"

"Yes, but are you hurt? You are covered in blood, boy. Is any of it yours?" Marshal pulled Will to his feet inspecting him. "What are you doing here? You do not even have armor on!" He wiped away at the blood to examine Will for a wound, but found only scratches.

Will still looked dazed. "I thought King Richard would kill King Philip and I…I…"

"Never mind." Marshal laughed with relief. "It would seem you take after your Uncle Richard after all."

"Yes, sir," Will replied. "I am sorry."

Marshal put his hand on Will's shoulder. "Where on earth did you get that sword you struck him with?"

Will ran a bloodied hand through his now grimy hair. "Um… there was a knight dead, I think, slumped over stuck in his saddle. His sword was there, and I just took it."

"You saved my life, Will." Marshal tried to help Will understand.

Behind him, Marshal's horse neighed, and Will saw the wounded animal. "Damn, your horse is injured." Will went to it, and Marshal followed, taken aback that Will cursed.

Together they examined the wound. "Thankfully, it only looks superficial. Fate is on our side," Marshal pronounced.

Will looked around and found his own horse still nearby. Indeed she was an amazing creature. He went to her and took the reins, bringing her back to Marshal. "Sir, you should be with the king. Take my horse, and I will take yours back to camp and see to her wounds. That is my duty."

Marshal took the reins from him. "Thank you, Will."

Will gave Marshal a quick bow and was off. Marshal knew he witnessed something that would change Will forever, but now he needed to do his duty to the king.

The pack train followed the army further down the river, and eventually the order came for them to make camp, but Anne was unable to glean any more information. Once her tent was pitched she waited with Blondel and Greta for news. She worried for Richard, for Philip, and for Will, whom she had not seen since he brought her the letter. Greta tried to do her best to distract Anne, but it was no use.

When night fell Anne ceased her pacing, sitting down on her bed instead. She buried her face in her hands and silently prayed. She was so focused on her litanies that she didn't hear the announcement of the king. She looked up as he entered her tent. "Richard!"

She rushed to him not caring that he was covered in dust, dirt, sweat, and dried blood. He put up his hands to stop her. As he plucked off his gloves, he turned to his page and ordered, "Fetch me some clean clothes, boy."

Anne poured water into a basin and set it on her small traveling table for Richard. He began stripping off his armor, and Anne joined him. The armor was too heavy to lift and she just left it in a pile. Greta attempted to gather it up, but it proved too much for her, and Blondel pitched in to help the ladies.

Richard stripped down to his braises, and the page had still not returned, so he splashed water on his face, and through his hair. In the basin, the water quickly turned a brown blackish-red colour, and, as Richard dried his face, Greta emptied the basin, and Anne refilled it again. Richard continued to clean himself, and Anne stood next to him afraid to ask her questions, afraid of the answers. She handed him another clean linen and he dried his face again. He tossed the linen down on the table and leaned against it. Sensing a question, he spoke, "Philip yet lives. He destroyed the bridge at Portjoie, and we could not pursue. Believe me, I would have... had he been in my hands... he will pay for this."

Anne let out the long breath. "Richard," she murmured.

The pageboy entered with clean clothing and helped Richard dress. Anne did not finish her question. Instead, she took the second bowl of water and emptied it outside the tent. When she came back inside, Richard was putting a belt on, and the page walked past her with the soiled clothing. Richard sat on Anne's bed and slipped on his shoes. He looked up at her standing there. "Are you alright? You look pale."

Finally she brought herself to ask the question. "Richard, where is Will? I have not seen him since he brought me Philip's letter."

"What?" Richard shot up. "Marshal was on Will's horse and said they traded because his was wounded, that Will brought the wounded animal back to camp."

Anne's eyes welled with tears. "I did not see him, and I have been watching like a hawk. Richard, where is my son?"

"Stay here," he commanded. "And, Blondel, stay with Anne." He bolted from the tent.

The moon shone brightly, reflecting on the dust that still hung in the air from the fall of the castle and the movement of men and horses. Soldiers still straggled into camp from the day's battle, and Richard pushed past them. He could not get to Marshal fast enough. At last he spotted him. "Marshal, where is Will?" he called out.

Marshal turned to Richard. "I was just looking for him, as I have not seen him or my horse."

"Will! Will!" Richard began calling. "Marshal, help me look."

One man bowed before the king. "Yes, your highness."

"No, not you!" Richard gruffed. "Will! Squire Will! Will de Marseilles! Has anyone seen my godson?"

Marshal went in the opposite direction from Richard, both men still searching for Will. Richard whipped around one way then the other, desperate to find him.

"My lord," Marshal called out as he returned to Richard. "One of the squires says he saw Will at the east end of camp where some of the horses are feeding."

"Thank you, Marshal." Richard started off toward the spot. "I shall go and get him myself."

"May I walk with you?" Marshal didn't wait for an answer but fell in step along side Richard.

"Hum," Richard grunted.

"Will saved my life today," Marshal informed him.

"What?" Richard stopped.

Marshal nodded and motioned as the two men continued on, he told Richard what happened on the battlefield. When Marshal finished, Richard replied, "Without armor, huh?"

Marshal could not help but chuckle. "Sounds familiar, no?"

They came upon the horses feeding, and Richard could see Marshal's steed with someone standing behind her. "Leave us," Richard whispered.

Once Marshal was gone, Richard made his way around to Marshal's horse. "Will?"

"Your highness!" Will was startled.

"Your mother is worried sick about you." Richard approached him.

Will laid his hand on the horse's neck. "I have put a poultice to her wounds, but I cannot convince her to eat or drink."

Richard examined the wound on the animal. "You have done a good job, Will. I think she will mend."

They stood in silence, and Richard could tell that Will felt troubled beyond the concern of the horse. "Marshal told me what happened today."

Will would not look at Richard. "How many people do you think my fa—*Castile*— has killed?"

"Ah. I do not know how many men he has killed, but I do know that there was honor in what you did today."

"It was not like I thought it would be." Will continued to

look ahead at the horse. "I have seen animals and even people die before but..." his voice trailed off.

Richard said nothing. He would let Will speak when he was ready. Instead he reached out and stroked the horse. In a moment, Will continued, "His eyes were open, and I saw something leave his eyes."

Will pulled his tunic away from his body, and Richard noticed that it was wet. "I did not want Mother to see the blood," Will explained.

Richard wanted to offer some words of wisdom; he felt it appropriate. "Will, you saved Marshal's life today. That knight had already killed him, and you snatched him away from death. Then he tried to kill you. Sometimes we have no choice. You were serving your master and the king. There is no shame in that. You behaved honorably and bravely, like a true knight."

Will shook his head. "I am not a knight, Uncle."

Will had not called Richard uncle in a long time. In fact, Richard could not recall Will addressing him that way since he returned from Crusade. "I think it is high time that we correct that technicality. Today you showed you have the mettle to be a knight." Richard motioned for Will to follow. "Come."

They headed back toward Anne's tent, and it wasn't long before they encountered Marshal. Richard slapped Marshal playfully on the shoulder. "Before this night is through, your squire will be Sir William."

"As you wish, my lord." Marshal smiled.

Richard began walking again. "Both of you go to my tent. Will, wash and change. Marshal, tell my page to find clean clothes for him. We will need some armor. For now, we will have to make do with what we can find until proper armor can be obtained. Oh, and we need a pair of spurs and a sword." Richard thought aloud. "Your mother, I know, has your grandsire's spurs and sword." He stopped walking. "I am not sure how your mother will react to this sudden news, but in order to get the sword, she will have to be told." He took in a deep breath. "I must be the one to tell her." He started walking again. "And someone find a priest."

Will whispered to Marshal, "Is the priest for me, or is the king going to confess his sins before he faces my mother, just in case?"

Marshal laughed. "The king is a brave man, Will."

Chapter Eighty

As Richard entered Anne's tent, she still paced back and forth. Before she could say anything, Richard informed her, "I have found Will and he is alright."

"Thank the Lord!" Every muscle in her face relaxed. Then she wondered aloud, "Where is he?"

Blondel and Greta left Richard and Anne alone. Richard continued, "He is in my tent cleaning up." Anxiously he shifted his weight. "My dear, you have your father's sword and spurs with you, correct?"

"Yes, in my trunk. Why do you ask?"

"Because I know how important he was to you, and I thought it would be nice for your son to be knighted with them." He scratched at his scalp hoping that just dropping a mere hint would be enough.

"Certainly, when the time comes." Anne did not move.

"The time has come." Richard grinned at her.

Anne narrowed her eyes and tipped her head to the side.

"Will is in my tent preparing to be knighted as we speak." Richard inched closer to Anne while he anticipated her arguments. "I know you . . . we were perhaps looking for another year, but he did something today that was brave and honorable. It shows he has the valor of a knight." Anne's confused look turned to incredulous. "Your son saved Marshal's life today."

"What? Marshal? Was he riding into battle with Marshal?"

Richard decided to omit certain facts. "The details are not important at the moment. What is important is that his time has come."

"Richard, he is fifteen," Anne protested.

"True. He is fifteen and he deserves this honor." Richard reached out and took Anne's hands.

"To whom will he swear an oath of loyalty? Has that been considered?" Anne stepped back from Richard.

"Well, to me." Richard shrugged. "The consolation that Hohenstaufen gave me was that I would be crowned King of Provence. The territory consists of Provence, Vienne, Viennois, Narbonne, Lyon to the Alps, and . . . Marseilles. I have not pursued it, as I have had other matters on my mind of late."

Anne asked quietly, "Does that mean you plan to carry through and be crowned King of Provence?"

Richard nodded his reply.

"Technically, that would make you lord over Marseilles— my king." Anne held her chin high as she looked through the tent opening.

"Indeed."

Anne stood up straight and in a proud tone declared, "I do not think you understand the dynamic here. We have not had a king ruling Marseilles for many years now. We are strong and independent, and we will not take easily to an outside lord."

"Yes, my dear. What do you think attracted me to both you and your city?"

Anne went on without answering his question. "Many men have claimed to be the heir of the old Kingdom of Lower Burgundy, but their claims are just that, claims. Nothing more than a mark on a sheepskin."

"Hohenstaufen's claim is from his mother, who was the heir to Burgundy."

"While everyone else has been busy arguing about who is lord of the region, we have become accustomed to governing ourselves, and we do quite well at that. King of Provence is just another title. It wields no real power over Marseilles, Richard. I know you. You are not the type to settle for a title without allegiance of subjects. Will is the heir of Marseilles, and if he swears an oath to you, her people will not take to it kindly."

"I do not seek to conquer," Richard tried to explain. "I wish to protect, Anne."

"There have been many acts committed under the guise of protection that have led to subjugation."

"Well then, who would you have him swear his allegiance to?"

Anne threw up her hands. "I do not know!"

"Anne, by God's right hand," Richard rumbled as he raised his own hand. "I vow that as long as there is breath in my body I will do all I can to aid you and Will to make Marseilles strong and free from outside rule."

Anne looked deep into his eyes and studied them. "Richard, knight my son with his grandsire's sword and spurs."

Richard's face let go of the argument, and he kissed her lightly. "As you command, *my* lady."

Anne patted Richard on the front of his shoulders to break from his embrace. She moved across the tent to her large chest. "You will have to forgive me." She began to empty the contents looking for the sword and spurs. "I know you are in a rush, but the items are in the bottom."

"There is little time, but time enough," the king said in a vain attempt to slow the pile growing in front of the trunk. "At dawn we will march south, so we must forgo many of the formalities. Will must receive communion, though."

"Oh," Anne struggled with the sword, "here they are."

"Here let me help you." Richard aided her as she removed the weapon from the box.

The tent door flapped open and Will marched forward with Marshal close behind. Now much cleaner, Will stopped just inside the doorway, uncertain if he should proceed. "It is alright, Will. Your mother knows our secret." Richard winked.

Anne stood looking at her son dressed in a light coloured, clean tunic that was at least a year too big for him, and proper black hose. He needed a belt, but that would come in the ceremony. As she studied him, he looked like a stranger. Anne did not remember when he grew so tall, his face thinned, his feet and hands become so large. "I am so proud of you, Will." She went to her son and embraced him.

"Thank you, Mother," he whispered.

Running her fingers through his hair, she sighed. "I suppose we shall have to cut your hair. Heaven knows, a young man knighted at fifteen can use the humility."

Richard chuckled behind her. It was customary to cut the squire's hair when he became a knight to promote humility, yet he knew that Anne was teasing him and not referring to Will. "That is why God created strong willed, stubborn women," Richard returned.

"Sir Marshal?" Will turned to his mentor.

Anne did not give Marshal a chance to respond. "I would like to do it, if I may."

"I think that would be splendid." Richard interjected. "I shall go see to the final preparation and Marshal can assist me." Richard thought Anne would like a few moments alone with Will. "There are some shears in my tent. I will tell Greta to fetch them." He gestured to Marshal, and the two men left the tent.

While Greta retrieved the shears, Anne found a chair for Will. It was too low, but it would have to do. "Here you are, Sir Will." Anne motioned for him to take a seat.

Will obeyed and sat. She took a hunk of hair from near the top of her son's head and put it between her fingers. As she held the shears in the other hand, she hesitated. "It is alright, Mother," the boy tried to reassure her. "I am nervous too, but it will grow back."

"It is not just your hair that I am worried about, Will." She spoke in a quiet but kind voice.

Will looked up at his mother standing behind him. "Mother, you have done everything you can. You have taught me well, and so has Uncle Richard, and Sir Marshal, and Etienne, and Nanette." He looked straight ahead again and with determination declared, "I will honor *my* knighthood, unlike other men you've known."

"I know you will. Though you are becoming a man, a good man," she added, "I cannot help but wish you were that little boy with a wooden sword tucked into his belt, giving Marguerite instructions on how to play a dragon."

Will laughed. "Would it help if I sang the song about the crocodile and the monkey?"

"No." Anne shook her head. "Uncle Richard has been doing too much of that lately." She looked down at Will's dark, curly soft hair that was just slightly longer than his ears, and took firmer hold of the hunk of hair. "I dare say this first snip will be the hardest."

She paused for a moment, his hair felt silken between her fingers, and there was a touch of some fragrance in it. *Peaches.* Here, at long last, through all of this time, Anne's father was beside her. *But of course*, she thought, as tears filled her eyes. *Of course he would come to see his grandson.* Her hand began to shake as much as her chin, but she knew that if she gave way she would never be able to cut Will's hair. She took in a protracted breath and clamped the shears together. Soft black curls floated gently down to the ground around Will where they lay still. She was glad that there was no mirror in front of Will, not because she did not wish him to see himself, but because she did not wish him to see any tears that might escape her control.

When at last Will was sheared, Anne dusted the hair off his shoulders and back. "There now, do not tell any sheep who cut your hair, else they shall all be frightened of my handiwork and me," she teased.

"I am sure it is fine." Will stood up and brushed some more hair to the floor. "Well, I suppose I should go now." He turned to leave.

"Will, wait!" Anne stopped him. She embraced him, noting again he was taller than her now.

With a gentle pat to his mother's back, Will tried to reassure her. "It is alright, Mother."

Will's back was turned to the tent door, and over his shoulder Anne saw Marshal appear in the doorway. She drew her son even closer. "Will you must always remember that the blood that runs through you is noble. You come from proud and strong families. No one can take that from you." She drew back and looked into his eyes. "Never, and I mean never be ashamed of where you come from."

"Yes, Mother."

"Will." Marshal beckoned. "It is time."

Will kissed his mother on the cheek, then beaming with pride and excitement left the tent. She watched him go, happy to know generations were together.

Since Anne's return, Richard always insisted his tent be pitched next to hers. Often the tents were close enough that sometimes Anne could hear snatches of conversation. Sitting down in the chair that Will just occupied she now listened for sounds from the king's tent. Without much effort, she could tell that Richard was outside his tent and conjectured that Will must be inside the tent at confession preparing to receive communion. In her mind, she could see Richard standing there with Marshal posted next to him.

After a while, Anne heard tramping back and forth and recognised Richard's footfall. For a moment, she considered joining Richard, but decided against it, more content to be alone now.

"God's legs!" Richard exclaimed loud enough to be clearly heard. "He is fifteen! How much could he possibly have to confess? Let us get on with it!"

Anne smiled to herself, and after Richard's comment she heard the voice of the priest say, "Sire, we are ready."

Continuing to sit in the chair, Anne strained to hear what was said next door, but she could only hear murmurs, the cadence of sentences rising and falling marked by periods of metal being moved about as various pieces of armor, belts, spurs, and other knightly accoutrements were presented to her son. Next she heard the lower tones of the men as they spoke, and the higher pitch of Will's responses. Richard's voice sounded for what seemed to be at least a minute, and she was certain that it was Richard because the tone resembled his. Then the pop of a slap, the collee, seemed to echo across to her tent. She had never actually witnessed a knighting ceremony before, but she knew what that meant. The accolade was given so that Will would not forget the oaths he took, and to symbolize the last slap he would he receive from a man that would not be reciprocated. More than that, it meant that Will was now a knight, and as such, considered a man with all the rights and regulations that came with the title of knight.

Anne looked down at her feet and noticed the large piles of hair that lay there. Plucking a section of curls, she laid it on her small desk and opened her coffer. Inside she found a piece of old ribbon and bound the lock of hair together with it. With tenderness, she placed it in the top compartment of her small casket and shut the lid.

Chapter Eighty-one

At dawn, Richard pursued Philip further south, learning that Philip retreated to his castle at Gisors. While in pursuit, Richard became ill with fever, so he returned to Vaudreuil, determined to rebuild it and fortify the territory he was winning back.

The night Richard knighted Will, he gave orders to begin reconstruction on the castle. By the time he returned reconstruction had begun. The outer walls sustained the heaviest damage, but the keep itself only needed minor repairs. It was sound enough to house the king, his officials, and of course, Anne.

From his window, Richard oversaw the efforts of restoration, but before long his fever worsened. After much pleading on Anne's part, Richard retired to his bed, but his men moved it to the window so he could view the construction.

The fever seemed to worsen and then slacken only to return with more vigor, and Marchadeus tried to attend the king closely. However, Richard preferred Anne to be with him. Marchadeus returned for periodic inspection. Anne attend him while disguising her anxiety. Richard's page was posted at the door ready to retrieve anything the king might need. Marshal became Richard's eyes and ears over the construction while continuing to work on military strategy and facilitating negotiations with Philip.

On one of Richard's better mornings Marshal informed them Gustave had arrived from Marseilles.

"Gustave has come?" queried Anne. "I am not sure if this is good news or ill."

"I have shown your secretary to your chamber, Lady Anne."

"Thank you, Marshal, I will see him shortly," Anne replied.

"Oh, and here is a letter he bid me give you, and there is another one for his highness as well." Marshal handed both letters to Richard, then promptly left the room.

Richard sat by the fire in a large chair, wrapped in a light blue fur lined robe. Anne took a smaller blanket from the bed and laid it across his shoulders. "It is too drafty in here," she remarked.

Richard responded lightheartedly, "Of course it is drafty. That cousin of yours left gaping holes in my castle."

"Think of it as a favor, dear. You would have remodeled it anyway, so Philip just gave you a head start." She wrinkled her nose at him.

Richard chuckled causing him to go into a coughing fit. Anne brought him a warm cup of wine. "Thank you," he managed.

Anne pulled the blanket back onto Richard's shoulders. "I wish you would let your surgeon attend you more. Marchadeus may be a Jew, but he is extremely skilled in his art."

"True, Marchadeus is one of the best, but he is not nearly as pleasant to look at. I prefer you, my sweet Annie." Richard flashed her one of his *I'm innocent* grins.

Anne rolled her eyes at him. Richard looked down at his lap and saw the letters there. "Here is your letter, and here is mine." He handed Anne her letter. "Damn, mine is from Joanna."

Anne sat next to him on the wide arm of his chair. "She must be ecstatic about her betrothal to Toulouse. I hear it is true love."

"It will be an important alliance for me." Richard did not feel like opening his sister's letter just yet, so he put it back on his lap and wrapped his arm around Anne's waist while she opened her letter.

"It is from Etienne, and about time too. I have not heard from him since I sent word that I was with you." She read on in silence.

Leaning his head against her, Richard closed his eyes, but Anne let out a long sigh and brought the letter back down to her lap. "Not bad news, I hope."

"Nanette," Anne whispered. "She fell asleep in her favourite chair and never awakened. Etienne says they found her in the evening with the most peaceful, contented look upon her face."

"Then she is with God." Richard offered comfort.

After a thoughtful pause, Anne said, "I hope that she has found her husband. Unlike so many, Nanette found love in her marriage, but did not enjoy it nearly long enough. She always told me, though, not to worry, that God grants true love to reunite in the life to come."

While Anne continued to read the letter to herself, Richard mulled the thought over and decided he agreed with Nanette. He reasoned that if God knew men, and called men to account for their sins, then men would remember their sins; therefore, they would remember those they knew and those they loved. If the reward for faithfulness was eternal happiness, then surely men must be allowed to spend eternity with those they loved. Without loved ones, there could be no happiness.

Deep in thought, Richard felt Anne's body tense. At last she shot up and crossed herself. "Merciful Lord in heaven," she mumbled.

"Anne what is it?"

Anne's eyes were wide. "Oh, Richard, Mathias."

"What of Mathias?" Richard prickled at the mention of the abbot. "Last I heard the—*he* was in Dieppe."

"Yes, and while there, somehow he convinced Castile to dine with him. Only, he served Castile poison." Anne trembled.

"Mathias killed Castile?" Now Richard rose to his feet. "Unbelievable!"

Anne continued. "Etienne says that all the clergy traveling with Mathias were part of the conspiracy against Castile, and that Mathias himself tempered the poison." Anne read aloud from the letter.

Overcome by the sin of murder, Abbot Mathias ate heartily of the poisoned food and devoured the toxic wine..."

Anne could read no further, and dropped the letter. Instantly Richard held her in his arms. "Go! Bring Lady Anne's secretary to my chamber. I wish him to confirm this," Richard ordered his page. He caressed Anne's hair. "The abbot made a difficult choice. We all wanted Castile dead."

"Mathias committed murder for me, and now he is dead by his own hand."

"Anne, it is not your fault; you cannot blame yourself."

"Eternal damnation, Richard." Anne buried her head in the soft shoulder of his robe.

Gustave arrived quickly and the page showed him in. "Your highness, my lady." He gave a low bow.

Anne looked over at her secretary. She had not seen him since she left Cyprus, and now crow's feet sprouted from his eyes. "Gustave." Richard spoke before she had a chance. "Tell us what you know of the abbot."

"Abbot Mathias?" Gustave looked at the distraught Anne. "But my lady, Mathias did everything he could. Why are you not happy for him? I have never seen him so contented."

"You saw the body then?" Richard demanded.

"No, your highness, no one did for certain. The priests left him under the docks and when they returned the body was gone. God willing, he washed out to sea with the tide. Do not fear, my lady. You are safe with the king." Gustave pulled out his handkerchief and wiped his brow.

"Why would his companions leave the abbot under the docks?" Anne was incredulous.

"Oh, pardon me, my lady. They left Castile under the docks." Gustave wiped his brow again.

Richard broke in, "You are too confusing, man. Abbot Mathias killed Castile, and then himself, correct?"

"Oh!" Gustave's eyes widened with understanding. "No, not exactly. The abbot's companions found him unconscious but still alive. He flirted with death, but death did not win. The brethren were worried that perhaps Castile survived too, so they returned to the docks to finish the job, but he was gone."

"So the bastard is alive. What of the other bastard, Castile?" Richard's tone was short.

"Castile ingested large amounts of poison, and it is highly probable his body washed out to sea. Abbot Mathias is alive, but he will never walk again. The poison robbed him of the use of his legs."

"Poor Mathias." Anne shook her head.

"Surely Etienne explained all this in his letter," Gustave questioned.

"Forgive me, Gustave, I should have read the entire letter, but I became so distressed upon reading that the abbot harmed himself, that I could not bear to read more." Anne snatched the letter from the floor where it fell.

"My lady, the abbot returned to Marseilles. I saw him myself just before I left," Gustave offered.

"You say he cannot walk?" Richard sat back down in his chair.

"Your highness." Gustave bowed to Richard again. "'Tis true. The poison robbed him of the use of his legs." Gustave held up a hand. "But do not fret, Lady Anne. I spoke with him privately. Now, there is a soul truly devoted to God, if ever I met one. Abbot Mathias is not the same man we once knew. His has been an interesting path to God, and he will tell you that himself. Mathias tells it as he fell in love, joined the church for worldly gain, committed a sin for love, and to save his city, and now he has found God."

Deciding she would read the rest of the letter and see what Etienne had to say, Anne folded it back up. "And yet, still there is the possibility that Castile lives."

"Yes, but rather a slight one. The poison did much harm to the abbot's body, and he only partook of the leftovers. I do not think you should worry about Castile, my lady."

"I agree." Richard reached out and took Anne's hand. "Even if Castile somehow survived, he would be a fool to come after you or Will. He would have to cross my lands or Philip's. Doing either would bring certain death for him."

"True, but I think it best we not tell Will about this, just yet. Let us wait until we have more solid information." Anne looked at Gustave who fidgeted.

"Anne, dear, your secretary looks as though he is about to burst." Richard rubbed his aching temples.

"Gustave, is there something more?" Anne questioned.

"Your highness, my lady, I am most anxious to go over some papers with Lady Anne."

"Go on then. I want to sleep now anyway, and there is no sense in you sitting here." Richard winked at Anne.

"I shall return shortly." She kissed him on the cheek before she and Gustave took their leave.

Alone now, Richard stretched out his feet, and brushed something on the floor. It was the letter from Joanna that fell from his lap. He picked it up, and with a long sigh broke the seal. What could Joanna possibly want now? Had he not given in on the subject of Toulouse?

Eager to return to Richard, Anne finished with Gustave as quickly as she could. She spent the majority of the time allaying Gustave's fears that a major cataclysm would befall the trade routes. Anne assured him they must continue to foster the alliances that her father so carefully formed, and she tried to maintain.

When at last Anne was able to return to Richard's chamber, what she found shocked her. Richard, out of bed, strode around giving orders as though he had never been sick, and most confusing of all, the orders to pack. "Are we going somewhere, my lord?" Anne took in the chaos surrounding her, and Richard dressed for travel.

"Anne!" Richard greeted her with a kiss. "*I* am going to Le Mans."

Anne could tell by his *I* that he was going without her, and her heart sank when she heard the destination, Le Mans where Berengaria resided. "But you are not well," Anne stammered.

"Well enough," he assured her as he looked into her pleading eyes. "Leave us," he ordered those in the room.

Once they were alone Anne dared to protest more forcefully. "Richard, I do not think you are well enough to travel. You should remain here while you mend."

"My sister has given me a gift, and I must go and use it." Richard put on his gloves.

"I do not understand what you mean. What kind of gift did Joanna give you?"

"I cannot explain it all right now, but believe me—"

"Richard! You cannot be so reckless with your health," Anne interrupted him.

Instead of becoming angry with her, Richard reached out and brushed some hair from her face. "You have not had an easy day, and I understand that. I know that Le Mans is the last place you want me to go right now. Trust me, Anne, just trust me."

Anne felt her panic melt. Something inside assured her that Richard's errand was for the best. "How long will you be gone?"

"I hope not much more than a fortnight." Richard caught sight of his ring around Anne's neck and he remembered their parting in Poitiers. "Marshal and Will shall remain here with you, and I am taking Mercadier with me."

"I am not sure that gives me any peace of mind."

Richard chuckled. "I will hurry back so swiftly that you will scarcely have time to miss me." He kissed her. "I must be on the road at once. The sooner I leave; the sooner I return."

Before Anne could respond, Richard bounded for the door and was gone. Standing alone in his chamber, Anne worried what could possibly be so important that Richard would leave her here at Vaudreuil and go to Le Mans where he kept his wife.

Chapter Eighty-two

From her bedchamber, Berengaria could hear the trumpets announce the King's arrival at Le Mans. She flushed with sudden excitement, then deflated just as quickly when she wondered if Anne accompanied him. "Do not just stand there gawking, Lucinda! Help me dress!" Berengaria snapped at her lady. "I must be a vision of perfection for the king."

Berengaria's lady sprang into action, but the queen could not decide which gown to wear. When she heard noises coming from the floors below, she hastily snatched a crystal blue gown that played off the colour of her eyes. As Lucinda laced up the gown, Berengaria heard heavy footsteps coming down the corridor, and she knew that she missed her opportunity to greet Richard as a proper queen. Just as Lucinda finished the last tie, the door to her bedchamber flew open, and Richard swept into the room. Flopping down in a chair, he ordered the servants standing about, "Leave us."

They bowed themselves out of the room, and the royal couple was alone. "My lord…" Berengaria began.

"Have a seat." Richard interrupted her.

Berengaria obeyed and sat in chair opposite Richard. He pulled off his gloves and laid them on the small table next to his chair, all the while studying his wife. A smile crept across his face.

"You are merry, my lord." The look on his face made her nervous.

A soft knock sounded on the door. "Come," Richard called out.

Berengaria's lady Lucinda entered carrying a galipot of wine and two goblets. She set them on the table next to Richard, and left the room. Richard unfastened the fermail on his cape, pushing it from his shoulders, and it fell to the floor in a soft, rolling thump. "You are no doubt wondering why I am here."

"I am humbled by your visit." Berengaria was just grateful he was here. She had not seen Richard since she left Acre.

"I have not been feeling well as of late."

"My lord, are you ill? How can I serve you?" Berengaria showed genuine concern.

"Sometime back, I was in Nottingham, and a strange old hermit accosted me." Richard began his story.

"I heard rumors of the encounter," Berengaria confessed.

"Then you also know that he warned me to denounce my wicked ways, and return to my wife; that I should become one flesh with her, forsaking all others." Richard poured himself a goblet of wine.

Berengaria's pulse quickened. "My lord, I am but your humble wife."

"Are you now?" Richard raised his eyebrows. "Well, I laughed at the hermit, holy man, or whatever you wish to call him. Then, when I fell ill many at my court, assumed it was because of my *sinful* ways. Sickness can be a consequence of sin, so I am told. Many assume I am here to repent of my sins and be healed."

"And are you here for that purpose?" Berengaria wanted to reach out and touch him.

Richard gave a low laugh. "I am here to purge myself of something. Tell me, how did you get that hermit to deliver his diatribe to me? Had I not been in such a generous mood, he could have easily paid for it with his life."

Berengaria went from hopeful to furious in an instant. "I did no such thing."

"Come now, you can tell me." Richard winked, but was met with a glare of anger. "No, then? Let me guess, did you pay him? Probably not. What would a hermit want with gold? You must have promised to keep him from harm somehow."

"Sire, I never set foot in England."

"As if that would somehow make a difference. You could have sent someone on your behalf. I think you perfectly capable of this kind of deception."

Berengaria rose to her feet. "Have you come here just to make ill founded accusations against me after all that I have suffered in your name? Your Anne is not the only woman who put herself at risk for your sake. I am your queen, and I am your people's queen. I would not have needed to pay the hermit! People take it that we have not produced an heir as proof of your wanton ways, and it is not as though you have made a concerted effort!"

"Ha! Sit down, sit down. Let the people think that I am here mending my ways."

Berengaria did as she was told. Thoughts of the years his mother spent in prison flowed through her head, and she worried Richard would do the same to her if she continued to yell at him. "I am sorry for my impertinence, your highness," she mumbled.

"Berengaria, Berengaria, Princess of Navarre." Richard sighed. "My queen."

His happy tone confused her. "What is your will, my lord?"

"My will?" He snickered. "Here," he poured her some wine, "drink this."

With caution, Berengaria took the cup, but did not drink. Richard took a long swig from his goblet and swallowed with a loud gulp. "What is the matter? Do not tell me you do not want any. It is delicious."

"I have lost my desire for wine." Berengaria set the goblet on the table.

Richard shrugged. "Pity. I had this brought in special from Toulouse. I heard you were particularly fond of this singular wine."

Berengaria felt as though her ears were on fire. She knew she was red from head to toe, but could not bring herself to speak. Silently she wondered if her lady talked about what happened in Toulouse.

Richard did not attempt to hide his smile. "By the by, your lady Lucinda is now going to be part of my household. I brought you a new lady, Ines, and she is downstairs waiting to serve you as we speak."

Berengaria swallowed hard. "What have I done to raise your ire so, my lord?"

"I think you know the answer to that, and it is nothing to do with the hermit." Richard poured himself some more wine. "This is good wine. No wonder you became so fond of it."

"My lord…" Berengaria started but was unable to finish.

"Lost for words, eh?" Richard taunted. "Very well, let me help you. When you were in Toulouse, you received a visit from a certain sworn enemy of your husband's."

Berengaria shook. "I beg—"

"No, no, no. Wait; I am not finished," he interrupted her. "If that were not enough, you spent time completely alone with said man. Again, I repeat, alone, behind closed doors."

Bursting into tears, Berengaria dropped to her knees bumping the table. Her goblet of wine tumbled to the floor spilling its contents on her dress and the rug beneath them. "My lord, you must believe me. I would never do anything to dishonor you!" She sobbed.

"Yet you are ruining my rug and a dress that must have cost a farm." Richard pointed to the spill.

Desperate, Berengaria tried to sop up the wine with her gown. "You are my lord and my king," she cried.

"I pay for your gowns as well." Richard remained in his chair.

"Please, in humility, I beg of you," Berengaria was wild-eyed. "Castile is the brother-in-law of the man who served as my escort to safety. I could not deny him an audience. He plied me with drink until I lost leave of my senses. I sent the servants away because I did not wish them to wag their tongues and spread rumors and lies regarding your household. My lady was outside the chamber door the entire time. I do not remember what happened after that. If anything, I was taken advantage of. It is not my fault. I would never break my marital vows."

"In my experience even when one is drunk, one does not do anything that is entirely against their nature. Wine only lifts the gates to action," Richard observed.

"No!" Berengaria sobbed. "I would never do such a thing of my own free will." Berengaria knew the penalty for a queen who committed adultery was death. Visions of Guinevere tied to the stake flashed through her head, and Berengaria knew she had no Lancelot to her rescue.

"Perhaps. But even if nothing happened, you gave the appearance that something did, and I cannot ignore that."

Berengaria dared to look up at her husband. Inside she seethed with hatred for Castile and Anne. It was not fair that her husband could have as many mistresses as he wished, but here she was in this predicament. She knew the only way to save her neck was to beg. "Have mercy, my lord. What can I do to gain your forgiveness?"

"To begin with, sit up and stop groveling," Richard pulled her to her feet. "Here, wipe your face and listen very carefully, Berengaria." He handed her a handkerchief. "Now, as far as anyone else is concerned, this trip to Le Mans is an attempt to produce an heir to the throne. As you stated before, I have not made much of an effort at that. However, there must be the appearance that I have. You will not say otherwise. Do you understand?"

Berengaria nodded. Richard continued, "When I leave here, I will be sending emissaries to the pope. England needs an heir, and my wife is barren. I cannot possibly think of returning to the Holy Land until England has an heir." The realization of what he was saying began to show on Berengaria's face. "Yes." Richard nodded. "I want an annulment, and you will not fight me on this."

"Dear God in heaven." Berengaria sank back into her chair.

"It will not be as bad as you think. You will retire to a convent, any of your choosing, and you will go peacefully. I also expect you to testify, if necessary, that we have failed all efforts to produce an heir. That is not a lie, but you will omit the fact that there has really not been an effort. You will relinquish your title as queen of England, and any claim to that title. Furthermore, you will not seek help from your brother. You will inform him you are satisfied with this annulment, and all you wish for is to join a sisterhood."

"What if I choose not to comply?"

"The choice is yours, but should you chose not to, I will expose you for an adulteress. The shame alone will be horrendous; then there is the fact that the people of England will demand justice."

Berengaria knew she had no choice. She was beaten, crushed. Although her head bowed in defeat, she still stared at the crest on Richard's chest as if to bore a hole out the backside of the chair. "I will do as you wish, my lord."

"Do not look at me like that Berengaria. You know as well as I, this is for the best." Richard stood up. "I think I shall go to my chamber now. I am famished."

"You are staying here?" Berengaria's head shot up.

"Why, yes. I will be here for about a fortnight. We will hold court together, and we will be the perfection of marital bliss." Richard snatched his gloves from the table. "I shall send up your new lady and tell the others that you are feeling tired and need some rest this afternoon. Oh, and take no thought of revenge against your former lady. She remained faithful to you; it was my sister who delivered the information of your treachery to me." Richard left his wife alone in her empty chamber.

Chapter Eighty-three

"Absolutely not!" Anne sat across the table from Will.

Mother and son shared a light evening meal together in Anne's chamber. His dogs, Nanna and Sigurd, flanked Will on either side, their ears perked up at the sound of anger in the voices around them.

"Mother, I am a knight now," Will protested.

"I am well aware of that, Will," Anne retorted, "but you are still fifteen."

"Marshal only asked me to accompany him to England, not Crusade."

"England is a broad term for going to tournaments and competitions, you mean," Anne grumbled. Taking a firmer tone, she continued, "You are the heir to Marseilles, not anything in England. If you go anywhere, you are going south."

"Alright," Will's voice grew louder as he stood up. "I'll go south then," he barked, throwing his hands in the air.

"No you will not!" Anne matched him. "Not until I know for certain that Castile is dead."

"What?" Will stammered, holding up his hands as if to stop the news. "Castile is dead?" He dropped his arms to his side, and face flushed. "He is dead? My blood-father dead, and you believe me to be so much a child I could not hear, *or bear* the news?"

She regretted saying anything about Castile and bit her tongue for spite. "It is a rumor," she offered meekly in a quiet voice, "not yet confirmed."

"Mother, whether or not it is true should not matter. I am a knight now, not your little boy."

"Knights do not shout at their mothers. You do not see Uncle Richard yelling at his mother do you?" Anne snapped.

Will held his right hand in a fist so tight that his knuckles turned white, and he held his left against his forehead, pulling back his hair. "His mother does not treat him like a little child!" He shouted, chopping the air with his right hand at each beat. "When Uncle Richard's father treated him like a child, Richard went to war against him."

"That is different."

"Why? Because you spent how many years in prison as a result?" Will aimed to wound now.

"That is enough, young man! Do not speak to me of prisons, for you certainly know nothing about it. Your Uncle Richard gave you a great honor, and this is how you behave?"

"I am a knight!"

Anne stepped into her son's face and snarled, "Then act like a knight."

Will's face turned pale, stung by her words. He took in a deep breath to calm himself. They both sat back at the table before he continued. "That is what I am trying to do, Mother. I need to go out there," he pointed to the window over Anne's shoulder, "and prove myself, in battle or tournament. You want me to rule Marseilles; then I must prove I can defend her. You say you want me to marry in a good match, but what father is going to agree to an alliance with a knight by title only?"

"You have plenty of opportunity to ride into battle here with Richard," Anne argued.

"Don't you understand? Right now I am seen only as the king's godson. I need to gain merit on my own without any help from Uncle Richard."

"What about Uncle Richard?" Richard's voice sounded. Ursula bounded into the room before Richard, and the three dogs began to wrestle with one another. Anne and Will made to get up. "No, stay seated."

"We did not know you had returned, my lord." Anne narrowed her eyes at Will.

"Just now." Even if he hadn't heard them from the hallway, Richard knew from the contortions of their bodies that Ann and Will were arguing. He looked down at the table. "Oh, good, food. I am half starved."

"You can have mine. I have not even touched it. I am not hungry." Will pushed himself away from the table.

"Nonsense." Richard laughed. "I have never met a young

man of your age who is not hungry." He looked from Will to Anne, but neither one relaxed at his jest. With a long sigh Richard sat down at the table. "Alright then. Why are we cross tonight?"

"I am not cross." Anne shook her head.

"Then I suppose those raised voices I heard were coming from the dogs?" Richard resorted to sarcasm.

Will folded his arms and leaned against the wall. "She has been impossible ever since you left for Le Mans."

"Damn it, Will!" Anne sprang to her feet.

The king chuckled. "I do believe that is the first time I heard you swear in a long time, my dear!" Richard laid his gloves on the table next to Will's plate of untouched food.

"That has nothing to do with it," Anne growled. "Will wants to go to England with Marshal when he leaves here."

"I need to go to tournaments there. I have to establish my own reputation," Will countered.

"You also have a duty to keep yourself safe so you can one day rule Marseilles. Tournaments are dangerous." Anne shook her head.

"That apple looks delicious." Trying to distract her, Richard pointed to the red fruit on her plate. Anne picked it up and tossed it to him.

"How am I supposed to gain a reputation as a worthy knight if I am not allowed to prove myself?" Will struggled not to shout at his mother.

Richard bit into the apple. Anne did not keep her voice down. "Duty, Will! Duty! You have a duty to Marseilles!"

"Do you not see that is the reason I must go!" Will stood up straight.

Richard swallowed and put up his hands. "Rome and Carthage shall cease their hostilities. Will, you have a valid point, but so does your mother. One thing I can tell you is that shouting will not resolve this matter."

"I am sorry, your highness," Will apologized.

"Perhaps you ought to go simmer down somewhere, then you can continue this conversation later," Richard advised.

"Yes, my lord." Will obeyed, with Nanna and Sigurd following after him.

Ursula followed her parents, but stopped at her master's side, looking up longingly at Richard. "Sit," Richard commanded the dog. With a sour look on her face Anne ambled to her seat. "I meant the dog, not you," Richard said. "Unless, of course, you wish to sit." Anne said nothing to Richard so he continued, "So, Will wants to go with Marshal?"

"You are sending Marshal to England to look after affairs of state, not be a nursemaid to my son while he runs around from tournament to tournament," Anne huffed.

"I understand why Will wants to go. I remember very similar conversations with my father. I also understand why you want to keep him here. Think of this. Will is a knight now, and as such, has certain expectations to meet. He needs to make a name for himself. My first line of attack in any battle is my reputation."

Anne started, "Richard…"

He didn't let her finish. "Anne, he came to you for your blessing. That is more courtesy than many would show. He is embarking on a new venture in his life, and he wants to know he has your support."

"I will consider it," Anne grumped.

"Do not wait too long, or he will be gone." Richard tried to reach out and touch her, but Anne withdrew her hands from the table and placed them on her lap. "Will is right. You are in a foul mood."

"I am just tired; that is all." Anne tried to dismiss his comment. "Besides, I promised Gustave that I would draft a letter with him."

"Tonight?" Richard knew she really didn't need to work on the letter that badly, but he reined in his temper. "Dear, please do not be sullen."

"I am sorry." She looked down as she apologized.

Richard bent down so he could meet her line of sight. "I swear to you, I did not lay so much as a finger on her."

"Not even to heal yourself?"

"What do you mean?"

"Richard." Anne sighed. "I heard all about the hermit's warning."

"Since when do you put your faith in rumors or superstitions?" He winked at her. "I cannot tell you everything just yet. There are too many variables to sort out, but I have put in motion something that will be beneficial to us. All I ask is that you trust me a little longer. When the time is right, I will reveal all."

Anne regarded him for a moment, then responded with caution, "Very well."

"Thank you." He pressed his hands together as if in prayer. "Thank you, sweetheart."

"Just remember that I am trusting you."

"I shall not forget." He looked down at the plate of food in front of him. "Will really didn't want any of this?"

"No. I am afraid our argument chased away his appetite."

"Well, I am not going to let such a meal go to waste." Richard began to eat.

"Pray, excuse me. I do need to speak with Gustave."

Richard nodded. Before Anne left the room, she grazed his cheek with a kiss.

Both monarchs felt pressure as everywhere the balance of power seemed to shift. In Outremer, their nephew, Henry, crowned King of Jerusalem, died in a fall from one of the upper windows in his castle at Acre. Saladin succumbed to a fever while in Damascus shortly after Richard left. Then, Leopold of Austria's horse fell on him and crushed his foot. He died of gangrene. Hohenstaufen died while on campaign to conquer Sicily, and Richard's nephew,

Matilda's son, Otto of Brunswick was named the new Holy Roman Emperor.

Richard and Philip's soldiers roamed the countryside taking up the practice of popping out their enemies' eyes. Each side claimed the other side started it. Regardless, it only made peace harder to achieve.

Philip himself gave Richard plenty of reasons to be angry, but one especially when he convinced Richard's nephew and heir, Arthur of Brittany to defect. It was reminiscent of the strategy Philip used with Henry's sons.

Richard wanted to make one last push against Philip before winter set in. He started with the French Vexin at Dangu. Conquering the fortress there and two others at Courcelles and Boury, along with Seri-fontaine, made the net around Philip at Mante all the tighter.

Philip did not believe that Dangu had fallen completely and wanting to move fast, took only three hundred knights, men-at-arms, and a light load of commissary wagons to see the situation for himself.

Mercadier brought the news the French were on the move to Richard's war council. "And, as you have commanded, your highness, with the bridges destroyed, their best route will be via Gisors, then across the Epte, and on to Dangu."

"We'll have him then, Mercadier. God and my right will be restored. Ha!" Richard bounced his fist off the table. "That shall be our countersign for the day."

Richard ordered a small force of foot soldiers be positioned at the bridge over the River Epte on the road from the castle at Gisors. When Philip's cavalry appeared, Richard's were commanded to feint, allowing Philip's force to cross, then the rest of the foot soldiers would come out of the hedge rows and seal off the bridge. Meanwhile, Richard and his knights would surprise them. The main body of footman would seal the crossing of the bridge and attack the French rear.

From his hiding spot in the hedge, Richard watched as the French troops made their way down the road. His heart pounded in his chest as he watched the columns of soldiers moving along, flags flapping in the breeze, dust rising in their wake in the late summer sun. He could easily tell that his troops outnumbered Philip's. Confidence flooded his body. "It looks like you could have followed them for another hour, Mercadier." Richard chuckled. "Tell all men to hold their positions. The knights will this day earn their place and go first. The foot soliders still should seal off the bridge to prevent their escape, but wait for the command."

As the column of Philip's soldiers swayed back and forth marching from the castle, Richard fought against his desire to pounce until his instinct revealed the perfect moment. Holding his right arm at the square, he watched the enemy's movement with hawk-like eyes. "God and my right!" Richard cried. A cheer went up and they were at full charge in an instant.

The suddenness of the attack bred confusion amongst Philip's men as realization grasped them that Richard and his men were not two days away at Dangu as expected. They were here, right here, attacking.

Philip saw the tide of Richard's cavalry rush upon and engulf his own men. Half dozen knights formed around Philip to protect their king. The infantry bore the brunt of the charge.

While wheeling his horse, Philip caught sight of Richard, fully armored, atop a black horse, charging the line with a lance, his red robes like fire in the wind. Then he saw the chevrons of de Montmorency, de Rusci, and de Gileval line up, all charge at the English king, and all three fall. Richard dropped his broken lance, grabbed his sword, and looking up, caught Philip's gaze, pointing his sword at him. At that instant, Philip knew being taken would mean excruciating humiliation, imprisonment, or worse. For a split second he felt the muscles give way to his dark desire of vengeance, preparing to charge straight at his vassal, and unleash every thought of anger, hatred, and jealousy through his own sword. Between himself and Richard was a mass of flesh and metal, and he calculated the fastest path. He saw Richard's cavalry slaughtering his sergents like so many beeves.

Duty is incumbent upon us all, no matter our station. The pawn, the knight, the castle, and even the queen owe their duty to the king. The king is in duty bound to God and his kingdom. It has always been thus, and must ever be, so long as a king reigns.

Anne's words stopped Philip from launching himself toward Richard. She was not there; she did not need to be. Her talk of duty echoing in his head reined him in. "Damn, damn, damn!" For the sake of his kingdom, Philip turned his horse around. "To the castle," he shouted, as he charged off.

Richard gave chase, fighting his way through the blockade of the rear guard defending the escape of their king, ready to die if necessary. He lost sight of Philip in the clouds of dust that seemed as thick as a curtain.

There were some who did not choose valor and instead of standing their ground, fled with the king. Philip and his company rode pell-mell for the castle. When they came to the River Epte, they saw Richard's foot soldiers in formation, closing off the escape. Racing as hard as they could, a large group of knights charged for the bridge before it could be sealed off. Some stopped to defend it from each direction, while sixty charged across, forcing them together like funneling the river through a bottle. The king and two-dozen knights followed in short order onto the bridge, pushing and shoving to get across. In front of Philip, Norbert shouted at the men to make way for their king, even beaning a foot soldier or two on the head with his mace.

Philip neared half way across the bridge when a groan and crack of thunder rose above the madness. His men in front of him began to fly into dust. Before he had time to react, he and his horse tumbled downward. Instinctively, he turned his shoulder to brace his fall, only to plunge headlong into the murky river.

The water stung as Philip hit, and the shock of the cold on the hot September day made him scream, losing all his breath. He gasped for air, but took in only water. It burnt his throat and stung his nostrils. Philip tore at his armor, pulling off his helmet. All around him, limbs of flailing men and horses churning the turbid water made it impossible to see. Not completely understanding what was going on, he felt upside down in water, his legs above him. He waved them back and forth to see if he was right, and could feel them move without resistance. He tried to push himself out to no avail. His coat seemed to be holding him from either falling all the way or pulling himself out. Images flashed before his eyes punctuated by the chaos of those struggling for life. Philip thought of that meeting when he convinced Richard to come to Paris with him, of the first time he met Anne, and how ironically those events occurred at Gisors. Anne's devotion to duty sparked in him again. Philip's son was still young and it would not take much for Richard to maneuver his way around such a young king.

So, this is how it ends, he thought to himself. *Philip, King of France by the Grace of God. Dead, not in battle, but drowned in the River Epte, upside down, while fleeing from the King of England.*

Brown blurs with flashes of light and muffled screams of men and cries of horses played with the king's senses. *Chaos*, was all he could think. *Chaos!* Then he felt someone grabbed his right ankle, and he moved it to tell whomever it was that he was still alive. Suddenly he felt several hands grasp his legs and pull. *That won't work*, he thought. Then a splash and someone grabbed him around the waist, holding him tight, and making a sawing motion. All at once, there was a brilliant light, and he heard someone shout "Highness!" Several pairs of hands grabbed at his wrists and arms from above.

Philip opened his mouth to purge the water. He coughed

and gasped, taking in life giving air. In his disorientation, he felt as though he was flying, then he hit something hard and fell back on it. Now he was aware that several different men were speeding him away. "To the castle," the man at his right hand yelled. "God save the king!"

Philip's senses reeled, and he was unable to control them. He struggled to sit up to cough out water, but the jostling made it impossible. He began to gag, then someone shouted a halt, and the men lowered him. In convulsion, Philip turned on his right and disgorged himself on a man in full mail, then blackness enveloped him.

Chapter Eighty-four

From the other side of the bridge, Richard watched the structure collapse and Philip tumble in. His reaction surprised himself. After all that passed between them, it would only be natural to feel hope, elation, or at least relief, as he watched his enemy fall. Instead, an unexpected feeling of anxiety and even regret took hold in him. Holding his breath, he stood in his stirrups to see if Philip resurfaced. The moment between when Philip went into the water and his men first tried to pull him out seemed to last an hour to Richard. As he watched Philip sink back into the water, he was sure his heart would burst through his chest. "Damn you, Philip!" He muttered. "Not like this! Not like this!"

Amongst the broken timbers and planks, Richard could see a man double over and tear off his coat and hauberk in one, grab a dagger from a fellow soldier to cut the knots on his brigandine, stripping off everything until he was nude, then jump in the murk after his king. It was difficult to make sense of all the bodies writhing in the water. Without thinking, Richard thrust himself forward toward the scene of carnage. His men took this as a sign to advance, and they amplified their efforts. Richard charged on, but stopped short when he saw Philip pulled from the water at last. A sense of relief washed over him, and Richard turned his attention to those around him. The French were subdued or captured. On this side of the bridge the battle was over, his men already pillaging what the French army left behind.

Richard had not brought materials for a siege, so he ordered his men to take the prisoners and spoils back to Dangu. Turning his horse, he spotted Marshal and Will. Will made his way over to Richard. "Your highness!" Will shouted with a large smile. "We have captured a chest of the King of France and the royal seal within it!"

Pleased, Richard ordered, "By God's arm, Sir Will! What fantastic news. Keep it safe, son, and tell Marshal to return to Dangu."

"Yes, my lord." Smiling up at his godfather, Will nodded. "It shall be done."

To Richard's left, Mercadier rode up with a prisoner bound by the hands, struggling to keep up with the horse. Stopping in front of Richard, Mercadier's three-day growth of beard twisted into an odd grin that resembled more of a vengeful grimace than smile. "Your highness, I bring you a gift." He yanked the man on the end of his tether to his knees.

The man kneeling before Richard was none other than the Bishop of Beauvais dressed in armor. "This day, God smiles upon England. He has gifted me a holy man dressed for battle," Richard scoffed.

"What would you know of God and holy men?" Beauvais sneered.

"I know that you are no more a man of God than the horse of Troy was a gift from Poseidon." Richard leaned down to see the bishop more closely. He was filthy and covered with splotches of blood and dirt. "At last you show your true self on the outside."

"I am a servant of God and His Holiness in Rome. Do you dare take me prisoner?" Beauvais remained defiant.

"You are a man of war, dressed for war," Richard responded with no qualms. "Mercadier, see to it that our prisoner is shown all the *niceties* that befall his sort of personage."

"With pleasure, your highness." Mercadier jerked on the cord, and this time Beauvais almost fell on his face. "Come on you!" He shouted at the hapless Beauvais and turned toward Dangu.

Richard took one last look around. "By God, what a glorious day." He smiled and spurred his horse toward Dangu where Anne waited for him.

When Philip awoke, he was clean, dry, warm, and safe in bed, but the images from the river still clung to his brain. With a shiver, he sat up and looked around. He was in the castle of Gisors. He listened for the sounds of siege outside. Had Richard followed him there to claim the castle? All seemed quiet except for the snores coming from Dreux de Mello, Philip's constable, as he slept in a chair in the corner. Philip was jealous that his commander of the armies could sleep so soundly and irritated Norbert was not there.

Philip coughed and de Mello only stirred. De Mello had been Philip's constable for about a year before Richard returned from Speyer. He was a fierce man on the field of battle and highly skilled at leading an army, but de Mello had the uncanny ability to fall into a deep sleep at the end of the day, as if nothing bothered him. Waking him until morning could prove difficult. Rolling his eyes, Philip called out, "De Mello." The constable sat up, but his eyes remained closed. "De Mello!" Philip took a more forceful tone even though his voice sounded hoarse.

"Your highness." This time de Mello sprang from his chair and into an automatic bowing position.

"Where is my page? I wish to dress." Philip scowled.

"I sent the boy away to get some sleep, your highness." In a flash, the drowsy look vanished from de Mello's face.

Philip swung his legs over the bed. "Well, then, I suppose you drew the short straw, and you are here to report the casualties."

"Yes, my lord. Twenty-two knights drowned." De Mello didn't flinch. Not even his grey moustache twitched as he delivered the news.

Philip stood up and stretched. "Is that all? I should think us very lucky 'twas not more."

De Mello's expression remained emotionless. "King Richard captured around two-hundred knights, along with the royal seal and the Bishop of Beauvais."

Putting his hand on his mouth, Philip shook his head. "God in heaven! Two-hundred knights captured, twenty-two dead in the river. We left Gisors with only three-hundred, Beauvais, and the royal seal. England must be celebrating this day. Now there will be thousands upon thousands of blind soldiers roaming the countryside. What a collection of eyes he must have now. It is fortunate that France still has Gisors, and you know how badly the devil wants that. I can commission another seal, but Richard cannot make another Gisors. And as for that cousin of mine, on one hand, I am angry he let himself be captured, but make no bones about it, he deserves it. May the Lord have mercy on him— Richard will not."

"Taking a bishop captive could certainly cause problems for a king," de Mello pointed out.

"Yes, it can." Philip gave de Mello a crooked smile. "Where *is* Norbert?"

"Your highness…" de Mello stroked his beard, the only sign of emotion he had showed thus far. "Sire, Norbert tried to pull you from the water. When you slipped from his grasp, he dove in after you." De Mello paused. "Sir Norbert is amongst the drowned."

Philip sank back down onto the bed. "Norbert? Drowned? He must have been the one who pushed me from underneath."

Philip's body shook and his face turned a dull gray. "Has his body been recovered?"

"No, my lord."

"Find it!" He shouted, springing back to his feet. "Leave me, and find his body! Leave me now!"

De Mello did not need to be told twice. He bowed to the king and hurried away. Philip wanted to throw something, hit, break, destroy, but in his choler he could not convince his arms to move. All he could do was bellow, "His blood shall be avenged, Richard, and if I have to deliver you to the devil myself, you will burn in the fires of hell!"

When Richard returned to Dangu, Anne was praying in the village church. The noise of his arrival compelled her to end her supplications and rush outside. He caught sight of her coming from the building and turned his horse to meet her. The tide of the returning army continued passing him to their camp around the chateau. Holding her hand up to shield her eyes from the sun, she greeted him. "Your highness."

"Do you mean to tell me I have ridden all this way to find you have been at prayer?" He grinned down at her.

"Where else should I be when your soul is involved?" Anne returned with her own jest.

"If it is my soul you pray for, I doubt you will be returning to the chateau anytime soon."

"Prayer can only do so much." She shrugged.

"Ha! Indeed! Lady Anne, you could make the devil himself act civilized."

"Perhaps I already have." She winked. "If it pleases you, I think I shall return to the chateau now."

"God's legs, of course it pleases me." He looked around. "But where is your horse?"

She tipped her head to the side. "I walked."

"Walked, huh?" He moved his left foot from the stirrup and extended his arm to her. "Forgive me, but I am too tired to walk back to the chateau fully armored, and my civilized sensibilities could not allow you to walk by yourself."

"I do not wish to trouble the king's conscience." She took his arm and stuck her small slipper shod foot into the stirrup.

Richard helped her swing onto the horse behind him. "Sorry, I am a bit dusty from the road."

With a gentle embrace, she wrapped her arms around his waist, but not too tightly, because even with a surcoat on over it, mail was not comfortable to press against, and she didn't want her dress to be stained with oil. "I do not mind."

Taking the reins in his right hand, he placed his left over hers and moved his horse forward at a leisurely pace. "Have you seen Will yet?"

"No, but I could tell by your expression when you arrived that he was fine, so I did not worry."

"Will is better than fine. He and Marshal are safeguarding some important documents." A hint of mischief lingered in his voice.

"What documents did you take with you?"

Richard gave a mock sigh. "Oh, they are not mine. They belong to Philip, and they were in his chest we captured, along with his royal seal."

"That should make him rather cross, I would wager."

"That is not all. We have around two-hundred of his knights, and the bridge to Gisors collapsed." Richard's tone turned serious. "Just as Philip crossed the Epte River, it fell." Richard added quickly, "Philip was pulled from the river soaked through, but alive." Anne's arms tensed around his middle, but she did not say anything. After a moment of silence Richard asked, "So, tell me, were your prayers answered?"

"I fear that sometimes my prayers confuse God." She relaxed the muscles in her arms.

"Why is that?"

Despite the dust, oil and armor, Anne leaned closer to Richard. "When you are gone, I pray for your safe return and Will's."

"Naturally."

"But I also pray for Philip's safety. I cannot help it. He has been a comfort to me when I needed it."

"I see." Richard supposed she referred to when they were in Messina and when Anne returned to Marseilles.

"The thing of it is," Anne continued, "you are both so determined to drive the other off a cliff and straight into the pits of hell that it seems one or the other of you is bound for a fiery reward."

"Perhaps we both are." Richard caught sight of something out of the corner of his eye. "Maybe you should not waste your time on prayers for us. There are others who could use prayers when it comes to their fate, like your other cousin Philip for example."

"What do you mean?" Anne sat up taller again.

"If you look off to your right there," he indicated the direction with his head, "you shall see the Bishop of Beauvais."

Ahead of her and to her right, Anne saw her cousin, the Bishop of Beauvais, the cause of much trouble for both herself, and Richard. She never told Richard what passed between bishop and herself because Richard already wanted to unseam him. The bishop was tied fast, riding inside a little cart with a defiant expression on his face. "Bad bit of luck for the bishop." She grimaced.

"Indeed, but I do not think that he has been able to grasp the severity of his situation yet. He convinced himself that because he *pretends* to be a holy man, I will release him. The bastard dressed in full battle armor, and played the role of soldier when Mercadier took him."

"He is lucky to have lived this long." Anne watched the

bishop who seemed to sense her looking at him, and he looked back at her, pleading with his eyes.

"My first instinct was to flay him alive, but that would have not been painful enough." Richard also noticed the Bishop looking at Anne. "Mercadier tells me the bishop has begged leave to speak with you."

"I meant it was not only a wonder that you have not harmed him, but that Philip did not punish him." Anne broke eye contact with her cousin in the cart.

They were at the chateau now, and Richard steered the horse through the rows of tents to the entrance of the fortress. "Do not forget, Beauvais was instrumental in making my life in Germany as difficult as possible, and that was good for Philip. I also think he was not punished for giving your name to Hohenstaufen, and yes, he was the one who gave your name to Hohenstaufen, no matter how much he protests, because Philip wanted that annulment from that Danish princess, and Beauvais would grant it for him."

"I will see Beauvais." Anne gave a curt nod.

"What?" Richard nearly halted the horse.

"I want to hear from his own lips how he can call himself a man of God and behave like he does." Anne narrowed her eyes.

"There is no way that I will allow him anywhere near you. Besides, we are at the chateau now, I am hungry, and my men are craving a celebration."

Chapter Eighty-five

A roar of cheers rose from the hall of Dangu Chateau as Richard's men celebrated their victory. The hall at Dangu was not nearly as grand as others they had known, but that didn't seem to matter to the revelers. As Richard addressed the assembled, Anne took the opportunity to slip away. She knew Richard might be upset, but she was compelled to face Beauvais herself.

The more valuable prisoners were being kept in the lowest level of the chateau's keep in a wine cellar hastily converted to a well-guarded, makeshift holding cell. As she descended the stairs, the stench of sweaty men and dirt accosted her nose. The prisoners were shackled together. Beauvais was in the middle, and Mercadier guarded his prize. The sight of the mercenary irritated Anne, but she would not let him dissuade her. Mercadier caught sight of her. "Lady Anne?"

"Mercadier." She nodded. "I am here to see Beauvais."

His eyes narrowed with suspicion. "The Bishop of Beauvais?"

"Is there any other man here called Beauvais?" She addressed the row of prisoners.

Beauvais rose to his feet. Mercadier grumped at Anne, "Do you want me to loose him?"

"Not entirely, but I do wish to speak to my cousin, and I require some semblance of privacy. Unloose him from the line; then bind his hands, hobble his feet, and bring him to me." She looked around and saw a kind of alcove by the entrance to the room formed in part by barrels. "Over there." She pointed.

"What does the king say about this?" Mercadier challenged her.

Folding her arms, Anne spoke with exasperation, "What do you think the king has to say about this? Now, you can go ask him if you want to, but I suspect that will just raise his ire at being second guessed."

Mercadier looked at Beauvais behind him then back at Anne. "Alright, but I'm warning you, I will hold you responsible if anything goes wrong."

"What could possibly go wrong? You are here to protect him." Anne quipped as she removed herself to the alcove.

Mercadier knew her last comment referred to Poitiers when

he *had* failed to protect her. "What was I supposed to do, go against a king and lose my head?" he mumbled.

Anne heard Mercadier, but ignored him. As she listened, the guards shifted their prisoners, and she second-guessed herself, her purpose. Then the memory of Beauvais came back to her, and her face flushed hot. Before long, Beauvais was at her feet, kneeling before her. "Lady Anne—cousin."

She let loose an angry sigh. She spoke softly so that others could not hear, "Get up, man. Do you want the others to see you begging before a woman?"

Obeying, Beauvais rose to his feet. He looked much older than he did in Speyer. His hair was cut short and had turned completely gray. The wrinkles around his eyes made his face look harsher. "Lady Anne, my dear cousin, I simply humble myself before you. I know the last time we spoke in Speyer, you were not entirely convinced of my intentions, and I wish you to know that I only…"

"How many times have you called me a whore?" Anne interrupted him.

"My lady," Beauvais stammered. "Have you ever heard me call you such a thing?"

"Do you think that you would have to say it to my face? The implications you made in Speyer clearly showed what you think that I am. I am certain the word, *whore* has escaped your lips when talking of me." She looked down her nose at him, as though he were a debased criminal. Beauvais opened his mouth to speak again, but Anne put up her hand to stop him. "Let me guess what you are going to say. You are going to protest your innocence, just as you protested your innocence to King Philip when you were accused of involving me with Richard's ransom. Or, perhaps, you were going to speak more of Christian tenets, especially of forgiveness, and remind me we are related and blood, after all, is a binding element between people."

"My lady, I humble myself before you," Beauvais pleaded.

"Be honest with yourself, *Bishop*. The only reason you escaped King Philip's wrath is because you had something he desperately wanted. You had the power to grant him an annulment. Your sense of family was no help to me in Speyer; it will be of no help to you here. As for what passed between you and Richard, that is his business and none of mine. From the sounds of it, he would have you drawn and quartered, but doesn't because that could only be relished once."

"I am a man of God, and doing harm to me would have repercussions." Beauvais stood up taller.

"Damn your repercussions. If you are looking for help from our cousin, we shall see how desperately Philip wants you back. Maybe he will want you to perform a new marriage for him while his other is still in question. Lord knows, you would do it for him."

"I already have."

"Oh, but of course," Anne mocked. "You weave such an intricate mess."

Beauvais held his hands out to her in supplication. "Will you do nothing for me? Will you not pray for me as I have so often prayed for you?"

"I will pray that God will be merciful to you because I doubt Richard will be. Here," she place something in the palm of his hand and wrapped his fingers around it. "Your prayers would be better spent on yourself than on me. Pray, Bishop, Pray." She moved beyond the barrels and shouted to Mercadier, "I am done with the Bishop."

Beauvais looked in his hand, and in his palm was the crude wooden cross he gave Anne in Speyer.

As Anne climbed the stairs, disappointment overwhelmed her. She found no satisfaction in confronting Beauvais, but wondered if she would have if she had jammed the cross in his neck. She decided she truly hated the man, even if it was a sin and rationalized that God could not like him much either. From the sound of it, she could tell the men were still making merry, and the wine had taken effect. They were louder now. She had no wish to return to the hall, so she went straight to her chamber.

There was no sign of Greta when Anne reached the chamber door, and peevishly she shoved it open. Her thoughts were still on Beauvais below and she did not notice that someone was already in the room. "Welcome back." Facing the doorway, he sat in a chair with his stocking feet propped up on her bed.

Anne jumped at the sound of his voice. "Richard! You startled me!" She closed the door behind her.

"So, how was your visit with the bishop?" He took his feet off the bed. She looked at him like a cat caught with a canary in its mouth. "Anne." His laugh rumbled softly across the room. "You disappeared, and earlier I could tell by the look in your eye you had something to settle with Beauvais. Tell me, did you give him a solid tongue lashing or just go straight for the dagger?"

Anne was trying to remain calm, but she felt like a pot of boiling oil about to simmer over. "Neither," she snapped.

"Neither?" Richard raised his eyebrows.

"Beauvais is a twisted, self-righteous, sanctimonious bastard!" She raised her voice.

"I will not argue with you there."

"You had just left Speyer when he . . . he came to *minister* to me." Anne shook like she had just seen something repulsive.

"By God! I will slit his throat!" Richard jumped to his feet.

"You will do no such thing!" Anne shouted. "Now, sit down. It is my turn to fly off the handle. You always get to bluster about as if someone is poking you with an iron. Besides, he did not do *that*." She was surprised by her disrespectful attitude towards Richard. She looked away from him. "I am sorry."

Richard spoke in a quiet voice, "You never told me about this."

Anne went to her small dressing table. "There is nothing to

tell." She yanked at her wimple, but it wouldn't come easily so she jerked harder, and the material ripped.

Richard went to her to help. "Stop. It is caught on a hairpin."

"I can take off my own wimple." Her words were brusque.

"I am well aware of that. Clearly there is something to tell about him. What is it?" Richard unhooked the linen from the bodkin.

"No. I am just tired, that is all," Anne insisted, "and I hate this stupid contraption!" She wadded up her wimple, and tossed it on the table.

"Anne, there is something you need to say, and I need to hear it."

With a fierce look in her eyes, Anne turned to face him. Her disheveled hair added to her wild appearance. "As I said, there is nothing to tell."

"Oh, yes there is." Richard knew he could match her in stubbornness. "We have never talked about Speyer. From the time I found you in that peasant hovel until you came to my room, you barely spoke to me. You were thin, frail, and shaking like a leaf. Somehow you managed to compose yourself, probably for Will, but I can tell that deep down you have something to say." He placed his hands on her shoulders. "I laid awake many a night, sick with guilt about all that happened to you on my account, worried that you will…"

"Will what? Blow away like a leaf?" Anne shook herself loose and moved towards the bed. Her anger spilled out in tears. "You just do not understand!"

Richard took a deep breath. "And how can I when you refuse to tell me what it is that I am supposed to understand?"

"You want to know what happened, do you?" She screamed back at him. "Well, let me share some of nightmares with you. Castile almost lost the race to take me. Your mother and I did not share a bed in Salisbury just to keep from freezing. The stinking filthy men there did not dare touch a queen, but her lady was another matter. There were times I had to hide in the stables, or even up in the rafters. Every time the sun rose I thanked God that I lived another day without being violated and prayed that day would not be the one. I cannot begin to number the times I was fondled when they thought your mother was not looking. I survived all those years with my virtue only to have Castile rob it!"

"Anne, I had no idea."

"Of course, you had no idea. At least I should hope! Richard, I know what you suffered in Speyer was horrible, and the thought of you imprisoned hurt me beyond description. Please do not think that I am trying to cheapen what you went through. I am not trying to be a martyr, but both times when I was imprisoned I fought every day not just to survive, but to survive without being… being…." She didn't finish, but only balled up her fists and groaned.

Richard moved toward her but held back. "I cannot tell you how much I worried about that very thing."

"You have worried?" She gave a contorted laugh.

Turning around twice as though she were looking for something, she stopped, and plucked her shoes from her feet. Without warning she flung one at the wall near Richard. She raised the other shoe as if to throw it as well. "Anne, what are you doing?"

"I am throwing my shoes. What does it look like I am doing?" She gritted her teeth.

"Why?"

She lowered the shoe. "Because I thought it would make me feel better." She raised it back up in a brisk motion. "I am irate! I am irate that bastard downstairs treated you the way he did, manipulated Hohenstaufen, made your time in prison miserable, and went stark raving religious mad on me! I am incensed that Castile might still be out there, and there is nothing I can do about it, that I am called your whore when I have done nothing but deny my desires!"

A dam broke and there was no stopping her now. "All I ever wanted was to marry someone who would make my father proud, love Marseilles, be honorable, and kind to me. I had *no* pretensions that I would marry for love, but I hoped at least to find a friend in my husband. I wanted to have children, several, grow old and die in Marseilles surrounded by my children and grandchildren. And after I am gone I wanted it to be said that I was honest and fair, kind hearted, wise, and people would tell of the honorable, good life I lived. Look at me now, married to a fiend, and known far and wide as the English king's whore. Oh, and I am not stupid; there are many who would have challenged my inheritance to Marseilles had it not been for the fact they were afraid you wanted it or my crazed but skilled husband would take it from them, destroying it if necessary. I have done nothing for Marseilles, but hurt her. Their abbot possibly committed murder on my account!"

Tears continued to pour down her face, and she gripped the shoe more tightly. "Then there is this whole matter with Will. I do not want him to go. He is my son, my only heir. Other mothers have sons to spare; I do not. He must go back to Marseilles and do for her what I could not, but how can he do that without proving himself a worthy knight? What if something happens to him, and I cannot be there? Then again, a knight who is followed around by his mother is hardly a knight at all. I know he has to prove himself, but it makes me angry, and angry that it needs to be done, and angry that I am angry about it." She burst into a fresh bout of tears.

"Anne, you are no whore," he offered.

"I know that, but that is how everyone sees me!"

Richard grimmaced. She had moved onto crying about Will, but now she would no doubt rant about being called that nasty name even more. "Not everyone." He tried to be pragmatic.

"Yes, everyone!" Anne was not ready to be sensible.

"Alright, dear, now you are being irrational." Richard

spoke with more force.

"No! I am downright livid at this whole situation. Oh, and I am sick to death of this never-ending quarrel between you and Philip. I saw it coming a long time ago, and it is never going to end. You will both be dead and buried, and it will still be going on. And speaking of death," Anne barely drew in a breath as she continued, "every time you or Will ride out of here I am terrified it is that last time I will see you. What if you do not come back? What if Castile does? What if I lose Will?" She stooped down and retrieved her shoe, then hurled it at her trunk. "And why the hell does throwing things not make me fell better?"

Anne sank down on the bed in a sobbing heap with her face buried in the coverings. Richard hesitated at first, not sure what to do. For a split second he though about leaving the room, but he knew that was not the right choice. He didn't run away in battle, and he would not run away now. Cautiously he made his way to the bed. Sitting down next to Anne he reached out and stroked her back. He didn't say anything. Anne muttered something about Will and her father that he couldn't understand.

Almost as sudden as the flood of tears started, the sobbing ended, and Anne pushed herself into a sitting position. "I am sorry. I do not know what came over me."

"It sounds to me as if seeing Beauvais tonight was a spark that lit the tinder."

"Richard, why does God punish us? I have tried everything I could to fulfil my duty and to serve Him; and you, you went all the way to the Holy Land where Jerusalem was dangled in front of you. He has given us this," she motioned back and forth between them, "but I feel like a child. A pretty little toy has been placed in front of me, and every time I reach out to it, I am slapped away and told I am a sinner, made to feel evil. In the end I will always be just the king's whore. Berengaria is revered for her patience, and long-suffering while her errant husband dallies with me." Anne started to cry again, but this time the tears just rolled down her cheeks; the pitch of her voice did not rise. "I would go to hell for you if need be, Richard."

He drew her to him, and she buried her face in his chest. "I think," he whispered, "you already have."

Chapter Eighty-six

Richard and Philip agreed to another truce. Philip needed time to recuperate, and strengthen his army before Richard went on the offensive again. Richard thought a break in the fighting would ease Anne's stress.

The pope sent Peter of Capua to facilitate the negotiations between Philip and Richard, but the negotiations almost broke down when he made the mistake of asking Richard to free the Bishop of Beauvais. Peter of Capua fled the English king's court after Richard threatened to castrate him. After a few days, Richard's temper cooled, and he agreed to a truce with Philip because he saw it as a sign of Philip's weakening resolve. Besides, it was only a truce and not meant to put a permanent seal on any boundaries. Richard could keep the lands he conquered or retaken from Philip. Richard got everything in Normandy but the Norman Vexin. The pope's emissary was nowhere to be seen at the treaty signing; neither were the kings. They sent personal representatives to do the work, which allowed Richard to concentrate on bringing his new plans to fruition.

Richard sent the Bishop of Beauvais to the stronghold of Rouen to await his fate, making sure the accommodations were much like those he had suffered in Speyer. Both Richard and Anne found it amusing that Philip was not the one requesting the release of Beauvais, but Peter of Capua.

Anne spent much of the time in Rouen or Vaudreuil, while Richard traveled south to Les Andelys. She did not know why he went there other than he made some sort of arrangement with the Bishop of Rouen regarding church property. Anne decided not to pester Richard about it. She promised to trust him, and she resolved to do just that, even though it proved difficult.

Marshal left for England shortly after the battle at Gisors, taking Will. After much careful thought, Anne bid her son farewell. She remembered Richard was about the same age when he felt it necessary to show his father, even by force, that he had honor and courage, deserving all the rites associated with knighthood. In the end, she gave her son a parting kiss on the cheek, then retired to her room to be alone. Richard remained close to her for the next few days. Since she showed no signs of melancholy, he headed south again leaving her at Rouen.

Time passed like this and life fell into a rhythm of negotiation and diplomatic cavortings. Winter gave way to spring, and spring opened up to summer. Late summer settled on the land again. Late summer was the season of Richard's first coronation, the season of his birth, in more ways than one, the season when fate introduced Richard to Anne. This late summer Richard told Anne he would to introduce her to something else.

Richard returned to Rouen late one night and crept into Anne's room. His eyes shone with the excitement of a child when he told her he would be going south again the next day, but this time, he wanted her with him.

They left Rouen early the next morning, traveling by river, but Richard would not tell Anne their exact destination. He promised to do so at the right time. Anne was growing tired of this game, but could not bring herself to be angry with him; he was too blithe. The late summer weather was beautiful, the sky crystal blue with only thins wisps of clouds. The breeze gently frolicked through the trees, down the bank, and across the river while the sun seemed to wrap itself around the band of travelers.

Taking advantage of the warmth of the day, Anne sat on the deck of the barge, cushions surrounding her. The lazy splash of water lapped against the boat as it glided southward. The late afternoon haze made Anne drowsy, so she leaned against the railing of the ship, and let its soft movement lull her to sleep. Anne did not know how long she slept, but something tender brushed against her cheek, and she opened her eyes. A smile spread across her face as she realized Richard just kissed her. "I was having such a pleasant nap," she whispered. "But I do not mind waking for that."

"Look up there." He pointed beyond her.

She turned following where his finger pointed and saw before her a massive citadel overlooking the river below. "A castle?" Its size and presence were impressive. She stood up and felt dizzy looking up at the structure.

Richard beamed with pride. "I call her Chateau Gaillard."

Anne gave him a crocked smile. "*Saucy castle*, eh? Now, to whom would it be saucy, I wonder?"

"Do not be mean now." He smiled. "Look at her! She is my creation. I designed everything right down to the tassels on the draperies."

"Congratulations, my lord. You have a beautiful daughter." Anne bobbed her head in a quick bow.

"Yes, a daughter of twelve months. Beat that if you can." Richard leaned against the railing admiring the sight of his castle above them.

Anne shook her head in wonder. "How did you keep this from me?"

"That was quite a feat, I can tell you. I do not know which was harder—building the castle or keeping it from you. I feared your beloved cousin might tell you."

"With good reason. We are only five miles from his castle at Gaillon. No doubt he knows what you have been up to here."

Richard chuckled. "Rumor has it Philip claims he will take this castle even if it is made of iron."

"Surely he will try."

"And I would defend it, even if the walls were made of butter." Richard pointed to a bridge that crossed the river. "It all starts here. I can blockade the river. Nothing can go up it, and especially go beyond this point to Rouen, unless I desire it."

The significance of the location for military purposes dawned on Anne. She knew that this was an ideal spot to build such a citadel. Still, Richard's quick mind for such matters never failed to amaze her, even after all these years. "So, this little fishing village today, and the Vexin tomorrow?" She wrapped her arms around his left arm in a playful hug.

The barge made its way to dock at the little village. "This is only the beginning," Richard told her. "Now, there is a dock just below the castle, but I want you to see everything." He acted giddy, like a lad who just kissed his first maid.

When the vessel docked, Richard helped Anne disembark, and horses waited to convey the royal party to the castle. As they made their way through the village, Richard busied himself pointing out places of interest to her. The beginnings of a cathedral sprouted to life. "They call it Saint Sauveur," he related.

Everywhere around them villagers poured out into the streets, cheering the king and his entourage. A proud Richard explained, "Many in this town helped provide the labor for the chateau. This little town has actually grown along with the castle."

"They seem rather fond of you." Anne gave him a sly wink.

"They will love you, Lady Anne." Longingly, Richard looked at her, and Anne raised her eyebrows.

A deep ditch surrounded the entire complex of Gaillard, skirted with a wooden palisade that must have taken an entire forest to create. Above the brown palisade, the white limestone walls of the castle gleamed against the azure sky. Richard led them to the bridge into the first bailey, located at the right corner. As they drew nearer, Anne counted five strong towers in the outer bailey; a curtain wall connecting them, which came to a point forming the shape of a triangle. Only this side of the castle was not naturally defended. Richard began a commentary on his new castle bragging as if she were a child. "Those walls are twelve feet thick and thirty feet high."

"Any invader would find it no small task just to breech the outer walls let alone take this castle. I've never seen her like before. She is absolutely astounding." Richard's imposing reputation lived before her eyes in this castle.

The horses clamored onto the bridge and the group crossed it high above the ditch. As they rode underneath the portcullis, Anne noticed the arrow slits and defensive holes in the perfect positions to fire away at an invader unlucky enough to be trapped between the outer and inner portcullis.

When they cleared the gatehouse and entered the outer court, Ursula came bounding to Richard to greet him. Richard leapt from his horse and gave the dog a friendly pat on the head. "Yes, yes. I brought our Lady Anne home." Turning back to Anne, he reached out and helped her from her horse.

Once she was on the ground, Anne took a better look around. Stable boys took the horses and headed toward the stable. The outer court held the stables and Anne could hear the clang of a blacksmith's hammer. High above them battlements of crenellated parapets topped walls with expertly spaced merlons to fire on the enemy from, and embrasures to dodge incoming assaults from below. She still looked up as Richard took her hand and began to pull her deeper into the complex. "Come, you will have plenty of time to explore every nook and cranny, but I still have much to show you."

Between the outer and middle courts, stood walls to protect a passageway with another portcullis. They crossed this on foot and emerged into the middle bailey. Richard motioned back over his shoulder. "The defences are strongest on the south end. Up here," he pointed forward, "you could not ask for a better fortification than the cliffs and the river below."

The middle bailey was as impressive as the outer bailey.

Inside the middle bailey wall had rounding buttresses topped with battlements with machicolations. The lower part of the wall sloped outward making it even more difficult for an invader to assault. Anne pointed up at the machicolations that looked like little boxes of stone extending from the walls above. "I have not seen those before."

"No, I got the idea in Outremer. They are wonderful for the defender. See, because they extend beyond the wall defenders can drop boiling liquid or shoot down through the holes in the floor." Richard explained as they continued to walk.

"Remind me never to attack this castle." Anne grinned at him.

Anne stopped walking next to a large well and peered over the edge into it. Deep and dark, it looked almost as if it went down to the river three-hundred feet below. There was no doubt in her mind that it sunk deep enough to provide water, even in the event of a long siege.

The sounds of more construction drew her attention to the left. Sensing he blocked her view, Richard took a step back. The outer walls of a small chapel had been erected and men were at the top working on a roof for the structure. "It is not the grandest chapel, but it will be used. More about that later, though."

This time Ursula seemed to lead the way as she bounded up and down before them. The middle and inner bailey were separated by a twenty-foot deep dry moat. A drawbridge led to the inner bailey of the castle, the entrance through a causeway carved out of solid rock. Here there was yet another portcullis both inner and outer. Anne doubted that an intruder could make it this far anyway. On the end of the inner portcullis stood an iron gateway at the bottom of steep stairs carved into the rock.

They ascended the stairs, and now were face to face with the keep. The keep was the most unique structure Anne had even seen. The back of the circular keep faced the cliff, with the front end jutting out into the yard in the shape of a right angle. Passing a second well, she gained a better view. The lower part of these walls sloped outward, and they were also ringed with machicolations. A tower crowned the very top of the keep.

The keep's bottom floor had only arrow slits, no windows. Entrance to the keep could only be obtained by climbing a steep wooden staircase that led to a small easy to defend door. In case of an emergency, the stairs could be burnt to prevent entry. This first level had only one small window. "And this is truly astonishing, Richard." Anne felt awed by the sheer might of the citadel.

Richard guided her along up the stairs and into the keep. "The keep is mainly for defence purposes, but let me show you where I intend to hold court."

Quickly he escorted her through several rooms, rattling off their functions. When he came to the throne room, he stopped, and proclaimed, "Now, this is where I shall hold my court."

Opposite the door, steps led up to a large window with a throne placed in front of it. "Reigning over your court from here?" Anne made her way to the bottom of the steps. "That will surely make an impression on those below. The light of heaven beaming down on your shoulders." Anne looked back at Richard, as she whispered, "Arthur returned from Avalon."

"Exactly what I was thinking!"

Anne glanced around the room. "Richard I have not noticed a single fireplace in the keep."

"I do not intend the keep as living quarters." He shrugged.

"Oh?"

"Let me show you the living quarters." He extended his hand to her, and Anne took it.

As they exited the keep, Richard pointed out the postern gate. It opened onto the sheer cliff below, the only access by a rope ladder. Just north of the keep, Richard led her into a multi-story building he called the manor house. When they entered, they found themselves in the great hall. At the far end was a raised dais for the head table. The hall was not as large as the hall in Poitiers or even

Marseilles, but it radiated an inviting quality, unlike the rest of the citadel. Anne looked up where two, large chandeliers cast their soft golden glow throughout the room.

To the right of the dais, a staircase led to the second floor and a balcony above. From the balcony hung banners emblazoned with Richard's livery. Richard pointed to the door on the left of the dais. "That leads to the kitchens, and up there are the bed chambers."

Anne followed him up the stairs. They traversed the balcony, then entered a hallway. Richard took her to the third door on the right and opened it. "You must see this room." He pulled her into it, and shut the door behind them, so they would be alone. "There, that is better, no one to bother us." Ursula managed to squeeze into the room before Richard shut the door. She lumbered over to the fireplace and plopped down in front of it.

The splendor of the room took Anne's breath away. Opposite the door was a fireplace adorned with Richard's crest carved into the facing. On either side of the fireplace, two small niches framed mullioned windows. Plush crimson and gold curtains were drawn back to reveal the contents of the spaces. The one on the left contained a washbasin and stand, while the one on the right held a window seat. The stone benches were lined with soft alluring cushions, their deep green, blue and gold colours complementing those of the drapes. On tiptoes, Anne peered out the window on the left to see a stunning view of the river and cliffs below.

Turning back around she saw the walls lined with vividly coloured tapestries, themed with depictions of unicorns, garden, and maidens. The walls that were not covered with tapestries had decorative stone flush work. Brilliantly coloured paintings of King Arthur, his knights, Lancelot, Guineverre, and most prominently, Tristan and Isolde crowned the room. The smell of fresh, varnished wood and paint tickled her nose as she slowly turned to take them all in.

The bed stood against the east wall, decorated with two sets of curtains. The heavier crimson and gold outer set was pulled back to reveal the gossamer inner layer. Even from behind the bed curtains, Anne could see an embroidered baldaquin at the head of the bed. Luxuriant bed coverings seemed to call out to a weary body to lie down and become encased in their supple forms. Anne turned back to Richard who stood with his arms behind his back rocking back and forth on his toes. "Richard, this is beyond magnificent. This is truly a chamber fit for a king."

"Do you really think so?" Richard beamed.

"Yes!" She nodded, trying to take in the whole room again, the blue, gold, green, red, and a splash of purple, hues of colour that played off one another lending brilliance to the atmosphere.

"I am glad," Richard spoke again to get her attention. "Because this is not my bedchamber. It is yours."

"Mine?" Anne swiftly turned to face him.

"Yes, take a look in the corner." Richard pointed to Anne's trunk. The room itself distracted her so much, she hadn't even noticed. "Peel back the bed curtain there and have a closer inspection," he prodded her.

With hesitant steps, Anne approached the bed and drew one of the curtains aside. It did not take her long to notice the linen coverings on the pillows embroidered with pale green A's. Turning back to Richard, Anne was unable to conjure any words.

"Alright, I confess." Richard threw up his hands in a mocking gesture. "My quarters have an outer chamber as well as a bed chamber. They are slightly bigger than yours."

"Richard, this is…" Anne could not finish.

Richard tossed his cap onto the cushions of the window

seat. "When I first began to make plans for Gaillard, the location was perfect, strategically. Then something began to eat at me as the walls went up. Right now, indeed for much of the time you have known me, you have lived in a tent, not always certain where your bed would be at night. Many nights you did not even have a genuine ceiling overhead. While it is true you have Marseilles, in a sense, you have given up your physical home there for me, and what have you got for it?"

"No, Richard, it is…" Anne protested.

He cut her off. "I wanted to give you something. I wanted to give you refuge where your bed would always be in the same place—well, unless you do not like where it is in the room."

Anne beckoned him to her with her forefinger. Like a nervous child he obeyed. Throwing her arms around his neck, she kissed him. "I would make my home in a mud puddle if it meant I could be with you."

He kissed her back. "Let us keep you out of as many mud puddles as possible."

"Do not misunderstand me, I would prefer this room to a mud puddle." She winked at him.

"Anne, I want you to run this household like Marseilles. Rule over it with all your wisdom and wiles." They were nose tip to nose tip now.

From the doorway came a little cough that startled Anne. Richard turned to see who it was. "Ah, come." He motioned to the man. "Anne, I would like you to meet Sir William FitzAlan. He is my castellan here."

Slightly shorter than Richard, FitzAlan had dirty blonde hair and blue eyes. He gave a respectful bow. "Your highness, welcome to Chateau Gaillard, my lady."

"As mistress of the house, what is your first command?" Richard threw open his arms.

Anne looked with searching eyes from Richard to the castellan. "I stand ready for your command, Lady Anne," FitzAlan assured her.

Anne looked at Richard while she spoke. "I would love for Gaillard to be a place of music, poetry and laughter, like your court at Poitiers."

"It shall be as you wish," Richard replied, and then turned to the castellan. "FitzAlan, music, poetry, and laughter. That sounds like a fine place to begin. Round up Blondel and anyone else around here you can think of. Lady Anne and I will be coming down to the great hall shortly."

FitzAlan smiled at both of them. "Yes, my lord." Then he scurried off.

Anne removed her traveling cloak and laid it next to Richard's cap on the window cushions. Around them, servants brought other articles into the room, her secretary and dressing table. "Thank you for this, Richard."

"Put that there," Richard ordered two men who carried her secretary to move it closer to the window. Turning his attention back to Anne, he motioned around the room. "This is only the beginning."

Anne tipped her head to one side and wondered aloud. "You keep saying that. Do not tell me you have built more castles like this one."

"Oh, no. Gaillard is one of a kind. I started to build this castle to defend what was mine, *do my duty*; but just as happened all those years ago, you crept in, and I changed the plans. I have much more in store for you, My Sweet Annie. I have so many plans."

Anne tried not to wrinkle her nose when he called her, 'Sweet Annie.' She never really liked it, but knew he did. "Are you going to share those plans with me?"

"Not just yet, but soon." He kissed her on the forehead. "For now, I shall change out of this dusty traveling garb and meet you here to go down to the hall." Richard looked around the room taking in a deep breath. Across his face flashed a look of euphoria as he imagined all that he planned taking place in this room. Then giving Anne another light kiss, he left the room.

Early the next morning, Richard woke Anne and asked her to meet him in the outer bailey. She found her new bed soft and luxuriant, and was loath to leave it, but she relented for Richard. When she arrived in the outer courtyard, Richard waited there with horses saddled and ready. Without question, she allowed him to help her onto her horse. "Are you ready then?" he asked as he mounted his own.

"Hunting? Before breakfast?" Anne stifled a yawn.

"Perhaps, or being hunted, it all depends upon the actions of my quarry." He raised one eyebrow. "Besides, we will eat breakfast on the way."

Anne's stomach growled at the mention of food. Looking around, she noticed Richard's sergeant at arms were also ready, only today there were only a half dozen or so. "Shall we?" She winked at Richard, anxious to get going to the food.

Richard, giving his horse a soft kick, answered her question, and they headed out of the castle walls to the village below. They rode through the town below just as the inhabitants were waking. Those who were out and about, sleepily wondered at the king passing by on his horse so early in the morning and tried their best to make a hasty bow.

They rode straight to the bridge and across the river. On the other side were cultivated fields. A little road traversed the outskirts of the fields and Richard steered onto it. Few peasants worked in the fields as it was not quite harvest season, but some were up early to beat the heat of the day. As the king and his group rode by, they ceased their work to watch, giving a bow as appropriate.

On a little rise just above the river, an area to the left of the road was cordoned off with a stonewall nine feet high. Richard stopped his horse in front of the iron gate that served as an entrance. Beyond the gate Anne could see a beautifully landscaped garden. "This was here before I even started construction on the chateau. I was very taken with this little spot." Richard slid from his horse and helped Anne from hers.

"It looks like a lovely garden." Anne commented.

Placing his left hand on the small of her back Richard opened the gate with his right. As they stepped through the gate, Anne noticed seven young peach tree in the centre. A floral lined gravel path led to the small orchard. Underneath the trees, a table was set up with breakfast spread on it. "This is my favourite part of the garden." Richard pointed to the peach trees.

Without a word, Anne took the path to the trees, skirted around the table of breakfast, removed her glove and laid her hand on the trunk of the nearest tree. "Peach trees," she whispered. Her gaze followed the lines of the trunk up into the branches. "There is fruit on the tree!"

Grinning, Richard placed his hand over hers. "I had these trees planted as soon as construction began on the castle. We built the walls with extra stone to protect this little garden." He slid his hand from hers and softly patted the trunk of the tree. "They are young trees but will become even stronger. I am pleased at how quickly they have produced fruit." Examining a peach more carefully he pronounced, "I would say that in about three weeks the fruit should be ready to harvest. In the spring you can gather blossoms to spread in the river. They will find their way to Will, or your father, or whomever you desire."

Anne shook her head and smiled. "So many surprises, Richard."

"Yes, well, are you hungry?" He moved away from the tree toward the table.

"Oh yes!" Anne followed.

They sat down at the table for a meal together in a garden underneath seven peach trees.

Gaillard impressed Philip, but not in the same way it did Anne. To begin with, he had not laid eyes on the castle, but relied on reports from others. He reasoned that the reports he got were not accurate, because those doing the reporting did not want to incur the wrath of the king. He decided the citadel must be a stronghold like no other. That wasn't what really irked him, though. To be sure, it was a massive castle, built only five miles from one of his own. But from Richard, he could expect no less. Thinking about Anne gnawed at him, or the fact she was there at Gaillard. In a way, it was as if Richard built the fortress to hide her away like stories of maidens trapped in towers. Would it be his job, to rescue his cousin? If he did, would she come of her own accord? That would remain to be seen.

Chapter Eighty-seven

The iron gate to the garden creaked as Richard opened it.

He followed the pebble-paved path towards the centre of the garden where he knew he would find Anne. In the last few weeks, she spent more time here in the garden, enjoying it before the weather turned cold. Indeed, she sat in a cross frame chair sewing. Beneath her feet a blanket was spread out, and at the edge Anne neatly placed her shoes, her bare toes peaking out from under the hem of her dress. A gentle breeze wound its way through the garden making the light that speckled through the leaves above her dance about and spark the auburn in her hair. Soon the lush green leaves above her would turn to the golden colours of autumn, but now the trees were laden with their heavy fruit ready to harvest.

The crunch of the pebbles alerted her that someone was close; she looked up and smiled when she saw Richard. He paused to take in the sight before him. "Good afternoon," Anne broke the silent spell. "Have you concluded your court business for the day?"

Richard gave a nod. Walking to the edge of the blanket, he peered down at her. "Greta told me you were here, so I decided to join you." Looking around he questioned, "Are you alone?"

She just put a pin in her mouth when he asked the question. "Um hum," she confirmed.

"Where is your guard?" Richard took off his riding gloves and tucked them into his belt.

Anne removed the pin from her mouth, and tucked it in a cushion lying on top of her sewing basket. "I made Mercadier stand down wind over in the northeast corner with the little old man who tends the garden." She added, "Close enough if he is needed, but far enough that I do not have to smell him."

Richard chuckled to himself. Anne really didn't like Mercadier, but he was good at keeping her safe. "Baldwin is returning to court now that his wife had her second baby, a girl this time."

"I look forward to seeing Baldwin again." Anne smiled.

Pointing to the material in her hand Richard queried, "What are you doing there?"

Holding it up before her, she wrinkled her nose at it. "I am attempting to finish this tunic for Will before he comes."

"I thought he was coming with Marshal, and I do not expect them until late November or even early December. It is only September, dear." Richard looked up at the fruit above him.

"I just do not want to leave it until the last minute." Anne put the material aside on top of her basket.

Reaching up, Richard plucked a lush looking peach from

the tree. He flopped down on his side in front of Anne, and took a bite. Anne slid out of the chair and sat before him. She twisted around to push the chair off the blanket and give them more room.

"Anne," Richard spoke her name in a hushed voice.

"Hum?" She still fiddled with the chair. At last she had it where she wanted it.

"Marry me, Anne." Richard took another bite of the peach.

Acting as if nothing was said, Anne turned her attention from the chair. "Here." She reached into her basket, and retrieved a handkerchief. She blotted up some peach juice that trickled onto his beard. "Peaches can be so messy."

"Anne," Richard repeated, "marry me."

Still, Anne acted as if he hadn't said anything. She gave him a quick kiss on the lips and playfully tugged at his whiskers. "I am convinced that you only grow these things to irritate me."

Richard sat up straight and tossed the rest of peach aside. Anne reached out to scratch his beard again, but he grasped her hand. "Anne, I am not in jest. I want you to marry me."

Anne wrinkled her brow at him. "Has the sun made you lose your memory? We are married... to different people."

"Anne, I want to marry *you*." Richard looked deep into her eyes. Anne inhaled to speak, but he placed a finger over her lips. "Before you speak, hear what I have to say."

"Alright," she agreed.

"For some time now, I have been telling you I have plans in the works, and I revealed many of them to you. However, those plans are more than just a castle. This afternoon I received word the pope is sending an emissary to meet with me, and he should be here about the same time as Will." Richard took in a deep breath, crossed his legs in front of him and continued on. "Do you remember that letter I received from Joanna, when I suddenly left for Le Mans?"

Anne clenched her jaw and nodded.

"In that letter, Joanna told me about a meeting Berengaria

had with none other than Castile. As if that were not bad enough, this meeting happened behind closed doors. Very suspicious. I went to Le Mans to confront Berengaria about this. Now, I cannot be certain they did anything, but nevertheless the suggestion of it is very strong. In short, I asked the pope for an annulment on the grounds that my wife is barren, and my kingdom needs an heir. Berengaria has agreed to annulment on the condition that I do not expose her deed. If I did, the law of the land is… well, you know. She has even convinced her brother that it is for the best. I will let her keep the income from her dowager lands, and she is to retire to the convent of her choosing." He paused, waiting for Anne to say something. When she said nothing, he continued.

"Alright, so that takes care of my marriage. As far as yours is concerned, the pope is ready to declare you a widow based on testimony that Abbot Mathias has provided, and the fact that no one has heard from or seen Castile, not even his own family. By you being a widow, Will's legitimacy is not in question, whereas with an annulment…" He searched her face for some sign of emotion, but he could not discern any. "The pope is very agreeable to grant my annulment, and I know you would miss your dear cousin, but I am willing to let the Bishop of Beauvais go free to sweeten the deal. Pope Innocent wants me to go back to the Holy Land, which I intended to do eventually, but I am not about to do that without an heir. It is all but done. I did not tell you any of this before, because I wanted to be certain."

Surprising Richard, Anne jumped to her feet, and turned her back on him. She gripped the top of the chair with her right hand, and wrapped the other around her waist, but she moved no further away.

"Anne, listen to me, dearest. For years we have talked about duty, and we can still fulfil it. Our duty can become the same. I know it is not normal to marry for love, but remember back in Sicily when you asked me what was so wrong with two people being in love and by some miracle both free to marry each other?

Well, what *is* wrong with it? We can do this Anne." Still she said nothing. "Anne, please say something."

Slowly Anne turned around to face him, her left hand balled up on her hip, and her right still clutching the top of the chair. Tears ran down her face, and he thought he angered her. Then she spoke, "Do you think this is really possible?" Her voice cracked. "Be honest with me, Richard."

"Absolutely." He got to his feet. "By Christmas, both of us will be free of any marital obligation." He dared move closer now.

"The emissary is on his way?" She looked pensive.

"As we stand here in this very garden, things are in motion. The pope has told his emissary to proceed as long as we can agree to the terms of release for Beauvais, and a date for my return to Outremer." Richard reached out and brushed the tears from her cheeks with the back of his hand.

A smile spread across her face. "We can do this? We can really do this? Berengaria will give you up?"

"She does not have a choice, and yes, this is possible. Everything is not solidly into place yet, though." He tried to look serious.

"What else is needed?" She frowned.

"The bride's family has to agree to the wedding, and you know how they can be." He narrowed his eyes.

"I do not think you will have any trouble convincing Will. My cousin, Philip, on the other hand..." She teased him back.

"We just will not tell him until the deed is done. Besides, technically you will be a widow, and since you are in my lands, you are in my custody; therefore, I can marry you to whomever I wish."

"Then let us give Philip a gray hair or two." She laughed.

"Or two? Why not the whole head of hair?" His laughter rolled throughout the garden. "Oh, I have to sit down." He landed back on the blanket.

"Is something wrong?" Anne knelt beside him.

"No, but I must tell you that was rather frightening. I was not certain how you would react, and I would be lying if I said I was not nervous."

She leaned over to him. "I would be lying if I said I am not scared, but as long as we are in this together..." She didn't finish but kissed him.

He pressed her backward onto the blanket, returning her kiss, enjoying the moment. Suddenly, he stopped. "I think that as soon as the final agreement is made with the emissary we should marry. Even if the chapel is not finished, we could marry there. Not even an hour should go by between the two events."

Anne giggled. "Why such haste, my lord?"

Richard placed his hand on her stomach. "This time next year, I hope for a son, and such a son he will be. You know, I should like a daughter as well. Heaven help me if she is like her mother."

"Richard, you forget, I... we, are not as young as we used to be," she chided.

"Well, you are not as old as my mother was when she bore John. Still, we do not have any time to waste, as we will want more than one son. Perhaps we should get started right now. In fact, this moment will do!" He bent down to kiss her again.

She put both of her hands on his chest. "Now Richard, I do not want there to be any question of our son's legitimacy. We can, I think, wait just a little longer, for the sake of our son."

"Damn." He smiled and groaned at the same time. "You will not wait until the last minute to make a tunic, but a baby is a different matter."

"Indeed it is." She sat up.

"Fine, you win this match," he relented. "But do not get used to it."

"Oh, I already am."

"Oh really?" He made to kiss her again, but she dodged him.

Anne smelled him before she saw him. "Mercadier," she whispered.

Irritated, Richard turned around. "What is it?"

"Your highness, Sir FitzAlan is looking for you." An embarrassed Mercadier could not seem to look the king in the eyes.

Before Richard could react, Anne kissed him on the cheek, and whispered in his ear, "It is alright; I will go with you."

Richard got to his feet. "Lady Anne and I are going back to the chateau now." He pulled Anne to her feet. "See that the lady's things are brought for her."

"Yes, my lord." Mercadier bowed his head.

Richard began to walk past Mercadier but stopped, speaking out of the corner of his mouth, "For heaven sake's man, take a bath!" He turned back to Anne, extended his arm, and led her from the garden.

In a deep state of sleep, Anne did not hear Richard enter her room. When her senses alerted her that someone was there, she sprang up. In her dazed state she could have sworn Richard opened the door, then leapt across the room like a large cat, landing on her bed. "Wrong?" She managed to squeeze out.

"Nothing, cannot sleep," came his reply.

Anne lay back down with a groan and rolled over on her side facing away from him. "Honestly, sweetheart, I killed the monster under your bed with my dagger, and we ate his liver last week, remember?"

"Yes, his liver was the only edible part, the rest of him was tough and stringy." He snuggled down next to her. "There is another monster; there always is, you know."

She tugged at the covers. "Yes, but I am not going to stab Philip, and as for eating him? Well, that is just poor form."

"This monster is not Philip, and this one has laid eggs." Richard tugged back at the blankets.

"This is a problem then. Here we thought all along this monster was male. Now we must feel like fools." She yanked the blankets hard enough to leave him without any.

"Will," Richard mumbled as he recaptured the covers.

Anne rolled over to face him. "Are you saying Will has laid eggs?"

"Thank heaven, no. That would certainly be a problem. My brain has been hatching all these plans, and now that I see them coming to fruition, it just will not stop!" Like an actor playing a role, Richard flopped onto his back. "But I have been thinking about Will."

Anne propped herself up on one elbow. "Alright, I am awake and listening."

"So, if you are declared a widow, that leaves it so Will is unquestionably legitimate, yes?"

"Yes."

"You also want him to marry well and have been in negotiations with the Doria and Lomellini families of Genoa, correct?" Richard asked, holding up each hand to represent the two families.

"Right."

"Vassalo Lumello's daughter is the more desirous union, is it not?"

"Right again." Anne yawned.

"In my estimation, if Will actually held the title of Viscount of Marseilles, *he* would be more desirable." Richard made the declaration as if he had solved some important matter of Christendom.

"You mean?"

"Yes! Invest him as Viscount. He is certainly old enough and ready. Do it before we marry; that way there will be no disputating his inheritance. Then he can make the best match possible." He gave a mock sigh. "Sometimes I amaze myself with my brilliance!"

As Anne thought about what he just said, Richard folded his arms with a satisfactory thump. Anne replied, "I suppose it could be done. We could tell him of it when he arrives for Christmas. Of course there will be some logistics to work out. Do we go south to see him invested? Can you leave Normandy with Philip about? You two do have a treaty but…" She didn't finish the thought. "Marseilles would be the best place."

Richard gave a great yawn and rolled on his side and stretched out. "I am exhausted. Thank you for this little chat," he said with a kiss. "You have slain the monster once again, and I shall sleep now." He got up out of the bed.

"Not so fast, my lord!" Anne tossed a pillow at him.

"What was that for?" He easily caught it.

"Well, now I am wide awake!"

"And I have got your pillow." Richard raised his eyebrows.

"Richard." She motioned with her finger for him to come to her.

"Not until our wedding night, dear." He turned and swiftly left the room.

"That is not what I meant. I would like my pillow back!" She called after him.

He reopened the door and stuck his head in only long enough to tease. "Not until our wedding night."

Anne gave the door a dirty look. She would not be going back to sleep; now the monster lodged under her bed.

Chapter Eighty-eight

Will felt as though some creature stirred about in his stomach. He had been dressed and ready for the joust for at least an hour. After dismissing his page, Will tried to mentally prepare himself. Now he stood before his horse, the same black destrier Richard gave him, stroking her neck. Since leaving Richard's court, he won other horses, but this one he trusted most.

Sigurd and Nanna lay close by happily dozing. In unison, the duo bolted to their feet and Sigurd gave a low growl. "There he is," Abram's voice sounded behind Will. "Damn dogs. They don't seem to like anybody." Abram scowled.

Will turned around. "You should not startle them, Abram."

Abram gave a shrug. He was the squire Will sparred with the day Will received the destrier. Recently, Marshal knighted Abram, but the title of knighthood only seemed to add swagger to his step. "You ready?"

"I guess." Will examined the cinch strap on his saddle.

"Marshal has planted himself in the stands. We should be grateful he doesn't compete anymore. Gives the rest of us poor saps a chance." Abram leaned against the rails dividing the stalls. "I guess we're also lucky to be summoned to Galliard with him."

"I suppose." Will kept his answers short, hoping to give Abram the hint he did not wish to continue the conversation.

"Are you really going to use those spurs," Abram asked, pointing to Will's ankles. "They are so old."

Will turned his back on Abram, hiding the irritation on his face. "They will do." The spurs were his grandsire's and he could not think of using any others.

Abram clapped him on the shoulder. "Don't be nervous. You will do just fine, much better than I did."

The image of Abram's joust revisited Will's mind. Abram lost, but something about it didn't seem quite right to Will. "Yes, what did happen out there?" Will turned back around to face Abram.

Abram shrugged. "I leaned right when I should have leaned left. Like I said though, you'll do much better."

A cold burst of wind filled the stables causing them both to shiver. "Weather is turning," Will commented.

"I'm grateful the good weather lasted this long, long enough for one more tournament before winter." A noise behind them distracted Abram.

Two giggling young ladies passed by the open door of the stables. As they walked by, they peeked in at the knights while trying to maintain the correct balance of conspicuousness. Will smiled at the attention, but rolled his eyes at the silliness and turned back to adjusting his saddle.

"As I was saying," Abram continued, "you need not worry about this afternoon. You are a born natural at this."

"Thank you for your confidence," Will spoke in soft tones.

"I just hope you will be generous with your old sparing mate." Abram gave him a wink.

The two girls circled back around and walked past the open door again. This time Abram acknowledged them with a smile. This sent the girls into a fresh spasm of laughing, as they moved on. "You mean them?" Will mouthed.

Abram gave Will a sly look. "You are the hero of the day. Don't you notice all these women fawning around after you?"

"You are imagining things, Abram." Will blushed.

"Oh, I'll tell you what I'm imagining." Abram looked back towards the door and licked his lips.

"Abram," Will took a firmer tone, "I have a joust to worry about right now. The last thing I need is girls complicating it all."

"Fine, Adam. If you won't partake of the fruit, I will. I do hope at least one of them is a virgin. There is nothing like a virgin."

Will shuddered at Abram's comment. "Then you had better go after your prey, Master Serpent, before you lose the trail."

"Right! I'll see you later then?"

"Yes," Will lied. He had no intention of being anywhere near Abram.

"Good luck, Ssssssir," Abram hissed as he jogged out of the barn after the young ladies.

Will tried to forget Abram's intrusion, but it was hard. Turning to Sigurd and Nanna, he grumped, "Next time bite him in the ass, you two."

That day the joust proved most entertaining, and many people braved the chill to watch. The peasants seemed to melt into the earth because their clothes were so drab as they lined the perimeter to watch. Unlike the reserved but colourful nobility seated in the stands, the peasants cheered, booed, and hissed all to show their support for their favourite knight. Amongst the peasants, a man wove his way through to get a better view. He wore a mud brown

cloak with the hood up over his head. This was not unusual. Both peasant and noble alike wrapped themselves in cloaks to fend off the chill. The man's cloak didn't look any different than any of the others. What made people notice him were his mannerisms, and his turn of phrase. He spoke very little, but when he made a request to move about in the crowd, his manner of speech made him sound out of place, more like he belonged in one of the seats above, not tramping about in the mud.

Several contenders competed, and the man watched each of them intently, studying the moves of each. When Sir William de Marseilles took the field, the man became even more intense, if that was possible. However, no one really noticed. They were all too focused on Sir William as he was a favourite. Had anyone taken their eyes off the joust and noticed the man, they would have seen into the recess of his hood, how his eyes narrowed, and his jaw clenched causing the scar on his face to whiten.

As the two riders hurled themselves toward one another, the man's eyes darted back and forth between them. The horses' hooves thundered, then came the crack of lances clashing. Sir William's opponent scored, but William was still mounted. The man knew where contact was made would leave a nasty bruise for William. His upper arm would be sore for a few days, but the pain had not taken effect yet, and William would be able to continue. The crowd roared their encouragement as the two riders prepared to make another run at each other.

The man with the scar held his breath as the two knights shot off again towards each other. This time Sir William gave off what sounded like a low growl, the kind of growl the man with the scar knew he himself had made before. There came another crash of contact followed by the thud of a man hitting the ground hard. Sir William had unhorsed his opponent. A smile spread across the face of the man stretching his scar into an even more bizarre shape. He clapped his hands together loudly three times and let out a triumphant, "Brilliant!" Then to himself, he whispered, "That's *my* son."

Anne was nervous. In fact she couldn't remember the last time she felt this anxious. That afternoon, word came that the pope's emissary would be arriving tomorrow, or the next day at the latest. He would travel from Le Mans where he interviewed Berengaria. There was much at stake with the interview.

All along, Richard and Anne prepared for the emissary's arrival, but now that he was so close, Anne sent the castle into a new frenzy of activity. Everything that could be cleaned was cleaned. She ordered fresh rushes brought in and threatened to make everyone, including the dogs, bathe. Richard pointed out that this was an impossible task, and if the emissary came and saw everyone at court had bathed then surely he would think something amiss. Anne relented and only asked a few of the more important members of court to bathe. Luckily for Mercadier, Richard sent him to Rouen, so the mercenary escaped a thorough scrubbing.

When evening fell, Anne retired to her room, much to the relief of many in the court. She hoped to get some rest before the long days ahead. As had become their custom, Richard joined her there. Both tried to relax but were preoccupied. Anne sent Greta away, and they were alone except for Ursula who happily dozed by the small fire in the grate. As she sat in front of her little dressing table, Anne brushed out her hair, and Richard watched her from his seat on the window cushions. He came to enjoy these quiet times and thought he could enjoy them even more once the business with the emissary concluded.

The glow from the fire played with the auburn in Anne's hair, and her silhouette stood out against the light. Richard enjoyed watching her; he could not help himself. She moved her hair to one side, and Richard could see the skin on her cheek illuminated with an ethereal radiance that awakened longings in him he fought hard to repress.

He looked around for something to distract him. Anne's lute was propped up on the window seat cushions in the corner. Snatching it up he began to pick at the strings. The sound made Anne smile. "I have not heard you play in so long," she said. "What has it been? Years now?" She set down her brush.

He didn't look up at her; he couldn't just yet. "Well, I hope you are not too disappointed, dear; I fear it has been quite a while, and I am somewhat rusty."

She rose from her chair and took a seat next to him at the window. He wished she wouldn't. That only made it harder. "I do not mind the rusty or crusty. I am just glad to hear you play at all." She grinned up at him.

He could not really reply. She was so close that it would

take little movement to press himself up against her, but he feared if he touched her it would be too hard to stay in control. He focused his attention once more on the lute. Next to him, Anne let out a long sigh he not only heard but felt. Without her speaking the words, he knew her thoughts. "Do not worry. Berengaria will keep her end of the arrangement. Remember, she does not have much of a choice."

At this, Anne sidled up next to him and asked, "How did you know that was what I was thinking?"

Her touch made him keenly aware this was a battle he was losing. He set the lute back in the corner and put his arm around Anne. She placed her head on his shoulder and closed her eyes. With his other hand he took hers, and played with her fingers. She opened her eyes but did not protest, so he continued. Shifting so that she faced him more, she nuzzled his neck with her nose and lightly brushed her lips over his earlobe. Without resisting, he turned to face her, and just as their lips met there was a knock at the door. "Send them away," Anne whispered.

"This is your room," he teased.

"You are the king," she reminded him.

"Not now," he called out to the door, never taking his eyes off her.

The knock came again, only this time more insistent. Anne buried her head in his chest, and he felt her laugh. "Promise me when we are married that you will always send them away."

"Of that you can be certain." He kissed the top her head.

Again the knock sounded, but this time the urgency seemed to escalate to a fury. Anne withdrew from his arms. "Come," they both called out together. She left the window seat to stand by the fireplace.

The door flew open and FitzAlan marched in. When he caught site of the king's angry face he gulped. "FitzAlan, what possessed you to try to bang down Lady Anne's door?"

"My humblest apologies, your highness, Lady Anne. There

is...something has happened..." FitzAlan tried to explain.

"God's legs, not the emissary." Richard jumped to his feet.

Before FitzAlan could answer, a knight burst into the room and knelt before Richard. "I humbly beg your forgiveness, your highness. Sir Marshal sent me."

Now Anne recognised the knight as Abram, the one who sparred with Will so often. Her heart thumped loudly in her chest. "Abram, is it?"

"Yes, my lady." From Abram's disheveled appearance revealed he just ended a long ride.

"Is there something the matter with Sir Marshal?" Richard raised his voice.

"No, your highness, but I am afraid that Will—Sir William was wounded." Abram kept his eyes on Anne.

Anne's eyes grew wide with fear, and she took a step closer to the messenger to hear him better. Richard went to her side. "What do you mean Sir William was wounded? Speak, boy."

Abram seemed flustered, but he tried to explain, "He was in a tournament." Anne moaned, and Abram put up his hands. "But he won the joust, sire. After the joust, someone attacked him in the stables. When I went to congratulate him," tears welled up in Abram's eyes, "I found him there. His horse gone, his dogs gone, his page nowhere to be seen."

Anne sank down to the floor, and sensing something wrong, Ursula crept over and laid her head in Anne's lap. "How badly is he hurt?" Richard shouted, as he knelt down beside Anne.

"From what I could tell, he took a blow to the head. I do not know how bad it is. There was a great amount of blood, but that does not necessarily mean it is a bad wound. Head wounds can bleed heavily causing more alarm than anything else." Abram swallowed hard. "As soon as I was able to alert Sir Marshal, the surgeon was sent for, but I did not stay. I took to the road at once, as I knew you would want to know. I haven't stopped since I left."

"Where is he now?" Anne managed to ask, her face ghostly

white.

"At Vaudreuil, my lady," Abram answered.

Anne shot up from the floor startling everyone in the room, including the dog. "I must go to him." She went straight to her trunk and flung it open.

"Not at night, we won't." Richard could tell that she was on the verge of leaving rational thought behind. He turned to the two men, "FitzAlan, please see to it that Sir Abram and his horse have something to eat and some rest."

"If it pleases you, your highness," Abram pleaded, "I would like to return to Le Vaudreuil."

"Good lad." Richard nodded, but his attention focused on the figure of Anne standing before her trunk. "Now, if you will please excuse us. Oh, FitzAlan, please send Anne's lady to her."

"Yes, your highness." FitzAlan beckoned Abram. "If you will follow me, sir."

"My lord," Abram spoke quietly. "We cannot take the river. A barge sunk where the river narrows at Le Mesnil, and the river is impassable."

Richard nodded, then watched the two men leave. He closed the door behind them. His own head spun. Will was the closest thing he had to a son, and Richard felt the grip of fear closing in on him. He would have to stave it off. "Anne?" She had not moved.

At the sound of his voice, she shook her head. "What are we going to do?"

"We are going to go to Will. That is what we are going to do, and we will see he is fine." Richard tried to sound confident. "But we will not travel at night. The land may be mine, but we are far too close to Philip to be moving at night. Come the blue line of morning, we will be on our way."

"The pope's emissary will be here on the morrow or surely the next." She spoke what he was thinking.

He placed his arms around her shoulders. "I know, and to

not be here would be a great slight to him. After all we have done, we cannot afford to slight him." Gently he rubbed her arms. "Right now, you should pack. Do not worry yourself with the emissary. Leave that to me." He gave her a kiss on the back of the head.

"I am going to leave at first light," she pronounced.

"I," Richard repeated. "Not we?"

"I think we both know that it would be best for you to remain here. You said it yourself. We cannot afford to insult the emissary." Anne tried to put on a brave face.

Richard ran his fingers through his hair and scratched at the top of his head. "Anne, I do not want you going off by yourself."

Anne grimmaced. "There really is not any other option, now is there? I am going to go to my son, and you need to be here when the emissary arrives. It is for the best."

Richard knew what she proposed was rational, but he wasn't ready to give in just yet. "No. Philip is out there."

"Philip?" She scoffed. "I hardly think that he would harm me."

Richard grew edgy, "Will may not be of my blood, but…"

She didn't let him finish. "I know. Besides, as soon as the emissary gets here, you can explain the situation then join us." Anne went back to packing her trunk.

"I do not like it," he complained.

"Neither do I!" She snapped. "Neither do I. Richard, my son is wounded, and I do not know how badly. I am leaving first thing in the morning to go him."

"I will not have it."

"Then what is your solution? If you can think of a way that we can go to my son and it can be done without offending the emissary, then by all means what is it?"

"I do not know!"

Anne turned around to face him. "I would gladly submit to any escort of your choosing, even Mercadier."

"Mercadier is not here. I sent him to Rouen on an errand."

Richard crossed his arms and looked down at her. As he did, he saw the determination in her eyes. Her solution was, under the circumstances, the most reasonable one. "Loading onto a barge, just to unload again would cost valuable time. I suggest the overland route."

"Besides, who would be looking for travelers going that way?" She suggested.

Richard rubbed at his right temple with his thumb. "Continue packing. I will be back."

Picking up some necessaries from her dressing table, Anne said nothing else as Richard left the room.

Richard did not return to Anne's room for the space of three hours. When he finally made his way back, a flurry of people whom Anne had clearly put to work, were coming and going from the room. As Richard entered the room, he heard Anne giving Greta instructions. "We will be leaving at first light. I think you have done all you can right now, so you should go and get some rest."

Greta nodded, and she gave Richard a curtsy on her way out the door. "You look pretty tired yourself," Richard remarked as Anne knelt before her trunk, placing some last minute additions inside its now nearly filled main compartment.

"I will be fine," she assured him.

"Remember the Templar Gerard? As luck would have it, he and two other Templars arrived tonight hoping to meet with the pope's emissary. Anyway, he agreed to escort you." Richard's tone was more subdued.

"Thank heaven for that. At least we were lucky there." Anne knew Richard still distressed over not going with her. "Would you be so kind as to hand me the casket on my desk, please?"

Richard took the fancy little box off her desk. It contained so many items that were important to her. Handing it to Anne, Richard worried aloud, "Promise me that you will not take any unnecessary risks."

"This coming from the man who rode into battle how many times without his armor?"

"Damn Baldwin. He might not have a tongue the next time you see him." Richard sat down on Anne's bed as she flipped open the lid on the casket.

As she searched around she tried to keep the conversation pleasant. "It will be nice to see that silver tongue serpent again."

"Yes," Richard mused.

Suddenly Anne stopped her rummaging. He fingers came upon a small soft cloth tied with a bit of ribbon. She froze. The little package contained Will's hair that she snipped the evening he was knighted. Richard noticed her abrupt change. "Anne?" She didn't answer, remaining frozen. "Anne, are you alright?" Now he could hear her crying, and he knelt beside her.

Anne opened the little packet of hair, and explained to Richard, "This is Will's."

"I remember the first time I saw Will. He terrified me." Richard put his arms around her. "Imagine that, the great Richard, *Coeur de Lion*, frightened by a baby."

She threw her arms around his neck. "I am so scared for him...*for us*."

"It will be alright. Will cannot have been wounded that badly, or Marshal would have sent a written message as well." He caressed her back and tried to soothe her. "Will is a strong, good man now. He will be fine."

Anne drew herself away from him and shook her head, "I did not want him. I mean, when I was pregnant with him, I was so angry, and all I knew was that I did not want that baby. Is God punishing me now?"

He took her face in his hands. "Anne, do not ever think like that. You love Will. We both love Will more than either of us could have ever dreamt. You have been and continue to be a good mother to your son. I have never seen you regret that you brought him into the world." He released her and took the little packet, rolling it up, and tying the ribbon back around it. "The morning after he was born, I remember looking at him, and I could not believe what I saw. His eyes were just like yours. The similarity was uncanny. Right then I knew he would become what he is today. His future will be extraordinary."

"Thank you." Anne placed the packet back in the top of her casket.

Richard propped himself up with his back against her trunk, and stretched out his legs in front of him. Anne twisted around, and sat next to him. He put his arm around her and she laid her head against him. "All will be well," he whispered.

At dawn, as Richard looked tired as he emerged into the courtyard of the outer bailey. Dark circles formed under his eyes, but neither he nor Anne were concerned with sleep. They spoke very little to each other as the final pieces of baggage were loaded onto a cart and Anne prepared to take her leave.

Greta, Anne's escort of ten men, Gerard, and his two companions already waited on their horses. Preparing to mount her own horse, Anne reached down and pulled up the hem of her skirt, but Richard put his hand on the small of her back and she let it fall again. "I still do not like this," he whispered in her ear.

Anne spoke over her shoulder, "If the emissary arrives early enough, perhaps you could meet us this evening." She sounded hopeful.

Gerard tried to reassure the king. "Your highness, I will see to Lady Anne's safety. My life for hers."

"Faithful Templar, I do not want

your life; I want hers protected." Richard managed a smile at Gerard.

Anne tugged her hem up again. "Daylight grows, my dear, and I must go."

With his hand about her waist, Richard turned Anne around to face him. Unabashed even though there were onlookers, he kissed her full on the lips. "I will see you within a few days," he promised. Then he helped her onto her horse. Anne tucked her token, the red kerchief, into Richard's shirt and rode out the portcullis gate.

From the battlements, Richard watched her ride away until the forms of her party melted with others coming and going from the village.

Chapter Eighty-nine

Anne rode next to Greta. Her lady slept only an hour or two as they prepared to leave at dawn. It was late morning now, and as the horses plodded on, the rocking seemed to work a drowsy spell on Greta. Anne could tell she kept nodding off. Even though she had not slept at all, Anne felt wide-awake with thoughts of her wounded son waiting for her to come to him.

Next to Anne, Greta swayed in her saddle, and jerked herself awake. "Steady there, Greta." Anne put a hand on the lady's shoulder. "I'm sorry, my lady." Greta yawned.

"I understand. It was a long night for us all," Anne replied with a nod.

Anne returned to thoughts of Will. At the front of the column, Gerard and Abram seemed deep in conversation. Abram was animated, as though he were trying to convince the Templar of something.

The man-at-arms in front of her fell before Anne realized that an arrow had pierced his neck. Greta screamed and pulled up hard on the reins of her horse. More arrows flew around them now, and the soldiers scrambled to take up a defensive position. Greta's horse was spooked, and she lost control of the animal. "Lady Anne!" Greta reached out.

Anne caught Greta's arm for an instant, but the terrified horse shook off its rider and bolted. Awkwardly, Greta landed in a heap. Leaping to the ground, Anne went to Greta, but she could not feel her breathing. "Greta!" Anne tried to revive her. "Greta!" Anne shook her. "Greta!"

Someone grabbed her arm. "Come, Lady Anne."

Turning, Anne realized it was Gerard. "My Lady, Greta," she pleaded.

Gerard reached down and quickly examined Greta. "Come." He took a firm hold of Anne's arm pulling her to her feet.

"But Greta," she protested.

"Her neck is broken," Gerard gruffed as he yanked Anne towards the cart. "Keep your head down."

Chaos surrounded them. Pushing her behind the cart, Gerard placed himself in front of Anne. "Who is it?" Anne sank back against the cart. It lurched forward and Anne understood the donkey was still harnessed on the other end.

Gerard scanned around. "It isn't King Philip. They look like bandits." He looked around again. "Stay behind me."

Gerard moved around the cart to the front. Without explanation he slapped the donkey until the frightened beast started forward at a run, the cart bouncing behind it. The instant the cart was gone, Gerard wrapped his arm around Anne, and steered her away from the road and into the trees, his sword drawn at the ready. "Hopefully they will go for the cart. Keep to the woods," he whispered.

No sooner had they entered the thicket of trees than another volley of arrows flew towards them. They were running straight into a trio of crossbowman. Gerard veered them left, away from the bowmen and further into the woods.

Anne felt a sting just below her collarbone that went all the way through her right breast to her back. She stumbled to her knees and came face to shaft with a bolt protruding from her body. Gerard tripped on her feet and landed next to her with a thump that sent up a cloud of dirt and dust, and his sword flying. Afraid the arrow would go further in, Anne rolled over onto her back.

A crossbowman inched toward her with his weapon at the ready. "My God! You fool! What have you done?" A voice screeched from behind him. An instant later the bowman's head exploded in pink mist as a spiked mace slammed into it.

Gerard struggled to regain his footing and lunged toward Anne to protect her. Still dazed, Anne heard the sickening crunch of bones as the mace landed on Gerard's back, and instantly his legs went limp. Gerard looked up at Anne in pain. "Run!" he groaned.

Fear petrified Anne. Gerard tried to reach for his sword, but the man with the mace kicked it out of the Templar's reach. Gerard clawed at the earth trying to propel himself forward. Before he had a chance to escape, the man behind him picked up Gerard's own sword and stabbed the Templar in the back, pinning him to the earth. Writhing in pain, Gerard twisted his body. Anne tried to look away; she could not bear to watch, but it was too late. She saw Gerard's helmet plucked from his head, and the man grabbed him by the hair. In one swift move he slit the Templar's throat and leapt out of the way of the blood spatter. Now Anne looked up at the man's face, and the first thing she saw was an unmistakable scar.

Castile plodded toward his wife, the dagger still dripping with blood in his right hand, his shoes and leggings spotted in red, the gurgling sounds of the dying Gerard behind him. Anne tried to crawl backwards away from him, but a sharp pain seized her, as the arrow seemed to move about inside her flesh. "Stop! Don't move! You'll only make it worse!" Castile ordered. "Abram, get over here!"

"Abram?" Anne repeated the name.

Castile knelt beside her and tried to examine the wound. Anne made a quick move to get away, but the combination of pain and Castile's strong hands holding her arms down made it impossible. "Hold still, damn it!" He shouted. "I swear on the lives of all the saints you were not to be harmed, Anne." He lifted his dagger towards Anne and she flinched. "Bastard!" He spat in the direction of the crossbowman. "He paid for his mistake with his life, didn't he?" Carefully Castile used his dagger to rip the fabric of her dress away from the wound. "Damn it! Abram!" He shouted again, the veins in his neck standing out.

Anne heard the tramping of boots as Abram came running. "My lord, we have lost all but you, me, and one crossbowman." He sounded winded.

"And the lady's escort?" Castile still picked away at the fabric.

"All dead." Abram looked at the two bodies lying close by. "I guess the bowman is dead as well."

"Damnable bastard hit her with an arrow. He was probably aiming for that templar son-of-a bitch."

"What shall we do?" Abram asked.

"Well, we shall get it out, you ass. She's no good to me dead." He sheathed his dagger. "If she dies, the boy inherits it all." Castile prodded the wound.

Anne struggled. "Do not touch me, you fiends and traitors!" She kicked at Castile.

"Hold her down," he commanded as he straddled her legs.

Abram sheathed his sword and came behind Anne, placing his hands firmly on both her arms, causing her to scream in pain. She was pinned to the ground. "Should we break the shoulder and push it through?" Abram looked at Castile.

"No," he shook his head. "I do not think the arrow is not so deep that I cannot pull it out."

"No, please!" Anne pleaded. "Please, just let me go."

"Anne, the arrow has got to come out." Castile spoke with

surprising tenderness. "Hold her steady."

"Yes, sir." Abram pressed down harder on Anne.

Taking in a deep breath, Castile repositioned himself, clamping his legs tighter around hers. Firmly, he gripped the arrow just above the skin. He relaxed his fingers and then tightened them again. He took another deep breath. "On my count of three," he said. "One." And he pulled at the arrow.

Anne felt pain and pressure unlike anything she had ever experienced. She tried hard not to scream because she didn't want Castile to derive any satisfaction, but the intensity overwhelmed her, and she cried out. Suddenly the tugging stopped and Castile bellowed, "Shit! Shit! Shit!"

Anne looked into Castile's eyes and saw the same anger she saw long ago in Poitiers when he threw her up against a wall and cursed her. Anne's face was wet and she realized she was crying. She wanted to struggle against the men who held her, but there was no strength left in her body.

"What now?" Abram whispered, his eyes wide with fear.

"The shaft broke. We'll have to dig it out." With the back of his hand, Castile wiped sweat from his forehead. He tossed the shaft of the arrow away. "Shit! Shit! Shit! All I've got is this damned dagger. Shit! This is going to be messy!"

"Oh, no, please no." Anne found new strength. "Castile, you do not know what you are doing. Please, I beg you. If you want me to live, get me to a surgeon."

"Cannot do that." Castile shook his head. "You'll try to escape. I know you."

"I cannot run anywhere," she sobbed. As Castile unsheathed his dagger again, Anne fought back with the only weapon she had. She screamed at him and spit in his face. "Leave it alone!"

As if from nowhere a sword suddenly pointed directly at the back of Castile's neck. "You will do as the lady says."

In disbelief Anne looked up to see a man-at-arms standing

there. Castile and Abram were so focused on her, they had not heard or seen the men approach. The man-at-arms wore Philip's livery.

Behind her, someone yanked Abram to his feet. "Now get up slowly," the soldier commanded Castile.

Ready to strike, two more French men-at-arms pointed their swords at Castile. Castile dropped his dagger and held out his palms to show he meant no harm. He eased himself to his feet. "Good sirs, you are mistaken. This is my wife. We were traveling and set upon by bandits. My wife was wounded, and I am trying to remove the arrow." The soldier signaled with his head and men moved in, binding both Castile and Abram.

"Sir, please help me. I am cousin to King Philip. These men were trying to kidnap me." Anne reached out to the soldier.

"Fear not, Lady Anne." He spoke to Anne, but didn't take his eyes off of Castile. "We came upon your smashed cart, and I recognised your trunk."

"My trunk?"

"Yes, I've had the misfortune of having to haul it around before. I am Grimaud." Both Castile and Abram were bound, and one soldier gave Castile a harsh shove away from Anne. "Tie their feet as well. There will be no escape." Grimaud shouted another order. Then he pointed to two of the other soldiers. "Athos and Bazin, go inform the king what happened." He lowered his sword so as to not look so threatening to Anne.

"King Philip is here?" Anne's head realed.

"Yes, my lady. He is across the river right now. We," he nodded in the direction of his comrades, "are doing reconnaissance against King Rich—" Grimaud stopped and raised his sword as if afraid of just the name alone.

Anne understood that the man-at-arms thought Richard might be close by. "King Richard is at Gaillard," she assured him. "I was traveling to Vaudreuil because my son has been wounded there."

"Are you in pain Lady Anne?" Grimaud asked.

Before she could answer Castile chimed in, "Of course she's in pain. She was hit by an arrow, you dolt."

"That's enough," Grimaud snarled at Castile. "Throw a rope over one of those branches, and put the other end around his neck so that he doesn't wander. And do the same with the other bastard over that branch," he shouted and pointed at the same time.

The French men-at-arms made quick work of their task as Grimaud knelt down beside Anne. "I was a page at court when you and then Duke Richard visited Paris." He called over his shoulder, "Retrieve the lady's trunk." Looking back at Anne, he gave her a small smile. "Let's see if we can't make you more comfortable."

"Thank you, sir," Anne whispered.

"Don't worry, the king will know what to do." Grimaud tried to comfort her. "In the meantime," he took off his cloak and surcoat, "this will have to do." Bundling up his surcoat, he carefully placed it beneath her head, and the cloak he laid on top of her.

Anne looked beyond him, and Grimaud turned to follow her gaze. She looked at Gerard's body lying there still and dead. She closed her eyes. Grimaud pointed to the bodies of the Templar and the bowman, and the soldiers carried them away.

Suddenly Castile screeched, "That is my wife and you have no right to hold me."

"That rope is too low!" Grimaud snapped.

Turning her head, Anne could see Castile with a noose around his neck that lifted him to his toes. Grimaud moved to block her view of the fracas. "Are you thirsty, my lady?" He tried to distract her further.

"All I want is to go to Will," she moaned. It grew harder to keep the pain to herself, so she closed her eyes.

"Oh, merciful God in heaven!" Philip blanched at the sight

of the blood both on Anne and the ground surrounding them.

"Your highness, what are you doing here?" She tried to sound cheerful to hide the pain she pain felt.

"How could Richard send you off like this?" Philip's face flushed with anger.

"Will, my lord. Will was wounded at Verneuil, and I was on my way to him when we were ambushed."

"Where is Richard?" Philip loosened Anne's wimple to make her more comfortable.

"At Galliard concluding some business. He was to follow tomorrow." Anne did not explain the business, nor did Philip ask.

Philip examined the wound but continued to talk in hope of distracting her. "Why did you not take the river?"

"We were told it was impassible at Le Mesnil due to a barge sinking. Cousin, my Will is hurt. I must go to him," she pleaded.

"Will is fine!" Castile's voice came from behind Philip, flat on his feet again. "Last time I saw *my* son, he had barely a scratch on him."

"Is that Castile?" Philip whispered through gritted teeth.

Anne could only nod as tears filled her eyes. Turning his head, Philip shouted at Castile, "Unless you wish to be a poached egg, you will shut your damn mouth. You do not have long to live, and your breath is wasted."

"Will," Anne sobbed.

Philip rose to his feet and motioned for Abram to be brought to him. The men-at-arms untied him from the tree and shoved him, forcing the knight to his knees before the king. "Explain!" Philip growled.

With a bowed head Abram began his story. "Your highness, Sir Wiliam is safe. At this moment he is probably on the river traveling to Chateau Galliard with Sir Marshal."

Philip took a firm stance in front of Abram, his legs spread at shoulder width, his right hand ready to pull his sword from its sheath at an instant. "And how do you know this?" Abram mumbled something unintelligible and Philip bellowed, "Stand up, and speak up!"

Stumbling, Abram rose to his feet, his hands still tied behind his back. "Sire, this is all Castile's doing. He bribed me to lure Lady Anne here with false news of her son." Abram leaned to the right, straining to speak over Philip's shoulder to Anne. "Will is safe and very much unharmed."

Anne turned her head away from them. Now she believed that Will was safe, and that knowledge was enough for the moment. Again she closed her eyes. Grimuad knelt down beside her again. "My lord, she fainted."

Philip didn't take his eyes off of Abram. "How much did Castile pay you?"

"My lord, I was beguiled…" Abram stammered.

"Oh come now! You have crossed into the realm of mercenary. Do not be ashamed of your wages!" Philip gave Abram a sardonic smile.

Abram looked down at the ground. "I am not from a wealthy family."

"That is not what I asked!" Philip barked at him.

"Castile has yet to pay me. He promised me a high position in his household."

So swift was Philip that Abram did not see the sword until the king's motion was complete. Wide eyed and horrified, Abram looked up at Philip. "I hope it was worth your life." Philip reached out and grasped Abram's sleeve, wiping his blood from the blade. The knight crumpled to the ground in a heap twitching and gurgling. "Get him out of here before she wakes up," Philip commanded. He pointed his sword at Castile. "Now you and I will speak."

Chapter Ninety

When Anne's eyes fluttered opened, she could see Philip's intense blue eyes. Brushing her hair away from her face, he knelt on the opposite side from her wound this time. "You were out for a moment, dear."

Suddenly Anne realized what woke her as she felt a sharp pain at her wound. She jumped at the pain. There was another man examining it, and she could tell by his biretta he was probably a surgeon. Philip tried to distract her, and he took her hand. "Anne, this is my surgeon, Lorenz. He is the best France has ever seen."

As if from nowhere, the surgeon produced an arrow spoon and Anne's eyes widened. "No!" She jerked away from the surgeon, but the movement caused her more pain.

"Anne, dearest," Philip tried to soothe her, "it has got to come out."

"Please my lord, I beg you. I just want to go home." Tears spilled onto her eyelashes and down her cheeks.

With tender strokes, Philip smoothed her hair back again and wiped her face. "I am afraid Marseilles is out of the question."

"No." She shook her head. "Galliard."

Instantly Philip flushed at the mention of that place, and he found he could not speak. His surgeon came to his aid. "Lady Anne, we cannot move you until the bolt is out. Moving you could force it to move about, do more damage, even embed itself further into your shoulder."

"I want to go home." She pleaded with the surgeon now.

"No." Philip's voice cracked. "Anne, Gaillon is the closest castle, much closer that Galliard."

"Am I your prisoner, my lord?" Anne narrowed her eyes at him.

"Do not be ridiculous," he scoffed.

"But am I? If I go with you to Gaillon, will I ever be free to leave?"

"If you go back to Galliard, *he* will never let you leave. He will lock you away in his stronghold." Philip's tone grew dark.

"My lord," the surgeon kindly interrupted. "May I speak to you regarding the lady's condition a moment?"

Philip gave Anne a tender look. "I will return shortly." He got to his feet and followed the surgeon until they were out of hearing range. Anne strained to hear, but it was futile. She saw the surgeon speaking, then Philip looked over at her and nodded with an anxious face.

With caution, Philip moved back toward her and took up his same position opposite her wound. "Cousin, please," Anne pleaded again.

"I will not have you moved before the arrow is out." He took in a deep breath to calm himself. "However, Lorenz convinced me that once the arrow is out, if your condition allows it, you may return to Galliard."

She reached her hand out to him, and he grasped it. "Thank you, sire, thank you."

The surgeon was next to her again. "This will hurt, my lady. I am sorry for that, and sorry about the conditions as well." He unrolled a bundle containing his tools and laid them out neatly next to her.

"It cannot be helped." Anne looked away from the surgeon's instruments.

Lorenz looked up and nodded to two men at arms who to assist. "No!" Philip held out his hand to stop them. "I shall hold her."

Anne paid little attention as Philip took up the position where the surgeon directed him. Instead, she closed her eyes and tried to concentrate on pleasant thoughts of Will and Richard. She pictured the little peach orchard and Richard sitting there underneath the trees waiting for her with his wide grin.

Her amiable thoughts were assaulted as the pain in her shoulder took hold of her entire body.

Anne felt a cold rough hand on her forehead. She tried to push it away, but the hand did not move, so she opened her eyes. It was Lorenz. "You fainted, Lady Anne," he explained.

"The arrow is out," Philip whispered in her left ear.

Anne looked down and saw her shoulder bandaged in linen. The surgeon finished gathering up his tools and moved away from her. "I will leave you alone for a moment."

Philip drew in a deep breath. "I have sent for a barge to take you to Galliard." There was a deep pain in his eyes.

"Thank you," she whispered. Next to her she could feel Philip trembling.

"I will not be going to Galliard with you. If I were to show up there with you in this condition, Richard would stab first, and ask questions of my dying corpse."

It was late night now, and a chill had set in the late October air. That was not why Philip trembled, and Anne could tell. "What is wrong, my lord?" She laid her hand on his.

"Anne, if you go to Galliard, I will never see you again." He reached out and touched her face.

"Do you have such little faith in your surgeon?"

"My surgeon has nothing to do with it." He glanced away in the direction of Lorenz.

Trying to move, she winced at the pain. "I do not know the prognosis. I fainted."

"As I said, the arrow is out. Now we just keep a watchful eye for putrification," he explained.

"We?" She queried.

"I will keep my word about Galliard." He frowned.

"Then I shall see you before long. After all, there is always some new treaty to negotiate or war to fight between you two."

Philip shook his head with fervor. "He will never let you out of his sight again, not after this. I certainly would not. Damn him! What could possibly be so important that he would let you go off like this at such a dangerous time?"

"An emissary from the pope is coming to discuss the release of our cousin, the bishop," she explained.

"Release Beauvais? Why would he do that?" Philip snorted.

"My lord, I was to be declared a widow upon Beauvais' release."

Philip looked over at the bound Castile then back at Anne. "Oh, I see. And Berengaria?"

"Annulment," Anne whispered.

Philip looked pensive. The silence made Anne even more uncomfortable. She feared that perhaps he would now change his mind and not send her Galliard. Just as she was ready to remind him that she had been honest with him, Philip spoke again. "I did want to run Castile through myself, but I do not think I shall. If Richard wants you a widow, let him do it himself."

"It is likely that he will."

Philip looked back at her. "Anne, do you remember all those years ago when we played that match of chess?"

"We played that game many times, my lord." Another sharp pain shot through Anne's shoulder as she moved too much.

"This was the first time we played chess, in Paris."

"I think I remember."

"Well, during that game we had a frank discussion about Richard. I told you then I thought it would kill him if he lost you."

"I remember, vaguely." She looked away from Philip.

"I have a confession to make." Philip lightly touched Anne's good shoulder.

"Are you telling me you are keeping me in some kind of odd scheme to kill Richard?" She raised her eyebrows.

Philip nervously laughed. "No, I'm telling you I already tried that, and it did not work."

"Of course, it did not work; it is a ridiculous notion," Anne scoffed.

Philip ignored her last comment. "I saw what Henry did, the chink in Richard's armor Henry used. I also saw how effective it was, so I decided to exploit it myself. Anne, I used you to get what I wanted from Richard or to get to him."

"I know."

Philip squirmed. "It did not work because I had not realized that I would care for you so deeply."

Lorenz appeared from behind Philip. "Sire, the litter is ready."

Anne felt grateful for the distraction because the conversation had taken an uncomfortable course. "If you will be so kind as to help me to my feet, I think I can walk."

"Easy now." Philip helped her to a sitting position. When she tried to rise too quickly, he urged her, "Slowly, cousin."

Anne groaned and her head drooped. Without a word, Philip gathered her in his arms and picked her up. She leaned her head towards his shoulder, but she quickly realized she could not hold it upright and let it fall against him. Philip liked the way her soft hair brushed his chin, her body pressed up against his and wished that it was not out of necessity that she was in his arms. Her head dropped more, and he realized she fainted again.

When Anne woke, she was on Philip's barge lying on a makeshift bed. Philip knelt next to her. "She is awake," he called to his surgeon. He turned back to her. "I am sending Lorenz with you to *Galliard*." He emphasized the last word.

"Thank you," she mouthed.

Then Philip did something that surprised even himself. He kissed her. When he slowly withdrew his lips, he pressed his forehead against hers. Anne could feel hot tears on her face; she wasn't sure if they were hers or his. "I am sorry, so very sorry," he whispered.

"It is alright. Richard need never know," she assured him.

"No, not for the kiss. That I do not regret, but for

everything else. I have wronged you in so many ways, Anne. Can you forgive me, really forgive me for everything? I would not blame you if you wanted to see me writhe in the pits of hell for all that I have done."

"Complete absolution is not mine to give. You must go to God for that. But what is in my power to forgive, I gladly do." With her good arm, she reached up placing her hand on his cheek. "I ask only that you make amends with Richard."

Turning his head, he kissed the palm of her hand. "Here." He closed her fingers around something.

Anne could see the ribbon that held Richard's ring spilling out between her fingers. Curiously she looked back at Philip. "We had to cut it off when we took the arrow out. I was tempted to keep it, but as I have never seen you without it..." He shrugged. "See what I mean about my plan not working."

Anne smiled and nodded.

He bent close to her ear and whispered. "I love you, Anne."

"I love you too, cousin," she whispered back.

Although she had not intended it, the word cousin stung him the most. "Sire," Lorenz spoke from behind Philip. "Now that the lady is awake, we must be on our way."

Philip gave Anne a quick kiss on the forehead and then stood. He turned back and began to disembark, but stopped short. Turning around, he grinned at her. "If he keeps you locked up in that damned fortress of his, I will take it brick by brick to get you out." "Even if it were made of iron?" Anne tried to raise her eyebrows.

"Especially if it were made of iron. That would be more entertaining." He gave her a wink and left the barge.

From the shore, Philip watched as the barge carried Anne up the river towards Galliard.

Chapter Ninety-one

Richard lost patience. The emissary took too long, so he decided to ride out and meet him. It didn't take long to find the emissary's party.

The emissary turned out to be a rotund cardinal, all the better for Richard. With a cardinal's authority no one would question his annulment. Before long, Richard convinced the cardinal that he rode out to meet him as a grand welcoming gesture.

As they rode back to Galliard, Richard found the cardinal amiable and easy to talk to, so Richard explained the situation with Will and Anne. The Cardinal readily agreed that on the morrow, they should leave for Vaudreuil.

Richard's next strategy was to entertain the cardinal with stories from crusade. These were meant not only pass the time, but subtly remind the emissary of all Richard had done for God and the church. Richard was so entrenched in his story, he did not see Blondel riding pell mell until he was almost upon them. When Blondel reined to a stop, Richard noticed his minstrel's distraught countenance. He thought of Will, and his stomach lurched. "God's legs, Blondel!"

"Pray, please pardon my intrusion, your highness, your eminence." Blondel was winded and had difficulty speaking.

The cardinal also noticed Blondel's distress. "What is it, my son?"

"It is Lady Anne, my lord," Blondel managed. "There has been some sort of accident."

Blondel and the others found it difficult to keep up with Richard as he dashed back to Galliard. Richard refused to slow down even enough for Blondel to explain. He rode his horse through the outer and middle baileys, and then sprang from his horse sprinting for the inner bailey.

Just as he reached Anne's chamber door, his surgeon, Marchadeus, left the room. "Your highness!"

Richard pushed passed him and flung the door open so hard that it sent a crack through the room causing everyone to jump. "Anne!"

Anne lay on the bed surrounded by a crowd of people, Philip's surgeon Lorenz amongst them discussing her condition. They made way for Richard. "In the name of all that is holy, what happened?"

She spoke in a calm and quiet voice. "I am alright Richard. Will is safe as well."

"Alright, my ass. You look awful, and your dress is torn, your arm in a sling, and your shoulder bandaged."

Lorenz tried to explain. "Your highness, Raymond of Castile set a trap for Lady Anne, and in the melee she was shot in the shoulder."

"*Castile!*" Richard's face contorted. In a rage, he turned on Lorenz. "And who the hell are you?"

"Sire," Marchadeus broke in. "He is personal surgeon to the King of France, and I might add, a very skillful one at that. He removed the arrow head."

"The arrow head?"

"Yes, the shaft broke off when Castile tried to remove it. King Philip sent him to aid Lady Anne." Marchadeus nodded.

"What? Philip? What does Philip have to do with this?" Richard yelled.

"I believe the surgeons were about to examine my wound. I will explain it all while they do." Anne hinted for Richard to move.

Richard understood and went around to the other side of the bed taking Anne's hand. With difficulty, Anne explained the situation for Richard while the surgeons examined her wound. Her voice faltered at times as the pain shot through her. Richard stole looks at the wound to ascertain the damage for himself. She finished her story before they completed their examination.

Richard said nothing. He studied her wound and listened to the whispering surgeons.

At last, they began to apply a clean bandage. Richard looked back at Anne's face. Her pale colour and tight lips told him she was in pain and trying hard to hide it. He stroked her face with his fingertips, and she closed her eyes. "Get some rest if you can, sweetheart." He brushed his lips against hers then motioned the two surgeons to the far corner of the room.

"Well?" Richard spoke with an edge, but still kept the volume to a whisper.

Lorenz answered, "Removing the head was difficult, and when the shaft broke, it splintered. I think I got as many as possible, but there may be more. It is hard to see."

Richard folded his arms. "Will she recover?"

"Sire, I will do my utmost toward that end. We must monitor her carefully."

"Thank you." It wasn't the news Richard wanted to hear.

He moved a chair closer to Anne's bed and sat down. Without opening her eyes, Anne reached out and took his hand. He scooted the chair closer, leaned over, and placed his head next to her shoulder.

Even the sheer magnificence of Galliard hadn't been enough to rid Will of a gnawing feeling that plagued him. Abram's disappearance, although not terribly surprising, was unsettling. Marshal looked for him only find out Abram was last seen leaving Vaudreuil with a band of mercenaries. Marshal was furious, and it would be better for Abram if Marshal were never to see him again. Will felt both anger and disgust at Abram's behavior. It wasn't as if Abram was the most honorable person to begin with, but still the whole situation bothered Will.

With his thoughts lost on Abram, Will followed Marshal into the outer bailey of the fortress. He noticed something different, but not the splendor or ingenious design of Galliard. No matter where it lodged, Richard's court always had a certain pleasant air about it. Something was wrong. A subdued atmosphere stretched over the grounds of the castle. As those in the outer bailey went about their work, they used hushed voices as if afraid to wake a sleeping giant or speak their thoughts aloud. Marshal and his men dismounted from their horses.

Just as Will thought to ask a nearby stable boy for information, he saw Blondel jogging toward them. The weather was cold, too cold, and Blondel wasn't even wearing a cap let alone a cloak. "Sir Marshal, Sir Will," Blondel called out, but not in his usual lithe tone.

Marshal noticed it, too. "What is the matter Blondel?"

Blondel was direct. "My lords, Lady Anne has been injured."

Will's feet seemed frozen in place. While Blondel explained what happened, Will stood rooted to the spot. He struggled to listen to Blondel explain the failed kidnapping plot. "And Abram?" He heard Marshal ask Blondel.

"Dead. King Philip unseamed him from hip to shoulder," Blondel answered.

"Where is my mother?" Will didn't realize he spoke through clenched teeth.

"This way," Blondel said, motioning for him to follow.

Blondel led them through the middle bailey and the inner court to the manor house, but Will didn't notice any of it. He could only think of his injured mother, and as he passed the keep, he knew his father was in some dungeon cell there.

A small group, including the surgeons, gathered outside Anne's chamber door, at the ready should their assistance be needed. When Will approached, they parted to make way. He took off his spurs, so they would not make noise and opened the door. Marshal stayed in the hall to allow the young knight time with his mother.

Anne lay on the bed with her eyes closed, and Richard slept in a chair next to the bed on the side closest to the fire. Will wasn't sure what to do because he didn't want to wake either of them. Just as he contemplated slipping back out into the hall, Anne stirred and opened her eyes. Upon seeing, Will a pained smile spread across her face. She motioned him to come to the bed. Obeying, he knelt down next to her. "I am so relieved to see you," she whispered.

Will took her hand and noticed it felt unusually hot. He brushed her cheek with the back of his hand to feel if just her hand was hot. "I am here now, Mother." Her face felt hot, too. "You are feverish," he whispered. "I should get the surgeon."

"No." She shook her head. "Don't wake the king. He hasn't slept much; he hasn't left my side. Besides, the fire is warm in here."

Will knew that it wasn't the fire, but he also knew that calling in a surgeon against his mother's wishes could make her angry, which would only worsen her condition. In his chair, Richard stirred, trying for a more comfortable position, but he didn't wake. Anne looked over at him, and tears came to her eyes. "He could not have loved you any greater if you were his son."

"There have been many times I wished for it." That brought the image of Will's own father to his mind. He hadn't seen Castile since he was a boy, and only through a grimy window in the Jewish Quarter.

"Oh, Will." Anne reached up and touched her son's face. "I am so glad you are here and safe."

Will looked at this mother's face, pale almost to the point of a greenish-yellow hue. "Mother, I am so very sorry. I..."

"Sh," Anne interrupted him. "I will have none of that from you. You are not to blame."

"I should say not." Richard awoke and sat up straight now.

"How long have you been listening?" Anne tilted her head toward him.

"Not long enough to know if you have told him or not."

Richard stretched.

"Told me what, sire?"

"Your mother and I feel that it is time you be invested as Viscount of Marseilles."

Will couldn't help but notice Richard made it sound like a joint decision. He voiced a different concern. "Does this mean that... that you are not expected to recover?"

"No! Oh, no, sweetheart." Anne reached for his hand again, and he took it wincing at the heat. "This was decided weeks ago."

"You see, Will," Richard took over, "my marriage is to be annulled, and your mother is to be declared a widow."

"But I don't understand. Blondel said my father is alive—a prisoner, but alive." Will furrowed his brow.

"Yes, dear, that was the plan until a few days ago." Anne couldn't look at Richard. They had not talked of Castile's fate.

"Castile has debts to pay." A dark shadow crossed Richard's face. "Your mother will be a widow soon."

"Oh." Will fidgeted in his seat.

"But enough of that. Our Will is back, returning with glory." Richard beamed at him with pride. "We have been hearing reports of your feats."

Will blushed. "I am sure these reports are exaggerated, my lord."

"I highly doubt it. After all, you have been taught by the best." Richard dismissed Will's humility with the wave of a hand.

"Fortune was very kind to me when you took me under your wing," Will answered, taking his eyes from his mother for a moment.

"Yes, it certainly was, but I was talking about Marshal." Richard winked.

Will felt his mother's grip slacken, and he looked down at her with alarm. "Mother?"

"I am sorry, dearest. I am feeling sleepy, but I do not want to go to sleep with you here. I have waited too long to see you. I want to hear all about… everything."

"I promise you will." Will released her hand. "For now, you should rest."

"No, no. There will be time to rest later," she protested.

"Will is right, Anne. Rest now. We will stay here." Richard rose and leaned over kissing her on the forehead. "Come Will, you must be starving."

While Richard drew Will to the window seat, Anne relented and closed her eyes. "She is burning with fever," Will whispered.

Richard gave a long sigh, and sunk down on the cushions. "I felt that when I kissed her."

"And what is that spice smell?"

"Oil of oregano." Richard grimaced. "I first encountered it on crusade. It seems to help fight putrification, but it burns like hellfire, so the physicians have been rather sparing with it."

"What do they say?"

"Not much. We just have to keep watch and pray." Richard motioned for Will to take a seat.

They were quiet, both lost in contemplation. After a few moments, Will said, "Sire, are you going to kill Castile?"

"Will, the pope sent an emissary, and the cardinal was ready to declare your mother a widow. Now Castile is here in the flesh. We could ask for an annulment, but then your inheritance would be in question. Your mother worked so hard to insure your inheritance."

"I see." Will spoke to the floor, not wanting Richard to see the guilt he felt.

Richard leaned forward. "There are rumors that while Castile was in Outremer, he converted to Islam to save his neck. The cardinal is going to question him, and witnesses against Castile are lining up."

"Do I still look much like him?" The question was out before Will realized.

"Not as much anymore. He is old and scarred from an ill-used life." Will turned an angry shade of red. "There is some wine over there. Help yourself," Richard pointed. "If your page is outside, tell him to bring something to eat."

"Yes, my lord." Will made for the wine.

Alone in the room with Anne, Richard jerked awake. He fell asleep while sitting on the widow cushions, his head leaning up against the cool glass of the window; night pressed against the other side. He looked around the room and rubbed his cheek. Anne was in a fitful sleep. In a haze, he rubbed his eyes. It seemed like months since Anne returned to Gailliard, wounded. It was dark outside, but the days and nights all seemed to be running together. In reality it had been just less than a fortnight.

When the surgeons examined Anne earlier that evening, her situation did not look hopeful. Anne twitched and moaned, but remained asleep. Now, Richard went to her bedside; he wanted to see the wound for himself without anyone to tell him this or that. Gingerly he pulled the bandage back until he could see it with his own eyes. He had seen his share of wounds on the battlefields and knew the signs of serious trouble. Despite the best efforts of the surgeons the puss that oozed from it told him of danger. He could have convinced himself that the puss only drained the putrid humors, but the smell that emanated from the wound was unmistakable, and he wondered if the surgeons ceasing the application of the oil of oregano had been the right choice. It burnt her, but Richard had heard wonders about its correct application in Cyprus. He replaced the bandage with clean linen and then pulled a chair up on the other side of the bed. Slumping down into the chair, he dropped his head into his hands.

At length, he felt someone playing with his hair. Anne wound her fingers through it. He looked up at her and asked, "How are you feeling?"

"Richard," her voice was weak and hoarse. "I want to ask you to do something for me."

"Yes, anything."

"Promise me that you will make amends with Philip."

Richard exhaled sharply. "Anne, we already have a truce."

"I mean a real truce. Remember there was some friendship there once."

"Perhaps." Richard shrugged.

Anne licked her dry lips, and a tear trickled down her cheek. "We almost got to be together, really honestly together, no shame, no looking over our shoulders, wondering when Castile would pop up, one and the same in purpose."

"What are you talking about? We are. The cardinal has agreed to the annulment, and you will be a confirmed widow very soon. Why, I can have it all done in an instant. If you like I shall send for the cardinal in to marry us right now."

"I am surprised you did not wring Castile's neck with your bare hands already."

"That would mean I would have to leave you, and I won't, not even for a moment, not until you are feeling better."

With difficulty Anne swallowed. "Is the cardinal nearby?"

"Yes," Richard nodded. "Would you have me bring him here?"

"I wish to make confession." She looked deep into his eyes trying to tell him what she couldn't say aloud.

Richard stroked her face. "There will be plenty of time for that."

"Possibly, but just in case." She gave a weak smile.

Deep in thought, Richard continued to caress her face. "You promised you would never leave me, Anne. Remember?"

"I intend to keep that promise." Fingers shaking with the effort, she reached up to stop his hands. "Richard, there are things around us that cannot always be seen with the eye or heard with ears."

"I only know how to see with my eyes and hear with my ears," Richard protested.

"You will learn." Anne closed her eyes, then pleaded, "Please Richard, if not the cardinal, then some other priest." She opened her eyes. "I must make confession so that we may be together in the next world. God knows we have done our duty, and I have faith that we will be together. Long ago you said we would find a way. Neither one of us imagined this would be the path."

"No. I will not have you talking like this, Anne. We shall be together in this world *and* the next." Richard shook his head.

"Either way, I must see a priest."

For a moment, Richard studied her. Her face was sallow. Yet, in her eyes, he still saw his Anne. Her eyes spoke to him again, so he went to the door and motioned. The cardinal waited outside the chamber. Out of concern, he came to see what assistance he could offer. When he entered the chamber, the air was thick and heavy. It enveloped his senses like a blanket of lead. He didn't waste time but went straight to Anne and listened as she whispered confession in his ear. Richard took up his seat at the window, never taking his eyes off Anne.

When at last Anne finished her confession, Richard resumed his place next to her and the cardinal took a seat at the window. Night continued on its path at an agonizing, slow pace, and Anne fell into another tumultuous sleep.

Three hours later, Will entered. Richard was aware the surgeons came in with him, and someone else, but he didn't bother to look. While he stared intently at Anne, a pair of firm hands laid themselves on his shoulders. "How is she doing, my lord?" It was Baldwin.

Richard ignored the question. "It is about damn time you got here." Emotion flooded the king, his throat tightened, and he fought not to let tears fall.

"If I remember correctly, you were the one to insist that I bring my wife and children. Traveling with a woman can be painstakingly slow." Baldwin rolled his blue eyes, but seeing his friend's face, he softly added, "Except with Anne."

Richard found he couldn't speak, so he just nodded. Baldwin understood. "My lord, there is a knight here who claims to be Will. Now, I know that cannot possibly be our Will."

Will forced a weak smile at Baldwin's good nature. "I know it is hard to believe, your grace."

"The imposter speaks!" Baldwin feigned surprise.

"'Tis true. That is our Will." Richard could see the misery past Will's smile.

"Good lord! What has Anne been feeding him?" Baldwin gave a quiet chuckle.

At the sound of her name, Anne's eyes flew open. She looked around at those in the room and made a low groaning sound. The disconcerting sound made Baldwin jumped back and Will rush to the bed. "Anne, I am here," Richard tried to soothe her. "And look, see who else has come." He motioned Baldwin forward.

Anne's wild eyes flashed about, and she shrank away from Richard. On impulse Richard reached out to her again, but she moved further away from him. "Do something!" He snapped at Marchadeus.

The surgeon Lorenz dabbed Anne's forehead with a cool cloth. "She is confused. The fever is affecting her mind."

"Mother," Will called out to her.

Anne clutched at the covers and drew them to her chin. "I do not think she knows who we are." Marchadeus gave Will a sympathetic pat on the shoulder.

Will panicked. He turned to Richard. "Surely she knows you."

"We should give her some space." Lorenz urged them to move away from the bed.

"I think the room is too crowded." Baldwin ushered most of them out.

Only Richard, Will, Lorenz, and the cardinal remained. Weary-faced Anne watched them leave. After a few moments, her grip on the covers loosened, and her eyes closed. She fell into a jerky, fitful state somewhere between consciousness and sleep.

As the first streaks of dawn began to lighten red on the horizon, Richard resumed his position next to Anne. Will now sat in a chair at the foot of the bed. The sweet pungent smell of incense did its best to break through the thick air, but it wasn't strong enough.

Anne settled on her back and rolled her head to the side toward Richard. She lay still now. With a gasp, she sucked in some air and opened her eyes, the mad look gone from her eyes, replaced with a lucid pain. Kneeling down, Richard put his face next to hers. He could tell she couldn't speak. Again she tried to speak with her eyes. He reached out and touched her cheek, her breathing shallow.

"My dearest Lady Anne, stay with me," he whispered his plea. Slowly her eyes sank back closed. "Please do not leave me. Stay with me." He could no longer feel her breathing. "You promised." He took a deep breath and held it down, pushing on his lungs as hard as he could.

Without saying a word Lorenz picked up a small mirror that lay on Anne's dressing table. He placed it in front of Anne's mouth and nose. Will couldn't bear to watch. With his arms, he buried his head in the foot of the bed.

Richard released his breath, and scanned Lorenz's face for any sign of hope. There was none. Lorenz shook his head with profound sadness. "Anne." The name choked in Richard's throat. He gathered her up in his arms and kissed her forehead. "Oh, God in heaven, I love you, Anne."

Chapter Ninety-two

Richard's sobs proved too much for Will. He fled the

room.

Marshal and Baldwin, along with others waited outside Anne's chamber. When Will burst through the door, his expression said enough. Baldwin tried to lay his hand on Will's shoulder, but Will knocked it away, his face twisted in rage. "Will?"

"It is over," Will growled.

Baldwin tried to calm the young man. "Will . . ." he didn't finish.

Will moved forward, and Baldwin reached out to stop him. "Let him go." Marshal stopped Baldwin.

Will exited the manor house shouting in a low, tired voice, "Where are the dungeons? Someone tell me! Where are the damn dungeons?"

A little old man carrying bundled wood pointed the way with a shaking finger, and Will bounded down the steps. The guard recognised Will and didn't try to restrain him. "Castile?" Will felt as though his head would explode. "Open the cell of Castile!" he demanded.

"Begging your pardon, sir, I cannot," replied the guard.

"I said open this cell, or I'll split you in two!"

"I cannot open the cell except upon order of the king himself."

"Son, I am here," a voice called from the farthest cell.

Will rushed to the cell, small, and cramped, with only enough room for a man to walk about four steps from end to end. In the left corner sat a bucket, and in the opposite one, straw and rags piled up for a bed. The whole place stank of moldy straw and urine. Will thought it a fitting place for such a man to be. He let loose and spat on Castile.

"She is dead, and now so are you, you God damned monster!"

"Anne!" Castile gasped.

The look of grief on Castile's face surprised Will, but did nothing to quash his rage. Will reached through the bars and grabbed Castile by the tunic, yanking him against the bars. "You will not mourn her! You murdered her!"

"No, the crossbowman's false aim killed her. I killed him for it." Castile remained calm.

"And what the hell was the bowman doing there?" Will slammed his father against the bars again.

The force made Castile's forehead to split open, spattering a bit of blood in Will's eyes, causing him to release Castile. "Will, I loved your mother." Castile's voice remained steady as he wiped blood away.

"That is a lie, and we both know it." Will narrowed his eyes.

"Think about it for just a minute, Will. You have only been told what Richard wanted you to hear. He loved her, too. I just never could express my love as eloquently as he."

"Richard never would have done to her what you did."

"Richard kept my wife and child from me." Castile raised his voice. "I did not even know I had a son until I heard it from some stranger in Acre. Imagine what that was like for me. I wanted to come to you, to know *my* son."

"You are no father to me! Any blood of yours that ever ran in my veins I have pissed out!" Will's exclamation echoed through the dungeon.

"Look at yourself, Will. You look just like me. That black curly hair; that is from me, your nose, cheekbones, forehead, all of it. Look," Castile held up his hand. "Our hands are even the same shape and size. You are as tall as me now."

"Half of Outremer looks like you!" Will snapped.

"Will, I was at Verneuil. I saw you do things, make gestures, even lean in your saddle the way I do. Those are things that cannot be taught. I gave you those things."

"My mother gave me life."

"Your mother never would have given you life, if it had not been for me." Castile held up his bloodied sleeve. "My blood is in you, Son. I know you came here with every intention of spilling my guts, but remember it will not only be my blood that turns the floor crimson; it will be yours as well."

Will stepped back from the cell. "Your time will come, Castile, and I hope to be the one to send you to hell. You have been no more father to me than the rats you share your cell with. I damn you." Will left his father in the dungeon cell.

Castile's words echoed in Will's head as he searched for a place to be alone. He made his way to the stable and his horse. Sigurd, Nanna, and Ursula were also there, all three rolling around playing with each other. Will envied them. They didn't know what just happened. They would never feel the kind of pain he felt.

Will did not know how long he stayed there in the stable, sitting on a bale of hay, going over in his mind what Castile said. He looked down at his hands, felt his face, and ran his hands through his hair. That only tortured him more.

A noise sounded behind him, and Will just assumed it was the dogs. "Will." Marshal found him.

Will stood. "Sir."

"Will, I know that right now you do not wish to be bothered, but it is the king."

Will hadn't thought about Richard, only about himself. "I am sure he is...is...is the king summoning me?"

Marshal shook his head with deep sadness. "The king will not speak to anybody. He has not left her side. We need to know what you wish us to do with your mother's remains. Do you want them returned to Marseilles?"

"The king will want to decide that, I am sure." Will gave a shrug.

"He is not in the frame of mind to decide anything right now," Marshal replied.

"Alright." Will walked past Marshal, left the stable, and

noticed the sun was halfway on its course of the day.

He went back to his mother's chamber. A large group still gathered in the hall. "Will, I am so sorry." Baldwin spoke first.

"The king will not speak?" Will looked around at the others.

Several of them shook their heads or looked away from Will. Baldwin answered, "No, he just sits there, holding her hand. We have all tried. Even the cardinal has tried, but he will not say a word."

Will didn't wait to be told more. He opened the door and entered the chamber.

The curtains were closed, and only one candle burnt. Richard still sat in the chair, his back to the door. Will closed the door, but Richard didn't move. "My lord?"

Richard said nothing, nor did he stir. Will paused, trying to think what his mother would do in this situation. He cleared his throat and spoke again. "Sire, I am making arrangements to leave at dawn. I will bury her in Marseilles." Richard twitched, so Will continued. "I think it would be fitting to bury her there, next to my grandsire, don't you?"

Will moved closer to Richard. Richard's strange behavior made Will even more uncomfortable. "Uncle." Will struggled to keep his own emotions in check.

The sound of Will calling him uncle roused Richard. He turned and looked up at his godson. "She is cold now."

"Then it is time to bury her."

Richard shook his head. "Not in Marseilles, not that far away."

"I noticed a little chapel here," Will offered.

"That was to be our wedding chapel." Richard fought to restrain his tears.

"She would like to remain close to you, I am sure." Will wanted to offer comfort but did not know how.

"She promised that she would." Richard grasped Anne's

hand more tightly.

"Shall I tell them to come and prepare the body?"

Richard rose part way from his chair, kissing her forehead one last time. When he finished, he nodded to Will.

Will stood next to Richard and watched as the men carried his mother from the room. As Baldwin and Marshal lifted her onto the stretcher, Will cried out, "Wait! Where is her ring? I have never seen her without it."

"Sir, your mother's jewelry is in her little casket on the desk," Lorenz informed him.

Will went to the casket and opened it. On top lay the ring on the ribbon. He plucked it up and took it over to his mother. As he placed it on her neck he said, "There now. That is much better."

When her body was gone from the room, Will softly asked, "Uncle, what will be done with Castile?"

Richard turned and looked at Will. The first things he saw were Will's eyes. They were the same hazel eyes that hours ago had tried to speak to him. Will's eyes spoke to him now. "He is yours," Richard said without emotion. "Do with him as you will."

The night after Anne was buried, Will had a dream. In his dream, his mother stood on her cliff high above the sea at Marseilles. She pointed to the distant ocean and Will looked. A little boat rocked about in the waves. Suddenly he was on the boat, along with Richard and Castile. A storm raged around them spraying each man with rain and seawater. They shouted at one another, arguing over something that each claimed belonged to them, Will assumed his mother. "I love her!" Castile yelled.

"Liar, you never loved her!" Will shouted at Castile, but neither man seemed to hear his words.

"Will should have been my son," screamed Richard with water running off his face.

"He will never be your son," Castile scoffed.

Without warning, Richard stabbed Castile with a dagger. Again and again he drove it into his enemy. Castile collapsed on the deck of the ship and crimson blood blended with the water in little streams that led to Will's feet. Will's gaze followed the trail of blood, and then he realized that the blood on the deck was mixing with his own that now trickled from his body. He looked to the spot where Castile fell, but there was no body there. In the exact places where Richard stabbed Castile, Will's own body now bled.

Will woke with a start, covered in sweat. Just to assure himself that it was a dream he looked around the room. He was not on a boat. To calm himself he concentrated on taking deep breaths. Will now knew what his father's fate would be.

"Where is the king?" Marshal asked Baldwin. Baldwin stood next to the well in the middle bailey.

"I have a pretty good guess." Baldwin gazed toward the chapel.

"He cannot live in there," Marshal protested.

"Give him time, Marshal. The cardinal talked with him last night."

"And did he make any progress?"

Baldwin shrugged. "He didn't really say, but at least Richard didn't throw him out like the rest of us."

Marshal glared at the chapel, as if it caused all the trouble. "Will reached a decision."

"It's about time. So, how does he die then?" Baldwin found it hard to restrain himself and not run Castile through.

"He will tell only the king." Marshal pulled his cloak around him to protect against the cold. "He wants to tell both Richard and Castile at the same time."

"Then we must convince the king to leave the chapel. It wouldn't be proper to kill him in a chapel." Baldwin sighed.

Marshal nodded, and Baldwin set off to enter the chapel.

Baldwin traveled through the little entryway wide enough to be a small hall, pausing at the chapel door to touch Anne's hatchment hanging there, the crest of red with the brilliant yellow sunburst. Closing his eyes and taking in a deep breath, he continued on into the chapel itself where Richard sat on the floor, his back against the wall next to Anne's grave. With muted steps, Baldwin strode down the nave, crossed himself at the altar, then turned to Richard. "Sire, I am sorry to disturb you."

"Then do not." Richard wouldn't even look up at Baldwin.

"We are all worried about you, my lord." Baldwin squatted down so he could be eye level with Richard. "Will reached a decision about Castile."

Richard ignored the comment about Will. "I have been thinking, there are probably many who would say that I am sick, diseased with love."

"I do not know." Baldwin shrugged.

"It is rather funny how love is equated with sickness. I do believe the person who called it a disease never felt the happiness and joy that love renders to its victim."

"Perhaps." Baldwin thought of his own wife.

"Still, I loved her beyond all reason." Richard looked into Baldwin's blue eyes. "Was that wrong?"

"I do not think so. Regardless, you cannot live out the rest of your days here in this chapel," Baldwin urged.

Richard let loose with an odd laugh. "Oh, Baldwin, Baldwin, there is a world between sleep and reason. It is there I wish to reside, for in that kingdom all is well. It is as if I can go around a corner and there she will be. There she is not lost to me. The danger is in getting there though, because you must first sleep. In sleep come the dreams, the awful images as your mind tries to settle out your troubles. But then for a moment, a delicious tranquil moment, you linger in the most pleasant state ever to be known. Alas, no matter how hard you try to cling to it, desire it, wish for it, fight for it, the time will pass. You are left with only the harsh knowledge of cruel, cold, calculating reality— a heavy emptiness of the soul, a painful longing for the world between sleep and reason."

Baldwin reached out and skimmed the edge of her grave with his finger. "What would Anne have you do?"

"Duty," Richard whispered.

"Honor her memory; do not wallow it in." Baldwin stood back up. "Do your duty, Richard. Your Will is waiting for you." Baldwin left Richard in the chapel.

At the well, Baldwin and Marshal waited to see if Richard would leave. Their efforts were rewarded when the door cracked open and Richard exited the building. "Shall I call Will to the manor?" Baldwin asked.

"No. To the battlements," said Richard.

They both knew that the wound must still be too sore to go past her room. At least he left the chapel.

Richard looked out from the battlements on the north side of the citadel that overlooked the cliffs and the river below. The cold November wind whipped around him, but he found the pain comforting. He gazed at the jagged rocks below. Closing his eyes he imagined himself falling from the battlements, the wind rushing passed him, flying to a welcome end. "Uncle," Will's voice brought him back from his thoughts, and Richard opened his eyes.

Will stood there along with Baldwin, Marshal, and four guards leading a bound Castile. They stopped and stood facing Richard. "You have made your choice?" It sounded more like a statement than a question.

Will nodded and gestured for Castile to be brought forward. "Raymond of Castile…"

"Son…" Castile interrupted him.

"That will be quite enough!" Will had his back to the river

with Castile on one side and Richard on the other.

"You can deny it all you want, but you are my son," Castile argued. "He may have raised you, but that is because I never had the chance." He threw his head toward Richard.

"Enough!" Baldwin moved towards Castile, but Will blocked him.

Castile continued, "I loved you from the moment I first found out I had a son. I left Acre in search of you. I found you too, but your mother cast me out. That was not enough to keep *you* away, was it? Will, the first time I saw your face, you peered at me through a window in the Jewish quarter. Do you remember?"

"You may have given me my life but nothing else." Will's face reddened with anger.

"Are you prepared to take mine? You accused me of being base and vile, yet you are ready to strike down your own father?" Castile seemed to forget he was well bound and guarded. "Perhaps you learnt something from your Uncle Richard after all."

"How dare you?" Baldwin pushed Castile to the ground.

Raymond had a twisted smile on his face. "You forget, sir, that your friend and I are both the sons of kings. What are you a son of?"

Richard finally spoke, but to Will. "I cannot tell you how many times I wished that you were my flesh and blood son, Will. If I learnt anything in all my years, it is that sometimes there is a bond that can be stronger than blood." He glanced at Marshal, then looked back at Will. "God knows I could not have loved you any more if you were my flesh and blood than I do already."

"Pick him up," Will ordered.

Two guards placed Castile on his feet. "Pronounce your sentence, Will, if you can. Say the words aloud, and see if they roll easily off your tongue."

"I will not kill you," Will announced. "You have killed yourself."

Castile gave his son a puzzled look. "Oh, I see. Let the

executioner do it for you then."

Will shook his head. "No. You will leave this place alive."

Baldwin gave an audible gasp. Marshal folded his arms and watched Richard for a sign. Castile held his head high. "Blood and family in the end."

Will put up his hand. "You will leave the castle immediately after you have been branded on your forehead as a coward; your head shaved to cleanse you of vanity; your right eye plucked out for having seen more years than it should have; and your right hand cut off for having stolen my mother's life and her virtue. You shall be without money or friends, having never had either of your own, and without a tongue so that you may never again use it to lie to others, and twist them to do evil. You will be at the mercy of those around you. You will learn what it truly is to be alone in the world. If God is willing, you will be shown the mercy that you failed to show my mother. You took my mother's life, but you gave me mine. I will not take yours."

Will gave a nod to the guards and they begin to unbind Castile's hand to cut it off. One took a dagger out preparing to liberate Castile of an eye. Will turned to leave, but the noise of a scuffle made him turn around. Somehow Castile wriggled free of the guards, and had one of their swords. He charged at Richard, but Marshal and Baldwin were too fast. "Let him loose!" Richard's voice boomed above the others, taking everyone by surprise.

"Sire?" Baldwin sputtered.

"I said turn him loose!" He spoke to Castile now. "Do you really think that you can do me any harm? You have taken her from me. There is nothing else you can do to me!" He shook with rage. "By God's wounds, turn him loose!"

Baldwin released Castile first, and Marshal followed. They both remained close enough, just in case. Richard backed up ten paces. "Here now, you can have a good run at me." A shocked Castile remained in place. "Nobody touch him. If anyone stops him, I will hang you from these walls myself. Come on now, you son of a whore. Do it!" Richard threw off his cloak. "You have wanted to for years, Castile, dreamt of it, I am sure!" He spread his arms wide. "I welcome it!"

Castile turned around to Will. "You say you will not kill me, but you have condemned me to death."

"It is true, you will die. We all will, someday. But I have not done it. Your blood will not be on my hands."

Castile looked back and forth between his son and Richard. His hand tightened around the grip of the sword, and he locked eyes with Richard. With a growl, the same growl Will made at the tournament, Castile ran at Richard. Richard remained steady with his arms open waiting for the moment of impact, but it did not come. Just before he reached Richard, Castile leapt over the battlements.

In astonishment, everyone ran to the edge and saw Castile's twisted mangled corpse crushed on the jagged rocks below. Even from that height Will could see the crimson stained rocks and plants about the body. To his left Baldwin whispered, "A coward to the last."

They all looked to Richard who took in the sight below. "Let the scavengers see to their own dead." The king turned and left the battlements.

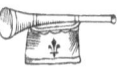

A click sounded behind Breton, and the door to the chapel began to open. At the sound of it, the gathered men in the hall got to their feet. King Philip stood in the doorway. "Breton, what is the meaning of this?" His blue eyes seemed to bore into each man.

Breton jumped to his feet. For the first time it crossed his mind that Philip would not want the story told. "Sire, I was just talking with the men here about duty."

"Well, I should think sitting here is not exactly fulfiling any duty," Philip scolded, though his voice did not sound angry.

The men stood and scattered in different directions. "My lord, the castellan wishes to see you," Breton informed Philip.

"Then we should grant him an audience." Philip left the chapel as well.

Bogis remained there at his post. As he watched Philip go, he thought to himself that somehow his king looked different.

Chapter Ninety-three

Upon being released from his duty, Bogis inquired which room in the manor house once belonged to Anne. He felt a burning curiosity to see it. After receiving directions, he found his way to the chamber.

The room was no longer used as a bedchamber because Richard locked it after Anne died. When John took possession of the castle, he ordered it open again and joked he would use it to house his mistresses. However, when the castellan opened it, anyone who entered was penetrated with an eerie feeling. No one stayed in the room long. Eventually they used it to store weapons and miscellaneous goods in case the need came to supply the postern gate.

Now, as Bogis stood in the doorway, he could see where supplies had been retrieved in a hasty manner, and many odds and ends were scattered about. With a feeling of awe, he stepped in the chamber and looked around. The layout of the room was just as Breton described it. The faded paintings with their figures from the Arthurian tales still ringed the top of the room. Next to the fireplace were two niches that once had curtains framing them. Only a single tattered curtain remained over one, the other held a bricked over window, nothing more than an arrow slit. The brown stones did not come close to matching the original gray colour.

Bogis couldn't see clearly into the one on the right because of the curtain, and he wondered if it was bricked up too. He couldn't be certain, but it almost seemed as if the curtain moved, or flickered. Avoiding the discarded, broken pieces of weapons and furniture that lay about, he made his way to the curtain, and slid it to the side. No one hid behind it; not that he expected someone to be there, exactly. Bogis dismissed his thoughts as foolish fancies, fueled by superstitious stories.

The window was still there, flanked by the window seat. Finding a hook on the wall, Bogis tucked the curtain behind it and took a seat. As he sat, he imagined the hard, cold stone seats covered with soft luxurious cushions, the walls of the room draped with brilliantly coloured tapestries, a supple rug covering the now bare floor, and a bed surrounded by majestic red curtains. Even in its haggard state, Bogis found the room impressive.

Looking out the window, he gazed down to the river. The steep cliffs descended to meet the river, and Bogis could not help but imagine the decaying body of Castile sprawled below while buzzards circled and pecked at it. Castile's eyes were plucked out after all.

With a shudder, Bogis turned away from the window, leaning back against the wall. He looked at the seat opposite him and wondered how many pleasant hours Anne and Richard spent in this very room.

"Tell me, Bogis, does this room make you uneasy?" Bogis, lost in his thoughts, did not see the king in the doorway.

Bogis jumped to his feet and gave the king a bow. Philip motioned for him to sit back down. "Your highness, I find it badly in need of repairs."

"Obviously, but you did not answer my question." Philip chided Bogis while making his way across the room.

"Perhaps a little," Bogis confessed.

Philip squatted down and examined a broken arrowhead that lay on the floor. "Despite its current condition, I find it an alluring place." He stood back up, dropped the arrowhead, and dusted his hands off, looking around again. "Those idiots left much useful surplus in here. It is not exactly the best location to resupply the postern gate."

"That it is not," Bogis agreed.

Philip took a seat opposite Bogis. "I hear Breton spun a tale for you and the others outside the chapel."

"Yes, my lord."

"Bogis, I know you did not particularly care for your assignment, but now you know why I trusted you with it. I commend your performance. Lesser men would have left their post for the fight."

"Thank you, sire." Bogis didn't want to look Philip in the eye.

"I think I shall restore this room," Philip pronounced in a merry tone of voice.

"Your highness, may I ask you a question?" Bogis was astonished the words came out of his mouth so quickly.

"You may ask." Bogis hesitated. "Well?" Philip prodded.

Bogis swallowed. "I was wondering how it is Father Breton knew so many details? I know he could have learnt much from you, but he told us things that only King Richard and Lady Anne could have known."

"Ah." Philip folded his arms across his chest. "It sounds as though Breton left some details about himself out of his discourse. Father Breton used to be Richard's personal priest. He knew us all from the time we were young." Philip paused briefly. "You see, he was with Richard at Chalus. Richard lingered for many days and he spent many hours in confession to Breton. Father Breton brought me the news of Richard's death."

Bogis knew the story of Richard's death but didn't interrupt the king as he retold it. Philip shook his head. "That fool went there to recover a treasure. Mercadier was the one who talked Richard into it. 'Twas another one of those impulsive moments Anne said would kill him. Mercadier argued that as the Viscount of Limoges' overlord, the treasure belonged to Richard, and he must assert his authority over Aquitaine, not to be seen as weakened by his recent loss. Chalus was on Limoges' lands. Mercadier dared to say it was what Anne would have wanted."

"But you do not believe that is the reason Richard went to Chalus then?" Bogis observed.

"No, not completely." Philip unfolded his arms. "Richard started a siege there during Lent. Only a man who has lost leave of his senses starts a siege during Lent, but it was not really much of an army to defeat. One evening Richard and Mercadier decided to do their own reconnaissance and a little target practice with their crossbows. Richard felt secure and, once again, went out without his armor, only a helmet. Up on the battlements a lone defender, a boy really, using a pan as a shield took aim at Richard. Richard decided to applaud the boy's gusto instead of raising his shield. The boy let lose another arrow, and, as you know, the arrow lodged into Richard's shoulder." Philip shifted in his seat.

"Richard pretended it was nothing and returned to his tent. He did not wish to alarm his men. Once back in the tent, Mercadier tried to pry the arrow out, but only succeeded in breaking the shaft. His surgeon, Marchadeus dug out the rest. Odd isn't it, after what happened to Anne?" Philip didn't wait for Bogis to reply. "When gangrene set in, Richard knew it meant death. Perhaps, that is what he wanted. Taken down by a mere boy..." Philip's voice trailed off.

After a moment, he cleared his throat. "On his death bed, Richard took his final communion. He told Breton he had not taken communion for seven years because he did not want to taint the sacrament with the hatred between us. He also pardoned the boy who shot him. Perhaps Richard thought it a favor. The boy didn't remain so lucky, because Mercadier and the others had the boy flayed alive after Richard died. They also executed Marchadeus for not extracting the arrowhead cleanly. The outpouring of their grief and anguish was absolute and genuine. His people loved their king."

Bogis tried to say something to comfort his king. "Your subjects love their king. Look what they have done for you here."

Philip continued on as though he hadn't heard Bogis' comment. "Queen Eleanor was there when he died. They took Richard's body to Fontevrault for burial. Berengaria came. She was hysterical and couldn't even be persuaded to leave her room for the funeral mass. Personally, I wonder which she was more upset about, losing Richard or the title. She is still fighting with John for her allowance as Dowager. The last we heard, she took the case before a high court of the church because some in the church do not recognise her as Richard's widow.

"Then there is Queen Eleanor. I am told she is on her deathbed as we speak. I hope she does not hear of this castle falling to me before she dies. I truly feel sorry for her. She lost both her children so close together. First Joanna, then a couple of weeks later Richard." "Joanna?" Bogis whispered, trying to remember what happened to her.

Philip reminded him. "It would seem that Joanna's love match with Toulouse took a nasty turn. He is a cruel man. Poor Joanna was caught in a mysterious fire while trying to escape from Toulouse. Pregnant and severely burnt, she made her way to her mother at Fontevrault where she languished. Just before the baby was born, the abbot allowed Joanna to take vows and become a nun. Joanna died shortly after she delivered."

"Poor Joanna." Bogis was amazed at the new sympathy he felt for this family he had always been taught to hate. He couldn't help but think of how Philip had been smitten with Joanna at one time.

"Well, both children were buried in Fontevrault. Richard requested to be buried at his father's feet to atone for his wrongs. He wanted his heart and entrails to be buried here at Galliard next to Anne, but the people of Rouen, stole them, and buried them at the ancient seat of the Dukes of Normandy."

Philip wrinkled his nose. "I am told that John was so drunk

he giggled and talked all through his entire coronation ceremony, even dropped the scepter, and thought it all a great joke." Philip's face flushed with anger, but with some effort, he regained control. "On the other hand, Richard would be proud of Will. The boy has become a powerful viscount. He even managed to stamp out an attempt by the Bishop of Marseilles to seize power. It really is too bad that Will was not Richard's son and heir, for the people of England, I mean. Alas, they are stuck with John."

"I dare say every Duke of Normandy stirs in his grave at the actions of John, and every King of England for that matter." John was the one person from the family toward whom Bogis felt absolutely no sympathy. "Rouen will be next, sire. Galliard is just the beginning."

Philip stood, walked to the fireplace, and shifted the dust and ash with the toe of his boot. "I did not invade these lands just to add to my domains; I did it to preserve them and the memory of their masters, and of my friends." Philip turned and directed his gaze at his field marshal. "Bogis, loyalty, honor, devotion to duty, friendship, and honest, pure, genuine love are qualities that are hard to find in people. I believe it is a gift to know someone who truly possesses them. Imagine my surprise when I found them in a woman. No wonder Richard loved her so. How could he not?"

Bogis dared to ask the king another question. "Do you think they are finally together and that you will see them again in the life to come?"

A smile spread across Philip's face. "Even though I am a king, it is not in my power to grant absolution. That right is God's alone."

Philip exited the room, leaving Bogis to ponder by himself. "I pray they have found peace." Bogis spoke to the empty room and then followed his king.

Epilogue

Philip remained at Galliard for only a few days. He needed to return to Paris, and he asked Bogis to accompany him. The deck of the king's barge was crowded with advisors, soldiers, and a few priests as it set sail on the Seine.

As the barge began to move, Bogis looked up at the castle on the hill. It seemed different than before. He could not quite identify what made it so, but it was more than the French flags flying from the walls. With a sigh of wonder, he turned around and saw Philip swamped by his advisors. Behind them, the flags on the ship rippled in the constant breeze.

Without warning, everything became still. The flags lay limp, and even the ship seemed to remain in place. The peculiar atmosphere caught the attention of others on the boat, and all fell silent. Philip left the circle of men around him and walked to the front of the barge to investigate.

Then a sudden fierce gale rocked the barge. Bogis glanced up at the flags to determine the direction, but they blew every which way. The wind swirled around them, and there came a sound with it like a roar of the surf breaking on the ocean shore. As abruptly as it started, it stopped.

The men exchanged looks of amazement. As Bogis looked at King Philip, he noticed something falling from the sky. Looking up, he could not believe what he saw. It was too early in the season, impossible. He closed his eyes and opened them again, but the phenomenon remained. The sky rained peach blossoms. Thousands of peach blossoms floated about, carried on a gentle breeze. Everyone on the barge remained speechless as the flowers drifted onto the men, the deck, and fell in the river beside the barge. Bogis looked to Philip again. A smile slowly spread across the king's face. Laughing, Philip knelt down, scooped up a handful of peach blossoms and placed them in the pouch hanging from his belt.

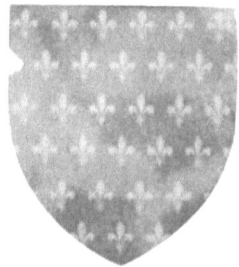

Dramatis Personae

Richard~ *Duke of Aquitaine, Count of Poitou*

- Eleanor~ *Queen of England, Richard's mother*
- Henry II~ *King of England, Richard's father*
- Young Henry, Geoffrey, John~ *Richard's brothers*
- Matilda, Joanna~ *Richard's sisters*
- Marie~ *Countess of Champagne, Richard's & Philip's half sister*
- Henry of Champagne~ *Marie's son, nephew to Richard & Philip*
- Andrew de Chauvigny, Baldwin of BeThune~ *Richard's companions*
- Blondel~ *Richard's troubadour*
- Marshal~ *Henry's steward*
- Henry the Lion~ *Duke of Saxony, Richard's brother-in-law, vassal to the Holy Roman Emperor*
- Rosamund de Clifford~ *Henry's mistress*
- Arthur of Brittany~ *Geoffrey's son, & Richard's heir*
- Otto of Brunswick~ *Matilda's son, Richard's trusted nephew*
- Marchadets~ *Richard's physician*

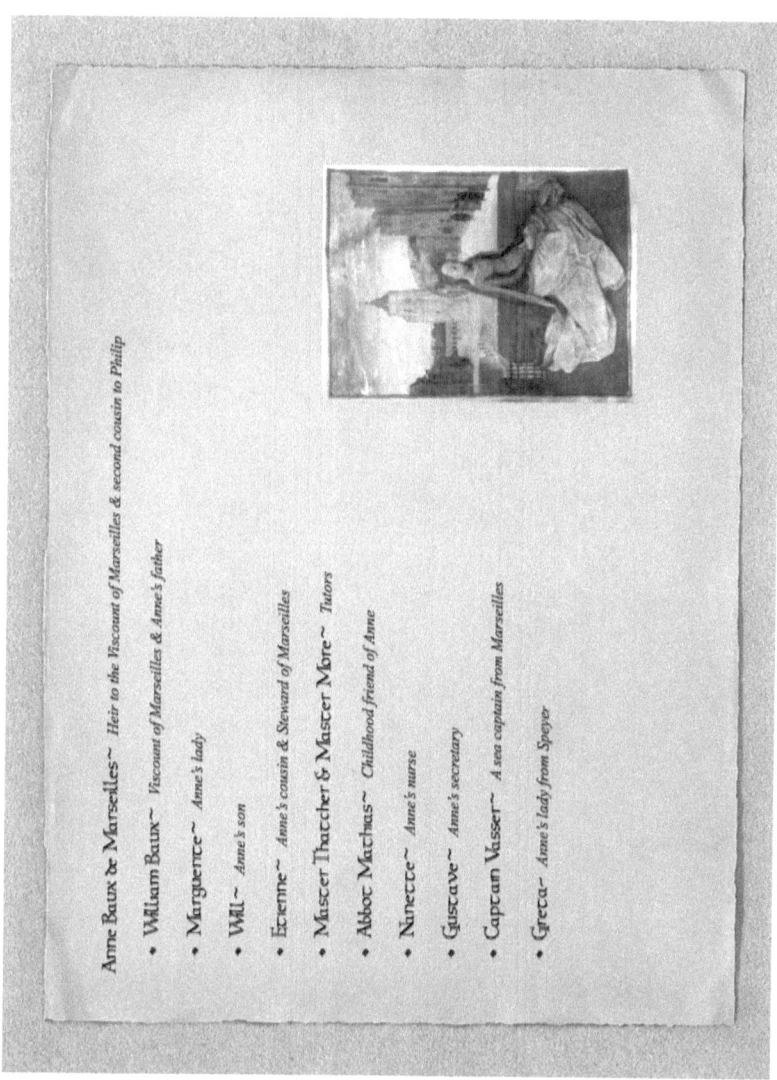

Anne Baux de Marseilles~ *Heir to the Viscount of Marseilles & second cousin to Philip*

- William Baux~ *Viscount of Marseilles & Anne's father*

- Marguerite~ *Anne's lady*

- Will~ *Anne's son*

- Etienne~ *Anne's cousin & Steward of Marseilles*

- Master Thatcher & Master More~ *Tutors*

- Abbot Mathas~ *Childhood friend of Anne*

- Ninette~ *Anne's nurse*

- Gustave~ *Anne's secretary*

- Captain Vasser~ *A sea captain from Marseilles*

- Greta~ *Anne's lady from Speyer*

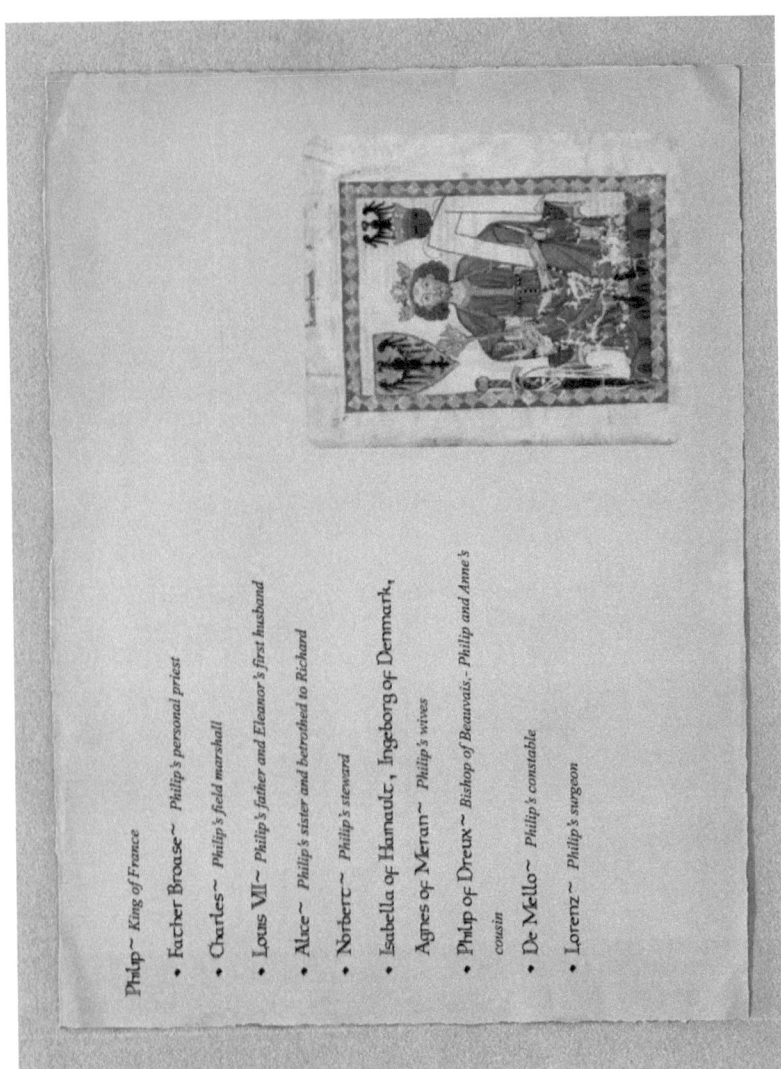

Philip~ *King of France*

- Father Broase~ *Philip's personal priest*
- Charles~ *Philip's field marshall*
- Louis VII~ *Philip's father and Eleanor's first husband*
- Alice~ *Philip's sister and betrothed to Richard*
- Norbert~ *Philip's steward*
- Isabella of Hainault, Ingeborg of Denmark, Agnes of Meran~ *Philip's wives*
- Philip of Dreux~ *Bishop of Beauvais - Philip and Anne's cousin*
- De Mello~ *Philip's constable*
- Lorenz~ *Philip's surgeon*

Others

- Raymond of Castile~ *Prince of Castile, suitor to Anne*
- Taillebourg~ *Baron of Taillebourg castle*
- Jacob of Orleans, Rabbi Isaac~ *Jewish leaders in London*
- Luigi~ *Jewish merchant from Provence*
- Johan de la Pumeria~ *Boy hired as an interpreter*
- Franz Rolf and Peter~ *Guards in the Holy Roman Emperor's court*
- Tancred of Lecce~ *Usurper to the throne of Sicily*
- Guy de Lusignan~ *Former King of Jerusalem*
- Isaac Comnenus~ *Tyrant ruler of Cyprus*
- Conrad of Montferrat~ *Contender for the throne of Jerusalem*
- Leopold ~ *Duke of Austria*
- Saladin~ *King of the Saracens*
- Al Adil~ *Saladin's brother*

- Balin of Belin~ *Baron of the Kingdom of Jerusalem*
- Gerard of Clairvaux~ *Templar knight*
- Henry Hohenstaufen~ *Holy Roman Emperor*
- Empress Constance~ *Hohenstaufen's wife*
- Chancellor Martin~ *Hohenstaufen's chancellor*
- Berta ~ *Servant to Empress Constance*
- Alfonso VIII~ *Raymond of Castile's brother*
- Alfonso the Troubadour~ *King of Aragon, Raymond's brother-in-law*
- Raymond V ~ *Count of Toulouse*

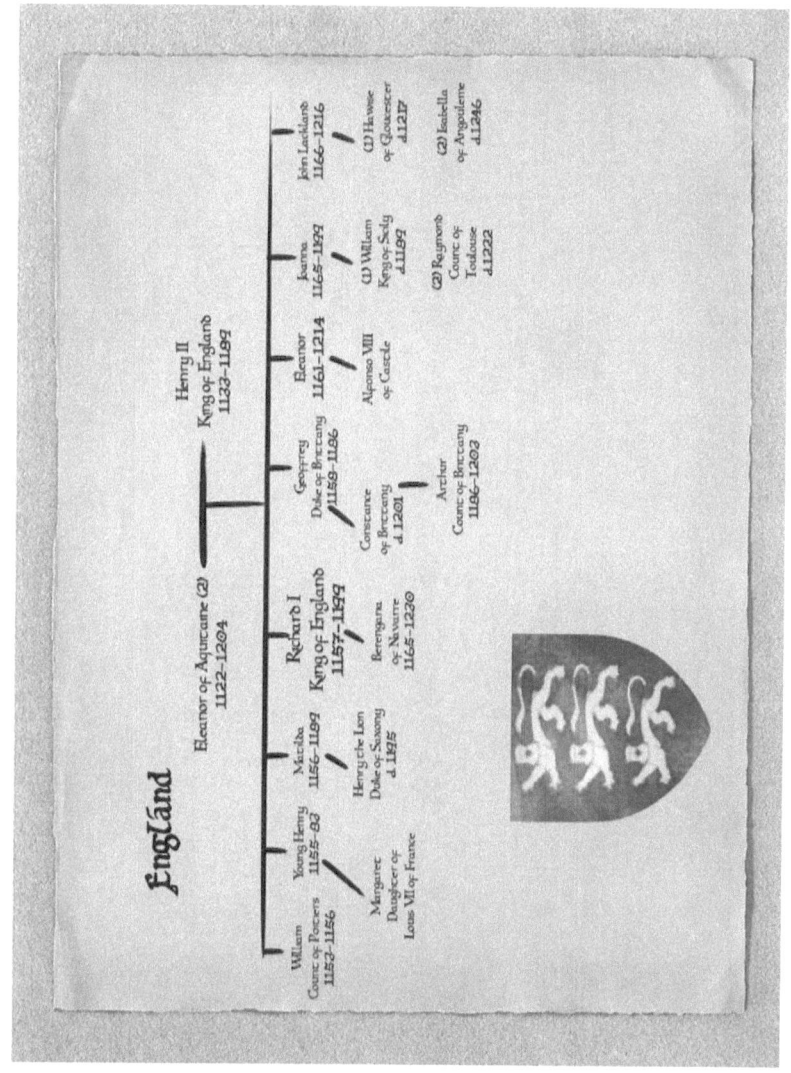

England

Eleanor of Aquitaine (2)
1122-1204

Henry II
King of England
1133-1189

William
Count of Poitiers
1153-1156

Young Henry 1155-83

Margaret
Daughter of
Louis VII of France

Matilda
1156-1189

Henry the Lion
Duke of Saxony
d.1195

Richard I
King of England
1157-1199

Berengaria
of Navarre
1165-1230

Geoffrey
Duke of Brittany
1158-1186

Constance
of Brittany
d.1201

Arthur
Count of Brittany
1186-1203

Eleanor
1161-1214

Alfonso VIII
of Castile

Joanna
1165-1199

(1) William
King of Sicily
d.1189

(2) Raymond
Count of
Toulouse
d.1222

John Lackland
1166-1216

(1) Hawise
of Gloucester
d.1217

(2) Isabella
of Angouleme
d.1246

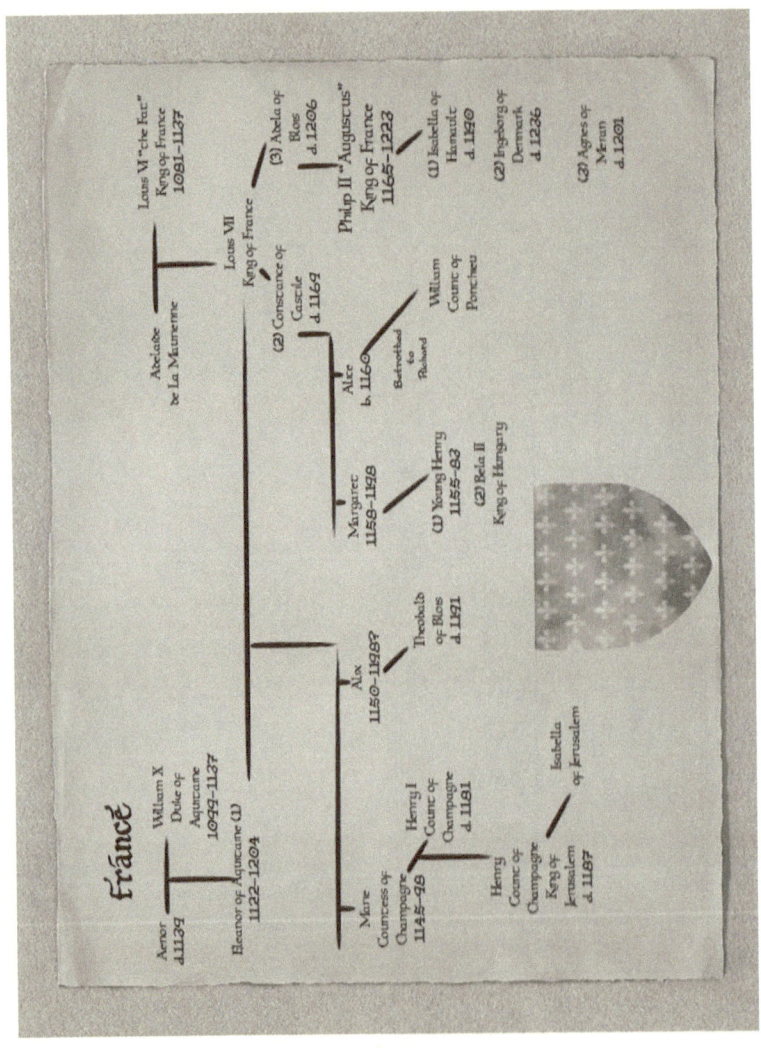

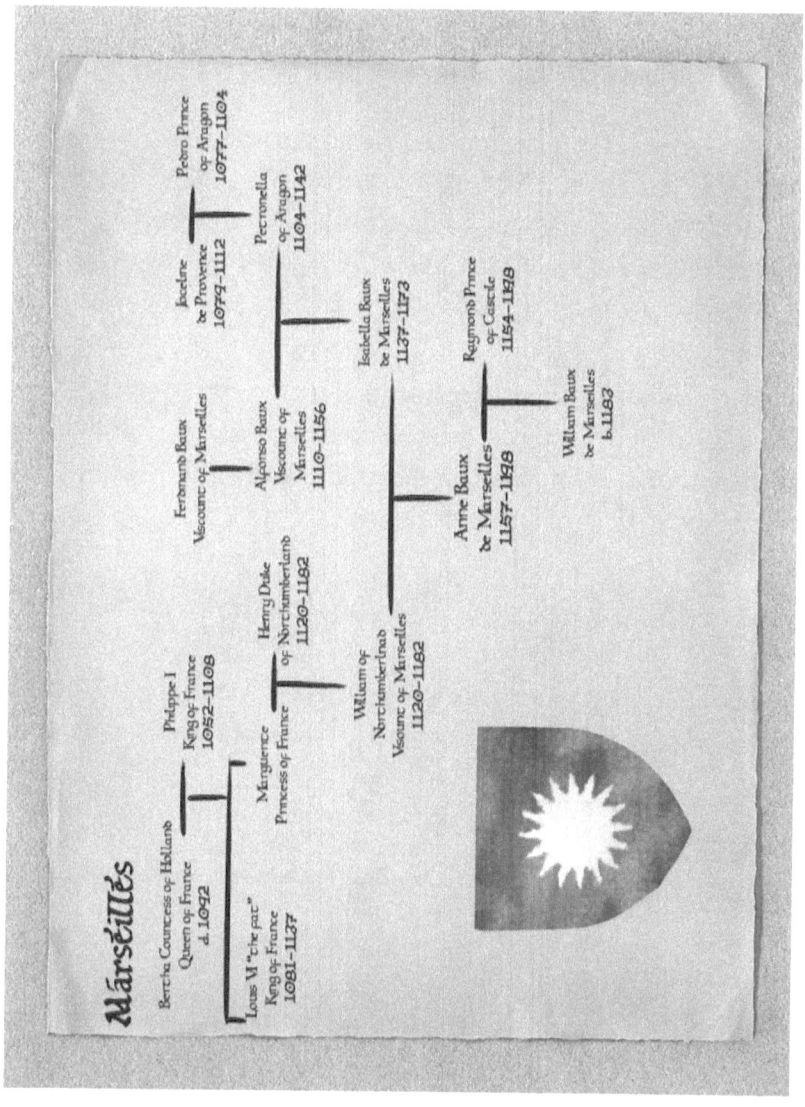

ABOUT THE AUTHOR

Shalisse Lewis is a graduate of Southern Utah University with a BS degree in History, and a double minor in English and secondary education. After college, she traveled from Omaha, Nebraska to Salt Lake City via wagon train- just to see what it was like.

She is a collector of stories. In addition, she loves all things historical, her job, gets excited about teaching Shakespeare, is addicted to chocolate, married, has kids, an English mastiff, and loves to learn.